Lost Lands
of
Witch World

Lost Lands of Witch World

∞

Comprising
Three Against the Witch World,
Warlock of the Witch World,
and *Sorceress of the Witch World*

ANDRE NORTON

With an Introduction by Mercedes Lackey

A Tom Doherty Associates Book
New York

This is a work of fiction. All the characters and events portrayed in this novel are either fictitious or are used fictitiously.

LOST LANDS OF WITCH WORLD

Edited by James Frenkel

A Tor Book
Published by Tom Doherty Associates, LLC
175 Fifth Avenue
New York, NY 10010

www.tor.com

Tor® is a registered trademark of Tom Doherty Associates, LLC.

LIBRARY OF CONGRESS CATALOGING-IN-PUBLICATION DATA

Norton, Andre.
    Lost lands of Witch World / Andre Norton.—1st ed.
        p. cm.
    "A Tom Doherty Associates book."
    Contents: Three against the Witch World—Warlock of the Witch World—Sorceress of the Witch World.
    ISBN 0-765-30052-4 (acid-free paper)
    EAN 978-0765-30052-2
    1. Witch World (Imaginary place)—Fiction. 2. Fantasy fiction, American. I. Title.

PS3527.O625A6 2004
813'.52—dc22

                                                                    2003071153

First Edition: June 2004

Printed in the United States of America

0 9 8 7 6 5 4 3 2 1

Contents

Introduction
Andre Norton's *Witch World*:
An Appreciation

O nce upon a time, in the 1950s and early 1960s, the only category in the "imaginative fiction" genre was science fiction. Never mind that there was a rich heritage of fantasy fiction ranging from the Middle Ages onward; in the bookstores (and for book buyers) it was all lumped under the heading of Science Fiction. And, to tell the truth, the pickings available to those who appreciated fantasy were pretty slender. There were Robert E Howard's Conan stories and the many imitators of those stories, of course, if you wanted Iron-Thewed Manly Fiction. There were reprints of Edgar Rice Burroughs and his ilk from the days of the pulps. But for those whose tastes ran to something more concerned with magic and wonder, well, there wasn't a lot in the paperback section. Tolkien's Lord of the Rings trilogy had just become available, both in the pirated Ace edition (heavily edited) and the Ballantine version (which had Tolkien's blessing). There was T. H. White's *The Once and Future King,* which had finally gone into paperback because of Lerner and Lowe's musical, *Camelot,* which was based upon it. But there was precious little else for someone stuck in small-town America or the endless tract houses of suburbia, as I was.

For readers in the big cities, things were not nearly so bleak. If you had access to a really good big-city or university library, you might be able to find C. S. Lewis's The Chronicles of Narnia in the children's section, as well as the works of George MacDonald, or at least *The Princess and the Goblin.* You might even be able to find the great Edwardian and Victorian fantasists, such as Lord Dunsany. If you were a science fiction cognoscente, you might have in your magazine collection C.L. Moore's Jirel of Joiry stories, and in fact the magazines *Amazing, Astounding,* and *The Magazine of Fantasy and Science Fiction* occasionally printed a fantasy tale.

But for the most part, for those of us whose reading consisted of what we could find at the corner drugstore, with rare forays into a "real" bookstore, anything that might be described as fantasy was generally science fiction in a different costume. Magic was almost always psychic powers with other names. Occasionally you could find a gothic romance with magical trappings—in fact, the late Fritz Leiber's *Conjure Wife* was marketed that way. Such a rare find was treasured indeed and required a lot of digging.

Then came the year 1963, and a slim little book from Ace called *Witch World* by Andre Norton, and everything changed. Perhaps not so strangely, the fact that a change was in the air was hardly obvious, not even to those who saw the book. It's difficult to see change when you are on top of it—often it is only apparent in retrospect.

Science fiction fans had known all about Andre Norton for some time; her novels *Daybreak 2250 A.D., The Last Planet,* and especially *Beast Master* were staples in any collection. She had been writing and publishing books since 1935, although she didn't start to become a big name in science fiction until the early 1950s; she had a solid reputation for producing consistently great stories and a long, long list of books in her backlist (some forty-five books in all by 1963).

In fact, C. J. Cherryh later said of her, "I've seen a complete collection of Andre Norton's books and it haunts me to this day, sort of like the sight of an unscalable Everest."

Miss Norton was prolific, and she was *good*—and by 1963 most people knew, thanks to a little Author's Note in the front of the books, that the masculine "Andre" was the *nom de plume* of the very feminine lady born Alice Mary Norton (who is, by the way, no relation to the lady of the same name who published the Borrowers books for children). When Andre first presented her books to publishers, she was advised that "science fiction is a boy's genre" and that "boys won't read books written by women," hence the name change, which she made legal in 1934. Well, boys *did* read her books, and girls, and people who were decidedly older than "boys" and "girls." She wrote in several genres—western, juvenile historical, and even gothics—but the genres that she loved most, and did the majority of her work in, were science fiction and fantasy.

At any rate, Andre had a respected name in science fiction, and was popular enough that her titles made it to corner drugstore racks everywhere. I already was an avid devourer of her work, as *Beast Master* was the second science fiction book I ever read (I believe I was about eleven at the time), and it led to my combing the shelves of the Science Fiction section of my local library for her works. She was among the few—such as Isaac Asimov, Poul Anderson, Ray Bradbury, Robert Heinlein, and H. G. Wells—whose works were popular enough that libraries purchased them in special hardbound editions. How could I not enjoy her work? Here were incredible, wild, exotic worlds where being different was special. Heady stuff for a bookish kid who was very definitely "different."

That was where I first encountered *Beast Master,* in fact, and if all you know about that story is the regrettable and eminently forgettable movies and television series, then believe me, you don't have any idea of what wonderful books it, and its sequel, *Lord of Thunder,* are. To begin with, these are real science fiction masterpieces with never a fur loincloth in sight. They feature Native Americans (not vanilla Caucasians) as the heroes, something that was totally unheard of at the time, and Andre Norton carefully researched the Navaho culture to bring her high-tech, psionic warrior, Hosteen Storm, to life. His Beast Team, genetically engineered before there was a term for such things, is composed of meerkats (*not* ferrets), a cougar, and the creature that truly enthralled me, an African Black Eagle (*not* a Redtailed Hawk, nor a Harris Hawk, nor any other bird of prey, short of an owl, that the cheapskate movie producers had on hand). Go read the books; you will soon understand why Andre insisted that her name be removed from the movie, and why she regards the sale of those rights as the worst mistake she ever made.

But I digress. Needless to say, Andre Norton was very familiar to me, and I soon went through every Norton book in the library. Then I canvassed the drugstore, then made twice-yearly forays to Chicago and the only "real" bookstore I knew of, Krochs. Finally, in desperation, I began *mail ordering* volumes from the backs of existing books. This might seem irredeemably quaint in these days of amazon.com and Web sites, but in those days people generally didn't mail order anything, unless it was in a catalog from a major department store like Sears, Montgomery Ward, or the like. I would save money from my allowance (fifty cents a week), put together four or five dollars, and, with grave trepidation, put it in an envelope to Ace Books. Six or eight weeks later, a brown-paper-wrapped package would arrive, holding treasure. I still have my original forty-cents copy of *Witch World,* purchased at Krochs. On the list of books in the back, I put tick marks for the books I didn't have yet and wrote little numbers beside them for the ones I wanted first. My book also had an Antioch Bookplate in medieval illumination style with my name on it in the front.

I bought a lot of those books—always trying, being as frugal as possible, to get the books at thirty cents each before the price went up to thirty-five or forty. After all, my fifty-cents-per-week allowance had to stretch as far as I could make it go—not only to buy science fiction books but Christmas and birthday presents, records (classical and folk), and after Beatlemania hit me in late 1964, fan magazines and still more records.

At any rate, here was *Witch World,* in my hot little thirteen-year-old hands. Let me quote the blurb on the back:

BY THE AUTHOR OF DAYBREAK 2250 A.D. For the myriads of Andre Norton readers, those who know Norton's books to be the tops in science-adventure, *WITCH WORLD* will prove to be a special treat. It's an all-original novel about a weird, adventure-filled planet where certain of the laws of nature operate differently—in fact, certain types of "magic" apparently work. Into this far-out space world, an Earthman is sent to test his skill against this new type of science. *Witch World* is high adventure in super-science, witchcraft, and fantasy-romance that will remind you of the best of such varied writers as Burroughs, Tolkien, and Brackett—and yet remains ANDRE NORTON in top form!

Now, by now you should have noticed that the word *fantasy* appears only once in that blurb, and that, if you were not already aware of the fact that it really was a fantasy, you could be forgiven for assuming this was another of Andre's space-faring tales. The fact is, it was marketed as science fiction; even the cover (by the great Jack Gaughan) would make you think that was what it was—the art prominently featured a man wearing a helmet that appeared to be a cross between the head of a hawk and the head of a toucan. He was carrying what looked, for all intents and purposes, to be a classic ray gun. True, the three men behind him had swords, spears, and shields, but they were in the background. The *ray gun* was in the foreground. From the perspective of 2003, I still wonder about this decision, which persisted into the late 1960s. What was so difficult about the word *fantasy*? Why did the publishers shy away from using it? Were they afraid that it would somehow be dismissed as another Conan clone?

But from the moment you read the first page, you knew you had something different.

The hero was a shadowy man with a shadowy past, Simon Tregarth, on the run in some unspecified, modern city, being hunted down by a hit man named "Sammy" (never seen), sent by one "Hanson" (also never seen), for some unspecified, but clearly terrible, affront. Whoever he was, Simon Tregarth was clearly dangerous, clearly competent, and his services (also unspecified but darkly hinted at) came at a high price, for he had something like twenty thousand 1963 dollars in his pocket (that would be enough to buy a new car, a house, a vacation home, a boat, and still have half left over). In short, it started rather like a James Bond novel. And within a few pages, you also knew that Simon Tregarth, though he trafficked with bad men and considered the money he made to be dirty, was, at heart, a man of honor. He had been tricked into the position he was in, his fall from grace engineered by the unscrupulous, and he continued because he had no other choice.

But he is intercepted over his (presumably last) dinner by a mysterious gentleman, Dr. Jorge Petronius, a man who has a reputation for making hunted people vanish. Simon is very well aware of this reputation, so he listens as Petronius tells him a strange story of menhirs, ancient magic, and the Siege Perilous, which he claims can open to a man the world he has been unconsciously searching for all his life. He styles himself the Guardian of the Siege Perilous—the latest of many. He offers Tregarth the use of the Siege Perilous. Being desperate, Tregarth takes his offer and the seat upon the Siege—and at dawn, a new world opens to him.

And that is where the book takes an abrupt departure from everything that Andre Norton had written before this.

Oh, there were some superficial trappings of science fiction—the "dart guns" used by Estcarp and other nations of the world, and some few similar bits and bobs. The ultimate enemy in the book does turn out to be the Kolder, a nasty set of aliens, who have wrenched open a way to their world with the goal of con-quering the one that harbors Estcarp. And certainly Simon Tregarth himself speculates that *some* of the "magic" might be psychic in nature, because the Witches of Estcarp do use telepathy and some other powers that might be called "psionic."

But there is magic, *real* magic in play here, for not only is it magic that opens the gate to another world, but within nine pages after their meeting, the hunted Witch that Simon rescues from men and hounds calls up a lightning storm that kills every one of her hunters. She does this using nothing more than a drop of her blood and a mysterious cloudy gemstone she wears around her neck.

By this time readers had figured out that this was nothing like science fiction. What was more, they liked it.

I certainly did; here, in a pure adventure story, was not only fantasy, but some-thing new to me, at least—not a hero, but a fantasy *heroine.* The unnamed Witch that Simon encounters within moments of his entry into Witch World is a woman in command of herself, competent to a fault, and possessed of her own sort of power that does not depend on swords or guns. And Estcarp, unlike the iron-fisted kingdoms of the Conan stories, was a matriarchy. Women had power here and were perfectly capable of ruling their kingdom without benefit of a king. Forget Conan; he'd find himself out-maneuvered in five minutes by the Witches of Estcarp, shown the door, and left standing outside, scratching his head and wondering what had happened. Our first look at the Witches of Estcarp is sym-pathetic, although the Witches have scant use for one of their sex who shares her gift and power and gives it up to live a life with a mere man.

It got better. A quarter into the book we encounter Loyse of Verlaine, the feisty young heiress to the wealthy wrecker-duchy, who is about to be bound in ax-marriage to the ruler of Kars. She appears to be a classic Gothic heroine; slight, pale, unpretty, unregarded, the pawn of her stepfather's plans. She is even presented in the classic Gothic setting—the storm-wracked castle tower over-looking a cliff and an angry sea.

In fact, she is nothing like that helpless maiden. She has had a plan all along, and proceeds to not only escape her bondage by her own wits and courage but to take the captive Witch with her. All by herself—no hero required.

It's time for a little perspective here. Nineteen sixty-three had far more in common with the stodgy and uptight fifties than the swinging sixties. There were a lot of things that "nice" girls "didn't" do, and I'm not talking about sex. Girls were supposed to be passive. Girls didn't have adventures. Girls didn't take the initiative. Try renting one of the classic old science fiction movies, like *Them,* and you'll see what I mean—the female scientist plays second fiddle to her father, totters around on high heels in a skirt too narrow to permit a reasonable stride, and requires an untrained military officer to do her observations in the giant ant nest for her. The women in science fiction books were mostly similar. They existed as foils for the young heroes. When they had any power whatsoever, they were generally evil and existed only to be put in their place by the heroes— or else, to fall in love with them and see the evil of their ways.

Andre Norton's women of *Witch World* were the antithesis of what girls were "supposed" to be like.

I seem to recall buying *Witch World* in May of 1963, so at that point in time, JFK and Pope John XXIII were still alive. Martin Luther King Jr. had not yet made his famous "I have a dream" speech. The cost of a first-class stamp was five cents. The Beatles were just beginning their rise to popularity in the U.K.; over here, no one had ever heard of them. Rock and roll was hardly mainstream; it still had something of a tainted image. In those days (unlike now, when a top twenty song will show up as Muzak within six months), if you had played a rock hit in a grocery store, you might have been lynched. Instead, the Grammy for that year went to "I Left My Heart in San Francisco," and Bible-school classes were burning Elvis Presley records as being "detrimental to the morals of youth" (sound familiar?).

At the time, I was into folk music, myself; I would listen to a folk music show that was on after 10:00 P.M. on radio station WLS—secretly, because I wasn't supposed to be up that late. This, by the way, was an AM station—no one had ever heard of FM. Peter, Paul, and Mary had been recording for just under three years. WLS played the real stuff: the protest songs, the things that had been banned from many radio stations, such as Pete Seeger, Bob Dylan, and the Weavers—in 1963 McCarthyism was making its last gasp, but it was still there.

The big movie of the year was *Lawrence of Arabia,* which starred an unknown fellow by the name of Peter O'Toole. It aired in what is now "the director's cut" so long it required an intermission.

Not even science fiction writers envisaged PCs, CDs, VCRs, DVDs, or the the Internet. We were more afraid of ICBMs than disease—plague was a thing of the past, and no one could imagine that there would ever be another disease that science couldn't find a cure for. But on the pessimistic side, the Cuban Missile Crisis had only just been sorted out, and *On the Beach* and nuclear holocaust seemed not only likely, but probable; many of Andre Norton's books took place in a post-nuclear-war world. Many science fiction authors were in the Ban the Bomb movement and wrote openly antiwar stories. Unlike those in more visible genres, their activism was ignored. After all, "everyone knew" that science fiction was nothing but escapist trash read by bespectacled boys in short pants.

Transistors were the highest tech available. Man had not only not gone to the moon, he had barely taken the first steps into orbit. My father worked on one of the first commercial computers—it occupied the space of a ten thousand-square-foot building and produced the computing power of one of today's credit-card-sized calculators.

This was the year that Sylvia Plath published *The Bell Jar* and Betty Friedan produced *The Feminine Mystique,* but neither book, so seminal to the budding Women's Liberation movement, made any impression in the suburbs where I lived. Far more important to the housewives where I lived was the new program on National Educational Television (not yet called PBS), *The French Chef,* with Julia Child. What went on the dinner table and could be used to impress Father's business colleagues was supposed to be more important that what Mother or Sister might be thinking or feeling. I had vaguely heard of *The Feminine Mystique* but only because comedians on the Johnny Carson show made jokes, calling it *The Feminine Mistake.* I had never heard of Sylvia Plath, and I doubt if I could have gotten my hands on a copy of either book.

Oh, there was feminist science fiction, but it was highbrow stuff and not really accessible to a thirteen-year-old—okay, a *bright* thirteen-year-old, but still, my brain wasn't entirely up to it, and my hovering-on-puberty body wasn't at all comfortable with some of the concepts being bruited about. And most of it wasn't being published where I could get my hands on it.

This was accessible, enjoyable, exciting. Girls who did not wait around to be rescued but dealt with their intolerable situations by themselves. Women who wielded executive power without turning a hair, and men (or at least, the men of Estcarp) who were fine with that.

But outside of Estcarp, the men weren't "fine" with that, which made it a lot more like the world I knew, and somehow, that made the rest of Witch World even more fascinating. Okay, the Witches were cool and something to aspire to, but Loyse was a girl not unlike me. She was smart; but she hid how smart she was. She knew that she had to escape her situation if she wasn't to be made into something less than a serf, but she was clever and planned well in advance. On the very eve of her marriage-by-proxy, she disguised herself as a boy with clothing, arms, and armor she had purloined while pretending to select wedding goods, and escaped through secret tunnels that she had personally discovered. Now Loyse was someone I could identify with.

I was hooked. I tore through the book, discovering that it remained a mix of fantasy and science fiction, with the great enemies behind everything, the Kolder, revealed as alien invaders, masters of high technology that was complete anathema to Witch World. Now, technology as the enemy as well as the savior of mankind was not new—science fiction writers were way ahead of the mainstream in creating tales of technological dystopias. But this was the first time that I had ever read a glorification of a fantastical, medieval setting set up in stark contrast to a hideous technological nightmare that threatened to overwhelm it. Medievalism was somehow always "barbaric" in the science fiction I had read, even the dystopian science fiction. "Civilization" was always rooted in modernism, and science, not magic, saved the day, even in a dystopia—unless, of course, there wasn't really supposed to be a happy ending (as was the case in Orwell's *1984* or Huxley's *Brave New World*).

Witch World was different. This was a revelation, an epiphany. I reread it over and over, not the least because at the end of the book it was very clear that there was more, much more, to come. I was used to books that finished their stories in one volume. The day of trilogies, tetralogies, and series books had yet to come. There were Tolkien's trilogy, and the Conan series, Edgar Rice Burroughs, and a few others—but not much more. Just as there was not much in the way of fantasy available, there were not many sequels, either. Andre Norton took a bold step in that direction with *Witch World,* which brought an end to a chapter, but by no means the entire story, of her creation.

It was a gamble, but it certainly paid off. *Witch World* was followed in 1964 by *Web of the Witch World.*

Once again, it was billed as science fiction, not fantasy—though I must admit that the technological elements are much more in evidence. Here is that original cover blurb:

> Simon Tregarth, whose own Earthly prowess had won him a throne and a witch-wife in an alien world, knew that both triumphs were precarious as long as the super-science of Kolder held a foothold on that planet. And his premonitions were right when those invaders from another dimension made their final diabolical strike for total conquest. Andre Norton's *WEB OF THE WITCH WORLD* is a terrific novel of scientific marvel, other-world color, and sword-and-sorcery action that will thrill and delight every reader.

In the manner of blurbs everywhere, in the inside cover blurb the witch Jaelithe had suddenly become a "princess" and Simon had a "throne"—which probably came as a surprise to Norton and to anyone who expected an Edgar Rice Burroughs pastiche. It wasn't anything of the sort, obviously, and in the course of the story Andre Norton gracefully tackled another aspect of the lot of a woman who stands up in her own light—the need and the desire for freedom within a partnership of marriage, and how both partners must compromise within freedom. Were you to have told this to the average teenager who was powering his or her way through the book, that reader would have stared at you in blank astonishment. It simply would never have occurred to the young readers of this book that there was anything there but a fantastic story. The best in science fiction and fantasy is always subversive, whether the subversiveness is overt or covert, and in *Web of the Witch World* Andre Norton proved that she has always been a mistress of the covert variety. Here was a topic that feminist literature had only begun to explore—the frustration of a woman trying to force herself into a role for which she was ill-equipped out of love—suddenly presented with the opportunity to have her old life back. But at what cost?

For Jaelithe suddenly discovers she has *not* lost her witch powers when she married and mated with Simon. In fact, she discovers that she has entirely new powers shared with him.

And Loyse finds herself the prisoner of the man she had been forced to wed and had discarded.

And behind it all are the machinations of the Kolder. Jaelithe must learn a new sort of power. Simon must learn how to allow his wife to be herself. Only then can they defeat the Kolder, for united they are infinitely more than the sum of their abilities.

Along with the times, Andre Norton's work was a-changing.

Nineteen sixty-five brought *Three Against the Witch World* and the beginning of a new branch to the story, that of Simon and Jaelithe's three children, Kyllan, Kemoc, and Kaththea—wizard, warrior, and witch. All these books had cover art and frontispieces by Jack Gaughan; in Andre's home in Tennessee is a real treasure, a huge piece of drawing paper covered with the sketches Jack made as Andre described her world and the people in it. There are the Witches, the Falconers, the Kolder and their dreadful machines. It is an amazing piece.

The blurb for *Three Against the Witch World* admits that the novel is a fantasy:

> North, East, South, West . . . the offspring of Simon Tregarth, half earthling, half witch-brood, realized that they alone could perceive the four directions—for everyone else, there was no East! It was a blank in legend and history. And when new menaces threatened, the Tregarths realized that in that mental barrier there lay the key to all their world . . . somewhere to the unknown eastward must lie the sorcery that had secretly molded their destinies!

At long last . . . perhaps thanks to the increasing popularity of the Lord of the Rings trilogy, which was now widely available in its legitimate and unabridged Ballantine version—the publishers were willing to allow the Witch World books out of the science fiction disguise. There are *no* elements of science fiction in this book. The Kolder are barely mentioned. Simon and Jaelithe are absentee parents, caught up in defending Estcarp, when Simon himself vanishes, and Jaelithe uses her magic to find and join him—somewhere (we don't learn where for several books to come). Kars rises up as the enemy to strike Estcarp, and the Witches must use the most extreme measures to keep them out, summoning enough magic to make the very land bar the enemy passage.

And for the first time, Andre Norton touches on the theme of what can happen when anyone who holds power does so without willingness to compromise—for the Witches of Estcarp, mired in their old ways and unwilling to acknowledge anything new or different, are offended that Simon and Jaelithe continue to exercise magic together, and appalled that their children, female *and* male, also do so. And in so doing, the Witches themselves become an enemy of another sort, one that is harder to deal with—the enemy that is a part of you. They attempt to force the sister, Kaththea, into their ranks, defying the wishes of her parents who forbade any such thing. Escape is the only option here, as Kyllan, Kemoc, and Kaththea seek to flee into the East that only they can see, without knowing *why* the East is forbidden to those of the Old Race.

What they find is the land of Escore, where legends walk—and where *their* kind is legend. They have gone from one peril into another, into a land where, in the long past, those who had sought after power for the sake of power had unleashed an evil that still lingered. An ancient and uneasy balance had been struck between good and evil in Escore, and the three out of Estcarp are the straw that unbalances it and brings war again.

Andre Norton had no need to make copies of the formula that made The Lord of the Rings a success; she had long since become a master of the craft of storytelling, and the Witch World books go on a path all their own. This book is all about the abuse of power and its consequences. You see that in the "present" as the Witches abuse their power and drive the triplets into Escore. You see it in the past, in Escore, where abuse of power has already created great and terrible evil. It is also about making the wrong kind of compromise—a compromise with evil, which only allows evil to grow stronger. I should be remiss if I failed to mention that this book and the other two of the set are told in that most difficult of "voices," first person, from the viewpoint of the eldest of the triplets, the warrior Kyllan.

Once again, the ending of the book only ends a chapter; there is going to be a war in Escore of good against evil. Some of the Old Race—families, with women and children—come to join in that war and perhaps make a place for themselves when—if—the war is won. It is clear that there is much more to come.

But not immediately. Nineteen sixty-five also saw yet another branch from the *Witch World* tree. *The Year of the Unicorn,* which also had interior art by Gaughan, showed readers that there was more to Witch World than Simon and Jaelithe and their offspring, that the Kolder threatened not just Estcarp but an entire world, giving us two linked and yet separate storylines—Estcarp and Escore, and High Hallack and the Dales. Alas, it also brought a step backward, for there is not a single word about *fantasy* in the blurb—no, Gillan of the Dales faces a *super-science challenge.*

And by this time, Andre Norton established that series books were not only possible but profitable. The series has been in production for forty years now, and I do not believe that any of the books has ever been out of print for very long.

I should also point out something else; these books were all written long before the advent of personal computers—which meant every draft had to be handwritten, transcribed, typed, and retyped. It took *forever*—and yet Andre Norton was producing no fewer than three and as many as five books a year, plus short fiction. Now *that* is the definition of *prolific.*

For instance: 1963, the year that *Witch World* was published, also saw publication of *Judgment on Janus* and *Key Out of Time.* Nineteen sixty-four brought *Web of the Witch World, Ordeal in Otherwhere,* and *Night of Masks.* Nineteen sixty-five meant a whopping five books in publication—two Witch World books and also *Quest Crosstime, Steel Magic,* and *The X Factor.* One has to wonder what Andre would have produced had computers been available.

Three Against the Witch World was followed by *Warlock of the Witch World.* As *Three Against the Witch World* is told from Kyllan's viewpoint, *Warlock of the Witch World* comes from Kemoc's. And here is a new theme—that a clever, evil man can wear a face that fools anyone who doesn't examine him and his deeds closely. Kaththea consorts with someone who is thought to be a friend, only to discover that he is the enemy. She does so partly because he is accepted by the People of the Green Silences, and partly because he offers something she wants badly. She walks into the situation with the best of intentions, but by willfully refusing to see the signs of trouble is herself corrupted, and nearly brings disaster down on everything and everyone she cares for.

Sorceress of the Witch World, told from Kaththea's viewpoint, brought this storyline to a close in 1968. In trying to save Kaththea, Kemoc had struck her with half-learned magic, and as a consequence she has been stripped of all her magical learning. Unfortunately, this leaves her vulnerable to evil influence, with her powers crippled. She intends to go back to Estcarp to try and find help. Instead, fate has other plans, bringing her into another part of Escore, where she must use what she learned so painfully about evil masquerading as good to decide whether or not the ancient power she finds there is boon or bane. The themes in this book are sophisticated and complex, and there are few easy answers. Kaththea is abducted by nomadic hunters—she is forced to become the apprentice to their Wise Woman, who herself is of witchblood out of Estcarp and has served in that capacity for several of the short-lived nomads' generations. The Wise Woman binds Kaththea to these people—yet she does so out of her own sense of obligation and duty, and a desperate need to find someone who can protect them. Kaththea concentrates so much on finding a way to break that obligation that she fails to watch for danger despite being told that raiders are a hazard. As a consequence, the tribe that is depending on her is slaughtered. She escapes, but how much of that doom is *she* responsible for? Her mistakes nearly brought disaster when she sought out great power previously—her desire for an equal partnership, like her parents and brothers have found, made her blind to the faults in a masquerading enemy. Dare she trust herself again when presented with a similar situation? Kaththea has to overcome the dark places in her own heart and find the courage to face her own demons. Andre Norton accomplishes all of this with an economy of language that still astonishes me. Kaththea is a whole, living, breathing person, with faults and virtues—someone who makes many fantasy heroines look like cardboard cutouts.

The blurb for this book wavers between fantasy and science fiction:

"I am one of three, three who once became one when there was need: Kyllan the warrior, Kemoc the seer-warlock, Kaththea the witch. So my mother had named us at our single birthing; so we were." Thus opens the final saga of Andre Norton's already classic WITCH WORLD novels. *SORCERESS OF THE WITCH WORLD* is the dramatic and fabulous novel of Kaththea, sister-witch-protectress, daughter of an Earthman and an Estcarp Wise Woman. Kaththea's destiny had yet to be resolved, and in her efforts to regain her knowledge of the forbidden sciences of that strange world we are drawn into a series of adventures which put a fitting and breathtaking climax to this series. It is a full-length novel, complete in itself, of fantastic adventures among strange races and on alien worlds, of high magic and low, and of wizardry and super-science.

Once again, the publisher seemed afraid to name this book for what it was—pure fantasy. And although the blurb would seem to indicate that this sixth book meant the end of the series, this was far from the case. There were many more books to come, thirty-five in all thus far, although they were to appear under the imprints of no less than five different publishers. This series has a life of its own, and Andre Norton created a world with the depth and breadth in it to play host to myriad tales.

Furthermore, this series has exerted an influence far out of proportion to the books' modest size. In an age when contracts routinely call for works of not less than 120,000 words, and when books of double and even triple that length are printed every month, these 60,000-word gems are the treasured prizes of many a collection. Not only are first printings, yellowing and often falling to pieces, lovingly encased in acid-free plastic envelopes and stored carefully upright in boxes and bookcases all over the country, but the words inside those covers resonate with readers every day. Not just readers, either—I can't think of any fantasy writer of my acquaintance who *doesn't* list Andre Norton's Witch World series as one of his or her primal influences. Her peers acknowledged that when she was presented with a Nebula Grand Master Award in 1984. She also has received the Grand Master of Fantasy award in 1977 at the World Science Fiction Convention, the Balrog Fantasy Award for Lifetime Achievement in 1979, the Fritz Leiber Award *and* the E. E. Smith (Skylark) Award in 1983, the Jules Verne Award in 1984, The Howard (World Fantasy) Award in 1987, the SF Bookclub Award for Best Book of the Year in 1991, and in 1998 another World Fantasy award, this time for Lifetime Achievement. These are in addition to so many other awards that it would take an entire page to list them all. In a time when books seem to be considered important only when they hit bestseller status on the *New York Times* list, and little attention is paid to volumes that aren't issued first in hardcover printing numbers of 250,000, this level of acclaim may seem unlikely. Nevertheless, I can assure you that nearly every SF and fantasy professional acknowledges these books as seminal.

The only exceptions to this may be those who have come to the genre considering themselves to be "mainstream" authors who are only using the fantasy genre as a vehicle for their own particular messages.

And this is their loss. Andre Norton long ago perfected the art of embedding theme and message in pure story, never sacrificing the tale for the sake of making a point. In Heinlein's words, she was *not* one of those who "sold their birthright for a pot of message." And in giving us amazing stories, she serves as an ongoing inspiration for more than one generation of fantasy writers.

It was certainly true for me, and in more ways than just one. Not only was I enthralled and inspired by the books, I was given inspiration by the author. The Witch World books proved several things to me.

The first was that fantasy was just as valid a genre as science fiction. This seems like a nonissue in 2003, when fantasy titles outnumber science fiction titles three to one. From the 1963 perspective, it appeared that science fiction was the king, that it was getting more and more technically oriented with every passing year, and that soon one would have to have a Ph.D. in physics to be able to write books that publishers and the public would accept. In 1965 it seemed that while one might not have to have a Ph.D. in physics, the way of the future was in literary science fiction, for which I was ill suited. But there were the Witch World books, doing well, prospering—giving me hope that what I liked might also be what other people would like.

The second was that heroines were as important and as valid as heroes. Again, this seems obvious now—it wasn't then, when publishers were convinced that only boys read these books, and that boys would revolt in droves if girls were anything but props for the heroes.

The third was that you didn't have to be male to write science fiction books. Andre Norton was the first author in the genre who I *knew* was female. Yes, there were others, and plenty of them—C. L. Moore, Leigh Brackett, Marion Zimmer Bradley—but Andre was the first whom *I was aware of*. To me, that meant that I, too, could write science fiction and fantasy.

Last of all, you didn't have to be an Oxford don or some sophisticated creature from Greenwich Village to write a fantasy series. In fact, you could be a perfectly ordinary American female librarian living in Cleveland, Ohio, and write amazing books.

So not only were the heroines of Andre Norton's Witch World books accessible to a young teenaged girl living in Indiana, not only were they women she could identify with, but the *author* was someone she could hope to emulate. She wasn't a Leigh Brackett, living in Hollywood and writing movie scripts for the likes of John Wayne. She wasn't J.R.R. Tolkien, professor at far-off Oxford; she was someone just like people I knew—and yet she wrote these amazing stories. And if she could, maybe so could I.

And there are countless others who have thought the same, and have gone and done it. That is what makes these books so special, and why they hold a revered place in the hearts of plenty of writers—and with the publication of this compilation, probably will continue to do so for decades to come.

These books are definitely masterpieces of their kind—keeping in mind that a *masterpiece* is not the culmination of a career, but a work from the hand of a master of the craft. The characters are real and seem alive in a way that should serve as an example to other writers who have expended a lot more energy and word-count but have failed to achieve the same level of creativity. The books are the sort that readers go back to time and time again, long after other books have been sent to Goodwill or the used-book store. They serve as testaments to the right to be different, and as such have given comfort to thousands of teenagers over the past four decades. They celebrated ethnicity—Andre's heroes and heroines have been Navaho, Sioux, Chinese, Japanese, African, Apache, and races with green and blue skin color, even in the time before the Civil Rights movement. They celebrate intelligence and courage. They are groundbreaking because they not only paved the way for fantasy to be accepted in its own right, but they also paved the way for other women to be accepted in the field. I think it is safe to say that not only did the Witch World books inspire and influence (particularly female) writers who have themselves often paid tribute to that fact, but had it not been for Andre Norton and the Witch World books, writers like J. K. Rowling would have had a much tougher job in getting *their* books in print.

The Witch World books still speak to me at fifty-three as eloquently as they spoke to me at thirteen; rereading my first editions was a joy. I believe that these books will do the same for you. Enjoy.

Mercedes Lackey

Three Against
the
Witch World

I

∞

$\mathcal{I}$ am no song-smith to forge a blade of chant to send men roaring into battle, as the bards of the Sulcar ships do when those sea-serpents nose into enemy ports. Nor can I use words with care as men carve out stones for the building of a strong, years-standing keep wall, that those generations following may wonder at their industry and skill. Yet when a man passes through great times, or faces action such as few dream on, there awakes within him the desire to set down, even limpingly, his part in those acts so that those who come after him to warm his high seat, lift his sword, light the fire on his hearth, may better understand what he and his fellows wrought that they might do these same things after the passing of time.

Thus do I write out the truth of the Three against Estcarp, and what chanced when they ventured to break a spell which had lain more than a thousand years on the Old Race, to darken minds and blot out the past. Three of us in the beginning, only three, Kyllan, Kemoc, and Kaththea. We were not fully of the Old Race, and in that lay both our sorrow and our salvation. From the hours of our birth we were set apart, for we were the House of Tregarth.

Our mother was the Lady Jaelithe who had been a Woman of Power, one of the Witches, able to summon, send and use forces beyond common reckoning. But it was also true that, contrary to all former knowledge, though she lay with our father, the Lord Warder Simon, and brought forth us three in a single birth, yet she lost not that gift which cannot be measured by sight nor touch.

And, though the Council never returned to her her Jewel, forfeited at the hour of her marriage, yet they were also forced to admit that she was still a Witch, though not one of their fellowship.

And he who was our father was also not to be measured by any of the age-old laws and customs. For he was out of another age and time, entering into Estcarp by one of the Gates. In his world he had been a warrior, one giving orders to be obeyed by other men. But he fell into a trap of ill fortune, and those who were his enemies sniffed at his heels in such numbers that he could not stand and meet them blade to blade. Thus he was hunted until he found the Gate and came into Estcarp, and so also into the war against the Kolder.

But by him and my mother there came also the end of Kolder. And the House of Tregarth thereafter had no little honor. For Simon and the Lady Jaelithe went up against the Kolder in their own secret place, and closed *their* Gate through which the scourge had come upon us. And of this there has already been sung many songs.

But though the Kolder evil was gone, the stain lingered and Estcarp continued to gasp for life as her enemies, ringing her about, nibbled eternally at her tattered borders. This was a twilight world, for which would come no morning, and we were born into the dusk of life.

Our triple birth was without precedent among the Old Race. When our mother was brought to bed on the last day of the dying year, she sang warrior spells, determined that that one who would enter into life would be a fighter such as was needed in this dark hour. Thus came I, crying as if already all the sorrows of a dim and forbidding future shadowed me.

Yet my mother's labor was not at an end. And there was such concern for her that I was hurriedly tended and put to one side. Her travail continued through the hours, until it would seem that she and that other life, still within her, would depart through the last gate of all.

Then there came a stranger of the Ward Keep, a woman walking on her own two dusty feet. In the courtyard she lifted up her voice, saying she was one sent and that her mission lay with the Lady Jaelithe. By that time so great was my father's fear that he ordered her brought in.

From under her cloak she drew a sword, the blade of it bright in the light, a glittering, icy thing, cold with the burden of killing metal. Holding this before my mother's eyes, she began to chant, and from that moment it was as if all the anxious ones gathered in that chamber were bound with ties they could not break. But the Lady Jaelithe rose out of the sea of pain and haunted dreams which held her, and she too gave voice. Wild raving they thought those words of hers as she said:

"Warrior, sage, witch—three—one—I will this! Each a gift. Together—one and great—apart far less!"

And in the second hour of the new year there came forth my brother, and then my sister, close together as if they were linked by a tie. But so great was my mother's exhaustion that her life was feared for. The woman who had made the birth magic put aside the sword quickly and took up the children as if that was her full right—and, because of my mother's collapse, none disputed her.

Thus Anghart of the Falconer village became our nurse and foster mother and had the first shaping of us in this world. She was an exile from her people, since she had revolted against their harsh code and departed by night from their woman village. For the Falconers, those strange fighting men, had their own customs, unnatural in the eyes of the Old Race whose women hold great power and authority. So repugnant were these customs to the Witches of Estcarp that they had refused the Falconers settlement land when they had come, centuries earlier, from over seas. Thus now the Hold of the Falconers was in the high mountains, a no-man's land border country between Estcarp and Karsten.

Among this people the males dwelt apart, living only for war and raiding, having more affection and kinship with their scout hawks then they did with their women. The latter were quartered in valley villages, to which certain selected men went at seasons to establish that their race did not die out. But upon the birth of children there was a ruthless judging, and Anghart's newly born son had been slain, since he had a crippled foot. So she came to the South Keep, but why she chose that day and hour, and seemed to have foreknowledge of our mother's need, she never said. Nor did any choose to ask her, for to most in the Keep she turned a grim, closed face.

But to us she was warmth, and love, and the mother the Lady Jaelithe could not be. Since from the hour of the last birth my mother sank into a trance of sorts and thus she lay day after day, eating when food was put in her mouth, aware of nothing about her. And this passed for several months. My father appealed to the Witches, but in return he received only a cold message—that Jaelithe had seen fit to follow her own path always, and that they did not meddle in the matters of fate, nor could they reach one who had gone long and far down an alien way.

Upon this saying my father grew silent and grim in his turn. He led his Borderers out on wild forays, showing a love of steel play and bloodletting new to him. And they said to him that he was willfully seeking yet another road and that led to the Black Gate. Of us he took no note, save to ask from time to time how we fared—absently, as if our welfare was that of strangers, no real concern to him.

It was heading into another year when the Lady Jaelithe at last roused. Then she was still weak and slipped easily into sleep when overtired. Also she seemed shadowed, as if some unhappiness she could not name haunted her mind. At length this wore away and there was a lightsome time, if brief, when the Seneschal Koris and his wife, the Lady Loyse, came to South Keep at the waning of the year to make merry, since the almost ceaseless war had been brought to an uneasy truce and for the first time in years there was no flame nor fast riding along either border, neither north to face the wolves of Alizon nor south where the anarchy in Karsten was a constant boil and bubble of raid and counter-raid.

But that was only a short breathing space. For it was four months into the new year when the threat of Pagar came into being. Karsten had been a wide battle field for many lords and would-be rulers since Duke Yvian had been killed during the Kolder war. To that wracked duchy the Lady Loyse had a claim. Wedded by force—axe marriage—to the Duke, she had never ruled. But on his death she might have raised his standard. However, there was no tie between her and a country in which she had suffered much. Loving Koris, she had thankfully tossed away any rights over Karsten. And the policy of Estcarp, to hold and maintain the old kingdom, not to carry war to its neighbors, suited her well. Also Koris and Simon, both bolstering as well as they could the dwindling might of the Old Race, saw no advantage in embroilment aboard, but much gain in the anarchy which would keep one of their enemies employed elsewhere.

Now what they had forseen came to pass. Starting as a small holder in the far south, Pagar of Geen began to gather followers and establish himself, first as a lord of two southern provinces, then acclaimed by the men of the city of Kars of their own free will, the ruined merchants there willing to declare for anyone likely to reestablish peace. By the end of our birth year Pagar was strong enough to risk battle against a confederation of rivals. And four months later he was proclaimed Duke, even along the border.

He came to rule in a country devasted by the worst sort of war, a civil struggle. His followers were a motley and hard-to-control crew. Many were mercenaries, and the loot which had drawn them under his banner must now be replaced by wages or they would go elsewhere to plunder.

Thus Pagar did as my father and Koris had expected: he looked outside his borders for a cause to unite his followers and provide the means for rebuilding his duchy. And where he looked was north. Estcarp had always been feared. Yvian, under the suggestion of the Kolder, had out-lawed and massacred those of the Old Race who had founded Karsten in days so far distant that no man could name the date. They had died—hard—or they had fled, across the mountains to their kin. And behind they left a burden of guilt and fear. None in Karsten ever really believed that Estcarp would not some day move to avenge those deaths. Now Pagar need only play slightly on that emotion and he had a crusade to occupy his fighters and unite the duchy firmly behind him.

Still, Estcarp was a formidable foe and one Pagar desired to test somewhat before he committed himself. Not only were the Old Race dour and respected fighting men, but the Witches of Estcarp used the Power in ways no outsider could understand, and which were the more dreaded for that very reason. In addition there was a firm and unbreakable alliance between Estcarp and the Sulcarmen— those dreaded sea rovers who already had raided Alizon into a truce and a sullen licking of sore wounds. They were as ready to turn their serpent ships southward and bite along Karsten's open coast line, and that would arouse the merchants of Kars to rebellion.

So Pagar had to prepare his holy war quietly. Border raiding began that summer, but never in such strength that the Falconers and the Borderers my father commanded could not easily control. Yet many small raids, even though easily beaten back, can gnaw at the warding forces. A few men lost here, one or two there—the sum mounts and is a steady drain. As my father early knew.

Estcarp's answer was loosing of the Sulcar fleets. And that did give Pagar to think. Hostovrul gathered twenty ships, rode out a storm by spectacular seamanship, and broke the river patrol, to raid into Kars itself, with such success that he left the new Duke unsteady for another full year. And then there was an insurrection in the south whence Pagar had come, led by his own half-brother, to keep the Duke further engaged. Thus three years, maybe more, were won from the threat of chaos, and the twilight of Estcarp did not slide into night as quickly as the Old Race had feared.

During these years of maneuvering the three of us were taken from the fortress of our birth—but not to Es, for both our father and mother held aloof from the city where the Council reigned. The Lady Loyse established a home in a small manor-garth of Etsford, and welcomed us into her household. Anghart was still the center of our lives, and she made an acceptable alliance with the mistress of Etsford based on mutual regard and respect. For the Lady Loyse had adventured, disguised as a blank shield mercenary, into the heart of enemy territory when she and my mother had been ranged against all the might of Kars and Duke Yvian.

Upon her long delayed recovery the Lady Jaelithe assumed once more her duties with my father as vice-warder. Together they had control of the Power, not after the same fashion as the Witches, but in another way. And I know now that the Witches were both jealous and suspicious of the gift so shared, though it was used only for the good of the Old Race and Estcarp. The Wise Ones found such talent unnatural in a man and secretly always reckoned my mother the less because of her uniting with Simon. At this time the Council appeared to have no interest in us children. In fact their attitude might be more termed a deliberate ignoring of our existence. Kaththea was not subjected to examination for inherited Power talent as were all girls of the Old Race before they were six.

I do not remember my mother much from those years. She would descend upon the manor, trailed by fighters from the Border forces—of much greater interest to me, for my first crawl across the floor took me to lay a baby's hand on the polished hilt of a sword. Her visits were very few, my father's even less; they could not often be spared from the patrol along the south border. We turned to Anghart for all answers to childish problems, and held the Lady Loyse in affection. To our mother was given respect and awe, and our father had much the same recognition. He was not a man who was easy with children, I believe, and perhaps he unconsciously held against us the suffering our birth had caused his wife who was the one person he held extremely dear.

If we did not have a closeknit relationship with our parents, we made up for that with a tight bond among the three of us. Yet in nature we were different. As my mother had wished, I was first a warrior, that being my approach to life. Kemoc was a thinker—presented with any problem his was not the response of outright and immediate action, but rather a considered examination and inquiry into its nature. Very early he began his questions, and when he found no one could give him all the answers he wished, he strove to discover the learning which would.

Kaththea felt the deeper. She had a great oneness, not only with us, but things about us—animals, people, even the countryside. Oftentimes her instinct topped my force of action or Kemoc's considered reasoning.

I cannot remember the first time we realized that we, too, possessed a gift of the Power. We need not be together, or even miles close, to be in communication. And when the need was we seemed a single person—I the arms for action, Kemoc the brain, Kaththea the heart and controlled emotion. But some wariness kept us from revealing this to those about us. Though I do not doubt that Anghart was well aware of our so-knitted strength.

We were about six when Kemoc and I were given small, specially forged swords, dart guns suited to our child hands, and began the profession of arms which all of the Old Race must follow during this eventide. Our tutor was a Sulcarman, crippled in a sea fight, sent by our father to give us the best training possible. He was a master of most weapons, was Otkell, having been one of Hostovrul's officers during the raid on Kars. Though neither of us took to the use of the axe, to Otkell's disappointment, both Kemoc and I learned other weapon play with a rapidity which pleased our instructor; and he was not in any way easy with us.

It was during the summer of our twelfth year that we rode on our first foray. By that time Pagar had reduced his unruly duchy to order and was prepared once more to try his luck north. The Sulcar fleet was raiding Alizon, his agents must have reported that. So he sent flying columns north through the mountains, in simultaneous clawing attacks at five different places.

The Falconers took out one of these, the Borderers two more. But the remaining two bands made their way into valley land which the enemy had never reached before. Cut off from any retreat they fought like wild beasts, intent on inflicting all the damage they could before they were dragged down.

So it was that a handful of these madmen reached Es River and captured a boat, putting her crew to the sword. They came downstream with some cunning, perhaps in a very vain hope of reaching the sea. But the hunt was up and a warship was in position at the river's mouth to cut then off.

They beached their stolen boat not five miles from Etsford and the whole of the manpower from the farms around turned out in a hunt. Otkell refused to take us along, an order we took in ill part. But the small force he led was not an hour gone when Kaththea intercepted a message. It came so sharply into her mind that she held her head and cried out as she stood between us on the watch walk of the center tower. It was a Witch sending, not aimed at a girl child a few miles away, but for one of the trained Old Race. And a portion of its demand for speedy aid reached us in turn through our sister.

We did not question the rightness of our answer as we rode forth, having to take our horses by stealth. And there was no leaving Kaththea behind—not only was she our directional guide, but we three had become a larger one in that moment on the tower walk.

Three children rode out of Etsford. But we were not ordinary children as we worked our way across country and approached a place where the wild wolves from Karsten had holed up with a captive for bargaining. Battle fortune does exist. We say this captain or that is a "lucky" man, for he loses few men, and is to be found at the right place at the right moment. Some of this is strategy and skill, intelligence and training serving as extra weapons. But other men equally well trained and endowed are never so favored by seeming chance. Battle fortune rode with us that day. For we found the wolves' den, and we picked off the guards there—five of them, all trained and desperate fighters—so that a woman, bloodstained, bound, yet proud and unbending, came out alive.

Her gray robe we knew. But her searching stare, her compelling measurement made us uneasy, and in some manner broke the oneness of our tie. Then I realized that she had dismissed Kemoc and me, and her attention was focused on Kaththea, and by that direct study we were all threatened. And, young as I was, I knew we had no defense against this peril.

Otkell did not allow our breech of discipline to pass, in spite of our success. Kemoc and I bore body smarts which lasted a few days. But we were glad because the Witch was swiftly gone out of our lives again, having spent but a single night at Etsford.

It was only much later, when we had lost the first battle of our personal struggle, that we learned what had followed upon that visit—that the Witches had ordered Kaththea to their testing and that our parents had refused, and that the Council had had to accept that refusal for a time. Though they were not in any way defeated by it. For the Witches never believed in hasty action and were willing to make time their ally.

Time was to serve them so. Simon Tregarth put to sea two years later on a Sulcar ship, his purpose an inspection of certain islands reported newly fortified in a strange way by Alizon. There was a hint of possible Kolder revival there. Neither he nor his ship were heard from again.

Since we had known so little of our father, his loss made small change in our lives—until our mother came to Etsford. This time it was not for a short visit: she came with her personal escort to stay.

She spoke little, looked out overmuch—not on the country, but to that which we could not see. For some months she shut herself up for hours at a time in one of the tower rooms, accompanied by the Lady Loyse. And from such periods the Lady Loyse would emerge whitefaced and stumbling, as if she had been drained of vital energy, while my mother grew thinner, her features sharper, her gaze more abstracted.

Then one day she summoned the three of us into the tower room. There was a gloom in that place, even though three windows were open on a fine summer day. She gestured with a fingertip and curtains fell over two of those windows, as if the fabric obeyed her will, leaving open only that to the north. With a fingertip again she traced certain dimly-seen lines on the floor and they flared into flickering life, making a design. Then, without a word, she motioned us to stand on portions of that pattern while she tossed dried herbs on a small brazier. Smoke curled up and around to hide us each from the other. But in that moment we were instantly one again, as we had ever been when threatened.

Then—it is hard to set this into words that can be understood by those who have not experienced it—we were aimed, sent, as one might shoot a dart or strike with a sword. And in that shooting I lost all sense of time, or distance, or identity. There was a purpose and a will and in that I was swallowed up beyond any protesting.

Afterwards we stood again in that room, facing our mother—no longer a woman abstracted and remote, but alive. She held out her hands to us, and there were tears running down her sunken cheeks.

"As we gave you life," she said, "so have you returned that gift, oh, my children!"

She took a small vial from the table and threw its contents upon the now dying coals in the brazier.

There was a flash of fire and in that moved things. But the nature of them, or what they did, I could not say. They were gone again and I was blinking, no longer a part, but myself alone.

Now my mother no longer smiled, but was intent. And that intentness was no longer concentrated upon her own concerns, but upon the three of us.

"Thus it must be: I go my way, and you take another road. What I can do, I shall—believe that, my children! It is not the fault of any of us that our destiny is so riven apart. I am going to seek your father—for he still lives—elsewhere. You have another fate before you. Use what is bred in you and it shall be a sword which never breaks nor fails, a shield which will ever cover you. Perhaps, in the end, we shall find our separate roads are one after all. Which would be good fortune past all telling!"

II

It was thus that our mother rode out of our lives on a hot midsummer morning when the dust rose in yellow puffs under the hooves of the mounts and the sky was cloudless. We watched her go from the walk on the tower. Twice she looked back and up, and the last time she raised her hand in a warrior's salute—to which Kemoc and I made fitting return in formal fashion, the brilliant sun mirroring on the blades of our drawn swords. But Kaththea, between us, shivered as if chill fingers of an outseason wind touched her. And Kemoc's left hand sought hers, to cover it where fingers gripped the parapet.

"I saw him," she said, "when she drew upon us in the search—I saw him—all alone—there were rocks, tall rocks and curling water—" This time her shudder shook her whole thin frame.

"Where?" Kemoc demanded.

Our sister shook her head. "I cannot tell, but it was far—and more than distance of land and sea lies between."

"Not enough to keep her from the searching," I said as I sheathed my sword. There was a sense of loss in me, but who can measure the loss of what one has never had? My mother and father dwelt inwardly together in a world they had made their own, unlike most other husbands and wives I had noted. To them that world was complete and all others were interlopers. There was *no* Power, good or evil, which could hold the Lady Jaelithe from her present quest as long as breath was in her. And had we offered aid in her search, she would have put us aside.

"We are together." Kemoc had picked my thought out of my skull, as was common with us.

"For how long?" Again Kaththea shivered and we turned quickly to her, my hand again to weapon hilt, Kemoc's on her shoulder.

"You mean?" he asked, but I thought that I had the answer.

"Seeresses ride with warriors. You need not remain here when Otkell allows us to join the Borderers!"

"Seeresses!" she repeated with emphasis. Kemoc's hold on her grew tighter, and then I, too, understood.

"The Witches will not take you for training! Our parents forbade it."

"Our parents are no longer here to speak!" Kemoc flung at me.

Then fear claimed us. For the training of a Witch was not like a warrior's daily use of sword, dart gun, or axe. She went away from all those of her blood, to a distant place of mysteries, there to abide for years. When she returned she no longer recognized kin of blood, only kinship with those of her calling. If they took Kaththea from us to become one of their gray robed ranks she might be lost forever. And what Kemoc had said was very true—with Simon and the Lady Jaelithe gone, who remained who could put a strong barrier between our sister and the desires of the Council?

Thus from that hour our life lay under a shadow. And the fear strengthened the bond between us into a tight ring. We knew each other's feelings, though I had less skill than Kemoc and Kaththea. But days passed, and life continued as it always had. Since no fear remains sharp unless it is fed by new alarms, we relaxed.

We did not know then that our mother had wrought for us as best she could before she departed from Estcarp. For she went to Koris and had him swear on the Axe of Volt—that supernatural weapon only he could wield and which had come to him directly from the dead hand of one who might be less than a god but who had certainly been more than human—swear that he would protect us from the wiles of the Council. Thus he took oath and we lived at Etsford as always.

Years passed and now the raids from Karsten grew more continuous. Pagar returned to his old policy of wearing us down. He met a flat defeat in the spring of the year we counted seventeen winters behind us, the larger force he had sent going to their deaths in a pass. And in that battle Kemoc and I had a part, being numbered among the scouts who combed the ridges to harry fugitives. We found war to be a dark and ugly business, but our breed continued to survive so, and when one has no choice one turns to the sword.

It was mid-afternoon as we cantered along a trail when the summons came. Kaththea might have stood before me, crying out in terror. For though my eyes did not see her, yet her voice rang not only in my ears, but through my body. And I heard Kemoc shout, then his mount jostled mine as I also used spurs.

Our commander was Dermont, an exile from Karsten who had joined the Borderers when my father first organized that force. He reined around to front us. There was no expression on his dark face, but so efficiently did he block passage that even our determination was stayed.

"What do you?" he asked.

"We ride," I answered, and I knew that I would cut down even him, should he hold that barrier of man and horse against us. "It is a sending—our sister is in danger!"

His gaze searched my eyes, and he read the truth in what I said. Then he reined to the left, opening the way to us.

"Ride!" It was both permission and an order.

How much did he know of what chanced? If he was aware, he did not agree with it. And perchance he was willing to let us make our try, for, young as we were, we had not been the least of those who had followed him uncomplaining through hard days and weary nights.

Ride we did, twice swapping mounts in camps where we left the impression we rode on orders. Gallop, walk, gallop, doze in the saddle in turns during the walking. A haze of time passed—too much time. Then Etsford was a shadow in a wide expanse of fields where grain had been lately harvested. What we had feared most was not to be seen—there was no sign of raiders. Fire and sword had not bitten here. Yet we had no lightening of our burden.

Dimly, through the ringing in my ears, I heard the horn alert of the tower watchman as we spurred down the road, urging our weary mounts to a last burst of speed. We were white with dust but the House badge on the breasts of our surcoats could be read, and we had passed the spell barrier with no hurt, so they would know we were friends.

My horse stumbled as we came into the court and I struggled to free my stiff feet from the stirrups and dismount before he went to his knees. Kemoc was a little before me, already staggering on his two feet to the door of the Hall.

She was standing there, her two hands bracing her strong body so that she met us on her feet by one last effort of will. Not Kaththea, but Anghart. And at the look in her eyes Kemoc wavered to a halt, so that I charged into him, and we held to one another. My brother spoke first:

"She is gone—they have taken her!"

Anghart nodded—very slowly, as if the motion of her head was almost too hard an effort. Her long braids fell forward, their brown now heavily streaked with white. And her face!—she was an old woman, and a broken one, from whom all will to live had been torn. For torn it had been. This was a stroke of the Power; in that instant we both recognized it. Anghart had stood between her nursling and the will of a Witch, pitting her unaided human strength and energy against a force greater than any material weapon.

"She—is—gone—" Her words were without inflection, gray ghosts of speech from the mouth of death. "They have set a wall about her. To ride after—is—death."

We did not want to believe, but belief was forced upon us. The Witches had taken our sister and shut her off from us by a force which would kill spirit and body together, should we follow. Our deaths could avail Kaththea nothing. Kemoc clutched at my arm until his nails bit into my skin. I wanted to beat back at him, smash flesh and bone—tear—rend— Perhaps the physical weakness left from our long ride was our salvation at that moment. For when Kemoc flung his arm across his face with a terrible cry and collapsed against me, his weight bore us both to the ground.

Anghard died within the hour. I think that she had held on to life with her two hands because she waited for us. But before her spirit went forth, she spoke to us again, and, the first shock being past, those words had meaning and a certain small comfort to us.

"You are warriors." Her eyes went from Kemoc to me and then back to my brother's white and misery-ravaged face. "Those Wise Ones think of warriors only as force of action. They disdain them at heart. Now they will expect a storming of their gates for our dear one. But—give them outward acceptance now and they will, in time, believe in it."

"And in the meantime," Kemoc said bitterly, "they will work upon her, fashioning from Kaththea one of their nameless Women of Power!"

Anghart frowned. "Do you hold your sister so low, then? She is no small maid to be molded easily into their pattern. I think that these Witches shall find her far more than they expect, perhaps to their undoing. But this is not the hour—when they are expecting trouble—to give it to them."

There is this about warrior training: it gives one a measure of control. And since we had always looked to Anghart for wisdom from our childhood, we accepted what she told us now. But, though we accepted, we neither forgot nor forgave. In those hours we cut the remaining bonds which tied us in personal allegiance to the Council.

If at that moment it seemed lesser, there was more ill news. Koris of Gorm, he who had been all these years to most of Estcarp an indestructable buttress and support, lay in the south sorely wounded. To him had gone the Lady Loyse, thus opening the door for Kaththea's taking. So all the safe supports which had based our small world were at once swept away.

"What do we now?" Kemoc asked of me in the night hours when we had taken Anghart to her last bed of all, and then sat together in a shadow-cornered room, eating of food which had no taste.

"We go back—"

"To the troop? To defend those who have done this thing?"

"Something of that, but more of this, in the eyes of all we are green youths. As Anghart said, they will expect us to engage in some rash action and that they will be prepared to counter. But—"

His eyes were now agleam. "Do not say of yourself again, brother, that you do not think deeply. You are right, very right! We are but children in their eyes, and good children accept the dictates of their elders. So we play that role. Also—" He hesitated and then continued, "There is this—we can learn more of this trade they have bred us to—this use of arms against a pressing enemy—and in addition seek learning in other directions—"

"If you mean the Power, we are men, and they hold it is for the use of women only."

"True enough. But there is more than one kind of Power. Did our father not have his own version of it? The Witches could not deny that, though they would have liked to. All knowledge is not bound up in their own tight little package. Have you not heard of Lormt?"

At first the name meant nothing to me. And then I recalled a half-heard conversation between Dermont and one of the men who had been with him since he had fled Karsten. Lormt—a repository of records, ancient chronicles.

"But what have we to learn from the records of old families?"

Kemoc smiled. "There may be other material there of service to us. Kyllan," he spoke sharply, as one giving an order, "think of the east!"

I blinked. His command was foolish. East—what was east?—why should I think of the east? East—east—I hunched my shoulders, alerted by an odd tingle along the nerves. East— There was the north where lay Alizon ready to spring at our throats, and south where Karsten now worried our flanks, and west where lay the ocean roamed by Sulcar ships, with any number of islands and unknown lands beyond the horizon's rim, such as the land where Simon and Jaelithe had found the true Kolder nest. But to the east there was only a blank—nothing at all—

"And tell me the why of that!" Kemoc demanded. "This land has an eastern border too, but have you ever heard any speech of it? Think, now—what lies to the east?"

I closed my eyes to picture a map of Estcarp as I had seen it many times in use in the field. Mountains—?

"Mountains?" I repeated hesitantly.

"And beyond those?"

"Only mountains, on every map nothing else!" I was certain now.

"Why?"

Why? He was very right. He had maps showing far north, far south, beyond our boundaries, in every detail. We had ocean charts drawn by the Sulcar. We had nothing—nothing at all for the east. And that very absence of fact was noteworthy.

"They cannot even think of the east," Kemoc continued.

"What!"

"It is very true. Question anyone, over a map, of the east. They cannot discuss it."

"*Will* not, maybe. But—"

"No." Kemoc was definite. "*Cannot.* They are mind-blocked against the east. I am ready to swear to that."

"Then—but why?"

"That we must learn. Do you not see, Kyllan, we cannot stay in Estcarp—not if we free Kaththea. The Witches will never allow her out of their hold willingly. And where could we go? Alizon or Karsten would welcome us—as prisoners. The House of Tregarth is too well known. And the Sulcarmen would not aid us when the Witches were our enemies. But suppose we vanish into a country or place they refuse to admit has existence—"

"Yes!"

But it was so perfect an answer that I mistrusted it. Behind the smiling face of fortune often hides the cracked countenance of ill luck.

"If there is a block in their minds, there is a reason for it, a very good one."

"Which I do not deny. It is up to us to discover what it is, and why, and if it can be turned to our purpose."

"But if them, why not us—?" I began, and then answered my question with another: "Because of our half-blood?"

"I think so. Let us go to Lormt and perhaps we'll have more than one explanation."

I got to my feet. Suddenly the need to do something, for positive action, was plain to me. "And how do we manage that? Do you suppose that the Council will allow us to roam about Estcarp under the circumstances? I thought you had agreed that we should be obedient, return to the company, act as if we acknowledged defeat."

Kemoc sighed. "Do you not find it hard to be young, brother?" he asked. "Of course we shall be watched. We do not know how much they suspect that we are bound to Kaththea in thought contact. Surely our bolting here at her message will tell them something of that. I—I have not reached her since." He did not look to me to see if I could give a different report. It had never been put into words with us but we all knew that between Kemoc and Kaththea the communication ties were far more secure; it was as if the time gap between our births had set me a little apart from the other two.

"Kemoc—the tower room! Where our mother—" Remembrance of that time when I had been a part of a questing was not good, but I would will myself into that joyfully if it would avail us now. Only he was already shaking his head.

"Our mother was an adept, with years of use of the full Power behind her. We have not the skill, the knowledge, the strength for that road, not now. But what we have we shall build upon. As for Lormt—well, I believe that willing can also open gates. Perhaps not yet—but there will be a road to Lormt for us."

Was it a flash of foreknowledge which made me correct him?

"For you. Lormt is yours, I am sure, Kemoc."

We did not tarry at Etsford; there was nothing any longer to hold us. Otkell had commanded the small force to escort the Lady Loyse to South Keep. And not one among the handful of retainers left there had the authority or reason to stay us when we announced our return to our company. But as we rode the next day we were at work inwardly—striving to communicate, to speak by thought, with a determination we had never really given to such exercises before. Without guidance or training we struggled to strengthen what talent we had.

And during the months which followed we kept at that task which was hidden from our camp fellows. But hide it we were sure we must. No effort on our part ever awoke a response from Kaththea, though we were informed that she had entered the completely cloistered dwelling of the novices of the Power.

Some side issues of our talent did manifest themselves. Kemoc discovered that his will, applied to learning, could implant much in his memory from a single listening, or sighting, and that he might pick out of other minds such information. The questioning of prisoners was increasingly left to him. Dermont may have guessed the reason for Kemoc's success in that direction, but he did not comment upon it.

While I had no such contribution to make to our mountain missions, I was aware, slowly, of another reach of whatever lay within me that was an inheritance from my parents. And this took the form of kinship with animals. Horses I knew probably as no other warrior of the forces. The wild things of the wilderness I could draw to me or send on their way merely by concentrating upon them. The mastery of horses I put to good use, but the other was not a matter of much moment.

As to Kemoc's desire to get to Lormt, there seemed to be no way to achieve that. The scrimmages along the border grew in intensity and we were absorbed into the guerrilla tactics. As the outlook for Estcarp grew darker we were all aware that it was only a matter of time before we would be fugitives in an overrun land. Koris did not recover swiftly from his wounding, and when he did, he was a maimed man, unable to again raise Valt's Axe. We heard the story of how he made a mysterious trip into the sea cliffs of the south and returned thereafter without his superweapon. From that moment his luck was left behind also, and his men suffered one defeat upon the heels of another.

For months Pagar played with us, as if he did not want to quite deliver the finishing blow, but amused himself in this feinting. There was talk of Sulcar ships departing with some of the Old Race aboard. Yet I am sure that what really delayed the final push of our enemies was their age-old fear of the Power and what might chance should the Witches loose on them all that might be so aimed. For no one, even among us, *knew* exactly what the Power might do if a whole nation of Witches willed it into action. It might burn out Estcarp, but it could also take with it the rest of our world.

It was at the beginning of the second year after Kaththea was taken that the road to Lormt opened for Kemoc, but not in a fashion we would have wished. He was trapped in an ambush and his right hand and arm so mangled that it would be long before he could freely use them, if ever he did again. As we sat together before they took him away for treatment we had our last words together:

"Healing is fast, if willed. And add your will to mine, Brother," he told me briskly, though his eyes were pain shadowed. "I shall heal as swiftly as I can, and then—"

He need put no more into words.

"Time may turn against us," I warned him. "Karsten can press home at anytime. Do we have even hours left?"

"I will not think of that. What I do, you shall know! I cannot believe that this chance shall be denied us!"

I was not alone as I had feared I might be when Kemoc was borne off slung in a horse litter. We had wrought well, for he was in my mind, even as I was in his. And the distance between us only thinned that bond a little, making us expend more effort. I knew when he went to Lormt. Then he warned me that we must cut contact, unless the need was great, for at Lormt he found or detected influences which tasted of the Power and these he thought perhaps a danger.

Then—for months—silence.

Still I rode with the Borderers, and now, young as I was, I headed my own small command. Uniting us was a comradeship forged of danger, and I had my friends. But still I always knew that that other bond was the stronger, and, should either Kaththea or Kemoc summon, I would be ahorse and gone, uncaring. Fearing just that, I began to train my own replacement and did not allow myself to become too involved in any matter beyond my regular duties. I fought, skulked, waited . . . and it seemed that the waiting was sometimes longer than my endurance.

III

$\mathcal{W}$e were as lean and vicious as those hounds the Riders of Alizon trained for the hunting of men, and, like those fleet beasts, we coursed through the narrow valleys and over mountains, faintly surprised each night that we still sat the saddle or tramped the narrow trails of the heights, and again in the morning when we awoke in our concealed camps, able to greet the dawn alive.

If Alizon and Karsten had made common cause, as all these years we had looked to them to do, Estcarp would have been cracked, crunched, and swallowed up. But it would seem that Pagar had no wish to drink cup-brotherhood with Facellian of Alizon—the why might stem from many causes. Perhaps the heart of those was some use of the Power which we did not detect. For we *did* know that the Witches of the Council had their own way of dealing with a few men, whereas the Power weakened and lost control when it was spread too thin, or when it was put to a prolonged use. For such an effort needed the life force of many adepts working together, and would leave them drained for a perilous space thereafter.

However, it was that very act which they determined upon in the late summer of the second year after Kemoc left us. Orders came by sending to every post, no matter how remote, or how mobile the men who held it. And rumor followed directly behind, as is the way in armies. We were to withdraw, out of the mountains, down from the foothills, gather onto the plains of Estcarp, leaving the ground we had defended so long bare of all who wore Estcarp's badge.

To the outer eye it was the folly of one wit-struck, but rumor had it that we were setting a trap, such a trap as our world had not seen—that the Witches, alarmed at the constant drain of our manpower in these endless engagements, were to concentrate their forces in a gamble which would either teach Pagar a lesson he would never forget, or let us all go down to a single defeat in place of this slow bloodletting.

But we were also ordered to retreat with skulker's skill so that it would be a little time before their raiders would discover that the mountains were empty, the passes free. Thus we flitted back, company by company, squad by squad, with a screen of rear guard behind us. And it was a week or more of redeployment before the Old Race were all in the low lands.

Pagar's men were cautious at first. Too many times had they been slashed in ambushes and attacks. But they scouted, they explored, and then they began to come. A Sulcar fleet gathered in the great bay into which emptied the Es River, some of the ships anchoring even at haunted Gorm, where no man lived unless under orders because of the terror that the Kolders had wrought there, others in the very river mouth. And the tale was that should our present plan fail, the remnants of the Old Race, those who could make it, would be taken aboard that fleet for a last escape by sea.

But that story, we thought, was only for the ears of any spies Alizon and Karsten might have among us. For this move was one born of extreme desperation, and we did not believe the Council were fools. Perhaps the story did bring the Karsten Army at a faster trot via the cleared passes, for they began to pour up into the hills and mountains in an unending river of fighting men.

Chance led my own company to within a few miles of Etsford, and we built our fire and set up a picket line in the later afternoon. The horses were restless, and as I walked among them, striving to sense the reason for their nervousness, I felt it also—a hovering feeling, perhaps not of doom, but of gathering pressure, of a juggling of the balance of nature. So that which was right and proper was now askew, and growing more so by the second, a sucking out of the land and those on it, man and animal, of some inner strength—

An ingathering! Out of nowhere came that thought and I knew it for the truth. That which was the life of Estcarp itself was being drawn in upon some central core—readied—

I reached the horses with what quieting influence I had, but I was very aware now of that sucking. No bird sound broke the oppressive silence, not a leaf or blade of grass moved under any touch of wind, and the heat was a heavy, sullen cover over us. Through that dead calm of waiting, perhaps the more acute because of it, flashed an alert to strike me like a Karstenian dart.

—Kyllan—Etsford—now!

That unspoken summons was the same forceful call for help as the cry from Kaththea had been years earlier. I swung bareback on the horse I held lightly by the mane, jerked free his picket rope. Then I was riding, at a gallop, to the manor which had been our home. There was shouting behind, but I did not look back. I sent a thought ahead:

Kemoc—what is it?

Come! Imperative, no explanation.

The sense of deadening, of withdrawal, held about me as we pounded down the road. Nothing moved in all that land save ourselves, and it was wrong. Yet that wrongness was outside my private concern and I would not yield to it.

There was the watch tower of the manor, but no flag hung limp in the stifling air. I could sight no sentry manning the walk, nor any sign of life about the walls. Then I faced a gate ajar enough to make entrance for a single rider.

Kemoc awaited me in the door of the hall as Anghart had done on the other day. But he was not Power blasted, half dying; he was vividly alive. So much so that his life force was fire, battling against the strangeness of the day and hour, so that just looking upon him I was a man who, facing his enemy alone, hears the battle cry of a comrade coming swiftly to share shields. There was no need for speech either of lip or mind. We—how shall I say it?—flowed together in a way past describing, and that which had been cut apart was partially healed. But only partially—for there was that third portion still lacking.

"In time—" He motioned towards the interior of the hall.

I loosed the horse and it trotted for the stable as if a groom were leading it by the reins. Then we were under the roof of Etsford once more. It was now an empty place, all those small things which marked daily living gone. I knew that the Lady Loyse now shared quarters with Koris in a border keep. Yet I looked about me, somehow seeking all that had once been ours.

There was a bench by the end of the great table and there Kemoc had put our food, traveler's cakes, and fruit from manor trees. But I did not hunger for that, and for my other hunger I had some appeasement.

"It has been a long time," my brother spoke aloud. "To find a key for such a lock takes searching."

I did not need to ask had he been successful: his triumph shone in his eyes.

"Tonight the Witches make their move against Karsten." Kemoc strode back and forth as if he could not sit still, though I dropped upon the bench, the oppression of the air making me feel even more drained.

"And in three days"—he spun around to face me—"they would set the Witch oath on Kaththea!"

My breath came out in a hiss, not unlike the first battle challenge of one of the high snow cats. This was the point of no return. Either she was brought forth from whatever bonds they had laid upon her before that hour, or she would be absorbed into their whole and lost to us.

"You have a plan." I did not make a question of that.

He shrugged. "As good a one as we shall ever have, or so I think. We shall take her forth from the Place of Wisdom and ride—east!"

Simple words, but the action they evoked was another thing. To get a selected one out of the Place of Wisdom was as great a feat as the walking into Kars to bring out Pagar.

As I thought that, Kemoc smiled. He brought up his hand between us. There was a ridge of scar red and rough across its surface and when he tried to flex his fingers, two of them remained stiff and outthrust.

"This was my key to Lormt; I used it well. Also I have used what lies here— to some purpose." He tapped those stiffened fingers against his forehead where the black hair we three shared fell in an unruly curling lock. "There was knowledge at Lormt, very old, veiled in much legend, but I scraped it bare. We shall have such a bolt hole for escape as they will not dream we dare use. As for the Place of Wisdom—"

I smiled then, without humor. "Yes? What is your answer to the safeguards set about that? It will not matter who or what we are, if we are taken within a mile of that without authorization. And it is said that the guards employed are not men to be countered with any weapon we know."

"Do not be too sure of that, brother. The guards may not be men—in that, I believe you speak the truth. But neither are we weaponless. And tomorrow those guards may not be as great as they have been in all other years. You know what will happen in the hours of dark tonight?"

"The Council will move to war—"

"Yes, but how? I tell you, they attempt now the greatest use of the Power that has been tried in generations. They return to what they did once before—in the east!"

"In the east? And that?"

"They will make the moutains to walk, and the land itself answer their will. It is their final throw in the battle against extinction."

"But—can they do that?" The Power could create illusions; it could further communications; it could kill—within narrow range. But that it could accomplish what Kemoc suggested, as if he were assured of its success, I did not quite believe.

"They did it once, and they will try again. But to do so they must build up such a reserve of energy as will sap their resources for some time. I would not wonder if some of them die. Perhaps few may live past the in-gathering and channeling of such force. Thus all the guards they have put on their secret places will be drained and we can win past them."

"You say they did this once in the east?"

"Yes." He had gone back to his striding. "The Old Race were not born in Estcarp—they came across the moutains, or from that direction, so many lifetimes ago that there is no true reckoning. They fled some danger there, and behind them the Power raised mountains, altered the land, walled them away. Then there was a block in their minds, nurtured for some generations until it became an integral part of the race. Tell me, have you found anyone who can speak of the east?"

I had never dared.

Since Kemoc's first uncovering of the puzzle, I had never dared press that too strongly among the Borderers, for fear of arousing suspicion. But it was true, no one ever spoke of the east and should I in devious ways lead to that subject they were as blank of thoughts as if that point of the compass had no existence.

"If what they fled was so terrible that they must take such precautions—" I began.

"Dare we face it now? A thousand years or more lies between that time and now. The Old Race are not what they were then. Any fire burns very low and finally to extinction. I know this, that the three of us will be hunted with greater fury than any Karstenian spy or Alizon Rider, more than any Kolder, if any such still live in this time and world. But not one of them will follow us east."

"We are half of the Old Race—can we break this block to take the trail?"

"That we shall not know until we try. But we can think of it and talk of it, as they cannot. Why, I discovered at Lormt that even the keeper of the old archives did not believe those significant legends which existed. He was not aware of scrolls I consulted, even when I had them spread in plain sight."

Kemoc was convincing. And reckless as the plan was, it was the only one. But there were miles between us and the Place of Wisdom; we had better be on our way. I said as much.

"I have five mounts of the Torgian breed," he replied. "Two here and ready, three others hidden for our last lap of the escape."

He mind-read my astonishment and respect, and laughed. "Oh, it took some doing. They were bought separately over a year's time under other names."

"But how could you know this chance would come?"

"I did not. But I believed that we would have some chance, and I was to be ready for it. You are right, brother: it is time to mount and ride—before the lash of the fury the Wise Women raise may snap back at us."

Torgian horses are from the high moors bordering on the secret marshes of Tor. They are noted for both speed and endurance, a coupling of qualities not always found in the same animal. And they are so highly prized that to gather five of them was a feat I had not thought possible for any individual. For most of them were kept under the control of the Seneschal himself. They were not much to look at, being usually dun colored, with dark manes and coats which did not take a gloss no matter how carefully they were groomed. But for heart, stamina and speed they had no match.

Kemoc had them both saddled with those light saddles used by anti-raider patrols along the seashore. But they were affected by the general eeriness of this night, dancing a little as we swung up, which was not their usual manner. We walked them out across the courtyard and beyond the wall. The sun was almost down, but the sky it bannered held a gathering of purple-black clouds in odd shapes, and these solidified into a threatening band of duskiness . . . while the land beneath lay in the same frightening silence.

My brother had left nothing to chance, which included his having scouted the fastest route. Yet this night even Torgian horses could not keep a swift pace. It was as if we rode through knee-deep, ever-shifting sand which sucked each hoof as it was placed, keeping us to a bare trot when every nerve demanded a full gallop. The clouds which had overshadowed the sunset thickened into a cover through which neither star nor moon shone.

And now a weird embellishment was added to the landscape. I had once ridden along the Tor marsh and seen those eerie lights native to that forbidden country glow and dim over its mist-ridden surface. Now such wan gleams began to touch here and there about us—on the tip of a tree branch, the crown of a bush, along a vine wreathing a wall. The very alienness heightened the general apprehension which strove to overwhelm us.

Our sense of anticipation grew moment by moment. And the Torgians reacted to it, snorting and rearing. I called to Kemoc:

"If we force them on now, they will panic!"

I had been trying to hold them under mental control for the past half mile, but I could do it no longer. We dropped out of our saddles, and I stood between the two mounts, one hand on each strong neck, striving with all I possessed to keep them from bolting. Then Kemoc's mind joined with mine, giving me added assistance, and the horses, still snorting, their eyes rolling, foam in sticky strings about their jaws, trembled but stood firm.

While I was so concentrating upon that task I had not seen beyond, and now I was shocked by a sharp flash of fire across the sky. There was, in answer, an ominous grumbling unlike any natural thunder I had ever heard before. And it was not born in the sky above, but out of the ground under us, for that shuddered. The horses screamed, but they did not try to bolt. They crowded under my hold even as I clung to them, dimly feeling in that contact an anchor in a world gone mad.

Those wan lights sprinkled here and there flamed higher, sent sharp points of pallid radiance skyward. Again the crack of lightning, a reply from the earth under us. A long moment of utter silence, then fury such as no man could imagine broke over and around us.

The earth heaved in long rolls, as if under its once stable surface waves moved towards the southern highlands. Wind which had been missing all day burst into frantic life, whipping the candled trees and bushes, tearing the air from our nostrils. One could not fight this—one lost his very identity in such an alien storm. We could only endure and hope, very faintly hope, that we could outlast the raving elements of earth, fire, air, and then water. For there was rain—or could you truly name such stinging lashes of water rain?

If the force of that storm drove us nearly witless, what must it have been like in those heights where it was brought to a climax? Mountains walked that night, lost themselves in vast waves of earth which ate away their sides, changed lowlands to highlands, and reversed the process by quake, slide, every violent action that could be evoked. The barrier formed by nature between Estcarp and Karsten, which we had kept fortified for years, was wrung, squeezed, wrought by a force which was initiated by human will, and once begun there was no altering of that destructive pattern.

Mind to mind, hand to hand, Kemoc and I made one during that terror. Afterwards we could piece together but a little of the night. Truly it was the end of a world—hearing and sight were soon torn from us, touch only remained and we clung to that sense with a fierce intensity, lest, losing it, we might lose all else, including that which made us what we were.

There was an end—though we had not dared to hope there could ever be. Dark as the matted clouds were over us, still there was light, gray as the tree candles, yet it was a light of the day rather than the weird glow of the storm. We still stood on the road, Kemoc and I and the horses, as if we had been frozen so amid the wild breakage of nature. The ground was solid under our feet, and a measure of sanity had returned, so that our minds might crawl slowly out of the hiding holes we had burrowed within ourselves.

Surprisingly, there was little storm wrack about us. A few branches down, the surface of the road wet and shining. As one we looked to the south. There the clouds were still thick, no gray relieved their night black, and now and again I thought I still saw the spark of lightning.

"What—?" Kemoc began, and then shook his head.

We did not question that the Council had used the Power as never before had it been done in Estcarp. I had very little doubt that Pagar was at last stopped. To be caught in the mountains during that!

I smoothed the wet, tangled mane of my mount. He snorted, stamped, waking out of some ill dream. As I got to saddle I could only marvel at our survival, which still seemed like a miracle.

Kemoc had also mounted.

This is our hour!

Mind contact seemed proper, as if whatever we attempted now might awaken some of the force not yet exhausted. We gave the Torgians light rein and this time they broke into their normal, country-covering pace. The day lightened and suddenly a bird broke the cloak of silence with a questioning note. All the pressure and drain had vanished; we were freed and the road was before us, with time now our worst enemy.

From the main highway Kemoc swung off along a lesser way, and here the debris of the storm slowed our pace. But we kept going, speeding up wherever we had an open space.

Whether we went by obscure paths, or whether the whole of Estcarp lay exhausted from shock that day, we did not know. But we saw no one, not even in the fields about the isolated farms. We might have ridden through a deserted country. And thus fortune favored us.

At nightfall we reached the farmstead with signs of long neglect where we could eat. Turning the Torgians into pasture, we saddled their three fellows Kemoc had left in waiting there. Then we took turns at a quick snatch of sleep. The moon was well up, not blanketed this time, when Kemoc's touch awakened me.

"This is *the* hour," he half-whispered.

And later, as we slid from the saddles and looked down into a hollow where a grove surrounded an age-darkened building, he did not have to add:

"This is the Place!"

IV

The longer I studied the building in the cup and its surroundings, the more I was conscious of a strange shifting, a rippling—as if between it and us hung a nearly invisible curtain. Distortion of shadow and light, of which I could not quite be certain, blurred a tree, elongated a bush, made even stone waver and move. Yet in another instant all was clear again.

Kemoc held out his maimed hand and my fingers closed about it. Instantly I was drawn into his mind, with an intensity I had not before known. He launched a probe, straight through all that moon and night-cloaked scene, down into the heart of the Place itself.

There was resistance, a wall as defensive to our attack as might be the stronghold of Es to the prick of a single dart gun. Kemoc withdrew speedily, only to launch for a second time his invisible spear, this time with more force, enough to make me gasp as it drained energy from me in one great gulp.

This time we hit that wall, yes, but we went through it, straight on. And then— It was like throwing a very dry branch on a fire—a blaze, fierce, welcoming, rejoicing, feeding—Kaththea! If I had ever faintly believed during the hours we had been riding that she might be changed, that perhaps she would not welcome our interference—I need not have. This was recognition, welcome, a wild desire to be free, all in one. Then, after that first moment of reply, swift apprehension and warning.

She could not give us any accurate idea of which lay between us, other than what we could see for ourselves. But that there were guards, and not human warriors, she knew. Also she dared not move to meet us, and warned off any contact by mind, lest those warders be alarmed. Thus she abruptly broke our thread of communication.

"So be it," Kemoc said softly.

I broke his hold, my hand reaching for sword hilt. Yet I knew that steel would have no part in any fight we faced this night.

"To the left, passing under the trees, then a quick run for the wall at that point—" My scouting knowledge took over, seeing each feature of that oddly fluid ground which could be put to our use.

"Yes. . . ."

Kemoc allowed me the lead, deferring to my scout craft. But he was no tyro at this game either, and we flitted down the slope with all the skill we could summon. I discovered that to glance ahead quickly and then away after a single second or so of regard cleared my sight, made that wavering less distracting.

We reached the edge of the wood and the outer defense of the Place fronted us. It was as if we had run full face into a rampart of glass. To the sight there was nothing, not even anything to touch when I struck out—but we could not stir a step ahead.

"Mind—think it away!" Kemoc said, not as if to me, but in self-encouragement.

It was hard to make that switch, from action of body to that of mind. But I willed myself forward, told myself that there was no wall, nothing but the earth, the trees growing out of it, the night—even if that night was nowhere as empty as it seemed.

Slowly we advanced, shoving with our wills against the barrier. I shall always believe that Kemoc was right about the effort of mountain turning exhausting the Power. For suddenly that invisible wall gave way, as a dam might suddenly burst agape before the pressure of a flood force. We went forward a few paces at a stumbling run.

"Only the first—"

I did not need that warning from Kemoc. Any defenses set about this heart center of Power would be the most intricate and best known to the Witches. To cheer when one has made a first small assault into a minor victory would be folly indeed.

There was movement among the trees. Again my hand went to weapon hilt. This was tangible—I could see the glint of moonlight on metal, and hear the footsteps of those who came.

Borderers! Here—? The hawk-crested helmet of a Falconer, the winged one of a Sulcarman, our own smooth caps—And then, where faces showed at all beneath that varied headgear they began to glow palely, making plain the features.

Dermont, Jorth, Nikon—I knew these every one, had ridden with them, shared shields in hot, quick attacks, lain beside them at countless camp fires. Yet now they all turned to me grim faces set with aversion, loathing, and from them came a wave of hatred and disgust, naming me traitor, back fighter. In me flowered the belief that they were right, that it was fit duty for them to cut me down as I stood, so vile a thing had I become. My hand dropped from my sword and I wanted to kneel before them in the dust and—

Kyllan!

Through the wave of guilt and shame rising to drown me that cry cut as might the bow of a serpent ship. Logic and reason battled emotion. They were *not* there, all these comrades-in-arms, judging me to my death. And I was not what they judged me. Though the belief was a smothering weight, I fought it, again willing it away with the same determination as that with which I had fought the invisible wall.

Dermont was before me. The glitter in his eyes was righteous rage, and his dart gun was aimed straight at my throat. But—Dermont was *not* there—he had no place—he was rightfully a tree, a bush, distorted by my own mind which the Power turned against me. I saw the small jerk of his gun as he fired. He *was not* there!

There was no prick of dart—no line of men—no shine of moon on metal! I heard a small, smothered sound from Kemoc.

"So passes their second defense." But his voice was as shaken as I felt.

We went on. I wondered how those guardians had known enough of us to front me with the phantoms of just those men. Then Kemoc laughed, startling me to hear it in that time and place.

"Do you not see, brother?" He had picked the question out of my mind to answer in words. "They merely supply the impulse, you the actors for its carrying out."

I was irritated that I had not realized that as quickly as he. Hallucinations were the stock in trade of the Witches, and hallucinations grow from seed in a man's own brain.

We were under the real walls, honest stone; we could touch and feel the darkness. I wondered at the fact that there had been no more assaults against us.

"They cannot be so easily conquered."

Again Kemoc laughed. "I knew you would not underrate them, Kyllan. The worst should still lie before us."

I stood face against the wall while Kemoc mounted my shoulder and climbed to the top. Then with a hand hold and a pull from his cloak I joined him. We crouched there, looking down into the garden. One side was the wall on which we balanced, the other three sides the building. There was a stillness there, too, a waiting. Yet in the moonlight we could see that the garden was a very fair one.

A fountain played, with small musical sounds, to feed an oval pool, and the fragrance of flowers and scented herbs arose about us. Scent—my mind caught at that: there were herbs the aroma of which could stupefy or drug a man, leaving him open to control by another's desire. I was wary of those flowers.

"I do not think so." Again Kemoc answered my thought. "This is their own dwelling, where they train for the Power. They dare not, for their own safety, play such tricks here." Deliberately he bent his head, drawing in deep breaths, as if testing.

"No—that we do not have to fear." He dropped to the ground and I followed, willing at this time to take such reassurance. But where in that dark bulk of building could we find Kaththea, without arousing all who dwelt there?

"Could we summon her?"

"No!" Kemoc's voice crackled with anger. "No summonings here—they would know of it instantly. That, too, is one of their tools, and they would react to it."

But he seemed as uncertain of the next move as was I. There was the building, utterly dark. And it held rooms we could not number, nor dared we explore them. Now—

Movement again, a shadow which was lighter than the pool of dark marking a door across from which we stood. I froze in an old night fighting trick, using immobility for a type of concealment. Someone was coming into the garden, walking with quiet assurance, obviously not expecting any trouble.

Only great good fortune kept me from speech as she moved into the open moonlight. Dark hair, lying in long, loose strands about her shoulders, her face upraised to the light as if she wished her features clearly seen. A girl's face, yet older, marked now by experience such as she had not known when last I had seen her. Kaththea had solved our riddle—she was coming to meet us!

Kemoc started forward, his hands outstretched. It was my turn to know—to guess—I caught him back. All my scout's instincts rebelled against his smooth solution. Dermont I had seen, and now Kaththea—and she might be no more true than that other. Was she not in our minds, to be easily summoned out?

She smiled and her beauty was such as to catch a man's heart. Slender, tall, her silken black hair in vivid contrast to her pale skin, her body moving with the grace of one who makes walking a formal dance. She held out her hands, her eyes alight, her welcome so plain and warm.

Kemoc pushed at my hold. He did not look at me; his attention was all hers.

"Kemoc!" Her voice was very low, hardly more than a whisper, singing in welcome, longing, joy. . . .

Yet still I held him fast, and he swung in my hold, his eyes angry.

"Kaththea! Let me go, Kyllan!"

"Kaththea—perhaps." I do not know what guiding prudence held me to that small particle of disbelief. But either he did not hear, or did not wish to understand.

She was close now, and flowers bent their heads as the hem of her gray robe brushed them. But so had I heard the jingle of metal and the sound of footsteps that were not back in the woods. How could I provide a test which would prove this mirage or truth?

"Kemoc—" Again that half whisper. Yet I was here also. Always there had been that tighter bond between the two of them, yet now her eyes were only for him, she spoke only his name—she did not seem to see me. Why?

"Kaththea?" Suiting my own voice to her low tone, I made her name into a question.

Her eyes did not falter; she never looked to me nor seemed to know I was there. At that moment Kemoc twisted out of my grip, and his went out to catch hers, pulling her to him in a quick embrace. Over his shoulder her eyes looked into mine, still unseeing, and her lips curved in the same set smile.

My questioning had become certainty. If this was a woman and not hallucination, she was playing a game. Yet when we had sought my sister by mind she had been welcoming. And I could not believe that the emotion we had met in that brief contact had been a lie. Could one lie with thoughts? I was sure I could not, though what the Witches might be able to accomplish I had no idea.

"Come!" His arm about her waist Kemoc was pushing her before him toward the wall. I moved—this might be a mistake, but better to learn now when we could retrieve our errors.

"Kemoc, listen!" My grip on his shoulder was no light one this time, and I had the greater strength, which I was willing to use.

He struggled for his freedom, dropping his hold on the girl. And his anger was growing with a rapidity which was not normal.

"I do not think this is Kaththea." I said slowly, with all the emphasis I could give to my words. And she just stood there, still smiling, her attention on him as if I were invisible.

"Kemoc—" His name with the same inflection, no word of protest to me.

"You are mad!" My brother's face was white with anger. He was a man bewitched.

Bewitched! Could I reach him with sense now—in time? I brought his arm up behind his back in a lock and held him so, then pulled him around to face the smiling girl. So holding him in spite of his struggles, I spoke again into his ear.

"Look at her, man! Look at her very well!"

He could not free himself, and look he did. Slowly he stopped struggling, and I hoped my fight won. Kaththea, smiling, undisturbed, now and again uttering his name as if she had only that one word to speak.

"What—what is she?"

I loosed him when he asked that. He knew now, was ready to accept the truth. But what *was* the truth? At our discovery she had not vanished away as had the warriors. I touched her arm—that was flesh beneath my fingers, warm, apparently living. So real a hallucination was beyond any I had seen before.

"I do not know what she is—save she is not who we seek here."

"If we had taken her and gone—" Kemoc paused.

"Yes. That would have served their purposes very well. But if this is counterfeit; where is the real?"

It was as if Kemoc had been shocked into inspired thinking by the closeness of his error.

"This—this one came from there." He pointed to the doorway. "Thus in the opposite direction lies, I think, what we seek."

He sounded too sure, yet I had no better reason or direction in which to look.

"Kemoc—" Her hands were out again. She was watching him and edging to the wall, subtly urging him to that way of escape.

He shivered, drew away. "Kyllan, hurry—we have to hurry!"

Turning his back on her, my brother ran towards the building, and I followed, fearing that any moment a cry of alarm would be voiced behind us, that the surrogate for our sister would utter a warning.

There was another door, and Kemoc, a little before me, put his hand to it. I expected bolts or bars and wondered how we could deal with such. But the panel swung inward readily enough and Kemoc peered into the dark.

"Hold to my belt," he ordered. And there was such certainty in his voice that I obeyed. So linked, we moved into a dark which was complete.

Yet Kemoc walked with quick sure steps, as if he could see every foot of the way. My shoulder brushed against the side of another doorway. Kemoc turned to the left. I felt about with my other hand, touched a surface not too far away, and ran fingertips along it as we moved. A hallway, I thought.

Then Kemoc halted, turned sharply to the right, and there was the sound of another door opening. Sudden light, gray and dim, but light. We stood on the threshold of a small, cell-like room, I looking over Kemoc's shoulder. On the edge of a narrow bed she sat, waiting for us.

There was none of the serene, smiling, untroubled beauty that the girl in the garden had worn. Experience showed on this girl's face also, but with it anxiety, strain, a wearing down of the body by the spirit. Beauty, too, but a beauty which was worn unconsciously and not as a weapon. Her lips parted, formed two names silently. Then Kaththea was on her feet, running to us, a hand for each.

"Haste, oh, haste!" Her voice was the thinnest of whispers. "We have so little time!"

This time there was no need for warning. I had Kaththea in my arms, no simulacrum of my sister. Then she crowded past us and took the lead back through the dark, drawing us with her at a run. We burst into the free night of the garden. I half expected Kaththea to meet her double, but there was no one there.

Back over the wall and into the wood we went, her frantic haste now spurring us. She held the long skirts of her robe high, dragging them with sharp jerks from the bushes where they appeared to catch and hold unnaturally. We strove not to use care now, only speed. And we were all gasping as we came out of the hollow to where our Torgians waited.

Just as we reached the saddles a deep boom welled from the building in the cup. It held a little of the earth-thunder we had heard during the mountain moving. Our horses screamed shrilly, as if they feared another such upheaval of their normal world. As we started off at a wild gallop I listened for any other sounds—shouts of some pursuit, another thunder roar. But there was nothing.

Not in the least reassured, I called to Kaththea:

"What will they send after us?"

Her hair whipped back, her face a white oval, she turned to answer me. "Not—warriors—" she gasped. "They have other servants—but tonight—they are limited."

Even Torgians could not stand the pace we had set in fleeing the valley of the Place. I was aware that the horses were disturbed, and that this uneasiness was fast approaching panic. Yet the reason for that was not plain since we should be out of the influence of the Place by now. With all the talent I had I strove to quiet their minds, to bring them again to sane balance.

"Rein in!" I ordered. "They will run themselves blind—rein in!"

I had no fears for Kemoc's horsemanship. But of Kathea's I was not so sure. While the Witches did not ignore the body in their training and exploration of the mind, I did not know how cloistered my sister had been during these past years, how able to control her mount.

The Torgians fought for the bits, strove to continue their headlong run, but between our strength on the reins, and my own efforts, they began to yield and we were slowing our pace when there was an ear-splitting squawl from before us. The cry of a snow cat, once heard, is never to be mistaken. They are the undisputed kings of the high valleys and the peaks. Though what one could be doing this far from its native hunting grounds, I did not understand. Unless the orders which had brought us from the border lands had been accompanied by some unknown commands which had moved the animals also, spreading them into territory they had not known before.

My mount reared and screamed, lashing out with front hooves as if the cat had materialized beneath its nose. And Kemoc fought a like battle. But the Torgian my sister rode swung about and bolted the way we had come, at the same breakneck pace which had started us off on this wild ride. I spurred after her, striving to reach the mind of her mount, with no effect, since it was now filled with witless terror. All I could read there was that it imagined the snow cat behind it preparing for a fatal leap to bring it down.

My horse fought me, but I drove savagely into its brain and did what I had never presumed to do before—I took over, pressing my wishes so deeply that nothing was left of its own identity for the present. We caught up with Kaththea and I stretched my control to the other horse—not with such success, since I also had to hold my own, but enough to eject from its brain the fear of imminent cat attack.

We turned to see Kemoc pounding up through the moonlight. I spoke between set teeth: "We may not be able to keep the horses!"

"Was that an attack?" Kemoc demanded.

"I think so. Let us ride while we can."

Ride we did through the waning hours of the night, Kemoc in the lead over the trail he had long ago marked. I brought up the rear, trying to keep ever alert to any new onslaught against our mounts or us. I ached with the weariness of the double strain, I who had believed myself fine trained to the peak of endurance, such as only the fighting men of these later days of Estcarp were called upon to face. Kaththea rode in silence, yet she was ever a source of sustenance to us both.

V

*T*here was light ahead—could that mark dawn? But dawn was not red and yellow, did not flicker and reach—

Fire! A line of fire across our path. Kemoc drew rein and Kaththea pulled level with him, and a moment later I brought up beside them. That ominous line ahead stretched across our way as far as the eye could see. Under us the horses were restive again, snorting, flinging up their heads. To force them into that would not be possible.

Kaththea's head turned slowly from left to right, her eyes surveying the fire as if seeking some gate. Then she made a small sound, close to laughter.

"Do they deem me so poor a thing?" she demanded, not of us, but of the night shadows before her. "I cannot believe that—or this."

"Illusion?" asked Kemoc.

If it were an illusion it was a very realistic one. I could smell the smoke, hear the crackle of flames. But my sister nodded. Now she looked to me.

"You have a fire striker—make me a torch."

I dared not dismount, lest my Torgian break and run. It was hard to hold him to a stand, but I urged him to the left and leaned in the saddle to jerk at a spindly bush, which luckily yielded to my pull. Thrusting this into Kemoc's hold, I fumbled one-handedly at my belt pouch, dragging forth the snapper to give a fire-starting spark.

The vegetation did not want to catch, but persistence won and finally a line of flame smoldered sullenly. Kaththea took the bunch of burning twigs and whirled it through the air until the fire was well alight. Then she put her horse forward. Again it was my will which sent the animals in. Kaththea's strange weapon was flung out and away, falling well ahead of us, to catch, so that a second fire spread from it.

They were burning towards each other, as if some magnetism existed pulling them into union. But as the first line reached the one my sister had kindled—it was gone! There remained only the now smoldering swath from the torch lighting. Kaththea laughed again, and this time there was real amusement in the sound.

"Play of children!" she called. "Can you not bring better to front us, ones of great wisdom?"

Kemoc gave a quick exclamation and rode to her, his crooked hand out.

"Do not provoke!" he ordered. "We have been very lucky."

As she looked to him, and beyond to me, her eyes were shining. She had an otherness in her face which put a curtain between us.

"You do not understand," she replied almost coldly. "It is best that we face—now—the worst they can summon up against us, rather than later when their power has strengthened and we are wearied. Thus it is well to challenge them, and not wait to do battle when *they* wish!"

Her words made sense to me. But I think that Kemoc still thought this unnecessary recklessness. And for that reason, I, too, began to wonder. For it could well be that our sister, out of her prison, might find freedom so fine a draft that she was not steady in her thinking.

She turned her head a small space farther, giving me her full attention.

"No, Kyllan, I am not drunk with freedom as a six-months Sulcar sailor greets wine the first hour off ship's decking! Though I could well be. Give me this much credit: I know well those I have lived among. We could not have done this thing tonight had they not lost much of their strength through the sending to the mountains. I could meet their worst before they recover—lest they crush us later. So—"

She began to chant, dropping the reins to free her hands for the making of gestures. And oddly enough the Torgian stood rock still under her as if no longer a creature of flesh and bone. The words were very old. Now and again I caught one which had some meaning, a far-off ancestor of one in daily use, but the majority of them were as a tongue foreign to me.

Her words might be foreign but the sense behind them had meaning. I have waited out the suspense of ambush, the lurking fore-terror of a stealthy advance into enemy-held territory, wherein each rock can give hiding place to death. I knew of old that prickle along the spine, that chill of nerve. Where I had met that with action, now I had to sit, waiting only for the doing—of what, I did not know. And I found this much harder than any such wait before.

Kaththea was challenging the Power itself, summoning up some counter-force of her own to draw it like a magnet, as her real fire had drawn that of illusion. But could she triumph now? All my respect and awe of the Witches' abilities argued that she could not. I waited, tense, for the very world to erupt around us.

But what came in answer to my sister's chant was no ground-twisting blow, no hallucination or illusion. It had no visible presence, no outward manifestation. It was—anger. Black, terrible anger—an emotion which was in itself a weapon to batter the mind, crush all identity beneath its icy weight.

Kyllan—Kemoc!

Sluggishly I answered that call to contact. We were not one, but three that had become one. Clumsily perhaps, not too smooth-fitting in our union, yet we were one—to stand against how many? But with that uniting came also Kaththea's assurance. We did not need to attack; our only purpose was defense. If we could hold, and hold, and continue to hold, we had a chance of winning. It was like one of the wrestling bouts in the camps wherein a man sets the whole of his strength against that of another.

I lost all knowledge of myself, Kyllan Tregarth, Captain of Scouts, seated ahorse in the night in a fire scorched clearing. I was no one—only something. Then, through that which was iron endurance, came a message:

Relax.

Without question I obeyed. The answering pressure came down—flat, hard, crushing—

Unite—hold!

We almost failed. But as a wrestler could use an unorthodox move to unsteady his opponent, so had my sister chosen the time and the maneuver. We threw the enemy off balance, even as she had hoped. The crushing descent met once more a sturdy resistance. Its steady push broke a little, wavered. Then came battering blows, one after another, but even I could sense that each one was slower, less strong. At last they came no more.

We glanced from one to the other, again ourselves, three in three bodies, not one in a place where bodies were naught.

Kemoc spoke first: "For a space—"

Kaththea nodded. "For a space—and how long I do not know. But perhaps we have won enough time."

True morning was graying the sky as we rode. But the Torgians were no longer fresh, and we dared not push the pace. We ate in the saddle, the journey bread of the army. And we did not talk much, saving all energy for what might lie ahead.

There were the eastern mountains making a great ridge against the sky, dark and threatening. And I knew that, miles distant though they were, these were the final wall between Estcarp and the unknown. What lay behind them? From all that Kemoc had learned in Lormt, there had once been some danger past all our present reckoning. Was he right—had the toll of years lessened that danger? Or were we riding from a peril we did know into danger we did not, and which would be even greater?

The day wore on. We kept to the cover of wasteland when we could. In our favor was the fact that here the farms were very few and far apart. Most of the ground was abandoned to second-growth woodlands. Fewer and fewer were the signs that man had ever planted his rule here.

Still the mountains loomed. Even though we plodded ever towards foothills we seemed to approach no closer. They might have been fixed on some huge platform which moved at a speed equal to ours always ahead. I waited throughout that whole day for another contest of wills, or some sign the hunt was up behind us. For I did not really believe that the Power was so exhausted they could not bring us up short and hold us captive while they sent their ministers to take us bodily prisoner.

Yet we rode untroubled. We halted to rest the horses, to take short naps with one always on watch, and we rode again. And we saw nothing save now and then a curious animal peering through some screen of bush. It was wrong, all wrong; every scout instinct belabored me with that. We would have trouble, we must have trouble—

"There may be this," Kemoc cut into my thoughts, "—they do not realize that we are not blocked against the east, so they believe that we ride now into a trap without an exit—save back into their hands."

That made sense. Yet I dared not wholly accept it. And, as we camped that night, without fire, on the bank of a rock-strewn, mountain-born stream, I still kept watch with the feeling that I would be easier in my mind if an attack did come.

"To think so, Kyllan"—that was Kaththea, gazing up at me from where she knelt at the streamside washing her face—"is to open you to attack. A man's uncertainty is a lever they may use to overset him."

"We cannot go without taking precautions," I countered.

"Yes. And thus always they will have a small door open. But it is a door which we may not close—you are most right, brother. Tell me, where do you look for any true hiding place?"

With that she surprised me. What had she thought—that we had taken her from the Place only to ride blindly about the countryside with no foreplan?

Kaththea laughed. "No, Kyllan, I do not think so meanly of your intelligence. That you have a plan, I knew from the moment you called to me from outside the walls of the Place. I know it has something to do with these mountains we seek so wearily. But now is the time to tell the what and the why."

"Kemoc has planned it, let him—"

She shook drops of water from her hands and wiped them on sun-dried grass from the stream bank. "Then Kemoc must tell me the whole."

As we sat together, chewing on the sustaining but insipid food, he laid before her the whole story of what he had discovered at Lormt. She listened without question until had done, and then she nodded.

"I can give you this further proof of your mystery, brother. For the past hour, before we reached this spot, I was riding blind—"

"What do you mean?"

She met my eyes gravely. "Just what I said, Kyllan. I rode through a mist. Oh, it was broken now and then—I could make out a tree, a bush, rocks. But for the most part it was a fog."

"But you said nothing!"

"No, because watching the two of you, I knew it must be some form of illusion which did not trouble you." She wrapped the part of cake she still held in its protecting napkin and restored it to saddle bag. "And it was also not born of anything they had unleashed against us. You say we do not have this block about the east because we are of mixed heritage. That is good sense. But it would also seem that my witch training mayhap has produced a measure of it to confuse me. Perhaps had I taken the oath and become wholly one of them I could not pierce it at all."

"What if it gets worse for you?" I blurted out my growing concern.

"Then you shall lead me," she returned tranquilly. "If it is some long ago induced blank-out, I do not believe it will last—except over the barrier itself,
through the mountains. But now I also agree with you, Kemoc. They will relax
their hunt, for they will confidently believe that we shall be turned back. They do
not realize that at least two of us can go clearsighted into their nothingness!"

I could not share her confidence completely, but also I had learned as a Borderer
that worry over what might be never added a single second to a man's life, nor
changed his future for well or ill. I had not encountered Kaththea's mist, nor had
Kemoc. And her explanation for that was reasonable. But could we continue to be
so free? Trailing over mountain tracks with impaired vision was a desperate thing.

Kemoc asked a question forming in my own mind. "This mist—of what manner is it? And you say . . . not complete?"

Kaththea shook her head. "No, and sometimes I think it is a matter of will. If
I fasten on something which is only a shadow and sharpen my will, I see it the
clearer. But that requires a concentration which might work against us."

"How so?" I demanded.

"Because I must listen—"

"Listen?" My head came up and now I strained to hear too.

"Not with ears," she replied quickly, "but with the inner hearing. They are not
moving against us now; they are content to wait. But will they remain so the farther we go eastward, when they at last know that we are not contained by their
long set boundries? Do not think they will ever give up."

"Has there ever before been one who refused witchhood, I wonder?" Kemoc
asked musingly. "The Council must be as startled by your flight as if one of the
stones of Es City spoke out against them. But why should they wish to keep you
against your will?"

"It is simple enough—I am not of their same pattern. At first they did not push
too hard to have me because of that very thing. There were those in the Council
who believed I would be a disrupting influence should they strive to make me
one with them. Then, as the menace of Karsten grew worse, they were ready to
grasp at any promise, no matter how small, of adding in some way to the sum total of the Power. Thus, they would have me to study, to see if through me any new
gates might be opened, that the basic amount of their long treasured force be increased. But as long as I would not take the oath, become one with them in a surrendering of self, they could not use me as they wished. Yet I could not delay
such a step too long. There was this—" She paused, her eyes dropped to the
hands which had rested lazily in her lap. Now those long fingers curled, came together as if protecting something in their cupped palms. "I wanted—some of
what they had to offer, that I wanted! Every part of me thirsted for their knowledge, for I knew that I could work wonders also. Then would come to me the
thought that if I chose their path, so must I cut away part of my life. Do you think
that one who has been three can happily be alone? Thus I turned and dodged,

would not answer when they asked of me this thing. And at last came the time when they would risk all against Karsten.

"They spoke plainly to me—to use the Power in a unification of all their selves meant an ending for some. Many would die, did die, burnt out by making of themselves vessels to hold the energy until it could be aimed and loosed. They had to have replacements and no longer would the choice be left to me. And now, with their ranks so depleted, neither will they allow me to go, if they can prevent it. Also—" Now she raised her eyes to look at us directly. "They will deal with you, the both of you, ruthlessly. They always secretly mistrusted and feared our father; I learned that when I was first among them. It is not natural, according to their belief, that a man should hold even a small portion of the Power. And they more than mistrusted our mother for the talent that she built with our father's aid when by all rights she should have lost her witchship in lying with a man. This they considered an abomination, a thing against all nature. They know you have some gift. After this past night and day, they will be even more certain of that— with good cause to dislike what they have learned. No normal man could have entered the Place, and he certainly could not have won free of it again. Of course, their safeguards there were depleted, yet they were such as would have been death to any male fully of the Old Race. Thus—you are not to be trusted, you are a menace, to be removed!"

"Kaththea, who was the girl, the one in the garden?" Kemoc asked suddenly. "Girl?"

"You and yet not you," he answered. "I believed in her—would have taken her and gone. Kyllan would not let me. Why?" He turned now to me. "What was it that made you suspect her?"

"No more than a feeling at first. Then—she was like one made for a purpose. She fastened upon you, as if she wished to hold you—"

"She looked like me?" Kaththea asked.

"Very much, save she was too serene. She smiled always. She lacked"—and I knew I had hit upon the truth—"she lacked humanity."

"A simulacrum! Then they *did* expect you, or some attempt to reach me! But it takes long and long to make one of those. I wonder which one of the novices it really was?"

"Shape changing?" Kemoc said.

"Yes. But more intricate, since she was designed to deceive such as you, who had mind contact—or did they know that much of us? Yes, they must have! Oh, that proves it—they must be very sure now that you are the enemy. And I wonder how much longer we have before they realize we are not in any trap, and so move after us?"

To that question we had no answer. But it left us with little peace of mind. The stream tinkled and burbled through the dark, and we could hear the sound of the hobbled Torgians at graze. And we set up watches turn and turn about.

The morning came and this one was clear and bright for Kemoc and me—
though Kaththea admitted that the fog was heavy for her, and that she had a disturbing disorientation when we began our ride into the foothills. At last she
begged us to tie her to her saddle and lead her mount as the overwhelming desire
to turn back was growing so strong she feared she could not control it.

We, too, had a measure of unease. There was a distortion of sight at times
which was like that we had experienced looking down into the valley of the
Place. And the sensation of moving into some dark and unpleasant surprise was
haunting, but not to the point that it had any effect upon our determination.

But we did as Kaththea asked and at intervals she struggled against the ties we
put on her, once crying out that directly before us was sudden death in the form
of a deep chasm—though that was not true. Finally she shut her eyes and had us
lay a bandage over them, saying that once shut into her own mind in that fashion,
she was better able to combat the waves of panic.

The faint trace of road had long since vanished. We went by the easiest riding
we could pick through true wilderness. I had lived much among mountains, but
the weirdly broken ways we now followed were strange to nature, and I thought I
knew the reason. Just as the mountains of the south had been toppled and turned,
so, too, had these heights.

It was evening of the second day since we had left the streamside when we
reached the end of open ways. Before us now lay heights a determined man
might climb on foot, but not on horseback. We faced that fact bleakly.

"Why do you stop?" Kaththea wanted to know.

"The way runs out; there is only climbing ahead."

"Wait!" She leaned down from her saddle. "Loose my hands!"

There was such urgency in that that Kemoc hastened to obey. As if she could see
in spite of the blindfold, her fingers moved surely out, touched his brows, slid down
to the eyes he blinked shut. For a long moment she held them so before she spoke:

"Turn, face where we must go."

With her touch still on his closed eyes, my brother moved his head slowly to
the left, facing the cliff face.

"Yes, oh, yes! Thus I can see it!" There was excitement and relief in
Kaththea's voice. "This is the way we must go, then?"

But how could we? Kemoc and I could have done it, though I wondered about
his maimed hand. But to take Kaththea bound and blindfolded—that was impossible.

"I do not think you need to take me so," she answered my silent doubts.
"Leave me thus for tonight, let me gather all my powers, and then, with the
dawn—let us try. There will be an end to the block, of that I am sure."

But her certainty was not mine. Perhaps with the dawn, instead of climbing,
we would have to backtrack, to seek out another way up through the tortured debris of this ancient battlefield.

VI

I could not sleep, though there was need for it in my body—to which my mind would not yield. Finally I slipped from my blanket and went to where Kemoc sat sentry.

"Nothing," he answered my question before it was voiced. "Perhaps we are so far into the debatable land we need not fear pursuit."

"I wish I knew at whose boundary we are," I said. And my eyes were for the heights that we must dare tomorrow.

"Friend or enemy?" In the moonlight his hand moved so there was a glint of light from the grip of the dart gun lying unholstered on his knee.

"And that—" I gestured to the weapon. "We have but two extra belts of darts. Steel may have to serve us in the end."

Kemoc flexed his hand and those stiff fingers did not curl with their fellows. "If you are thinking of this, brother, do not underrate me. I have learned other things besides the lore of Lormt. If a man determines enough he can change one hand for the other. Tomorrow I will belt on a blade for the left hand."

"I have the feeling that what we win beyond will be sword-taken."

"In that you may be very right. But better land sword-taken than what lies behind us now."

I gazed about. The moon was bright, so bright it seemed uncannily so. We were in a valley between two ridges. And Kemoc had his post on a ledge a little more than a man's height above the valley floor. Yet here our sight was restricted as to what lay above us, or farther down the cut of our back trail. And this blindness worried me.

"I want to see from up there," I told him.

In the brightness of the moon I did not fear trouble, the slope being rough enough to afford good hand and toe holds. Once on the crest I looked to the west. We had been climbing all day as we worked our way through the foothills. The tree growth was sparse now and I had a clear sight. With the long seeing lenses from my service belt I searched our back trail.

They were distant, those pricks of light in the night. No effort had been taken to conceal them; rather they had been lit to let us know we were awaited. I counted some twenty fires and smiled wryly. So much did those who sent those waiting sentries respect the three of us. Judging by Borderer practices there must be well over a hundred men so encamped, waiting. How many of them were those with whom Kemoc and I had ridden? Were any drawn from my own small command? Freed from the necessity of southward patrols they could be used thus.

But we were not yet in a trap. I pivoted to study the cliff wall which now fronted us. As far as the glass advanced my own sight north and south there appeared no easier way up. And would those others, back there, remain at the line they had drawn, or come after us?

I dropped to Kemoc's perch.

"So they are there. . . ."

Mind contact passed news swiftly.

"I make it at least a full field company, if we go by fire count. Maybe more."

"It would seem there is a vow we shall be taken. But I doubt if they will sniff this far in after us."

"I could sight no better climbing place."

There was no need to put the rest of my worry into words: he shared it fully already. But now he gave me a short reply.

"Do not believe that she will not climb, Kyllan."

"But if she does so blind?"

"Two of us, the saddle ropes, and mind contact which will give her sight? We may be slow, but we shall go. And you shall fuzz the back trail, Kyllan, even as it has just crossed your mind to do."

I laughed. "Why do we bother with speech? You know my thoughts as I think them—"

He interrupted, his words sober: "Do I? Do you know mine?"

I considered. He was right, at least as far as I was concerned. I had contact, could communicate with him and with Kathea, but it was a come and go matter and, as I knew, mostly when we were intent upon a mutual problem. Unless he willed it, Kemoc's personal thoughts were not mine.

"Nor yours mine," he replied promptly. "We may be one in will when necessary, but still we are three individuals with separate thoughts, separate needs, and perhaps separate fates also."

"That is good!" I said without thinking.

"It could not be otherwise, or we would be as the non-men the Kolder used to do their labor and their fighting—those bodies who obeyed, though mind and spirit were dead. It is enough to open one surface of our thoughts to one another when we must, but for the test—it is our own."

"Tomorrow, if I blaze our trail up there and keep my mind open, can Kaththea see thus, even if she goes blinded?"

"So is my hope. But this is also the truth, brother, that such an open mind must be held so by will, and this will add to the strain of the climb. I do not think you can do this for long; we shall have to divide it between us. And"—again he flexed his scarred hand in the moonlight—"do not believe that in this either shall I be found wanting. Crooked and stiff as these fingers are, yet my bone and flesh have learned to obey me!"

That I did not doubt either. Kemoc got to his feet, holstering his gun, and I took his place so that he might rest. We had already agreed that Kaththea would not be one of this night's sentries, since it was her task to wrestle with the block her witch training had set upon her.

As I watched, the very brilliance of the vale began to have its effect. There was a kind of dazzlement about the pallid light, akin to the subtle distortion we had noticed earlier, and I was so inwardly warned against any long study. There was that here which could evoke glamourie—the visionary state into which the half-learned in any magic could easily slip, to be lost in their own visions. And I wanted no such ensorcelment.

At length I dropped from Kemoc's ledge and took to active sentry patrol, keeping on my feet, taking care not to look too long at any rock, bush or stretch of ground. Thus I came to where the Torgians browsed. They moved slowly, and a quick reading of their minds showed me a dulling of their kind of thought. Yet undue fatigue would not normally have brought them to such a state. Perhaps the same block which acted upon the Old Race held in small part for their animals also.

We could not take them with us. And still there was a way they could continue to serve us. It did not take me long to strip off their hobbles. Then I saddled them and set on bridle and bit, looping the reins about the saddle horns. As I worked they became more alert.

As I was about to set on them my last commands, there was a stir behind me. I turned, hand going to my gun. Kaththea was in the open, her hands tugging at the band she herself had fastened to blind her eyes after we had eaten our meal. At a last tug that gave way and she stared in my direction as a short-sighted person might peer.

"What—?" I began, then her hand came up in an impatient gesture.

"There is more which can be done to carry through your scheme, brother," she said softly. "Horses should have riders."

"Dummies? Yes, I had thought of that, but the materials for the making of such are lacking."

"For materials there is not much needed to induce illusion."

"But you have no Jewel of Power," I protested. "How can you build one of the strong illusions?"

She was frowning a little. "It may well be that I cannot, but I shall not be sure until I try. Our mother surrendered her Jewel upon her marriage day, yet thereafter she accomplished much without it. Mayhap the Jewel is not quite as much the focus of the Power as the Wise Women will have us believe. Oh, I am very young in their learning as they count such things, but also am I certain that there has been no proper measurement of what *can* be wrought by wish, will and the Power. If one is content to use a tool then one shall never know what one can do without it. Now, here—" She plucked a curled, silvery leaf from a nearby bush. "Lay upon this some hairs from your head, Kyllan—and pluck them from the roots, for they must be living hairs. Also, moisten them with spittle from your mouth."

Her tone summoned obedience. I took off my helm, and my forehead and throat, about which its mail veil had been wreathed, felt naked and chill in the night breeze. I plucked the hair she wished, and the separate threads curled about my fingers, for it had gone unclipped for some time. Then I spat upon the leaf and laid the hair therein, even as Kaththea was doing in another such improvised carrier.

She crossed to Kemoc and awakened him to do likewise. Then she held the three leaves on her palm and walked to the horses. With her right hand she rolled the first leaf and its strange burden into a spill, all the time her lips murmuring sounds I could not make into any real word. The spill she tucked between the knotted reins and the saddle horn, taking great care as to its wedging. And this she did also with the others. Then she stood aside and raised her hands to her mouth as half open fists. Through these trumpets of flesh and bone she sang, first in a low semi-whisper, then louder and louder. And the rhythm of those sounds became a part of me, until I felt them in the beat of my heart, the throb of my pulses. While the brilliance of the moonlight was a flashing glare, its light condensed to where we stood.

Kaththea's song ended abruptly, on a broken note. "Now! Give your commands, brother—send them forth!"

The orders I set in the Torgians' befogged brains sent them moving down the vale, away from us, in the direction of that fire line. And as they so left us I will always believe that I saw the misty forms in those saddles, a swirl of something to form three riders, nor did I wonder who those riders would seem to be.

"It would appear, sister, that the half has not been told concerning the powers of Witches," Kemoc commented.

Kaththea swayed and caught at his arm, so that he gave her his support.

"Witchery has its prices." She smiled upon us wanly. "But I believe that this has bought us time—more than just a night. And now we may rest in peace."

We half-carried her between us to the blanket-branch bed we had earlier made her, and, as she lay with closed eyes, Kemoc looked to me. There was no need for a reading of minds between us—to attempt the mountain climb tomorrow was beyond the borders of reasonable risk. If those who tended those watchfires did not advance and Kaththea's magic bought us more time, we need not push.

Dawn found me back on the lookout ridge. The fires still burned, more difficult to see with the coming of light. I searched for the horses. It was a long and anxious moment before my lenses picked them up, moving across an open glade. And I was startled. There were riders in those saddles, and they would truly have deceived me had I been on scout. They would be watching, those others, and they would see their prey returning. How good the illusion would be at close quarters, I could not guess. But for the time we were covered.

Kemoc joined me and we took turns watching the horses, until a fold in the earth concealed them from us. Then we went down to inspect the cliff wall. It was rough enough to promise adequate holds, and not far from the top was a ledge of some depth to afford a resting place. As to what lay beyond its crests we did not know, but neither could we say that we would be faced by something we could not surmount.

For that day we rested in camp, sleeping so deeply in turn that no dreams troubled us. And Kaththea recovered that strength which had been drawn from her in the weaving of illusion. At the first shadow of night I climbed the ridge again. This time there was no sparkle of watch-fires, nor did we sight any later in the night. What this could mean might be either of two things: Kaththea's painfully wrought illusions might have provided the waiting company with prisoners for a space—or they had speedily discovered the trickery, struck camp, and were moving on. Yet a most painstaking use of the lenses, studying each bit of cover which might attract a stalking hunt, showed nothing amiss.

"I think they are truly gone," Kaththea said with a confidence I did not altogether share. "But it does not matter. In the morning we shall go also, up and back—there." She pointed to the mountain.

And in the morning we did go. Our provisions, weapons and blankets were made into packs which Kemoc and I shouldered. And roped between us both was Kaththea, her hands free, no weight upon her. She had discarded the eye bandage, but still kept her eyes closed, striving to "see" through mind contact, since she was still in the confusing fog.

It was slow work, that upward pull, and I found it doubly hard when I had to concentrate not only on my own efforts, but as an aid for Kaththea. She showed a surprising dexterity in spite of her self-imposed blindness, never fumbling or missing a hold I pictured in my mind. But when we reached the ledge I was so weak with fatigue I feared it was not in me to pull up the last short way. Kemoc reached across Kaththea as she crouched between us, his hand falling on my shaking knee.

"The rest to me," he stated as one who would not be denied.

Nor could I have fought him for that danger. I was too spent to risk their safety on my own fast failing strength. So from the rest we reversed and my brother took the lead, his face as rigid with concentration as mine must have been. For I discovered my chin stiff, my jaw aching with pressure when I had come to those moments of relaxation.

It was lucky that I had given way to Kemoc, for the last part of that climb was a nightmare. I forced my trembling body to the effort, knowing well the danger of pulling back upon the rope and distracting Kaththea. But there came an end and we were on a space almost wide enough to be a plateau.

There was a cold wind here which dried our sweat, chilled us. So we pressed on hurriedly to where two peaks jutted skyward, a shadowed cleft between them. And when we entered that slash Kaththea suddenly flung back her head and opened her eyes, giving a small but joyful cry. We did not need any words to know that her blindness was gone.

The cleft we entered intensified the cold of those heights. Kemoc scuffed a boot toe through a patch of white and I saw that he had kicked up snow. Yet this was summer and the heat of the year had weighed heavily on us below. We stopped to undo our packs and bring out the blankets, pulling them cloakwise about our shoulders. That helped in a small measure as we came to the end of the cleft and looked down—into the world of the unknown.

Our first impression was one of stark disbelief. There was a kind of wrongness about the broken land which receded down and down from our present perch, into a misty lowland so hidden we could not tell whether land or water, or both, lay far below. All I could think of was a piece of cloth which had been soaked in thin mud and then twisted by hand before being allowed to dry, so that a thousand wrinkles ran this way and that without sane purpose. I had thought that I knew mountain country, but this cut up land was worse than the foothills we had passed.

Kaththea was breathing deeply, not just as one who would fill her lungs, but as if she could separate some one scent from many, and identify it, as a hound or a snow cat could identify a hunting trace.

"There is that here—" she began, and then hesitated. "No, I make no judgments. But this land has felt the lash of a fury which was man-born and not the stroke of nature. Only that was long and long ago, and the destruction is under mend. Let us get from this place; I do not like my winds ice-tipped."

In one way the broken nature of the descent served us well—for while the finding of the way was time consuming, yet the terrain was so rough here there were natural stairways of rock to be discovered. Since Kaththea was now sure of her sight, we made far better time than we had on the other side of the mountain.

However, the mist which choked the lower lands still curtained them from us, and that did not inspire confidence. There was this also: on the other side of the mountain, broken as the way had been, there had been life. I had seen fresh tracks of animals, and we had noted birds, even though their number had been few. But here were no such signs of life. We were down from the bare rock and into the first circle of vegetation to find that this had a strange look. The green of the narrow bush leaves was lighter in shade than that we had always known, and the very shape of the leaves had a shriveled appearance as if they had been born from blighted seeds.

It was when we came out at the head of a valley that I called a halt. The territory below was even more unbelievable than that we had sighted from the pass. At first I could not really tell the nature of what I looked upon. Then, glancing about me, the sight of seedlings spreading from that growth gave me the answer to that choked gap. They must be trees, for no bush grew to such a height, but they were no normal tree. And they must have grown so for centuries of time, for they completely filled the valley, their tips reaching only a few feet below the rocky point on which we now stood.

Sometime in the distant past they had begun as might any normal tree, but when their boles had reached perhaps ten feet above the ground surface they had taken a sharp bend left or right. After proceeding in that new direction for some feet, they again pointed skyward, to repeat the process again and again, lacing a vast criss-cross of such branched levels, with the true ground of the valley far below. To cross this we would have to walk the branches, for the woven growth gave no chance of penetration any lower, which meant balancing from limb to limb, with fear that a slip meant either a bone-breaking fall or even impalement on one of those shooting uptips.

I edged back from our vantage point. "For this I want a full day."

Kaththea shaded her eyes from the last sun rays, reflected glitteringly from some quartz in the rocks. "That is truth. But it is cold here—where can we shelter?"

Kemoc found protection, a crevice about which we piled other stones until the three of us, huddling closely into that crack, could endure the chill. There was wood, but none of us suggested a fire. Who knew what eyes might pick up a spark on a mountain side where no spark should rightly be, or what might be drawn to investigate such a phenomenon? Kemoc and I had lain rough before, and Kaththea made no complaint, we putting her between us and bringing the blankets about us all.

If the mountain had seemed dead, a lifeless world in daytime, that was not true at night. There was the wail of a snow cat that had missed its kill, and a hooting from the air over the choked valley.

But nothing came near us as we dozed, awoke to listen, and then slept again through a night which also was different this side of the mountain—one far too long.

VII

*I*n the early morning we ate the last crumbs of journey bread, and discovered there were only a few sips of water left in the saddle bottles we had filled at the streamside. Kemoc shook his bag over his hand.

"It would seem we now have another very good reason to push on," he remarked.

I ran my tongue over my lip and tried to think back to the last really filling meal I had eaten. That was hard doing, for I had lived more or less on emergency rations since Kemoc's summons had taken me from camp. We had seen no trace of game—yet a snow cat had yowled in the night and one of those hunters would not be prowling a preyless land. I visualized a prong-buck steak or even a grass burrower, sizzling on a spit over a fire. And that provided me impetus to approach the verge and survey the springy bough road we must travel.

We made what precautions we could, using the rope once again to unite us, so that a slip need not be fatal. But it was not with any great confidence that any of us faced that crossing. We could not aim straight for the other rim, but had to angle down the length of the branch-filled cut in order to keep moving east to the presumed lowlands. The mist still clung there and we could only hope that there *were* lowlands to be found.

I had always held that I had a good head for heights, but in my mountaineering I had trod on solid stone and earth, not on a footing which swayed and dipped, giving to my weight with every step. And I was almost a few feet out on that surface when I discovered, almost to my undoing, that this weird valley had inhabitants.

There was a sharp chattering cry; and from the upthrust branch tip, to which I had just reached a hand for a supporting grip, burst a thing which swooped on skin wings and skittered ahead to disappear again into the masking foliage.

Kaththea gave a startled cry and I found my hold on the branch very necessary, for I was almost unbalanced by my start. So our advance became even more slow.

Three times more we sent flitters flying from our path. Once we needed to make an exhausting detour when we sighted another and more frightening inhabitant of this treetop maze; a scaled thing which watched us unblinkingly, a narrow forked tongue flickering from its green lips—for it was colored much like the silver-green of the leaves among which it lay. It was not a serpent, for it had small limbs and clawed feet with which to cling, yet it was elongated of body, and its whole appearance was malefic. Nor did it fear us in the least.

All time has an end. Sweating, weary from tension to the point of swimming heads and shaking bodies, we made the last step from the quivering boughs to the solid rock of the valley rim. Kaththea dropped to the ground, panting. All of us bore raw scratches and the red marks left by lashing branches. While our field uniforms were sturdy enough to withstand hard usage, Kaththea's robe was torn in many places, and there were bits of broken twig snarled in hair ends which had escaped from the kerchief into which she had knotted them before beginning that journey.

"I would seem to be one of the Moss Ones," she commented with a small slightly uncertain smile.

I looked back at the way we had come. "This is proper country for such," I said idly. Then silence drew my attention back to my companions. Both of them were staring at me with an intensity which had no connection with what I had just said, or so I thought, but as if I had uttered some profound fact.

"Moss Ones," Kaththea repeated.

"The Krogan, the Thas, the People of Green Silences, the Flannan," Kemoc added.

"But those are legend—tales to amuse children, to frighten the naughty, or to amuse," I protested.

"They are those who are foreign to Estcarp," Kaththea pointed out. "What of Volt? He, too, was dismissed as legend until Koris and our father found his Hole and him waiting. And did not Koris bring forth from there that great axe, which was only legend too? And the sea serpent of Sulcar song—not even the most learned ever said that that was only fantasy."

"But women of moss who seek a human mother to nurse their children and who pay in pale gold and good fortune, beings who fly on wings and torment those who strive to learn their secrets, creatures who dwell blindly underground and are to be feared lest they draw a man after them into eternal darkness, and people akin to trees with powers over all growth . . ." I recalled scraps and bits of those tales, told to amuse with laughter, or bring delightful shivers up the back of those who listened to terror while sitting snug and secure by a winter fire in a strongly held manor.

"Those stories are as old as Estcarp," Kemoc said, "and perhaps they reach beyond Estcarp . . . to some other place."

"We have enough to face without evoking phantoms," I snapped. "Do not put one behind each bush for us now."

Yet one could not stifle the working of imagination and this was the type of land which could give rise to such legends. Always, too, there was the reality of Volt which my father had helped to prove. And, as we advanced, my mind kept returning to sift old memories for descriptions of those fantastic beings in the stories.

We were definitely on a down slope, though the broken character of the land continued. Now our greatest need was for water. Though the vegetation grew heavily hereabouts, we came across no stream nor spring, and the growing heat of the day added to our discomfort. The mist still clung, and thus at times we could see only a short distance ahead. And that mist had a steamy quality, making us long to throw aside our helms and mail which weighed so heavy.

I do not know just when I became aware that we were not alone in that steam wreathed wildness. Perhaps fatigue and the need for water had dulled my scouting sense. But it grew on me that we were under observation. And so sure was I of that, that I waved my companions to cover in the thicket and drew my dart gun as I studied the half-concealed landscape.

"It is there . . . somewhere." Kemoc had his weapon in hand also.

Kaththea sat with closed eyes, her lips parted a little, her whole attitude one of listening, perhaps not with the ears, but with a deeper sense.

"I cannot touch it," she said in a whisper. "There is not contact—"

"Now it is gone!" I was as sure of that as if I had seen the lurker flitting away as the skinned flapped things had done in the tree valley. I beckoned them on, having now only the desire to put distance between us and whatever had skulked in our wake.

As we moved into yet lower land the mist disappeared. Here the trees and high brush gave way to wide, open glades. Many of these were carpeted by thick, springy growth of gray moss. And I had a faint distaste for walking on it, though it cushioned the step and made the going more comfortable.

Bird calls sounded, and we saw small creatures in the moss lands. There was a chance for hunting now, but water remained our major desire. Then we came upon our first trace of man—a crumbling wall, more than half buried or tumbled from its estate as boundary for a field. The growth it guarded was tall grass, but here and there showed the yellow-ripe head of a grain stalk, wizened and small, reverting to the wild grass from which it had evolved. Once this had been a farm.

We took one side of that wall for a guide and so came into the open. The heat of the sun added to our distress but a farm meant water somewhere near. Kaththea stumbled and caught at the wall.

"I am sorry," her voice was low and strained. "I do not think I can go much farther."

She was right. Yet to separate in this place of danger . . .

Kemoc supported her. "Over there." He pointed to where a stand of trees grew to offer a patch of shade. When we reached those we discovered another piece of good fortune, for there was a fruit-laden vine on the wall. The red globes it bore I recognized as a species of grape, tart and mouth-puckering even when ripe as these were, but to be welcomed now for the moisture they held. Kemoc began to pick all within reach, passing his harvest to Kaththea.

"There is water somewhere, and we must have it." I dropped my pack, checked again the loading of my dart gun, then slung the straps of two of the saddle bottles over my shoulder.

"Kyllan!" Kaththea swallowed a mouthful of pulp hurriedly. "Keep in mind touch!"

But Kemoc shook his head. "I think not—unless you need us. There is no need to arouse anything."

So he felt it too, the sensation that we did not walk through an empty world, that there was here that which was aware of us, waiting, measuring, studying. . . .

"I will think of water, and water only." I do not know just why that assertion seemed important. But I did walk away from them concentrating on a spring, a stream, building up in my mind a vivid mental picture of what I sought.

The walled field was separated from another of its kind; perhaps the gap between them marked some roadway long since overgrown. I caught sight, in the second enclosure, of a prong-horn family group at graze. The buck was larger than any of his species I had known in Estcarp, standing some four feet at the shoulder, his horns a ruddy pair of intricate spirals in the sunlight. He had three does, their lesser horns glistening black, lacking the ringing of the male's. And there were four fawns and an almost grown yearling. The latter was my prize.

Darts are noiseless save for the faint hiss of their ejection. The yearling gave a convulsive leap and fell. For a second or two its companions lifted their heads to regard the fallen with round-eyed stares. Then they took fright and headed in great bounds for the far end of the ancient field, while I leaped the wall and went to my kill.

It was while I was butchering that the sound of water reached my ears, the steady, rippling gurgle of what could only be a swiftly flowing stream. Having made a bundle of meat inside the green hide, I shouldered the package and followed that sound.

Not a stream, but a river, was what I slid down a high bank to find. There was a good current, and a scattering of large rocks around which the water washed with some force.

I ran forward and knelt to drink from my cupped hands. The flood was mountain born, for it was cold, and it was good to fill my mouth and then splash it over my bared head, upon my sweating face. For a long moment or two I was content merely to revel in the touch of water, the wonderful taste of water. Then I rinsed out the saddle bottles, filled each to the brim and hammered in their stoppers, making certain not to lose a drop.

Food and drink—and Kaththea and Kemoc waiting for both. With the heavy bottles dragging at my side, and the prong-horn meat on my shoulder, I started to retrace my trail. But to climb the bank at this point, so burdened, would not be easy. I needed two hands—thus I moved to the right, seeking a gap in the earth barrier.

What I came upon in rounding a stream curve was another reminder that this land had once been peopled. But this was no ruins of a house, nor any building I could recognize. There was a platform of massive blocks, now over-grown in parts with grass and moss. And rising from the sturdy base a series of pillars— not set in aisles, but in concentric circles. I doubted, after surveying them, whether they had ever supported any roofing. And the reason for such an erection was baffling. It was plain curiosity which betrayed me, for I stepped from raw earth onto the platform, and walked between two of the nearest pillars.

Then . . . I was marching at a slow, set pace around the circle, and I could not break free. Round and round, spiraling ever to the middle of the maze. From that core came forth—not a greeting—but a kind of gloating recognition that prey was advancing to its maw, a lapping tongue from which my whole nature revolted. A complete and loathsome evil as if I had been licked by a black foulness whose traces still befouled my shrinking skin.

The attack was so utterly racking that I think I cried out, shaken past the point of courage. And if I screamed with throat and tongue, so did I scream with mind, reaching for any help which might exist, in a blindly terrified call for aid.

That came—I was not alone. Strength flowed in, made union with me, tightened to hold against the licking of what dwelt in this stone web. There was another contact and that touch snapped. Satisfaction and desire became anger. I set my hand to the pillar, pulled myself backward, broke the pattern of my steady march.

Pillar hold by pillar hold I retreated, and in me held that defense against the raging entity I could not see. Rage fed upon frustration and bafflement. And then the confidence began to fray. The thing that lurked here had been bloated with constant success; it had not met any counter to its power. And that fact that it could not sweep me in easily for its feeding now worried it.

I had clawed my way to the outer row of the pillar circle when it launched one last attack. Black—I could *see* the wave of black foulness flowing towards me. I think I cried out again, as I threw myself on with a last surge of energy. My foot caught, and I was falling—into the dark, the black, the very opposite of all that life meant to me.

I was vilely ill—of that I was conscious first, as if there were some substance in my body now being violently rejected by my flesh. And I was retching miserably as I opened my eyes, to find Kemoc supporting me through those wrenching spasms. For the time, only my illness was real. Then, as my brother lowered me to the ground, I levered myself up, to stare wildly about, fearful that I still lay within the pillar way.

But around me was open field, clean and wide under a late afternoon sun which held no hint of any threatening shadows. As Kaththea leaned over me to hold one of the water bottles to my lips I tried to raise my hand to her and found that gesture was beyond my power.

Her face had a strange, closed look; her mouth was set. Beyond her Kemoc was on one knee, his eyes roving, as if he feared attack.

"Evil—" Kaththea cradled my heavy head on her arm. "But thank the Power it was tied to its own sink hole! There is indeed peril in this land. The stench of it hangs to warn us. . . ."

"How did I get here?" I whispered.

"When it took you—or strove to take you—you summoned. And we came. When you reeled out of that trap we brought you away, lest it have greater range than its own cold web—but it did not." She raised her head, looked from side to side; her nostrils expanded as she drew in deep breaths of the warm air. "This is sweet and clean, and wishes hurt to nothing—empty of all threat. Yet there you stumbled on a pocket of evil, very ancient evil, and where there is one we are likely to find another."

"What kind of evil?" I asked. "Kolder—?" Even as I gave the name of that old arch enemy, I was sure it did not answer what I had stumbled upon by the river.

"I never knew Kolder, but I do not think this is of that ilk. This is evil, as of . . . the Power!" She gazed down at me as if she herself could not believe in what she said.

Kemoc broke in sharply: "That is a contradiction which cannot stand!"

"So would I have said before today. Yet, I tell you, this was born not from any alien force, but in a twisted way from what we have known all our lives. Can I not recognize my learning, my weapons, even when distorted and debased?

Distorted and debased is this thing, and for that reason perhaps the greater menace to us, as it carries in it a minute particle of the familiar. What happened here to turn all we know utterly vile?"

But there was no reply for her. She rested the palm of her hand flat against my forehead, and stooped far over me so that her eyes looked directly into mine. Again from her lips came a low chant, and her actions drew out of me, mind and body, the rest of the wrenching nausea and terrible revulsion, leaving only the warning memory of what had happened and must never happen so again.

A measure of my energy restored, we went on. The open field had been security of a kind, but with night so close upon us we wanted shelter. Thus we followed the walls until we came to a small rise with on it a mound of stones, some of which still held together in an angle of what once might have been the corner of a building.

Together Kemoc and I worked to loosen more and build up a barricade before that triangular space while Kaththea roamed about the rise gathering sticks, and now and then breaking off a bit of growing thing. When she returned she was lighter of countenance.

"There is no rank smell here—rather, once there must have dwelt nearby one who followed the healing arts. Herbs will grow without tending, once they are well rooted. And look what I have found." She spread out her harvest on top of a squared block of stone.

"This"—one finger touched a slip of what could be fern—"is saxfage, which gives sweet sleep to the fevered. And this"—a stem with four trifid leaves—"langlorn, which brightens the mind and clears the senses. Best of all, which may be the reason that the other fair herbs have continued to grow—Illbane—Spirit Flower."

That I knew of, since it was the old, old custom even in Estcarp to plant such about a doorway in spring, harvest its white flowers in the fall and dry them, to wreath above the main entrance to any house and stable. Such action brought good luck, prevented the entrance of ill fortune, and also had an older meaning—that any power of evil be baffled by its scent. For it was the nature of the plant that, picked or broken, its aromatic odor lingered for a long time.

Kaththea built a fire, laying her pieces with the care of one constructing a work of significance. When I would have protested such revealment of our presence, Kemoc shook his head, laying fingertip to lips in warning. Then, when she had her sticks laid, she crushed between her palms the saxfage and langlorn, working the mass into the midst of the wood. Last of all she carefully broke two blossoms from her spray of Illbane and added those also. Taking up the stem with its remaining tip cluster of flowers, she began to walk back and forth along our small barricade, brushing the stones we had set there with it, then planting the bruised spray among the rocks as a small banner.

"Light the fire," she bade us. "It will not betray; rather, it will guard this night.

For nothing which is truly of the dark will find in it, smoke and flame, that which it can face."

So I set spark and the flames arose. The smoke was spiced with the smell of herbs. And shortly thereafter came another fine aroma as we toasted fresh meat on spits of wood. Perhaps Kaththea had indeed wrought strong magic, for I no longer felt that eyes saw, ears listened, that we were over-watched in this strange land.

VIII

We slept well that night, too deep for the troubling of dreams, to awake rested and clear-eyed, with only memory's warning against what must walk here. But Kaththea must have awakened the first, for when I roused she knelt, her crossed arms on our barrier, gazing out into the morning land. There was no sun, only clouds prolonging the half-light of the early hours into the day.

She turned her head as I stirred. "Kyllan, what do you make of that?"

My gaze followed her pointing finger. There was a copse of trees some distance away and from beyond that a glow reached the sky. Not the red of fire flame, but a greenish radiance, which clearly was from no natural cause.

"It remains always the same, neither waning nor waxing."

"A beacon of sorts?" I hazarded.

"Perhaps. But to summon—or to guide—what? I do not remember that we saw it last night. But I have listened and there is naught to hear."

I knew that she had not listened with her ears, but with her seer-trained inner sense.

"Kaththea—"

She turned her head to look at me.

"This land may be full of such traps as I blundered into. There may be good reason why it was closed and is closed to those of our mother's blood."

"All that is true. Yet it has come to me that there was a purpose beyond our own wills guiding us here, Kyllan. Save for such plague spots as you found, this is a fair land. Look about you. Even under the shadow of the clouds, do you not find it in you to have a liking for these fields?"

She was right. There was an odd drawing in me, a desire to walk those ancient, overgrown fields, even to thrust my hands deep into their waiting soil. I wanted to fling off the heaviness of helm and mail, to run joyously free and unburdened, with the wind about me and a fresh land under my feet. I had not felt so since I had been a small boy already under the hammer of Otkell's discipline.

Kaththea nodded. "You see? Can you turn your back on all this merely because it suffers from some disease? We can beware of the places of evil, and make the best of those of good. I tell you such herbs as I harvested last night cannot grow where all is befouled by the Powers of the Dark."

"No matter how fair a land," Kemoc said from behind us, "a man must have two things—a shelter and a supply of food. I do not believe this is what we want for a home roof-tree or hall. And for awhile we must turn hunters for food. Also, I would like to know a little more of our neighbors."

With that I agreed. It is always best to be sure that any shadow pooled behind a tree is only shadow and not sheltering some unpleasant surprise.

We ate more of the meat and drank the tart vine fruit, and then we prepared to journey on. Though before Kaththea left the hill she again plucked a selection of herbs, bagging them in a strip torn from the hem of her robe, which she now proceeded to shorten to only slightly below knee length.

The gleam, still faintly visible because of the clouds, drew us. But we went warily, taking to the cover of the woods. Kaththea reported no troublesome scents and the small copse seemed normal with birds and other wild life. This woods was not too wide and finally we reached a fringe of brush on its far side. Here again was open country and through it wound the river. In a curve of that stream stood the first real structure we had seen this side of the mountains. And it was familiar in shape—one of the watch-tower-guard-keeps, such as we had been housed in many times in Estcarp. From the slit windows of the third and fourth levels issued the light, and more was diffused from the crown, where were the only evidence of age, a few stones missing from parapet gaps.

Looking upon it I had not the slightest desire to explore further. It had not met us with an active slap of evil such as I had met in the stone web . . . but there was an eerie sense of withdrawal, a signpost without words to ward off the coming of men. Whatever walked there might not be actively antagonistic to our species, but neither would we be welcomed by it. As to how I knew this, I cannot explain. But Kemoc agreed with me.

Kaththea centered upon it her "seeing," then shook her head. "There is no penetration of mind, and I would not try in body. Let be what lies there, if anything does. There are and have always been forces which are not actively good or evil—they can kill or cure. But to meddle with them is risky; it is best not to awaken them."

Still I had a distaste for being observed by anything or anyone manning that post. The others agreed to slip back into the wood and circle under its cover to the river. We kept downstream from the site of the pillar web, Kaththea sniffing the wind for any warning of ill.

Though it did not rain, yet the gloom of the clouds continued as we followed the stream for a guide. And this country was more wooded and therefore dark. Then I sighted the fresh tracks of one of the large, flightless birds which are esteemed excellent eating in Estcarp. They being most wary, I thought it best to hunt alone, promising faithfully that I would not fall under any enticement because of curiosity. I stripped off pack and water bottle, and even my helm, lest its chain mail throat scarf give forth some small clink of noise.

It was plain that the birds fed in beds of riverside wild grain, but tall reeds arose nearby, promising cover. However, I was not to reach my quarry. Warning came in a movement across the stream.

Drift from past high water had gathered on a sand bank there, piling up a causeway. In and among that tangle were slinking shadows—black, agile, so swift of movement that I could not truly make out what manner of creature they were. Yet the very stealth of their approach, the concentration of their numbers, was a warning. As if they knew or sensed my uneasiness, they came the faster, more and more of them. The first plunged into the water, its narrow snout cutting a V across the current.

Only the swiftness of the current delayed their determination, carrying them well downstream. Yet I was certain they would make a landing there somewhere. And they were not hunting the birds, but me!

Trouble—head for the open—the nearest field.

As I thought that alarm I got to my feet and ran for the open. The slinking advance of these things needed cover; in the open they could be met more effectively.

Kemoc acknowledged and signaled me to the right. Now I slowed my retreat, walking backwards, having no wish to be rushed from behind. And my precautions proved to be well taken when the first of that black pack darted from a bush to the massive roots of a fallen tree in my sight a few moments later.

I was moving through shoulder high bush, and this was unpleasant country through which to be so stalked. There were too many excellent sites for ambush. Animals! Perhaps I had been too shocked from my experience with the web thing. I had been able to control animals before, so there was no reason why I might not again. I sent an exploring thought to what lurked behind the tree roots.

No animal—no normal animal! What? A red madness of kill, kill, tear and devour—an insanity which was not animal, but raw fury combined with cunning on another level. There was no control for this, only revulsion and the fear that the sane can feel for the chaotic depths of complete unbalance! Again I had erred, for my contact aroused them even more, flamed their hunger to a higher pitch. Also there were many—too many—

I wanted to run, to burst through the brush which was now a prison restraining me to be pulled down and slain at their pleasure. But I forced myself to move slowly, dart gun ready, watching for any slinker that came within range.

The bushes became smaller . . . then I was free, out in a wide stretch of open. Some distance away Kemoc and Kaththea moved, heading for the very center of that space. But with the pack coming . . . How could we stand them all off?

In my eagerness to reach the others I stumbled and went down. I heard Kaththea cry out, and flung myself over, to see the black creatures flow eagerly toward me. They ran silently, not as hounds that give tongue in the hunt, and that silence added to their uncanniness.

They were short of leg, though that did not impair their speed, and their bodies were sleekly furred, very lithe and agile. Their heads were narrow, pointing sharply to muzzles where yellow fangs showed against their dark hides. Their eyes were small specks of red fire.

Since I dared not take time to get to my feet I fired as I lay. The leader of that pack curled up, biting savagely at a dart in its shoulder. Yet even in pain and rage the thing made no outcry. However, the mishap of their leader gave the rest of the pack pause. They scattered back into cover, leaving the writhing wounded one behind until its struggles were stilled.

I ran for where Kaththea and Kemoc stood.

Kemoc was waiting with ready gun. "Hunters," he said. "Where did they come from?"

"They crossed the river," I panted. "I have never seen their kind before—"

"Haven't you?" Kaththea held her bundle of herbs pressed tight against her breast as if in those withering bits of twig, leaf and stem she had a shield to withstand all danger. "They are rasti."

"Rasti?" How could one associate a rodent perhaps as long as a mid-finger with these three-foot, insane hunters? Yet, when I considered the appearance of the creatures, perhaps not true rasti, but of the same family, grown to gigantic proportions for their species and with even worse ferocity than their midget brethren displayed. To so identify them removed some of the fear of the unknown that had been part of their impact upon me.

"And rasti are not so easily turned from any prey," Kemoc pointed out. "Have you never seen them drag down a fowl in a hill-protected farmyard?"

I had once, and that memory made me flinch. Circling—yes, they were beginning to circle us now, as they had that doomed fowl on that long past day. More and more of them squirmed out of the wood, bellies flat to earth as if they were snakes rather than warm-blooded furred things.

No need to warn Kemoc—he was firing. Three black things leaped in the air, beat at and clawed the ground. But a gun can continue to fire only as long as it is loaded. How long could our limited supply of darts last? We had our swords, but to wait until rasti came into range for cutting work was to open our defense to only one probable end.

"I cannot—the Power will not work against them!" Kaththea's voice was shrill. "They have nothing I can reach!"

"These will reach them!" I fired again, striving to pick the best shot possible. But it seemed that nature was ranged against us now in more than one fashion. For the darkness of the clouds approached night and suddenly a downpour of rain burst upon us, with force enough to buffet our bodies. However, it did not make our enemy retreat.

"Wait—look there!"

I missed my shot at Kemoc's cry and snarled at him as a snow cat might after an aborted hunting leap. Then I saw what was coming. A horse—at least in this gloom it seemed to be a horse—pounded on at a gallop. And on it was a rider. The figure came up between us and the rasti pack. Then my eyes were dazzled by a burst of white, searing light. It seemed that that rider called down lightning to serve as a lash with which to beat the earth about the skulking hunters.

Three times that lash fell, blinding us. Then I caught a dim sight of mount and rider galloping on, lost in the wood once again, while from the earth where that strange weapon had smote arose smoking trails of vapor. Nothing else moved.

Without a word Kemoc and I caught Kaththea between us and ran—away from that place, out of the open and the pouring rain. We gained the shelter of a tree and crouched together as if we were all one.

I heard Kaththea speak close to my ear. "That—that was of the Power—and for good, not ill. But it did not answer me!" Her bewilderment held a note of hurt. "Listen"—her fingers gripped both of us— "I have remembered something. Running water—if we can find the place in the midst of running water, and bless it, then we are safe."

"Those rasti swam the river," I protested.

"True. But we were not in the midst of running water on a blessed place. We must find such."

I had no wish to return to the river; as far as I could see most of the evil we had met with so far had been connected with that stretch of water. It would be better to try and follow the rider—

"Come!" Kaththea urged us out into the fury of the storm. "I tell you, this dark, together with wind and water, may release other things—we must find a safe place."

I was unconvinced, but I also knew that no argument of mine would make any impression on her. And Kemoc advanced no protest. We went on, the rain beating us, as that rider had lashed the ground which now showed great slashes of seared black vegetation and earth. At least I was able to convince Kaththea to head in the direction where the rider had disappeared.

Here the wooded land was less densely grown. I thought we had stumbled on some track or road, for we found the footing easier. And that track did bring us to the river. Kaththea could have claimed foresight, for there, in the midst of the rain-pitted and rising river, was an islet of rock. Drift had caught at one end, and a point in the center made a natural watchtower.

"We had better get over before the water is any higher," Kemoc said.

Whether we might or not, burdened with packs and weapons, I was not sure. Kaththea broke from us, was already wading through the shallows. She was waist deep and battling the pull of the current before we reached her. The fact that we entered the stream above the narrow tip of the island was in our favor, as the current bore us down upon it and we crawled out on the tip very little wetter than the rain had already left us.

Nature had fashioned an easily defended keep, with a rock-walled space for a hall and the watch point above. A short survey proved we had come ashore on the only place possible for a landing. Elsewhere the rocks gave no foothold, but reared up small cliffs from the water's foaming edge. Should the rasti come after us, we would have only a narrow strip to defend, so they could not possibly draw their fatal ring.

"This is a free place, not touched by any ill," Kaththea told us. "Now I shall seal it so." From her packet of herbs she brought out a stalk of Illbane, crushing it tightly in her fist, then holding her hand to her lips while she alternately breathed upon and chanted over what she held. At length she went forward on hands and knees, scrubbing the mass of vegetation into the rocky way up which we had come from the water. Then she was back with us, leaning against a stone, limp as one spent after hours of hard labor.

The violence of the rain did not long continue, though the river water continued to boil about our refuge. Storm gusts receded into a drizzle, which at length pattered into silence.

Speculation concerning the rider who had saved us continued to excise most of my thought. Kaththea had declared the stranger to be one who used the Power rightly, if not in her way. That other had not replied to my sister's attempt for communication, but that did not mean enmity. The fact that such service had been rendered spoke of good will. Thus far we had come across no other sign of any natives. Unless one could count the horror of the web, and that which *might* have garrisoned the watch-keep as inhabitants.

My glimpse of the rider had been so limited by the gloom and the storm that I was sure only that he had a reasonably human shape, that he was a horseman of no mean ability, and that he had known exactly how to put rasti to rout. Beyond that was ignorance.

But the thought of horses in this land also gave me material to chew upon. Since I had bestrode my first pony when I had had no more than four summers behind me, I have never willingly gone afoot. After we had left the Torgians on the other side of the range a kind of loss had plagued me. Now—if there were mounts to be had in this land the sooner we obtained them the better! Mounted, we need not have feared the rasti.

Tomorrow we must hunt in our turn, trace that galloping rescuer, and learn what manner of men shared this wilderness. . . .

Look! Be quiet—

Two orders, one beamed over the other in Kemoc's haste.

Out over the surface of the turbulent stream, a bird wheeled, dipped and soared. There was a shimmer to its wings, a glint which I had never seen reflected from feathers before, as it approached our refuge.

Food. . . .

Kemoc's suggestion made me aware of hunger. We did not lack water this time, but we did food—our packet of prong-horn meat having been lost in the rasti hunt. Unless we could hook some stream dweller out of the flood, we would fast this night. The bird was large enough to provide a scanty meal. But to shoot it unless directly overhead would send it down to be swept away by the current.

My brother drew his gun, then Kaththea's hand shot forward, slapping down his. "No!" she cried aloud.

Closer the bird swung; then, after a downward plunge, it settled on the rocks of our refuge and began to sidle around that rough way in our direction.

The shimmering quality of its plumage was even more pronounced at close range, white and pure, yet overlaid with radiant sheen. Bill and feet were a clear, bright red, the eyes dark and large. It halted and folded its wings, sat watching us as if awaiting some meaningful move on our part. All idea of feeding on the creature faded rapidly from my mind.

Kaththea studied it as intently as the bird appeared to be observing us. Then, lifting her right hand, our sister tossed a small crumpled leaf at the winged visitor. The long neck twisted and the head darted forward; bright eyes inspected her offering.

The shimmering became even brighter. My sister uttered some words in a tone of command, brought her hands together with a sharp clap. There was a shimmer of mist, then it cleared before us. The bird was gone—what teetered on a rock perch was still winged but no bird.

IX

*F*lannan!" I whispered, unable to believe that my eyes were not bedazzled by some sorcery.

The creature might not be the ethereal thing legend has reported in tales, but it was not a bird and it did have characteristics which were akin—outwardly—to the human.

The feet were still clawed and red, yet they were not the stick-proportions of a true bird; the body had taken on a humanoid shape with arms showing beneath the half spread wings, and tiny hands at the end of those arms. The neck might still be long and supple, but the head it supported, though centered by a jutting beak, held a recognizable face. The white shimmering feathers clothed it, save for feet, arms and hands.

It was blinking rapidly and those tiny hands lifted in a gesture toward Kaththea as if warding off some blow it feared.

Flannan, the air-borne race. . . . My memory presented gleanings from half a hundred old stories, and I thought fleetingly that perhaps it was well for us now that we had all had a liking in childhood for listening to old legends. The Flannan were friendly to man after a somewhat skittish fashion, for they quickly lost interest in any project, had small powers of concentration, and were very apt to leave any undertaking far from finished. The heroes and heroines of many stories had come to grief by depending upon a Flannan past its desire to render aid. However, never had it made any alliance with dark forces.

Kaththea began a crooning sing-song, close to a bird's trill. The Flannan sidled a little closer, its long neck twisting. Then its beak opened and it trilled back. My sister frowned, was silent a moment before she replied—to be interrupted by a trill in higher note. A pause, then it sang longer, and this time I was sure that sound held the rasp of impatience.

"It responds," Kaththea told us, "to the invocation of shared power, but I cannot read its answer. And I do not believe that it practices shape changing of its own accord."

"Sent to spy on us?" Kemoc wondered.

"Perhaps."

"Then it could guide us to the one who sent it!" I was still thinking of the rider.

Kaththea laughed. "Only if it wishes, unless you can grow wings and take to the air in its wake."

She brought out her packet of herbs and picked free Illbane. On the palm of her hand she held it towards the Flannan. The creature looked from the withered herb to Kaththea, plainly in question. A little of my sister's frown lightened.

"At least legend holds true so far. This is not the messenger of any ill force. So—" Once again she broke into song, this time slowly, with space between notes.

The Flannan cocked its head in a bird-like pose. When it trilled in reply, its answer, too, was slower, so that I was able to detect individual notes. Once or twice Kaththea nodded as if she had caught one she could translate.

"It was sent to watch us. This is a land where evil interlocks with good, and the pools of evil may overflow from time to time. Its message is for us to retreat, to return whence we came."

"Who sent it?" My demand was blunt.

Kaththea trilled. The Flannan's long neck curved, it looked to me, and I could read nothing, not even interest, in that regard. It made no answer. Kaththea repeated her query, this time sharply. When it remained silent, she traced a symbol by fingertip in the air between them.

The reaction to this was startling. There was a squawk, and the half-human aspect of the Flannan vanished. We saw a bird once more. It spread wings and took off flying three times counterclockwise about the islet, while each time it passed us it shrieked. My sister's eyes were ablaze and her hands moved in a series of sharp gestures as she chanted some words in the seer tongue. The bird faltered and squawked again, then flew straight as a dart's flight north.

"So—well, that will not work!" Kaththea broke out. "I may not be a sworn witch, but I have more Power than a thrice-circle set by such as *that* can confine!"

"What was it trying to do?" I asked.

"A piece of very elementary magic." My sister made a sound close to a snort of contempt. "It was laying a thrice-circle to keep us pinned on this spot. If that is the best the one who sent it can do, then we can beat it on all points."

"When it went north, could it have been returning to the one who sent it?" Kemoc put my own question aloud.

"I think so. It is the nature of the Flannan not to be able to hold any purpose long in mind. And the fact that I defeated it could send it back to the source in panic."

"Then north lies what we seek."

"Northward went the rider also," I added.

"And north would take us once more past the web, and the silent keep, and perhaps other pitfalls. There must come a time when we have clear sight . . ." There was an odd note of hesitation in her voice, drawing our attention to her.

Kaththea stared down at her hands, as I had seen her sit before, cupping in their apparent emptiness something in which she could read the future, and it would seem that was not a bright one.

"To be only half of a thing is never easy," she continued. "This we have always known. I did not take the oath and I have never worn the Jewel of the sisterhood. Yet, save for those two things, I am a witch. There is one other step I did not take, which was forbidden to one not sworn and bound by seer oaths. Yet now this might serve, even save us."

"No!" Kemoc knew, though I did not, what she hinted. His hands went to cup her chin, bringing up her head so that he might look straight into her eyes. *"No!"* he repeated, with such force that his cry might have been a battle shout.

"So we continue to walk into hidden peril, when by so much we may be able to guard, and guide?" she asked.

"And you would do this thing, knowing all the danger which lies in it? We have no time for rank folly either, Kaththea. Think—how many even of the sisterhood have taken this grave step? And when it is done they must have the aid of the Power to the highest degree. And—"

"And, and, and!" she interrupted him. "Do not believe all you have heard, Kemoc. It is the nature of any organization of Wise Ones that they make mysteries to awe those who have not their gifts. Yes, it is true that few Witches now have this aid, but in Estcarp there was little reason for it. What need had they to explore? They knew their country intimately, both as it was and as it had been for countless years. They have not ventured for centuries into territory so strange they must have a delegate. It was our father and mother, not the Witches, who went up against the Kolder. And in their time the Kolder sealed off Gorm. But here is no alien force, only that which we know in part. Though it may be warped or changed in some particulars. Thus no better aid could we summon—"

"What does she mean?" I appealed to Kemoc.

"A Familiar's birth," he replied. His face was as set as it had been on that ride to bring Kaththea forth from the Place.

"A Familiar?" I did not yet know what he meant. What was a Familiar?

Kaththea raised her hands and took Kemoc's wrists so that she could set aside his grasp on her chin. She did not look at me when she answered, but at him as if she would impose her will so that he could not deny her desire.

"I must make a servant, Kyllan. One which will explore not this country as we see it, walk it, sense it, but who can return to the past and witness what chanced here and what can be done in the present for our preservation."

"And how must she do this?" Kemoc burst out hotly. "As a woman gives birth to a child, so must she in a measure create a being, though this will be born of her mind and spirit, not her flesh! It can be a deadly thing!"

"All birth lays a risk on someone," Kaththea's quiet tone was in such contrast to his anger that it carried more emphasis. "And—if you are both willing—I shall have more than myself to call upon. Never before in Estcarp have there been three like us—is that not so? We can be one after a fashion when there is need. What if we now unite so and will with me—will not the risk be so much the lessened? I would not try this alone, that I swear to you in all truth. Only if you will consent freely and willingly to my aid will this be my path."

"And you think that there is a true need for such an act?" I asked.

"It is a choice between walking into a pit as blindly as I crossed the mountains, or going clear-eyed. The seeds of all perils which lurk here were sown in the past, and time has both nourished and mutated them. But should we dig up those seeds and understand the reason for their sowing, then we can also take guard against the fruit they have borne through the years."

"I will not!" Kemoc was vehement.

"Kemoc . . ." She had not loosed her hold on his hands, and now she spread out the scarred and stiff-fingered one, smoothing its ridged flesh. "Did you say 'I will not' when you went into the fight wherein you got this?"

"But that was far different! I was a man, a warrior—it was my strength against that of those I faced—"

"Why count me as less than yourself?" she countered. "Perhaps my battles may not be fought with dart gun and sword blade, but I have been under as severe a discipline these six years as any warrior could ever know. And I have in that time been set against such enemies as perhaps you cannot even conceive. Nor am I saying now in false confidence that I can do this thing alone—I know that is not the truth. I am bidding you to a fight, to stand with me, which is an easier thing than willing you to stand aside and do nothing while watching another take risks."

His set lips did not relax, but he did not protest again, and I knew that she had won. Perhaps I had not fought on his side because I did not know the danger into which she would venture, but my ignorance was also trust in her. At moments such as these she was no young girl: instead she put on such a robe of authority that the matter of years did not mean much and she was our elder.

"When?" Kemoc surrendered with that word.

"What better time than here and now? Though first we must eat and drink. Strength of body means backing for strength of mind and will."

"The drinking is easy, but the eating . . ." Kemoc looked a little brighter, as if he had discovered in this mundane need an argument for abandoning the whole project.

"Kyllan will provide." Again she did not look at me. But I knew what must be done. And this I had never tried before, save when I had approached it with the Torgians.

When one has even a small share of talent or reflection of the Power, one also knows that there are bounds set upon its use. And to willfully break one such for one's own benefit exacts a price in return. Never since the time I had first learned I could control the minds of beasts had I ever used that to facilitate hunting. I had not sent the Torgians away in peril when I had dispatched them from our camp. Several times I had deterred wild things from attacking or trailing men. But to summon a creature to death for my profit, I sensed, was one of the forbidden things.

But now that was just what I must do, for the good Kaththea would accomplish. Silently I took upon myself the full responsibility for my act, lest the backlash of this perversion of the Power fall upon my sister's sorcery. Then I set myself, intently, to seek and draw the food we must have.

Fish and reptiles, as I had long ago learned, had minds so apart from human kind that they could not be compelled to action—though, in the case of some reptiles, a withdrawing could be urged. But a mammal could be so brought to us. Prong-horns could swim. . . . Mentally I built up as vivid a picture of a prong-horn as memory and imagination combined could create. Holding such a picture then, I cast out my thin line, seeking contact. Never before I tried to do this thing, for I had dealt with beasts directly under eye, or knew, from other evidence, were nearby. This seeking for no particular animal, but only one of a species, might fail.

But it did not. My spinning thought made contact—and instantly I impressed will, needing to move swiftly to control the animal. Moments later a young prong-horn leaped down the river bank in full sight. I brought it out into the flood at the same angle we had used so that the current would bear it to the islet.

"No!" I forbade Kemoc's use of his gun. The kill was my responsibility in all ways; none of the guilt must go to another. I awaited the animal I had forced to swim to its death, and all I could offer it was a quick, clean end.

Kaththea watched me closely as I dragged up the body. Out of my troubled mind I asked her:

"Will this in any way lessen the Power?"

She shook her head, but there was a shadow in her eyes. "We need only strength of body, Kyllan. But yet . . . you have taken upon yourself a burden. And how great will be your payment, I cannot reckon."

A lessening of my talent, I thought, and put it to mind that I must not trust that in any crisis until I was sure of the extent of my loss. Nor did I take into consideration that this was not Estcarp, that those rules which conditioned witchery in that land might not hold here where the Power had been set adrift into other ways.

We made a fire of drift and ate, forcing ourselves past the first satisfying of hunger, as flames must consume fuel for some necessary degree of heat.

"It is near to night." Kemoc thrust a stick which had spitted meat into the heart of the fire. "Should this not wait upon daybreak? Ours is a force fed by light. Such summoning at the wrong time might bring instead a Power of the dark."

"This is a thing which, begun at sunset, is well begun. If a Familiar be sent forth by the mid-hour of the night, it may rove the farther. Not always are light and dark so opposed, one to the other," Kaththea returned. "Now listen well, for once I have begun this I cannot tell you aught, or explain. We shall clasp hands, and you must join minds as well. Pay no heed to anything my body may do, save do not loose our hand clasp. Above all, no matter what may come, stay with me!"

We needed to make no promises as to that. I feared now for her, as Kemoc did. She was very young for all her seeress training. And, though she seemed very sure of her powers, yet she might also have the overconfidence of the warrior who has not yet been tried in his first ambush.

The clouds which had overhung the day lifted at sunset, and my sister drew us around to face those brilliant flags in the sky, so that we could also see the mountains over which we had come into this haunted land. We joined hands and then minds.

For me it was like that time when our mother had so drawn upon the three of us in her search for our father. There was first the loss of identity, with the knowledge that I must not fight that loss though it went against every instinct of self-preservation. After that—a kind of flowing back and forth, in and out . . . a weaving . . . of what?

I do not know how long that period lasted, but I emerged suddenly, my hand jerking wildly. Kaththea was gasping, moaning, her body moved now and again in convulsive shudders. I caught at her shoulder with my free hand, trying to steady her. Then I heard a cry from Kemoc as he came to my aid.

She gave small, sharp ejaculations of pain. And at intervals she writhed so that we could hardly keep the hold we had promised her we would not break. To make it more difficult, I was tired and drained of strength, so that I had to force myself to every movement.

Her eyes were shut. I thought that she must be elsewhere, her body remaining to fight against what she willed it to do. In the light of the now dying fire her face was not only pale, but faintly luminescent, so that we missed no outward sign of her torment.

The end came with a last sharp outcry and arching of her body. From her sprang a dart of—was it flame? Perhaps the size of my hand, it stood upright, sharply brilliant. Then it swayed a little, as might a candle flame in a breeze. Kaththea shuddered again and opened her eyes to look upon what she had brought forth. The flame shape changed, put forth small pinions of light, and became a slender wand between those wings. Kaththea sighed and then said weakly:

"It is not like—"

"Evil?" Kemoc demanded sharply.

"No. But the form is different. That which is here has had a hand in its making. Form does not matter, though. Now—"

With our arms about her in support, she leaned forward to address the winged wand as she had spoken to the Flannan. In our minds we read the meaning of those unknown words. She was repeating ancient formulae, putting this child, or more-than-child, of hers under obedience, setting it to the task it must do.

Back and forth it swayed as she spoke. Her words might have been wind bending it to and fro. Then she finished and it stood still and upright. Her last command came dart-swift:

"Go!"

It was gone and we sat in the dark. Kaththea withdrew her hands from ours and pressed them down upon her body as if striving to soothe an ache.

I threw wood on the fire. As the flames climbed, her face showed in their light sunken, old, with a cast of suffering I had seen on men sore wounded. Kemoc cried out and drew her to him, so that her head rested on his shoulder, and his cheeks were wet with more than the sweat called forth by our efforts to feed her energy.

She raised her hand slowly and touched his face. "It is over and we have wrought together very well, my brothers! Our child searches time and space, being bound by neither, and what it learns will serve us well. I do not guess this; I know it. Now, let us sleep. . . ."

Kaththea slept, and Kemoc also. But though I was weary yet still there was a restlessness within me. Fear for Kaththea, no—her travail was over, and anything which could have been perilous for her must already have struck during that struggle. Wariness of attack now? I thought not: we were on safe ground for this night. My own guilt? Perhaps. But for that I would not disturb the others. In due time I would pay for what I had done; for the present it would be best to put it out of mind.

I settled down on my blanket, shut my eyes, and strove to invite sleep. Then I started up on one elbow, awake—to listen to a long familiar sound through the night. Not too far away a horse had neighed!

X

I heard the sound of hooves pounding turf. And did I or did I not sight the flash of lightning whip on the far shore of the river, that from which the rasti had swum for their attack? But lastly I fixed my mind on the thought of horses and what those might mean to us. In me grew the determination that with the coming of morning light I would go exploring. . . .

As if that decision were an answer to allay my uneasiness, I slept. For the sounds of the hunt, if hunt it could be, died away, while the murmur of the river made a sound to soothe overwrought nerves.

Though I was the last to sleep, I was the first to wake. Our fire had smoldered into dead ash and the dawn was cold, with damp eddying from the water to touch us with moist fingers. I pulled the rest of the bleached wood we had gathered and coaxed a new blaze into life. It was while I knelt so that I saw him—coming down to the water to drink.

Torgians were the finest steeds of Estcarp, but they were not beautiful. Their coats never gleamed, for all the grooming a man could give, nor were they large in frame. But here, raising a dripping muzzle from the water's edge, was such a mount as a man may dream of all his days, yet never see save in those dreams. Big of frame, yet slender of leg, arched of neck, with a black coat which shone like a polished sword blade, a mane and tail rippling as might a maiden's hair—

And once I looked upon that stallion I knew such a longing as I could not stifle. Head raised he faced me across that current. There was no fear in him; curiosity, yes, but no fear. He was of the wild, and I thought he had never had reason to believe that his will could be subordinated to that of any creature.

For a long moment he stood so, studying me as I moved to the narrow end of the islet. And then, dismissing me as harmless, he drank again, before moving a little into the river, as if he enjoyed the feel of the water about his legs. Looking upon him, his beauty and his proud freedom, I was lost.

Without thought I tried contact, striving to win him so to wait for me, to listen to my desire. Head flung up, he snorted, retreated a step or two for the bank from which he had come. He was curious, yet a little wary. Then I touched what could only be a dim memory—of a rider he had once had . . .

On the shore he waited, watched, as I plunged into the stream, helmless, without the mail or weapons I had laid aside. I swam for the shore and still the stallion stood to watch me, now and then pawing the earth a little impatiently, tossing his head so that the silky mane fluttered out, or flicking his long tail.

He would stand for me! I exulted in my triumph—he was mine! My fears of losing my gift had been foolish; never had my ability to contact an animal mind been so sharp and so quickly successful. With such a horse as this the world was mine! There was only the stallion and me in the early morning—

I waded ashore, unheeding water-soaked garments and the chill of the wind, intent only on the great and wonderful animal waiting for me—for *me!* He lowered his noble head to blow into the palm I held out to him. Then he allowed me to run my hands along his shoulders. He was mine as securely as if I had followed the ancient craft of training wherein a cake of oats and honey carried against my skin for three days and then moistened with my spittle had been given him to eat. Between us there was a bond of no breaking. That was so clear to me that I had no hesitation in mounting him bareback, and he suffered me to do so.

He began to trot and I gloried in the strong motion of his body, the even pacing. In all my years I had never bestrode such force, dignity, beauty, authority. It carried with it an intoxication greater than any wine a man might savor. This—this was being a king, a godling out of early mists of forgotten time.

Behind us was the river, before us an open world. Just the two of us, free and alone. A faint questioning rose somewhere deep within me. Two of us?—away from the river? But there was something back there, something of importance. Under me that mighty body tensed, began to gallop. I twined my fingers deep in the flowing mane which whipped at my face, and knew a wonderful exultation as we pounded on across a plain.

There was sunlight now, and still the stallion ran effortlessly, as if those muscles could know no fatigue. I believed he could keep to that flight for hours. But my first exultation paled as the light brightened. The river . . . I glanced over my shoulder—than dim line far behind marked it. The river . . . and on it . . .

In my mind there was a click. Kaththea! Kemoc! How, why had I come to do this? Back—I must head back there. Without bit or rein I should use my mind to control the stallion, return him to the river. I set my wish upon him—

No effect. Under me that powerful body still galloped away from the river, into the unknown. I thrust again, harder now as my faint discomfort became active alarm. Yet there was no lessening of speed, no turning. Then I strove to take entire control wholly, as I had with the Torgians and the prong-horn I had brought to its death.

It was as if I walked across a crust beneath which bubbled a far different substance. If one did not test the crust it served for a footing, but to strike hard upon it carried one to what lay below. And in those seconds I learned the truth. If what I rode carried to my eyes and my surface probing the form of a stallion, it was in reality a very different creature. What it was I could not tell, save that it was wholly alien to all I knew or wished to know.

And also I believed that I had as much chance of controlling it by my will as I had of containing the full flood of the river in my two hands. I had not mastered a free running horse; I had been taken in as clever a net as had ever been laid for a half-bewitched man, for that I must have been from my first sighting of this beast.

Perhaps I could throw myself from its back, though its pace, now certainly swifter than any set by a real horse, could mean injury, even death, to follow such a try at escape. Where was it taking me, and for what purpose? I strove frantically to pierce below the horse level of its mind. There was a strong compulsion, yes. I was to be entrapped and then delivered—where and to whom?

Through my own folly this had come upon me. But the peril at the end could be more than mine alone, for what if the other two could then be reached through me? That enchantment which had held from my sighting of the horse was breaking fast, cracked by shock and fear.

With me they would possess a lever to use against Kaththea and Kemoc. *They*—who or what were *they?* Who *were* the rulers of this land, and what did they want with us? That the force which had taken me so was not beneficent I was well aware. This was merely another part of that which had tried to trap me in the stone web. And this time I must not summon any aid, lest that recoil upon those I wanted least to harm.

The plain over which we sped did have an end. A dark line of trees appeared to spring out of the ground, so fast was our pace. They were oddly pallid trees, their green bleached, their trunks and limbs gray, as if life had somehow been slowly sucked out of them. And from this gaunt forest came an effluvium of ancient evil, worn and very old, but still abiding as a stench.

There was a road through that wood, and the stallion's hooves rang on its pavement as if he were shod with steel. It did not run straight, but wove in and out. And now I had no desire to leap from my seat, for I believed that more than just clean death awaited any who touched this leached ground.

On and on pounded my mount. I no longer strove to contact its mind; rather did I husband what strength I possessed in perhaps a vain hope that there would be some second allowed me in which I could use every bit of my talent in a last stroke for freedom. And I tried to develop a crust of my own, an outer covering of despair, so that whatever intelligence might be in command would believe I was indeed now its full captive.

Always I had been one who depended upon action of body more than of mind, and this new form of warfare did not come easily. For some men fear ignites and enrages, it does not dampen nor subdue, and so it is with me. I must now curb my burning desire to strike out, and instead harbor all my ability to do so against a time when I might have at least the smallest of chances.

We came through the wood, but still we kept to the road. Now before us was a city, towers, walls. . . . Yet it was not a city of the living as I knew life. From it spread an aura of cold, of utter negation of my kind of living and being. As I stared at it I knew that once I was borne within those gray walls Kyllan Tregarth as he now was would cease to be.

Not only did my inborn rejection of death arm me then, but also the remembrance of those I had betrayed by my yielding to this enchantment. I must make my move—now!

I struck, deep down, through the vanishing crust, into the will of the thing which had captured me. *My will now,* not to turn, to reach safety for myself, but to avoid what lay before me as the final end. If I would die it would be a death of my choosing.

Perhaps I had played my part so well I had deceived that which would compel me to its own ends, or perhaps it had no real knowledge of my species. It must have relaxed its strongest force, for I succeeded in part. That steady stride faltered, and the stallion turned from the city road. I held to my purpose, despite a boiling up of that other will. Then came a petulant flash of anger which reached me almost as if I understood words shouted at me from the walls now to my left. Very well, if I would have it so, then it would let me choose—

And in that was a hint of the wearing of age on the force in command. For, angered by defiance, it was willing to sacrifice a pawn that might be of greater value alive.

The stallion ran smoothly and I had no doubts at all that I rode to my death. But no man dies tamely and I would not yield where any chance of a fight remained. There was a flash in the sky as a bird flapped overhead. The shimmer about it— Flannan! That same one that had visited us on the islet? What was its purpose?

It made a sudden dart and the stallion veered, voicing at the same time a scream of rage, though he did not abate his pace. Again and again the bird dived, to change the path of the animal, until we headed north, away from the city, on ground which climbed to heights forest cloaked and dark against the sky, but green and good, with some of the withered evil of that other wood.

Once the stallion was headed in this direction the Flannan flew above us, keeping a watchful eye upon our going. And in me a small, very small hope was kindled, a fire which a breath could have puffed into nothingness. The Flannan served good, or at least was an ally, and by so much had it challenged that other Power in this land. Thus by a fraction had I the aid of something which might be well disposed to me.

In my need I strove to communicate with any such unknown friend, using the link sense I shared with those of my triple birth. But I was not seer trained; I had no hope of contact. Then I feared lest I endanger those who I hoped were still safe. Only one short cast did I make before I busied myself with thoughts of what I could do for myself.

We were running into broken ground, not quite as twisted and torn as the foothills of the western range, but still cut by sharp bitten ravines and craggy outcroppings. It was no country into which one should penetrate at a wild run. When I tried to reach the stallion's consciousness I found nothing now, only the command to run and run which I could not break.

The end came as we reached the top of a rise, where our path was a narrow one between cliffside wall and a drop into nothingness. In that moment my hope was extinguished, for the Flannan made another of those darts, the stallion leaped, and we were falling—

All men speculate sometime during their lives on the nature of death. Perhaps this is not so common while we are young, but if a man is a warrior there is always the prospect of ending at the point of every sword he must face. Thus he cannot push from him the wonder of what will become of that which is truly him, once that sword may open the final gate.

There are believers who hold to them the promise of another world beyond that gate, in which there is a reckoning and payment on both sides of the scale, for the good and the ill they have wrought in their lifetimes. And others select endless sleep and nothingness as their portion.

But I had not thought that pain, torment so racking that it filled the entire world, was what ate on one when life was passed. For I was pain—all pain—a shrieking madness of it in which I no longer had a body, was only fire ever burning, never quenched. Then that passed and I knew that I had a body, and that body was the fuel of the flame which burned.

Later, I could see . . . and there was sky over me, blue as ever the sky of life had been. A broken branch showed a freshly-splintered end against the sky. But always the abiding pain was a cover over and about me, shutting off the reality of branch and sky.

Pain—and then a small thought creeping through the pain, a dim feeling that this was not the mercy of death, that that was yet to come and I had life still to suffer. I closed my eyes against the sky and the branch and willed with all left in me, in that small place yet free from the crowding pain, that death would come and soon.

After awhile there was a little dulling of the pain and I opened my eyes, hoping this meant death was indeed close, for I knew that sometimes there was an end to agony when a man neared his departure. On the branch now perched a bird—not the Flannan, but a true bird with brilliantly blue-green feathers. It peered down at me and then raised its head and gave out a clear call. And I wondered dully if so fair a thing could be an eater of carrion, akin to those black ill-omened gleaners of the battlefields.

The pain was still a part of me, yet between it and me there was a cushioning cloud. I tried to turn my head, but no nerve nor muscle obeyed my will. The sky, the branch, the peering bird: that was what my world had become. But the sky was very blue, the bird was beautiful, and the pain less. . . .

As I had heard the bird call, so now I heard another sound. Hooves! The stallion! But I could not be charmed onto his back now; in that much had I escaped the trap. The pound of hooves on earth stopped. Now came another noise. . . . But that did not matter; nothing mattered—save that the pain was less.

I looked up into a face which came between me and the branch.

How can I describe a dream in clumsy words? Are there ever creatures fashioned of mist and cloud, lacking the solid harshness of our own species? A wraith from beyond that gate now opening for me—?

Pain, sudden and sharp, bore me once more into torment. I screamed and heard that cry ring in my own ears. There was a cool touch on my head and from that spread a measure of curtain once more between me and red agony. I gasped and spun out into darkness.

But I was not to have that respite for long. Once more I came into consciousness. This time neither branch nor bird nor wraith face was over me, though the sky was still blue. But pain was with me. And it exploded in hot darts as there was movement over and about me where someone subjected my broken body to further torment.

I whimpered and begged, my voice a quavering ghost which was not heeded by my torturer. My head was raised, propped so, and forcing my eyes open I strove to see who wished me such ill.

Perhaps it was the pain which made that whole picture wavery and indistinct. I lay bare of body, and what I saw of that body my mind flinched from recording—broken bones must have been the least of the injuries. But much was hidden beneath red mud and the rest was being speedily covered in the same fashion.

It was hard in my dizzy state to see the workers. At least two of them were animals, bringing up the mud with front paws, patting it down in mounds over my helpless and broken limbs. Another had a scaled skin which gave off sparkling glints in the sunlight. But the fourth, she who put on the first layer with infinite care . . .

My wraith? Just as the Flannan's feathered wings had shimmered, so did her body outline fade and melt. Sometimes she was a shadow, then substance. And whether that was because of my own condition or an aspect of her nature I did not know. But that she would do me well instead of ill I dimly guessed.

They worked with a swift concentration and deftness, covering from sight the ruin of torn flesh and broken bones. Not as one would bury a spirit-discarded body, but as those who labor on a task of some delicacy and much need.

Yet none of them looked into my eyes, nor showed in any way that they knew I was aware of what they did. After a time this came to disturb me, leading me to wonder if I were indeed seeing this, or whether it was all born of some pain-rooted hallucination.

It was not until she who led that strange company reached the last packing of mud under my chin and smoothed it over with her hands that she did at last look into my eyes. And even so close a view between us brought no lasting certainty of her true countenance. Always did it seem to flow or change, so that sometimes her hair was dark, her face of one shape, her eyes of one color, and the next she was light of hair, different of eye, changed as to chin line—as if, in one woman, many faces had been blended, with the power of changing from one to another at her will or the onlooker's fancy. And this was so bewildering a thing that I closed my eyes.

But I felt a cool touch on my cheek and then the pressure of fingertips on my forehead growing stronger. There was a soft singing which was like my sister's voice when weaving a spell, and yet again unlike, in that it held a trilling like a bird's note, rising and falling. But from that touch spread a cooling, a soothing throughout my head and then down into my body, putting up a barrier against the pain which was now a dim, far-off thing, no longer really a part of me. And as the singing continued it seemed that I did not lay buried in mud for some unknown reason, but that I floated in a place which had no relation to time or space as I knew those to exist.

There were powers and forces in that place beyond measurement by human means, and they moved about on incomprehensible duties. But that it all had meaning I also knew. Twice did I return to my body, open my eyes and gaze into that face which was never the same. And once behind it was night sky and moonlight, and once again blue, with drifting white clouds.

Both times did the touch and the singing send me out once more into the other places beyond the boundaries of our world. Dimly I knew that this was not the death I had sought during the time of my agony, but rather a renewing of life.

Then for the third time I awoke, and this time I was alone. And my mind was clear as it had not been since that dawn when I had looked at the stallion by the river. My head was still supported so that I could look down my body mounded by clay. It had hardened and baked, with here and there a crack in its surface. But there were no fingers on my flesh, no voice singing. And this bothered me, first dimly and then with growing unease. I strove to turn my head, to see more of where I lay, imprisoned in the earth.

XI

*T*here was a curving wall to my left, and, a little way from that saucer-like slope, a pool which bubbled lazily, a pool of the same red mud hardened upon my body. I turned my head slowly to the left: again there was the wall and farther beyond another pool, its thick substance churning. It was day—light enough, though there were clouds veiling the sun. I could hear the soft plop-plop as the pool blew bubbles and they broke.

Then came another sound, a plaintive mewling which held in it such a burden of pain that it awoke my own memories, hazy though they now tended to be. On the rim of the saucer something stirred and pulled itself laboriously along. It gathered in a back-arched hump and each movement was so constrained and awkward that I knew the creature was sorely injured.

It slid over the concave slope, uttering a sharp yowl of hurt. A snow cat! The beautiful gray-white of its thick fur was dabbled with blood. There was an oozing rent in its side, so deep I thought I could see the white of bone laid bare. But still the cat crawled, its eyes fixed on the nearest pool, uttering its plaint. With a last effort of what must have been dying energy it rolled into the soft mud, plastering its hurt and most of its body. Then it lay still, now facing me, panting, its tongue lolling from its jaws, and it no longer cried.

I might have believed the cat dead, save that the heavy panting continued. It did not move again, lying half in the pool of mud as if utterly spent.

My range of vision was very limited; whatever braced my head to give it to me was not high. But I could see other pools in this depression. And by some of them were mounds which could mark other sufferers who had dragged their hurts hither.

Then I realized that all my pain was gone. I had no desire to move, to break the dried covering which immobilized me. For I felt languidly at ease, soothed, a kind of well-being flowing through my body.

There were a number of tracks in the dried mud about me, even prints left in that mounded over my body. I tried to see them more clearly. Had it been truth and not a dream, that half-memory of lying here torn and broken while two furred and one scaled creature had worked to pack me under the direction of an ever-changing wrath? But all trace of the latter were missing, save for a hand print which was left impressed, sharp and clear, over the region of my heart.

Slender fingers, narrow palm—yes it was human, no animal pad nor reptile foot. And I tried to remember more clearly the wraith who had been one woman and then another in a bewildering medley of shimmering forms.

The snow cat's eyes were closed, but it still breathed. Along its body the mud was already hardening into a protective crust. How long—for the first time the idea of time itself returned to me. Kaththea—Kemoc! How long had it been since I had ridden away from them on that devil's lure?

My languid acceptance broke as the need for action worked in me. I strove to move. There was no yielding of the dried mud. I was a helpless prisoner, encased in stone hard material! And that discovery banished all my waking content.

I do not know why I did not call aloud, but it never occurred to me to do so. Instead I used the mind call, not to those I had deserted during my bewitchment, but to the wraith, she who might not have any existence at all save in my pain world.

What would you do with me?

There was a scurry. A thing which glinted with rainbow colors skittered across the basin, reared up on hind legs to survey me with bright beads of eyes. It was not any creature I had known in Estcarp, nor was it from one of the legends. Lizard, yes, but more than a mere green-gold reptile. Beautiful in its way. It had paused at my buried feet; now it gave a little leap to the mound which encased me and ran, on its hind legs, up to my head. There it stopped to examine me searchingly. And I knew there was intelligence of a sort in its narrow, pike-crested head.

"Greeting, sword brother." The words came out of me unthinkingly.

It whistled back, an odd noise to issue from that scaled throat. Then it was gone, a green-gold streak heading up and over the rim of the saucer.

Oddly enough its coming and going allayed my first dismay at finding myself a prisoner. The lizard had certainly not meant me harm and neither, I was certain, had those who had left me here. That was apparent by my own present feeling of well-being, and by the actions of the sorely hurt snow cat. This was a place of healing to which an animal would drag itself if it could. And those virtues had been applied to me . . . by whom? The lizard, the furred ones . . . the wraith. . . . yes, surely the wraith!

Though I could not smell sorcery as Kaththea could, I was sure no evil abode here—that it was an oasis of some Power. And I was alive only because I had been brought into its beneficent influence. Now I knew by a tingling of my skin, a prickling of my scalp, a little like that excitement which eats one before the order to advance comes, that there was something on the way.

Several of the lizards sped down the saucer side, and behind them, at a less frantic pace, came two of the furred beasts, their hides also of a blue-green shade. Their narrow heads and plumed tails were those of a tree-dwelling animal I knew, but they were much larger than their brothers of Estcarp.

Behind this advance guard and out-scouts she came, walking with a lithesome stride. Her dark hair hung loose about her shoulders—but *was* it dark? Did it glint with a red hue? Or was it light and fair? To me it seemed all that at one and the same time. She wore a tunic of green-blue close-fitting her body, leaving arms and legs bare. And this garment was girdled by a broad belt of green-blue gems set thickly in pale gold, flexible to her movements. About each slender wrist was a wide band of the same gems, and she carried by a shoulder strap a quiver of arrows, all tipped with blue-green feathers, and a bow of the pale gold color.

One could be far more certain of her garments than of her, since, though I struggled to focus on her face and that floating cloud of hair, I could not be sure of what I saw, that some haze of change did not ever hold between us. Even as she knelt beside me that disorientation held.

"Who are you?" I asked that baldly, for my inability to see her clearly irked me.

Amazingly, I heard her laugh. Her hand touched my cheek, moved to my forehead, and under that touch my vision cleared. I saw her face—or one face—sharply and distinctly.

The features of the Old Race are never to be mistaken: the delicate bones, the pointed chin, the small mouth, larger eyes, arched brows. And she possessed these, making such beauty as to awe a man. But there was also about her a modification which hinted at the unhuman as I knew human. That did not matter—not in the least did it matter.

A warrior knows women. I was no Falconer to foreswear such companion-ship. But it is also true that some appetites run less deeply with the Old Race. Perhaps the very ancientness of their blood and the fact that the witch gift has set a wedge between male and female makes this so. I had never looked upon any woman whom I wanted for more than a passing hour of pleasure such as the Free Companions of the Sulcar give, finding equal enjoyment of such play. But it was no passing desire which awoke in me as I gazed at that face. No, this was some-thing different, a heightening of the excitement which had built in me as I had sensed her coming, a thing I had never known before.

She laughed and then fell sober once again, her eyes holding mine in a lock which was not quite the communication I wished.

"Rather—who are you?" Her demand was swift, almost roughly spoken.

"Kyllan of the House of Tregarth, out of Estcarp," I replied formally, as I might on delivering a challenge. What was it between us? I could not quite un-derstand. "And you?" For the second time I asked, and now my tone pressed for her reply.

"I have many names, Kyllan of the House of Tregarth, out of Estcarp." She was mocking me, but I did not accept that mockery.

"Tell me one, or two, or all."

"You are a brave man," her silken mockery continued. "In my own time and place. I am not one to be lightly named."

"Nor will I do it lightly." From whence had come this word play new to me?

She was silent. Her fingers twitched as if she would lift them from my fore-head. And that I feared, lest my clear sight of her be so spoiled.

"I am Dahaun, also am I Morquant, and some say Lady of the Green—"

"—Silences," I finished for her as she paused. Legend—no! She was alive; I felt the pressure and coolness of her flesh against mine.

"So you know me after all, Kyllan of the House of Tregarth."

"I have heard the old legends—"

"Legends?" Laughter bubbled once again from her. "But a legend is a tale which may or may not hold a core of truth. I dwell in the here and now. Estcarp—and where is Estcarp, bold warrior, that you know of Dahaun as a legend?"

"To the west, over the mountains—"

She snatched her hand away, as if the touch burnt her fingertips. Once more distortion made her waver in my sight.

"Am I suddenly made so into a monster?" I asked of the silence fallen be-tween us.

"I do not know—are you?" Then her hand was back, and once more she was clear to see. "No, you are not—though what you are I do not know either. That Which Dwells Apart strove to take you with the Keplian, but you were not swallowed up. You fought in a way new to me, stranger. And then I read you for a force of good, not ill. Yet the mountains and what lie behind them are a barrier through which only ill may seep—or so say *our* legends. Why did you come, Kyllan of the House of Tregarth, out of Estcarp?"

I had no wish to dissemble with her: between us must be only the truth as well as I could give it.

"For refuge."

"And what do you flee, stranger? What ill have you wrought behind you that you must run from wrath?"

"The ill of not being as our fellows—"

"Yes, you are not one but three—and yet, also one. . . ."

Her words aroused memory. "Kaththea! Kemoc? What—?"

"What has happened to them since you would go ariding the Keplian, thus foolishly surrendering yourself to the very power you would fight? They have taken their own road, Kyllan. This sister of yours has done that which has troubled the land. We do not easily take Witches to our bosoms here, warrior. In the past that served us ill. Were she older in magic, then she would not have been so eager to trouble dark pools which should be left undisturbed in the shadows. So far she has not met that which she cannot face with her own shield and armor. But that state of affairs will not last long—not here in Escore."

"But you are a Wise One." I was as certain of that as if I saw the Witch Jewel on her breast, yet I also knew that she was not of the same breed as the rulers of Estcarp.

"There are many kinds of wisdom, as you well know already. Long ago, roads branched here in Escore, and we Green People chose to walk in different ways. Some led us very far apart from one another. But also through the years we learned to balance good against ill, so that there was no inequality to draw new witchcraft in. To do so, even on the side of good, will evoke change, and change may awaken things which have long slumbered, to the ill of all. This has your sister done—as an unthinking child might smite the surface of a pool with a stick, sending ripples running, annoying some monster at ease in the depths. Yet . . ." She pursed her lips as if about to give judgment, and in that small movement lost more of the strangeness which separated us, so that I saw her as a girl, like Kaththea. "Yet, we can not deny to her the right of what she has done; we only wish she had done it elsewhere!" Again Dahaun smiled. "Now, Kyllan of Tregarth, we have immediate things to see to."

Her hand went from my head to the baked clay over my chest. Down the center of that she scratched a line with the nail of her forefinger, again marking such along my arms and legs.

The creatures that had accompanied her thereupon set to work, clawing away along those lines, working with a speed and diligence which suggested this was a task they had performed many times before. Dahaun got to her feet and crossed to the snow cat, stooping to examine the drying mud, stroking the head of the creature between the eyes and up behind the ears.

Speedy as her servants were, it took them some time to chip me out of my covering. But finally I was able to rise out of the depression which was the shape of my body. My limbs were whole, although scarred with marks of almost healed hurts I would have thought no man could survive.

"Death is powerless here, if you can reach this place," said Dahaun.

"And how *did* I reach this place, lady?"

"By the aid of many strengths, to which you are now beholden, warrior."

"I acknowledge all debts," I said, giving the formal reply. But I spoke a little absently, since I looked down upon my nakedness and wondered if I was to go so bare.

"Another debt also I lay upon you." Amusement became a small trill of laughter. "What you seek now, stranger, you shall find up there."

She had not moved to leave the wounded cat, merely waved me to the saucer's rim. The ground was soft underfoot as I hurried up the slope, a couple of the lizards flashing along.

There was grass here, tall as my knees, soft and green, and by two rock pillars a bundle of nearly the same color. I pulled at a belt which held it together and inspected my new wardrobe. The outer wrapping was a green cloak, within garments which seemed at first well tanned and very supple leather, and which I then decided were some unknown material. There were breeches, with attached leggings and booted feet sections, the soles soft and earth-feeling. Above the waist I donned a sleeveless jerkin which latched halfway down my chest by a metal clasp set with one of the blue-green gems Dahaun favored. The belt supported not a sword, but a metal rod about as long as my forearm and a finger span thick. If it was a weapon, it was like none I had seen before.

The clothing fitted as if it had been cut and sewn for me alone, and gave a marvelous freedom to my body, such as was lacking in the mail and leather of Estcarp. Yet I found my hands were going ever to feel for the arms I did not wear: the sword and dart gun which had been my tools for so long.

With the cloak over my arm I strode back to the edge of the saucer. Now that I could look down upon it I saw that the area was larger than I had thought. A dozen or more of the mud pools were scattered haphazardly about it, and more than one had a patient immobilized—though all of these were animals or birds.

Dahaun still knelt, stroking the snow cat's head. But now she looked up and waved with her other hand and a moment later arose and came to join me, surveying me with a frankly appraising stare.

"You are a proper Green Man, Kyllan of the House of Tregarth."

"A Green Man?"

It did not seem so difficult now for me to read her features, though I still could not have given a positive name to the color of her hair or eyes.

"The Green People." She pointed to the cloak I held. "Though this is only their outer skin that you wear, and not our true semblance. However, it will serve you for what needs be done." She put her half closed fist to her mouth as had my sister when engaged in sorcery, but the sound she uttered was a clear call, not unlike the high note of a verge horn.

A drumming of hooves brought me around, my hand seeking a weapon I no longer had. Sense told me this was not the stallion that had been my undoing, yet that sound now made my flesh creep.

They came out of the green shadow of a copse, shoulder to shoulder, cantering easily and matching their paces. They were bare of saddle or bridle, but only in that were they like the stallion. For they had not the appearance of true horses at all. More closely allied to the prong-horns, yet not them either, they were as large as a normal mount, but their tails were brushes of fluff they kept clipped tight against their haunches as they moved. There was no mane, but a topknot of fluffy longer hair on the crest of each skull, right above a horn which curved gracefully in a gleaming red arc. In color they were a sleek, roan red, with a creamy underbody. And for all their strangeness I found them most beautiful.

Coming to a stop before Dahaun, they swung their heads about to regard me with large yellow eyes. As with the lizard, they shared a spark of what I realized was intelligence.

"Shabra, Shabrina," Dahaun said gravely in introduction, and those proud horned heads inclined to me in dignified recognition of their naming.

Out of the grass burst one of the lizards, running to Dahaun, who stopped to catch it up. It sped up her arm to her shoulder, settling there in her hair.

"Shabra will bear you." One of the horned ones moved to me. "You need have no fears of *this* mount."

"He will take me to the river?"

"To those who seek you," she replied obliquely. "Fortune attend you—good, not ill."

I do not know why I had expected her to come with me, but I was startled at the suggestion she would not. So abrupt a parting was like the slicing of a rope upon which one's safety depended.

"You—you do not ride with me?"

She was already astride her mount. Now she favored me with one of those long, measuring stares.

"Why?"

To that I had no answer but the simple truth. "Because I cannot leave you so—"

"You feel your debt weighing heavily?"

"If owing one's life is a debt, yes—but there is more. Also, even if there was no debt, still I would seek your road."

"To do this you are not free."

I nodded. "In this I am not free—you need not remind me of that, lady. You owe me no debt—the choice is yours."

She played with one of the long tresses of hair hanging so long as to brush the gems on her belt.

"Well said." Plainly something amused her and I was not altogether sure I cared for her laughter now. "Also, I begin to think that having seen one out of Estcarp, I would see more—this sister of yours who may have stirred up too much for all of us. So I choose your road . . . for this time. HO!" She gave a cry and her mount leaped with a great bound.

I scrambled up on Shabra and fought to keep my seat as he lunged to catch up with his mate. Sun broke through clouds to light us, and as it touched Dahaun she was no longer dusky. The hair streaming behind her in the wind was the same pale gold of her belt and wristlets, and she blazed with a great surge of light and life.

XII

*T*here was a thing loping awkwardly in a parallel course towards us. Sometimes it ran limpingly on three legs, a forelimb held upcurved; again, stumbling and bent over, on two. Dahaun checked her mount and waited for the creature to approach. It lifted a narrow head, showed fangs in a snarl. There were patches of foam at the corners of its black lips, matting the brindle fur on its neck and shoulders, while the forelimb it upheld ended in a red blob of mangled flesh.

It growled, walked stiff-legged, striving to pass Dahaun at a distance. As I rode to join her, my hair stirred a little at skull base. For this was not animal, but something which was an unholy mingling of species—wolf and man.

"By the pact." Its words were a coughing growl and it made a half gesture with its wounded paw-hand.

"By the pact," Dahaun acknowledged. "Strange, Fikkold, for *you* to seek what lies here. Have matters gone so badly that the dark must seek the light for succor?"

The creature snarled again, its eyes gleaming, yellow-red pits of that evil against which all clean human flesh and spirit revolts.

"There will come a time—" it spat.

"Yes, there will come a time, Fikkold, when we shall test Powers, not in small strikes against each other, but in open battle. But it would appear that you have already done battle, and not to benefit for you."

Those yellow-red eyes shifted away from Dahaun, as if they could not bear to look too long at the golden glory she had become. Now they fastened on me. The twisted snarl was more acute. Fikkold hunched his shoulders as if he wished to spring to bring me down. My hand sought the blade I did not wear.

Dahaun spoke sharply. "You have claimed the right, Fikkold; do you now step beyond that right?"

The wolf-man relaxed. A red tongue licked between those fanged jaws.

"So you make one with these, Morquant?" he asked in return. "That will be pleasant hearing for the Gray Ones, and That Which Is Apart. No, I do not step beyond the right, but perchance you have crossed another barrier. And if you make common cause with these, ride swift, Green Lady, for they need all the aid possible."

With a last snarl in my direction, Fikkold went on, staggering, weaving toward the mud pools, his blood-streaming paw pressed tight to his furred breast.

But what he had hinted at, that Kaththea and Kemoc might be in active danger, sent me pounding along his back trail.

"No!" Dahaun pulled up beside me. "No! Never ride so along a were-trail. To follow it straightly leaves your own track open for them. Cross it, thus. . . ."

She cantered in a criss-cross pattern, back and forth across the blood-spotted track the wounded Fikkold had left. And, though I grudged the time such a complicated maneuver cost us, I did likewise.

"Did he speak the truth?" I asked as I drew level with her again.

"Yes, for in this case the truth would please Fikkold." She frowned. "And if they felt strong enough to meet in an open fight with Power such as your sister can shape and mould, then the balance is surely upset and things move here which have not stirred in years upon long years! It is time we knew what or who is aligned. . . ."

She set her hand to her mouth again as she had when she had summoned the horned ones to our service. But no audible sound issued between her fingers. In my head was that sound, shrill, painful. Both our mounts flung high their heads and gave voice to coughing grunts.

I was not too surprised at the shimmer of a Flannan in its bird shape appearing before us. It flapped about Dahaun as she rode. A moment later she looked to me, her face troubled.

"Fikkold spoke the truth, but it is a worse truth than I thought, Kyllan. Those of your blood have been trapped in one of the Silent Places and the thrice circle laid upon them, such as no witch, lest she be more powerful than your sister, may break. Thus can they be held until the death of their bodies—and even beyond—"

I had faced death for myself, and had come to accept the fact that perhaps I had taken the last sword blow. But for Kaththea and Kemoc I would *not* accept this—not while I still breathed, walked, had hands to hold weapons or to use bare. Of this I did not speak, but the resolution filled me in a hot surge of rage and determination. And more strongly was I pledged to this because of my folly and desertion by the river.

"I knew you would feel so," she said. "But more than strength of body, will of mind, desire of heart, will you need for this. Where are your weapons?"

"I shall find such!" I told her between set teeth.

"There is one." Dahaun pointed to the rod which hung as a sword from my borrowed belt. "Whether it will answer you. I know not. It was forged for another hand and mind. Try it. It is a force whip—use it as you would a lash."

I remembered the crackling fire with which the unknown rider had beaten off the rasti and I jerked the rod from its sling, to use it as she suggested, as if a thong depended from its tip.

There was a flash of fire crackling against the ground to sear and blacken. I shouted in triumph. Dahaun smiled at me across that burned strip.

"It would seem that we are not so different after all, Kyllan of the House of Tregarth, out of Estcarp. So you do not ride barehanded, nor, perhaps, will you fight alone. For that, we must see. But to summon aid will take time, and that runs fast for those you would succor. Also, it will need persuasion such as you can not provide. Thus we part here warrior. Follow the blood trail, to do what you must do. I go to other labors."

She was at a gallop before I could speak, her horned one keeping a speed I do not believe even the stallion could have equaled. Before me lay the back trail of the werewolf for my guide.

I followed Dahaun's instructions and continued to crisscross those tracks, but at a steady, ground-eating pace. We descended from that high ground into which the stallion had carried me, away from the healthy country. I did not sight that bleached wood, nor the city, unless a distant gray shadow to my left was a glimpse of that, but there were other places Shabra avoided, sometimes leaving the trail to detour about them—a setting of rocks, an off-color splotch of vegetation and the like. I trusted to my mount's decision in such matters, for it was plain this part of the country was a stronghold of those forces against which my kind were eternally arrayed.

Shabra slowed pace. I marveled at how far Fikkold had come with his spouting wound. A flock of black winged things arose from a tangle of brush and twisted trees, circled above us, crying raucously.

"Whip!"

Out of nowhere came that warning. Then I saw Shabra turn his head, and knew that the alarm came from the one who carried me. I gave a sharp jerk to the weapon. A light flash snapped out. One of the black things screeched, somersaulted in the air and fell. The rest broke, flew for a distance, and then reformed with the cunning of an advance guard, to try once more to complete their circle. Three times they attempted that, and each time the lash drove them off, broke their pattern. From the last attack they flew before us, as if determining somewhere on ahead to lay an ambush.

We were still going down slope. Here the grass in the open spaces was coarser and darker than that of the upper country. And in places it was broken and stamped flat as if a host had gone this way. My scout training asserted control. To ride face on into impossible odds was no way to provide help for those I sought. Tentatively I thought this at Shabra.

They know you come. You cannot hide from those who hold this land.

The answer came clearly and promptly. I was ready to accept any help from my mount which he had ready to offer.

His pace had dropped to a walk. He held his head high, his wide nostrils drawing in and expelling the air in audible sniffs, as if by this sense he could detect what lay ahead. Abandoning the blood trail which had guided us to this point, he swung to the right on a course which angled sharply from the one we had followed.

Along the pillar way. Peace holds there in part.

Shabra's explanation meant nothing to me, but that he was willing to risk this route did. I could not scent anything in the air, though I strove to. But there was something else—a weight upon the spirit, a darkening of the mind, which grew as we advanced, until it was a burden on me.

We came out on the rim of another slope and below lay open country with, not too far away, the line of the river. In that plains land was a circle of menhirs, not concentric rings as had been the stone web, but a single line of rough pillars, two of which had fallen and lay pointing outward. They encircled or guarded a platform of stone of a slate-blue color. And on that platform were the two I sought. While outside the ring of menhirs, a motley pack of creatures crawled, prowled, sniffed. Black blots of rasti slithered in and out, visible where the grass was well trampled. Several werewolves paced, sometimes on four feet, other times erect. The black birds wheeled and dipped. An armorplated thing raised a ghastly head and clawed forefeet now and then. And white blobs of mist gathered, drifted, thickened and thinned. But all these moved outside the ring of stones, and they avoided the two which had fallen outward, leaving a goodly space free about those as they continued their siege.

From the circle led two paths of pillars, one from the direction of the river, one marching up the hill to my right. Of these, many had fallen, some were broken, even blackened, as if they had been lightning struck.

Shabra trotted to the line near us. Again he began an in and out advance. Those broken and blackened stones he leaped or passed with speed; by the others he modified his pace. But back and forth, in and out, he worked down to the besieged circle.

Kyllan! Greeting, recognition from the two I sought.

Then: *Take care! To your left—*

There was an upheaval among the watchers, and one of the armored monsters came at a clumsy run. It opened its mouth to puff foul and stinking breath at us. I swished the whip and the lightning curled about the scaled barrel just behind the head. But that did not slow the thing. Next I laid the lash of energy across its head and eyes. It gave an explosive grunt and plowed ahead.

Hold! Not Kemoc nor Kaththea, but Shabra, warning.

Under me the horned one bunched muscle, leaped, plowed to a halt by a standing stone. The armored thing came on, to be hurled back as if it had run headfirst into a wall that even its bulk could not breach. Its coughing roar grew louder as it kept on stupidly attempting to reach us. Now some of the other attackers gathered to join it. A wolf-man, striding on two feet, yellow-red eyes cunning and intelligent, rasti a-boil, a drifting blob of mist—

Hold!

I gripped Shabra as tightly with my knees as I could, and kept a left-handed hold on the curve of his neck while I held ready the whip with my right. He made a dart past one of the shattered pillars while I lashed at the mist curling in at us. There was a burst of brilliant fire. The thing, whatever it might have been, ignited from the whip's force. Rasti squalled as it puffed out to catch two of them in its throes.

We were in another of the pools of safety by a standing stone. The space ahead was not too wide, but midpoint there was a fallen pillar, and there gathered rasti and wolfmen. The mist drifted back from any contact with the weapon I carried.

Come—now!

That was Kaththea. She stood on the blue block, her hands to her mouth as she chanted. Though the meaning of what she sang did not reach me, I felt a response in my body, a rising surge of strength. The horned one sprang, breaking into a run. I lashed out on either side, not with any aim, but to clear our path.

I heard growling from a hairy wolf throat. One of the were-things sprang, striving to drag me from Shabra's back. I stiff-armed it, my blow striking, by good fortune alone, beneath its jaw. But it left a dripping slash along my arm. Somehow I managed to cling to both my seat on the horned one and the whip. Then we were within the circle. And outside, the howls of that weird pack arose in a discordant chorus.

Shabra trotted to the blue stone. Kemoc half lay, half sat there, with his back supported by a shrunken pack. His helm was gone, his arm bandaged. And in his hand was the hilt of a sword, its blade broken into a narrow sliver. Kaththea still stood on the stone, her hands now at her breast. She was gaunt, as if from months of ill foraging, her beauty worn to a dying shadow, her spirit so outgoing through its sheath of flesh that I was frightened to look upon her. I slid from Shabra's back and came to them, dropping the whip unknowingly, my hands out to give them all that I had, of my own strength, comfort—whatever they could draw from me.

Kemoc greeted me with a faint, very faint stretch of lips, the merest shadow of his one-time smile.

"Welcome back, brother. I might have known that a fight would draw you when all else failed."

Kaththea came to the edge of the rock and half jumped, half fell into my arms.

For a long moment she clung to me, no Wise Woman, no Witch, but only my sister, who had been sorely frightened and yet found the need to put aside that fear. She raised her head, her eyes closed.

"Power." Her lips shaped the word rather than spoke it clearly aloud. "You have lain in the shadow of Power. When—where?" Eagerness overrode her fatigue.

Kemoc stirred and pulled himself up. He was studying me, intently from head to foot, his gaze lingering on my chest where the tunic gaped and the just healed scars from my hurts were still plain to read.

"It would seem that this is not your first battle, brother. But—now it would be well to tend to this—" He gestured to the gash the werewolf had opened on my arm. Kaththea pushed away from me with a little cry of concern.

I felt no pain. Perhaps whatever virtue lay in the healing mud held for a while in the bodies of those so treated. For when Kaththea examined the hurt the edges of the wound were closed and I bled no longer.

"Who has been your aid, my brother?" she asked as she worked.

"The Lady of Green Silence."

My sister raised her head and stared at me as one who seeks for signs of jesting.

"She also calls herself Dahaun and Morquant," I added.

"Morquant!" Kaththea seized upon the second of those names. "Of the Green Ones, the forest born! We must know more, we must!" She moved her hands as if wringing speech from silence.

"You have learned nothing?" Far ago now was that night we had wrought magic that Kaththea's spirit messenger might cross time. "What happened? How and why have you come here?"

Kemoc answered first. "As to your first question, we have learned that trouble arises swiftly hereabouts. We left the islet because—" He hesitated, his eyes avoiding mine.

I gave him the rest: "Because you sought one whose folly had made him easy prey for the enemy? Is that not the right of it?"

And he respected me enough not to give any comforting lie.

"Yes. Kaththea—when we awoke, she knew, and through her did I also, that evil had come to you."

Kaththea asked softly. "Had you not thrown open the gate to it when you used your gift in an ill fashion, even if the result was for our good? We knew not how you had been taken from us, only that this was so. And that we must find you."

"But the Familiar—you needed to await its return."

She smiled at my protest. "Not so. Where I am, there it will come—though that has not yet happened. We found your trail—or at least a trail of active evil. But where it led"—she shivered—"there we dared not follow—not without such safeguards for our inner selves that I did not have the knowledge to weave. Then those came a-hunting, and we ran before them. But this is a holy place in which that kind can not venture. So we took refuge here, only to discover that we had trapped ourselves, for they have woven their net outside and we are within two walls, one built by the enemy."

Then she sighed and swayed so that I threw out an arm to support her. Her eyes closed and she leaned back against me as Kemoc made plain the rest of their plight.

"I do not suppose, brother, that you carry any food? It has been three days since we have eaten. There was dew on the stone this morning, enough to quench our thirst a little. But water in such small amounts does little for the filling of an empty belly!"

"I won in with this," I touched the whip with my toe. "It can cut us a passage out—"

Kemoc shook his head. "We have not the strength nor the quickness for such a fight now. Also, they have a counterspell to strip Kaththea of all Power if she ventures forth."

But I refused to accept that. "With Kaththea on Shabra, and you and I running—it is worth the try!" But I knew that he was right. Outside the protection of the circle stones we could not out-run and out-fight that pack, now padding, trotting, drifting about, waiting for us to try such desperate measures. In addition both Kemoc and Kaththea had said they were immured here by magic.

"Oh!" In my grasp Kaththea shuddered, shaking as she had on the night she had brought forth the Familiar. She opened her eyes and looked before her with a wide, unseeing stare.

"To the stone with her!" Kemoc cried. "It holds the most virtue in this place."

There was a blanket on the stone, as if perhaps during the night they had rested there together. I swung her pitifully light body up to lie on that, and then scrambled to her side, pulling Kemoc after me. She still moaned a little, her hands moving restlessly back and forth, sometimes lifting up as if she sought to pluck something from the air.

The din which had followed my entrance into the circle had died away. Those creatures paraded in utter silence now, so that Kaththea's small plaints could be heard.

One of those reaching hands caught at Kemoc's scarred fingers, clasped and tightened. His thought sped to me and I took her other hand. We were linked now as we had been on that night.

Expectancy awoke in me. There was a glow in the air above the blue block. The glow grew brighter, formed an image, a winged wand, looking solid and distinct.

For a moment we saw it so, and then, as a dart, it dropped in a streak of white fire. Kaththea's back arched and she gave a great cry, as her messenger returned to that which had given it birth. She was quiet but not silent—not to our minds—for as she learned so did we also, and for us rock, day and world vanished as that knowledge unfolded.

XIII

*I*t was a strange sight we had, operating on two levels. First it was as if we hung in the sky above this land as it had once been, all its fields, woods, streams and mountains spread below us. And it was a fair land then, holding no shadows, no spots of corruption. Also it was a well-peopled land, with garths and manors serene and safe. There were three cities—no, four . . . for in the foothills of the mountains was a collection of tall towers apart in use and spirit from the rest. Men and women of the Old Race went about, content and untroubled.

Also there were others, partly of the Old Race, partly of a yet older stock. And these had gifts which led them to be revered. There was a golden light on this land and it drew us as if we rode at twilight through the wind and dark of a coming storm, to see before us the guest lights of a manor wherein dwelt the best of friends. Yes, it drew us, yet we could not accept what it promised, for between us lay the barrier of time.

Then that all encompassing vision narrowed, and we watched the coming of change. There were Wise Women here, but they did not rule so autocratically as they did in Estcarp. For not only did the women of this land have the gift of Power—among them were men who could also walk with spirits.

How did the ill begin? With good intentions, not by any active evil. A handful of seekers after knowledge experimented with Powers they thought they understood. And their discoveries, feeding upon them in turn, altered subtly spirit, mind, and sometimes even body. Power for its results was what first they sought, but then, inevitably, it was Power for the sake of power alone. They did not accept gradual changes; they began to force them.

Years sped as might the moments of an hour. There was the rise of the brother-sisterhood, first secretly, then in the open, dedicated to experimentation, with volunteers, then with those forced to their purposes. Children, animals, things were born which were not as their parents had been. Some were harmless, even of great beauty and an aid to all. But that kind became fewer and fewer. At first those that were distorted, ill-conceived, were destroyed. Then it was proposed that they be kept, studied, examined. Later yet their makers released them, that they might be observed in freedom.

And, as the corruption spread and befouled those who dabbled in it, these monstrosities were used! Nor did the users and the makers any longer place bonds on the fashioning of such dark servants and weapons.

So began a struggle, to eclipse the fast fading brightness of the land. There was a party of the Old Race, as yet unshadowed by the evil flowering among their kind. At first they sounded war horns, gathering a host to put down the enemy. But they had waited far too long; they were as a dipper of water against the ocean. War brought them bitter defeat and the prospect of being utterly lost in the ocean of defilement which was turning their homeland into a morass wherein no decent thing might find existence.

There were leaders who argued that it was better to perish in war than to live under the hand of the enemy, taking with them all that they held dear, so that death would in fact be safety from that which threatened more than the body. And there were many who supported them in that. We watched households go into their manors, take comfort together, and then bring down upon themselves a blotting out by raw forces they deliberately summoned and did not try to control.

But others held to a faith that the end was not yet for them and their kind. Against the array of the Enemy they were a pitifully few in number. But among them were some wielders of the Power such as even their opponents might well fear. And these ordered an ingathering of those willing to try another road.

There was this about the Old Race: they were deeply rooted in their own country, drawing from the land a recharging of energy and life force. Never had they been wanderers, rovers, seekers of the physical unknown—though they moved afar in mind and spirit. And to leave the land was almost as hard as death. Still they were minded to try this. And they set out for the west and what might lie across the bordering mountains there.

They did not go without trouble. The crooked servants of the Enemy harassed their train, harried them by night and day. They lost men, women, families— some to death, some otherwise. Yet they held to their purpose. Through the mountains they fought their way. And once beyond those barriers, they turned and wrought such havoc against the land that it closed the road behind them for century upon century.

Left to itself, evil boiled and spread out in greedy freedom. But it was not entire master in the land, even though what challenged it lay very low, making no move in those first years to betray its presence. The Old Race had not taken with it any of the creatures that had been born of experimentation, not even those attuned to good rather than ill. A few of these were strong, and they withdrew to the waste spaces and there disguised themselves against detection. There were also those who were not of the Old Race in whole, but part more ancient yet. And these were so united to the land that it was their life base.

There were only a handful of these, yet they were held in awe and shunned by the new rulers. For, though they had not stirred against evil, nor actively aided good, yet they had such forces under their command as could not be reckoned by evil. These too withdrew to the wild, and in time they attracted to them the created ones in loose alliance. But evil ruled totally except in these wastes.

Time flowed as the river current. Those who were drunk with power arose to greater and greater extravagances in its use. Quarreling, they turned upon one another, so that the countryside was wracked with strange and terrible wars, fought with energies and inhuman, demonic things. Struggles lasted so for centuries, but there were drastic defeats, completely wiping out one force or the other. Thus the more outwardly aggressive ate up each other. Then there were those who turned their backs upon the world as it was and ventured farther and farther into weird realms they broke open for exploration. Of these few ever returned. So did the long toll of years bring a measure of quietude to the riven land.

There were still powers of evil, but the majority of them, satiated by countless tastings and explorations, were lulled into a kind of abstracted existence in which they floated unmoved and unmoving. Now those in the wastes ventured forth, a creeping at first, wary, ready to retreat. For they only tested evil in small ways, not battles.

In time they held again half the land, always taking cautiously, never offering direct opposition when one of the evil ones was aroused to active retaliation. And this had gone on so long it was the accepted way of life.

Then—into this balanced land we had come, and we saw in part what our coming had done. Magic summoned magic, aroused more than one of the dreaming evils into languid action. Yet against the least of these, alone, we were as helpless as the dust the wind whirls before it. As for now the evil was old, withdrawn, yet still a little rooted to this plane. Were we greater than we were— only a little greater—it could be utterly driven forth into that world, or worlds, which it now roved, doors sealed behind it, the land free and golden, and open for our kind once again.

I opened my eyes to meet Kemoc's.

"So now we know," he said quietly. "And are no better for that knowing. The Council, in our position, could overcome this. We have not a single chance! And it was—*is*—so fair a land!"

I shared that nostalgic longing for the country we had seen at the beginning of that time flight. All my life I had lived under the cloud of war and trouble. And I had faced from a child the knowledge that I was living in the end days of a civilization which had no hope. Therefore to have seen what we had been shown was doubly bitter. And to realize there was nothing we could do—not even to save ourselves—was more than bitter.

Kaththea stirred in our hold. Her eyes opened. Tears gathered, flowed to her thin cheeks.

"So beautiful! So warm, so good!" she whispered. "And if—if we only had the Power—we could bring it back!"

"If we had wings," I said harshly, "we could fly out of here!" I gazed over my shoulder at what lay beyond our protecting ring of stones.

The creatures of the dark still prowled there. And I knew, without needing the telling, they would continue to do so, until there came an end to us and all the slight danger to their overlords which we represented.

It was growing dark and, while I knew that the pillars would keep them at a distance, yet I was also haunted by the knowledge that with the night their true world began, that they would be strengthened by so much. I was hungry and if I felt thus, how much more must Kaththea and Kemoc be in need of food. To stay here, waiting for death—that could not be my way!

Again I thought of Shabra. He had brought me safely in—could be get out again? And doing so, might he serve as a messenger? Could or would Dahaun do aught to aid us now? She had said she was going for help, but hours had passed since then and none had come. It could well be that she had failed in the persuasion she had said she must use. Once more the thought of Kaththea on the horned one, Kemoc and I to flank her in a break out crossed my mind . . . only to be answered by my sister's weak voice:

"Have you forgotten? They have set a witch bar. But you and Kemoc—perhaps that will not encompass you—"

Our combined dissent was quick and hot. As three we would escape or not at all.

"There is no way left to fight them with the Power?"

She shook her head. "Already I have done too much. My acts troubled the quiet here and aroused that which hunts us now. A child playing with a sword cuts itself because it had neither the skill nor strength to use such a weapon properly. There is only this, my brothers: that which sits out there cannot take us. For which we should give thanks, for if it could we would not face clean death of body, but that which is far worse!"

Remembering what I had learned as the stallion bore me towards that city of dread silence, I understood. Yet I was not meant to await death, clean or otherwise, without a struggle. And all I had now was a very faint hope that a wraith girl, who had saved my life and then ridden from me, would redeem a half promise she had made.

I covered my eyes with my hands and strove with every bit of any small power I had to fix upon her face, to somehow reach her, to learn if I could in any way find hope. For if I could not, then I must turn to some desperate and doubtless fatal move of my own.

But those features of many changes could not be so pinned in mind for a real picture. All the vision faces she had shown me spun elusively, sometimes singly for an instant, sometimes superimposed one on the other. Dahaun was not one of the created ones, produced by a whim of the Old Race; she was one of those who had stood apart, being of yet more ancient blood, and in her the human portion was the lesser.

There was a snort from Shabra. With the coming of evening a pale luminescence fingered up the menhirs. About them swirled threads of light, twining about them as planted vines might seek support on such rough stone. Also the blue platform on which we now rested had its measure of such spectral radiance.

By the light I saw the horned one face about, head up, nostrils expanded. Then, with a toss of head so that his red horn caught the light, he voiced a cry, not unlike the challenge of a fighting stallion.

I almost expected to see that black thing which had entrapped me come pacing along with the other besiegers. But Shabra's answer came in another form— a crackle of fire on the crest of the slope down which the line of pillars marched. There was no mistaking its source—the lash of an energy whip!

Dahaun! I put into that silent call all my need.

No answer, save once more the whip cracked an arc of raw lightning in the sky. A bush flamed where its tip must have stuck the ground. And from outside the circle arose a concentrated, growling roar from the things who kept sentry duty there.

Shabra—I reached for contact. *Who rides there?*

Be still! Would you have the Dark Ones know? It was a sharp rebuke.

I was startled. This was no contact with any animal; this was equal chiding equal, or perhaps even an adult rebuking a child. I might have ridden Shabra to this place, but his function was not only that of mount. And now I caught a flash of amusement at my surprise. Then his mind was closed to me as a door might be locked and barred to any entrance.

Kaththea grasped my arm and Kemoc's and pulled herself up.

"There are forces on the move," she said. But something in the curling light about the pillars bedazzled our eyes to anything which lay beyond. We could hear the evil host but we could no longer see it. No more whip cracks broke the night.

"Can you reach—have any contact at all?" Kemoc demanded.

"No, I must not. I could disturb, awaken—Our power is a mixture. Ceremonial magic comes from ritual, from study, used by those who learn as scholars and priestesses. True witchcraft is older, more primitive, allied with nature, not truly bound by our standards of good and evil. In Estcarp we have united the two, but always give the greater weight to magic, not witchcraft. Here magic went utterly wrong and crooked, becoming a twisted, wicked thing. But witchcraft stepped aside and walks in its earlier guise. Thus when I strove to use what I knew I drew magic, yes, but I used a force which had been distorted. What may work in our favor is witchcraft, and of that I have no mastery. Tell me, quickly, Kyllan, of this Lady of Green Silences and how you met with her!"

With my attention half for anything which might move outside the lights of the menhirs, I told my story—and more slowly of what had happened after my awaking in the mud basin.

"Natural forces," Kaththea broke in. "Shape changing—because she has Power which adapts—"

"How do you mean?" I had not guessed that my sister, never having seen Dahaun, could yet explain some of her mystery.

"The Green Silences—the woodlands—have always had their guardians and inhabitants. And their magic is of wind, water, earth and sky—literally of those. Not as we witches use them, imposing our will for a space, either in illusion or for destruction, but with the rhythm and flow of nature. They will use a storm, yes, but they do not summon one. They can use the rushing current of a river, but within its boundaries. All animals and birds, even plants, will obey them—unless such are already in the service of evil, and thus corrupt. They take on the coloring of their surroundings. If they wish, you can not see them among trees, in water, nor even in the open. And they cannot live among stone walls, nor in places wherein only men dwell, or they wither and die. Because they are of the very stuff of life, so they are feared by the forces of destruction. But also they will be wary of the risking of life. In some ways they are indeed more powerful than we, in spite of all our centuries of magic; yet in others they are more vulnerable. Their like does not exist in Estcarp; they could not make the break to leave this land in which they are rooted. But still we had our legends of their kind—"

"Legends centuries old," I interrupted. "Dahaun—she can not *be* that Lady of those—"

"Perhaps an office descending in some ancient line, the name with it. Morquant is one of the names by which we evoke wind magic, yet you say she gave it as her own. Also, note that unlike a sworn witch she gives you her name freely, proving that she has no fear of so delivering herself into your hands. Only her kind are so above the threat of counter-spell."

There was a trill overhead. Startled, we looked up at a blue-green bird such as had been with me during my hours of pain. Three times it circled us, trilling in short bursts of clear, sweet notes. Kaththea gasped, her grip tightening to dig nails into my shoulder, her face becoming even more pale. She whispered:

"They—they are indeed great! I have been—silenced!"

"Silenced?" Kemoc echoed.

"I cannot use spells. Should I strive to use an incantation it would not make sense! Kyllan—why? Why would they do this thing? I am now open to what lies out there. Kyllan, they wish us ill, not well! They have chosen this time to stand with evil!"

She pulled away from me and clung to Kemoc. Over her bowed shoulders he gazed hostilely at me, as he had never done before.

Nor could I deny that he might have some cause for such judgment. I had returned to them through the agency of this force which now acted against Kaththea, to take from her what might be her only defense. And I had come charging in blindly, not to bring them any real succor, perhaps merely to direct a final blow. Yet a large part of me would not accept that measurement of what was happening here, even though I could not give any reason for still believing that we had hope for aid.

The prowlers were growing bolder. A lean wolf head was clearly outlined in the light from a menhir; a vast armored paw, talons outspread, waved in another direction. Kaththea raised her head from Kemoc's shoulder. There was now fear in her eyes.

"The lights—look to the lights!"

Until her cry I had not noted the change. When we had awakened from the time spell those wreathing threads had been of a blue shade, akin in color to the rock platform they ringed. Now they were smoky, yellowish, giving one an unpleasant sensation when looked at too closely. That change in them appeared to summon the attackers. More and more faces and paws were visible by their glare. Our besiegers were drawing in closely.

Shabra stamped a forehoof, and the impact on the ground had the thud of hand against war drum, booming unnaturally in the air. Kaththea's throat worked convulsively, as if she were trying to speak; her head turned from side to side, and her hands arose before her by visible effort, as if she struggled against bonds. They jerked, twitched, rebels against her will. And I knew that she was fighting to use her own craft—without avail.

The horned one began to trot around with the blue stone the core of his circle. His trot became a canter, then sped to a gallop. Now he gave voice in a series of sharp barking cries. Still more faces of evil were plain in the yellow light.

Then I sighted something else, something I had to stare at a long second before I could believe in what my eyes reported. Shabra might not be running on trampled grass, but hock high in a flowing, deep green stream of water. There was a rippling out and away from his circling, gathering impetus as he passed. Not light, nor mist, but a flowing—of what, I could not say. And, under us, the blue stone was growing warm. From its four corners spiraled tendrils of blue which arched over to touch that flowing green, and were swallowed, blue to green. And the green swept on, a little faster, towards the smoky yellow of the pillars. Round and round Shabra galloped.

I dared not watch him, for his circling made me light-headed. The edge of the green flow lapped at the roots of the menhirs. There followed an explosion of light, as had when my whip had cut at the mist thing. Eyes dazzled, I blinked and rubbed, striving to clear my sight.

Before me the menhirs were no longer a smoky yellow, but each a towering green candle, so lost in light that their rugged outlines vanished. No more did the sentries stare hungrily at us from between them.

The columns began to pulse in waves, as the light mounted higher and higher. But it proved a barrier to our sight of all that lay beyond. We did not see; we heard —a crying, the sound of running. . . . It was the breaking of the siege! I got to my feet, jumped from the platform, sought for the whip I had dropped hours earlier.

Magic, perhaps not that which we knew, but still magic, had come to our aid. Whip in hand I strained to see beyond the pillar light.

"Dahaun!" I did not shout, I whispered, but that I would be answered I was almost sure.

XIV

*T*hey appeared suddenly between two of the candled menhirs—not as if they had ridden into view, but flashed from the air itself. No longer was Dahaun blonde or dusky; her hair flowed as green as the flood about Shabra's hooves, her skin had a verdant caste, and the others with her were of a like coloring.

They swung whip stocks idly, the flashing lashes not in evidence. But Dahaun carried her bow, strung and ready for action. Now she fitted arrow to string, aimed skyward and shot.

We did not see the passing of that, but we heard sound, for it sang, almost as had the bird earlier, up and up, over our heads, its call growing fainter as if vanishing into the immensity of the night sky, never to return. Then, from some lofty point, there burst a rain of fire, splashing in green glitter widely between us and the real stars, and these flakes drifted down, glimmering as they fell. Still those three sat their mounts, gazing soberly at us.

Those who accompanied Dahaun were both men, human to the most part, save that among the loose curls on their temples showed curved horns, not as long or as arching as those on their mounts, and of an ivory shade. They wore the same clothing as she had brought to me at the mud basin, but their cloaks were hooked on their shoulders and swung out behind them.

There was none of that flickering instability about their features which Dahaun possessed, but a kind of withdrawn, almost chilling expression, freezing masculine beauty into a rigidly aloof pattern to put a barrier between us.

Come! Her summons was imperious, demanding.

That was what part of me wanted. But older ties held. I turned and reached out a hand to Kaththea. Then they stood beside me, my brother and sister, facing those others who made no move to pass between the menhirs to us. In a flash I knew without being told that they could not—that what made this a place of refuge for us locked them out.

One of Dahaun's companions snapped his whip impatiently, and sparks cracked in the air.

"Come!" This time she called the summons aloud. "We have little time. That which prowls is routed only for a space."

With my arm about my sister's shoulders, Kemoc on her other side, I walked towards them. Then I saw that Dahaun's eyes were not for me any more; they were on Kaththea, and that between those two met and mingled a current.

Dahaun leaned forward on her horned one. She had shouldered her bow and now one hand came fully into the green glow. With deliberation her fingers moved, outlining a pattern which continued to shine as lines in the air. Kaththea's arm raised by vast and wearying effort which I shared through contact. Quickly I willed strength to her, as did Kemoc. Her fingers spread slowly, so slowly, but in turn she sketched lines—lines which burned blue after the fashion of the block behind us, not green like those of Dahaun.

I heard a quick exclamation from one of Dahaun's excorts.

"Come—sister—" The hand with which she had sketched that sign Dahaun now held out to Kaththea. And I heard a small sigh of relief from my sister.

We passed between the green-lit stones, feeling a tingling throughout our bodies. Small sparks flashed from our skins. I sensed a stir on my scalp as if my hair moved from its roots. Then Dahaun's hand clasped tight about my sister's.

"Give her up to me!" she ordered. "We must ride, and swiftly!"

I mounted then on Shabra, Kemoc behind me. Ride we did. Dahaun went first, her horned one skimming the ground at a pace which seemed to say that a double rider burden was nothing. Then came Kemoc and I, and the two whip swinging guards behind us.

As we left the blazing menhirs a kind of greenish haze accompanied us, and in a measure, at least for me, walled off clean sight of the countryside through which we traveled. Though I strained to see better, I could not sight more than would be visible to a man caught in a fog. And at last I gave up, knowing we must depend wholly upon Dahaun.

There was no uncertainty about her riding. And the first pace she set did not slacken. I began to marvel at the stamina of her horned mounts.

"Where do we go?" asked Kemoc.

"I do not know," I answered.

"It can be that we ride into yet deeper trouble," he commented.

"And maybe we do not! There is no evil in these—"

"Still I do not believe that those now riding rear guard look upon us with much favor."

"They came to save us."

But he was right. Dahaun had brought us out of the refuge which was also a prison; in that much she had favored us. But we could not be sure of what lay ahead.

Though I could not see our path, I believed we were headed back for the heights where lay the healing basin and perhaps the homeland of those who rode with us.

"I do not like to go thus blindly," Kemoc said. "But I do not think they use this screen to confuse *us*. This is a land through which we must feel our way, blinded by ignorance. Kyllan, if we have upset the balance of peace, what must we answer for—beyond our own lives?"

"Perhaps a world!" Yet looking back through time I could not see wherein we might have altered anything we had done, given no more foreknowledge than we held when we rode out of deserted Etsford.

I heard a soft laugh from my brother. "Very well, make it a world to be succored, Kyllan. Did not our parents go up against the Kolder blindly and with only the strength within them? Can we reckon outselves less than they? And we are three, not two. It is in my mind, brother, that we ride now to a hosting—and with such company as shall suit us well."

On and on we rode, and within the envelope of haze perhaps time as well as space was distorted. Yet I thought that outside that the night passed.

The mist began to fade slowly. Trees, brush, outcrops were more visible in it. And they were illumined by dawn light. Then there came a time when the first rays of the sun were bright as we rode into a pass between two crags. Beneath the hooves of the horned ones was a leveled road. And, on either hand, set into the rock walls of the cut, were symbols which looked vaguely familiar to me, but which I could not read. But I heard a small hiss from Kemoc at my back.

"Euthayan!"

"What?"

"A word of power—I found it among the most ancient screeds at Lormt. This must be a well guarded place, Kyllan—no hostile force can pass such safety devices."

The rows of those symbols ended; we were descending again and before us opened a wide basin, well wooded, yet with open glades too, and a silver river in a gentle curve along its bottom. At first glimpse my heart pounded. This was a small slice of that golden ancient land before the coming of ill to twist and foul it. There was that in the air which we drew into our lungs, in the wind which reached us, in all our eyes feasted upon, which soothed, heartened, turned ages back to an untroubled time of joy and freedom when the world was young and man had not yet sought that which would lead to his own undoing.

Neither was it an empty world. Birds of the blue-green plumage, shimmering Flannan, and others sailed above us. I saw two of the lizard folk sitting on top of a stone, their claw hands holding food, watching us as we passed. Horned ones without riders grazed in glades. And over it all was an aura of rightness such as I had never known in all my life.

We had slacked pace as we came through the corridor of the symbol signs, and now we ambled. Flowers bloomed along the edge of our road, as if gardeners kept that brilliant tapestry of verge. Then we entered an open space near the river, and saw the manor hall.

But this was no building—it was growth out of the soil, alive to shelter the living. Its walls were not quarried stone, nor dead, shaped timber, but trees or strong, tall brush of an unknown species, forming solid surfaces over which grew vines, flowers, leaves.

There was no defense wall, no courtyard. Its wide entrance was curtained by vines. And the roof was the most eye-catching of all, for it arose sharply to a center ridge, the whole thatched with feathers—the blue-green feathers of the birds we had already seen.

We dismounted and the horned ones trotted away on their own concerns, first down to the stream to drink. Dahaun set her arm about my sister's shoulders, drew and supported Kaththea to the doorway. We followed, more than a little wearied, in her wake.

Beyond the vine curtain was a hall, carpeted with tough moss. Screens, some woven of feathers and others of still flowering vines, cut the space about the walls into various alcoves and compartments. And there was a soft green light about us.

"Come—" One of the guards beckoned to Kemoc and me. Dahaun and Kaththea had already disappeared behind a screen. We went in the opposite direction and came to a place where the floor was hollowed out in a pool. Its water was thick and red, and I recognized the scent of it. These far more liquid contents were akin to the healing mud of the basin. Eagerly I stripped, Kemoc following my example. Together we sank into the stuff which drew all aches and pains from us, leaving us languid.

Then we ate, drowsily, of stubstances set before us in polished wooden bowls. Finally, we slept, on couches of dried moss. And I dreamed.

Here again was a golden land, not this into which our rescuers had brought us, but that earlier and wider territory at which we had looked through the eyes of the Familiar. And there stood manors in that land which I knew with an intimacy which could belong only to one who had lived within their walls. I rode in company with other men, men who wore faces which I knew—Borderers from the Estcarp mountains, men of the Old Race with whom I had feasted in the rare intervals when there was no active war, and even men and women I had known at Etsford.

And, in the strange manner of dreaming when many things may be mingled, I was sure that the threats which had been with me since my birth did not hold here, but that once more our people were strong, able, unbeset by those who would drag them and their whole civilization down into the dust of ending.

But with me also was a shadowy memory of a great trial and war which lay behind, and which we had survived through struggle and many defeats, to this final victory. And that dark war had been worth all it had cost, for what we had come to hold.

Then I awoke, and lay blinking at dusky shadows over my head. Yet I carried with me something from that dream, an idea which held the improbability of most dream action, yet which was very real to me, as if in my sleep some geas past my avoiding had been laid on me. As perhaps it had, for in this land were there not forces at work past our divining? I was sure in that hour as to what I must do—as if it were all action past; already laid out in words on some scroll of history.

Kemoc still lay on the neighboring couch, his face clear and untroubled in his sleep. For a moment I envied him, for it seemed that he was under no compulsion such as now moved me. I did not wake him, but dressed in the fresh clothing my host or hostess had left, and went past the screen, into the main hall.

Four of the lizards sat about a flat stone, their slender claws moving about tiny carved objects, no doubt playing a game. Their heads all turned at my coming and they favored me with those unwinking stares of their kind. And two others also looked at me. I raised my hand in a small salute of greeting to her who sat cross-legged on a wide cushion, a cup by her hand on a low table.

"Kyllan of the House of Tregarth, out of Estcarp." She made that both formal greeting and introduction. "Ethutur of the Green Silences."

He who was with her got lightly to his feet. He was as tall as I, his dark eyes meeting mine on a level. He wore the jerkin and breeches like mine, but, as with Dahaun, he had gemmed wristlets and belt in addition. His horns were longer, more in evidence, than those of the guards who had ridden with us from the menhir ring, but save for those he might have been any man of the Old Race. As to his age, I could make no guess. For he might have had a few more years than I counted, but meeting his eyes and what lay behind them, that I doubted. Here was one who had all the unobtrusive authority of he who has commanded men— or forces—for years, who had made decisions and ordered them, or carried them out for himself, abiding by the result without complaint or excuse. This was a leader such as I had known in Koris of the Axe, or my father, little as I could remember of Simon Tregarth.

His eyes measured me in return. But I had stood for appraisement before, and this was not as important to me as that which had carried over from my dream.

Then his hands came out, palm up. Without knowing the why of that gesture, mine moved to them, palm down, our flesh so meeting. Between us passed something else, not as strong a contact as I had with Kemoc and Kaththea, but some of the union. And in that I knew he accepted me—to a point.

Dahaun gazed from one to the other of us; then she smiled. Whether that was in relief as to how our meeting had gone, I could not tell, but she motioned me to another cushion, and poured golden liquid from a flagon into a cup for me.

"Kaththea?" I asked before I drank.

"She sleeps. She will need rest, for more than her body is tired. She tells me that she did not accept the oath of the Witches, but certainly she cannot be less than they. She has the Right, the Will, and the Strength to be a Doer rather than a Seeker."

"If she uses it rightly," Ethutur said, speaking for the first time.

I gave him a level glance across the rim of my goblet. "She has never used it wrongly."

Then he, too, smiled, and the lighting of his general somberness made him indeed a youth and not a war leader of too many strained years. "Never as you fear I meant," he agreed. "But this is not your land—the currents here are very swift and deep, and can be disastrous. Your sister will be the first to admit, when she knows it all, that a new kind of discipline must be exercised. However . . ." He paused, and then smiled again. "You do not really realize what your coming means to us, do you? We have walked a very narrow path between utter dark on one hand, and chaos on the other. Now forces are loosed to nudge us into peril. Chance may dictate that such a move will bring us through to new beginnings— or it may be the end of us. We have been weighing one fortune against another this day, Kyllan. Here in this valley we have our safety, hardwon, nursed through centuries. We have our allies—none to be despised—but we are few in number. Perhaps the enemy is also limited, but those who now serve them as hands and feet muster the greater."

"And what if your numbers were increased?"

He took up his cup from the table. "In what manner, friend? I tell you this, we do not recruit from other levels of existence! That was the root of all our present evils."

"No. What if your recruits be men of the Old Race—already seasoned warriors—what then?"

Dahaun moved a little on her cushion. "Men can be swayed by the Powers here—and what men do you speak of? All dwelling in Escore made their choice long ago. The handful who chose to stand with us are already one, our blood long since mingled so there is no pure Old Race to be found."

"Except in the west."

Now I had their full attention, though their faces were impassive, their thoughts well hidden from me. Was I indeed bewitched that a dream could possess me after this fashion? Or had I been granted a small bit of foreknowledge as a promise—and bait?

"The west is closed."

"Yet we three came that way."

"You are not of the fullblood either! Paths not closed to you might be closed to others."

"With a guide to whom such paths were open a party could win in."

"Why?" The one word from Ethutur was a bleak question.

"Listen—perhaps you do not know how it is there. We, too, have walked a narrow path such as yours . . ." Swiftly I told them of the twilight of Estcarp and what it would mean to all those who shared my blood.

"No!" Ethutur brought down his fist with such force on the top of the table that the goblets jumped. "We want no more Witches here! Magic will open doors to magic. We might as well cut our own throats and be done with it!"

"Who spoke of Witches?" I asked. "I would not seek out the Wise Ones—my life would be forfeit if I did so. But those who carry shields in Estcarp's service are not always one in thought with the Council. Why should they be, in their hearts, when the Witches close so many doors?" And once again I laid facts before them. That marriages were few since women with the Power did not easily lay aside their gift, and births even fewer. That many men went without woman or homeplace for all of their lives, and that this was not a thing which made for contentment.

"But if there is a war, they will have assigned their loyalty and you could not find followers," Ethutur objected. "Or those you could find would not be men to whom you could trust your unarmed back—"

"Now there may be an end to war—for a time. Such a blow as was dealt to Karsten in the mountains would also prove a shock to Alizon. I will not know unless I go to see."

"Why?" This time the question was Dahaun's, and I made frank answer.

"I do not know why I must do this, but that I am under geas of that I am sure. There is no turning for me from this road—"

"Geas!" She rose and came to kneel before me, her hands tight upon my shoulders as if she would hold me past all escape. Her eyes probed into mine, a kind of searching deeper than that Ethutur had used, deeper than I had thought possible. Then she sat back on her heels, loosing her grasp.

Turning her head she spoke to Ethutur. "He is right. He is under geas."

"How? This is clear land!" Ethutur was on his feet, staring about him as one who seeks an enemy.

"The land is clear; there has been no troubling. Therefore it must be a sending. . . ."

"From whence?"

"Who knows what happens when a balance swings? That this has happened we cannot question. But—to bear the burden of a geas is not easy, Kyllan of the House of Tregarth out of Estcarp."

"I did not believe that it would be so, lady," I replied.

XV

*W*e might be riding across a deserted land, we who had been harried and hunted before. No sign of that frightening crew that had besieged us in the menhir-guarded refuge showed; even their tracks had vanished from the soil. Yet I sensed our going was noted, assessed, perhaps wondered over, and this was only a short lull with very false peace.

Ethutur's men rode at my back, and, beside me, against my wishes, Dahaun who had taken no discouraging from that journey. Before us were the western mountains and the gateway between the lands.

We did not talk much—a few surface words now and then as she pointed out some landmark, either as a guide or a thing to beware in crossing the country, with always an unspoken assurance that I would return to have need of such information. But as I rode my own confidence was not as great. I was a man under compulsion—the way of it I did not understand. Because I would not have Kemoc and Kaththea join their fates to mine in this perilous business I had ridden while they still lay in healing slumber.

That night we camped among the trees which were not as fine or tall as those of the Green Valley, but were of the same species, thus friendly to those with me. This time I did not dream—or at least not to remember—yet with my morning waking the need for going was more deeply rooted, spurring me to speed. Dahaun rode on my right and this time she sang, soft and low, and now and then she was answered, by the green birds, or by Flannan in bird form.

She looked at me from the corners of her eyes and then smiled.

"We have our scouts also, man of war. And, even though they know their duty well, it sometimes goes even better if they are alerted. Tell me, Kyllan, what chances have you on this man quest of yours?"

I shrugged. "If matters rest as they did when I fled Estcarp, very few. But with an end made to any Karsten invasion, perhaps that has changed."

"You have those who will come to your horn—your own shield men?"

I was forced to shake my head. "I have no shields pledged to me as overlord, no. But the Borderers among whom I served are landless and homeless. Years ago they were thrice horned as outlaws in Karsten and escaped with only their lives and the bare steel in their hands. Odd, when we came hither we spoke of that—that it would be a land won by swords."

"By more than swords," she corrected me. "However, these landless warriors might well be reckless enough to follow such a quest. In the final saying most of us seek a place to set roots and raise house trees. Here they will pay sword weight instead of tribute. Yet—our seeking is based on guesses, Kyllan, and guesses are light things."

I would not look at her now. I had no dispute for what she said, and the closer we drew to a time of parting the more I rebelled against the invisible purpose which had been laid upon me. Why me? I had no power to command respect, no gift of words such as Kemoc could summon upon occasion. My position as eldest son of Tregarth was nothing to draw any support to my shield. Nor had I made a war name to gather any followers. So—why must I be driven back to a fruitless task?

"To break a geas . . ." Had she been reading my mind? For a second I resented, was ashamed of, what she might have picked from my thought.

"To break a geas, that is courting complete disaster."

"I know!" I interrupted her roughly. "And it can recoil on more than he who breaks it. I ride to the mountains, not from them, lady."

"But not in any helpful spirit." Her tone was a little cold. "Right thinking can draw good fortune, and the reverse is also true. Not that I believe you have any easy path. Nor do I understand why . . ." Her voice trailed into silence. When she spoke again her words were pitched lower, hurried. "I do not know what force can aid beyond the mountains. You leave those here who have reason to wish you well, would will what they can in your behalf. If you fall into danger—think on that, and on them. I can promise you nothing, for this is an untried, unmarked wilderness. But what can be done in your behalf, that I promise will be! And with your sister and brother—who knows indeed!"

She began to talk then of little things which were far apart from my purpose, things which opened for me small sunny vistas of her life as it had been before we came to break the uneasy peace of Escore. It was as if she took me by the hand and welcomed me into the great hall of her life, showing me most of its private rooms and treasures. And that was a gift beyond price, as I knew even as I accepted it, for now she was not the awesome controller of strange powers, but instead, a girl as my sister had been before the Wise Ones rift her from us and strove to remodel her into their own pattern.

Then in turn Dahaun coaxed memories from me. I told her of Etsford and our life there, more of that than of the hard years which followed when we rode mailed and armed about the grim business of war. And the sweet of those memories, even though it carried always a hint of bitter, relaxed me.

"Ah, Kyllan of the House of Tregarth," she said, "I think we two understand each other a little better. And that is to your liking, is it not?"

I felt the warmth of blood-flush rising up throat and cheek. "I cannot hide all thoughts, lady—"

"Is there a need to?" Her question was sober enough, yet under that soberness lurked amusement. "Has there been any need to since first we looked, really looked upon one another?"

She was not bold; it was fact she stated. Then there roused in me such fire that I clenched fists, fought myself, lest I reach for her in the instant, the need to have her in my arms nearly breaking all control. But that would be the false step, the wrong path for both of us. How did I reckon that? It was like the geas, knowledge out of nowhere yet not to be denied. And the hatred of my task grew with that constraint so holding me now.

"Yes—and yes—and yes!" she burst out, equaling my own inner turmoil. "Tell me—make me see what path you shall take when you leave us!" Thus she tried to cut that too taut cord between us.

I sought my memories on our trip over the mountains, recalling it all for her.

"You will be afoot in a wilderness." Dahaun put that into words as if it presented a problem for careful consideration.

I wore Kemoc's mail and helm, and carried his dart gun—though ammunition for that was near exhaustion. My sword and gun had been lost in their flight after leaving the river islet. Yes, I would be afoot and poorly armed in rough wilderness on the other side of the mountain. But how to better that position I could not see.

"Perhaps this is a test for us, to see how well any influence can cross the barrier." Dahaun flung back her head and trilled, her voice echoing. The ground eating pace of the horned ones had brought us very close to the climb of the heights.

A green bird planed down with hardly a beat of its wide wings. It chirped an answer and arose, on beating pinions, higher and higher, heading west. We watched it until it was beyond sight, yet Dahaun still glanced from time to time in its wake. Suddenly she gave a little cry of triumph.

"No barrier to that one! It is over the pass, winging out beyond. Now let us see if it can do anything more."

There came a moment, not too much later, when I swung down from Shabra's back, before me the trail out of Escore. Dahaun did not dismount, nor did her guard. But those sat a little apart, leaving us to a shared silence we dared not break. Then she raised her hand as she had done in her first meeting with Kaththea and sketched a burning symbol in the air. It blazed, dazzling my eyes, so that her features again shifted and changed, as they had not for many hours past.

And I brought my fist up as I would salute a war leader, before I swung around and began that climb with a burst of speed, aware that if I hesitated, or looked behind me, I would break. And that was not to be thought on, for all our sakes.

Nor did I look back as long as I thought I might see anything of Escore to lay ties upon me. But before I set out on the perilous swing across the tree limb valley, I took my last glance at this lost world, as one does when going into exile. I had not felt so torn when we had left Estcarp; this was different. But the mist curtain was closed, I could see nothing, and for that I was very glad.

I spent the night among the mountain rocks, and with the day began the descent up which Kemoc and I had brought Kaththea blindfolded. It was easier, that descent, since now I had only myself to think on. But I did not welcome traveling the broken lands on foot. There was a need to make plans. Those to whom I might appeal had been in camp on the plains when I set forth on my ride to join Kemoc at Etsford, but there was no reason to think that they would still be where I left them.

No Falconer would be tempted by what I had to offer. They lived for fighting, yes, supplying mercenaries for Estcarp and marines for the Sulcar ships. But they were rooted in their Eyrie in the mountains, wedded to their own warped customs and life. There would be no place for them in Escore.

Sulcarmen never ventured too far from the sea which was their life; they would be lost where no surf roared, no waves battered high. I had hopes only of the Old Race uprooted in the south. A few, very few, of the refugees from Karsten had been absorbed into Estcarp. The rest roved restlessly along the border, taking grim vengeance for the massacre of their blood. It had been close to twenty-five years since that happening, yet they would not forget nor really make one with Estcarp dwellers.

Karsten would never be theirs again. They had accepted that. But if I could offer them land of their own, even if they must take it by sword—I believed they might listen. It remained now to find them, and not *be* found by those who would deliver me forthwith to the justice of the Council.

I climbed the ridge from which I had sighted the campfires of those who had hunted us, and waited there until night fell, watching for any trace of continued sentry go there. But the land was dark, although that did not necessarily mean that it was unpatrolled. Kaththea's ruse with the Torgians—how well had that served us? I shrugged. Magic was no weapon for me. I had my gun, my wits, and the training drilled into me. With the morning I must put all to the test.

Even in the last rays of the sun and well into twilight I found myself watching for the bird Dahaun had dispatched across the mountains. Just what service that could perform I had no idea, but just seeing it would have meant much in that hour. But all the flying things I sighted were common to the land, and none flashed emerald.

In the early morning I started along the same trail which had brought us into that twisted land. Though I wanted to hasten, yet I knew the wisdom of checking landmarks, of not becoming entangled in the maze. So I went slowly, nursing my water bottle's contents and the supplies Dahaun had provided. Once I was trailed for a space by an upland wolf. But my gift held so that I suggested hunting elsewhere and was obeyed. That disorientation of sight which had been troubling when we had come this way was no longer a problem, so perhaps it only worked when one faced the east, not retreated from it.

I advanced upon the campfire sites, utilizing every scouting trick I knew. The fire scars were there, as well as the traces of more than a company of men, but now the land was empty, the hunters gone. Yet I went warily, taking no risks.

Two logs close together gave me a measure of shelter for the second night. I lay unable to sleep for a while, striving to picture in my mind a map of the countryside. Kemoc had guided us this way, but I had studied as I rode, making note of landmarks and the route. Hazy as I had been, I thought that I would have no great difficulty in winning westward to country where I would know every field, wood, and hill. Those were the fringe lands of deserted holdings where the dwindling population no longer lived, and where I could find shelter.

It came to me through the earth on which my head rested—a steady pound of hoof beat. Some patroller riding a set course? There was only one rider. And I lay in thick cover which only ill luck would lead him to explore.

The approaching horse neighed and then blew. And it *was* heading directly for my hiding place! At first I could not accept such incredible ill fortune. Then I squirmed out of my cramped bed and wriggled snakewise to the right; once behind brush, I got to my feet, my dart gun drawn. Again the horse nickered, something almost plaintive in the sound. I froze, for it had altered course, was still pointed to me, as if its rider could see me, naked of any cover, vividly plain in the moonlight!

Betrayed by some attribute of the Power? If so, turn, twist, run and hide as I would, I could be run down helplessly at the desire of the hunter. So being, it would be best to come into the open and face it boldly.

There was a rustling, the sound of the horse moving unerringly towards me, with no pretense of concealment. Which argued of a perfect confidence on the part of the rider. I kept to the shadow of the bush but my weapon was aimed at where the rider would face me.

But, though it wore saddle and bridle, and there was dried foam encrusted on its chest and about its jaws, the horse was riderless. Its eyes showed white, and it had the appearance of an animal that had stampeded and run in fight. As I stepped into the open it shied, but I had already established mind contact. It had bolted in panic, been driven by fear. But the cause of that fear was so ill defined and nebulous I could not identify it.

Now the horse stood with hanging head, while I caught the dangling reins. It could, of course, be part of a trap—but then I would have encountered some block in its mind, some trace, even negatively, of the setting of the trap. No, I felt it was safe, the four feet I needed to make me free of the country and give me that fraction more of security in a place where safety was rare.

I led it along, traveling to the south, and in it was a desire and liking for my company as if my presence banished the fear which had driven it. We worked our way slowly, keeping to cover, so setting some distance between us and the place to which the horse had come as if aimed. And all the time I kept mind contact, hoping to detect any hint if this was a capture scheme.

Finally I stripped off the saddle and bridle, put field hobbles on the horse and turned it loose for the rest of the night, while with the equipment I took cover in heavy brush. But this time I pillowed my head on the support of a saddle and tried to solve the puzzle of whence and why had come what I needed most—a horse. My thoughts kept circling back to Dahaun's winged messenger, and, improbable as it seemed, I could accept the idea that this was connected. Yet there had been no memory of a bird in the horse's mind.

My new mount was not by any means a Torgian, but its saddle was the light one of a border ride and there was an intricate crest set into the horn in silver lines. Sulcar crests were simple affairs, usually heads of animals, reptiles, birds or mythical creatures out of legend. Falconers, recognizing no families, used only their falcon badges with a small under-modification to denote their troop. This could only be the sign of one of the Old Race Houses, and, since such identification had fallen into disuse in Estcarp, it meant that this horse gear was the possession of one of those I sought, a refugee from Karsten.

There was an extremely simple way of proving the rightness of my guess.

Tomorrow morning I need only mount the animal I could see grazing in the moonlight, set in its mind the desire to return whence it had come and let it bear me to its master. Of course, to ride into a strange camp on a missing mount would be the act of a fool. But once in the vicinity of such a camp the mount could be turned loose as if it had only strayed and returned and I could make contact when and if I pleased.

Simple, yes, but once at that camp what brave arguments would I use? I perhaps a total stranger to all therein, striving to induce them to void their allegiance to Estcarp and ride into an unknown land on my word alone—the more so if they rode as blind as Kaththea had had to do! Simple to begin, but impossible to advance from that point.

If I could first contact men I knew, they might listen even if the fiat of outlawry had gone out against me. Men such as Dermont, and others who had served with me. But where to find them now in all the length of the south border country? Perhaps I could fashion a story to serve me in the camp from which the horse had come, discover from the men there where I could meet with my own late comrades.

No battle plan can be so meticulous that no ill fortune can not upset it. As small a thing as a storm-downed tree across a trail at the wrong time may wipe out the careful work of days, as I well knew. The "lucky" commander is the one who can improvise on a moment's notice, thus pulling victory out of the very claws of defeat. I had never commanded more than a small squad of scouts, nor had I before been called upon to make a decision which risked more than my own life. How could I induce older and more experienced men to trust in me? That was the growing doubt in my mind as I tried to sleep away the fatigue of the day, be fresh for the demands of the morrow.

Sleep I did, but that was a troubled dozing which did not leave me much rested. In the end I took my simple solution: work back to the camp from which the horse had come, free the animal without being seen, scout to see who might be bivouacked there. And that I did, turning the horse south at not more than a walking pace. One concession to caution I made: we kept to the best cover possible, avoiding any large stretch of open. Also I watched for green against the sky. Still haunting me was that thought—or was it a hope?—that Dahaun's messenger might be nearby.

We had left Estcarp in late summer, and surely we had not been long away, yet the appearance of the land and the chill in the air was that of autumn. And the wind was close to winter's blast. In the day I could now see the purple fringe of the mountains. And—nowhere along that broken fringe of peaks did I sight one that I could recognize, though I had studied that territory for most of my life. Truly the Power had wrought a great change, one such as stunned a man to think on. And I did not want any closer acquaintance with a land which had been so wrung and devastated.

But it was south that the horse went, and it was not long before we came into the fringe lands. Here there were raw pits in the earth from which upthrust the roots of fallen trees, debris of slides, and marks of fire in thick powdery ash. I dismounted, for the place was a trap in which a mount could easily take a false step and break a leg. And once, in impulse, I put my hand to a puddle of that ash, wind-gathered into a hollow, and marked my forehead and chest with a very old sign. For one of the guards against ill witchcraft was ash from honest wood fire, though that was a belief I had never put to test before.

The horse flung up its head and I caught its thought. This was home territory. Straightaway I loosened my hold on the reins, slapped the animal on the rump and bade it seek its master . . . while I slipped into a tangle of tree roots, to work my way stealthily to the top of a nearby ridge.

XVI

*W*hat I saw as I lay belly flat on the crest of the slope was no war camp. This was centered by a shelter built not for a day nor a week's occupancy, but more sturdily, to last at least a season—a stockade about it. Though that safeguard was not yet complete—logs were still waiting to be upended and set into place to close its perimeter.

There was a corral in which I counted more than twenty mounts and before which now stood the horse I had loosed, while its companions nickered a greeting. A man ran from among those busied with the stockade building to catch the reins of the strayed mount. He shouted.

I saw the saffron yellow of a woman's robe in the doorway of the half finished hall, and other colors behind her. The men had downed tools, were gathering around the horse. Old Race all of them, with here and there a lighter head which could mark one of Half-Sulcar strain. And they all wore the leather of fighting men. Whatever this household was now, I was ready to wager all that they had been Borderers not too long ago.

And as a Borderer I could well believe that, as peaceful and open as the scene below appeared from my perch, they had their sentinels and safeguards. So that to win down into their midst would tax any scout's ability. Yet to be found skulking here would do me no good.

The same intricate device as was set on the saddle horn had been freshly painted on the wall of the hall, but I did not recognize it. The only conclusion I dared draw was that the very presence of such a to-be-permanent holding here meant that the dwellers therein believed they had nothing to fear from the south, that Karsten had ceased to be an enemy.

Yet they fortified with a stockade, and they were working with a will to get that up before they finished the hall. Was that merely because they had lived in the midst of danger so long that they could not conceive of any house without such protection?

Now what should I do? This household had come into the wilderness by choice. They might be the very kind I sought. Yet I could not be sure.

Below, they continued to inspect the returned horse, almost as if it had materialized out of air before their eyes, going over the saddle searchingly before they took it off. Several of them gathered together, conferring. Then heads turned, to look to the slope on which I lay. I thought that they had not accepted the idea that the mount had returned of its own will.

The saffron-robed woman disappeared, came back again. In her arms were mail shirts, while behind her a slighter figure in a rose-red dress brought helms, their chain-mail throat scarves swinging.

As four of the workers armed themselves in practiced speed, a fifth put fingers to mouth and whistled shrilly. He was answered from at least five points, one of them behind and above me to the left! I flattened yet tighter to the ground. Had I already been sighted by that lookout? If so—why had he not already jumped me? If I had not yet been seen, then any move on my part might betray me at once. I was pinned. Perhaps I had made the wrong choice; to go boldly in would be better than to be caught spying.

I got to my feet, keeping my hands up, palms out before me, well away from my weapons belt. Then I began to walk down. They caught sight of me in seconds.

"Keep on, bold hero!" The voice behind me was sharp. "We like well to see open hands on those who come without verge horn warning."

I did not turn my head as I answered. "You have them in your sight now, sentry. There has been no war glove flung between us—"

"That is as it may be, warrior. Yet friend does not belly-creep upon friend after the manner of one come to collect a head and so enslave the ghost of the slain."

Head-collecting! Refuge holding right enough—not only that, but at least this sentry was one of the fanatics who had made a name for themselves, even in the tough Borderer companies, for the utter ferocity of their fighting. There were those come out of Karsten who had suffered so grievously that they had retreated into barbarian customs to allay, if anything ever could, their well-deep hatred.

I made no haste down that slope and to the holding. The man or men who had chosen to plant it here had an eye for the country. And, once the stockade was complete, they would be very snug against attack. They waited for me in the now gateless opening of that stockade, armed, helmed, though they had not yet drawn sword or gun.

The centermost wore insignia on the fore of his helm, set there in small yellow gem stones. He was a man of middle years, I believed, though with all of us of the Old Race the matter of age is hard to determine, for our life spans are long unless put to an end by violence, and the marks of age do not show until close to the end of that tale of years.

I halted some paces from him. My helm veil was thrown well back, giving him clear view of my features.

"To the House greeting, to those of the House good fortune, to the day a good dawn and sunset, to the endeavor good fortune without break." I gave the old formal greeting, then waited upon his answer, on which depended whether I could reckon myself tolerated, if not a guest, or find myself a prisoner.

There was something of the same searching measurement as Ethutur had used on me back in the Green Valley. A sword scar had left a white seam long his jaw line, and his mail, though well kept, had been mended on the shoulder with a patch of slightly larger links.

The silence lengthened. I heard a small scuffing behind me and guessed that the guard who had accompanied me was ready to spring at the Manor Lord's order. It was hard not to stand ready to my own defense, to hold my hands high and wait upon another's whim.

"The House of Dhulmat opens its gates to whom?"

I heard a choked sound, a bitten off protest from my guard. Again I was presented with a dilemma. To answer with my true name and family clan might condemn me if I had been outlawed, and I had no reason to believe that that had not been done. Yet if this holding already had its gate-crier in place, that protection device would detect a false name instantly as I passed it. I could retreat only to a very old custom, one which had been in abeyance in time of war. Whether it would have any force in the here and now I did not know.

"The House of Dhulmat, on which be the sun, the wind, and the good of wide harvest, opens gates to a geas-ordered man." It was the truth and in the far past it meant that I was under certain bounds of speech which none might question without bringing me into peril. I waited once more for the Lord to accept or deny me.

"Gates open to one swearing no threat against Dhulmat, man or clan, roof-tree, field, flock, herd, mount—" He intoned the words slowly as if he pulled them one by one from long buried memory.

I relaxed. That oath could I give without any reservations. He held out his sword blade point to me, a sign I accepted the death it promised were I foresworn. I went to one knee and laid my lips to the cold metal.

"No threat from me to man or clan, roof-tree, field, flock, herd or mount of the House of Dhulmat!"

He must have given some signal I did not detect, for the woman in saffron approached, bearing with both hands a goblet filled with a mixture of water, wine, milk, the true guesting cup. So I knew that here they clung to the old ways, perhaps the more because they had been rift from all which had once been home to them.

My host touched his lips to the edge of the goblet and handed it to me. I swallowed a mouthful and then dribbled a few drops to right and left, to the house and the land, before I passed it back, to go from hand to hand in that company, finally to the guard who now stepped up to my side, shooting me a still suspicious glance. He was a lean mountain wolf right enough, tough and hard as the steel he wore. I knew his like well.

Thus I came into the Manor of Dhulmat—or what was the germ of that manor-to-be. My host was the Lord Hervon, and, though he never said it, I could guess that he must once have been lord of a far larger land than this. The Lady Chriswitha who now headed his household was his second wife—for his first family had vanished during the horning in Karsten. But she had given him two daughters and a son, and both daughters had married landless men who had chosen to join the clan. These, with such shield men as had attached themselves to Hervon during the twenty years or more of border warfare, and the wives of such, had come here to found a new life.

"We marked this valley during patrol," Hervon told me as they put food before me, "and camped here many times during the years, raising part of this hall. You may not understand at your age, but a man needs a place to return to, and this was ours. So when the sealing of the mountains was done and we needed no longer bear swords south, then we were minded to set our hearthstone here."

How much dared I ask him concerning what had happened in Estcarp during the time I had been east of the mountains? Yet I had to know.

"Karsten is truly sealed?" I risked that much.

There was a grunt from the other man at the board—Godgar, who had played sentinel in the heights.

Hervon smiled thinly. "So it would seem. We have not yet any real news, but if any of Pagar's force survived that sealing, then he is not a human man. With their army gone and all passes closed, it will be long before they can move again. The Falconers still ride the mountains—where they may find passage, that is—and the eyes of their scout-hawks are ready to report any movement from that filth."

"But Alizon is not sealed," I ventured again.

This time Godgar gave a grating laugh. "Alizon? Those hounds have slunk back to their kennels in a hurry. They do not want to sniff the same kind of storm in *their* noses! For once the Power has been a—"

I saw Hervon shoot him a warning look and he was suddenly silent, flushing a little.

"Yes, the Power has wrought well," I interposed. "Thanks to the Wise Ones we have now a breathing spell."

"The Wise Ones." The Lady Chriswitha seated herself on the bench beside her lord. "But in such action they served themselves ill. The tidings are that they wrung the forces out of them, to their great hurt—many died and others are spent. If Alizon knew of this, surely they would not be so wary of us."

Hervon nodded. "Yes, so you do well, young man, to call this peace a breathing spell." His gaze dropped to the board before him. "Perhaps we waste our strength and our hopes in what we strive to do here now. It is very hard to lose all—"

His lady's hand fell over his in a warming clasp. Then her eyes went to the daughters at the other end of the hall, and those with them. And I was shaken, for, if by some miracle I could rouse such men as these to follow me to the east, what could I offer them save danger once more? Perhaps worse danger than these had fled when they came out of Karsten. Leave them be in their small, hard won time of peace. My memory of the golden land when it was free faded. Though nothing would lift from me the geas in this matter.

Godgar cleared his throat. "You, young man, where do you ride—or walk, since, though you wear horseman's boots, you come hither on your own two feet?"

And the compulsion which had brought me over the mountains set on me now an order for truth though I did not wish to speak in this place where peace was a birth of hope.

"I hunt men—"

"Men—not a man?" Hervon's eyebrows lifted. I thought he had credited me with some motive from his own past, the desire for private vengeance. For a feud vow, taken in the right time and place—or the wrong, depending upon how you looked on the matter—could also be a geas.

"Men—those willing to carve out a new future—" How could I put my mission into words without revealing too much to those inclined to betray me?

Godgar frowned. "You are no Sulcar recruiter for a raiding voyage. To venture this far inland when you could have men beyond counting along the river or in any port would be folly. And if it is foray against Alizon—the Seneschal has forbidden such, save under his own banner."

"No. I have fighting to offer, but not at sea nor in the north. I offer land—good land—to be sword bought. Where a son may uncover his father's fire to a higher blazing—"

The Lady Chriswitha had been watching me closely. Now she leaned forward a little, holding me with her gaze as if she were one of the Witches, able to pick true from false in my very brain.

"And where lies this land of yours, stranger?"

I wet my lips with tongue tip. This was the time of testing. "To the east," I said.

They were all blank of countenance. Did the block hold so tight that no thought of Escore could ever penetrate, that I could *not* arouse any of them even to think of such a journey?

"East?" She repeated that with complete incomprehension, as if I had used a word entirely without meaning. "East?" she said again, and this time it was a sharp-asked question.

This was a gamble, but all my life had been a wagering of one risk against another. I must learn here and now what luck I would have with any men such as these. Tell them the truth as we had discovered it, see if that truth would free them from the bonds tied long ago.

So I spoke of what Kemoc had discovered at Lormt, and of what we had found over the mountains sealed in that long ago. Yet in that telling I did not reveal my own identity, and it was that fact the Lady Chriswitha struck upon unerringly when I had done.

"If all this be so—then how is it that you went over these mountains you say we cannot remember, or are not allowed to remember, and which have been so long closed to us? Why did not such bonds hold you also?" Her suspicion was plain.

But her lord, as if he had not heard her, spoke now:

"This much is true, I have never thought of the east. In Karsten, yes, but here—no. It was as if that direction did not exist."

"The Lady has asked a question which needs an answer," growled Godgar from the other side. "I would like to hear it, too."

There could be no more disguise. To prove my truth I must tell all—the reason for my going eastward. And I put it directly.

"For two reasons did I go. I am outlawed, or believe that I am, and I am not fully of your blood."

"I knew it!" Godgar's fist raised menacingly, though he did not strike with it. "Outlawed, yet he tricked you into guesting him, Lord. And with such a guest bond does not hold. Cut him down, else he bring us new troubles!"

"Hold!" Hervon cut through that hot speech. "What name do you bear, outlaw? And talk of geas will not cover you now."

"I am Kyllan of the House of Tregarth."

For a second or two I thought that they did not know, that that name meant nothing here. Then Godgar roared in wrath and this time his fist sent me sprawling, my head ringing. I had no chance in my defense, for his men were in the hall and they piled on me before I could even gain my knees. Another blow sent me into darkness and I awoke, with an aching head and bruised body, to yet more darkness.

From very faint traces of light outlining a door—or at least an entrance—well above me and the feel of pounded, hardened earth under my body, my hands being locked in rope loops, I concluded that I now lay in a storage place which must antedate, maybe by several years, this half completed manor. I had helped to construct just such supply pits in the past, deep dug in the earth, floored and walled with stone if possible, if not with hardened clay, to be covered by a trap door.

Why did I still live? By rights they could have taken my life there in the hall. Apparently Godgar, at least, knew me for what I had been undoubtedly proclaimed. That they had not killed me at once probably meant they planned to deliver me to the authorities of the Council, and perhaps the first ending was the one I should desire the most.

As a recruiter I was a failure indeed. One can always see one's mistakes afterwards, as plain as the victors' shields hung on the outwalls of a conquered keep. But I had never claimed to be clever at such work. How long would I lie here? I believed this holding to be one far to the southeast, perhaps the only one now in this section of the country. Any messenger to the authorities might have more than a day's travel, even if he took extra mounts for relays. Unless, of course, there was an adept trained in sending somewhere in the neighborhood.

I squirmed around, though the movement added to the pain in my head, and I had to fight nausea. Whoever had tied that confining rope knew his business well. I stopped my fruitless struggling, since no energy of mine was going to free me. To free me—had I the slightest hope left?

But if I was going to be given up to the Council, there was something I must do, if I could, for others. Would the Witches ever dare to turn east? They might. Who can fore-tell any action when he has not even the dimmest of foresight? Those on the other side of the mountain must be warned.

Matter would not aid me—but mind? I concentrated, building my mental picture of Kaththea, straining to contact my sister wherever she might be. Faint— very faint—a stirring. But no more than that shadow of a shadow. Kemoc? Having tried the greater first, now I strove for the lesser. And this time received not even a shadow reply.

So much for our talent. Dahaun had been wrong when she had suggested I might communicate so in extremity. Dahaun? I set her in my mind as I had seen her last.

Shadow—deeper than shadow—not real contact as I had with brother and sister so that words and messages might pass from mind to mind, but enough to give warning. Instantly there was a beating at me in return—only it was as if someone shouted to me in a foreign tongue some frantic message which I could not understand. I lay gasping under the pressure of that unintelligible sending. It snapped, and was gone.

My breath came in fast, shallow gasps; my heart pounded as if I raced before some enemy host. There was a sound, but it was of this world and not from that place outside. The crack of light about the opening above grew larger and a ladder thudded down. They were coming for me. I braced myself for action which I must face.

A whisper of robes. I tried to hold my head higher. Why had the Lady Chriswitha come alone? The door fell behind her so that the gloom was again complete as she came to stand over me. I caught the scent of that sweet fern women use to lay between fresh washed garments.

She was stooping very close above me. "Tell me why you fled Estcarp."

There was urgency in her demand, but the way of it I did not understand. What made the reason of our escape of any importance now?

I told her the whole of it, making a terse statement of facts and fears as we three had known them. She listened without interruption, then:

"The rest of it. The lost land—the chance to bring it once more under our rule—?"

"Under the rule of good instead of evil, through a war," I corrected. Again I was puzzled, and asked:

"What matters all this to you, lady?"

"Perhaps nothing, or perhaps much. They have sent a messenger to the nearest ward keep, and it will go then by sending to Es Castle. Afterward—they will come for you."

"I had expected no less." I was glad my voice held steady when I said that.

Her robes swished. I knew she was turning away from me. But from the foot of the ladder she spoke once more:

"Not all minds are the same in some matters. Outlaws have been born because of laws not all hold by."

"What do you mean?"

She gave me no straight reply, only saying. "Good fortune go with you, Kyllan of Tregarth. You have given me much to think on."

I heard her climb the ladder, saw her raise the door. Then she was gone, leaving me in turn with things to think on—though to no profitable purpose.

XVII

*T*hey came for me at last, on a morning when there were clouds across the sky and the softness of coming rain in the air. There were Godgar and three others, but, to my surprise, no Council guard. I do not know how long I had lain in the store-pit. They had brought me food and drink, but those who came so singly would answer no questions. I had time for many thoughts, but there were no more dreams. Except those I wove deliberately when awake, riding the golden land with one—but there is no need to dwell upon those.

Now they produced a mount for me—a sorry animal, probably the worst of their stable—and they lashed me into the saddle as if they thought that I might suddenly produce the claw and fangs of a wolf-man. Save for these four there was no sign of life about the manor. That I wondered about . . . until my wonder became a tremor of uneasiness. It almost seemed that this expedition could be of Godgar's planning alone, and there had been nothing in his attitude since our first meeting to suggest that he designed any good end for me.

He took the fore in our ride out, my mount led by the rider just behind, the other two bringing up the rear. They were all older men, those guards, enough like their leader to have been fashioned in one dart stamper. And, while they did not use me with any unnecessary roughness, yet neither did I see any hope of escape.

We turned north as we came out on the manor road, which was no more than a track of beaten earth. The pace Godgar set was that of any routine patrol, not forced, yet designed to eat miles. I glanced over my shoulder at the manor. The matter of the Lady Chriswitha's visit still puzzled me. I had not dared to believe that anything in my favor might come of it. But still I thought that it had shown minds divided on some subjects within those half completed walls. But the manor might now be deserted.

None of the guards spoke, nor did I see any reason to ask questions. We merely rode, first under clouds, and then in the beginning of a drizzle which seemed to affect them no more than might the sun of a pleasant day.

In spite of the hopelessness of my situation I continued to study those who accompanied me, and the land about, trying to sight any chance for a break. My hands were bound before me to the high horn of my saddle, my feet lashed to the stirrups, the reins of my horse in the hands of him who rode before me. My helm was gone, though they had left me my mail shirt. There were no weapons in my belt. And the horse under me could be easily run down by any they bestrode.

As for the country, we were in open land where there was little or no cover. The grass, which brushed as high as our stirrups beyond the edge of the narrow road, was autumn yellowed. And the rain was chill. But there were inhabitants in the grass. I saw prong-horns race away, their great start-leaps carrying them well into the air. And birds flew—

I do not know why I began to watch the sky for any hint of green wings. It might be more probable for a Flannan to perch suddenly on the saddle horn above my tied hands. Yet each time I saw a bird I looked the closer.

Then Godgar reined up, waiting for my leader to catch level with him. He said something in a low voice and the rein passed from guard to commander, the relieved man spurring ahead, Godgar pulling at the reins until my horse was beside his. He had fastened his helm veil across his throat and chin as if we were about to go into battle, and over that half mask of tiny metallic links his eyes were hot.

"Who sent you, oath breaker? Who sent you to bring down the House of Dhulmat?"

His demand made no sense to me.

"I am neither oath-breaker, nor one who wishes ill to you and yours."

Tied as I was I could not escape the answering blow which made my head ring and swayed me in the saddle.

"We know ways to make a man talk," he snarled. "Karsten taught us much!"

"Perhaps you can make a man talk," I got out, "but this man does not know what you seek."

Luckily, though he had come to depend upon pain and force to support his orders, he had a measure of intelligence behind such brutality. Now he chose to use it.

"You go to the Council. If you are who you say, you know what they will do to you."

"Assuredly." To Godgar the warrior's creed was a living thing and part of that was a fatalistic acceptance of things as they were. I could do no more than summon that to my aid now.

"They will wring out of you all knowledge; thus we shall learn sooner or later what we want to know. Why not tell us now—who sent you to take refuge with Hervon and so blacken his name?"

"No one. I came by chance to—"

"Riding one of our horses, a mount that bolted without warning from our holding and returned two days later only a little before you? By your own telling, oath-breaker, you have consorted with witchery, so all could be of your doing. But the why of it? Why do you move against Hervon? We have no family-feud with you! Who told you to do this?"

"Any holding would have suited me," I said wearily. There was no way of making him believe that. He was determined that I meant ill to his lord. But that private feuds were still alive among the Old Race refugees was new to me. Apparently Godgar expected such now. "A geas was laid upon me in Escore, even as I told you. I was to recruit such of the Old Race as wanted to try to free the land from which they once sprang."

I half expected a second blow, a demand that I speak what he would consider the truth. But to my surprise, Godgar turned his head with deliberation and looked to the east. Then he laughed, a harsh bark.

"Did you think such a story would win you a fighting tail into nowhere, outlaw? Why, I could think of two handsful of words which would serve you better in Hervon's listening!"

"Have it your own way then," I told him, tired of argument. "This is the bare bones of it. My sister was forced to enter the Place of Wisdom against her will. She shared with me and my brother a gift. Through that she reached Kemoc before the time of her final Vow, for she would not be one of the Witches. We had her forth from the Place, since the safeguards of the Power were exhausted by the closing of the mountains. Having won her freedom we strove to preserve it by striking east, into the unknown. We crossed the forbidden passes, found Escore, and those there, both enemy and friend, with the need for men to fight on the side of good in a very old war. Through no wish of mine—that I shall swear to by any Sign or Name—it was laid upon me to come here, and seek out any willing to cross the mountains. More than that no wile nor force can learn from me, for that is the full truth!"

He no longer laughed; instead his eyes regarded me very narrowly over the veil of his helm.

"I have heard of the Warder of the South, of Simon Tregarth—"

"And of the Lady Jaelithe," I added for him. "And never has it been hidden that he was an outlander and held some of the Power—is that not so?"

He nodded reluctantly.

"Then can it also be beyond the bounds of belief that we, the flesh of their flesh, have also gifts not usual to others? We were born at one birth, and always have we been locked of spirit, and sometimes of mind. When Kaththea wanted to come forth from that Place, we could do nothing else than bring her. If that makes us meat for any man's sword, then that is the way matters stand."

This time Godgar made me no answer, but set his horse on, pulling sharply at the leading reins. We trotted down the rough road in a thick drizzle. Nor did he speak with me again throughout that long morning. We made a noonday stop in a place of rocks where an overhanging ledge gave shelter and there was a supply of wood laid up by a blackened ring of stones to mark a known camping place.

I walked stiffly when they had me down from my horse, for they left my legs free but not my hands. They produced journey bread, dried meat and fruit, little better than field rations. And they loosed my hands to eat, though one of them stood over me until I was done, then promptly applied the lashings again. But to my surprise they did not mount up after they had eaten. Instead one of them set a fire, which we had not needed for the cooking of food, taking what seemed to me unnecessary care in just how the wood was placed. Then, when light was put to that stack of wood, he took a stand to the right of it, a cloak in his hands.

Signaling! Though the code they used was none I knew from my scouting days. Blink, blink, blink, back and forth he snapped the cloak. I stared out on the gloomy country-side, straining to read anywhere along the darkened horizon an answer to those flashes. But without result.

However, my guards seemed satisfied. They kept the fire going, after letting it die down a little, sitting about it while their cloaks and surcoats steamed dry. I watched the sodden countryside. They were waiting—for whom and why?

Godgar cleared his throat, and the sound was loud in that place, for they had not spoken more than a few words since they had dismounted.

"We wait for those who will take you to deliver to the Council guards," he addressed me. "There will be no one then who can say that you sheltered with Hervon."

"As you yourself said, when they question me under the Power, the Wise Ones will know all." I could not understand why he tried the clumsy coverup of passing me from one party to another.

"Perhaps."

Then it came to me: there was one way in which I could not be questioned, and that was if I was delivered dead! If my body was so brought in by a middle party, there could be no connection then with Hervon's people.

"Why leave the throat cutting to another?" I asked then. "You have a sword to your hand."

When he did not reply I continued: "Or do you wear a rune sword which will flame out with blood on it—to be read thereafter by all men? Your lord was not one with you in this. He would not set point or edge to a man with tied wrists!"

Godgar stirred. His eyes were hot again; I had pricked him then. Hard as he was, old customs still held. And there flashed now into my mind, as if some voice spoke the words into my ears, an oath considered so potent and binding that no man who had ever borne a sword in war could break it.

"You know me—I am Kyllan of Tregarth. I have ridden with the Border Scouts—is that not fact? Have you heard any ill report of such riding?"

He might not understand the why of my asking, but he returned frankly enough:

"I have heard of you with the Scouts. You were a warrior—and a man—in those days."

"Then listen well, Godgar and you others—" I paused, and then spoke each word that followed with emphasis and measured slowness, as my sister might have delivered one of her chants to summon the Power.

"May I be slain by my own blade, struck by my own darts, if I ever meant any ill to those within the House of Dhulmat, or to any man of Estcarp."

They stared at me across their veils. I had given them the strongest assurance any of our calling might ever use. Would it hold?

They stirred uneasily, and their eyes went from me to each other. Godgar tugged at his helm veil, bringing it in a loose loop from his jaw as if he were about to eat once more.

"That was ill done!" he barked angrily.

"Ill done?" I shot back. "In what way, Godgar? I have given you Sword Oath that I mean you and yours no ill. What evil lies in that?"

Then I turned to his men. "Do you believe me?"

They hesitated, then he in the center spoke. "We believe because we must."

"Then where lies the ill doing?"

Godgar got to his feet and strode back and forth a few paces, his frown blackly heavy. He stopped and rounded on me.

"We have begun a thing for the sake of those to whom we owe allegiance. You are no one, nothing. Why must your fate be made now a shadow on our shield honor? What witchery have you used, outlaw?"

"No witchery, save that which you, and you"—I pointed to each—"and you, and you, Godgar, share with me. I am warrior bred; I did what I had to do in the support of my own allegiances. That put me outside the law of the Council. I came back here because I was laid under another command—the why of it and by whom I have no knowing. But that I meant ill by my coming no Power can prove, for it is not so."

"Too late." Another of the guards was standing, pointing into the open.

Dim as the clouds made the scene, the coming riders could be counted. Five . . . six of them.

Godgar nodded in their direction. "Those owe us a battle debt. But since you say you came to Hervon by chance, and have taken oath on it—well, they will turn you in living, not dead. With the Witches you can take your chances and those will not be bright. I—I am not honor broke in this, outlaw!"

"You are not honor broke," I agreed.

"Wait!"

He who had indicated the riders now spoke more sharply.

"What is—what is that?"

Between the distant riders and our shelter there was open country, covered only with the tall grass. It was at that grass he pointed now. It rippled, was like the sea with each wave troubled and wind tossed. And through it came such a regiment as no man among us had ever seen. Prong-horns, not leaping away in alarm, but gathering with purpose towards us. A shambling bear taking no notice, a grass cat—yellow-brown, but equal to his brothers of the snow lines—smaller things we could not distinguish save for the movement in the grass . . . all headed to us!

"What will they do?" Godgar was disconcerted as he would never have been to see an armed party about to attack. The very unnaturalness of this advance was unnerving.

I struggled to my feet and none reached a hand to stay me, for they were too awed by what they now witnessed.

As the grass was agitated by a gathering of four-footed inhabitants, so was the sky filled in turn. Birds came in flocks out of nowhere, and they swooped, called, strove to reach us under the ledge. These men had endured years of war such as only warrior blood could face, but this was against nature.

I struggled to contact the minds of those closing in upon us. I found that I could contact them, yes, and read their determination—but I could not control them in any manner.

I moved away from the others, who had drawn tightly under the protection of the ledge. The birds whirred, screamed, trilled about me, but they made no move to attack. Grass dwellers gathered about my feet, and wove circles, always facing—not me—but those who had brought me here. I began to walk, out into the open and the rain, away from Godgar and his men.

"Stand—or I shoot!"

I glanced back. His dart gun was out, aimed at me. Through the air came that which I had sought—blue-green, moving swiftly, straight for Godgar's head. He cried out, and ducked. I walked on, passing a grass cat growling deep in its throat and lashing its tail, looking not to me but to the men behind, past a prong-horn that snorted, struck the earth with blade-sharp hooves, past a gathering army in fur and feathers.

And always I probed, trying to find the will which had launched that army, which held them there. For that such existed I was certain. The horses that had carried us snorted, screamed, reared to break loose from their picket ropes and run, in wild galloping, from feline forms skulking about. I heard shouts behind me, but this time I did not turn to look. If I were to die by Godgar's darts, why face them? Better to walk towards freedom.

I discovered that walking with tied hands was not walking free. The rain had made the ground slippery, and I lost balance with my arms so tightly confined. I had to watch my footing as I went. Then I heard sounds from behind strange enough to make me look.

Just as I had walked away from the ledge, so after me stumbled and wavered my captors—not willingly, but under compulsion. For they were being herded by the animals and birds. What had become of their weapons I did not know, but their dart guns were gone. And, strangely enough, none had drawn steel. So they came, strained of face, staring of eye, men caught up in a nightmare of mad dreaming.

I had headed east, and so east we went in company, the birds always above, and always around us the host of animals large and small. Now they gave voice, squeaks, growls, snorts, almost as if they protested their use in this fashion—for being used they were. I glanced to where we had seen those other riders. There was no sign of them! Could they have been overwhelmed by the weird army?

Of all the marches I had made in a lifetime, that was the strangest. The creatures kept pace with me, and those after me, to the best of their ability. Though, after a space, the smaller ones fell behind, and only the larger beasts matched us. The birds went in flocks, wheeling and diving. But the blue-green one had once more vanished.

We plodded on, to what goal I had no idea, though not to return to Hervon's holding. Again and again I tried to reach by contact the control over that furred and feathered force. Finally in my mind the old march cadence began its well-known sing-song:

"Sky-earth-mountain-stone! Sword cuts to the bone!" Then I realized I was chanting that aloud and the clamor of beast and bird was stilled. Yet silent they marched with a determination not of their natures.

At length I paused and turned to face those behind me. They were pale under the brown weathering on their faces. And they met my gaze glassily, as men will front something over which they have no domination, against which they can make no true stand.

"Godgar!" I raised my voice sharply to shake him out of that ensorcellment. "Godgar, go from here by your path, as long as it leads back to the House of Dhulmat. As I have said, between us lies no feud, nor the need for any answer to be made to this day's work. If I wore a sword I would exchange it now for your blade in truce."

He had passed beyond anger, but he was not broken.

"Captain"—that address of respect came wryly from him—"if it is peace you offer, peace shall we take. But do those who walk with us also offer it?"

That I did not know either, but it must be tested. "Try them," I replied.

Then, watching warily their flankers, Godgar and his men started south. Slowly, with a semblance of reluctance, a way was opened to them. As he saw this, Godgar's shoulders went back a fraction more. He looked once more to me.

"This must be reported," he said.

"Let it be so," I answered.

"Wait!" He started towards me. A grass cat crouched, fangs bared, snarling. Godgar stopped short. "I mean you no ill. Walking with bound hands is hard; I would free you."

But the cat would have none of that, despite my silent command.

"It would seem that *our* oaths are not current coin here, Godgar. Go you in peace, and report as you must. And I say again—I hold no feud thought against you or yours."

He returned to his men and they walked south, behind them trailing a detachment of the creatures, as if they were to be escorted on their way. But for me there was another path—blue-green wings again in the air and a trill of song urging me along it.

XVIII

*I*t was a little later that I learned I was not being escorted, but after a manner herded also. For once Godgar and his men were out of sight. I paused, faced about—and looked into the snarling mask of a grass cat, behind it a prong-horn snorting and pawing earth. Ancient enemies, but now united in purpose. The cat growled; I wheeled to face east and the growling ceased. More and more of the furred company had fallen away from the body which had set us moving away from the ledge, but I still led a formidable force, mostly of larger creatures.

A trilling overhead—Dahaun's messenger circled there, urging me on, I thought. So I left the road, tramped on in the sodden grass which brushed wetly about me almost thigh high and sometimes concealed my escort altogether. When I was on the move once more, the bird flashed ahead.

Dahaun—had she followed across the mountains? But sense was against that. There was so close a tie between her race and Escore that they could not go out of that haunted land. Kemoc? But the command over this company of beasts and birds was not Kemoc's, nor Kaththea's, nor born of any magic ever brewed in Estcarp.

Ahead was the dark mass of broken mountains. This route would bring me into their foothills. I struggled against the cords about my wrists. Once into that rough country I would need use of my hands. The ties cut into my flesh and I felt the slipperiness of blood oozing from ridged cuts. Perhaps that loosened them sufficiently at last. For, in spite of menacing growls and snorts, I halted now and again to work with all my might at those circlets. Then, with a tearing of skin, I pulled one hand free and brought both before me, congested and purple, blood-stained. I wriggled fingers to restore circulation.

The rain had ceased but there was no lightening of the clouds, now that it was twilight. Not only the coming of dark in this wilderness plagued me, but fatigue had slowed my progress to a weary shuffle. I glanced behind. The head of a prong-horn buck was up, the eyes of a cat watched—but farther back. I took a step or so in their direction. Snarl and snort—warning me on. I could see other bodies crouched or erect in the grass. There was for me no road to the west.

They did not follow me, merely stood where they were now, a barrier before those lands where I might find others of my kind. Just as those hunters had been on my trail before, so now these were harrying me out of Estcarp.

Seeing a rocky outcrop not too far away, I made for that and sat down to rest aching feet. Riding boots had never been fashioned for steady hours of walking. I could spy those sentinels slipping along the ground if they were felines, treading on determined hooves for prong-horns. The heavily built bears had disappeared, perhaps unable to keep up. But for the others . . . we matched stares while I thought.

It would seem that someone or something wished to send me back to Escore. And I rebelled against such pressure. First send me to Estcarp on a fruitless mission, then drive me out again. I could see no sense in this, nor does any man take easily to the knowledge that he is only a piece on some gameboard, to be moved hither and thither for purposes which are none of his.

Dermont had told me once of a very ancient custom of Karsten, one which had fallen into disuse when the Old Race lost rule there and the newcomers from still farther south had overrun the land. But in dim history there had been a game played each decade. Carven pieces were set out on a marked board. At one side sat him who was deemed the greatest lord, on the other who was landless, followerless, the least, but who would dare the game. And the landless player represented the forces of disruption and ill luck, while the lord those of confidence and success. Thus they played, not only for all the great lord held, but also for the luck and fortune of the whole land. For, should the landless topple the lord, a period of chaos and change would ensue in the land.

Was such a game now in progress, with a living man—me—for one of its pieces? In Estcarp abode the settled state of things as they are, well established, even firmer now that Karsten had been dealt with. And uneasy Escore where old troubles stirred was the opposite. Perhaps behind that ancient game had lain some older truth well buried, that a more powerful action once known had been reduced to ritual at a gameboard.

So could I speculate, but I doubted that I would ever know how much of my guessing was the truth. I had certainly been moved into Estcarp, just as I was being moved out again. I shook my head, though only the beasts saw that gesture. Then I began to pull up the grass about my rock, making a nest bed. The one thing I *was* sure of was that I could go no farther now.

Though I lay in the open this was one night I felt no need for watch keeping. Perhaps I had been lifted out of the normal courses to the point where I no longer cared, or perhaps I was too tired and worn by what had chanced.

Thus I slept. And if I dreamed, I did not carry the memory of those dreams past my waking. But when I got stiffly to my feet from that mass of grass in the morning, I faced the mountains. This was right—if I were a piece on a gameboard, then I had been moved. I started off with empty hands, no food, and a hard climb before me. Twice I looked back. If my herders had kept vigil during the night that had not lasted until this hour. No sign of them was visible. Neither was there in me any need to go out once more into Estcarp.

During the day I was certainly one under some order, though I could not have put it into words. The broken mountains were my goal. Senseless, senseless, one part of my mind repeated over and over. Urge me in, bring me out—what had I accomplished? A meeting with refugees on a single holding, and on them I had made only a negative impression.

I thought I had been sent to recruit—but my feeble effort had not even begun that task. So—and that brought me up short as I halted on the verge of a mountain reaching ravine—so what *had* been the real reason for my return to Estcarp? I kicked viciously at a stone, sent it rolling from me with a sound to break the general silence.

A use for me—what? None that I could see, and my ignorance gnawed, plunging me into action, the only kind open to me now, the return overmountain. I scrambled down slope, began to run almost blindly, taking little heed of my body with my mind so bedeviled with frightening half-thoughts to which there were no sane answers.

A fall was the end of that witless race, witless because there was no escaping from fears I bore with me. I lay panting on the earth, beating my still swollen hands on the gravel until the pain of that contact shocked me back to quiet again.

Once the blood stopped pounding so heavily in my ears I heard the gurgle of water and I was drawn by that, my dry mouth gaping even before I reached a spring fed pool. I lapped up the fresh liquid as might one of the hunting cats. Water cold against my face restored more rational thinking. To run terror stricken was never an answer, so—yield to this mysterious ordering until more could be learned. I was far more a man when I left the spring. There was an explanation somewhere and it could only lie in Escore. For the beast army was not of Estcarp's devising. So the sooner I gained to Escore, that much earlier would I learn my place in the new scheme of things.

Hunger grew in me. It had been a long time since I had chewed those trail rations under the rock ledge. Yet nowhere in this wilderness was there food. But I had known hunger before and kept on the move in spite of its twinges. The mountains—could I find again that valley which led to our climb point? Sometimes when I looked about me, either that peculiar distortion which had plagued us before was in force, or else my lack of food worked upon my vision, for there was a disorientation to this land through which I moved.

Evening did not stop me, for the need of Escore had grown to an all-pervading urge. I stumbled on, in a narrow cut, but whether the right one I could not have said. And then—ahead was light! Stupidly I plowed to a halt and blinked. I had a dull fear that I had been forestalled, that I was awaited now by those who would cut me off, take me once more captive.

My mind worked so sluggishly that I could see no way out of such disaster. If I retreated it could only be back to the plains, or to be lost in the foothills where I could never find my way again.

Brother!

So deep was I sunk in my own inner pit that at first that mind call meant nothing. Then—then—Kemoc!

I do not believe that I shouted the name aloud as I began to run towards the fire—but in me was a welling fountain of recognition.

He came to meet me and I could not have made those last steps, few as they were, alone. Half guiding, half supporting, he brought me to his oasis of light and warmth. I leaned against a backing springy brush and held a small bowl, the warmth of its contents reaching my hands, the aroma making me eager to sip at a thick stew.

Kemoc—wearing the garb of Dahaun's people—even to the whip stock at his belt, yet looking as he had a hundred times before when we had shared patrol camps. And the familiarity of the scene was as soothing to my feeling of being under another's control, as the stew was to my hunger of body.

"You knew I was coming?" I broke the silence first, for he had allowed me those moments in which to soak up ease and reassurance.

"She did—The Lady of Green Silence." He sounded a little restrained and aloof. "She told us you were taken—"

"Yes."

"They would not let Kaththea try to aid you. They put a mind lock on her!" Now his constraint was hostile. "But they could not hold me. So having wrought their own magic, they allowed me to come to see how well it worked."

A small flash of insight—did Kemoc, also, feel that he was now moved by another's will?

"*Their* magic." The beasts—yes, that could well be Dahaun's magic.

"They were not sure it would work—not in Estcarp. But it seems that it did, since you are here. Kyllan, why did you go?" he demanded of me hotly.

"Because I had to." And I told him of what and how it had chanced with me since my awaking from that dream in the Green Valley. Nor did I hide from him my concern over being used by some unknown authority for a reason I did not understand.

"Dahaun?" Again that sharpness.

I shook my head. "No, she did not wish it. But I tell you, Kemoc, in all of this we play a game, and it is not of our choosing or understanding. Least of all do I know why I was sent here and then allowed—no, ordered—to return again!"

"They say there is an ingathering of forces in Escore, a rallying of evil—and they summon their people also. The time of truce is past; both move now to a trial of strength. And I tell you, brother, hard as this may be, still I welcome it. For I do not relish this play behind a screen."

"Kaththea—you say they have mind locked her."

"Only until she would agree not to use her Power. They said it would only further awaken all we have to fear. She waits with the others, up there." He gestured at the mountain wall behind him. "With the day we shall join them."

This night I did not sleep dreamlessly. Once more I rode the fields of Escore in another guise—mailed, armed, ready for bared swords or worse. And with me was a force of those to choose to share shields. Among them were faces I knew from the past, but not all from a distant past. For, mailed and armed as was the custom in times of great danger, I saw the Lady Chriswitha. Once she smiled at me before she rode on and others of the Old Race took her place. But always we traveled with danger to the right and left, and a kind of desperation eating at us. There was a banner fashioned like a huge green bird (or could it have been a real bird many times life size?) and the wind appeared to whip it so the wings were ever spread in flight. Always we bore with us an axe's weight of death, not tribute, to satisfy any dark overlord.

"Kyllan!" I awoke with Kemoc's hand on my shoulder, shaking me into consciousness.

"You had ill dreams," he told me.

"Perhaps ill, perhaps otherwise. You shall have your open battles, Kemoc, one after another of them. Whether we shall cleanse the land or be buried in it—" I shrugged. "At any rate we have our hands, and swords for them to use. Though it may be that time does not favor us."

For the second time we climbed the cliff out of Estcarp. And for all the urgency riding me I moved slowly. But when we had reached the crest, before we moved on to the pass, I turned, as did Kemoc. He had a distance lens to his eyes. Suddenly his body tensed and I knew he had sighted something.

"What is it?"

His answer was to pass the lenses to me. Trees and rocks leaped up at me. Among them men moved. So they were a-hunting on my track again? Well, that would not last; they would shy off from the forbidden lands as had those others. A large force—truly they wanted me badly.

Then I focused the glasses better and I saw one rider, another, a third. Unbelieving, I looked to Kemoc. He nodded, his surprise open to read on his face.

"You see truly, brother—those are in part women!"

"But—why? Wise Ones come to capture the fugitive for themselves?"

"What Wise One would bear a child in a riding cradle before her?"

I raised the lenses again, swept that company, found what he had earlier marked, a cloaked woman in the breeches meant for long and hard riding, but across her saddle the cradle of a child still too young to sit a pony.

"Some invasion—they being hunted before it—" I sought for the only explanation I could credit.

"I think not. They ride from the southwest. Invasion now would come only from Alizon in the north. No, I believe they are recruits—the recruits you were sent for, brother."

"That cannot be—women and children?" I protested. "And I told my story only at Hervon's manor where it was discredited when I named myself outlaw. There was no reason for them to—"

"No reason that you knew of," he corrected.

I do not know why at that moment I remembered something from my childhood. I had come into the hall at Etsford on one of those rare occasions when my father had visited us. Yes, it was the time that he had brought Otkell to be our tutor in arms. And he was speaking of something which had lately happened at Gorm. A Sulcar ship from overseas had drifted into harbor, all her crew dead on board. And in the Captain's cabin, written out in the log, the story of a plague picked up in a distant port, which spread from man to man. Those at Gorm towed the ship well to sea, set her afire to burn and sink, taking her dead with her. But all had come from one man, returning from shore leave with the seeds of death in him.

Supposing I had been sent to Estcarp carrying some such seed—not directly of disease and death, though the end result might well be the latter, but to infect those about me with the need to seek Escore? Wild as it was, that could be an explanation to answer more than one question.

Kemoc read it in my mind and now he took the lenses from me, to once more study those moving with such purpose towards us.

"They do not seem to be befogged, or otherwise blocked," he observed. "Your plague may already be well seated."

Women and children—no! A tail of fighting men, those with no ties who were long hardened by slim chances—that I had wished for. But to bring their families into the threat of shadowed Escore—*No!*

"It would appear that *someone* or *something* has plans for refounding a nation." Kemoc lowered the lenses.

"More players for the game!" I knew dull anger and also that such anger would not avail me. Nor would I take the lenses again as Kemoc held them out. This was my doing and I would have to answer for it.

"They cannot bring their mounts in," Kemoc said, becoming practical. I could almost have struck him for his quick acceptance of what was to come. "But with ropes their gear may be lifted, and they aided. Then, perhaps, horned ones waiting beyond the tree valley—"

"You are very sure they are coming to us," I shot at him.

"Because he is right!"

Kaththea stood behind us. Now she ran forward, her hand on my arm, on Kemoc's, linking us.

"Why?" Somewhere in her, I hoped, was an answer for me.

"Why do they come? Not all of them will, only those able to feel the call, the need. And why were you sent, Kyllan? Because you were the one of us who could best carry the seed of that call. In me the dream could not be set; I had too many Power safeguards implanted. In Kemoc also, for he was so close of mind that my block spread to him. So you had to be the carrier, the sower . . . and now comes the harvest!"

"To their deaths!"

"Some to death," my sister agreed. "But do not all living things abide with death from the first drawing of life breath? No man may order the hour of his dying if he travels by life's pattern. Nor can you bewail the chance, brother, which made you carry your dream into Estcarp. We stand in a time of chance and change, and move into new designs we do not understand. Play your life boldly as you always have. Do you blame the sword for killing? It is the hand and brain behind it which holds the responsibility!"

"And who is the hand and brain behind this?"

"Who can name the names of Eternal Ones?"

Her prompt reply startled me. That some still believed in those nameless forces beyond nature, man, or the world, I knew. That those of witch training would, I could not understand.

"Yes, Kyllan, the acquiring of learning does not mean the end of faith, even though some who stop too soon would swear that so. I do not know in *whose* pattern we begin to move now, nor do I deny that it may be a harsh one with sore troubles ahead. But we are caught in it and there is no turning back. Meanwhile, cease chewing fingers and become yourself!"

So was the incoming to Escore. And I, who had been challenging death since I first felt the weight of a sword above my hip, took on again that weight and others. For we did thereafter indeed buy Escore with steel, raw courage, and such witchery as was not tainted. And that winning is a marvelous tale which must have a full chronicle to itself. But this was the beginning of that tale, the sowing of the seed from which came later harvest—and it was the story of us three.

Warlock
of the
Witch World

I

∞

*J*t has been an oft-told story of our birthing that our mother, the Lady Jaelithe (she who put aside her witchhood in Estcarp to wed the outland warrior, Simon Tregarth), did demand of some Power she served certain gifts for us, whom she bore in great and painful travail. That she named my brother Kyllan, warrior, my sister Kaththea, witch (or one to control powers), and asked for me, wisdom. But it has been that my wisdom consists in knowing that I know very little, though the thirst for learning has ever been in me. Only, in spite of all my striving, I have done no more than nibble at the edges of knowledge's rich cake, liplicked the goblet rim of true wisdom. But perhaps to know one's limitations is, in itself, a kind of sagecraft.

In the beginning, when we were children, I did not lack fellowship, for we three, born at one birth (which in Estcarp was something hitherto unknown) were also one in spirit. Kyllan was formed for action, Kaththea for feeling, and I—supposedly—for thought. We worked together smoothly, and the bond between us was tight, as if it were wrought of flesh as well as of spirit. Then came that bleak day when Kaththea was rift from us by the Wise Women who kept the rule of the land. And for a period we lost her.

Still, in a war a man can lose himself, or be able to put aside one set of fears for another, living from each sun's rising to its setting, each dusk to dawn. And that we were forced to do. For Kyllan and I rode with the Borderers who kept a thin line of ever-ready defense between Estcarp and the darksome menace of Karsten.

Then luck deserted me in a single swing of a short sword, and I was swept from usefulness into that human wastage resulting from the chances of war. Yet, for this once, I welcomed such a respite, painful as it was for my body. For from it came the freeing of our sister from the bondage of the Witches.

Though my right hand was maimed, my warrior life apparently past, I waited hardly past the outward healing of my wound before I went to Lormt. For during my days in the mountains I had stumbled upon a curious piece of knowledge. Which was this—though those of Estcarp knew the south of their long enemy Karsten, and the north of Arizon, greedy too for their downfall, the western seas where their long-time allies, the Sulcar seamen, cut wave and harried shores halfway around our world, yet of the east was no mention among them. It was as if the world ended at a chain of mountains we could see on clear days. And in the minds of those with whom we rode there was, I came to be sure, a block against that direction, so for them the east did not exist.

Lormt was very old, even for Estcarp which has a history so buried in the dust of years that no modern searching can disinter its beginnings. Once perhaps it was a town, though for what purpose one should be set in that bleak country I could not guess. Now it is only a moldering handful of buildings, surrounded by crumbling ruins. But in it there are records of the Old Race, long forgotten; though there are those who tunnel molewise among them, copying and recopying what seems to them worth the preserving, the choice of what to save, theirs alone. When, perhaps in the next cupboard may lie, in near tattered scraps, something far more worth renewing.

There I sought out an answer to this mystery of the unknown east. For Kyllan and I had not surrendered (though outwardly those about us might have believed that we did) our hope of bringing Kaththea forth and reuniting our company of three. But to escape the wrath of the Council we needed a refuge—and this eastern mystery might offer such.

So in Lormt I found two tasks to occupy me through the months; one the searching of ancient manuscripts; the other of learning to be a warrior once again, though now my left hand must curve to the sword hilt. For in the twilight world in which we lived, when the sun of Estcarp was red on the horizon, half-slipped into the dark of night, no man could ride unarmed.

I discovered enough to make me sure that in the east did indeed lie our salvation—or at least a chance of escaping the wrath of the witches. Also, I became once more a warrior—of sorts.

The final blow, decided upon by the Council, to finish Karsten, gave us our chance. While the Witches drew all power to their bidding—to stir the mountains of the south as a cook would stir a pudding in the kettle—Kyllan and I met once more at Etsford, which had been home to us. And we rode together through a night of turmoil, to bring our sister out of the trap which had held her so long.

Then did we go east, to find Escore, that riven land from which the Old Race had come in the far, far past, where the powers of both good and ill had been unleashed to walk as they would, wearing strange guises. We strove with those powers, separately and together. Kyllan, having used part of his gift on our behalf, laid himself open to the possession of one of these forces, and, while the cost to him was high in peril and pain, it brought us to the People of Green Silences and into their sanctuary.

They were not wholly of our blood. Even as we were not wholly of the Old Race, sharing the inheritance from our father who had come from another space and time. Though they had in them some of the Old Race, yet for the rest they were older still, being akin to the land in a way which those of my blood are not. But then, in Escore there are many legends we had heard in our childhood which lived to walk, burrow, fly.

Then a geas was laid on Kyllan, by what Power we had no telling. And under it he went back across the mountains to Estcarp. From him spread a kind of need—I do not know the proper words for its description—which settled into some of the Old Race, who had been driven out of Karsten during the Kolder War and since had been a restless, homeless people. When he came back to us, they followed him.

Not only fighting men came so, but also their women and children, bringing all that they could to enable them to set up households in this new land. The Men of the Green Silences under Dahaun, their Lady (she who had succored Kyllan during his great peril), and Ethutur, their warlord, aided them over the cliffs and brought them to the safe Valley.

So much have I wrote in this chronicle, and perhaps it repeats what is already a too familiar tale. But it has been set upon me to add this to the record begun by Kyllan. This is my portion of the story, which stands a little apart from the history of the Great War, though it was a rightful place in that, since it helped in bringing about the final victory.

Rightfully, my adventure begins in the Valley—which was a lightsome place in which the heart could rejoice. Through the years the ones who dwelt there had set such Symbols and bonds about it that it remained free of all evil—a place in which a man could take his ease. I knew those Symbols from my studies at Lormt and I thought them high protection.

Peaceful as it was in the Valley, we could not give ourselves to rest there, for about us the whole of Escore was astir. Long ago this land had been riven time and time again with wars as great as those which now gnawed our homeland in the west. Here men and women had sought knowledge, and then passed beyond the bonds set by prudence for such seeking. There arose those who sought power for the sake of power alone; and from that always issues the Shadow which is darker than any night. There was a drawing apart and some of the Old Race retreated over the mountains, wrecking behind them all roads, closing their minds to the past.

Then the remnants warred, titanic and awful force against force, blasting and blighting. Some, such as the Green People, who abode still by laws, drew back into the places of wilderness. And to them came others—a handful of humans of good will; others who were the result of early experimentation by the dabblers in strange knowledge, yet were not evil, nor had been used for evil purposes.

But all these were too few and too weak to challenge the Great Ones, drunk with their controls of energies beyond our comprehending. So they lay very low and waited for the storms to sweep and ebb. Some of the Dark Ones destroyed each other in those blasting struggles. Others withdrew through Gates they had opened that led to other times and spaces—even as that gate through which my father had come into Estcarp. But all of their striving left behind pools of ancient evil, servants who were freed or abandoned. It was unknown, too, whether or not they might choose to return if something chanced to summon them.

When we first came into Escore, Kaththea had drawn upon her witch learning to save and aid us. In so doing she had broken the false calm which had long abode here. Things awoke and gathered, and the land was troubled, so that the Green People believed we were on the eve of new war. But this time we must fight or be utterly ground into powder between the millstones of the Dark.

Now came an in-gathering of all who were of the light, that we might plan against aroused evil. Ethutur had called this Council and we sat there, a strange mixture of peoples—or should I say, living creatures; for some in that assembly were not men at all—neither were they beasts.

Ethutur spoke for the Green People. To his right was a Renthan, who could and did bear men on occasion on his back, yet spoke with a voice when there was need; and captained a band of wily fighters—and that was Shapurn. On a large rock squatted a jewel-scaled lizard who used its front feet as hands and now fingered in its claws a cord on which were knotted at irregular intervals silver beads, as if these were reminders of points to be made in any discussion.

Beyond the lizard's rock was a helmed man whose like I had seen many times, and to his right and left sat a man and woman in stately cloaks-of-ceremony. This was Lord Hervon, who had come from the holding Kyllan had found in the hills, the Lady Chriswitha, and his Leader-of-forces, Godgar. Then there were Kyllan and Kaththea and Dahaun. Perched on another rock—thus giving him more presence in a company which towered above him physically—was Farfar the Flannan, with feathered, human shaped body, spreading bird wings, clawed feet. The Flannan was there for reasons of prestige only, since his people lacked the concentration to be reckoned among a fighting force, although they made good messengers.

On the other side were the newcomers. There was another bird-like form, but it had the head of a lizard, narrow, toothed of jaw, covered with red scales which glittered in the sun, in bright contrast to its blue-gray feathers. From time to time it spread its wings uneasily, darting the head from side to side, eyeing the company with sharp measurement. This was a Vrang from the Heights and Dahaun had greeted it with ceremony as "Vorlong, the Wing Beater."

Beyond that strange ally was more human appearing company, four of them. These were, we had been told before their arrival, descendants of the Old Race who had fled long ago into the hills and managed there to exist and carve out some small pockets of safety. Chief among them was a tall man with the dark, familiar features of the true blood. He had the seeming of a young man, but that could be deceptive, since the Old Race show no signs of aging until a few weeks before death—if any of them live to grow old, which in the past years few have. He was both comely and courtly of manner.

And I hated him.

Bound together as we three had been, in the past we had never reached out beyond for companionship. After Kaththea had been torn from us, still had Kyllan and I been so allied. Even so, there had been comrades in arms which had our liking, and some we viewed with distaste. But never in the past had I known such strong emotion as speared me through—save when I had cut down some Karsten raider. Yet then my hated had been more for what the foe represented than the man himself. Whereas this Dinzil out of the Heights I hated bitterly, coldly, and the reason I did not know. In fact, I was so startled by the emotion which filled me when Dahaun introduced us that I hesitated over the greeting words.

And it seemed to me in that moment that he knew what I felt and was amused—as one would be amused at some act of a child. Yet I was not a child, as Dinzil would speedily discover if the need arose.

If the need arose . . . I realized it was not hatred alone which shook me whenever I looked upon that smooth, handsome face, but also apprehension . . . as if, at any moment, this lord of the peaks would suddenly change from what he was to something very dangerous to us all. Still, reason told me, the Green People had welcomed him in friendship, regarded his arrival as a stroke of good fortune. Since they knew all the dangers of this land, surely they would not freely open their gates to one who carried with him the taint of evil.

Kaththea had insisted when we first crossed the fields and woods of Escore that she could smell out pockets of old dark magic as an ill stench. My nose did not so mark Dinzil. Yet inside of me some guardian stood to arms whenever I looked upon him.

He spoke well at our council, with good sense and showing a knowledge of warfare. Those other lords and warriors with him would now and then offer some comment which laid plain to us a past in which Dinzil had been the backbone of their country.

Ethutur brought out maps which were cunningly fashioned of dried leaves, the ribs and markings on them serving for points and divisions. These we passed from hand to hand while the Green People and the men from the Heights supplied pertinent comments, as did also the nonhumans. Vorlong was very emphatic in his warning of a certain line of hills which bore, he croaked in barely understandable speech, three circles of standing stones containing something so deadly that even to fly above them brought death. We marked out those danger spots which were known until all present recognized them.

I was smoothing out one of those maps when I felt a queer drawing. My scar-twisted right hand—of it I was seldom aware nowadays, since it had ceased to pain me and I had as much use of it as I could reestablish with exercise—drew my eyes from the lines on the gray-brown surface of the map. I studied it, puzzled, and then glanced up.

Dinzil—he was looking at my hand. Looking and smiling a small smile, but one which brought a flush to my face. I wanted to snatch my hand away, hide it behind me. Why? It was scarred in honorable war, not from any shameful thing. Yet shame spread from that scar merely because Dinzil regarded it so—as if anything which marred the symmetry of one's flesh was a deformity one should conceal from the world.

Then his eyes arose from my hand to meet mine, and again I thought I read amusement in them—the kind of amusement some men find in the misshapen. And he knew that I knew—yet that only added to his amusement.

I must warn them, I thought feverishly. *Kyllan—Kaththea*—Surely they could share my apprehension and vague suspicion of this man. Let us but get to ourselves again and I would bring them into my mind so they could be on their guard. On guard against what? And why? To that I had no answer.

My eyes went once more to the map. And now, with a kind of defiance, I used my ridged hand with its two stiffened fingers, to smooth it. In me anger was cold and deadly.

Ethutur spoke at last. "It is then decided that we send out the summons to the Krogan, the Thas—"

"Do not count upon them too much, my lord." That was Dinzil. "They are still neutral, yes. But it may well be their desire to remain so."

I heard an impatient exclamation from Dahaun. "If they believe that when battle is once enjoined they can be so, then they are fools!"

"In our eyes, perhaps," Dinzil answered her. "We look upon one side of a shield, my lady. They may not yet look upon the other. But neither do they wish to make such a choice at another's bidding. Knowing the Krogan at least, for we of the Heights have had some dealings with them in the past, we are also aware that if they are pushed they snap at the pusher. Therefore, approach them we must, but let it be done with no pressure. Give them time after the warn-sword is passed to hold their own council. Above all, do not show them an angry face if they say you nay. For this will not be a short struggle we now enter upon, but a long one. Those who stand uncommitted at its beginning, may be drawn in before its ending. If we would have them join behind our war horns, then leave them to their choices in their own time."

I saw Ethutur nod agreement, as did the others. We could not raise contrary voices, since this was their land and they knew it. But I thought it was never wise to war in a country where there are those uncommitted to either side, for a neutral can turn enemy suddenly and find an unprotected flank to attack.

"We send out the warn-sword to the Krogan, the Thas—the moss-ones?" Ethutur ended on a questioning note.

Dahaun laughed. "The moss-ones? Perhaps—if any can find them. But they follow too much their own ways. Those we can count upon wholly stand here and now—is that what you would tell us, Lord Dinzil?"

He shrugged. "Who am I to call the roll of those who walk apart from my own men, Lady? It is but proper caution to awake, or summon, naught but those we have had dealings with in the past. Change and counterchange have wrought deeply here. Perhaps even long ago friends are not now to be trusted. Yes, I would say that what army we can trust to the blooding stand now within this safe Valley of yours—or shall when we marshal all our forces. The hills shall be horned. To the low country, yours the summons."

I had not dared to call mind to mind in that assembly, so I was impatient for its breaking. As yet we had but small idea of what powers or gifts those about us had—so I would not so summon my kin. Thus it was much later that I tried to get speech with them apart. I had the first luck with Kyllan as he rode with Horvan to seek a camping place for the ones from over-mountain. But first I was beside Godgar, falling into talk concerning the border war. We found we had once served in the same section of knife-edged ridges, but at different times.

His type I knew well. They are born to war, sometimes having the spark of leadership in them. But more often they are content to come to the horn as shield men under a commander they respect. Such are the hard and unbreakable core of any good force, unhappy in peace, feeling perhaps unconsciously that their reason for life vanishes when the sword remains too long in the scabbard. He rode now as one who sniffs a scent upon the air, glancing from side to side, marking out the country for his memory as a scout, alert to all the tides of war.

Horvan found land to his liking and set about putting up tent shelters, though in the valley so mild was the air that one could well lay in the open with comfort. At last I was free to ride with Kyllan, and, avoiding mind touch here, I spoke to him of Dinzil.

I had spoken for some moments before I was aware of Kyllan's frown. I stopped, to look at him sharply. Then I did use the mind touch.

To discover with surprise—confusion—because I found something which at first I could not identify and then met—for the first time in our close-knit lives—refusal to believe! It was a shock, for Kyllan believed that I was now one looking for shadows under an open sun, trying to make trouble—

"No—not that!" His protest was quick as he followed my thought in turn. "But—what do you hold against this man? Save a feeling? If he wishes us ill—how could he pass the Symbols which seal the Valley? I do not think this place goes undefended against any who walk cloaked in the Great Shadow."

But how wrong he was—though we were not aware of it then.

What did I have to offer in proof of the rightness of my feeling? A look in a man's eyes? That feeling alone—yet such emotions were also our defenses here.

Kyllan nodded; his amazement was beginning to fade. But I closed my mind to him. I was like a child who has trustingly set hand to a coal, admiring its light without knowing of the danger. And then, burned, I regarded the world with newly awakened suspicion.

"I am warned," my brother assured me. But I felt he did not think it a true warning.

That night they had a feast—although not a joyful one, since the reason for the gathering was so grave. But they held to the bonds of high ceremony; perhaps because in such forms there was a kind of security. I had not spoken with Kaththea as I wished; I had waited too long, shaken after my attempt with Kyllan. Now it rested as a burden on me that she sat beside Dinzil at the board and he smiled much upon her. She smiled or laughed in return when he spoke.

"Are you always so silent, warrior with a stern face?"

I turned to look at Dahaun, she who can change at will to seem any fair one a man holds in mind. Now she was raven of hair with a faint touch of rose in her ivory cheeks. But in the sunset her hair had been copper-gold, her skin golden also. What would it be like, I wondered, to be so many in one?

"Do you dream now, Kemoc of the wise head?" she challenged and I came out of my bemusement.

"No good dream if I do, Lady."

The light challenge vanished; her eyes dropped from mine to the cup she held in her two hands. She moved it slightly and the purple liquid within it flowed from side to side.

"Look not in any foretelling mirror this night, Kemoc. Yet you have more than the shadow of a dream over you, to my thinking."

"I do."

Now why had I said that? Always had I kept my own counsel, or our own counsel, for we three-who-were-one shared. But was that still so? I looked again to my sister, who laughed with Dinzil, and to Kyllan, who was talking eagerly with Ethutur and Hervon as if he were a link between the two of them.

"Branch, hold not to the leaves," said Dahaun softly. "There comes a time when those must loose for the wind to bear them away. But new leaves grow in turn—"

I caught her meaning and flushed. That she and Kyllan had an understanding between them I had known for weeks. Nor had it hurt me that this was so. That there might come a day when Kaththea would step into a road wherein she would walk with another, that I also accepted. I did not resent it that Kaththea laughed this night and was more maiden than witch and sister. But I resented whom she laughed with!

"Kemoc—"

I glanced again to Dahaun and found her staring at me.

"Kemoc—what is it?"

"Lady—" I held her eyes but I did not try to reach her mind. "Look well to your walls. I am afraid."

"Of Dinzil? That he may take from you that which you have cherished?"

"Of Dinzil—what he may be."

She sipped from her cup, still watching me over its rim. "So, I shall look, warrior. I was ill-spoken, ill-thought, to put it to you as I did. This is no jealousy of close kin eating at you. You dislike him for himself. Why?"

"I do not know—I only feel."

Dahaun put down her cup. "And feelings can speak more truthfully than tongues. Be certain I shall watch—in more ways than one."

"For that I thank you, Lady," I said low-voiced.

"Ride hence with foreboding this much lightened, Kemoc," she replied. "And good luck ride with you, to right, to left, at your back—"

"But not before?" I raised my own cup to salute her.

"Ah, but you carry a sword before you, Kemoc."

Thus did Dahaun know what lay in my mind, and she believed. Yet still did I face the morning to come with a chill in me. For I was the one selected to ride to summon the Krogan, and Dinzil showed no sign of leaving the Valley himself.

II

*I*t was decided that the Green People, and we who were joined with them, must pass the warn-sword through the lowlands to such allies as they might deem possible of influencing. With Dahaun, Kyllan would ride to the Thas, that underground dwelling people of whom we had yet caught no sight. They were of the dusk and the night, though not one with the Shadow as far as was known. Ethutur and I would go to the Krogan, those who made the lakes, rivers, waterways of Escore their own. It was thought that the very sight of us from Estcarp might add to the serious meaning of our summoning.

We went forth in the early morning while Kyllan and Dahaun must wait for night and the placing of torches as a summons in a waste place. So they watched us go. Horses we no longer had; instead I bestrode one of Shapurn's people and Ethutur rode Shapurn himself. Large, or a hand's breadth larger than the cross-mountain mounts, these were, sleek of hide of a rich, roan red, with creamy underbody. Their tails were a fluff of cream they kept clamped tight against their haunches as they cantered, a tuft which was matched by a similar puff on the tops of their heads, beneath which a long, red horn slanted up and back in a graceful curve.

They wore no reins nor bridles, for they were not our servants, but rather fellow ambassadors who were gracious enough to lend us their strength to speed our journeying. And, with keener senses than ours, they were our scouts, alert to all dangers.

Ethutur wore the green of the Valley men, their most potent weapon, the force lash, clipped to his belt. But I went in leather and mail of Estcarp. It seemed a heavy weight across my shoulders, one which I had not noted for a long time.

But my helm, with its throat veil of fine chain weaving, I carried in my hand, baring my head to the soft dawn wind.

Though it had been autumn, close to the time of frosts, when we had come to Escore, yet it would seem that summer lingered longer here. We saw touches of yellow and red in leaf and bush as we passed—still, the wind was softer, the chill of early morning quickly gone.

"Be not deceived," Ethutur said now. Though little or no emotion ever broke the handsome perfection of his expression, yet now there was warning in his eyes. As in all the males of his race he showed the horns, ivory-white among the curls above his forehead. To a lesser degree he shared Dahaun's ability to change his coloring. Now in this early light his curls were dark, his face pale. But as the first sun reached to touch him, it was red locks and brown skin I saw.

"Be not deceived," he repeated. "There are traps upon traps, and the bait for some is very fair."

"As I have seen," I assured him.

Shapurn pulled a little ahead, turning from the road which led into the Valley. My mount followed his leader without any order I knew of passing between them. At first it seemed that we were going back up into the Heights, but having climbed for a short space, again we were on a downward slope. Narrow as this passage was, there were traces that this had once been a road of sorts. Blocks of stone protruded from the soil as broad steps which our four-footed companions took cautiously.

We came into a second valley, much choked with a growth of dark-leafed vegetation which was either stunted tree or tall bush. From this loomed masses of ancient masonry, tumbled and broken, but still with a semblance of walls.

Ethutur nodded to it. "HaHarc—"

"Which being?" I prompted when he said no more.

"A safe place once."

"Overrun by the Shadow?"

He shook his head. "The hills danced and it fell. But they danced to a strange piping that night. Let us hope that that secret is indeed lost to those we front now."

"How much of such knowledge does remain?" I asked, already sure men might only guess.

"Who knows? Many of the Great Ones destroyed themselves when they fought. Others went out through their gates to find new tests, new victories—or defeats—elsewhere. Some are so withdrawn from our kind now that what happens here holds no meaning for them. It is our hope that we face not the Great Ones of old, but those who were their lesser shield men, whom they long ago left behind. But never forget that those are formidable enough."

Having seen some, I was not likely to.

Our faint and ancient road took us through the edge of the tumbled ruins. They were well earth-buried, and trees had rooted themselves among those stones and died in turn. Time had lain long here since HaHarc had been shaken to its ending.

Then Shapurn turned left, again following the traces of an old way. We rode from the mouth of that haunted valley into a tall, grassed plain. Now the sun was well up and warm. Ethutur threw back his cloak. Resting across his thighs was the warn-sword—not fashioned of any steel but of white wood, with intricately carved runes running the length of its broad and edgeless blade. About its haft and guard were, twined and tied in fantastic knots, cords of red and green.

We were well out into the open when Shapurn threw high his head and halted, my own mount following his example. The nose flaps of the Renthan were spread wide; he turned his head from side to side in a slow sweep, questing for scent.

He spoke to our minds. "Gray Ones—"

I stared over the grass which rippled under the touch of the wind. It was tall enough to provide hiding for a creeping man. Since Kaththea and I had fled before a wild pack of mixed monstrosities, I had learned to distrust all landscape, no matter how innocent seeming.

"How do they cast?" Ethutur's thought and mine were almost the same.

"They prowl; they seek—"

"Us?"

Shapurn inhaled the breeze. "Not so. They are belly-lean; they hunt to fill themselves. Ah—they have started meat! Now they yammer on its trail."

Faintly I could hear it, too, a distant howl. Having been so hunted, I knew pity for the game they now ran. Ethutur showed a small trace of frown, a break in the usual calm of his face.

"Too close," he said aloud. "We must ride the borders more often." His hand went to the whipstock at his belt. But he did not draw that weapon. For as long as he carried the warn-sword he was barred from that by custom.

Shapurn broke into a trot, a pace my mount easily matched, crossing the open end of the plain with a speed not even one of the famed Torgian mounts of Estcarp could better. Then we were in a defile where bushes grew a thick curtain on either side of the way. There was a thin thread of stream curling a snake-path through sand and gravel, as if it were the ghost of a torrent which ran there at other seasons. I caught a glint from a pocket of pebbles, a flashing which could not be denied. Without thinking I swung down to pluck out of that drab nest a blue-green stone. It was one of those esteemed by the Valley people. Its like was set in the gemmed wristlets and belt Ethutur wore. Although this was rough and uncut, still it caught the sun and flashed sea fire in my palm.

Ethutur turned impatiently to look back, but when he saw what I held he gave an exclamation of surprise and pleasure.

"So! By so much does Fortune smile on us, Kemoc. It is a promise that ill does not intrude too far into this country—since such loses all fire when the

Shadow touches them. A gift to you from this land, and may it be of profit." He raised his right hand from the hilt of the warn-sword and made a gesture which I recognized from the crypts of Lormt to be one of well wishing.

It would seem that my finding of the jewel had heartened my companion, for now he began to talk. I listened, for all that he had to say concerning this country and its in-dwellers was of importance.

The Krogan, to whom we were bound, were another race born of early experiments on the part of the Great Ones. Initially of humankind, volunteers from among the experimenters, they had been mutated and altered to become water dwellers, though they could also exist for varying periods of time outside their aquatic world. However, during the devastation of Escore, they had withdrawn into those depths for safety, and now were seldom seen ashore. They sometimes inhabited islands in lakes, and came now and then on the banks of streams.

They had never been hostile to the Green People. In fact, in the past, they had sometimes united with them. Ethutur spoke of a time when they had loosed a flood for the taking of a particularly noxious nest of evil things which had holed up where riders from the Valley could not rout them. Ethutur now had hopes of binding them officially to our company. Hitherto any alliance had been loose and temporary. They would make excellent scouts, he pointed out, for water ran everywhere in this land; where it flowed, either the Krogan or the stream dwellers that served them could venture with ease.

As he talked we came out of the stream cut into a wide, marshy space. But the land had the look of drought. Marsh reeds and growth were sere and brown. Farther beyond were small hillocks in pools of water and those were still green. Farther the morass advanced until it touched a lake.

In spite of the sun over our heads a mist hovered over that lake. I thought I could see what might be islands, yet there was a wavering which was bewildering to the mind and made me uneasy. I remembered the Tor Fen of Estcarp in which dwelt that strange race which had held my father captive during the Kolder War. That, too, was a place of like mystery, and none ventured therein without the permission of its people . . . though that was seldom gotten.

The Renthan brought us to the edge of this bog. Ethutur slid from Shapurn's back and I also dismounted. The Green war-leader steadied the warn-sword across his left arm and raised his right hand to his mouth. Making a hollow trumpet of its flesh and bones he sent forth a call which rose and fell, then rose again with an inquiry in the sound.

We waited. I saw naught save the passing of large water insects which either flew above the reeds or ran across the surface of the pools, as if water under their feet was solid. There were no birds, nor even the tracks of any animal in the mud, which was long-dried and crumbling into a thick yellow dust about our boots.

Three times Ethutur called; each time we waited for an answer which did not come. Just as a shade of frown had earlier crossed his face, so did I now detect impatience there. But if he inwardly seethed at this delay, he gave no other sign of it.

Neither did he retreat from there. I began to wonder how long we would continue to stand, awaiting the capricious pleasure of what dwellers did make this swamp-lake their home.

It was not a sound which alerted me to their coming after his third summons, rather a troubling or stirring of the air. I have felt a similar thing at times with my mother and Kaththea. It is as if a creature with great confidence moves to some purpose. Now I glanced at Ethutur, content to take my cue from him. There was power here.

My companion held up the warn-sword to face the strip of bog and the lake it guarded. In the sun the red and green cords were brilliant, so dazzling they might have been woven of molten jewels. He did not call again, but only stood, holding out his credentials as envoy.

Beyond, where still living reeds curtained the edge of the lake, was movement which came from no passing wind. Out of the water arose, to stand knee deep in the flood, two figures.

As they came to us, moving swiftly and with ease through mud, pool, and reed thicket, I saw that they were manlike. They possessed legs and feet, save that those feet were webbed and wedge-form in shape. Their arms and hands were a match for my own, but the skin covering the flesh and firm bones was pallid under the sun and glistened when the light struck it.

Their heads were very human, too. But their hair was short and sleeked tight to their skulls and it was only a shade or two darker than their skin. On either side of their throats were circular spots which marked gills, now closed in the air.

They wore scanty waistcloths made of a scaled substance rippling with jeweled coloring. To the belts, which held those, were attached large shells which appeared to serve as pouches. In their web-fingered hands were staffs. Half the length was green and richly carved, the rest black and keen-pointed, to give one the impression of a wicked and deadly weapon. The Krogan carried those point down, to assure us of good intentions.

When they at last came to stand before us I saw that, human as they appeared from a distance, those eyes turned unblinkingly upon us were not man's eyes. There were no whites, only a deep green expanse from lid to lid—as the eyes of a snow cat.

"Ethutur." Instead of any greeting, the foremost of the two just repeated my companion's name.

"Orias?" His return was in a note of inquiry. Then he moved the warn-sword a fraction and again the color of its binding glowed brilliantly.

The Krogan stared at us and the sword. Then the leader beckoned. Gingerly we followed them back through the mud holes, jumping from tussock to tussock of coarse growth wherever that was possible. There was the smell of rotting stuff, which is normal in such places, and slime clung to our boots after only a few steps. But our guides appeared to be able to move through all this without carrying any smears.

We reached the edge of the lake and I wondered if they expected us now to wade in. But a shallow shadow shot from one of those barely seen islands, heading toward us. It turned out to be a boat, made of the skin of some type of water dweller pulled tight over a frame of bones cut and fitted together. Embarking in it was something of a feat. The Renthan did not even attempt that, but took to the water as did our guides and the Krogan who had towed the boat, the three water people pulling the craft after them.

As we approached the island I noted that unlike the unwholesome shore, it was ringed with a wide, silvery beach of clean sand. The stench of the bog was gone. Vegetation grew back of that sand, unlike I had seen elsewhere. The shoots rose well into the air and were soft plumes, such as the Sulcar traders sometimes brought from overseas. They did not have a green shade, but more of a muted silver tone, and here and there a frond had green or dull yellow flowers in lines along the upper portions of the main branches.

The beach itself was divided into neatly geometric patterns by the setting out of large shells and pale-colored rocks. Among these ran path-roads bordered with stake fences, ankle high, fashioned of bleached driftwood.

Our Krogan guides started along one of these roads and Ethutur and I fell in behind them. As we passed the marked parts of the beach, I saw that in those were small baskets and mats woven in delicate patterns. But of those to whom these belonged there was then no sign. We came into the shade of the plume trees and I smelled the perfume of the flowers. Also I caught glimpses of those we must have disturbed on the beach. More men, like unto our guides, and with them the women of their race. The hair of the latter flowed free save for bands of shells or reeds interwoven with flowers. They had garments of a softer substance than the scaled material, caught with shell clasps on their shoulders, confined with ornamented belts at their waists. Those robes were softly green, or yellow, or pink-gray. But we saw little of them, for they kept back among their farther trees.

When we came into the open again it was to front an outcrop of rock which perhaps once had been natural. But since it had been wrought upon by master carvers. Monsters with eyes of shell or dull gems leered and menaced. Some were more amusing than threatening with their grotesque grins. Two such guarded a flat shelf which served the Krogan chief for a chair-of-state.

He did not rise to greet us, and across his knees lay a spear staff similar to those his guards carried. His hand rested ready upon it and he did not reverse the point as we came to face him.

Ethutur drove the warn-sword point down into the soft sand earth, dropping his hand from its hilt when it stood firmly upright.

"Orias!" he said.

The Krogan leader was much like the two who had brought us here, except that a dark seam of some old scar ran along the side of his face from temple to jaw on the left, drawing down a little on the eye corner, so the lid remained almost closed.

"I see you, Ethutur. Why do I see you?" His voice was thin and, in my ears, toneless.

"Because of this—" Ethutur's fingers just touched the hilt of the warn-sword. "We would talk."

"Of a carrying of spears, and a beating of drums, and a killing," the Krogan interrupted him. "Stirred up by outlanders . . ." Now he turned his head so that he surveyed me squarely with his good eye. "They have awakened that which slept, these outlanders. Why do you take up their cause, Ethutur? Have you not past hard-won victories to nurse for your kind?"

"Victories won long ago do not mean that a man may hang his weapons to rust in the roof tree and never have need to draw them again," returned Ethutur levelly. "There are forces astir—no matter how awakened. The day draws near when men must hear the beating of the drums whether or no they would thrust fingers in their ears against such summoning. The men of the Heights, the Vrang, the Renthan, the Flamman, we of the Green Silences, those from overmountain, drink brother-drink now and close ranks. For in union we have a chance. While such begins to stir as promises no safety in sky, on land—" he paused and then added, "—or in water!"

"No one picks up the warn-sword in haste." I thought Orias used words to cloak thoughts. I did not try mind touch; it promised danger. The Krogan continued, "Nor does one man's answer cover that for all the water folk. We take counsel. You are free to remain on the visitor's isle."

Ethutur bowed his head. But he did not touch the sword, leaving it point-planted where it was. Back they took us through the plume wood and into the boat, drawing us to another island. Here was vegetation, but that of normal growth. There was a paved space of rock slabs and a hollow for a fire, with a pile of drift nearby. Ethutur and I brought out our supplies and ate. Afterward I wandered back to the shore and stared across at that silvery island. But the haze which might be born of some wizardry blurred its details. I believed I saw Krogan come out of the lake and return into it. But no one came near our island, or, if they did, we were not aware of it.

Ethutur would make no guess as to how Orias' council would decide. Several times he remarked that the Krogan were a law unto themselves, and, as Dinzil had warned, could not be influenced by outsiders. When he mentioned Dinzil my forebodings, which I had managed to push into the back of my mind, awoke. Deliberately I set about learning what I could concerning the war leader from the Heights.

He was of the Old Race, truly human as far as the Green People knew. His reputation in the field was firmly established. It seemed that he controlled powers of his own, having had for tutor in his childhood one of the few remaining wonder workers who had set a limit on his own studies and used what he learned for the preservation of the small portion of Escore into which he had fled. So high was Dinzil in Ethutur's respect that I did not venture to mention my own doubts; for what was feeling against such proofs?

There came no signal from the other isle. We ate again and rolled in our blankets for sleep. But with sleep there came to me such a dream of evil as brought me sitting up, cold and shivering, wet drops running down my cheeks to drip from my chin. I had had such a dream before Kaththea had been rift from us—so had I awakened then, unable to remember what I had dreamed, yet knowing it to be evil indeed.

I could not sleep again, nor could I disturb Ethutur with my restlessness. What I wanted most of all was to leave this island, strike out for the Valley to see for myself that no ill had chanced to those two who were the other parts of me. Greatly daring, I stole away from the campsite and went down to the shore, facing as I hoped in the direction of the Valley—though in this place I could not truly be sure of north, south, east or west.

Then I put my head in my hands, and I sent forth the call. For I *must* know. When there was no answer, I put to the full strength of my will and sent again.

Faint, very faint, came the answer. Kaththea . . . alarmed for me. Quickly I let her know that the danger was not mine, but that I feared for her or Kyllan. Then she replied that all was safe, that it must be some evil in the land between us. But she urged to cut the bond, lest it be seized upon by an ill force and used to seek me out. So sharp was she I did as she bade. But I was not satisfied; it was as if, though she reported all aright, it would not be so for long.

"Who are you, to call upon the spirit of another?"

I was so startled by that query out of the night that my sword flashed in the moonlight even as I turned. Then I dropped it, point to the ground, and watched her come into the open, her webbed feet noiseless on the sand. The waters of the lake had made her garment like unto a second skin, and she seemed very small and frail, her pallor a part of the moonlight. She brushed back wet strands of hair and tightened the shell band which held it out of her eyes.

"Why do you call?" As Orias, her voice lacked timbre, was soft and monotonous.

Though I am not one who naturally tells all to strangers, yet at that moment I spoke the truth.

"I dreamed evilly, as I have beforetimes in warning. I sought those I had reason to be concerned about, my sister and brother."

"I am Orsya, and you?" She did not comment upon my words; it was as if she needed at once some identification.

"Kemoc—Kemoc Tregarth out of Estcarp," I told her.

"Kemoc," she repeated. "Ah, yes, you are one of the outlanders who have come to make trouble. . . ."

"We did not come to make it," I corrected her. Somehow it was necessary to assure her of that. "We were fleeing trouble of our own, and we came over the mountains, not knowing what lay here. We meant no more than to find a refuge."

"Yet you have wrought disturbances." She picked up a pebble and tossed it into the lake. It splashed and ripples sped across the surface. "You have done things which could awake old evils. You would draw in the Krogan."

"Not I alone," I protested. "We shall stand together, all of us!"

"I do not think that Orias and the others will agree. No." She shook her head. Her hair, which seemed to dry very quickly in the open air, fanned out in a silver net about her. "You have had your journey here for naught, outlander."

Then she took a skip, a leap, and the water closed about her.

But she had the right of it. When we were ferried back to the plumed island in the morning the warn-sword was as Ethutur had planted it, untouched, bearing no added cords of agreement. Nor was Orias there. We faced an empty throne and the feeling that it was better for us to be gone from territory where we were not wanted.

III

*W*hat do we now?" I asked when the silent Krogan had brought us back to the swamp shore and were gone again into the lake before we could voice any farewell.

"Naught," Ethutur replied. "They have decided to remain neutral. I fear they will not find that so easy." He spoke absently and I saw that he watched the hills about us with a scout's eye.

I followed his gaze. There was nothing to see, or was there? The sun shown as it had the morning before, and the country appeared empty. Then I saw a black speck wing across the sky and behind it another.

"Mount!" Ethutur's voice was urgent. "The Rus fly. Indeed there must be a beating of the borders now!"

Shapurn and Shil, who trotted under my weight, picked a careful way along that nearly dry stream bed. But they were swifter than in their coming. I drew a deep breath. The corrupt miasma of the swamp still clung. I glanced at my boots to see if the slime spotted them, though we had wiped ourselves with withered grass.

No such traces on me, yet that breath of rottenness grew stronger as we rode. I watched the rises which fenced this water way. A man who has gone often to war, such as we knew along the border, develops senses of warning. The sun was hot and strong, yet a shadow stretched to touch us. I set my helm on my head in spite of the heat, threw the ends of its mail scarf about my throat. Also I loosened the sword which was a weight against my thigh.

Ever it seemed to me that that stench grew stronger, brought to us with every small puff of wind which found its way into that narrow ravine. No longer did Ethutur carry the warn-sword before him. Rather it was fastened to his belt, since his mission as envoy was done; he freed the stock of his force whip, holding it ready in his hand. It was as if an enemy massed unseen upon the heights above us.

Yet there was nothing we could see: only the smell and the warning within us. I marveled at the speed with which the Renthan bore us through that place which was a natural trap. Yet one part of my mind wondered why the trap was not sprung. The enemy were throwing away an advantage they might not find so easily again.

"Why?"

I saw Ethutur's lips fold tight and then he answered my unfinished question:

"Those who watch have not the strength to pull us down. But the Rus fly for reinforcements. If we can reach the open plain—"

We did that, coming to where the grass rippled grain-ripe and tall. But the plains were not empty. I saw those who gathered to dispute our passage. Some were old enemies I had fronted before. There were those unholy mixtures of men and beast who raised brindled, wolfish muzzles to catch our scent and had pricked ears to hear. About them the grass moved and I thought of the Rasti which could be in hiding there. Ethutur cracked his force whip, and the fire of its strike upon the earth was a flash bright enough to be seen even in the sunlight, leaving smoldering stubble behind.

I longed for the dart gun which had been mine over mountains. We had brought such weapons with us in flight, but long since their ammunition had been spent, which left them useless tubes. Now I had to wait until the enemy was sword-length for fighting.

The Gray Ones and their unseen allies—if the rippling covered the movements of the Rasti—did not attack. They had a deep respect for the force lash. But they circled about as at a distance. Their circle now lay between us to the entrance of the HaHarc road.

"They must not three time us!" Ethutur cried. Again my studies at Lormt came to my aid. If the enemy could put that running circle about us and hold it for a thrice running of all who made it a barrier, then they could put a willlock on us—even though they did not venture to attack openly the prisoners within it.

Shapurn and Shil ran. Again, as I settled my body to the rise and fall of those mighty muscles under me, I thought that no horse of Estcarp could match these. At the same time, though I am not learned in the Mysteries, I shouted aloud certain *words* from very ancient texts.

And as I did so, I was startled and almost stricken dumb. For—this I swear, though a man who has not seen such may disbelieve me—I *saw* those words as well as heard them! They were flaming fire arrows and they went before, as darts might have been shot from that weapon I no longer had. I will swear again that I saw them strike the ground where the Gray Ones ran and that light burst upon impact, even as the fire which came from Ethutur's lash.

There was sound, too; more than the mouthing I made, claps loud and clear. Then I heard a shrill, high screeching overhead as Ethutur called out something I did not understand. His head went back as one who searches danger in the sky. Then his lash curled up and that shrill, ear-tormenting screeching was cut in mid-note. From the sky fell something which struck the ground before us, and exploded in a puff of dark smoke which choked us with its foulness as, a moment later, Shapurn and Shil, unable to avoid it, rushed on through.

But of any body which might lie there, I saw no sign. Only the smoke and smell before we burst into the clean air.

Now I heard the howling of the Gray Ones and a squealing from the grass, which, once heard, could not be forgotten. Rasti ran here, right enough. They came upon us in a wave and Shapurn and Shil stamped and danced in fury, while Ethutur's lash cut again and again, firing the grass to clear us a path. We met the Gray Ones at the mouth of the HaHarc road and there we fought them. My blade cut flesh, jarred upon bone, and Shil screamed as raking claws and gnashing teeth tore his hide. Once more I hurled at them those *words* and saw them flinch from what became darts of flaming energy.

Then there came a *sound,* and before that all the other clamor of our fight was nothing. For it was a blow which appeared to fall upon us all equally. I clung, weak and deafened, to my seat on Shil's back. Dimly I saw Ethutur's arm drop limply to his side, the force lash dead, only the stock gripped in his fingers. But I also saw the Gray Ones reel back, the hand-paws pressed to their ears, their heads twisting to and fro as if in agony.

For how long we were so stricken I do not know. But at length my mind cleared and I felt Shil trembling under me. The Renthan took one step and then another, and I raised to see that he was following, as he had throughout that journey, his war chief Shapurn, and that other one was walking, one step at a time, down the road to HaHarc. On his back Ethutur sat with drooping head, as one who rode in a daze.

I wanted to turn my head and see if the enemy padded behind us. But trying, I found I could not. It was not that I was too weak; it was rather in some way all my muscles had been locked. When at last I was able to look behind I saw no sign of any pursuers. That stench which had been with us since we had left the lake was also gone. But there was another odor heavy on the air, a metallic scent I could not set name to.

When we were among the ruins Ethutur straightened and looked over his shoulder to meet my eyes. He was very pale, but there was a set to his features I had not seen before.

"Do not so again!" His words were an order.

"I do not know what—"

"You evoked ancient powers back there and were *answered*. Do not bring your witchcraft here, outlander. I had not believed that you might also evoke forces—"

"Nor did I," I answered truthfully. "And I do not know why I did what I did. I am no witch, but a warrior."

I could not quite believe in what had passed, even though I had been a part of it. For we were so confirmed in the belief, we of Estcarp, that only the Wise Women could control the unseen, or communicate with it, that this was unnatural. Although it was true that my father had certain gifts, which even the Witches had not been able to deny. With my mother, the Lady Jaelithe, he had shared strengths which were not of hand and body, but of mind and will.

But me, I wanted no more of this. For I had wisdom enough to know that experimenting with such matters, when one is untaught in the proper safeguards, is rank folly, liable to harm not only he who rashly tries it, but those about him. Ethutur could be sure I would not do so. Still I remembered that *sound,* which I could find no words to describe, and I wondered what it was and from whence it had come.

It seemed to be effective in protecting our back trail, for, though we took every precaution and backtracked to be sure, we had no pursuers. At last Ethutur was satisfied and we went up that stair road which led out of HaHarc to come again to the boundaries of the Valley.

As we rode between the carven stones, which had on them protective words, Ethutur paused now and then and made certain signs to each. Some I knew; others were strange to me. But I knew that he was relocking the guards of the Valley, alerting them. We came at last to the greatest of all, which was Euthayan. Deep graven it was, and inlaid in those cuts was a thread of green. Then did the warlord of the Valley turn to me with his second order:

"Go, lay your hands to that, your bare hands!"

I knew a small stir of anger, for his suspicion was plain. He believed that I was, or had become, that which the Valley dared no longer shelter for the good of those who dwelt there. But I did as he bade, slipped from Shil's sweaty back, went to lay my bare palms flat against that symbol which was so much a part of Power that no evil might look upon it, let alone touch it.

I was startled as my fingers touched cool stone, rough and gritty with windblown dust when first I set them upon that surface, yet under their tips there came a change. I saw, or seemed to see, those inlaid traces of green become brighter, while the stone grew warm. But I was not blasted, nor did any warning come— only the brightening of the green and the gentle warmth. I held my hands so and looked to Ethutur.

"Are you now satisfied that you do not harbor a traitor?" I asked.

But he was watching the stone and there was puzzlement in his eyes. He raised his hand and rubbed across them as if to clear away a mist. And he said:

"I do not know what we harbor in you, Kemoc. But it would seem that you do our company no ill. This I had to know." There was a note of apology in his voice.

"As your right." It was, of course, in spite of the smart to my pride. As warlord he had no right to bring into the Valley any weak link which might open it to the Great Shadow. And what did he know of we three from Estcarp, save what we have done since coming to Escore?

It was late afternoon when we came down to those houses of living vine and roofs of green-blue feathers. Along the way we picked up a company of Ethutur's men. But I did not see any of the hill men who had come with Dinzil. That gave me a feeling of relief.

When we swung off the Renthan in the open space where we had taken counsel earlier, we found a varied company awaiting us. Their faces were sober, their mood one of impatience. It was Dahaun who spoke first.

"There was—she seemed almost at a loss for words—"a Great Troubling. What happened? Or do you know?"

"Ask of Kemoc," Ethutur returned shortly and their attention fastened upon me. Kyllan looked surprised but Kaththea, at his side, was frowning slightly.

"I do not know," I told them. "We were about to be thrice-ringed by Gray Ones, together with Rasti. All I did, and why I cannot tell you, was speak words I had learned at Lormt. And then—then—

"You were *answered*." It was Kaththea who spoke. "Unwise, unwise to meddle when you are not trained in the Mysteries."

For the first time in my life I met in her—not the incredulity which Kyllan had earlier shown—but a turning from me, a closing of doors. Behind was some emotion I could not read. Was it that her long years of Witch training had set into her the belief they all shared, that no man was to usurp their dealing with the Invisible? If so, it was so unlike the Kaththea I knew that I could not accept it. Yet withdraw she had and I was too hurt to pursue her, or even question. I would not put it to the proof. Sometimes we cling to uncertainty, dreading fact.

I spoke then to Dahaun, rather than to my sister. "Be sure that I shall not try it again. I do not even know why I did it then."

She took a step forward and laid her hands on my shoulders. Then, as I was the taller, she looked up to meet my eyes. But she used words, not the mind touch, to answer me, because, I am sure, she wanted all those others to hear her.

"What lies within a man, strength, will, or gift, rises to the surface when need calls. That you were *answered* is a shock, for it was our belief that the Great Ones had sped from us long ago. But now you have taught us that they are not to be disregarded, and that is well worth our knowing. It is in my mind that you have done us a single service this day."

Her words appeared to ease the tension. Now Kyllan raised the question of how our mission to the Krogan fared. He frowned when he heard it was a failure. Then the war leader asked in turn concerning the Thas and Dahaun replied:

"They did not even come to answer the torch signal. So we can continue to guess whether their absence means neutrality, or whether they have allied themselves elsewhere."

"But there is other news," Kyllan offered. "The sentinels from the peaks have signaled that another party from overmountain comes into the foothills."

"Then they must be met with a guard to bring them here," Ethutur said, "It is my belief that the country is roused and the lesser ones of the shadow will do all they can to prevent our mustering of any force."

As I went to bathe in one of the renewing pools of the Green People, to put on the lighter clothing they wore, I still looked for Dinzil or any of his following. Kyllan came to sit upon a bench, watching me draw on breeches, latch the golden clasps of the jerkin across my breast.

Finally I brought my thought into the open. "I do not see Dinzil."

"He rode out before dawn. There is much to be done in raising the Heights. What of these Krogan?"

It seemed to me that Kyllan skirted the subject of Dinzil, was too quick to change the subject. But I followed his lead and told him all I had observed of the water people.

"Would they matter to us greatly?"

"Ethutur says they have ways of penetrating wherever there is water, they, or the creatures who give them allegiance. I saw no weapons except their spears. Yet those looked deadly. Who can say that they do not have other arms which were not shown? Ethutur believes they are still neutral. He accepted their decision without argument."

That had puzzled me, for my reading of him was that he had too much force of character to accept rebuffs tamely.

"He was bound by custom," Kyllan said. "There has been no compelling, nor pleading, between race and race after they fled into refuges. They have been content to go their own roads apart."

"Custom cannot save any of us now," I countered. "Which way did Dinzil ride?" Deliberately I came back to my own questioning. "Kyllan—you know how it has been with us always. Would I push this uneasiness if I were not convinced that it holds some danger for us three?"

He looked me eye to eye as Dahaun had done earlier, and we mind touched; I opened to him all my worries.

"I believe that you believe, brother."

"But—you do not?"

"Enough so that I shall hold watch and ward if he returns. But—this I must say to you, Kemoc—do not flutter those flags of war before our sister, not when they are to raise hosts to face in that direction!"

My hands tightened until my stiff fingers pointed palely.

"It is like that then." I did not ask a question; I stated a fact.

"She has clearly shown her liking. She will read ill will into any contrary urging, not against him, but against the one giving the warning. She has . . . changed." There was uncertainty in him also, a kind of bewilderment which was less than that pang I felt when she had closed her mind to me an hour earlier, yet which carried some of the same hurt.

"She is a maid, unwed. We knew that sometime she would look upon some man with eyes she did not turn to us. That we could face . . . but this man—no!" I said that as one swearing an oath. I knew that Kyllan heard it so, but he shook his head slowly.

"Over this we may have no control. He is a man esteemed, and he pleases her; that is to be seen by the least observant. Against that, you offer but a feeling of wrongness, which she and others may read as jealousy. You must have more proof."

He spoke the truth, but sometimes the truth is black hearing. So did it seem to me now. Again Kyllan picked up my thought.

"It is hard to believe that you summoned one of the Great Ones and was *answered*. We were schooled that such is impossible save for an adept. No man of Estcarp ever trod that path, so you can see that Kaththea finds it hard to accept. How *did* you do it?"

"I tell you, I do not know. Ethutur warned of thrice-ringing; we were riding to cut through before that happened." I spoke of seeing the words as fiery darts. And then that *sound* which had blasted at us all.

"Our mother asked wisdom for your share when she called our futures," he said thoughtfully when I was done. "It would seem that you *do* have some power. . . ."

I shook my head. "There is a vast difference between learning and wisdom, brother. Do not confuse the two. I called upon learning then, and without thinking. Perhaps that was folly—"

"Not altogether. It saved you; did it not? And, as Dahaun has said, it made known to us that certain forces are still at work here, powers long thought gone." He spread out his hands and regarded them thoughtfully. "For most of my life I have been at war. But before it was with steel and weapons known to me. This is a different war, and I am no worker of power—save that which lies within my own mind and body."

"Nor shall I be, henceforth!"

He shook his head. "Vow no vows upon that subject, Kemoc. We do not read the future—nor, I believe, would we really want to if we could. For I do not think it is in us to change what will come to pass. You shall do that which is set before you for the doing, as shall I, and every living thing within Escore. We shall go down to defeat, or ride to victory in the end, each playing his own ordained part."

I broke through his somber words. "You said that once you dreamed of this land at peace once more, and of holdings of our folk well planted here. Do you not remember?"

"Dreams are not the truth. Did you not dream a darker dream only a night ago?"

"Kaththea told you?"

"Yes. She believed it to be a seeking sent by some black power, a try at influencing you."

"And you?"

Kyllan got to his feet. "It can be that you are both right: That you had a forewarning; that it was twisted by some power. This is no country in which to dream. And no country to allow some comrades to ride into, unwarned, unarmed . . ."

So we went forth again in the dawn, Kyllan, I, Godgar and Horvan, and three of Ethutur's men, together with Dahaun. We rode to the mountains over which those we sought must come. Above our heads quested both Flannan and those birds who were the messengers and scouts for Dahaun. Their reports were of a land aroused. We caught sight of sentinels on high places. Some of them had the seeming of men, and some were clearly monsters. Whether they constituted the enemy now in force, or whether they answered to stronger leaders, being only hands, feet, eyes and ears for yet more powerful adversaries, we did not know.

We made detours around some places. There was a grove by the river which Dahaun made a wide arc to avoid, pausing to face it, her fingers in a vee before her mouth as she spat between them to right and left. Yet to my eyes it was a grove as fair as any in the Valley and I felt no uneasiness when I looked upon it. Varied and hidden indeed were the many traps for the innocent and unwary in Escore.

Two days it took us, even with the speed of the Renthans, to reach the place where we left the animals and climbed by foot to aid those of Estcarp. But that climb was not as demanding as it had been when we came into this land, for exploration along the mountain walls had found shorter and easier paths.

Those who came, moved apparently by that inner compulsion which Kyllan had sown unwittingly in Estcarp, were men from Borderer companies, among them those I knew, having served with them in the scouts. They rubbed their eyes a little dazedly, as men will when awakening from deep sleep, as they reached us. Then they shouted greetings and came eagerly to us, hands outstretched, not with the anger outlaws might expect.

Once more the past caught up with us—a past which seemed so far removed. We heard the news out of Estcarp that the Council, so weakened by the effort of churning the mountains against Karsten, held now only part power. For many had died in that battle, and Koris of Gorm, my father's long comrade, was now virtually the ruler. He was in the process of tightening control over what might otherwise have fallen into complete chaos.

These Borderers were of a patrol sent out to track us, for Koris stood to us as a father, and his wife, the Lady Loyse, was more mother than she who had had too many duties to claim that role with us. Thus, if we wished, we might return— our outlawry done. But Kyllan and I knew that we had left that road and there was no turning back.

The patrol had met with a household kin to Hervon's and the planted desire to ride east had spread to them. Now they listened in wonder to the tale Kyllan told, but for them there was no return either. Chance had served us very well in sending these war-tried men to join our ragged standards.

IV

*W*e came down into the lower lands with all the speed we could muster. There the Renthan and those from the Valley awaited us. It had been bright sunlight when we had begun that descent. But when we reached the meeting place clouds were gathering. Dahaun gave slight greeting to those from Estcarp— rather she turned her head from right to left, surveying the country. About her flew, constantly coming and going, her winged messengers.

In part Kyllan and I felt, too, a lowering of spirit and a chill which was not born of the cloud sky nor the rising winds. It was a foreboding which was folly to dismiss.

But those who had come overmountain were wearied, and among them were women and children for whom the climb and descent had been a trial of strength. We should camp soon.

"We must ride!" Dahaun's gesture brought up the Renthan. "This is no place in which to face the dark and that which may prowl there this night."

"And *what* may prowl?" demanded Kyllan.

"I do not know, for such lies now unseen to the eyes of my feathered ones. Yet that it comes, I have no doubt."

Nor did we. Even those from Estcarp, who had none of the gift, glanced now and then over their shoulders, and made a wall about their women folk. And I saw that the Borderers went helmed, their mail scarves fastened high.

"These cannot make the Valley without a rest," I warned Dahaun.

She nodded. "There is a place, not as far as I would like, but better than here."

She led us. Under the clouds, she was all sable and silver, no longer red and gold. We shared our mounts, taking up women and children with us for that riding. A little maid, her hair close braided beneath a scarlet hood, her gloved hands holding tightly to my sword belt, went with me on Shil.

"Please, lord, where do we ride?" Her voice was a clear pipe.

"To where the lady leads us." I gave her the truth. "This is her country and she knows it well. I am Kemoc Tregarth, and who are you?"

"Loelle, of the House of Mohakar, Lord Kemoc. Why do those birds fly with the lady? Ah, that is no bird, it—it is a little man!"

One of the Flannan beat wings, hovering shoulder high beside Dahaun, while she turned her head to look at him.

"A Flannan, Loelle. Have you not heard tales of them?"

I felt her grip grow tighter. "But those—those are tales, Lord Kemoc! Nurse Grenwel said they were but stories, not the truth!"

"In Escore, Loelle, many old stories are true. Now, hold tight—"

We had come to a level space and the Renthan burst into speed to shame any horse out of Estcarp, Dahaun setting the pace. That brooding menace I had felt in the foothills was almost tangible as the clouds gathered, twilight dark, over us.

Through that gloom were glimmers of light, reminding me of the ghostly "candles" we had seen on tree and bush that night when the Witches of Estcarp had readied their power for the mountain twisting. Pale, hardly to be distinguished from the general gloom, these clung to a rock, a bush, a twisted tree. Looking upon them, I knew that I did not want to see them any closer.

Once more the land began to rise, and on the crown of a small hill stood some stones. Not gray, but blue in hue, and they glowed. Once before had we refuged with such stones, when Kaththea and I had fled after Kyllan had disappeared, taking sanctuary in a place where a great altar of such blue had been our guard.

To this place Dahaun brought us. This was no standing circle of pillars about an altar stone, but rather scattered blocks, as if a building, once there, had been shattered into rubble. But the blue glow welcomed us and we slid down from the Renthan with a sense of freedom from that which had followed us from the mountain's foot.

Dahaun broke a branch from a bush which grew among the stones, and, holding that in her hand, she walked down the hill, to beat the leafy end against the ground. So she encircled the entire hill, appearing to draw some unseen protective barrier about it. Then, as she came back to us, she stopped now and again to pull leaves and twigs from plants.

When the Green Lady was back among us she had her cloak gathered to form a shallow bag and in that was her herb harvest. There had been a fire kindled in a sheltered spot between two stones and she stood by that, tossing into it first a pinch of this, and then three or four leaves of that. Smoke puffed out, bringing an aromatic scent. This Dahaun fanned so that it wreathed among our company.

As the smoke cleared and I could see better again, I noted the darkness had grown. In that unnatural twilight the "candles" were brighter. But the light burning in them did not spread far. It also seemed to me that there was movement beyond the hill, a stirring which could only be half seen, to vanish if one looked straightly at the suspected spot.

"Against what do we bare swords here, Kemoc?" It was Rothorf of Dolmain who came up beside me as I watched that interweaving which seemed so sinister.

"Strange things." I gave him the best answer that I could. He was one of the half-blood ones found among the Borderers. His mother had been of the Karsten refuges. Rescued by Sulcar seamen, she had later married into that seaborne race. But it was a mixture which had not proved too happy. When her sea lord had fallen in one of the raids along the coast of Alizor, she had returned to her own people. Her son had the frame of the bull-shouldered sea rovers and their fair hair, so that always among the Old Race he was marked. Inwardly he was of his mother's people, having no wish for the sea, but a love for the hills. Thus he had come to the Borderers and we had been blooded together in a raid before we were truly men.

"It is true then; this is a land bewitched." He asked no question, but made an observation.

"Yes. But once it was a fair land. By our efforts it may so be again. Yet it will be a long time—"

"Before we cleanse it?" he finished for me. "What manner of enemy do we front?" There was a briskness in that which returned me to the old days when Rothorf had looked upon maps in the hills and then waited for the orders to move out.

Uneasiness moved in me. These old comrades (drawn from a war, it was true, but a war which seemed simple beside the complexities which faced us here), would they be as children blundering among the dangers they could not foresee? What had we done to them? Kyllan, when he had returned from that geas sending into Estcarp, had reasoned so: that he was drawing after him those of his blood, perhaps untimely to their deaths. Now I knew what he had felt then.

"All manner, Rothorf, and some of which we have no knowledge." I spoke then of the Gray Ones and the Rasti, but also of such deceits as the Keplian-stallion which had nearly borne Kyllan to his death, and of the traps which awaited the over-curious and under-cautious. He listened to me gravely, not questioning anything I said, though much of it must have sounded wild.

"A place where legends walk," he commented at last. "It would seem we should search our memories of childhood tales to be warned. How far is it to this safe Valley of the Green Folk?"

"Another day's journey. We muster there."

"To attack where?"

I shook my head. "That we do not know. They still wish to bring to our warn-horn any uncommitted forces left."

We posted guards as the night drew in, the clouds bringing it early to us. No rain fell from them, though they looked heavy-bellied, as if they carried pent within them some tempest. I saw flashes of light about the hills, as bright and crackling as the force whips of the Green People, but knew them to be lightning, foretelling the storm which sullenly refused to break.

Kyllan was no more inclined to sleep than I and we paced around the ruins among which our people sheltered as if we walked sentry beats on the walls of Es City, constantly alert to the least suspicion of change beyond the perimeter Dahaun had drawn.

The Lady of Green Silences remained by the fire, having about her all the women and children, creating for them a pocket of safe feeling in which we caught glimpses of smiling faces and from which we heard soft laughter. I saw Loelle on Dahaun's lap, staring up into her face and listening to what she said as a thirsty child might drink crystal water from a bubbling spring.

There was such a spring among the ruins, fed into a very old and silted basin. It might have been the remains of a fountain which no longer proudly played, defeated by time.

We had shared out journey rations earlier. At last those about the fire rolled in cloaks and slept. Still the storm did not break, yet the threat held above us. Godgar tramped to where I stood behind an earth-buried rock staring down the slope. The gray candles grew more confusing to the eyes and I tried not to look at them. Yet still they drew my attention, and I found myself engaged in a small struggle not to stare at them.

"There is something brewing this night," Hervon's man told me, his voice harsh and heavy. "It is not the storm. This place may be good for defense, but I do not like to be driven to making a defense."

"Neither could we ride on through the dark, not in this country," I answered.

"That is so. There is something . . . Come you here with me and see."

I followed him to that basin where the spring bubbled. Going down on one knee, he gestured to the far side of that pool. There was enough light from the fire to show stones set there, as if at one time the basin had been broken at that point and then hurriedly built up again with rocks conveniently at hand. That they had served the purpose well was manifest in that there was no seepage from that place. But why this should so interest Godgar, I had no idea and looked to him questioningly.

"That was done, I think, for a purpose," he said.

"Why?"

In answer he beckoned me to come a little beyond the basin. Earth had drifted and tufts of grass rooted. But not enough to cover a slab of stone which was part of the small remaining fragment of pavement. Godgar dug about that stone with the point of his hunting knife, laying bare the cleavage between it and the pavement.

"I think that the water was made to pour down here."

"Why?"

"That I do not know. But it had great importance for those who did it. That basin was broken in haste. When it was patched again, it was not made to stand for all time, but so that it might be freed again."

"What meaning for us now?" I was impatient.

"Again—I do not know. Save that all things which are strange must be considered when men rest as we do this night. And—" He stopped suddenly. His hand had been resting on that block of stone and now he stared down at it wide-eyed. Then he threw himself on the ground and set his ear to the cold surface.

"Listen!" It was a command I obeyed, stretching my body on the ground so that my head might rest with his, ear on stone.

Sound or vibration, I could not say which. But it came from below. I made very sure I was not mistaken and then summoned Kyllan, and he in turn, Dahaun.

It was she who had an answer for us. "Thas, perhaps . . ." She knelt there, her fingertips resting on the slab. Her eyes were closed, as if she now called upon a different kind of sight to serve her. Then she shook her head slowly.

"What lies below the earth's surface is another world and not mine. This I say—something comes upon us from below. Fortune favors us with this much warning. I had not thought that the Thas would join the enemy. It may be that they are only curious, though why . . ." She shook her head. "To come secretly thus is not the way of a friend or a neutral."

"Your boundaries—" Kyllan broke in.

"Will hold against what walks the soil, but not under it. And look you—this stone is not of the blessed kind, but of another fashioning."

"The basin—" I got to my feet. "If it were once used to answer an attack from below as Godgar believes, why not again?"

"If they are only curious, then such a use would make enemies needlessly. But it is a thought to keep in mind. Let us inspect this water trap." Dahaun said.

She brought a brand from the fire and held it close so we could look upon the stones which had put a stopper in the broken basin. I believed that Godgar was right in his reconstruction of what had happened here long ago. It was plain that the basin wall had been shattered so that its contents could flow out at this point, and that the rebuilding of that break had been done with no idea of permanence.

"Strike it here and here," Godgar pointed out, "and it will give way again."

We went back to the stone. But this time we could hear no movement beneath it. Only, that unease which had been over me since we had come from the mountains increased a hundred-fold.

"Can the stone be sealed?" Kyllan looked to Dahaun.

"I do not know. To each his own power. The Thas can do much with earth, as the Krogan with water, and we with growing things." She picked up her torch and glanced at the place where the women and children were asleep. "I think we must be prepared. Get away from any standing stone which might be overthrown."

Godgar still squatted on his heels, his hands resting on the stone. Even as Dahaun went toward those who slept, he cried out. I think I must have echoed his cry, as did Kyllan, for the ground under us moved, slipping under our feet, carrying us with it. I caught at a stone, one of the blue ones, and held to it, as soil poured about my boots. I heard crashes and shouts from the camp, saw stones slide and bound downslope.

Something fell into the fire sending sparks and flaming pieces of wood scattering. I heard screaming. For a moment I could only hold to my rock, for under my kicking feet, as I tried to find some stable spot, the earth moved as the waters of the Krogan lake might have splashed and eddied.

Then I saw Kyllan using the point of his sword, dug into the shifting earth, to pull himself along. I followed his example, trying to reach the confusion marking our campsite.

"Ha—to me!" called Godgar. About him whirled other things, small flitting figures ringing him in, in a frenzy of attack. I cut and slashed, felt steel meet flesh and was not sure of what flesh. Then I saw Godgar stumble and go down, and things scurried to leap upon him as he fought to regain his feet. At those things I aimed strokes which sent them flying. Points of angry red sparked about us and I knew them for eyes. But in what faces those eyes were set, I could not see.

Godgar clawed at me and I used my maimed hand to draw him up.

"The pool—break the pool—drown them out—" He lurched from my hold toward the basin, fell there again, fumbling at the stones set in the break. Then I heard a sharp hammering even above the squealing of the things through which I waded to join him. There were sharp pains in my legs and thighs. I shook off a small body which leaped to plaster itself against my back and tried to overtopple me. But I reached Godgar and bent to pry at the stones.

Though we worked in the dark, fighting off the foul-smelling rabble which poured out of the earth, yet by some stroke of fortune one of us loosed the main stone of that barrier. There boiled out a flood which surprised me, since I had thought that not so much force would come from a pool fed by such a quiet and sluggish stream.

The squealing of our half-seen enemies rose to screams, as if they looked upon water as a danger even greater than that steel and fire we used against them. They fled, uttering their piercing cries, while the water dashed around us with the force of a strong river current. Surely more poured from there than had ever been pent in the basin.

Godgar cried out and tried to drag me to one isde. I looked over my shoulder. Visible, glowing with some of the blue light of the stones, a tall pillar of water rose even higher, its plume crest dashing down in the flood faster and faster. This fountaining had no relation now to the gurgling, puffing bubble which earlier fed the basin.

I saw small shaggy things caught in that overflow, whirled back and down, rammed by the water into the hole from which they must have emerged. For the flood sought the stone Godgar had earlier marked, or rather the dark pit that stone had capped, and now it poured hungrily into that cavity with the activity of a falls feeding a river.

We stumbled yet further back. The torrent of rushing water was now between us and the fire. The noise of its passing drowned all other sound. Something whirled along in it clutched at my leg, nearly toppling me. In instinctive reaction I struck down to free myself from that hold, but not before swift, sharp pain struck into my thigh and brought a cry out of me.

I could not rest my weight upon that wounded leg, but fell back against one of the blue stones, trying to feel in the dark the extent of the damage. But so tender was my flesh, that I could not bear the touch of my own fumbling examination. I could only hold to the rock, Godgar gasping and choking beside me, while the water continued to run from what seemed an inexhaustible source.

There were no more of the squealing things on our side of the stream. Now across the flood the fire flared again so we had a better measure of light. I could see men there and the gleam of swords. On the very edge of the flood, the water licking eagerly at it, lay a body, face turned up and eyes staring sightlessly straight at me.

I heard a cry from Godgar and would have echoed that had I not needed all my strength to cling to consciousness. For the pain from my thigh had become red torment such as no other wound I had ever taken.

The thing was small and twisted, its arms and legs, if those four limbs could be dignified by such human applications, were thin, covered with coarse bristles which made them resemble roots with a matting of finer fibers. In contrast the body was thick and bloated and of a white-gray which grew rapidly paler while we looked upon it. This, too, was covered with hair in shaggy patches, not like any hair I had ever seen on man or beast, but very coarse and upstanding from the hide.

It had very little neck; its skull seemed supported directly by wide bowed shoulders. The jaw and chin, and very little chin there was, jutted forward to a sharp point; the nose was a ridge joined to that vee of jaw, with two openings just above the lips. The eyes were deep sunk on either side of that ridge. It wore no clothing, nor was there any sign it was more than animal . . . yet I knew that it was.

"What is it?" Godgar asked.

"I do not know." Except, all my instincts told me, that it was one of the servants of evil, as were the Gray Ones and the Rasti.

"Look!" Godgar pointed. "The water—"

That fountain, which had stood so tall and poured forth such a volume of water, was dropping lower and lower as it continued to play. The flood which had cut us from the fire was growing narrower by the moment. I watched the dwindling dully, knowing that if I loosed my hold upon the rock which supported me I would fall. I doubted greatly that I could then rise once again. The river became a runnel; the runnel, a trickle.

"Kemoc!" I heard a cry raised from the fireside and tried to answer. It was Godgar's shout which brought them to us. With Kyllan's arm about me I fell forward, not only into his ward, but also into darkness in which pain was lost.

I roused, only too soon, to find Dahaun and my brother in counsel over me. It would seem, I understood with a kind of dreamy unconcern, that the wounds of the Thas—for it was those underground dwellers who had sprung the attack—were poisoned and that, though Dahaun could apply certain temporary measures to alleviate my pain, the healing must take place elsewhere.

I was not the only wounded. There were broken bones from the falling rocks, and several more poisoned cuts among the defenders. But mine was the deepest hurt and the one which might slow our retreat.

Kyllan spoke quickly—saying that he would stay with me until help could be sent. But, catching the look in Dahaun's eyes, I knew our peril, and, in this dreamy state where her remedies had placed me, I did not fear riding. This much I did foresee: that although the Thas attack had failed, mainly by reason of that extraordinary flood, it would not be the last. To be trapped away from the Valley meant defeat.

"Tie me on Shil." I managed to get out the words, though those sounded faint and far away in my own hearing. "We ride—or we die—as well we all know."

Dahaun looked deep into my eyes. "This is your will, Kemoc?"

"This is my will."

So at dawn we did ride, I bound to Shil as I had said. Dahaun had given me leaves to chew. The sour juices in my mouth were bitter, but they kept that barrier between me and pain, leaving me aware of it yet not subject to its tearing.

We traveled under clouds, still heavy with the storm which did not break. I went as a man might go in a dream, seeing here a bit sharply, there a fraction with a clear mind, then sliding once more into a haze.

It was when we came to the river that I awakened out of that state. Or was awakened—by a mind thrust, so keen, so inimical, that I gasped and tried to right myself on Shil's back. The Renthan gave a great trumpeting cry, whirled, to race away from our party, down the bank. I could do nothing to control our going. Behind sounded shouts, cries, the pounding of hooves in our wake.

As if he would escape any pursuit, Shil leaped from the bank into the river. Water closed over me as I struggled against the ties which kept me on the back of the plunging Renthan who seemed utterly mad.

Something gave and I was free, gasping and choking. I had been well taught to swim by Otkell, the crippled Sulcar warrior our father had sent to lesson us. But my wound had made of my left leg a part which would not answer the orders of my mind. Still gasping, choking, I came against a boulder and held to it despairingly. All mist had gone from my mind, and the fierce pain of my wound left me too weak to keep that grasp against the pull of the current.

A clutch on me from behind. Kyllan! I tried to say his name. But I could not shape it. I used mind touch. . . . To meeting nothing!

The grip was very strong, pulling me away from the rock anchorage, out into the current. I cried out, thrashed about with my arms, trying vainly to turn my head far enough to see who or what held me. But I continued to be borne along, my head a little above water, away from the bank and the shelter of the rocks.

I saw Kyllan, mounted on Shabrina, look straight at me, but there was no sign that he really saw me. I tried again to call . . . but there was no sound from my lips. With mind touch it was as if I beat against a high wall in which there was no opening.

Kyllan rode along the bank, still visibly searching. Yet I was there plain to see. Then fear closed upon me as I was drawn farther and farther away, leaving Kyllan and those who came after him. I saw Shil climb from the water and stand with hanging head. Then the bank curved and all of them were hidden from me, so I lost my last hope.

V

I was no longer carried along helplessly in a swift flowing flood, rather did I rest upon something stable and dry. Yet I did not at once open my eyes, moved by some primitive need for learning all that I could by my other senses before betraying the fact that I was conscious. The pain in my thigh gnawed and I was more and more aware of its torment. I fought against giving way to that, to hold my mind on other things.

Wind blew chill, making me shiver and shake. I pressed one hand against the surface on which I lay and felt gravel and sand. I listened; there was a gurgle not too far off which might be water, and a sighing which could be born of the passing of wind through vegetation. But that was the limit of the knowledge I gained.

I opened my eyes. Above, far above, still hung those thick clouds, turning day into twilight. But, cutting between those and me, was a branch, gray-white, bare of any foliage, standing as a stark and dreary monument to some long dead tree.

Now I pulled up my hands, struggled to brace myself higher. The world reeled back and forth sickeningly. I retched, turning my head weakly to let a water flood pour out of my mouth, my body wracked by the force of revulsion.

Once I had finished, I struggled up again, trying with fierce determination so that I might see where I lay. My resting place, I learned as I turned my head with great caution, moving only by force of will against the waves of nausea which continued to strike, was a scrap of beach, wet only a few inches away by the lapping of the river. To my right were boulders among which were caught bleached drift, marking the rise of old flooding.

My helm and sword were gone. The bandages Dahaun had set upon my wound were loosened and new stains grew there. But as far as I could see I was now alone. What or who had brought me along the current and away from my brother and friends, had not drowned me, but left me to what might be a far crueler fate, abandonment in this place where I was pinned by my wound from any try at escape.

But we are a stubborn race, we of Estcarp; my father was never known to accept without struggle any ill which fortune visited upon him. So, in spite of the pain it cost me, I managed to drag myself to a rock which might give me support. There I sweated and groaned as I pulled up to my feet, leaning heavily on the stone, to examine farther my situation. It was not one to encourage any man.

I was not on the river's bank, but rather on a small islet in the midst of its current. An islet which, by evidence about me, was at times completely overrun by water. Nothing grew here. There was only rock and pieces of drift wedged among the stones. It reminded me of that isle where we had taken refuge on the night when Kaththea had given birth to her familiar and sent it to range the past for our enlightenment. But then I had been whole, not only of body, but also in that we three had been closeknit to one purpose.

The shores on either side were high banked, and the current was swift. Had I been whole I would have thrown off my mail and dared to swim. Crippled as I now was, I had no chance.

Bracing myself closer to the rock, I twisted around to finger my bandage, trying to draw it tighter. The slightest touch made me flinch and grit my teeth, but I did what I could. The chill air still cut at me. It was as if the prolonged summer which abode in Escore was now changing into autumn. I longed for a fire and looked at the drift. There was a light-striker in my belt pouch. But such a fire might also be a beacon for the enemy.

Slowly I surveyed the banks. Ahead of my islet was another, larger, covered in places with green. A place which had a small promise of hospitality, better than this perch. I longed to reach it, but knew I could not fight the current.

Unless . . . Again I studied the piles of caught drift. Suppose I might put together a raft? Or perhaps, nothing as ambitious as a raft—a support to keep my head above water while the current took me somewhere downstream where I could swim to one shore or the other?

Then what? Weaponless, unable to do more than crawl, perhaps—easy meat for the Rasti, the Gray Ones or any other trouble roaming this land.

Yet, because it is born in our breed not to surrender without one last effort, I leaned over, as well as I could without losing my precarious balance, to pull to me those pieces of drift within my reach. My haul was disappointing; most were light sticks, so water-worn and dried they broke easily. There was one longer piece I essayed to use as a staff, hopping along by its aid. The pain and strain of such progress was so great, I had to rest, sweating and sick, between each step. The tiny beach was so small I could not go far. The rest of my water-washed perch was rock covered and I could not venture to climb over it.

Still I pulled and threw those pieces of drift I could reach into a pile on the beach and then eased myself down there. To tie this all together was a problem I could not solve at the moment. If I still had a knife with me I might have been able to slit tie strips from my clothing. But the knife, too, was gone, and the rocks afforded no vines to be put to such usage.

Perhaps, if I took off the leather under-jerkin which kept my mail from chafing breast and shoulders, I could make a kind of bag of that. Stuffed with the very dry drift, would it make a support? Would it float at all?

Things were a little hazy about me; my thinking no longer was connected. I held foggily to an idea, not certain it had any value. I was thirsty. Slowly I edged to where the river lapped the gravel and dipped my hand into the flood, bringing what I could cup in my palm's hollow up to my lips. It took many such handfuls to satisfy my longing. Then I splashed the liquid over my face. To my fingers my flesh felt hot and tight, and I thought I must have a fever.

I went back to fumbling with the buckles of my mail shirt, having to pause weakly many times in the business of getting it off. Now I was no longer cold, but hot . . . so hot I longed to lunge forward into the blessed coolness of that river.

Why had I taken off my mail . . . what was it I must do? I sat staring down at the folds of metal rings on my knees, trying to remember why it had been so important that I struggle so against my own weakness.

Jerkin . . . I plucked the latches of my leather undershirt. *Must take off jerkin.* But the smallest movement was now too hard, requiring such effort that I sat panting heavily between my attempts to free myself from that other garment.

Thirsty . . . water . . . I needed water. . . . Once more I hunched along, the gravel bruising and cutting my hands as I crawled, and came to the river. My hands went into the flood.

Out of the water arose a nightmare to front me!

It was fanged; a great gaping mouth stretched wide and ready to snap me in. For that moment I saw only the mouth and the teeth within it. I threw myself back and away, wrenching my wound so that I lost consciousness.

"—AWAKE!"

"Kyllan?"

"Awake! Dussa, let him wake!"

Cool wetness on my face. But that frantic cry did not ring in my ear; it was in my mind.

"Kyllan?"

"Wake you! If you would live, wake!"

Not Kyllan, not Kaththea. This was not the known mind touch. It was a thin, keening voice which hurt my brain as some sounds hurt the ears. I tried to flee it, but it held me fast.

"Wake!"

I opened my eyes, expecting somehow to see that monster from the river. But instead it was an oval face of pale, fair coloring, and around it tendrils of spun-silver hair dried, to spring into a floss cloud.

"Wake!" Hands on me, pulling me up.

"What—who—?"

She kept looking over her shoulder, as if she also feared what might emerge from the river. Her anxiety was plain. But to me it had little meaning, and when she looked back to me she frowned. Her thoughts were as sharp pointed knives to prick my swimming brain into action.

"We have little time. They make a bargain—with you for payment! Do you wish to be given to *those*?"

I blinked. But the urgency of her mind touch stirred within me the instinct for self-preservation that will keep a man going even when his conscious mind has retreated into non-thought. Clumsily I tried to answer to her tugging, somehow crawling to the river as she pulled and pushed me in that direction.

Then I remembered and tried to jerk out of her hold. "Thing—thing in there—"

Her grip tightened and she thought at me fiercely. "No longer. It will obey me. You must get away before *they* send for you."

So determined was her will that it overrode my small spark of rebellion and I lurched on. Then I was floundering in the water.

"On your back—over on your back," she ordered.

Somehow I did find myself on my back, and once more I was drawn along, my head held above the surface. We were headed downstream. My companion swam, but also used the current to aid our flight. For flight it was. My immersion cleared my thinking enough to let me know that we were in danger.

Then it began to rain; huge drops struck the surface about us. The clouds were at last loosing the burden with which they had so long threatened us. I closed my eyes against the beating, and I thought my companion's apprehension heightened.

"Must—must get ashore—before the floods came. . . ." I caught her hurried thought. Then she called a call so high in pitch it faded from my mental grasp. Shortly after, there was a burst of relief from her mind. Then followed her orders.

"We must go under water here. Take a deep breath and hold it when I say so."

My protest did not register with her. So when her order reached my mind I filled my lungs as best I might. There was abrupt darkness about us. We were not only submerged beneath the water, but must also come under some other roofing. There is a fear in this for my species, and perhaps I felt it the more since I was helpless. Did she realize I must breathe—breathe—*now!*

Then my face broke water, my nose and mouth open to the air. I gulped that in, and with it a strong animal scent, as if we transversed a burrow, yet water still lapped about us. It was dark, yet my companion advanced with confidence.

"Where are we?"

"In a runway to an aspt house. Ah, now we must crawl. Hold to my belt and come—"

Turning from my back was a task which left me sweating again, but turn I did in those cramped quarters. Her hands aided and guided me, setting my groping fingers in a belt with many sharp shells set along its surface. We crawled and came into a wide circular place which had ghostly light shifting from the upper portion of its dome.

The flooring under us was piled with dried rushes and bunches of leaves, while the walls of the dome were of dried mud mixed with more reeds, plastered into some smoothness. At the apex of that ceiling were small holes to give air, though that was heavily tainted with the strong animal odor. Light also came from another source: bits of vegetable matter had been wedged haphazardly into the walls and emitted a weird grayish radiance.

We were not alone in that domed room. Squatting across from us was a furred creature. It was large. If it had stood on its powerful hindfeet it might have just topped my shoulder. Its head was round, with no discernible ears, a wide mouth with noticeable, jutting teeth, and feet provided with long heavy claws. Had I fronted it in other company I might have watched it warily. But now it smoothed its fur with its paws, combing through that thickness with its claws. It did this almost absently, for its eyes were fixed upon the girl who had brought me. Though I could not catch their thought speech, I was sure they were communicating.

She was Orsya, but why she had brought me from the islet, and from what danger we fled, I had no idea. The furred owner of the house waddled to a hole and, ducking into it, was gone. Orsya turned her attention to me.

"Let me look upon your wound." It was an order rather than a request, but one I obeyed. For the raging pain Dahaun's treatment had reduced was fast returning, and I wondered how much more I could stand.

The Krogan girl brought out a knife and cut more of my breeches and the bandage I had knotted tighter. Though the light of our refuge seemed twilight to me, it apparently served her adequately. She examined my wound intently.

"It is better than I had hoped. The woodswoman knows her herbs," was Orsya's comment. "While her roots and leaves would not heal it, yet the poison has eaten no deeper. Now let us see what can be done."

I had raised myself on my elbows to watch her. Now, with a palm flat against my chest, she pushed me flat again.

"Rest—do not move! I shall speedily return."

As the animal, she crawled through that mud arch and I was left alone. The light-headedness which had come and gone upon the islet plagued me, and with it the pain in my thigh was a fire charring to the bone.

It seemed a very long time before she came back, and I needed all my small remaining stock of fortitude to endure it. I knew that I had a fever and it was increasingly hard to keep in touch with the world about me.

Orsya bent over my wound again; her touch was at first sheer agony as she coated torn flesh with a soft, wet substance she took from a shell box. Then a coolness spread from that coating, soothing, turning the torn flesh numb. Three times she spread the coating, each time waiting for a short interval before she applied the next layer. Then she put over it some wide leaves.

When she had finished she raised my heavy head and urged into my mouth some globules that burst as I bit down on them, filling my mouth with a salty, bitter fluid.

"Swallow!" she commanded.

In spite of my distaste, I did, though it was faintly nauseating and left my throat feeling raw. Water from a shell cup followed, before she settled me back on an improvised pillow of reeds scraped up from the floor.

I slept then, my last waking memory that of seeing Orsya curl up at the other side of the house. She held something between her hands; whatever that object was, it gave off flickers of light which ran hither and thither across the walls, for what purpose I could not guess.

When I awoke again I was alone. But my head was clear and the pain in my wound was only a suggestion of ache. Suddenly I wanted out—into the clear, clean air which did not carry the animal smell, wanted out enough so that, if I still had my sword, I might have been hacking at the walls which pent me there.

Only, when I tried to sit up, I discovered that the plaster Orsya had put on my thigh was now a great weight, its surface under my exploring hands, seemingly as hard as stone. It tied me as efficiently where I was as if she had left me in dungeon chains. But I did not have long to fret about that, for she crawled in from the tunnel, carrying something wrapped in a net.

For a moment she eyed me appraisingly. "It is well," she commented. "The poison no longer fills you. Now, eat, and so grow strong, for danger stalks this land, with net and spear, to take you."

Her net bag she put down and opened to show small leaf-wrapped parcels in it. Hunger—yes, I *was* hungry—with the hunger that follows involuntary fasting. I glanced at the parcels and knew I would not question flavor, nor source, that only the substance interested me.

There were small slivers of white meat, moist, and I believe, raw. Over these she scattered a flower-like dust from another packet. I ate eagerly, and found it good, where I had been prepared to overcome repugnance because of my need. There were four or five things which might have been roots, peeled and scraped, which had a sharp flavor, a little biting to the tongue. When I had finished, Orsya folded away the net.

"We must talk, man from overmountain. As I have said, you are not free from danger—but very far from safety. At least, beyond these walls you are. The Valley is far from here. Also, those who rode with you believe you dead."

"How did I get to that island?"

She had brought out a comb and drew it through her cloud of hair, smoothing and parting those filmy locks with a kind of unconscious sensual pleasure.

"Oboro was sent to take you, or one of you. The People—the Krogan as you earth walkers call us—are very frightened; and fear has made them angry against those they believe have brought them danger. No longer may it be in this land to answer no war horn except one's own. You and Ethutur came to Oaris and asked for our aid. But other, and greater, lords had come before you. After you were gone they sent such messengers as we did not dare to deny hearing.

"We want none of your wars; do you understand? None!" Her mind touch was a ringing shout in my brain. "Leave us to our lakes and pools, our rivers and streams. Leave us in peace!"

"Yet Oboro caught me—"

For a moment she did not answer, but busied herself ridding one long strand of hair of a tangle, as if that was the weightiest act in all the world. But I guessed that she hid behind her comb and combing as one might cower for refuge under the spreading limbs of a welcoming tree.

"You called upon water to war with the Thas—loosed one of the ancient weapons the Krogan once built for a lord long since dead. Now the Thas, and those who sent them, cry out upon my people, saying that in truth we have secretly allied ourselves to you. Those sent among us to see we do not do such a thing, they will take toll—"

"But why was I captured?"

"You are one of those who began the troubling, one who helped to loose the flood. You were wounded and so easy to capture," she replied frankly.

Suddenly I discovered that I was watching the rise and fall of that comb in her hair with a serious attention which woke an uneasiness in me. Reluctantly, and that reluctance alarmed me even more, I looked away from her, fixing my eyes on the dome wall above her head.

"So Oboro thought me easy prey—"

"Orias ordered that one of you be taken, if it were possible. He might use such a prisoner as a peace-offering to *those*. And mayhap, if he drove a good bargain, free us from their notice."

"But if it meant so much to your people, why did you rescue me?"

Her comb was still now. "Because what Orias ordered would bring trouble also. Perhaps worse trouble in the end. Is it not the truth, that you *spoke* and one of the Great Ones *answered?*"

"How—how did you know that?"

"Because we are who we are, man from overmountain. Once, very long and long ago, we had ancestors who were of your breed. But those chose to walk another road, and from that walking, little by little, were we born. But powers shaped us, and once we answered to their pull and sway. So when one of the Great Ones stirs, then all like unto us in this land knows it. And if you are one who will be *answered,* then you might loose upon us worse than *those* can summon in their turn."

"But Orias did not think so?"

"Orias believes what he was told—that only by chance did you hit upon some spell which moved a long closed gate. His informer also said better give you unto those who can force you to put such a key into their hands."

"No!"

"So say I also, man from overmountain."

"My name is Kemoc."

For the first time I saw her smile. "Kemoc, then. No, if you have such a spell, I would rather have it serve those you company with in the Valley, than others. Thus did I come to take you from the island."

"And this?" I looked about me.

"This is a winter dwelling for the aspt. Since they are of the rivers, so are they bidable when we approach them properly. But time passes and powers walk. I do not think it will be much longer that you dare an overland trip to the Valley. It is whispered that the Shadow forces will soon have that under siege."

I rapped my hand against the stone-hard covering of my wound. "How long must I be tied here?

Again she smiled and put away her comb. "For no longer than is needed to chip you free, Kemoc."

Chip she did, hammering with stone and the point of her knife. I thought that what she had plastered on me and left to dry must be the same healing mud as had brought my brother back from the edge of death. For when the last shards fell away there was no wound, but a half-healed scar seam, and I could move the limb with ease.

She took me out through the underwater tunnel and we sheltered warily in a thicket of reed growth, rooted where the water swirled. It was early morning and a mist clung to the surface of the river. Orsya sniffed, drawing deep breaths into her lungs and expelling them slowly, as if in that way she tested for some message which eluded me.

"The day will be fair," she announced. "That is good—clouds favor the Shadow; sun is the enemy to *those.*"

"Which way do I go?"

She shook her head at me. "Way *we* go, Kemoc. To let you blunder helplessly in this land is to pick a possel from its shell and throw it to a vuffle. We go by water."

Go by water we did, first swimming with the current of the river, and then against the push of ripples in a smaller side stream to the south. Although the land seemed open and smiling under the sun, yet I paid close attention to all Orsya's directions. We lay in a reed bank once—she underwater, I with a hollow reed in my mouth for air—while a small pack of Gray Ones lapped water and growled to one another within arms touching of our hiding place.

It was irking to my guide that I could not take wholly to the water as she was able, but needed air for my laboring lungs. I am sure she could have made that journey in a third less time than we took. At night we sheltered again in another river dweller's abandoned burrow, one not finished with the skill of the aspt dwelling, merely a hole cut in the bank.

There she spoke of her people and their like. I learned that she was the first daughter of Orias' elder sister, so by their way of ranking kinship, thought closer to him than his own children. She was more adventurous than most of her generation, having slipped away from her home on numerous occasions to explore waterways where only a few, if any, of the males had ever ventured. She hinted of strange finds in the mountains, and then said impatiently, that with the coming of war such searching must be abandoned. Mention of the war silenced her and she curled into sleep.

It was midmorning before the stream we had followed dwindled to a size so we could no longer swim. Then she motioned to the heights ahead and said:

"Guide your way by that peak, Kemoc. If you take care and make haste, you will reach your Valley by sundown. I can abide for short periods of time in the open air, but not for long. Thus, this is our parting place."

I tried to thank her. But what are adequate thanks for one's life? She smiled again and waved. Then she splashed back into the water and was gone before I could finish what I was stumbling over to say.

Setting my attention on the peak she had pointed out I began the last stage of my journey.

VI

*T*he winged sentries of the Valley had me in view long before I sighted them. A Flannan appeared out of nowhere to coast along over my head, then was gone with beating wings. I came up, not the road entrance I had known before, but a notch between two standing stones. Back door to the Green domain this might be, but here were also inscribed the Symbols on each wall. One of the lizard folk who helped patrol the heights peered down on me, jewel-eyed.

"Kemoc!"

Kyllan came running, throwing his arms about my shoulders, mind and eyes both meeting mine. In that moment our old closeness was as if it had never been broken.

It was like unto a high feast day as they brought me to the feather-roofed houses, asking questions all the way. But what I had to tell them of Krogan enmity made them quickly sober.

"This is ill hearing!" Dahaun had poured the guesting cup for me. Now she put the flagon back on the table as if she saw some evil picture. "With the Krogan ranged against us . . . water can be a bad weapon to face. But who can be these Great Ones of the Shadow whom Orias fears so much that he tries to buy their favor with a captive? The Krogan are not a timid folk. In the past they have been friends to us. Perhaps a seeking—"

Ethutur shook his head. "Not yet; not until we can learn in no other way. Remember, those who so *seek* may also find themselves the sought, if they are detected and the power on the other side is equal to, or greater than, their own."

In the first excitement of my return I had forgotten something, but no longer. Kaththea—where was my sister? I looked to Kyllan for an answer. Surely she was not avoiding me . . .?

He was quick with reassurance. "She rode east yesterday, when we believed you dead. It was her thought to go to a place, known here, where certain forces can be tapped; and where, with her witch knowledge, perhaps she could read your fate. Believe this, Kemoc; she was sure that you were not dead. For she said that she and I would know it if your life had been taken from you!"

I dropped my head into my hands. Suddenly it became so needful that I reach her, that I sent out a call, believing that here in the protected Valley, it could cause no harm. Kyllan's thought twined with mine, making it twofold as it went forth, joyfully seeking.

Into that seeking I poured more and more strength. I felt the tide of Kyllan's rise with it—out and out. . . . Yet there came no answer. It was not as if Kaththea was absorbed in some spell of her own, for still we would have touched her mind and been warned off. No, this was a total absense of all Kaththea meant to both of us—as total as if the walls of the Wise Women's Secret Place had once more closed about her.

Now my spear of thought grew swifter, shot in all directions. But there was no target, only that emptiness which in itself was ominous. I raised my head again from trembling hands and looked to Kyllan, saw the grayish shade beneath the weathering of his face and knew we were united in fear.

"Gone!" He said it first, in a whisper which still must have reached the ears of those about us, for they, too, looked startled and dismayed.

"Where?" To me that was most important. When I had called Kaththea from the island of the Krogan lake, her answer has been faint and hard to read, coming across miles of territory which the enemy held; still, I had reached her and she, me. In this protected Valley where there would be no barriers, I could not reach her at all.

I turned to Dahaun. "This place of power to which she went, where does it lie?"

"At the eastern tip of the Valley, up against the Heights."

The Heights—Dinzil! To me the answer was as plain as if written out in fiery runes across the air between us. My thought was clear to her.

"Why?"

So Dahaun did not dispute the possibility of my guess; she looked for a reason.

"Yes, why?" That was Kyllan. "Kaththea looked upon him with favor; that is true. But she would not go to him thus without speech between us, especially after saying that she wished to seek you through the power."

"Not willingly," I answered aloud, between set teeth.

Dahaun shook her head. "Not unwillingly, Kemoc. One with her powers could not be drawn unwillingly past our defenses. And those guard every gate of this Valley."

"I do not believe that she agreed—"

"How know you what arguments may have been used with her?" Kyllan asked.

I turned on him, and some of my fear became anger, to be directed at one within my reach: "Why did you not keep mind touch, to know what chanced with her?"

He flushed. But when he made answer he kept a rein on his temper. "Because she wished it so, saying she must hoard her energy to use in the seeing. She said that while she was learned in much, yet never had she taken the Witch Oath, nor received the Jewel, been admitted into full company. Thus she doubts at times and needs all her strength."

That sounded as Kaththea's own words, and I knew that he spoke the truth. Still . . . that he might have protected her, and had not, burned unfairly in me. I spoke now to Dahaun:

"Can Shil bear me to where Kaththea went?"

"I do not know. That he can go in that direction, yes. But whether you, who have little protection against the forces which gather there, can reach it, that is another question."

"Which only trial may answer! But let me try—"

Only I was not to have that chance. For, even before I finished speaking, one of the birds swooped down to perch on Dahaun's shoulder. Instead of the usual trilled greeting, its cries were a scream, plainly meant to announce some disaster. Ethutur and the rest were on their feet, crowding for the door. Dahaun looked to us from Estcarp.

"They move upon the Valley, even as the Krogan maid warned you, Kemoc."

So began our siege time and it was a bitter one. While the Symbols might bar the gates, yet there were miles of cliffs, and against those a motley crew of monsters climbed, flew, scrabbled to find a way at us. Storm clouds gathered about the rim we defended; wind and torrents of rain lashed at us. The gloom hid those who strove to make the ascent. The lightning strikes of the force whips were undistinguishable at times from the true lightning of the storm.

It was a wild series of battles. There would come lulls, even as the most vicious hurricanes know lulls. Then once more the rush, so we had to be on the alert, for we never knew when the next attack would muster.

Some of the enemy I had seen before. While the Rasti could not climb the cliffs, the Gray Ones put on their quasi-human shapes to find holes. There were other things . . . drifting mists which were perhaps the more feared by us from overmountain because they had no substance to be hewed by steel, nor shattered by dart . . . and vast, armored things prowling about the base of the cliffs, unable to climb, but digging with taloned paws at our natural wall with sullen ferocity.

Flying things fought airborne over our heads where Flannan, bird, Vrang of the peaks cut and slew in turn. It was a struggle out of a nightmare; even those among our recruits who had gone up against the frightening otherworld might of the Kolder long years past found this a more fearsome battle.

For how long we held that defense, I do not know, for day was nearly as darksome as night. When day came pillars of fire flamed green, high into the sky, from cressets along the cliff. In that light our adversaries seemed less inclined to press forward.

The Green People had their own magic that they called upon. Dahaun and others did not take actual part in the fighting, but summoned and marshaled forces which were not of any earth I had known.

I knew that the Lady of Green Silences feared the waters within the Valley, that some disaster might come from them since the Krogan were against us. But, though the lizard folk patrolled there, they found no sign that Orias had taken the field openly under the Shadow.

Once, when Ethutur spoke to a handful of the Old Race, he said, in a puzzled fashion, that all who had been sent against us were only the minor servants of evil and no Great One from the Shadow had given us a blow. This he thought sinister . . . unless the Great Ones had indeed withdrawn so far into their other worlds that they could not be easily summoned again.

We suffered losses in those grim hours. Godgar fell, taking with him a warrior's guard of the enemy. There were gaps in the ranks of the Green People also, and among their four-footed and winged allies. No one kept count of the casualties for there was no time to think of anything but dogged defense. Although Kyllan fought a distance from me, I knew all was still well with him. But, even through this, my thought for Kaththea was a gnawing. That she had gone out of the Valley, I was certain.

Some of the men from the Heights fought in our ranks. But among them Dinzil did not show. Nor did I expect him to, no matter what excuse his followers could offer for him.

Perhaps what Dahaun called down was what came to our succor at last. Or perhaps the enemy had just so many fangs, claws, bodies, and wills to throw against us, and those had become so thinned they were ready to retreat. But at last the clouds broke and the sun shone. Under that glory the hosts of the Shadow drew back. They took their dead with them, so we could not tell how great a toll we had exacted. However, they had been beaten this time, of that we were sure.

We took counsel then and knew that our own losses had not been light. Nor could we withstand many more such concentrated attacks. So in the breathing space now allowed us, we must fortify and scout, strike back where we could.

But I had another task. And so I told them.

Then Kyllan arose and said that this would be his road also: for the three of us were one, and when that bond was broken, then we were all lessened.

Then I spoke to him alone, saying that once before we had been parted, and he, the warrior, had held to his duty, when I had been maimed and Kaththea rift from us. Now, here again, was a time when we must be what we were called upon to be. Warrior he was, and in this place his skill was needed. But with me was Kaththea even closer linked, and upon me the need to go to her was the heavier.

I think Dahaun and Ethutur understood. But those from Estcarp did not. For, to them, long nurtured in the harshness of border war, the life of one woman weighed as nothing against the good of all. That she was a witch tipped the scales even more, for among those who fled from Karsten the Wise Ones were feared but not esteemed.

I expected no support. I took only a small supply of food, a sword, and a spark of hope, to travel east. Shil's strength was offered me, but I said I would ride only to the borders of the Valley; beyond that I risked no life save my own.

Kyllan parted from me reluctantly. I think—I know—that he was hurt by my frankness concerning the stronger bond between me and Kaththea, though he knew that I spoke the truth, and that his skill was needed here.

In the Valley it seemed that our bloody struggle, of the days just past, was an ugly dream. Shil went at a steady gallop along the river bottom. There were no traps here to be evaded and his going was swift and smooth. I saw the lizard sentries who still watched for any Krogan menace. I wondered about Orsya and what her people would do when they discovered, if they did, that she had freed me from the prison islet.

The wide grasslands and pleasant groves of the Valley gave way now to a landscape narrowing between slowly converging walls, wilder looking, with a predominance of rocky outcrops. I thought that the Valley must dwindle to a point ahead. In that point, according to Dahaun's directions, lay a little used, climbing way which led to the place where Kaththea had gone, to find that which even the Lady of Green Silences held in awe.

To each his or her own magic, as Dahaun had once said to me. The Valley's was of growth and life from the soil, the Thas' was of things underground, and the Krogan's of the water. I gathered from Dahaun that the place Kaththea had sought was akin to the powers of the air.

The Witches of Estcarp could control wind and rain and tempests, after a fashion. Perhaps my sister planned to draw upon such arts now. Only, if she had gone there with such intent, she had not succeeded.

Shil slowed pace, single-footed warily through a narrow slit between towering walls. No longer was the sun with me, though it was still some hours from setting. But here twilight abode.

Finally the Renthan halted.

"So far—no farther," came his thought.

A narrow path was before us, but I felt it, too . . . a distinct warn-off to the spirit. I dismounted and slung the strap of the supply bag across my shoulder.

"My thanks for your courtesy, swift-footed runner. Tell them all was well with me when we parted."

His head was up; he was searching the walls above and beyond. In my sight they were sheer reaches of rock, no place on their surfaces to shelter any would-be ambusher. I had a strong feeling also that this place would not welcome such forces as we had beaten back from the Valley. Shil blew from his nostrils, pawed the ground.

"There is the taste, the smell, the feel, of power here."

"But not of evil," I answered him.

He lowered his head so his golden eyes met mine.

"Some powers are beyond our measurement—for good or ill. He who goes this road walks blindfolded in the senses we know."

"I have no choice."

Once again he blew and tossed his head. "Go in strength, watch well your footing, and keep always alert with eye and ear. . . ."

He did not want to leave, but he could not pass some barrier there. Would it also stand against me? I went on with long strides, half expecting that I might find myself running into one of those force walls, such as had once been between us and the Secret Place where Kaththea was shut from the world. But there was nothing.

I looked back once and saw Shil still standing there, watching me. When I raised my hand in salute, once more he tossed his head in answer. Then I turned and kept my eyes only for the forward route, shutting out of mind what lay behind.

For a while the cut sloped gently upward and the footing was easy. Then

I came to the very tip point of that cut. The way was very narrow here. I could stretch forth my arms and have the fingers of each hand brush the walls. Before me was a stair. Plainly no act of nature, but the work of intelligence. On each of those steps were deep graven symbols. Some were of the protective kind of the Valley, but others were strange to me. I did not quite like setting bootsoles upon those marks, yet that I must do if I were to climb. So I went. Seven steps, a landing place the width of three steps, three steps, another such landing, then nine. . . . I could not see any natural reason for such an arrangement, unless the grouping had an occult meaning.

Gradually the stairway grew yet narrower, tapering from one landing to the next. When I was on the last flight there was barely room on each step for two feet set together. I found I made the climb one step at a time, placing my feet together before I raised one for the next step. There were thirteen in this last very narrow way. I found myself counting them under my breath as I went.

The symbols here were all strange: I discovered that I did not like to look at any of them very long. No trace of warning clung to them—I was sensitive enough to the evil of Escore to recognize that—rather it was as if they were never meant for eyes and brains such as mine to sight and understand.

I was tired, though I had not felt any fatigue when I had ridden down the Valley. This was a heaviness which weighted my limbs, made me gasp a little at each step, a need to rest between. My wound had healed fast and clean after Orsya's treatment. It was not that which affected me now, but rather an all-over heaviness of body, a corresponding darkness of spirit.

The stairs were behind me at last, and I stood on the top of the cliff wall of the Valley. Cut into the surface of the stone was a path. As the steps had narrowed little by little, this followed the opposite pattern: beginning no wider than that exit, spreading out, wedged-shaped, beyond to a place where stood a forest of pillars.

Night had come while I climbed and, though I wanted to go on, the weariness was now so heavy upon me I could pull myself no farther than to where I could rest my length in a slot of the road, wrapped in my cloak. So I slept, with no drowsy fall into slumber, but a swift extinction of consciousness. Had I wished, I could not have fought that sleep.

I awoke as swiftly, sat up stiffly, to flex my arms and legs. Dawn light struck here. I ate sparingly from the food Dahaun had packed for me, drank a mouthful of water from my bottle. I must guard well those supplies, she had warned me. For, in troubled lands where the Shadow reached, a man might be brought under evil influences should he eat of what he found growing ripe and ready to his plucking.

Once more I walked that wedge road. The pillars did not appear to be set in any order, nor did they carry any marks of tooling. They might rather have been the boles of petrified frees from which crowns and branches had long since been chipped away. So strong did this feeling of being in a stone forest grow, that

I kept glancing from side to side to see if those missing branches might still lie on the surface between the boles. But the rock was bare. As the wind arose and blew among those standing stones, I could plainly hear the sound present in a grove when a stout breeze sets leaves to rustling. I shut my eyes once and knew that I stood in a grove; yet when I opened them to look, I only gazed upon stone.

The rustling of the unseen wood grew louder, though the push of air against me was no more. There began a wailing, a keening, which were the cries of all the bereft of the world wailing their dead. That, too, died away, and then there was *sound*—words I thought—in no tongue known to me or any man of my kind. I did not *answer,* as had that Other I had provoked in the lowlands. No, these sounds were uttered in a space which might touch upon that in which I moved, but was not mine.

The very feeling of that awesome otherness was such that I did fall, or rather was crushed, to my knees, unable to even think of where that might be—or what lips uttered those *words*.

There followed silence as sharp as if a door had been shut, no wind, no wailing, only silence. I got to my feet and began to run on. So I came into an open space where the road ended, and I stood staring about me.

Stone and rock . . . Across that rock a splash of color, I went to that. It lay in a loose coil as if dropped only a moment earlier. I picked up a scarf, loose, silken, its fine threads catching on my scarred fingers' rough skin. It was green-blue, such a scarf as the women of the Valley wore about their shoulders in the evening. Kaththea had worn a like one when she had laughed with Dinzil at the feasting.

"Kaththea!" I felt it was wrong to raise my voice in that place, but I dared the mind call, as I stood running the soft length back and forth in my hands. "Kaththea! Where are you?"

Silence . . . that dead and awesome silence which had fallen in this place since the closing of the door. To my mind not the faintest answer, though I went seeking.

I coiled the scarf into a small handful and stowed it inside my jerkin to lie against my breast. It had been Kaththea's I was sure. Thus, perhaps, I could use it for a linkage, since a possession can be a draw point.

But where had she gone from here? Not back into the Valley . . . and the road to this haunted place ended here. If she had gone on, it was among those stone trees and there I would follow.

The road had been a sure guide, but once I left it behind and threaded a way among the standing stones, I found I had entered a maze. There was no point ahead I could fix upon as a goal, and, as I twisted and turned, I found myself heading back into the open space where I had found the scarf. On the second such return, I sat down.

That there was a spell set here I no longer doubted. It was meant to confuse mind and eye. To counter it, I closed my eyes upon those bewildering ranks of trees and concentrated on the days I had spent in Lormt. It had been so accepted that no male could use witch power, that no guardian-ship had been put on the records. It was true that most were written in such allegorical style, with so many obscure references to matters unknown, that those not carefully schooled in witch training could make little or nothing of them. At the time I had been searching there, my one desire was to find a refuge for us, and so I had paid little attention to other secrets.

But some of what I had pushed aside along the way lingered in mind. I had the words which had brought the *answer;* those I had no intention of trying again. Now I must bring to my need other knowledge.

There was a chance. I forced a picture from memory. A page of parchment covered with crabbed, archaic writing. Of the handful of words I had been able to read, perhaps a few would serve. How much power did I have in me? Was I one who had inherited the ability of my father to overstep the boundaries of my sex and be more gifted than other males of the Old Race?

I brought out that scarf I had carried. Now I began to knead and roll it between my fingers, twisting it slowly and with care into a cord. So soft was the material it was like a ribbon. Then I knotted the two ends and laid it down before me, so that what I had was a circle, very vivid against the stone.

Fixing my full attention on it as it lay there, I brought my will into use. I had no training in such matters. All I possessed was a memory of some lines on parchment, a driving need for success, and a will which might or might not be equal to the demand I made upon it.

Kaththea . . . in my mind I built the picture of Kaththea, perhaps not just as she was in life, but as she was to me. I concentrated upon that picture for a long time, trying to see her standing within that green circle. Then—now would come the test of what I knew, or what I might be.

I moved my hands slowly and I said aloud three words.

Hardly daring to breathe I watched and waited. The blue-green circlet trembled . . . one side across. Now it was a hoop balanced on its edge. It began to roll slowly, away from the open, out among the topless, branchless stone trees. I followed it, holding to the hope that I had now a guide.

VII

*B*ack and forth the hoop wove a path through the stone wood, and many times was I sure it turned upon itself to lead me in circles. Yet it was my only hope for passing through this ensorceled place. Sometimes I faced the now beaming sun, and then I would remember the old warnings: when a man's shadow lay behind him, so that he could not set eye upon it—that was the time when evil might creep upon him unawares. But, although this place was alien to me, I did not think of it as evil, rather as a barrier, set up to warn off or mislead those who had no kinship with it. We came at last to the other side of that pillared land and the hoop rolled into the open. It wobbled from side to side as if the energy which sustained it was failing. Yet still it rolled, and the path it followed was straight ahead; now there was no chiseled road, only rough rock worked by time and storms.

To the very end of this plateau the loop brought me before it collapsed, no longer anything but a silken cord. If what powers I had sought to fasten upon it had worked, then Kaththea had come this way. But why? And—how?

I picked up the scarf and once more folded it small, to put in my jerkin, as I moved along the edge of a drop, looking down. There was no visible means of descent; the break was sharp and deep.

When I was sure of that I retraced my steps to examine intently the spot where my hoop guide had fallen. The sun, though westering now, showed me scars on the rock. Something had rested there, under weight. I glanced to the opposite side of the chasm. There was a level space; there could have been a bridge across. But if so, that was gone. I rubbed my thigh where the wound was now but a memory and tried to measure by eye the distance between my stand and the other edge.

Only a desperate man would consider such a leap. But now, ridden by my fears, I was a desperate man. I drew my sword and tied it to the supply bag. By the strap I whirled this around my head twice and let it fly. I heard the clang of the blade against the rock, saw it come to rest a foot or so in from the lip of that other rim.

Next I shed my boots, to make them another bundle with my belt buckled about them, and flung them across that gulf. Under my bare feet the rock was warmed by the sun. I paced back toward the edge of the stone forest, though I did not venture in among those boles. Then I put my energy and determination to the test, racing for the edge of the cliff, arching out in a leap, not daring to let myself believe that I would do anything but land safely on the other side.

I sprawled forward, struck painfully, bruising my body with such force that I feared I might have broken bones. I lay there, the breath driven out of me, gasping, before I realized, with a leap of inner exultation, that I had indeed crossed. But I was sore, when I moved to sit up and look about me. I went limpingly when I once more drew on my boots and shouldered my pack.

The marks which had guided me on the other side were sharper to read here; there were scratches as if something had been dragged along the rock. For want of better track I followed those, to find, wedged in behind some rocks, my bridge; a thing made of three logs bound together with hide thongs. The fact that it had been hidden suggested that its makers thought to use it again and I wondered. Would they so have a secret way of reaching the Valley? And would it be in the best interests of those I had left behind to destroy the bridge here and now.

But how? I did not have the strength to maneuver it back and send it rolling into the gulf. To set it afire . . . that was beyond me. Also I doubted if those we feared could move easily through that stone wood.

Those who had hidden the bridge left other traces of their going. I had had good training as a scout in the mountains of Estcarp. These men—if they were men—had not hidden their trail. Hoofprints of Renthan—those were plain in a patch of earth. A tuft of fleece flagged me from a thorn bush, for this side of the gulf was not all rock. Things grew here, though the whipping wind and lack of good soil stunted that growth.

I followed the trail, easier to read in the soil, down a steep slope and into a wood of grotesquely twisted trees, which at first grew hardly higher than my own head. But, as I descended farther into their stand, they stood taller, though nonetheless crooked, until I was in a wood where sunlight did not pierce and I moved in a grayish gloom. Then I saw a thick moss depending from the limbs and crooked branches, so that, though these trees were scanty of leaf, yet they shut out light. Some of this moss dripped in long, swaying masses, as if tattered curtains hung between tree and tree. But the party whose traces I followed had broken away, pulling down some of this wiry vegetation so that it lay in heaps on the ground, giving forth a faintly spicy odor.

As the moss curtains hung from the trees, so did the ground give root to a similar growth. This was soft and springing under foot and from it, here and there, arose slender stems on which trembled, at my passing, pallid flowers. There were other lighter glimmers here and there along that mossy undergrowth. As the forest grew darker about me, so these did glow with a phosphorescent light. They were star-shaped with six points. When I bent more closely to them, they would fade, and all left to be seen was a kind of grayish web spun across the top of moss tendrils.

Night was coming, and I could not follow the trail in the dark. Nor had I any wish to camp in this place. So far I had not seen or heard life within the wood, but that did not rule out the possibility that some very unpleasant surprises might lurk here.

Yet I must find a place in which to rest, or else try to return back the way I had come. For the farther down-slope I went, the deeper became the moss-grown forest. I found myself pausing for long moments to listen intently. The faint breezes, which did manage to penetrate to this place, moved the tree-rooted vegetation so that there was always a low whispering. I thought it sounded eerily like half-heard words, broken speech, issuing from things which spied and followed as I went.

I stopped at last to look at one great tree which might, in spite of its gray-green curtains, provide a firm and safe wall for a man's back. Eat, drink and rest, I must. My bruised body was too tired to be forced along and I had no desire to blunder perhaps into a camp of the enemy.

The tree did provide a feeling of security as I sat with my back against it. Now, as the gloom deepened, the stars and the pale flowers were more noticeable. I was aware of an elusive fragrance, a pleasant scent carried by the sighing breeze.

I ate and drank with moderation. Luckily, the journey rations of the Green People had been long ago devised to give a maximum of nourishment to a minimum of bulk, so that a few mouthfuls sufficed a man for a day. Still one's stomach continued to want real food, chewed and swallowed for its filling. So I was vaguely dissatisfied, even though my mind told me I was well-fed on the crumbs I had licked from my fingers.

Just as, the night before, that climb up the stairs had wearied me past all previous acquaintance with fatigue, so now something of the same trembling weakness settled upon me as I sat there. It was rank folly to sleep . . . rank folly. . . . I remembered some inner warning trying to arouse me even as the waves of sleep rolled over me, and me, under them.

Water about me, rising higher and higher, choking me! I had lost Orsya, I was drowning in the river. . . .

Gasping, I awoke. Not water, no. But I was buried in drifts, waves of moss which rose to chin level, the end of the fronds weaving loosely about my head. Fear triggered my responses, my struggle to throw off that blanket. Yet, my legs and arms were now as tightly caught as if cords bound them. I could not even move away from the tree against which I had set my back, for now this tide of gray and green had lashed me to it! Would I indeed drown in it? I ducked, twisted and turned my head, and then I realized that the weaving fronds about my shoulders were not tightening about my head. While my movement was constricted, yet the fibers had not tightened to the point that either breathing or circulation was impaired. I was captive, but so far my life was not yet imperiled.

But that was small comfort. I rested my head against the tree trunk and gave up struggling. It was very dark now and the glow of the stars almost brilliant. Those caught my attention. I had not noted any particular pattern to their setting before, but now I saw two rows, leading from where I was imprisoned off to my left. Almost as if they had been deliberately set to mark a path! A path for who— or what?

The swish-swish of the tree-rooted moss whispered under some breeze. But I could hear no insect, no night hunter.

I turned my attention to the moss. The coarse strands about me were not of the ground growth, but that which was limb rooted. I could see by the aid of the phosphorescent stars that loops of it had loosened hold on branches to fall about the parent trunk and my body. Tales, told by the Sulcar rovers, of strange growths in far southern lands which had a taste for flesh and blood, which seized upon prey as might animal hunters, came far too easily to mind at that moment. Then, I discovered I could move a little in that cording, enough to change position slightly when I strove to favor, half-unconsciously, one of my worst bruises. It was as if what held me captive had picked the need for such easement out of my mind and responded to it.

Out of my mind? But that was wild—utterly wild! How could a plant read my thoughts? Or was it a plant? Oh, yes; leaf and fiber about me were vegetation. But could it be a tool—this prisoning mass—a tool in other hands?

"Who are you?" Deliberately I aimed that thought into the gloom. "Who are you? What would you do with me?"

I do not believe that I expected any answer. But—while I did not get an answer—I did tap *something!* Just as Orsya had slid off that beam used for contact between us when she spoke to the aspt, so did I now but touch for a second, to lose it again, some think-level. It was not like those of the Green People, or of the Krogan, being far less "human." Animal? Somehow, I did not believe so. I put all my concentration now, not into physical struggle against the moss, but into seeking.

"Who—are—you?"

Twice more that flicker of almost touch. Enough to keep me struggling. But it came and was lost again before I could even decide whether it was an upper band such as Orsya used, or a lower, in a level to which I had not delved before.

Light . . . it was much lighter . . . day coming? No—from those star-beacons to my left the light streamed in visible shafts of pearl glow. There was an expectancy about them, a waiting.

"Who—are—you?" This time I plunged, down the scale of mind bands, taking a chance that what I sought lay below and not above.

And I caught, held, though not long enough for a complete thought to pass between us. What burst at me in return was excitement, shock, and fear.

Fear I wanted least of all, for fear may drive the one afraid to violent action.

"Who are you?" Once more I hit that low level. But this time with no reaction; I touched no mind. It was as if that other, still afraid, had closed a door firmly against me.

The candles which had sprung from the stars continued to grow stronger. They were not akin to the weird gray lights which we had seen shine for evil, for they did not chill me. While sun did not shine, it was now coolly pale as if in the light of a cloudy day.

Up the path came a figure: small, yes, and hunched. But I did not feel about it as I had about those scuttling things of the dark, the Thas. This came very slowly, pausing now and then to eye me apprehensively. Fear—

When it came to stand between two of the nearer star candles I could see it better. It was as gray as the moss of the trees, and its long hair could hardly be told from that growth. When it put up gnarled hands to part and brush aside that hair in order to view me the better, I saw a small wrinkled face with a flattened nose and large eyes fringed in lashes which grew bushy and thick. Once more it made that sweeping motion to send cascades of hair back over its shoulders and I saw it was female. The large breasts and protruding stomach were only part covered by a kind of net woven of moss. In that were caught some of the fragrant flowers in what seemed to me a pitiful attempt at adornment.

Then memory awoke in me and I remembered more childhood tales. This was a Mosswife, who, according to legend, crept despairingly about the haunts of man, trying ever to win some attention from the other race. A Mosswife, reported the stories of old, yearned to have her children nursed and fostered by humankind. And if one would strike such a bargain, the Mosswife thereafter served him richly, giving secrets of hidden treasure and the like.

Legend reported them good, a shy people, meaning no ill, distressed when their uncouth appearance frightened or disgusted those they wanted to befriend or favor. How true was legend? It seemed I was to test that now.

The Mosswife advanced another hesitant step or two. She gave the appearance of age, but if that were so I could not tell. The memories I had of the tales always described them so. Also—that no Moss man had ever been sighted.

She stood and stared. I tried again to use mind touch, with no result. If it were she whom I had contacted earlier, she held her barrier against me now. But there flowed from her a kind of good will, a timid good will, as if she meant me no harm, but feared that I did not feel the same toward her.

I gave up trying to reach her by mind touch. Instead I spoke aloud, and into the tones of my voice I never tried harder to put that which would lead her to believe that I meant her no harm, that on the contrary I now looked to her for aid. Elsewhere in Escore we had discovered that the language of this land, though using different pronunciations and some archaic turns of speech, was still that of the Old Race, and we could be understood.

"Friend—" I schooled my voice to softness. "I am friend—friend to the Moss Folk."

She searched me with her eyes, holding mine in a steady gaze.

How did the old saying go: "Whole friend, half-friend, unfriend."

Though I did not repeat that aloud, I was willing to accept from her name of half-friend—if she did not think me unfriend.

I saw her puckered lips work as if she chewed upon the word before she spoke it aloud in turn.

"Friend—" Her voice was a whisper, not much louder than the wind whisper through the moss curtains.

Her stare still held me. Then, as a door opening, thought flowed into my mind.

"Who are you who follow a trail through the mossland?"

"I am Kemoc Tregarth from overmountain." But the designation which might mean something to others of Escore, meant nothing to her. "From the Valley of Green Silences," I added, and this did carry weight.

She mouthed a word again, and this time a flood of reassurance warmed me. For the word she said, though it was distorted by the sibilance of her whisper, was the badge of rightness in what might be a land of nameless evil—the ancient word of power:

"Euthayan."

I answered it quickly, by lip, not mind, so that she could be sure that I was one who could say such and not be blasted in the saying.

Her hands moved from the hold they had kept upon the mantle of her moss hair. They waved gently, as the breeze stirred banners on the trees. Following the bidding of those gestures, the moss strands binding me to the tree stirred, fell apart, loosing me, until I sat in a nest of fibers.

"Come!"

She beckoned and I got to my feet. Then she drew back a step as if the fact I towered over her was daunting. But, drawing her hair about her as one might draw a cloak, she turned and went down that path of the star candles.

Shouldering my pack, I followed. The candles continued to light our way, though outside the borders of their dim light the night pressed in and I thought we must still be a ways from dawn. Now those woods lamps were farther and farther apart, and paler. I hastened so as not to lose my guide. For all her stumpy frame and withered looking legs, she threaded this way very swiftly.

Heavier and heavier hung the moss curtains. Sometimes they appeared almost solid between the trees, too thick to be stirred by any wind. I realized these took the form of walls, that I might be passing among dwellings. My guide put out her hands and parted the substance of one such wall, again beckoned me to pass her in that entrance.

I came into a space under a very large tree. Its scaled bole was the center support of the house. The moss curtains formed the walls, and a moss carpet grew underfoot. There were stars of light set flat against the tree trunk, wreathed around it from the ground up to the branching of the first limbs. The light they gave was near to that of a fire.

On the moss sat my—hostesses? judges? captors? I knew not what they were, save they were Mosswives, so resembling she who had brought me that I could believe them all of one sisterhood. She who was closest to the star-studded tree gestured for me to sit. I put aside my pack and dropped, cross-legged.

Again there was a period of silent appraisal, just as there had been with my guide. Then she, whom I guessed was chief of that company, named first herself and then the others, in the formal manner followed by those country dwellers living far from the main life of Estcarp.

"Fuusu, Foruw, Frono, Fyngri, Fubbi—" Fubbi being she who had led me here.

"Kemoc Tregarth," I answered, as was proper. Then I added, which was of the custom of Estcarp, but not might be so here:

"No threat from me to the House of Fuusu and her sister, clan, or rooftree, harvest, flocks—"

If they did not understand my good-wish, they did the will behind it. For Fuusu made another sign, and Foruw, who sat upon her right, produced a cup of wood and poured into it a darkish liquid from a stone bottle. She touched her lips briefly to one side of the cup and then held it out.

Though I remembered Dahaun's injunction against drinking or eating in the wilds, I dared not refuse a sip from the guesting cup. I swallowed it a little fearfully. The stuff was sour and a little bitter. I was glad that I need not drink more of it. But I formally tipped the cup right and left, dribbled a few drops over its brim to the moss carpet, wishing thus luck on both house and land.

I put the cup down between us and waited politely for Fuusu to continue. I did not have to wait long.

"Where go you through the moss land, Kemoc Tregarth?" She stumbled a little over my name. "And why?"

"I seek one who has been taken from me, and the trail leads hither."

"There have been those who came and went."

"Went where?" I could not restrain my eagerness.

The Mosswife shook her head slowly. "Into hidden ways; they have set a blind spell on their going. None may follow."

Blind spell? I did not know what she meant. But perhaps she could tell me more. . . .

"There was a maiden with them?" I asked.

Fuusu nodded to Fubbi. "Let her answer; she saw their passing."

"There was a maiden, and others. A Great Dark One—"

A Great Dark One; the words repeated in my mind. Had I guessed wrong? Not Dinzil, but one of the enemy . . .?

"She was of the light, but she rode among dark ones. Hurry, hurry, hurry, they went. Then they took a hidden way and the blind spell was cast," Fubbi said.

"Can you show me this way?" I broke in with scant courtesy. Danger from Dinzil was one thing, but if Kaththea had been taken by one of the enemy . . .? Time—time was also now an enemy.

"I can show, but you will not be able to take that way."

I did not believe her. Perhaps I was over confident because I had already won so far with success. Her talk of a blind spell meant little.

"Show him," Fuusu ordered. "He will not believe until he sees."

I remembered to pay the proper farewells to Fuusu and her court, but once outside her tree house I was impatient to be gone. There was no longer a candle-lighted way, but Fubbi put out her hand to clasp mine. Against my flesh hers felt dry and hard, as might a harsh strand of moss, but her fingers gripped mine tightly and drew me on.

Without that guiding I could not have made my way through the moss-grown forest. At last it thinned somewhat and there was dawn light about us. It began to rain, the drops soaking into the moss tangles. I saw in patches of earth and torn moss the markings of Renthan hooves and knew I was again on the trail.

As the trees dwindled to bushes and the light grew stronger I saw a tall cliff of very dark rock. It veined with a wide banding of red and was unlike any rock I had seen elsewhere. The trail led directly to it—into it. Yet there was no door-way there, not the faintest sign of any archway. Nothing save the trail led into the stone, over which my questing fingers slid in vain.

I could not believe it. Yet the stone would not yield to my pushing and the prints, now crumbling in the rain's beat, led to that spot.

Fubbi had drawn her hair about her cloakwise, and the moisture dripped from it, so she was protected from the downpour. She watched me and I thought there was a spark of amusement within her eyes.

"They went through," I said aloud; perhaps I wanted her to deny it. Instead she repeated my words with assured finality. "They went through."

"To where?"

"Who knows? A spell to blind, to bind. Ask of Loskeetha and mayhap she will show you her futures."

"Loskeetha? Who is Loskeetha?"

Fubbi pivoted, one of her thin arms protruded from her cloak of hair to point yet farther east. "Loskeetha of the Garden of Stones, the Reader of Sands. If she will read, then mayhap you shall know."

Having given me so faint a clue, she drew all of herself back into the mass of hair, and padded away at a brisk trot, into the brush—to be at one with that before I could halt her.

VIII

*T*he rain was fast washing away the tracks of those who had ridden into the wall. I hunched my shoulders under its drive and looked back at the moss forest. But all within me rebelled against retreat. To the east then. Where was this Loskeetha and her Garden of Rocks? Legend did not identify her for me.

I took the edge of the black and red wall for my guide and tramped on, already well wet by the rain. If any road led this way it was not discernible to my eyes. What grew here were no longer trees, or even grass and brush, such as I had seen elsewhere: but, instead, low plants with thick, fleshy cushions of leaves and stems in one. These were sharply thorned, as I found to my discomfort, when

I skidded on some rain-slicked mud and stumbled against one. They were yellow in color and a few had centermost stalks upstanding, on which clustered small flowers, now tight closed. Pallid insects sheltered under those leaves and I disliked what I saw of them.

To avoid contact with this foliage, I wove an in and out track, for they grew thicker and thicker—taller, too—until those center flower stalks overtopped my head. A winged thing with a serpentine neck and reptilian appearance, though it was clothed in drab brown feathers, dropped from the sky and hung upside down on one of those stalks, feasting on the insects it plucked with tapping darts of its narrow head. It paused for only an instant as I passed, showing no fear of me, but staring with small, black beads of eyes in curiosity.

I liked its looks no better than I did of the territory in which it hunted. There was something alien here—another warn-off territory such as the stone forest had been. Yet I did not sense that this was an ensorceled place, rather one unkindly to my species.

The rain dripped and ran, puddling about some of the fleshy plants. I saw tendrils like blades of grass reach out to lie in those puddles, swell, carrying back a burden of water they sucked up. It seemed to me the thick leaves swelled in turn, storing up that moisture.

I was hungry, but I was in no mind to stop and eat in that place. So I quickened pace, hoping to get beyond the growths. Then I came to an abrupt end of planting. It was as if I faced an invisible wall: here, were the plants; beyond, smooth sand. So vivid was that impression that I put out my hand to feel before me. But it met only empty air. The rain about me cut small rivulets in the ground. But— over that sand no rain fell; the sand was unmarked.

I turned my head from left to right. On one side was the cliff wall of black and red. South lay a stretch of the cushion plants. Ahead, to my right, was a line of rocks fitted together into a wall, and between that and the cliff was the smooth sand and no rain.

I hesitated about venturing out on that unmarked surface. There are treacherous stretches about the Fens of Tor which look to the eye as firm as any sea strand. But let a body rest upon them and it is swallowed.

Looking about me, I found a stone as large as my hand. That, I tossed out, to lie upon the sand some lengths ahead. The stone did not sink. But—more weight? My sword, together with its scabbard, was heavier. I hurled it ahead.

The sword lay where it had fallen. Then I noted the other peculiarity of this ground. Ordinary sand would have been soft enough to let that weight of leather and metal sink in a little. But not this. It was as if the surface, which looked to be fine sand, was indeed a hard one. I knelt and put a fingertip cautiously upon it. It felt as soft as it looked, close to powdery, in fact. But, for all the pressure I could put into that fingertip, I could not push it below the surface.

So, at least it could be walked upon. Yet the wall which guarded it to the south had been set there with purpose. Whether this was the domain of Loskeetha, I did not know. But it looked promising.

I had ventured onto the sand, and stepped out of the storm into an unnatural complete dryness, with but a single stride.

I belted on my sword. There was a sharp turn to the north just ahead; both the cliff and the wall which paralleled it angled so I could not see what lay beyond. The wall was rough rocks. They varied in size from large boulders at the base, to quite small stones atop. They had been fitted together cunningly and with such care that I do not believe I could have put the point of my knife into any of the cracks.

At that angle I turned, to find myself looking down into a basin. The wall did not descend, but ran on to enclose three sides of that hollow, while the cliff formed the fourth. Not too far ahead was a sharp drop from the level on which I stood to the bottom. What lay therein drew my eyes. It was floored with sand: this was of a blue shade. Out of it arose rocks, solitary and rough shaped. They were set in no pattern I could follow, but the sand about them had been marked with long curving lines in and around the rocks.

As I continued to look at it, I had an odd sensation. I no longer surveyed rocks set in sand. No, I hung high above an ocean which assaulted islands, and yet never conquered those outposts of land. Or—yes, now I looked down, as might a spirit in the clouds, upon mountains which towered high above a plain; but the plain which supported their roots was a misty nothing. . . .

This was a world, but I was mightier than it. I could stride from island to island, giant tall and strong, to cross a sea in steps. I was one who would use a mountain for a stepping stone . . . I was greater—taller, stronger—than a whole world. . . .

"Are you, man? Look and tell me—are you?"

Did it ring in my ears or my head, that question?

I looked upon the islands in the sea, the mountains on the plain. Yes, I was! I was! I could set my boots there and there. I could stoop and pluck land from out of the sea and hurl it elsewhere. I could crumble a mountain with my heel.

"You could destroy then, man. But tell me; could you build again?"

My hands moved and I looked from the mountains and the islands to them. My left one moved easily, fingers curling and uncurling. But the right with its scar ridge, its stiffened bones . . .

I was no godling to remake a world at my fancy. I was a man, one Kemoc Tregarth. And the madness passed from me. Then I looked at the rocks and the sand and this time I held to sanity and forced upon my mind the knowledge of what they were and what I was.

"You are no giant, no godling then?" The voice out of nowhere was amused.

"I am not!" That amusement stung.

"Remember that, man. Now, why come you to disturb my days?"

I searched that valley of rocks and sand, to see no one. Yet I knew I was not alone.

"You—you are Loskeetha?" I asked of the emptiness.

"That is one of my names. Through the years one picks up many names from friends and unfriends. Since you call me that, the Mosswives must have said it to you. But I repeat; man, why come you here?"

"The Mosswife Fubbi—she said you might aid me."

"Aid you? Why, man? What tie have you with me—kinship? Well, and who were your father and mother?"

I found myself answering the invisible one literally. "My father is Simon Tregarth, Warden of the Marches of Estcarp, my mother the Lady Jaelithe, once of the Wise Ones."

"Warrior-witch, then. But neither kin to me! So you cannot claim favor because of kinship. Now, do you claim it by treaty? What treaty have you made with me, man out of Estcarp?"

"None." Still I searched for the speaker and irritation grew in me that I must stand here being questioned by a voice.

"No kin, no treaty. What then, man? Are you a trader, perhaps? What treasure have you brought me that I may give you something in return?"

Only stubbornness kept me there as a voice hammered each point sharply home.

"I am no trader," I answered.

"No, just one who sees himself as a giant fit to rule worlds," came back in scornful amusement. "Welladay, since it had been long since any have sought me for advice, that is what you really want; is it not, man? Then perhaps I should give it free of any ties, to one who is not kin, nor ally, nor is ready to pay for it. Come down, man. But do not venture out on that sea, lest you find it more than it seems, and you, less than you imagine yourself to be."

I advanced along the edge of the drop and now saw that there were holds for hands and feet which would take me to the floor of the basin. In addition, below was a path of lighter-hued sand, hugging the wall, which could be followed without stepping onto the blue.

So I descended and went along that path. Its end was a cave which might have been a freak of nature, but she who had her being there had made use of it for her own purposes. Its entrance was a crack in the cliff wall.

I called it cave, though it was not truly that, for it was open far above to a sliver of sky. Then I faced the source of the voice.

Perhaps Loskeetha and the Mosswives had shared a common ancestor long ago. She was as small and withered looking as they, but she did not go cloaked in a growth of hair. Instead what scanty locks she had, and they were indeed thin and few, were pulled into a standing knot on top of her head. Held by a ring of smoothly polished green stone. Bracelets of the same were about her bony wrists and ankles. For her clothing she had a sleeveless robe of some stuff which resembled the blue sand, as if the sand indeed had been plastered on a pliable surface and belted about her.

Very old and very frail she looked, until you met her eyes. Those showed neither age nor weakness, but were alive with that fierce gleam one sees in the eyes of a hill hawk. They were as green as her stone ornaments and, I will always believe, saw farther and deeper than any human eyes.

"Greeting, man." She was seated on a rock and before her was a depression in the sand, as if it cupped a pool of water, that held blue sand like unto that about the rocks in the outer basin.

"I am Kemoc Tregarth," I said, for her calling me "man" seemed to make me, even in my own eyes, less than I was.

She laughed then, silently, her whole small, wizened body quivering with amusement.

"Kemoc Tregarth," she repeated, and to my surprise her hand rose to her head in a gesture copying a scout's salute. "Kemoc Tregarth who rides—or now walks—into danger as a proper hero should. Yet I fear, Kemoc Tregarth, that you shall now find you have gone well along a path which will prove to be your undoing."

"Why?" I demanded of her bluntly.

"Why? Well, because you must decide this and that. And if you make the wrong decision, then all you wish, all you have been, all you might have been, will come to naught."

"You prophesy darkly, lady—" I had begun when she drew herself more erect, and sent one of those disconcertingly piercing glances flashing out at me.

"Lady," she mimicked. "I am Loskeetha, since that is the name you have hailed me by. I need no titles of courtesy or honor. Mind your tongue, Kemoc Tregarth; you speak to such as you have not fronted before, witch-warrior son that you be."

"I meant no disrespect."

"One can excuse ignorance," she returned with an arrogance to match the arrogance of the Wise Ones when dealing with males. "Yes, I can prophesy, after a fashion. What would you of me, a telling of your future? That is a small thing for which to come such a wild way, for there is but one end for any man—"

"I want to find my sister." I cut through her word play. "I traced her to a rock wall and Fubbi said she passed within, or through that, and a blind spell was laid there."

Loskeetha blinked and put her hands together, the fingers of each reaching to touch the bracelet about the opposite wrist, turning those stone rings around and around.

"A blind spell? Now which of the Great Ones, or would-be Great Ones has been meddling on the boundaries of Loskeetha's land? Well, that much will be easy to discover."

Loosing her clasp on her bracelets, she spread her hands out over the hollow filled with blue sand. She moved them quickly, once up and then down, as if to fan the grains below. They puffed up in a fountain, cascading back into the cup. No longer did it lie smooth. There were raised ridges on the surface and they made a picture—that of a tower. It was not unlike those we built for watchpoints along the Estcarpian border, save it had no windows.

"So—" Loskeetha considered the picture. "The Dark Tower it is. Well, time moves when a small man tries to walk in boots too large for him." She leaned forward again as if some thought had suddenly struck her and in that thought there was some faint alarm.

Once more she spread her hands wide and the fountain of sand rose and fell. This time the grains did not form a tower, but rather a complicated symbol, like unto one of the coats of arms those of the Old Race used. But that it was no heraldic device I was also sure, for it carried a hint of the Mysteries.

Loskeetha stared at it, one of her fingers raised a little as if with its tip she traced the intricate weaving of line upon line.

She did not look at me, and she spoke sharply with none of the embroidery of speech she had used before: "This sister of yours, is she a Witch?"

"She was Witch-trained in Estcarp, but she did not take the final vow nor put on the Jewel. She has some powers—"

"Perhaps more than she has shown. Listen well, Kemoc Tregarth. There have long been those in this land who have tried for power and pulled to them rulership over forces which do not answer lightly. This desire is born into some men and eats upon them as a fever, so that they will throw to it, as one throws wood upon a fire, everything they deem will bring them what they wish. Some rose high in their knowledge in the old days; they rent this land, even carrying their struggles into places you cannot dream of, for the Great Ones have gone, still the wish to be as them comes to men—men who know a little, scraps of old learning, a fragment here and there. They strive to patch these together, to make a whole to center about them.

"There is a man in these hills who has gone far along such a seeking road—"

"Dinzil!" I interrupted her.

"If you know, why, then, do you ask?"

"Because I did not know. I only felt that he was—"

"Removed from mankind?" she interrupted in turn. "So, you were able to sense what lies in him. But you are no witch, Kemoc Tregarth. Whatever you are, or what you may be in time, you are not your sister. However, Dinzil saw in her a tool to open farther his long sought road. She was trained but not sworn, thus she was vulnerable to what influence he could lay about her. Through her he will seek—"

"But she would not willingly—" I protested, refusing to accept an alliance between Kaththea and one who played with unleashed power.

"Will can be swallowed up. If he cannot enlist her willingly, still he believes he can use her for his key. And she is in the Dark Tower, which is the heart of his secret world."

"Where I shall follow . . ."

"You have seen the working of one blind spell. How think you to follow?" she asked.

"Fubbi said—"

"Fubbi!" She threw up her hands. "I am Loskeetha and my magic is of only one kind. I can read the future—or futures."

"The futures . . . ?"

"Yes. There are many 'ifs' in any life. Walk this road and meet a beggar, throw him a coin, and he will steal behind you and use a knife between your ribs for what else you carry. But go another road and your life will run for some years more. Yes, we have a choice of futures, but we make such choices blindly—and know not sometimes the reason for or the worth of the choice we have made."

"So you can see the future. In that seeing could you also show me the Dark Tower and the way thereto?" I only half believed her then, though I was sure she entirely believed herself.

"You wish to see your futures? How may I say without looking whether the Dark Tower lies within them? But this warning I will give you, though it is not laid upon me to do so. To read the futures may weaken your resolve."

Now that I did *not* believe. I shook my head. "I go after Kaththea, to that end I do not weaken."

"Be it on your own head, then, warrior who is no witch."

She reached out swiftly and caught both my hands, pulling them toward her with a sharp jerk which also brought me to my knees across the basin of blue sand. Then, keeping a tight grasp with her fingers about my wrists, she moved those hands in certain gestures and the sand fountained to make a picture. This was not a flat, two-dimensional showing such as had lain there before. Now it was as if I looked down into a living landscape, far below and small, as it had been in the Garden of Stones.

I myself was therein and before me a tall dark tower without windows. As I went toward it the wall reached out and engulfed me, but still I could see what happened. Kaththea was there. I caught her up to take her with me, but as I turned I fronted—not Dinzil—but a menacing shadow. Kaththea twisted and broke my hold and I saw a stricken look upon my face. Then—then I saw myself cut down Kaththea before she could join with that shadow!

My sharp cry of horror and denial still rang in my ears when the sand foun-tained again. This time I was in the Valley, riding with men I knew, to my right was Kyllan. We faced not the strange rabble we had beaten back from the walls but a shadow host. In the midst of them rode Kaththea, her eyes a-glitter, her hands upheld. From those burst sullen flashes of red which brought death to members of our company.

Then I saw myself ride forward and swing my sword, to throw it as a lance. It spun through the air and its heavy hilt struck my sister's skull. She fell, to be trampled by those she rode among.

Once more the sand fountained and cleared. I stood before the Dark Tower and from it ran Kaththea and this time I knew that she was not one of the enemy, but fleeing from them. But I saw the darkness wreathe about me. Blinded, I thrust out as if I fought with what I could not see. Kaththea, running to me for protec-tion, was again cut down. Then the mist went and I was left alone to face my deed.

Loskeetha released my hands. "Three futures—yet the same ending. You see that, but—listen well to this—not the decisions upon which it is based. For each of those comes from other happenings."

I awoke from my daze. "You mean it is not the last act, not my strokes, that re-ally kill Kaththea, but other things done or undone, which lead to that point? If those are not done, or undone, then Kaththea will not—will not—"

"Die at your hands? Yes."

It was my turn to catch at her wrists. But under my fingers those smooth stone bracelets turned seemingly of their own accord to break my grip.

"Tell me! Tell me what to do?"

"That is not my magic. What I can see, that I have shown you."

"Three futures, and they all end so. Can there be a fourth—one in which all goes well?"

"You have choices; make the right ones. If fortune favors you—who knows? I have read sands for men in the past and one or two—but only one or two—defeated the fates shown them."

"And . . . suppose I do nothing at all?" I asked slowly.

"You can slay yourself with that blade you seem so ready to use upon your sis-ter. But I do not think you have so reached the end to all hope as to do that, not yet. But, save for that, you will still have choices to make in each moment's breath, and you cannot help the making of them. Now will you know which are wrong and which are right."

"I can do this much. I can stay away from the Valley and the Dark Tower. I can find a place in this wilderness and stay—"

"Decision—there is a decision," Loskeetha said promptly. "Every decision has a future. Who can guess how it will be twisted to lead you to the end you fear. But, I am wearied, Kemoc Tregarth. No more can I show you, so . . ."

She clapped her hands together and that sharp sound echoed and reechoed in my ears. I blinked and shivered in a sudden blast of cold. I was on a mountainside. Below me was the cliff of red and black. It was raining and the wind was rising, and it was close to night. Shaken, hungry, cold and wet, I wavered along. Then there was a dark pit to my right and I half stumbled, half fell into a shadow cave. I crouched there, dazed.

Had there been a Loskeetha at all? And what of the three futures she had shown me? Decisions, each putting thread into a pattern. If she had really shown me the truth, how could I defeat fortune to build a fourth future?

I fumbled in my supply bag and brought forth some crumbling journey cake, ate it bit by bit to fill the aching void in my middle. I had chosen to eat. I had chosen to take refuge in this cave; had either choice led me a single step closer to one of the three futures?

Two had come at the Dark Tower, one in the Valley. Could I believe that if I stayed away from both those sites I could stave off or change the future? But, I did not even know where lay the Dark Tower. Suppose I blundered along among these hills and came across it unawares? The one decision I thought I could be sure of was not to return to the Valley.

Yet Loskeetha said small things could alter all.

I folded my arms across my knees and buried my face upon them. Was Loskeetha right? Could Kaththea's only safety lie in my turning my sword against myself?

In two of those futures Kaththea had been one of the forces of evil. In the Valley she killed her friends. In the Dark Tower it was my life she threatened. In the third, she fled, while I was the one bewitched. In two out of three Kaththea was no longer my sister, but a dark one. Was I betraying all I loved best in Kaththea by trying to save her body?

Decisions! Loskeetha had said one man, two, had defeated the possible futures. But if one did not know which decision—

I rolled my head back and forth across my arms. My thoughts beat in my brain. What if Loskeetha was not what she seemed, but another of the defenses Dinzil set up to protect his back trail? I had seen hallucinations wrought by the Witches of Estcarp; I had been duped by them. Loskeetha could be such an illusion, or the scenes she showed me illusion. How could I be sure?

My head ached as I leaned back against the wall of the cave. Night and rain made a dismal curtain. Sleep . . . if I could sleep. Another decision—leading where? But sleep I must.

IX

*I*t was an ill sleep, haunted by fell dreams, so that I roused sweating. Yet, in spite of my efforts, I would sleep again, only to face more monstrous terrors. Whether those were born of my own imagination or the pall which lay over the cave land, I did not know. But when I awoke with an aching head, which spun when I moved, in the gray morn, I still had not made my big decision. Stay here, imprisoned by my own will, until life left me. Dare to go ahead, with belief in the rightness of my cause to arm me with courage against the futures Loskeetha had shown me. Which?

If there was evil abroad in Escore, then there was also good. I thought on that dully. But to what force could I appeal now to my arming?

There were Names from petitions made in Estcarp. But such appeals were very old and had lost their meaning for most men. We had come to look to our own strength and the backing of the Wise Women for our salvation.

I still wore a sword; I had skill in its use. I had my Borderer's knowledge of war. But to me at that moment these seemed as nothing at all. For what I would go up against now was not to be vanquished by steel. So, what had I left? Scraps of ancient wisdom culled at Lormt, but so tattered by the passing of ages as to be no shield.

And always in my mind were the three pictures Loskeetha had shown me.

There was no rain now. Neither were there any sun banners painting the highlands of the east, rather a sullen lowering of clouds. Under that gloom the stretch of land I could see from the cave was stark and lifeless. What vegetation grew there was twisted, misshapen, faded of color. There were many outcroppings of rock. These, if one looked at them carefully, had an unpleasant aspect. It was easy to picture here a leering face, there a menacing taloned paw, a mouth with gaping, fanged jaws. These appeared to slide about just under the surface of the stone. One moment they were there, the next they were gone again—to reappear a short distance away. I wrenched my eyes from that, closed them to the gray day and tried to think. The thoughts which raced through my mind were not clear. It was as if I were in a cage and darted here and there, only to always face restraining bars.

I heard a thin wailing, such as I had heard in the stone forest where I had found Kaththea's scarf. Kaththea's scarf—my hand went to the front of my jerkin; its silken softness was between my fingers.

Kaththea—Kaththea thrice dead, and always by my hand. Was Loskeetha's magic the true sight? Or, as a small, nibbling suspicion told me, was she one of the safeguards used to befog the enemy trail?

I ate more of my rations, sipped from my flask. There was very little water left in it now. A man may endure hunger longer than he can thirst. I did not know if I would have the fortitude to stay here until death sought me out.

Nor would my nature allow me to take that do-nothing path, though it might be the highest wisdom. There was in me too much of my father, and perhaps my mother, both of whom marched to meet danger, not await its coming.

At last I crawled stiffly from that hole and looked about. I remembered, or thought I did, the look of the land about the Dark Tower in those two scenes Loskeetha's sand had painted for me. Around me now I saw no resemblance to that land. Not too far away, I could hear running water.

Danger in food, in drink, that was Dahaun's warning. But perhaps if I were to mix this water with that still remaining in my flask the danger would be lessened. Decision. . . .

I kept my head turned from the walls; the menaces which grew and dissolved there were sharper. Being sure they were illusion, I wanted none of them, lest rational thinking be disrupted.

The wailing wind in the heights tormented my ears with a keening which I would take sword-oath on was the cries of those pushed to some great extremity of terror, calling upon me for aid. Some of them seemed to be voices I knew. But, I told myself, wind around rocks can produce strange sounds.

I drew to mind odd bits of old lore. Some were of the Sulcar. It was their belief that a man would not fall in any fight unless he heard his name called aloud while the battle clamor still rang. So I found myself listening for the wind to sound some long wailing "Keeemooc."

There had been those, such as Aidan from the outback of Estcarp (where men followed the old ways more closely), who carried talismen. He had once shown me a stone with a perfect round hole in it, saying such given to one, by a woman who cared deeply, was great protection against an ill. Aidan—I had not thought of him for years. Where was Aidan now? Had he survived the border raiding, returned to the maid who had put that stone in his hand that it would keep him safe for her?

The cut I followed turned downward, leading into a wider valley. Here was more vegetation, and the shallow waters of a river I had heard before the wind raised such a doleful lament. I looked at the water. Then, with the reflexes taught me by the border years, I dropped instantly into cover among the boulders.

Not even the wind could drown out the new cries, nor the clash of metal. There was a fierce battle going on near the water's edge, even into the stream itself where the water was splashed high by the fighters. The Krogan had been trapped in a stream too shallow for them to swim. There were three of them, two men and a woman. Around and about them, apparently fighting on their side, were several furred creatures. Their opponents were a mixed force. I saw men, mailed and dark cloaked, striking out with steel, at the cornered Krogan. Farther upstream a squad of Thas rolled stones, and hurled earth into the water, trying to cut off more of the flow which might aid the aquatic race.

I saw one of the Krogan, his spear sheared off, collapse under a flashing blade. Then they had no hope at all, for, from the brush on the other bank, a second contingent of the enemy came. They held not swords but wands or staves, from which came flashes, not unlike the energy whips of the Green People. Animal and Krogan alike, they went down before those.

One of the swordsmen waded out into the water, kicked here and there at the bodies which were awash. Then he caught the floating hair of the woman, jerked up her head so that her face was fully exposed.

Orsya!

Still keeping that painful hold upon her hair, the man pulled her limp body ashore, dragged her out upon the sand and gravel. Those who held the wands made no move to join their allies. I saw a gesture or two pass between the parties and the wand people melted back into the brush.

The Thas came stumping down stream, uttering guttural cries, to fall upon the bodies still in the water. I have seen much brutality in war. But this was of no human knowing, yet I dared not look aside for Orsya still lay there and . . .

I do not know if the Krogan were dead when they fell. But the Thas made sure that they and their furred companions would not rise again. Having fed their fury, and yet remaining unappeased, they came to where Orsya lay, the swordsmen standing about her. He who must be the Thas leader stretched out filthy claws to hook in her garment to draw her out to be ravaged by his pack.

But one of the swordsmen swung a blade warningly and those paws were jerked back, though the Thas chief set up a yammering which out-noised the wind, his ire plain to read.

Again that blade swung, in a wider circle, and the Thas retreated. He mouthed louder cries, spit and gnashed his teeth, spittle flying from his wide mouth to fleck the hair on his flailing arms, his protruding barrel of chest and paunch.

At some order from the leader of the swordsmen, two of his fellows advanced on the Thas. They were confident, arrogant, contemptuous, and the earth burrowers stood their ground only for a moment or two. Then, scurrying, they snatched at what lay staining the stream red, and, carrying burdens no one would wish to look upon, they retreated upstream. Still their leader walked backward, thumping his chest to add a hollow roll to his chittering cries.

I found my hand on sword hilt as I watched one of the swordsmen pick up the light body of the Krogan girl and drape her over his shoulder. Surely she was not dead.

My other hand was on the boulder, drawing me up. There were five of them. Let the Thas get well away . . . then follow downstream . . . watch for my chance and . . .

I could not move!

Oh, I could stand upon my feet, finger my sword hilt, turn my head to stare after those who had taken Orsya with them. Watch them go openly and without any searching of the ground around them, as men who walk their own safe territory. That I could do. But follow—no!

It was the curse Loskeetha had laid upon me, or the curse I had laid upon myself which held me there. For this was a major decision, not such a one as seeking water to drink, walking among haunted rocks, venturing forth from the cave slit. This meant throwing luck stones against fate. If I did take that trail, skulk along behind the swordsmen, try to free Orsya, then I could well be setting my feet on a road which would lead inevitably to Kaththea's blood on my sword.

I owed my life to Orsya. What I owed to Kaththea I cannot find words to say. I was torn; ah, what a tearing that was. But it kept me from following the party which had the Krogan girl. I leaned, weak as one who had taken a death blow, against the rock behind which I had taken shelter, and watched them go. I continued to stare thereafter at the empty river valley when they had passed from sight.

Then something of those bonds broke and I came down to the place of slaying. One of the animals still lay, torn and frightfully mangled, in the wash at the stream's edge, and there were other gruesome reminders of what had been done there. Without knowing why I stooped and picked up one of the broken Krogan spears. Water ran down its shaft and over my scarred hand and stiffened fingers. I watched it drip so, dully.

Loskeetha had said, no man knew what small decision would lead to a greater and more fatal one. How very right! I had made the decision to come forth from the cave, another to seek water, now I faced a third and larger. The one I had tried to avoid was one I would have named days earlier must be taken or remain a foresworn coward. A curse laid upon me—and a cursed man moved under a shadow.

The Krogan spear slipped through fingers which could not grip its smooth shaft tightly enough, and clattered on the stones.

They had taken Orsya with them and she was not dead, of that I was sure. They had not left her to the Thas, yet they meant her no mercy, I was also sure. I walked here, breathed, could touch that broken weapon, feel—because Orsya had willed to make a decision. It must not have been an easy one, for she had gone against the will of her people.

"But, Kaththea," I said aloud. I think I meant it as an appeal, though to whom, I did not know.

Somewhere before me lay the Dark Tower; I must accept that. I had a part to be played there.

One man—two—had broken the alternate futures.

I watched the water glide by, muddied from the half dam the Thas had thrown up, stained still from what it washed here from sand and stone. Then, as one might break through a wall and see freedom, even with danger to come, I broke the spell—if spell it had been which had fallen on me in Loskeetha's Garden. To breathe, walk, live, were decisions of sorts. I could never escape them. But I could make the ones my heart, mind and training demanded of me. Those I must do with the wisdom granted me. Therefore, I must set aside this fear and do as I would have done before Loskeetha set her sand to making pictures.

I owed a deep debt to Orsya and that I would repay. If the Dark Tower lay ahead, that I would also face when the time came, with what courage I could summon.

I came away from that river point more nearly a whole man and not one who looked ever over his shoulder for the hunter sniffing at his tracks.

Putting my scout craft to work I went again to the ridge on this side of the valley. It was very rough ground, and could not have been better designed for my purposes. I was surefooted enough to make speed from one place of concealment to another, hurrying to catch up with the party who had Orsya. My growing fear now was that they might have had mounts and those I could not overtake.

So spurred, I might have taken reckless chances, but one warning kept tugging at my thoughts. Though the Thas had seemed to withdraw, they had done so in anger. It might be that they, too, would dog the victors in that clash of wills and so be going in my direction. Thus, I not only watched downslope and ahead for those I tracked, but paused now and again, chaffing at the need, to scout behind. If the Thas did skulk there I did not sight them.

Eventually I did find those I followed. There were now four of them and in the van walked the one who carried Orsya. She was still a limp and apparently lifeless burden. Only the fact that they did see fit to take her, was an indication that she was alive.

The party which had used the flashing wands made me wary. Against such weapons my sword was no defense. I longed for one of the dart guns. Might as well long for a squad so armed, as well!

At least there were no signs of any mounts awaiting the party. Perhaps the fifth man had gone ahead to get them.

I used a convenient ridge and ran at the best speed I could dare to use over rough ground. That burst, when I peered down again, had brought me almost level with the party and their prisoner. They had come to a halt. The leader allowed Orsya to fall to the ground with callous disregard. She sprawled on a patch of grass just as she landed. But the men went a step or two beyond and dropped down, to sit at their ease, apparently to wait.

It was still a dark and cloudy day. The brush and trees along the river could afford a number of lurking places. But to reach those I would have to retreat and cross higher up. I hesitated, fearing to lose sight of the quarry lest mounts would be brought and they would go.

Four men . . . But with only a sword and the resulting need for hand-to-hand combat, I could not hope to win against such odds. Small use would I be then to either Orsya or Kaththea.

Yet the river drew me. Looking at the currents I thought that it ran deeper here. If Orsya could be aroused, escape into it, she might have a chance. For she would have the advantage of being in an element more at home to her than to the enemy.

Sitting here answered no problems. I was driven by the need for action. One of the swordsmen had opened a bag, and passed rations to his comrades.

I slipped off my small shoulder pack. The cloak blanket which made its cover caught my eyes. Against this barren, gray-brown land, the soft green of the Valley's favorite coloring was very noticeable. I shook it free. Then I looked to the rocks above me. Could a man seem to be in two places?

With the cloak rolled again in a wad against my chest, I climbed up between two rocks. The wind . . . in so much was the wind favoring me.

I hacked at shrubs and broke off a mass of thick twigged branches, pushing these into the cloak and fastening it about the bundle as best I could with its throat buckle and the latches from my jerkin. At close sight it could not possibly deceive any one . . . but, perhaps, just at a distance with the further embellishment I could give it. Pushing and pulling I set that unwieldy package up between the rocks. I dared not wedge it too tightly lest it not give way when I wanted. My cord, a length hastily knotted of grass, would it hold at all?

Now I crawled downhill, gentling that grass thread behind me, fearing any moment to have it break apart in my hand. By some smile of fortune it did not. I measured with my eye the space of open ground between me and my goal. Given a stouter cord, a few other things I did *not* have, my chances would have doubled to perhaps fifty out of a hundred. But I had to be content with far less.

I opened my mouth. It had been years since I had tried this, in the days before I had taken my maiming wound. I had had no chance to practice.

Then I screamed. The sound came not from where I crouched, but from the spot where my stuffed cloak perched. So—I had not lost my skill at voice throwing! Once more I screeched, and the results were even better than I had dared to hope, since some echoing trick multipled and reinforced that cry until it appeared to come from more than one throat. I jerked my grass cord. It broke and the loose end came flying at me.

Only the strength of that jerk had been enough. The blob of green leaned, went toppling, to fall out of sight. I watched those below.

They were on their feet, weapons out, staring. Then the leader and another started for that spot where the cloak bundle had disappeared. The two remaining behind stepped closer together, their attention fixed on the heights, peering at the rocks there.

Now I snaked from one piece of cover to the next, using every bit of skill

I possessed. Once more I measured by eye. If I could continue to escape their notice for only a moment, to catch up Orsya. We would have a chance, thin, but still a chance, to get into the underbrush. This was the moment for my final move—

Once more I readied my lips. No scream this time, rather a sound like some unintelligible command, and it came from uphill beyond the two guards.

I was out and running. On sod my boots made no sound. But they turned and saw me. One shouted; both came on with bared weapons. I whirled my supply bag around my head and let it fly at the one farther away, then parried the leaping attack of the other, expecting at any moment to face two points at once. When the second did not come I concentrated upon the first.

He was good enough as a fighter, and he had the advantage of wearing mail. But he had not been schooled by the equal of Otkell, a Sulcar Marine, to whom there are no equals in tricky swordplay, since they learn to fight on board a heaving deck where skill is in high need.

Thus he took my point between his chin and the rise of his mail coat, for his helm had no evil of linked steel such as we wore in Estcarp. The fact that I fought left-handed had, I think, disconcerted him more than a little.

I looked for his fellow and saw that he lay prone a little farther off, not stirring. That my hastily thrown supply bag had done that, I could hardly believe. But I was in no mind to investigate. I caught up Orsya and crashed back into the bush, heading for the river. Behind me I heard cries; those who had gone upslope must be fast coming down again.

When I reached the bank I saw that my guess about the deeper water here had been right. There were no stones standing half dry in the sun, and the water was murky so I could not see the bottom. I took a deep breath and dived, bearing Orsya with me, hoping her gills would work automatically as we entered.

We were below surface in one great splash and I pulled her along to where a drift log plowed its butt into the bank. Under the bole of that we had a momentary hiding place. My hand was on her breast and I could feel the beating of her heart. I tucked her back with one hand and had to surface again, gasp for air. Then I saw a crevice between two waterlogged roots.

Moving about, I got into position, that crevice affording me a scrap of breathing room. My arms were locked about Orsya to keep her from drifting away with the pull of the water, the tree protecting us both above.

I could not see the bank, nor if they had tracked us here. For all I knew they might be waiting up there, ready to take us when those shallow gulps of air, all I could get, would not be enough.

Blind in a way, deaf also, I dared then to use the sense which in this land could be an invitation to disaster. I aimed mind touch at the Krogan girl.

"Orsya!"

There was no answer.

I strengthened that cry, though I was well aware that those who hunted us might well have the ability to track us so.

"Orsya!"

A flicker! Such a weak, trembling, flicker. But enough to make me try for the third time.

"Orsya!"

Fear—fear and hate! Blasting out along the touch with which I had reached her. My arm had just time to tighten about her firmly or she would have fought out of my hold.

"Orsya!" Not a summons now but a demand for her recognition.

It came quicker than I dared hope for. Her convulsive struggles stopped.

"What—what—?"

"Be still!" I put into that all the authority I could summon.

"We are hiding in the river. They search for us above."

I felt her thought groping, weakly, slowly, as if whatever had rendered her helpless for capture had slowed and deadened her mental processes.

"You are Kemoc. . . ."

"Yes."

"They trailed me, to take me back." She still thought in that slow, weakened fashion. "They found out—"

"That you freed me? What were they taking you back for—judgment?"

"No, I had already been judged, even though I was not there to answer. I think they meant to give me in place of you."

"Your own people!"

She was communicating more strongly now, with some of her old, firm flow. "Fear is a great governor of minds, Kemoc. I do not know what arguments the enemy may have used. There are very bad things which can be done by them."

"If the Krogan meant to give you up, then why—"

"Why were Orfons and Obbo attacked? I do not know. Mayhap the Sarn Riders are not of the same mind as those with whom Orias treated. This has always been so, Kemoc; such alliances do not hold long among those of the Shadow. An ally one day is a rival the next."

"These Sarn Riders, who are they?"

"A force which holds these hills. It is said they follow one of the Great Ones who has not altogether withdrawn from this world, and that their captains take orders from a strange mouth. Wait . . ."

Now it was she who ordered, and I who lay silent. I could breathe through my tiny root niche, but I was still blind. I could feel her body against mine and it was rigid with sudden tension.

X

*T*o wait blind the coming of danger is to await the full of a war ax when one stands a captive with bound hands. Orsya's mind touch was shut off. I thought she used that skill elsewhere, questing for danger, but of that I was not sure. It was all I could do to lie there.

Water splashed, washing me dangerously back and forth in my shallow hiding place. I gasped and choked as it filled my nose unexpectedly. This was no normal rippling of the river. How soon would their steel stab to spit us?

Orsya's hands fastened on my forearm. Her nails bit into my flesh. I read it as a warning. But still she did not use mind touch. Minutes drew hour long; those threatening waves subsided.

Tentatively my companion made contact: "They are gone, for now. But they will not give up the search."

"Dare we move?" I did not know how she could be so sure, but that she was, I accepted.

"You cannot take to the river deeps."

"But you can! Go, then. I am a scout and can easily throw off these bush-beaters." I tried to make my answer as certain as hers.

"The deeps lie downriver, they know that, and will be waiting."

"The Thas have left a half-dam above. There are no deeps to hide in there," I counterwarned. "Will you not have a better chance down than up?"

"You forget—my people also hunt me. Safety only lies where they do not go, where I was heading when they caught me."

"Where?"

"The river is shallow for a space, where the Thas and the Sarn forced us to a stand, but higher still it narrows and deepens again. Then it takes to underground ways. Wherever waters run the Krogan may go. I do not think the Sarn will follow that way, and while Thas lurk in burrows, still there are places they do not like." She hesitated. "I have found an old, old way, one made by those before us. There is a spell-laying there, but thin and tattered by the years, so if one is of strong will, one may penetrate it. But to sniff such will send a Thas squealing in flight, for it is a man spell, not one laid in their earth magic, but sealed with fire and air. Nor will the Sarn come, even if they find the gate, because it is guarded by one of the words of power. Of all that lies within I have no knowledge, save that such as we are not forbidden entrance. It will shelter us for a space."

"Yet upstream and past shallows," I reminded her. Though she offered me this shelter freely, yet I had Kaththea to think about now.

"It lies in the direction of the Dark Tower." Her simple answer to my thoughts at first did not make sense. Then I flinched.

"Why do you fear that?" Orsya's curiosity was as plain to me as my flare of fear must have been to her.

I told her, then, of Loskeetha and her sand reading, and of the three fates she had seen for the ending of my quest.

"Yet I believe that you cannot take any other path," Orsya replied. "The Dark Tower draws you as if it is a pull-spell. For it is not in you to turn your back upon her whom you seek, not even if you believe such a desertion may save you both. You are too close-knit, one to the other. You shall see the Dark Tower, but thereafter the fate may not lie in Loskeetha's reading at all. I have heard of her Garden of Stone and whispers concerning her sorcery. But in this land nothing is fixed and certain. For long ago all balances were set swinging this way and that. We can live but one day from dawn to sunset, one night from twilight to first dawn, and what lies ahead can change many times before we reach it."

"But Loskeetha said—decisions—the smallest decisions—"

"One has to make choices and abide by them. I know this much; any road to the Dark Tower is guarded, not only by things seen, but those unseen. I can offer you one path I believe that Dinzil and his men do not know."

There was logic in her saying. If that were the heart of Dinzil's holding, he would treat it to every defense. I could do much worse than accept her offer and go with the river. There would be trouble enough along that watery road to make a man keep his wits sharp, his eyes ever on watch.

We pulled out from under the drift refuge and, for as long as we could, we swam. If the enemy hunted, it was downstream. Orsya took the lead, using each promising overhang of bank, each large boulder or half submerged piece of drift for concealment from which to spy out clear passage beyond. We saw pronghorns come to the water to drink, and that was heartening. For those timid grazers would not seek the open if any men were about.

Finally the water grew too shallow and we must wade instead of swim. It was then that we came to the bloodstained place where Orsya's people had been attacked. Now it was twilight, gloom thickening into night. I was glad that she could not see, or did not seem to see, those stains and the carcass of the animal.

Night brought no halt as far as my companion was concerned. I was amazed at her energy, for I had thought that her hard usage at the hands of her captors would have left her weakened and not able to keep to such a steady pace.

We were well past the half dam that the Thas had made, and thereafter I tried to make my ears serve me, since my eyes could not penetrate the shadows. Now we went hand in hand to keep in touch. I heard sounds in plenty and some of them made me tense, since I could not believe they were of the normal night. But they drew no closer to where we crouched listening, and then we would venture on.

Orsya's prediction was right; the stream began to narrow and the waters arose to our middles. Here and there trails of phosphorescence in the form of bubbles spun in lines.

My companion might be tireless, but I was not. Though I did not like to admit my weakness, I began to believe there was a limit to the number of steps I could continue to take. Perhaps she read my mind; perhaps she was willing to admit that she was also not a thing forged from metal, such as the machines the Kolder used to do their bidding in the old days, but knew the fatigues and aches of flesh and bone.

Her grasp upon my hand brought us into a burrow, such as the one in which we had sheltered on our way back to the Valley. It had not been recently used, for there was no animal taint in it. It was barely large enough for both of us to crowd in very close together.

"Rest now," she told me. "There is still a long way upstream and I cannot mark my guide points in the night."

I had not thought I could sleep, but I did. Unlike the night before, my dreams were not haunted, nor could I remember dreaming at all. But I awoke hungry and thirsty. The last of my supplies had gone with the bag I had used as a weapon, and since that happening, now a day away, we had been so constantly on the move, I had forgotten food. Dahaun's warning would have to be disregarded now.

So close together had we slept that I could not alter position now without waking my burrow mate. She murmured sleepily as I slipped away, my gnawing hunger demanding that I do something about filling that far too empty middle.

I caught Orsya's thought. "What comes?"

"Nothing that I know. But we must have food."

"Surely." With far more ease she joined me in the river. The cliffs held away the direct rays of the rising sun, but the sky was light enough to let me believe the day would be a fair one.

"Ah." My companion waded along the shore. Then, as suddenly as if she had been seized by the ankles and pulled under, she was gone! I splashed after her, not knowing what I might find. Though I ducked where she had disappeared and tried to grope about with my hands I could not locate her. But I heard a soft laugh.

Orsya stood upright again, her hands busy stripping long brown stalks from a root. Those gone, she rubbed the root vigorously between her palms, and its covering came away, so what she finally held was an ovule of ivory white.

"Eat!" She held it out with no invitation but an order.

"Dahaun said—" I held that root, looking at it hesitatingly, but hungry.

"Well enough." Orsya nodded. "Yes, there is that to be found in these lands where the Shadow has long hovered, which will kill, or will-bind, or take away memory, even the mind. But this is no be-spelled trap but a clean offering of the earth and water. You may eat of it as freely as of anything in the Valley."

So encouraged, I bit into the root. It broke crisply under my teeth and it had a clean, slightly sweet taste. Orsya dived again but was back before I had chewed and swallowed the last of my root, having found it not only pleasant to taste, but that it had juice which quenched my thirst.

She peeled another and gave it to me, before she prepared two more for herself. The banks here were steeper and higher, the water steadily rising. We finished the last of our breakfast and then began to swim.

In this I was no match for Orsya, nor did I try to keep level with her, but conserved my strength, content to hold her in sight. Lucikly she paused to tread water now and then, looking about her for those guide marks she had mentioned the night before.

Once she motioned me toward the bank with a sharp gesture and on reaching me, gave a sharp jerk to my shoulder, ordering me to hold my breath. We went below surface.

"A Rus watcher on the heights," her thought explained. "They are keen-eyed, but water distorts all which lies within it. If the Rus drops no lower, I do not think we need fear."

A moment later her hold on me relaxed and I was able to break surface. But we kept close to the right-hand bank. This seemed to me as wild and desolate country as that which held Loskeetha's domain, even if it lacked the growth of strange fleshy-leaved plants, and our road was a waterway instead of rock.

Down the walls of the river banks looped vines, some thread-fine, others as thick as my wrist. Orsya's warning to me to avoid them was not needed, for they were so loathsome looking that no one could believe any virtue existed in them at all. They were a very pallid green with a sickly oversheen, as if they were wrought of some living rot. From them came such a stench of decay as to make one choke, dare he draw a heavy breath near them. I noticed that, though they tendriled down from above, as if seeking water, yet those strands which had touched the river surface were withered into thin skeletons. The more wholesome water must have killed them.

Things lived among those vines, though none of them did I ever see clearly. They moved in fluttering runs under the leaves, the shaking of the foliage marking their progress, but did not come into the light and air. Nor had I any desire that they do so.

"Ah, not far now." Orsya's thought carried a feeling of relief.

She treaded water where the river bank made an outward curve. The vines were less thick here and out of their noxious wreathing protruded a weatherworn lump. But was it a lump of rock? I reached Orsya and peered up in a more detailed examination.

Not a rock—some hand had worked there for a purpose. It had been, I thought, meant to be a head. But whether of man or animal, monster or spirit, no one now could say. There were two deep pits for eyes, and to see them from below as I did (the head being inclined so it looked down while we stared up) gave one a disturbing sensation that, from those holes, something still did measure all below.

"A watcher, not of our time, and one we need not fear, whatever once may have been its purpose. Now—" She swam but a short space on before she turned to me again.

"For a Krogan this would be no task, Kemoc. But for you . . ." She was plainly doubtful. "We must enter here under water, and for a space beyond remain so. I do not know how well equipped you may be for such a venture."

I flushed; it was plain she considered me the weaker party, one she must tend. Though logic told me that in the waterways she had the right of it, still my emotions could not be altogether governed by logic.

"Let us go!" I breathed deeply several times, expelling all I could from my lungs and refilling them. Orsya bobbed below, to search out that hidden entrance and see if it was still open. Now she reappeared just before me.

"Are you ready?"

"As I ever shall be."

I took the last breath and dived. Orsya's hand on my shoulder pointed me forward into darkness. I swam with what speed I could muster, my lungs bursting, the need for reaching the upper air so great it filled my world. Then I could stand it no longer and headed up. My shoulder, the back of my head, struck against solid rock. I kicked, sending my body on, felt my arm scrape painfully, and then—my head broke water, and I could breathe again!

But I was in utter darkness. And, as soon as my first gasps of relief were ended, I felt a rising unease. There was nothing but water about me, and the dark, pressing in thick and stifling in spite of the chill cold.

"Kemoc!"

"Here!" By so much had that terrible feeling of isolation and loss been broken.

Fingers scraped my upper arm and I knew she was close beside me. Her words pushed aside the dark and made this all a part of a real—if different—world again.

"This is a passage. Find a wall and use it for your guide," Orsya told me. "There are no more underground waterways—at least now as far as I was, when I first came here."

I splashed about until my outstretched fingertips touched rock.

"How did you come here—and why?"

"As you know, we communicate with other water dwellers. A Merfay told me of this and showed me the opening below. He came hither to hunt quasfi; there is a great colony who have taken shell rooting in here. A stream washes down and brings with it such food as the quasfi relish and these have grown to an unusual size. Since I have a liking for strange places I came to see, and found that I was not the first who was not Merfay or quasfi who traveled herein."

"What did you find, then?

"I leave that for you to see for yourself."

"You *can* see it? This dark is not everywhere?"

Again I heard her soft laughter. "There is more than one kind of candle, Kemoc from overmountain. There are even those suited to a place such as this."

But still a dark passage held us as we swam on. Then I became aware that the dark was not quite so thick beyond and that the graying gradually increased. It was not as bright as any torch or lamp, but compared to what we had come from, it was as passing from midnight to dawn.

Then we were out of the tunnel into a space so large, and yet so dim, that I could only guess at its size. A hollow mountain might have held it. The light was not diffused throughout, but spread in patches of radiance from underwater, approaching a short stretch of pebbled beach not too far away.

I swam for the beach. It presented to me such a promise of safety as I had not thought to find. As I waded out on it I saw that the light came from partly open shells which were in great clusters, rooted to the rocks under the surface.

"Quasfi," Orsya identified them. "To be relished not only by Merfays; but the deeper dwellers are more tasty."

She left in a dive which took her out of my sight. I stood dripping on that small patch of dry land and tried to learn more of this cavern. I could detect no sign of any intelligent remains here. Whatever Orsya promised to show me did not lie within my present range of vision.

The Krogan girl came out of the water, her hair plastered tight to her skull, her clothing as another skin on her body. She had a net bag in one hand—I was reminded of how she had carried one during our flight to the mountains—and from the bag glowed the light of the shellfish. But as she left the water it faded and by the time she joined me was almost gone.

In a very practical way she opened the shells with a knife she borrowed from me. A quick jab dispatched the creatures, and she offered one to me, its own outer covering serving as a plate.

Long ago I had learned that it was not good to be squeamish in such matters. When one was hungry, one ate, whatever one was lucky enough to find. The life of a Border scout did not provide dainty food, any more than it provides warm, soft beds, and uninterrupted sleep.

I ate. The meat was tough and one needed to chew it vigorously. The flavor was strange, not as satisfying as the taste of the roots. But neither was it too unpleasant, and looking at the wealth of quasfi beds about us, one could see starvation was no menace.

Orsya did not throw away the shells we emptied, but put them once more into her net, setting them therein with care, their inner surfaces pointing outward, small stones in the middle to keep them so. Having twisted, turned and repacked, she stood up.

"Are you ready?"

"Where do we go now?"

"Over there." She pointed, but now I could not say whether our direction led north or south, east or west.

Orsya waded into the water, having carefully made fast the net bag to her belt. As I followed more slowly I saw that once the bag dipped below the surface, it began to give out ghostly light as if the water had ignited the shells.

We headed away from the beach. There were fewer of the quasfi beds now, more dark patches. But under us the bottom was shelving and shortly thereafter we waded, water waist-high. I judged, since I saw cavern walls looming out into the half gloom, that we were now in a rift, leading back into the cliffs.

As the water fell to our knees, Orsya unhooked the bag from her belt and dragged it along at the end of one of its tie cords, being careful to let it go under the surface so its light continued.

The rift widened out again. Once more I saw the glimmer of living quasfi beds. But—I stopped short, straining.

Here were no rocky beaches providing the shellfish with housing space. Instead, they rooted on platforms on which towered, above the waterline, carved figures. These were set in two lines leading from where we stood to a bulk I could only half discern in the limited light.

Water lapped around their feet and lines of dead quasfi, their shells still cemented fast, strung about them, thigh-high, suggesting that in another time the statues had been even further submerged.

They were human of body, although some of the figures were so muffled in cloaks or long robes that their forms could only be guessed at.

Yes, human of body—but they had no faces! The heads set on those shoulders were blank of any carving, being only oval balls, though in each oval were deep eyepits, such eyepits as had marked the carving on the cliff outside.

"Come!" Still trailing her shell bag, Orsya moved forward down the avenue between those standing figures. She did not glance at them as she passed, but headed straight for the dark mass ahead.

But I had an odd feeling as I followed her that through each set of those eyepits, we were watched, remotely, detachedly, but still watched.

I stumbled, caught my balance and knew my feet were on underwater steps, which led up out of the flood. Before us was a wide platform and on it a building. So poor was the light that I could not be sure of its size. Darker gaps in its walls suggested windows and doors, but to explore it without proper lighting was folly. I said as much to Orsya. It was well out of the water and her quasfi shell lamp would not serve us here.

"No," she agreed, "but wait and see."

We stepped together from the top of that stair onto the platform. Once more I halted with a gasp of amazement.

Because, as our feet touched pavement, there came a glow from it, thin, hardly better than the radiance from the shells, but enough to make us sure of our footing.

"It is some magic of this place," Orsya told me. "Stoop—place your hands upon the stone."

I did as she bade, as she herself was doing. From the point where my flesh touched that stone (or was it stone?—the surface texture did not feel like it) light gleamed forth even brighter.

"Take off your boots!" She was hopping on one foot, pulling off her own tight foot covering. "It seems to kindle greater from the touch of skin upon it."

I was reluctant to follow her example, but when she went on confidently and then looked back in some surprise, I pulled off my light boots to carry them in one hand. She was right; as our bare feet crossed that smooth surface, the glow heightened, until we could really see something of the dark structure before us.

There were no panes in those windows; the doorway was a wide open portal. I wished that I had the sword I had dropped back by the river. Orsya had returned my knife to me and there was a good eight inches of well-tried blade, but in such a place imagination is quick to paint perils which could not be faced by so small a weapon.

I saw no carvings, no embellishments about the doorpost, nothing to break the severe look of the walls, save the stark openings of the windows. But, as we ventured inside, the light which followed the pacing of our feet, flared up to twice the brilliance. The room in which we stood was bare. Fronting us was a long wall, and set into that were ten openings. They had doors shut tight, nor could I see any latch, any way of opening them. Orsya crossed to the one directly facing us and put her hand against it, to find it immovable.

"I did not come so far before," she said. "There was an old warn-spell then— today it was gone."

"A warn-spell!" I was angered at the danger into which she had brought us. "And we come here without weapons—"

"A warn-spell very old," she returned. "It was one which answered to our protective words, not to *theirs*."

I must accept her explanation. But there was one way to test it. From left to right I looked along that row of closed doors. Then I spoke two *words* I had learned in Lormt.

XI

*T*hey were not Great Words, such as I had used when the power had *answered* me, but they would test and protect the tester.

As they echoed along that narrow room where we stood, the light under our feet blazed so high my eyes were dazzled for a moment and I heard Orsya cry out softly. Then followed on the roll of those *words* a crackling, a splintering, low and far off thunder. And in that new light I saw the door to which my companion had set her hands was now riven, falling apart in flakes. Orsya leaped back as they struck and crumbled into powdery debris.

Only that one door had been so affected. It was as if Orsya's touch had channeled whatever power the words had into striking there. I thought, though I could not be sure, for it all happened so quickly, that the breakage had come from the very point where her fingers rested.

Now came an *answer*—not such a one as had before, but a kind of chanting. It was quickly ended, and of it I understood not a word.

"What . . .?"

Orsya shook her head. "I do not know, though it is very old. Some of the sounds—" She shook her head again. "No, I do not know. It was a guard set, I believe, to answer such a coming as ours. What was opened to us, we need not now fear."

I did not share her certainty about that. I would have held her back as she went confidently through that door, but I was too far from her and she eluded my grasp easily. There was nothing left to do but follow.

The light enveloped us with a cloud of radiance, and was reflected by a blaze of glitter.

This was a square room, in its center a two-step dais on which stood a high-backed, wide-armed chair: the chair had an occupant. Memory stirred in me. That tale of how my father and Koris and the other survivors of shipwreck had found, high in a Karsten cliff, the hollowed tomb of the legended Volt, who had been seated so in a chair, his great ax across his knees. Koris had dared to claim that ax. After his taking of it, the remains of Volt had vanished into dust, as if he had waited only for the coming of some warrior bold enough, strong enough to wield a weapon which was forged not for human hands but for one deemed a half-god.

But this was no time-dried body which faced us. What it was I could not say, for I could not see it. A blue light veiled what rested in that chair so one was aware only of a form somewhere within. But it was not alive. This I knew was a tomb, even as Volt's rock hole had been.

One could have no fear, no feeling of morbidity about that mist in the chair. Rather there was a kind of welcome . . . I was startled when my thoughts read my feelings so.

"Who . . .?" Orsya took another step forward, a second, a third; now she was very close to the foot of the dais, staring up at that column of mist.

"Someone," the words came out of nowhere into my mind, surely Orsya had not sent them, "who means us no harm."

About the dais were piled small chests. Some of these had rotted and burst. From them trickled such treasures as I had never seen gathered in one place before. But my eyes came quickly to the first step where there lay by itself, very plain in that light, a sword.

My hand went out of itself, fingers flexing, reaching for the hilt. The blade did not have the blue cast of fine steel, but rather a golden glow—or perhaps that was only the reflection of the light in the room. Its hilt appeared to be cut from a single piece of yellow quartz in which small sparks of red, gold, and blue like unto the mist flashed, died, and flashed again. It was slightly longer, I thought, than the weapons I knew. But it showed no signs of any eating by time.

I wanted it more than anything I had ever wanted in my life before. That desire was as sharp in me as physical hunger, as the need for drink in a desert.

Had Koris felt this when he looked upon Volt's ax? If he had I did not wonder that he set hand to it. But Volt had not denied him in that taking. Would I—did I dare—to do the same here?

To rob the dead—that is a dire thing. Yet Koris had asked of Volt his ax and taken it, and thereafter wrought great things for his chosen people, using that weapon.

To take up a dead man's sword, that was to take to one a measure of him who had first carried it. The Sulcar believed that in the heat of battle a man using a dead man's sword can be possessed by the ghost, inspired either to such deeds as he would not dare alone, or driven to his fate if the ghost proved vengeful and jealous. Yet still Sulcarmen have been known to plunder tombs for none other than swords of story and fame: not in Estcarp, but in the northlands where once they had their home ports before they made their alliance with the Wise Women. They sang sagas of the deeds of such men and such swords.

I tried to fight that eating desire to take into my hand that hilt of gold. But there are some hungers which are greater than any reason, even for such as I who have tried all my life to put thought before action. And this time temptation won.

So I brushed past Orsya and went down on one knee. But the hand I put out to clasp that hilt was not the left, rather the maimed right: It went so naturally. Those fingers which could still move closed about the half. Yet, even as they did, for the last time prudence warned. I broke that queer eyelock which riveted my attention to the sword, looked up into the blue mist.

Within it was a core, a dim seen figure; that it did exist there was all of which I was sure. Koris had taken Volt's ax, but boldly, as a gift, not as one who plundered. Could I do less here and now?

I drew back my hand, though it was hard to break that hold, as if my fingers, against my will, decided to keep what they had grasped. Though I did not rise to my feet, I spoke aloud to what the mist cloaked.

"I am Kemoc Tregarth out of Estcarp, overmountain. I seek that which has been unlawfully taken; I have lost my sword in honorable battle. Do I go forth from here empty-handed, then already is my cause part lost. I claim no hero's name nor fame. But I can say these words and not be blasted—"

Those *words* from Lormt, which had opened to us this doorway, once again I spoke. But this time in no challenge or as a war cry, but rather as identification, so that this throne and its occupant, would know that I was not of the Shadow, but of those who raised shield against the Dark.

I do not know what I expected to follow my speaking. Anything might happen. That which sat within the blue might rise and welcome me, or strike me down. But there was nothing, no blaze of heightened radiance, not even an echo.

So I felt a little foolish. But not so much so that I did not hesitate to raise the hand, which had been curved about the hilt, to he or she who sat above, in the same salute I would have given a war leader.

Then I picked up the sword. It was not time marked. No rust pits marred its surface. Its point and edge were as sharp and clean as a man might wish. Again my scarred and stiffened hand closed about the hilt with an ease I had not known since the healing of that old wound.

I got to my feet and fumbled in my jerkin to bring out the scarf, now wet and like a string. This I looped to make an improvised baldric, since it would not fit into the empty scabbard at my belt.

"You have done what must be done." For the first time in long minutes Orsya's thoughts reached me. "We do not see the patterns woven by the Great Ones, only a thread now and then which belongs to us. You have taken on you more than a sword; may the bearing of both be not too heavy a burden."

I wondered if her people shared the Sulcar beliefs concerning dead men's weapons. But the blade did not seem heavy. Instead, handling it was fired with a sense of impatience new to me, a desire to push on, to hurry about my self-appointed task.

Already I had turned to the door. But Orsya did not follow me. Surprised, I glanced back. She was slowly circling the throne and the misty figure, surveying the moldering treasure boxes. Had she been emboldened by my appropriation of the sword to go hunting on her own? I would have protested but had a second thought. Orsya must do as she believed best, with no right of mine to question.

She was behind the throne now, and she lingered there. When she came forth she carried in her hand a short rod. It was cone shaped, rising to a sharp point at the tip she held upright, and it was not smooth, but ridged with corrugations which spiraled along its full length. In color it was ivory-white, and, when she moved her hand, I thought I saw a spark of white light or fire dance for a second on its point.

It was not long enough, nor shaped to suggest a weapon. Nor was it bejeweled, set into any precious base. What it was, or its purpose, I could not guess. But Orsya held it carefully as if it were to her as meaningful as the sword to me. Now she faced the misty figure. She did not kneel as I had to take the sword and make my half plea. She spoke—not by mind touch—in that curiously toneless audible speech of her people.

"I am Orsya of the Krogan, though they no longer own me as daughter or friend. I am one fit to hold what I have taken from its casket. Powers I have, if not great ones, and weapons I have, if they are not forged by fire out of molten metal. This I take because I know it for what it is, and what it may do, and because I am what I am, and I go where I go."

She lifted the cone-rod, holding it out between her and the shrouded one. This time it was no spark which showed at the tip, but a darting streak of white fire. Then she turned and came quickly to join me.

We did not speak as we went back to the platform outside, to look back along the road we had come, past those faceless statues with their holes for eyes. I was about to retrace our path, when Orsya stopped me with uplifted hand. Her head was forward a little, turning slowly from side to side, her nostrils expanded as if she were testing for some scent. But all I could sniff was that odd smell which hung about all these water-logged caverns. It was plain she was alerted by something I could not detect.

"What . . .?" I asked in a half-whisper.

"Thas," she replied in a sound as muted, "and something else."

I unslung the sword I had taken. Underground was the Thas' home. I and perhaps Orsya, would be at as great a disadvantage as I was underwater. I tried to pick up any scent in the air, but my sense was not as acute as hers.

"They come—that way." She pointed along the way of the statues with her cone-rod. "Let us go this—" Her choice ran to our right along the front of the building. I did not see how that could favor us, but Orsya had been here before, and there was a chance she knew more than she had shown me.

I put on my boots, even as she latched her scaled foot coverings. To dim the light of our going was a prudent move. Then we hurried past those blank oblongs of windows to the end.

The tomb had been constructed to the fore of the platform which ran on back for quite a distance more, to a shadow which might denote the wall of the cavern. Again Orsya held her head high, sniffing.

"Do you feel that air?" she asked aloud.

Even as she spoke, I did. There was a distinct inward flow of air current coming from the rear of the platform.

"Water—fresher water." She began to run while I lengthened stride to keep up with her.

As we retreated from the tomb, so did the light recede. Orsya's shell lamp was useless out of the water, and we headed into a dark which increased near to the thick black of that first passageway through which we had come. I listened, as we went, for any sound behind us. How about ahead? The Thas must burrow; what if they waited for us wherever Orsya led?

"No Thas." She picked up my thought. "I do not think that this is a place they have ever visited before. They leave their stench wherever they push their foul runways. But—I wish I knew what they brought with them, or what ranges before them now, for its like I have never scented."

We reached the end of the platform. Orsya moved beside me and there was a glow of light: enough to show that she had shed one foot covering and planted her flesh against the floor to give us that gleam.

The wall of the cavern was there, arching up and back over our heads. Between it and the platform was a channel in which ran water. This came from an archway to our right and gurgled on, to be lost in the dark. Orsya replaced her boot and that momentary glimpse was gone.

"That scarf—the one you use to sling the sword—hold one end; give me the other. Now get down into the water."

I did as she bade, feeling the sharp twitch as she gripped Kaththea's scarf, lowering myself gingerly into the water which I hoped was not deep enough to close over my head. But it was only waist-high. Once more immersed, Orsya's shell lamp came to life.

She headed for the archway. I discovered that this water had a current, and we were walking against that force. After a few moments I was aware of something else; the shell lamp was radiating a dimmer illumination and I feared that it was actually dying away. At my questioning Orsya confirmed that alarming fact. The quasfi shells did not hold their natural illumination for long after they were emptied of their indwellers. Soon the light would be completely exhausted.

"Do you know this way?" I asked, for reassurance.

She held the cone-rod tight against her breast with the scarf end, while with her free hand she scooped up a little of the water and touched her tongue tip to it. "No; but this is water which has run in the open air, under sun, and not too long ago. It will lead us out."

With that I had to be content.

The increasing dark was hard for me to take. Never have I favored underground ways, having to fight a feeling that around me walls were moving in to crush. Perhaps because we walked in water Orsya did not appear to be affected in the same way and I hid my feelings from her.

There was an urgent jerk on the scarf. I stopped, listened. She did not try to reach me by mind touch, rather did her hand slide down the scarf to close upon mine, and I did not need the cramping of her fingers to know this was a warning.

My senses in this deep hole might not be as acute as hers, but now I could hear it too; a splashing ahead. The last glimmer of our shell lamp was quenched and we were in the dark. I swung out my sword in a short arc ahead and to the right. Its point scraped wall and with that as my guide, I drew to it, bringing my companion with me, feeling somehow the safer with a solid surface to my side. In spite of my wishes to deny it, that splashing sounded nearer. What kind of monsters patrolled these darksome ways?

For the first time Orsya spoke. She was very close to me, so that her breath was against my cheek as she whispered:

"This is none of my knowing. I cannot reach it with a hail call. I do not know if it is of the water world at all."

"Thas?"

"No! Thas I know." There was loathing in that.

We listened. To retreat before it was still possible, but we might reach the cavern of the tomb, only to find Thas waiting for us. In that moment I longed for Kyllan's gift, for it was in him to touch and act upon the minds of beasts, bringing them under his will. He could have turned that splasher, sent it off from us—always supposing it *was* an animal and not some unknown abomination loosed by the Shadow in this place.

Suddenly Orsya's grip tightened. Though we now stood in utter dark, yet ahead were lights—two grayish disks just above water level. From them came a little diffused glimmering. Those disks were set in a line—

Eyes! But eyes which glowed, which were equal in size to the palm of my hand: eyes far enough apart to suggest a head of proportions beyond any beast I had ever seen!

I pushed Orsya against the wall behind me. The sword was in my maimed hand; now I tried to transfer it to my left. But found, to my dismay, that I could not clasp it as well, that even with my stiff fingers it was better in my right hand.

The eyes, which had been close to the surface of the water, now suddenly jerked aloft to a level above my own head. We heard a sibilant hissing as the thing came to a full stop. I had no doubt that it had sighted us, though the beams of light those eyes cast ahead did not reach to where we now stood.

Since the only target I had were those gray disks, those must be my point of attack. The hissing grew stronger. A fetid puff of air struck me full face, as if the creature had exhaled. I brought up the sword and, though I have used a blade since childhood, it seemed to me that never had I held one before which felt like an extension of my own body.

The eyes swung downward, and now, though still at water level, they were much closer. Again a puff of stinking breath.

"Kemoc!" Orsya's mind thrust was harsh. "The eyes—do not look into them—Ahh! Keep me . . . keep me with you . . ."

I felt her move stiffly, trying to break the pressure of my body, to slip from between me and the wall.

"It wills me to it! Keep me—" Now she cried aloud as if terror had filled her.

I dared not wait any longer. With a push from my shoulder I sent her stumbling back and heard a splash as she must have fallen into the water. But whatever compulsion those eyes exerted on her, they did not hold for me.

One could not rush nor leap through the current of this stream. It was rather like wading through slipping sand and I dared not lose my footing. Those eyes, at the level of my own waist . . . if the thing had a skull shaped in proportion to their size, its jaws must now be submerged.

"Sytry!"

That was no word of mine, but it had come out of me in a cry like unto a war shout. Then it was as if I were no longer Kemoc Tregarth, but another, one who knew such fighting and was not dismayed by either the dark or the nature of the unseen enemy. In my mind I seemed to stand aside and watch with a kind of awe the action of my body. Just as my maimed hand was put to use it had not known since that wound years ago, so did I thrust and spring in waves in which I had never been trained.

The golden sword went home in one of those gray disks. A bulk arose high, with a terrible scream to tear through one's head. But my hand held to hilt, and, though I was hurled away with a punishing stroke from what must be a great paw, yet I kept my weapon and struggled up to my feet again, back to the wall, facing straightly that bobbing single disk.

It struck at me and I flung out my arm, the sword straight pointed, in what I deemed a very short chance at any victory. My blade struck something hard, skidded down, to slash open that other disk. Then I was crushed back against the rock wall as a vast, scaled weight fell upon me. Had I been pinned below the surface of the stream I would have died, for that blow had enough force to drive both wits and breath out of me. When I struggled back to full consciousness I felt a weight across me waist-high, but it did not move.

Cautiously I used my left hand to explore: scaled skin, and under that the general shape of a limb, now inert. Revulsion set me to working for freedom. I wavered finally to my feet, the sword still in my hand as if nothing but my conscious will could ever dislodge it.

"Orsya! Orsya!"

I called first with voice and then mind. Had she been caught in the struggle, lay now perhaps crushed under the body of the thing I had apparently killed?

"Orsya!"

"Coming—" Mind touch and from some distance. I leaned against the wall and tried to explore by touch any damage I had taken in the encounter. My ribs and side were sore to any pressure, but I thought they were not broken. My jerkin was rent from one shoulder.

But I had been very lucky, too lucky to believe that it had been good fortune alone which had brought me through. Were the Sulcarmen right? When I had taken that sword into my hand, had I also taken into my body some essence of the one to whom it had once belonged? What meant the strange word I had hurled into that face (if the monster had a face) when I attacked? I would not lose it now . . . I never could. . . .

"Kemoc?"

"Here!"

She was coming. I put out my hands, touched skin and instantly her fingers were about my wrist in a fierce, hurting hold.

"I fell into the water; I think I was dazed. The current carried me back. What—what happened?"

"The thing is dead."

"You killed it!"

"The sword killed it. I was merely one who held it for the kill. But it seems we have picked a dangerous road. If we have met one such surprise, there may be others ahead."

"The Thas are coming—and with them that other . . ."

"What other?"

"I do not know. Save that it is of the Shadow. It is not even remotely human-kind and they even fear it, though they are bound to its company for the present."

So our road must still lie ahead. We struggled over the monster bulk of the dead thing. Behind it the waters of the stream arose, partly dammed by the body. Where the current had washed only a little above our knees, now it rose rapidly. We quickened pace for I feared it might choke the passage.

"The eyes—you said that the eyes drew you." I questioned as we went.

I read her surprise. "Did you not feel it? That there was naught to do but to surrender to it—to go to it as it wished? But, no, you could not, or you would not have fought! Truly, you have your own safeguards, overmountain man!"

As far as Orsya could explain, the gaze of the creature had overpowered her will, drawn her to it. I wondered if that was not the manner of its hunting in these dark passages, so that it brought its prey easily within reach. Yet my own immunization to the spell puzzled us both. It might have something to do with the sword. For, folly though it might be, I was convinced that the blade had in the past been used against just such a monster and what had come to me was a memory of that other battle.

To our relief the waters did not reach higher than our breasts; and I wondered what the Thas would make of that bulk stopped in the tunnel when they blundered into it.

The waterway opened into a pool and there was the splash of a falls. Light, daylight, though grayed and dim from the distance, danced down to show us those falls, laced with foam, which cascaded from an opening far above.

XII

*T*he spray from the falls was a mist of rain over us. But at least we could see. I drew Orsya with me back against the wall farthest from the falls, from where I could see best those openings (there were three of them) above us.

It was clear we could not climb near the falls; the rock was too much under the blanket of spray. The second opening was no good to us either, for it was in the roof of the cavern and only a winged man could reach it. So I studied the third.

It was a narrow slit, to the right of the falls, out of the direct force of the water for most of the climb.

But even if we could reach that opening to the outer world we did not know what awaited us on the far side, nor in what part of the country we would emerge. I said as much to Orsya, but she shook her head.

"We are in the highlands. You still have the Dark Tower ahead."

I could not see how she was so sure of our direction. But I did not argue about it.

"Can you climb?" Whether her webbed feet could find toeholds as easily as mine, I did not know.

"One does not know without trying," she said.

As I feared, even here the stone was slick with water. We were beyond all but the edge of the constant dampening of the spray and the wall was rough enough to give us purchase for our hands and feet, bared to grip more firmly. However, it was not a progress to be hurried.

I went first, testing each hold before I risked setting weight upon it. Now and then I glanced back to be sure Orsya was following. She did not seem in any distress, though she moved deliberately. About two thirds of the way up I came across a fault in the rock, hidden from below, a small shelf which could hardly be termed a ledge, but which would give us a resting place, sorely needed after those hours of flight.

I lay down on the ledge and reached my hands to Orsya, helping her up and over beside me in that narrow space. But her head turned to a very narrow crevice in the wall at our backs, her nostrils expanding as she tested the air.

"Thas!"

"Here?" This shelf was no place on which to face a fight. Nor did I want to start to climb again and be attacked from below.

"Not now," she reported after a moment. "But this crack leads to one of their burrows. We had better not linger."

She was right. The entrance to a Thas run was no place in which to take our ease—especially not when a slight push could send us both over and down. I got to my feet, tried to forget the pain in my shoulders, the aching weariness of my arms. Behind lay the longest stretch. *Keep my mind only on the few inches before me—the next hand hold—and then the one after that—*

It was a slowly rising agony, that last part of the climb. My maimed hand was numb. I could watch it move and hold, but I could not feel the stone beneath the awkward fingers. Always with me was the fear that that grasp could slip.

But that was the hand which I at last pushed through the opening into the outer world. The light was not that of the sun and I wondered if we were coming out into a storm. But, as I struggled through, I discovered we were still at the bottom of a rift. The stream which made the falls in the cavern poured along there. The rest was only rock walls and sand. I turned to draw Orsya up beside me.

We were a wild looking pair, our clothing tattered, with raw red scraps of skin on our arms and legs, along with dark bruises, the grime of mud and other signs of our journey. But the sheer relief of getting out of those ways made me feel light of head and heart—though some of that might have been due to lack of food.

Orsya went to the edge of the stream, fell on her knees by it, staring into the water intently, as Loskeetha might have consulted her bowl of sand. Then she made a quick dart with one hand and brought it up clasped about a wriggling, fighting creature which was so long and slim of body it seemed more snake than fish. She knocked this against a rock and left it there, then made another grab. Hungry as I was, I could not find any appetite for her catch. But she gathered them together carefully and put them in the bag from which she dumped the quasfi shells.

We started along the cut, I on the narrow bank, Orsya in the stream. Twice more she made a raid into the flood swirling about her feet and added to her bag.

Twilight was dim about us as the ravine widened out and vegetation and grass began to show in ragged clumps. We drew away from the water a little and I found a place where a boulder and part of an ancient slide from the heights, together with the cliff wall, gave us a corner of protection. Orsya borrowed my knife to work upon the fish, while I piled stones to add to our shelter.

I did not relish the thought of raw fish, but when she handed me some, I accepted it and tried not to think what I was eating. It was not as unpleasant as I had expected and, while I would not choose to live upon such foodstuffs, I could chew and swallow my share.

It was already dark, but Orsya brought out the cone-rod, unwrapping Kaththea's scarf. This she sat on the ground before us with much care.

When it stood point up to her satisfaction, she bent her head and breathed upon it. Then, with her hands she made certain signs, one or two of which I recognized, for I had seen Kaththea sketch their like. I knew better than to disturb her concentration at such a time. But I wondered what Orsya was, and if she were indeed the Krogan equivalent of a Wise Woman.

She sat back at last, rubbing her hands together as if they were either cold, or she would free them of something clinging to her skin.

"You may sleep without fear of surprise," came her thought. "We have such a guardian as had not been known since my mother's mother's mother's time."

I longed to ask her what manner of magic she had wrought. But the first law of power is that explanations must not be asked for—if they are volunteered, well and good. And, since she did not tell me, I could only wonder. Yet I believed in her promise of safety. This was good, for I do not think I could have stood any watch that night, my fatigue of mind and body was as a burden heavy enough to push me to earth.

When I awoke Orsya was not curled in sleep, but rather sat, her hands arched over the cone-rod, not quite touching it, her position being that of one who warms herself at a fire. She must have heard me stir, for she gave a start as one awakened out of deep thought and turned her head to look at me.

Her hair, well dried now, was a silvery cloud about her head and shoulders. Somehow at this moment she looked more unhuman, more alien, than she had since our first meeting by the guest isle.

"I have been screeing. . . . Eat." She nodded at what rested just beyond my hand. "And listen!"

There was about her such an air of command as I had seen in the Witches of Estcarp, and automatically I obeyed. Screeing? The term was new to me, but I thought she meant foreseeing, after Loskeetha's pattern, and I wanted no more of that.

Orsya read my thoughts and shook her head. "I deal not with futures, possible or impossible, but with dangers which walk this land. There is much abroad here—"

I glanced from her to the wider stretch of valley. There was nothing I could see except scanty growths of brush and the stream.

"The eyes of the head cannot be trusted here," she answered my thought once more. "Whatever you see, look twice, and thrice, and with the mind also."

"Illusions?" I guessed.

Orsya nodded. "Illusions. They are deft at weaving such, these who deal in the powers of the Shadow. Look now." She placed her right hand so that the point of the cone must touch the palm, then she leaned forward to touch my forehead.

I blinked, startled.

A rock not too far away was no longer a thing of rugged stone, but rather of warty gray hide, of large, questing eyes, of claws to tear.

"Look now upon your sword," Orsya's thought commanded.

I must have unconsciously reached for its hilt when I sighted the rock-monster. Along its blade red runes glowed; they might have been written in freshly shed blood. But they were in no language I knew.

"Illusion? Or is it really there? And, if it is, why does it not attack?"

"Because we have also a protection of illusion about us."

She raised her hand from the cone and I saw only a rock. "How long we can maintain our cover and—" She hesitated and then continued, "There is also this. We can go together only while we travel by water. I can not take wholly to land. Thus the last part of the journey will be yours."

"None of it need be yours," I told her swiftly. "You have the means to make yourself safe. Stay here—" I could not say "Stay here until I return," for I was sure that returning was not one of the things I could read into any future. This quest was mine alone and Orsya need not bear any of its burdens.

It was as if she neither heard my words, nor read them in my mind. Instead she had gone back to studying the cone-rod.

"The sword will warn you. It is not in my power to read its history, for it is of war and warriors. My gifts lie with the waters and, a little, of the earth across which they run. But there are tales which travel from one people to another across this riven land of ours. A blood runs on that blade when evil is nearby, as you have seen. Therefore, when we must part, you must use it as a touchstone to try the truth of what you see: the fair, the safe, those may seem foul or dangerous. The seeming foul may be harmless. Do not trust your unaided sight. Now, it is day—let us go."

"That thing out there—" I stood up, sword in hand, half expecting to see the rock turn into a monster ready to charge.

"It is a guardian, I think." Orsya was rewinding the cone in Kaththea's scarf. "Give me your hand, and walk softly with me in the stream. It may be able to sense that we pass, but it will not see us."

I kept my eyes upon that rock—fearing that the illusion might hold so that I could still be seeing it while what it covered was stalking us.

"Think not of it," she ordered. "And no more mind touch—such creatures cannot read it, but they are alerted by its use."

Hand in hand we hurried down to the stream and stepped into the water. As we had in the tunnels, we waded in a current which flowed with some power, and which reached our knees. I held the sword before me, watching the bared blade. The runes blazed as we passed the rock, and then they began to fade.

The second time that warning showed we were well out in the canyon valley. But this time the danger was visible: small, scuttling things moving around the open end of a cut in the cliff—Thas!

They were bringing forth baskets of earth and rocks, dumping it in piles, running back again in a fury of work. I felt Orsya's hand tighten about mine, read the wave of disgust which filled her.

We rounded a curve in the canyon and saw another portion of Thas labor. They were building a road with earth and rocks, angling it up along the side of the cliff. Among them were man-like figures wearing saffron yellow cloaks, and those carried staffs, but wore no swords. They were plainly in charge of the operation, ordering the Thas here and there, consulting maps or rolls of instructions. The reason for the labor was a mystery to me, but that it had great importance to the enemy was clear.

Orsya raised her fingers to her lips in warning, having dropped my hand for an instant. Then she snatched my fingers up again as if even so small a break between us might be disastrous. Silence, she had cautioned, and I gathered that stood for mind touch also.

Some distance away, more Thas worked along the river, some piling rock out in the stream bed, though they entered water with very visible reluctance and had to be constantly urged to it by two of the saffron robes who kept constant watch over their activities. How we were going to pass them if we kept to the water I did not see.

With my sword blade I motioned left. Orsya studied the ground there and then nodded. It seemed to me that our splashing progress out of the stream would surely alert the workers. But we gained the far bank unobserved.

I guessed that Orsya had by some means rendered us invisible to those workers. The illusion had protected us—so far. But I breathed more freely when we were in cover in broken country. The footing was less smooth, but this type of lurking was familiar to me. Threading in and out among the rocks and brush, we worked our way safely past the activity by the river. I wished I could learn the reason for it. That it meant no good to us I could guess.

"Listen; I will climb . . . see what lies ahead."

"Take care. When we are apart, the illusion does not cloak you."

"This is a game not unknown to me," I returned with confidence.

Orsya pushed back between two rocks, crouching down. I fastened the sword to my belt and began to climb behind a chimney, which was weather sculptured almost free of the cliff wall. I had nearly reached the perch I had selected when there was a whistling screech behind. Had that attacker not so made clear its intentions, I would have been easy prey. But at that cry I pushed away. My spine and shoulders were now firm against the parent cliff, so narrow was this portion of the break through which I crawled, though my feet were still in place on the chimney. I freed the sword as death on wings hurtled down at me.

It made one pass over the top of the chimney, screeching, and the wind of its wing flapping nearly upset my precarious balance. Then it circled and came back, landing on top of the chimney, striking down at me with a murderous beak. It had a long neck which was very supple. The head was small, and seemed mostly to be that beak, with eyes to guide its attack.

The runes on the sword blazed high as I brought the blade point up at the darting head. With my shoulders so wedged I could not strike freely. It seemed I was cornered, unable to either defend myself or retreat.

Again the beak reached for me. I tried to move the sword and the red runes on it dazzled my eyes. The blade touched something by pure fortune, for I could move it only a few inches either way. There was a screech broken off in mid-cry and that snake neck tossed. I saw that the beak had been slashed off close to its roots. The thing took to the air; cries came from it as it flew wildly back and forth, as if bereft of whatever wits it ever had. One of those swoops brought it crashing into the cliff wall and it hurtled, end over end, broken and writhing down to the ground below. I stared at the sword in unbelief. As it had when I had faced the monster in the tunnel, it answered some life or purpose of its own. I had certainly not aimed that blow, had tried feebly to use it in defense. What power-things had I brought out of that long sealed tomb?

Then my mind turned sharply to the present. Surely the cries of the winged thing would draw the attention of those working at the river. The sooner we were away from here the better. I pulled up to the perch and gave a hurried survey to what lay ahead.

The canyon opened on hilly country, less high than the heights behind us, but very broken and rough. I could see movement here and there, but a haze hid much of it. Farther to the left was the streak of what might be a road. But I did not sight any buildings. And the broken land promised lurking places in plenty.

I dared remain no longer to spy out the best route. However we went we would have to cross that road. Thinking about that I dropped from hold to hold, to find Orsya waiting for me at the foot of the chimney.

"Come!" She held out her hand. "They will come to see why the Rus cried. If they find it they will know strangers are abroad. I do not know if I can hold an illusion against searching."

"Do you know where the Dark Tower stands?" To venture just blindly on was utter folly.

"Only that it stands somewhere near. But you have a better guide than my scant knowledge."

"What?" I did not understand her.

"She whom you seek. If the tie is strong between you, open your mind and heart, and it will draw you."

"Perhaps they can detect us so." I remembered how Kaththea had once warned me against such seeking.

"If you use magic, perhaps. But use your heart hunger rather, Kemoc. You have said that you three are a part of a whole in a way which is to no other born. Therefore, think upon her, using no lore you have learned, but only your own longing."

"I do not know how." I could think of Kaththea, fear for her, long to see her—but was that what Orsya meant?

"Set aside your fears, for this land holds much which feeds happily on fears and will in turn use that to weaken you. Think rather of when you were all together and happy in that joining. Set her in your mind as she was in those days. Now this also will I tell you, Kemoc; beware of illusions. Fair may be foul, foul fair. . . ."

"You have said that before."

"And never can I say it enough. For danger from beast and weapon may walk this land, but greater danger than that we carry in our own minds."

We had been making our way along, shoulder to shoulder. Though Orsya spoke as one certain, yet still I shrank from trying as she had suggested, to find Kaththea in that fashion. Mind touch I knew, but this other kind of seeking was something new—unless it was like unto that which I had used to guide me through the bewildering stone forest. That magic in the scarf had worn away, but it had served its purpose. Could such be tried again?

Swiftly I told Orsya what I had in mind. She listened, and then looked, with narrowed, speculative eyes upon the scarf now wrapped about her cone-rod.

"To use magic within this land is perhaps the same as lighting a fire in a beacon basket to draw the attention of half the countryside. But there is this—the scarf has shrouded this for long now, and that will give it virtue. You might not be able to command that virtue. . . ." Now she turned that speculative look upon me. The question she asked next was one which I would never have expected to hear in that time and place, for it seemed to have no relation to what was to be done.

"Tell me, Kemoc; have you been with a woman and known her after the fashion of male and female?"

Startled, I answered, "Yes." That was long ago during border leaves and it might have happened to one who was no longer me.

"Then it would not work for you. But for me . . . What were the words you used to send the scarf seeking before?"

I repeated them slowly, in the softest of whispers. Her lips moved soundlessly as if she shaped those words. Then she nodded again.

"I cannot go far from the stream-side. Once we are in those broken lands we must find a place where I can shelter while you go ahead, if your path leads from the water. Then I shall lay a spell upon this. You must hold the picture of Kaththea in your mind. For her I have not seen, nor does there stretch any tie between us. Once that is done, the scarf may once more lead you—only, remember; it must be your heart and not your mind which sets it on its way. This"—she held the cone tighter to her breast—"cannot work for any save a virgin. Even if it is taken into another's hand some of its virtue will depart. For it is the horn of a unicorn, and it carries great power for those who can use it."

Only the top protruded from the wrapping of scarf, but I looked at that, startled. The forces which could be channeled through such rare objects were more than just legends. We still named our years for beasts of old—Firedrake, Griffin, and there was a Year of the Unicorn.

We made our way from one bit of cover to the next until we came to the road. Orsya put up her hand in warning, though I did not need that gesture, for the runes on the sword ran red. There was no way of passing over it, and we trailed impatiently along beside it until we came to where a stream cut across the land. There was no bridge to carry the road as one might suppose—rather the pavement ended abruptly on one bank to begin on the other, and Orsya smiled.

"So . . . as yet they have not mastered water."

"What is it?"

"Running water." She pointed to the stream. "Evil cannot cross it without some powerful, nature-twisting spell. They can build on one side and the other, but they cannot yet successfully span it. This is our road."

She splashed joyfully into the stream and perforce I followed. We kept well away from either bank, but as we passed the two ends of the road, my sword appeared to drip crimson drops, so shimmering were the runes.

Once beyond the road I wished to go ashore again, lest in the open river we be too visible, but Orsya insisted that our covering illusion held. We were still arguing the matter when she gave a little cry and pointed downstream, the way we had come. I turned my head.

There was something swimming there against the current, a vee of ripples, but nothing making them. I looked to the sword which I swung into readiness. The surface was cool and gray, no bloody runes along it. Yet something moved toward us at good speed and it was invisible.

XIII

*O*rsya took one step and then another toward that rippling in the water. I had the testimony of my blade that it was no danger, yet the unseen and unknown will always be feared, for that is inherent in us.

"Kofi!"

At my companion's hail, the vee of ripples veered, pointed to Orsya. Then there were splashings and movements in the water as if whatever swam there was now treading water.

"What is it?" I demanded.

"Merfay," she answered before her lips shaped soft twitterings, not akin to any speech I have ever heard. Nor did "Merfay" mean anything to me.

The invisible one swam forward again, splashing us with waves made in his passing. Orsya caught my hand once more.

"Come! Oh, this day we are favored! Kofi will lead us to a safe place."

"Can you see him—her—it?" I asked.

Her eyes went wide in surprise. "You do not?"

"Nothing but water rippling as if something swims there."

"But he is there—plain—"

Not to me. Nor have I ever heard of a Merfay.

Orsya shook her head. "They are like unto us in some instances, save smaller, and closer akin to the furred and finned ones than we. Mostly they dwell apart, not needing others. But Kofi—he is of like mind with me, one who explores beyond the haunts of his people. We have shared ventures in the past. He is not subject to the illusions, since his mind is so unique he cannot be so entrapped. He has roamed the water lands here for a space, watching to see what the enemies do. They are preparing for a great march of men, to the west—"

"The Valley!"

"Perhaps so. Yet, the hour has not yet come when they muster. They await some order or sending."

I thought of Dinzil and what Loskeetha said he might do, now that Kaththea was within his hands. The need to seek the Dark Tower, even though that seeking might lead to disaster, boiled within me. So that I quickened pace, pulling Orsya after me by our hand clasp. While ahead of us that guide I could only trace by ripples swam steadily onward.

More and more vegetation grew about. Orsya plundered here and there, finding more of those edible roots, cleaning them and storing them in her net bag. We munched some and they were better to me than the fish. Always the Merfay served as our scout. Once he (though it seemed odd to grant any identity to a wedge of ripples) made a wide detour about a block of stone which had fallen into the river. Orsya followed his lead, beckoning me well away from any contact with it.

As we passed, I saw that the stone had been dressed, and that once it might have been a pillar. There were others like it lying in confusion on the shore, as if they had been tumbled this way or that by some titanic blow of nature or man. They were not blue, as those in the haven experience had taught me to watch for, but rather a yellowish-gray, unpleasant to the eye.

"An ancient place of power," Orsya explained. "But no power we would wish to raise."

As we passed that place, I felt a clammy chill, or perhaps my imagination furnished that.

The brush became trees, weirdly leafed, resembling the blasted forests we had found on the Escore side of the churned mountains, where the witch power had set the ancient barrier between Estcarp, the refuge, and this country, the threat. Those leaves might have been living, still they had a skeleton look which made one think of ashes, of something long since dead and dry. The grass was a tall, sword-edged, spiky growth which could cut skin if one were unwary, and there were other nasty looking things which one certainly did not want to touch at all.

But among all this rank and poisoned vegetation, there were islets and ways which had normal-looking foliage growing. The unseen Kofi turned into a side stream, banked by such growth, leading to our left.

I was still hazy about directions. This territory beyond the Heights made one unsure of any north or south. But I thought now we might be heading once more east, so further and further into the unknown.

Splashing began ahead as the stream grew more shallow. It would seem Kofi now walked as we did. My boots were almost rotted on my feet, and I wondered at how I would replace them to go overland. Perhaps bindings cut from my jerkin would serve.

The trees here were of a species which grew thickly along waterways. They arched over our heads, meeting in a canopy which, while it did not shut out all light, kept away the sun. Within that tenting floated wisps of the haze I had seen from the survey point back in the hills.

"Good!" Orsya broke the quiet for the first time since we had left the main river. "Our thanks must be to Kofi."

Her ejaculation appeared to be caused by the rise of a humpbacked hillock in the midst of the stream. It was, in spite of the brush growth rooted on it, too symmetrical to be a product of nature. My companion identified it.

"Aspt house, and very large. We shall find an entrance along the bank. The stream must have shrunk much since this was built and abandoned."

A branch waved vigorously at the bank, not pulled by any wind. Orsya laughed.

"We see, Kofi. Thanks to you again," and then she twittered.

There was a hole there. I pulled out a tangle of roots and some stones before we could crawl within, to find ourselves in a very darkish chamber like the one where Orsya had tended my wound. Luckily there were holes in the roof, where portions of the covering had fallen away, so that I was not moving blind. Our guide had led us well; we could not have found a more snug or safe place in which to spend the fast approaching night.

A small pattering noise drew my attention to the opposite side of the chamber. Nothing—or did Kofi now share our quarters?

"Right!" Orsya answered my thoughts. "I wonder . . . yes, let us try."

She edged around behind me and leaned forward to place her two hands on my forehead just above my eyes. "Watch," she ordered, "and tell me if you now see aught."

I blinked and then blinked again. A wisp of mist against the dusk? No, it was not the floating mist which had found its way inside, rather it was a shape taking form. So, I saw Kofi.

He was small, about as tall as my mid-thigh. Unlike the aspts, he was humanoid in form. That is, he had four limbs, of which the upper two appeared to function as arms. He was like, yet unlike, the lizard folk of the Valley. Though his skin was scaled, his feet and hands were webbed as Orsya's, the webs extending close to the tips of the digits. His head was round, and seemed to have very little neck. Front and back his body was covered by a shell which was shaped in a wedge, wide at the top, narrowing to a point between his legs. When I turned my attention on him, his head snapped down into the shoulder part of that shield, so that only the snout and two eyes could be seen.

"Kofi." Orsya took away her hand and there was nothing to be seen.

I put out my right hand in the universal peace sign, holding it palm up and empty. For want of better reassurance to this strange water person I gave the formal greeting of the overmountain men.

"To Kofi of the river, greeting and peace from Kemoc Tregarth."

There was another faint sound. Then, for an instant, on the thick scar of my wound ridge I felt a delicate touch, as if one of those webbed hands had rested there in acknowledgment of understanding that I meant well and was no unfriend.

Orsya opened her net and divided the roots she had harvested along the river, setting aside a half dozen of them. We ate, but Kofi did not share; I asked why.

"He has gone hunting. He will hunt for more than that to fill his middle, for he will bring us news of aught which comes near this clean place."

She gathered up the roots she had put aside and said: "Put these in your belt pouch, Kemoc. They will furnish food when you may need it. This is truly a land where you must heed Dahaun's warning, and eat not, even when it might seem that you look upon food you know well. Now, let us rest. With the morning may come great demands upon us."

Whether Kofi came back to share our shelter, I do not know. But this night I did not sleep sound. There was an abiding sense of something lurking just beyond the borders of what I could see. Whether it was aware of me and waiting to attack, of that I was not sure. In fact, perhaps I would have been less uneasy had I been certain *that* was so.

Orsya appeared no better at resting than I. I heard her stirring about. Then I saw a faint white spark and guessed that she had once more set up the cone-rod and with it wrought such protective magic as she knew.

We were both up and eager to go when the first gray of dawn lit up the deserted house. She had once more wound Kaththea's scarf about the horn, and she tried to impart to that tie with my sister some virtue of her talisman.

"Kofi?" I looked to her for enlightenment.

"Waits us outside."

We came into a thick mist curtain. There was a splash in the reeds and Orsya turned her head to twitter. She listened and then looked to me.

"The Tower lies ahead. But you must leave the waterways to reach it and Kofi says it is spell-guarded. Most of the garrison who were once there have been sent away, and it is no longer warrior held, but protected in other ways. We can go with you to the beginning of the climb, but beyond that . . ." She shook her head. "Land for the Merfays is less hospitable even than it is for me. Without water I am only a burden. But what I can give you, I shall."

Once more the unseen Merfay splashed ahead of us. The mist was so thick that we were only shadows to one another as we moved. But the stream made a road we could not wander from. However, if this fog continued to hold elsewhere I did not see how I could find the Tower.

"Did I not say that this, and your heart"—Orsya held up an end of the scarf— "would be your guide? Wait and see before you despair."

Loskeetha's prophecies of death and disaster at the Tower . . . Perhaps I had escaped the third fate of the Valley meeting, but there remained the other two.

"No!" Orsya's thought struck sharply, to clash with those in my head. "Believe that you have no foreseen future, that you can control fate. Listen; if all else fails, and it seems that you have indeed to face what Loskeetha read in her sand, then— use the *words* which brought that *answer*. You can do no worse ill than Loskeetha showed you, and you may break fate by matching one power against another. It is a fearsome thing, but in times of great peril men will call upon any weapon."

The mist-filled world through which we moved held no sense of time. It was day because of the light, but how long since we had left our night's lodging, I could not tell. I was aware that the stream grew shallow, and that more and more reefs of rock broke it.

Orsya halted on one of these. "This is our parting place, Kemoc. Now—"

Slowly she unwound the scarf from the horn. Her mind was abruptly closed to me, but I think she was rapt for those moments in her own use of power, pouring into the scarf what she could to strengthen the tie between it and she who had once worn it. For a very long time it lay across her knees, with her hands—still holding the horn, as one might cup a lighted candle—resting on the bedraggled green stuff. Orsya's lips moved; she might have been chanting, without voicing aloud the words.

Then she made a scooping motion with the horn, caught its tip under the fabric and so flipped it over to me.

"What I can do, I have done. Think on your Kaththea, and see what comes of it. Remember, it must be the Kaththea with whom you were the most closely tied, even if she lives now only in the past."

I took up the length which was no longer whole, nor as bright in color as it had been when I had found it in the stone forest. I gathered it tightly in my closed fists while I did as she bade, or tried to.

How far back was the Kaththea with whom Kyllan and I had been truly one? Not in the Valley, nor during our journey into Escore, nor in those years when she had been in the Secret Place of the Wise Women, while Kyllan and I had plied our sword trade on the borders. So year by year I slipped back in time until I came to those days when we had been at Etsford, children still, when my mother had come riding with a stricken heart because Simon Tregarth, her lord, had vanished, no man knowing where, save that the sea had taken him.

Then we had been indeed one. I dragged from that well of memory the Kaththea I had known in those days before the discipline of the Wise Women had tried to mold her into their accepted image.

How true was my remembering I did not know, but that it was the way she seemed to me then, of that I was sure. I built her picture in my mind as vividly as I could. That was Kaththea who was the third part of something greater than any one of us. Kaththea to whom I was tied past any breaking of bonds.

Then the silken stuff I prisoned in my hand seemed to fight against the pressure of my fingers. I released it and a green rope coiled upward, swung down to the ground. This time it did not form a loop, but writhed as might a snake across the rock.

So intent was I upon following it that it was not until later I realized I had said no farewell to Orsya, nor was I even sure I could find again that reef-ridge in the stream where I had left her. But I knew without being told that if I allowed other thoughts to distract me from the remembered image of Kaththea I would lose this guide.

I climbed the bank, giving my green ribbon full attention. Above the cut of the stream the mist thinned. For a space there was good and wholesome foliage about me, as there had been all along the waterway. But that began to grow sparser. Then came herbage of another kind which had the noxious look of evil growth. I had taken time by the stream to reinforce my boots with strips cut from my jerkin, and now my upper body was bare to the chill which lingered over the land.

On wriggled the scarf and I followed. The ground rose steadily, but as yet the slope was not difficult to breast. I kept the sword in my hand, looking now and then to it for the glowing of the danger runes.

Orsya had masked us in illusion. That would not hold for me alone. But as yet the land seemed deserted; that in itself struck me as strange and sinister, as if I walked now into a trap, my way made easy until the lock of the cage clicked behind me.

Up and up, and colder the air I shivered in. Kaththea . . . I sought Kaththea. She was to me as a missing arm, a part lopped off to leave me crippled.

Then the sword blazed scarlet. Someone came running lightly through the last tatters of the mist. She whom I sought! But the sword was red—

"Brother!" Her hands reached for mine.

There had been another Kaththea who was illusion, who had almost tricked me once, in the garden of the Secret Place.

Or was this such a future as Loskeetha had seen. If I turned steel against this smiling girl, would my sister's blood flow over it?

Trust to the sword, Orsya had said. *Fair* is *foul* . . . if it says so.

"Kemoc!" Hands out . . . then that green ribbon flowed across the rock. She gave a croaking cry which could never rightfully burst from any human throat, as if that silken thing was a poisonous reptile. And I struck.

Blood fountained up to bathe the blade, showered in crimson drops over my hand. Where those drops touched my skin, fire ate. What lay writhing on the ground was a thing out of deep nightmare. It died still trying to reach me with great grasping claws.

Did he who ruled the Dark Tower know that I came? Or was the form this guard had used to mask its evil lifted just now from my mind? For the Kaththea who had run to meet me was the youthful Kaththea I thought on. I thrust the sword into the sand, whipping it back and forth to cleanse it of the smoking blood. The drops I smeared from my hand left blisters rising on the skin. Then I hurried to catch up with the green ribbon which had not paused.

It dropped over a bank into a road, rutted by use, and that not too long ago. To my unease the ribbon wriggled now in one of those ruts. But there was naught I could do, save follow, even though such a path must lead me directly to whatever guards Dinzil would have placed here.

Towering rocks walled in this way and, as it had been in the road away from Loskeetha, it seemed that things slid to peer, leer, threaten under the surface of the stone, to be sighted from the corners of one's eyes, to vanish when one looked directly.

I heard weeping as a low wail such as the wind might make, but it grew louder as I went. From the top of a rise I looked down into a cup, from which the road went up again on the far side. In that hollow was a woman of the Green People, her clothing rent from her, her bruised body lashed across a rock so that her spine was arched at a painful angle. She wailed and then babbled as might one who had passed too far the threshold of pain and terror.

The sword flamed—

Too good a touchstone was that for Dinzil's traps, or those I had met so far. It would be easy to pass this counterfeit of his devising, yet to leave a live enemy at my back—that was folly. So persuasive was the illusion that I had to force my hand to the use of the warning sword.

The woman vanished as blood ran. There was a man in her place, choking in death. Man? He had a human body, and human features, but what I saw in the hate-filled eyes he turned upon me, what he screamed as he died—those were not of mankind.

A dead monster, a dead seeming-man. Did Dinzil know when they died? Did I so alert him against my coming?

I pulled up to the top of the rise beyond the cup and saw it.

This was the Dark Tower of Loskeetha's pictures. I hesitated; two visions she had shown me. In one I would meet with some bewilderment before I reached the Tower and, during that, cut down Kaththea. Therefore, beware; watch for any troubling. . . .

The green ribbon flowed on to where that black finger pointed as if in defiance to the sky.

It was in truth, a dark tower. The stone of its walls was black; it had about it that suggestion of terrible age which was in Es City, in some of the places where the Wise Women carried out their sorceries. As if not only the years men knew had passed over it, but another withering and aging which was not of our reckoning.

There were no breaks in its surface, no sign of door or window. It stood on a mound covered with a thick growth of short grass, a gray grass. The road I followed ran only to the foot of that mound. There had been traffic on that road, yet those who used it might well have leaped forth from the ground at that spot; there were no signs they had ever passed over the grass.

I went forward slowly, alert always to any hint that Loskeetha's prophecy was about to be fulfilled. When I reached the mound I breathed easier. Two of her pictures had I now defeated, that of the Valley, and the fight before the Tower.

The scarf had paused before the mound side. One end of it arose to wave in the air, back and forth, as if it would climb that rise but dared not rest upon the grass. I saw that the runes were red when I pointed the sword at that slope.

I touched the scarf with the sword and was amazed as straightway the silk wreathed itself about the length of golden metal, writhed up over it to my arm, and there wrapped itself around and around flesh and muscle. There was a warmth to it which spread over my shoulder into the rest of my body.

But I was no nearer my goal, the interior of the Tower. Now I put the thought of Kaththea to the back of my mind while I considered the problem immediately before me. There was a spell here to which I had no key.

Or did I? There was one mentioned in old legends, but it was danger above danger to use it in such a place. For, while it opened the doors of the Shadow, or was said to do so, it also threw away some of the defenses of him who used it, rendering him easy prey.

How much can one trust legends? Since we had come into the fields of Esocre, we had come to believe that there was more truth than fantasy in the tales of Estcarp. I could take this road, knowing I had thrown away some shields, and prove whether or not this particular story was also true.

To linger here, hoping for blind chance to perhaps throw me a favor, was folly. I had no other key, so let me turn this one.

I set off to walk around that mound and Tower widdershins, against the light of the sun, open-eyed into the ways of those who served the Shadow. If I did it with my teeth set, my hand locked upon sword hilt, that was only return for the danger I was sure I faced.

Three, seven, nine, those are the numbers which have power in them. One of those three I was sure I must use now. Three times I walked that ringing, from the road's end to the road's end. Nothing happened.

Four times more I made that journey. The warmth from the scarf was in me; the sword showed the only danger was on the mound.

Three and seven had not availed me; now I must try nine. When I came to the road's end for the ninth time, there was at last an answer. The grass vanished in a shifting the eye could not follow. My door was open and it led, not to the tower above, but into the mound on which that sat. An open door in which no guardian stood—who knew what waited inside?

Holding the sword before me, fully expecting to see it burst into fiery runes, I advanced step by cautious step. But the warning I thought to see did not come. Before me was a passage with unbroken walls having a cold gray glimmer. That passage ran on and on.

I walked, my eyes going from wall to sword, to wall again, seeking a door, a stair, some way into the tower above. While there was none of that shifting movement under the surface here, as there had been on the rocks without, still there was an odd, distracting distortion when one looked too long at those walls, a queer sickening feeling.

How long did that passage run? It seemed to me that I had traveled leagues and that I ached with weariness, yet dared not vary my pace nor sit to rest in such a place. At last there was an archway and through it I came into a round room which might indeed have marked the foundation of the tower. There were other doors here, set about the walls, so that if similar passages to that I had followed ran from them, they would be spoked as a wheel. But there were no stairs, no way aloft.

I moved about that round chamber, trying each door. They had neither handles nor latches; not one gave, even when I put my shoulder to them in full strength. There was only the road I had come from.

Then I went to the middle of the room. I could retreat without accomplishing anything. So far Loskeetha's third future had not materialized. There was no sign of Kaththea, nor of any shadow form to which she could betray me.

Kaththea! I laid my left hand over the binding of the scarf about my upper arm. Into my mind I resummoned the memory of Kaththea. Under my touch the tie stirred, began to unwind. I withdrew my fingers but continued to remember. The ribbon length crept down, wreathing about the sword to reach the pavement.

XIV

I had expected my silken guide to seek out one of those barred doors. Instead it drew in tight coils to the mid-point of the chamber, almost at my feet, and one end pointed up, to the roof. I leaned back, but to my eyes there was no hint of any opening there.

Illusion? This was a place in which illusion was a weapon. What was the answer to illusion? Suddenly I thought of those scraps netted in Lormt. To use counter-magic here was to open my defenses further, yet there was nothing else I could do. The sword was an emblem of power; how much power, I could not guess. But it would provide, or I hoped it would, the spark I needed. I closed my eyes and held the sword high, pressing its blade to my face, so that I felt the metal touch my eye-lids.

I did not say those ancient words aloud in this place, rather I thought them slowly, picturing them in my mind as I had seen them on that crumpled, time-worn parchment.

Three there were, and then three more. Then after them the mind picture of a certain symbol. I put down the sword and opened my eyes, to see how well I had wrought.

There was a stair before me, a ladder of stone blocks. Up it went the scarf. So . . . by this much had my learning worked; I had my door into the Dark Tower. I began to climb, watching the sword for warning of ill to come. But, as in the passage and the room below, there was no sign of glowing runes.

Up and up went that steep stair. Though I had seen a ceiling over my head when I stood below, yet now it seemed that that was also an illusion: that there were no floors above, only this stair leading up and up.

Though I could see the stone steps immediately before me, farther ahead they were concealed by a shifting. Fearing giddiness on such a steep perch, I dared not watch them.

The scarf continued to rise confidently ahead. Around the stair there was a sense of open space in which that core of stone ladder was the only secure thing. Thus I could look neither to left nor right, lest light-headedness assault me.

Under my breath I muttered some of those words of power. The sensation that I might lose my balance at every step and go spinning off one side or the other, into that nothingness, grew stronger, until it was close to torment.

But there did come at last an end to the stair. I emerged through a well opening, to stand in a circular chamber, not unlike the one in which the stair was rooted, save that it was smaller. The scarf coiled there, one end aloft like the head of a reptile, weaving back and forth.

There were doorways here, also, but these portals were open, with no locked barriers. Only, each of them opened upon nothingness! Not fog, nor mist, but upon open space. When I had glanced at them I sat down on the floor, my sword across my knees, unable to move because of the panic which comes to all of us with a dream of falling. For those doorways drew, beckoned, and I was afraid as I had never been before.

What kind of a place that was I did not know. But that it was an entrance way into areas where my kind was not meant to venture, of that I was convinced. Yet the scarf brought me here.

Kaththea! I closed my eyes, fastened my will upon a mind picture, put my desire into it. Then I opened my eyes again. The scarf—it was no longer coiled—moved toward one of those portals open upon nothingness.

I thought this was another illusion, that the scarf had at last betrayed me, and once more I applied the ritual which had freed my sight below. I raised the sword to my eyes and repeated the potent charm.

When I looked again, there was no change. The scarf was coiled before the doorway directly before me; it fluttered one end up and down as it had when it had come to the mound and dared not touch the evil grass there.

I could not get to my feet, so little did I now trust my sense of balance. I crawled on hands and knees, pushing the sword before me. Then I was behind that questing scarf facing nothingness. In that moment I almost broke, being sure that it was not in me to go through that door into whatever lay beyond.

My hand went out and fell upon the scarf and once more that wreathed about my hand and wrist, moved up my arm. In my despair I voiced a call:

"Kaththea!"

As I had set my will on the scarf, so did I now bend it. I had used mind touch all my life, but this time I put into it all my energy. The effort left me weak and gasping, as if I had run clad in full mail to the top of a hill and then plunged at once into fierce swordplay.

I lay flat upon the floor of that chamber, my forehead on the blade of the sword. Perhaps it was the virtue in that which helped me now. For faint, very faint, and from far off, came an answer:

"Kemoc?" No louder than a sigh. Yet it was an answer, and there could be no illusion in it.

So . . . she still lived, even though she might be pent in this place. To reach her I must—*must*—go through that door. In that moment I was not sure I could force myself to do so.

What had I to serve me? The scarf which Orsya had bespelled for me, the sword which had not been forged by my race, some words which might summon help, or call down doom. . . . I was a blind man, wandering unguided.

I began to crawl; it was beyond my strength to stand erect and march as a man should. As I crawled part of me, deep inside, shrieked and struggled against such folly, such willed self-destruction. For it hammered in my brain that to go into such a place without mighty protection was advancing to certain death, and not only that of the body.

Now that I was on the very threshold of that doorway, I had to shut my eyes. To look upon that nothingness churned all the thoughts in a man's brain and made him mad.

My will gave me the last thrust through—over—

This was the old nightmare—falling, falling, falling . . .

Not only my thoughts were twisted—pain—such agony as a man cannot bear, I felt. Yet I did not escape into unconsciousness—I fell—and felt.

I was no man now, only a thing which cried, screamed, whimpered, suffered.

Color, burst of wild color—What was color?

Crawling . . . across a flat surface. Great sweeps of that raw, eye-hurting color bursting in explosive action from surface to over head. A dull drone of noise . . . crawl . . .

My eyes were full of tears; they were also full of fire which burnt back into my head.

MY? Who was *my*? What was *my*?

Crawl on . . . keep moving. Shut eyes against another violent blast of flaming color. Do not cease to crawl—Why?

It is hard to put into words what possessed that "my" in that time. I cannot tell how long it took for a small sense of identity to seep back to that thing which crawled, wept, flinched from every burst of the earth-sky flames. But come it did—first as dim questions, then as fragmentary answers.

There came a time when I stopped crawling, looking with my watering eyes at what had become my body. I was not—a man!

Green-gray, warty hide with straggling patches of hair-fine tendrils of flesh growing out of it. My hands were paws, webbed, thickened; my feet like them. I tried to straighten my back, found that my head was set forward between high, hunched shoulders. But around my right arm was wound a strip of green flame— flame? Slowly I raised one of those misshapen paws and touched it. It had no substance, being a mist, into which my paw sank.

But that movement, the sight of the band, awoke in me a greater stirring of memory. Scarf—but there had been something else—a sword! The word slipping into my sluggish mind acted as a key to turn a lock, open a coffer from which flooded full memory.

The sword! I looked about me frantically; I dared not lose the sword!

There was no sword. But on the ground before me, that stony surface splotched with searing color, was a shaft of golden light. As did the green mist about my arm, it too soothed my irritated eyes. I reached for it. Again my paw sank into light and fear struck at me. I could no longer hold it!

But I must! I opened and closed that paw as best I could. It swept back and forth through the shaft of light, grasping nothing. I pounded my paws on the rocky floor in fear and rage. Pain came from that. A thick, greenish fluid oozed from the bruises. I folded them against the distorted barrel which was now my chest and rocked back and forth, moaning with a mouth I could guess was of no human shape.

How had that shaft come here? I had been crawling when my wits began to return to me. I had not carried the sword, yet there it lay. Therefore it had somehow come with me, though I had not borne it.

I rubbed the back of the warty paw across my face to clear away the sticky tears, shrinking from that touch of unwholesome flesh against flesh. There was one way to learn how that shaft had come with me, and that was to travel on and see what happened. But not crawling—no! This hideous form which I looked upon was not my own, though I seemed now to inhabit it. But I was a man, and as a man I would now go to meet the unknown on my feet—so much had resolution returned to me.

But to get onto those paw feet and then balance erect was a labor which seemed almost beyond my determination to accomplish. My hunched back pushed my torso so far forward that I was top-heavy. I could not screw up my head to see more than a few steps ahead. I tried to learn more of this body. The hunched back, the thick shoulders tapered to abnormally slender loins and legs. Cautiously I raised a paw to touch my face, almost afraid of what that examination would tell me. My mouth appeared to be a wide gash with little lip, in it teeth which were sharply pointed fangs.

My nose had ceased to exist; in its place was a single gash which served as a nostril. There was no hair on my head, but a ragged growth of flesh stretched from ear to ear in a quivering band. The ears were very large, though lobeless.

In truth, I was such a monster as to send any but the stoutest of heart screaming from a first meeting.

Flinging out my arms to balance the top-heavy weight of flesh and bone, I took one unsteady step and then another, as one who walks a narrow and perilous bridge above a gulf. The shaft of light moved, always the same distance ahead of my tottering advance.

Heartened by that, for I thought that the sword, even in this strange new form, was the best talisman I could have, I practiced walking. I discovered that a slow shuffle would carry me along.

Along—where?

I had come into this hellish place seeking Kaththea. Kaththea! Glancing down at the loathsome body I now had, I recoiled from the thought that if it had fared so with me, then it must also have been with my sister. Where was this place? Surely far outside the boundaries laid upon any normal world known to human kind.

If the Dark Tower guarded a gate, and it would appear that was so, I did not believe that Dinzil had meant for Kaththea never to return. Loskeetha had said Dinzil looked upon Kaththea as a means of gaining mastery over new forces. He would not willingly lose such a key.

If he had not taken steps from which there was no retreat.

I paused, strained to lift my monster head the higher in order to see what might lie ahead. There was no horizon in this place, nothing but the eternal explosions of color and the hard ground over which I moved so slowly.

The colors . . . perhaps I was growing more accustomed to them. My eyes did not water so much, neither was the pain so sharp when I looked about me. I began to count and found they followed a pattern. The pattern they followed was the old one: three, seven, nine. Not only could I count that between bursts, but certain colors showed in flashes of the same grouping. Thus what abode here was in tune to a power.

But I must have a guide.

"Kaththea!"

Just as once I had seen certain *words* take shape and fly visibly before me, so now in this place I saw my sister's name do likewise. Brightly green as the scarf which was now a ring of light, it took wing, speeding to the right of my path.

I shuffled to follow it. Then it was hidden in a burst of purple fire, a fountain of angry crimson.

"Kaththea!"

Another bird-thought skimming ahead. Under my feet the gold of the sword moved with me. I put my hand-paw once more to the band of the scarf.

"Kaththea!"

Bird-thoughts flying, if they only would continue to lead me! Yet she did not answer, and I could only trust that what I followed was the truth and not bait for a trap.

I saw nothing but the springing flashes, the ground under my feet, until, when a spout of dark blue shot high, I sighted a massive bulk a little to the left of the path the winged thoughts set me.

It was a sullen crimson in color, its hue not affected by the constant play of contrasting shades. I thought it first a rocky outcrop, and then some very rudely wrought and ancient statue.

It crouched upon wide haunches, its hands upon the ground on either side just beyond the upjutting of its knees, its head turned a little to watch in the direction my thoughts flew. It was obscenely female, huge pendulous breasts flowing over its knees. But the face was unfinished—there was no mouth, no nose, only pits for eyes. From those pits flowed steadily two streams of darker red, like unto blood, which dripped and stained the rest of its body. In size it was twice, three times, that of the body I now wore. From it spread such a dampening of the spirit that I nearly wilted under that blow, which was not to the body, but the soul.

Whatever it might once have been, it was now a prisoner, and the agony of its spirit was a shadow over the land on which it crouched. I shuddered away from it, yet did I turn twice to look back. Monstrous though it was, it stirred my pity.

The last time I turned, I forced up one of my paws. I tried to mouth aloud what I would say. But human words could not be shaped by the guise I wore. So I thought, the very old words which we had used many times along the border, to wish to rest those who had been shield mates and sword brothers in our company. For I knew no other comfort for the suffering spirit.

"Earth take that which is of earth. Water, accept that of water, and that which is now freed, let it *be* free, to follow the High Path—Sytry willing—"

Those last two words, they were not of my belief. But I had only a moment to think that. For once more I saw thoughts speed through the air, not green this time, but golden, the golden of the sword. They flew to that crouching red thing which wept blood. Then they were gone as if they had entered it, some in the featureless head, some in the body.

There was no sound, only a wave of feeling. But I was buffeted by it to the ground as a man may be beaten down by a storm of great force. I lay under it, fighting to hold my own identity intact. Then it was gone, and I pulled once more to my hands and knees. That what had wept was crumbling, falling apart, as unbaked clay will yield to water. Swiftly it went, until there was nothing left but a heaped pile of red dust.

Shaking, I got clumsily to my feet. Something lay there. Startled, I saw that the light which had traveled with me had taken on a more substantial form. Once again it had the outline of a sword. When I went painfully back down on one knee to grasp it, I discovered that, while I could move it a little way, I still could not pick it up.

Once more I stood as erect as I could, for the first time becoming aware of another change. There was an alteration in the feeling of this land, a kind of troubling. I began to wonder if, in my pity, I had not done something which would bring on me such notice as no traveler here would care to court.

"Kaththea!"

I sent the thought and tried to speed the pace of my shuffle, also puzzling as to why my sword had changed.

Sytry willing—The words I had used from no memory of my own. Further back, when I had fought the monster in the underground channel—what had I called on? Sytry! Was it a *name* or a *word* of power? There was a way to test that. I came to a stop, staring down at that gold shaftblade.

In the Name of Sytry! I thought. *Be you again a weapon* to *my hand, a thing of power!*

There was no buffeting wind of emotion this time. Rather a trembling which shook my body as if some invisible thing shook me to and fro. A flash of light exploded, to dance wildly along the length of the sword, making it blaze until I shut my eyes and uttered a beastly kind of mewling sound. But when I forced them open again—

The sword—no light beam now—but seemingly a weapon as complete and concrete as that which I had carried out of the tomb. I was on my knees where that shaking fit had left me; for the third time I reached for the hilt. It was hard to flex my paw about it, yet I did so. From that grip a new kind of strength flowed up my arm into me.

Who was Sytry? Or what? In this place it had some governance. Would it also restore my own form so that I could go into battle, if need be, as one in his proper body?

In the Name of Sytry, I tried that thought, *let me be as the man I was*—

I waited for that shaking, for some sign that the spell would work again. But nothing came; I did not alter. Then I got wearily to my feet. The sword was a thing of Sytry; I was not. I should not have hoped it would be so.

"Kaththea!"

Once more I loosed the winged thought and continued on this endless journey across space, bound by no dimensions known to me. Though my shuffle was hardly more than a painful hobble, I did make progress. Some time later I saw looming in the flashes of color something else above the surface of the plain. This was no giant hunched figure but a band of light which did not leap and die, but was constant. Great gems cut in facets to reflect might have looked so, for these were diamond shaped, one narrow point rooted in the ground. Again the system of numbering prevailed—three yellow, seven purple, nine red—making a wall to rise well above my bowed head.

Yet my thoughts sped over that wall; for whom I sought must be behind it. I came to it, moved right for many steps, and then went in the opposite direction.

Both ways the wall continued on and on as far as I could see. There was no climbing it, for the surface was slick; there was nothing for my poorly coordinated paws to cling to.

I squatted down before one of the red stones, my weariness a great aching in my bones. It would seem I had come to the end of my journey. As I sat there, I slid the flat of my paw back and forth across the blade of the sword. No runes blazed there; it was as if they had never been. The metal was cool, somehow reassuring. I continued to finger it as I stared at the stones.

The narrow points . . . how were they based? Set immovable in the surface of this land? Now on my hands and knees I crawled to the place where I could examine the setting carefully. Yes, the wall was not an integral part of the ground; there was a thin line. To me that seemed the only part to attack.

My only tool was the sword. Almost I feared to put it to such a test. To break the blade—what would I have left? On the other hand, what would an intact sword profit me if this was indeed the end of my quest?

My clumsy movements made it a far harder business than was necessary, as I began to pick and dig with the point at that juncture between the red stone and the ground. I tried to search my memory for anything out of Lormt which might now lend me strength, either of arm or purpose. But to think of Lormt was also a struggle, and when I did so, my arm grew weary at once and I missed my aim.

Lormt, then, was no aid. What of Sytry?

For the first time the sword hit true, just where I had wished to aim it!

"By the power of Sytry, under the Name of Sytry." I paused and then experimented. Three times I repeated that name in my mind and then gave a thanks word, seven times, and again thanks, and at last nine times—

The sword was out of my awkward grasp. It stood erect at an angle, to work in sharp picks and jabs as I wanted. There was a humming along the gem wall, a buzzing—it filled my head. I raised my paws to my ears, tried to blanket out that sound. Still the sword worked on.

Now small fragments, chips of red glitter, flew splinter-like to the ground. Some of them cut my warty hide. Yet I dared not take my paws from my ears to shield myself. The sword moved faster, a blur of light. Sometimes in my teary sight it was no longer a sword but a dart of pure force.

The tall stone shivered, trembled. Now the sword rose in the air, turned to a horizontal position and launched itself straight at the side of the diamond about halfway up. The stone cracked at impact, crashed down into crimson shards. The splintering spread to its two neighbors, so they, too, fell apart in a rain of vicious fragments. Along that wall the breakage continued to spread.

I did not wait to see how far it would carry. I got to my feet and held out my right paw. Back through the air swung the sword, to fit itself there securely. Then, wincing at the cuts that carpet gave me, I crossed the broken barrier into a vastly different place.

Alien had been the world of color: This had a superficial resemblance to the lands I knew. At first I thought that perhaps I had been returned to Escore. Before me ran a road among rocks, and down this road I had gone trailing behind a green scarf which moved, a ribbon-serpent, to the Dark Tower.

As I stepped onto that rutted way I saw that any resemblance was indeed only superficial, since there was no stability to anything there. Rocks melted into ground and grew again in another place. The road flowed and I struggled through it knee-deep, as I had walked streams with Orsya. Those things I had sensed being below the surface of rocks, now showed themselves plainly, so I must keep my eyes from looking at them or be lost in madness.

There was only one stable thing in all this—the sword. When I looked upon it for a space and then to what lay before me, that too was solid, had some security, if only for a small fraction of time.

I came to a dip which had been the dell in which I slew the guard. But this brimmed with a bubbling, stinking stuff which might be poisonous mud. There was no way for me to go except down into it.

XV

*B*ubbles rose to the surface of that slime pit and burst, releasing fetid puffs of gas. Swim? Could I put this twisted body of mine to such effort? I tried with my teary eyes to discover footing which might lie either to the left or the right. But in both directions was only that shifting which was so confusing; I quickly looked away.

If I were to go it must be by this road. Once more I put my paw to the scarf about my warty skin. Then I gripped the sword as tightly as I could and went down into that mass of half-liquid corruption. It was too thick for swimming. I sank into it slowly, though I flailed with my arms, kicked those weaker legs and feet.

I was not engulfed as I had feared. My desperate struggles brought me some progress, though it was so slow! The sickening fumes made my head light, kept the tears flowing from my eyes.

It was a little time before I noticed that where the sword rested a path opened through the stuff. Once aware of that I applied the blade with cutting strokes, carving a slit through it.

At long last there was a rock ledge facing me and I pulled out on stable land, though the mess sucked avidly at my body as if it would not let me go. I had to turn and cut with what strength I could still muster to free myself.

Then I lay full length on that rock, breathing in great gasps, even though the major part of each breath I drew was the foul gas from the bubbles. Up . . . an inner warning pricked at me . . . up and away.

Once more I was reduced to crawling, leaving smears from my caked body on the rock. Up . . . still that inner urge was a lash, growing in intensity.

I heard a sound from the morass behind, louder than the bursting of those bubbles, more akin to the sucking which had come from my own struggles. My paws gripped again and pulled feebly, bringing up the weight of my heavy body. The sword I held between my fangs, cutting my lips when I moved them incautiously, but in such safety as I could devise.

The sucking sound was closer, but I could not yet turn my head. Fear lent the last impetus to reach the top of the rise, to drag myself along the lip. Then, somehow, I hunched to my knees, swung my body around.

They were coming through the muck with a speed I could not equal. There were two of them and—

Spent with my efforts to reach this point I could not get to my feet unaided. But I wriggled to one of the stones and with its help was somehow erect again, my back against it, facing those things.

They were gray and warty of skin; they had heavy arms and thick shoulders, toad faces (though the mouths were fanged). Ridges of ragged flesh arose across their skulls from one great ear to the other. These were kinsmen of the body I inhabited!

Their gashes of mouths opened as they yammered in no understandable speech. Each carried in his hand an ax, as mighty of blade as that of Volt which I had seen often in Koris' keeping, but far shorter of haft. It was plain they were hunting me.

There was no running from this, nor would I, I believe, even if I could force my weary body to the effort. The axes resembled those used by Sulcar borderers, which could be used either as a hand weapon, or to be thrown from a distance, with fatal results if the axman was expert. Whether these toadmen were, I did not know. But in such cases it is always best to give high credit to your foe's fighting prowess rather than underrate him.

I had the sword and for that to be effective I must wait until they were closer. If they were going to throw those axes, I did not believe it was possible for them to do so while they pushed through the mud. If I retreated no farther from the rim, I could dispute their landing, giving me one small advantage.

But I was so slow of body, so worn from my push through that fetid hole, that I could not move fast. I might not even leave the support of the rock against which I had set my back. When I brought up my sword in a swing meant to suggest defense, my arm answered my will so reluctantly that I felt this was indeed a fight already decided in favor of the enemy.

"Sytry!" I tried to raise the hilt to the level of my lips, the point thrusting at whatever sky this space owned. "Steel, I hold by that Name, battle I do, in that Name. Whatever favor cometh from powers I know not, yet are of the White and not the Shadow, let it rest upon me now! For I have that to do which has not been done, and there is yet a road before me—" A jumble of thoughts, ill chosen, but in that moment the most I could muster to express a plea of which I was not sure anyone, or anything, would heed.

If I could have taken only two steps forward, thrust while they were still scrambling up out of the mud, then I would have had a small advantage. But I knew that effort was not in me. Take those two steps and I would not meet them on my feet, but groveling before them, my neck bent and ready for the fall of their axes.

They must have believed me easy prey, or else they were so slow of wit that they knew only one method of attack and that a forward run, weapons aloft, yammering out what might have been war cries. I tried to swing the sword as I would have done had I had my normal body.

Its hilt loosened in my hold, spun out of my grasp, and hurled on through the air. Once more it no longer appeared a sword, but rather a flash of golden light. So swift was its passage that my eyes could not follow it, to see what it wrought in my defense. What I afterwards witnessed were wounds gaping beneath the lower jaws of the toadmen, pumping forth purplish liquid; saw them stumble and sprawl forward, sliding across the stone, their axes, falling from paws suddenly lax, striking ringingly, while I cowered back against my support, gaping foolishly.

There was another ring, louder than the axes had made, almost bell-like in tone. The sword lay there, no longer a flashing fury of destruction. I pushed away from my support, tottered to it. But the effort of stooping to pick it up made me topple and fall in turn. For a moment or two I lay there, the steel of the blade under my body. From its touch against my noisome skin spread, first a kind of warmth and then, following that, a renewal of strength. So heartened I braced myself up on my forepaws.

Where the bodies of the toadmen had lain puffed a shimmering fog of blackish motes, as soot might rise from the disturbance of a place where many fires had burned and then been quenched. And, as soot, the particles settled again to the surface of the rock, ringing—

Not the toad bodies I had seen fall to the strokes of the sword, but two lighter frames, so close to skeletons that one could see the bones plainly through the too tightly stretched skin. These, in spite of the extreme emaciation, were those of normal human kind!

The strength which had come out of the blade was in me, so I got to my feet, shuffled through the black dust to the nearest of those skeleton-men. His features were very sharp in his skull face. Looking upon him I thought that once he must have been of the Old Race or kindred blood. Death had broken some ensorcelment and returned him to his true self. Death? I glanced down at my own paws, the warty skin on my arms. Was death the *only* way of return?

The skeleton was changing again, falling into dust, as had the weeping, female thing on the other side of the gem wall. The other followed it into nothingness.

I turned my back on them as quickly as I could, faced in the other direction, to see as I expected that I would, the rise of a tower upon a mound, waiting for me even as its twin had before.

This one loomed very black and harsh, with more of a distinct outline and clarity of bulk than anything else I had seen in this eerie other world. The mound on which it was based was also dark.

Once more I walked the road into which my paw feet sank, and which was a river, but not of water. When I came to the foot of the mound there was no need to work any spell to open a door, for there it gaped, very black, already waiting. I thought "Kaththea!" to see it wing in before me, quickly vanishing in the gloom.

With the sword hilt grasped in both paws, I lumbered unsteadily on, past the portal of the mound, to enter this Dark Tower. Would it also have a staircase and doorways into more distorted worlds?

The black-dark which had seemed so thick when looking in from outside was here enlightened by a glimmer of yellowish-gray. I realized that was shed by my own body. By it I caught glimpses of floor and walls, all of huge blocks of black stone, close set. Again the walls ran without doors, to bring me into a circular room from which a stair climbed. But this was not shrouded in any spell, nor were there any other doors about that room.

My paw feet were not made for use on stairways. Once more I had to grip the sword between my teeth, go on all fours, aware that any side slip would send me crashing down upon the hard pavement below. So I went very slowly.

Then my head emerged into a lighter place, no hint of which had reached below that opening. It was as if I came into a place of ghosts. But they were not of things which had once lived and breathed. The thin, cloudy, half pictures I saw were of furnishings. There were chairs, a table which supported many jars, flasks, and tubing I did not understand. Against the walls were chests and cabinets with closed doors. All as insubstantial as river mist, yet plain to trace against the stone.

I put one paw to the edge of the table. It touched no surface, but passed easily through in a sweep which met no resistance.

There was another stairway leading aloft. This was not in the center of the room, but curled up against the wall. However it was stone and solid, not like the ghost furnishings. I shuffled to it. Since the incline here was not so steep, I managed to take it step by step, still standing, slipping my body painfully along the wall as far from the unguarded outer edge as I could get.

No sound; the tower was wrapped in silence. I tried not to make any noise, but in that I was not too successful. Even my heavy breathing stirred the air loudly enough, I feared, to alert any who walked sentry here.

There was another room above, and once more the dim, misty furnishings ringed me around. Here was a table with two chairs drawn up to it, and it was set as if for a meal. Mist goblets and plates at each place.

I swallowed. Since I had left Orsya—centuries ago—I had not eaten. Until I saw that table I had not thought of food. But now, in an instant, hunger was a pain in me. Where would I find food? What food did this toad body need for nourishment? Unwillingly I remembered those skeleton bodies. Had they gone famishing until their deaths?

There was some pretension in the furnishing of this chamber. Cobweb tapestry cloaked the walls. So thin was it, I could not detect any pattern. There were chests with the suggestion of carving on their fronts, the kind of work one might see in a manor house.

Once more another flight of stairs urged me up and on. Laboriously I climbed. Here the way was shut against me at the top by a trapdoor. I steadied my back as best I could against the wall, put the sword between my teeth, and pushed up against it with all the strength I could summon.

It yielded, rising, to fall back against the floor above with a crash which was doubly startling in the silence. I followed as quickly as I could, sure that must rouse any who sheltered here.

"Welcome—bold hero!"

I strained my head up and back on those crooked shoulders, trying to see.

Dinzil—yes, Dinzil!

But not in any disfiguring toad man disguise. He was as tall, as strong, as fair of face, as when I saw him last in the Valley. But added to that a vitality, as if in him some fire burned high, not consuming the flesh which held it, but giving an energy and force such as human kind did not know. To look upon him dazzled my eyes, and the tears dripped fast down my distorted jaws, but still I held that gaze. For hate can be a force to strengthen one, and I knew that all the hate that I had tasted before in my life was nothing to the emotion now in me.

He stood with his hands on his hips, and he was laughing—silently, his amusement a lash of contempt and scorn.

"Kemoc of Tregarth, one of the Three—I bid you welcome. Though it would seem that you have lost something, and gained something—not for the rest of your spirit, nor to delight the eyes of those—if there now are any—who look upon you with kindliness. Would you see what those would see? Behold!"

He clicked his lips and straightway there appeared before me a burnished surface on which was painfully clear what must be my reflection. But the shock was perhaps not what he had expected, since I had already known of my changed body. Perhaps my composure startled Dinzil a little, if he were still able to be touched by human emotions.

"They say," he smiled again, "there are places where what a man sees is not his outer form, but the inner; the thing he himself has fashioned through the years by his ill desires, his hidden lusts, the evil he has thought on doing but not had the courage to act upon. Do you recognize your inner self now—when it is turned to outer—Kemoc Tregarth, renegade from overmountain?"

I was past such needling.

Kaththea! I thought that not at him, but as I had before, sending it seeking. Here, what showed as that thought was no longer a bright green flying thing, but rather a bird sore hurt, fluttering, trying to reach a goal, but hindered from it.

I saw Dinzil turn his head, follow it. There was startlement in his eyes for an instant. He swept up his hand in a forbidding gesture and the thought-bird vanished. Now he looked to me again and he was no longer amused.

"It seems that I have underrated you, my misshapen hero. I will admit, I wondered how you could come this road without misstepping somewhere along the way. So you still have the power to find Kaththea, have you?" He appeared to think for a moment and then brought his hands together in a sharp clap, laughing once more.

"Very well. I have weaknesses; one of them is for heroes. Such constancy and devotion must be rewarded. Also, it will be amusing to see if your tie is strong enough to really show you Kaththea."

He said a *word*, raised both hands over his head and plunged them down. There was a whirling about me, with nothing to cling to—

We stood in the round chamber. On the floor lay the trapdoor I had pushed back. It was as it had been, save that all which had been ghostly was now solid. The tapestries on the wall were woven in time faded colors, but jewels and metallic threads gave them sparkling life. The chairs, a chest or two, were heavily carved and plainly old. Dinzil still fronted me and now he made mock reverence.

"Welcome, welcome. I would give you the guesting cup, my poor hero, but I fear what you would quaff from it in this place would be the death of you. And that is not my wish—not yet. But we tarry too long. You have not come a-guesting—have you?—but to see another."

He turned his head a little from me and I followed his glance. There was a small table and on either side of it stood a sconce as tall as a man, in which candies burned, with a mirror between. Before that mirror, as if someone sat there, a comb with a jeweled back moved slowly up and down, in the motions of one smoothing long, loose locks of hair. But that was all, just the moving comb.

I shuffled toward the mirror and table. My thought went out in a sharp call: "Kaththea!"

Did she in truth sit there, unseen by me? Or was that moving comb but a trick Dinzil used for my torment?

In the glass I saw something. But it was my toad self pictured there, no reflection of the beauty which was my sister's.

The comb fell to the floor. There came out of nothingness such a scream of terror as I have never heard. Dinzil threw out his arms, folded them about something invisible to me.

Yet all of this could be his trickery and no truth.

"Kaththea!" Once more I called, mind to mind.

"Evil!" That was no answer, but a feeling of loathing strong as any physical blow, and following it, *words,* some of which I knew. She was using a spell. Dinzil did not trick me; no one but Kaththea could do this.

"Evil indeed, my love." Dinzil spoke as one soothing a child. "This thing would have you believe it is Kemoc come seeking you. Hush; waste not your wisdom which cannot harm a thing of this place."

"Kaththea!" To the mind call I added two *words.* If she was not entirely lost to all she had been, then those would assure her that nothing of the Shadow stood here, but one of the light.

"Evil!" Again that blast against me. Stronger this time. But not buttressed with any word of power. "Send it hence, Dinzil!" that voice which was my sister's cried out of empty air. "Send it hence! To look upon it chills my heart!"

"So be it, my love!" He loosed his hold on that invisible body and then raised his hands once more and spoke a *word.* We whirled, to come again into the room furnished in mist.

"She has chosen, has she not, my hero? Let me show you something."

Once more he brought out of nothingness that mirror. But this time it did not reflect me, or the room. There was a thing—female—akin to the monstrous weeper. That is, part of it was. But on the twisted shoulders of that foul body sat my sister's head; over those shoulders and sagging breasts flowed her hair. Her hands were not paws but white and human.

"This is Kaththea as she now is."

My hate for him was a poison rising in my throat. He must have known, for his hand moved and I was planted to the floor as if roots sealed my paws to the stone.

"You see in me one who can vanquish the dangers of this place. I am Dinzil; I remain Dinzil. Slowly Kaththea is learning. When she is wholly as I am, then will she be wholly Kaththea here as well as in your own world—outwardly. She learns well and fast. All women shrink from the monstrous. I let her see a little of her present self—not telling her, of course, that she was the one upon whose form she looked, but letting her think that that is what might happen unless she speedily puts to use the safeguards I could teach her. Since then she has been most biddable. No, you are more than I thought you, Kemoc Tregarth. I had believed that most of the power was your sister's. However, one must not lightly toss aside any potential weapon without considering carefully the possibilities for future use. So—we shall put you in safe keeping until I can make a decision."

Once more his signs and the warping. Then I was in a stone-walled cell, where only the yellowish aura given off by my body provided the light. The walls about me looked solid, with no break in them. I crouched down in the middle of that small, cold space and tried to think.

Hero—Dinzil had been derisive when he named me that, and rightly so. I had done naught to defend myself, to reach Kaththea, save what my enemy had

forced upon me. The battle had been no battle at all, but a pitifully inept encounter which had gone exactly as Dinzil wished.

But to con the unhappy past was no good stepping-stone to any future. That
Dinzil had powers I had known since I had begun this so far ineffective quest. On
my side were only the facts that I had won to the Tower, which he had not expected, that I still had the sword. Ha—I held the sword across my knees. Had
Dinzil let me keep that weapon because he scorned the use of steel, or had he
seen it at all?

That speculation lingered. Suppose to Dinzil the sword had been as invisible as
Kaththea had been to me! Why? Or why had I not tested it upon him when we
met? It was, looking back, as if I had been in bonds of a kind, unable to raise hand
against him.

The Tower was his fortress. It could have safeguards in plenty, none of which
were wrought of stone, steel, or even things visible. I could have been subject to
them from the time I entered the mound door.

I had not once thought of using the sword, not until this moment when Dinzil
must believe me safely caged. The sword had picked away the support of the
gem stone wall. Could it do as well against the stones of my present prison?

Once free—if I were still in the tower—what could I do? Kaththea had fled
from me to Dinzil. She had not accepted my call of identity. And she was already
under the change Dinzil had set upon her. That thing he had showed me—now
I wished it was wholly monster, knowing what the changes meant.

Kaththea had knowledge out of Estcarp. But much of the lore of the Wise
Women could be only used by a virgin. They had held it against my mother that
she had managed to retain her power even after she had wedded my father. Dinzil
could not make her wholly his without destroying her usefulness.

Dear one—the words he had used to soothe her. . . . My rage was choking;
my paw closed tight upon the sword hilt. Then the other arose to touch the band
of light which had been Kaththea's, on which Orsya had set magic of her own.

That had been woman's magic also. It had served me, but from the outside,
not the in. What had Orsya said? *Seek with the heart—*

The heart . . . What had I used to set the scarf seeking? Not Kaththea as she
was but as she had been, before any magic save that which was born in us—
which we used as naturally as we breathed, slept, walked, talked—was known
to us.

I could not really touch the scarf which was now only a band of light. But I put
my toad paw firmly into the glow, kept the other on the sword hilt. I began to
make magic—not Dinzil's, not any of this land, nor of Escore, but of the past.
I sent back my mind, far, far back, to the first memory which had been mine, and
Kyllan's and Kaththea's. We were on a furry rug before a fire which sent sparks
flying upward now and then.

Anghart, who had been our foster mother, spun and the thread came smoothly between her fingers, her skillful everybusy fingers. Kaththea's thought reached me—

"There is a fairy wood, and there are fairy birds in the trees—"

Looking into the fire, I saw it as she did.

Then Kyllan thought: *"Here comes our father riding with his men."*

And flames rode manwise on some mountain horses.

"Mountains beyond—" That had been my addition, little guessing then how mountains beyond would change our lives. No, do not think of what happened later. Keep memory clean and clear!

Anghart had looked down on us; very big Anghart had seemed then.

"So quiet; so quiet. Listen; I will tell you of the hoarfrost spirit and how Samsaw tricked it—"

But we had not been quiet; we had been talking to one another in our own way. Even then we knew that that was something those about us did not do and we kept it for our secret.

Memory after memory I pulled from my mind, trying to recall each small detail to make a vivid picture. Once we rode in the spring fields. Kyllan broke a branch from the Tansen tree, and its white flowers with their pink centers gave forth the sweetest fragrance. I had caught up flowering grass and made of it a crown. We had put them, crown on head, scepter in hand, on Kaththea, and told her she was like unto the Lady Bruthe, who was so fair that even the flowers blushed that they could not but equal her.

"I remember—"

It had stolen so into my thought weaving that at first I was not aware. Then I took tight rein upon my emotions. Immediately I summoned up another memory and another. She who had been so drawn now joined with me. Together we knitted a tapestry of how it had been with us. I did not venture to approach her along that line of memory, only bind her tighter to me in the sharing.

"You—you are Kemoc?"

It was she who broke the spell with a tentative, uneasy question.

"I am Kemoc." I acknowledged that, but not more.

XVI

*I*f you be Kemoc"—there was rising tension in her thought—"then this is no land for you! Get you forth before ill comes. You do not know what happens to those who do not have the proper safeguards. I have seen—monstrous things!"

She had seen what Dinzil had taken good care to show her. "Dinzil!" Her thoughts ran even louder. "Dinzil will protect you; use the counterspells—"

So was she caught in his net that she turned instantly to him when there was need for aid.

"I have come for you, Kaththea." I told her the simple truth. If she had not gone too far down that road on which he had set her feet, then I might reach her, even as the memories I had spun had drawn her.

"But why?" There was a simplicity in that question which was not of the sister I had known. She had never been one to lean upon another, but held to her own mind. This was a different Kaththea.

I tried to make my thoughts simple, to keep her holding that slender tie between us: "Did you believe that we would let you go, uncaring what chanced with you?"

"But you knew!" her retort was swift. "You knew that I had gone to a place of power, to learn that which would make us all safe against the Shadow. And I am learning, Kemoc, much more than the Wise Women ever dreamed of. They are really small-minded, timid. They but peer through doors which they dare not enter. I marvel that we are in any awe of them."

"There is knowledge and knowledge. You yourself said that once upon a time, Kaththea. Some can pass through man and come into flower—some men cannot hold, unless they change."

"Men, yes!" she caught me up. "But I am of the Witches of Estcarp, who are adepts. What man cannot hope to do we can! And when I have garnered what I came here to find, then I shall return and you will rejoice at what I bring with me."

Loskeetha's third picture. Suddenly that was vivid in my mind and I saw it as sharply as it had appeared in the sand bowl. There rode the hosts of the Shadow and among them Kaththea, hurling her bolts of force against us, her kin.

"No!" Kaththea's cry of denial was sharp. "That is a weaving of evil, not a true foretelling. You have been deceived; you believe that I—one of the Three—could do so? Dinzil has said—"

She hesitated and I prompted her. "Dinzil has said—what?"

But she did not answer at once, and when she did there was in her reply a coolness, such as had been in her in the Valley.

"You wish me to have no true friends, but to keep me to yourself. Kyllan, he is larger of heart; he knows we shall still be united, even though we walk apart. But you will not admit it; you would prison me in bonds of your choosing."

"This Dinzil has said, and you believe?" He had been wily, but what else might I have expected? This was an argument, my own actions to free her would bolster, past my being able to refute.

"You do not like Dinzil. He has other unfriends. He did not need to tell me this; I had already seen it in you, in others of the Valley. Yet now he strives to gather such power as will deliver all of them. Do they believe they can turn sword steel and a few mutterings of lesser learning against the Great Ones whom rebellion in Escore now rouse? It takes forces beyond most men's knowledge to face those."

"Dinzil can summon such forces, control them?"

"With my aid, yes!" There was an arrogance, a pride in that which might have had roots in the confidence of the Kaththea I had known, but which had grown to turn her stranger.

"Go back, Kemoc. I know you love me, though that love is a thing of fetters for me. Because you came in love, I wish you well. Dinzil will see that you return to the world suited to you. Tell them there that we come with such powers behind us that the Shadow, seeing what marches with us, shall be routed before the first blow is struck."

I shut my mind to her words, to this Kaththea who was the monster Dinzil had shown me. Deliberately and with all the energy I could summon, I thought again of the Kaththea I had known and loved, who had been a part of me—

"Kemoc!" The arrogance had gone out of that cry; it was one of pain. "Kemoc, what would you do? Stop, stop! You lay your fetters on me again and it takes strength, such strength to break them. That strength I must save for the tasks set me here."

I thought. Kaththea who was young of heart, clean of heart, happy, danced in a green meadow and charmed birds out of the sky to come to her singing. . . . Kaththea, laughing, put up her hand to break off a dripping icicle from the eave edge and suck it, while before her the land was frost and snow, yet gem-beautiful under a winter sun. She took the icicle from her lips to trill a call, to be answered by the snow hawk. . . . Kaththea diving cleanly into the river flood to swim with us, but forgetting all contest when she found a watercub tangled in a reed bed, freeing the captive tenderly. . . . Kaththea in the firelight, sitting between us, listening to Anghart's tales . . .

"Stop!" Weaker that plea. I pushed it from me, concentrated on the pictures, on my touch upon the two talismen I trusted in this place which Dinzil believed he ruled.

Kaththea running lightly between us to the harvest field where we worked under the sun with all the manor folk to bind the grain. Kaththea chosen to take the Feast bowl to greet passing strangers that day, to gather the Earthtithe after the old custom, bringing it back jingling and ringing, laughing at her success because a whole troop of Borderers had passed and each had tossed a coin into it.

But never Kaththea in use of her power—never that! For to be Kaththea of the power was to open the door to this Kaththea of the here and now, whom I did not know, whom I feared.

"Kemoc—Kemoc, where are you?"

For a second or two I thought that was the cry of the Kaththea of my memories; for it was young, and strangely uncertain, almost lost.

I opened my eyes and looked about me. Where *was* I? In some place Dinzil deemed safe keeping. But now my confidence rose. I might have little on which to base that confidence. But when a man reaches a point which seems to have no future at all, then he can make a firm stand. In such stands are weak causes sometimes won, simply because there is nothing left to fear.

"Kemoc, please—where are you?"

"With you, soon," I made answer. I did not know if I spoke the truth.

I struggled to my feet, held the sword. "Kaththea!" Once more I sent the winged thought. It flew to the wall immediately before me, was gone. I walked to the wall.

Stone, solid under my touch. But still my confidence held. I set the sword point to the stone, and once more made my reckless magic. For I combined the word "Sytry" which was the sword key, with the phrases out of Lormt.

The hilt in my paw burned. But in spite of the pain I held it steady. The point chewed at a line between two of those blocks. Began to chew, that is, but as I continued to recite those names the stone itself yielded to my weapon, which cut as it had cleared my path through the mud pit. I came out of the prison where Dinzil had put me, and once more I stood in the underground chamber from which raised the stair into the Dark Tower.

Once more I climbed, coming into the first chamber. But now the furnishings were more substantial, less ghosts of themselves. When I put out a paw to touch one I almost dropped the sword. Had I put forth a paw—or a man's hand? Now I could see fingers! Then once more they were hidden in monster flesh—to appear again—back and forth.

I was shaken. The creature Dinzil had shown me and said was Kaththea on this plane—woman's head and hands combined with loathsome body. She had used her hands, her head, to work forces here. He had said—when she was all human seeming again—then she would be completely sealed to his purposes. Now—I brought forth my other hand to look upon it. Yes, there, too, was a flow from hand to paw. Still the paw had greater substance; the hand was but a ghost.

Using magic here, had that linked me to the world of the Shadow, brought about that change? Yet there was nothing else I could have done. I crept up the next flight of stairs to the dining room. Again firmer lines, colors I could now see. Kaththea, would she still be invisible to me, and I the monster who roused only fear in her?

The last stair. At its top the door was this time open to me. If Dinzil once more waited he would have the advantage, but that was a risk I must escape. I raised the sword before me. Never in this other world had the runes blazed to warn me, but now so great was my dependence upon it that I had as much confidence in it as a commander in the field has upon long tried and tested scouts.

At least I had not been blasted as I moved. Laboriously I gained the top of the stairs. There was the mirrored table. Almost I expected to see the comb in action. But to my first inspection the room was empty of any life save my own.

"Kaththea!" I summoned sharply. My winged word sped for the darksome other side of that chamber where tapestry hung. Then out of the gloom shuffled the thing Dinzil had shown me—save that now the hands hung white and distinct from the swollen wrists, and the head was more misty, looming behind it an ovoid such as matched the weeper of the plain.

Her gait was as shuffling as my own, and there was a frozen horror on her face—as one who faces a nightmare come to stalking life.

"No!" Her protest was shrill, near to a shriek.

Even if I would now lose her, I could take but one step. "As this place shows me—I am Kemoc!"

"But Dinzil said— You are not evil; you cannot be so loathsome. I know you—your thoughts, what lies within you—"

I remembered Dinzil's spiteful suggestion that this plane turned a man inside out, showing his spirit. But that I did not accept. If he had said the same words to her, I must break that belief and speedily, lest we both be lost.

"Think for yourself. Do not take Dinzil's thoughts for your own!"

Had I gone too far, so that, under his spell, she would turn again to believe I spoke out of jealousy?

Then I put out one of those paws which tried to be hands now and again. I saw her gaze fasten on it, her eyes widen. So much had I made her attend to me. I raised the paw, tried to touch her. She shivered away, yet I persevered and caught firm hold on her, pulling her around to stand before that mirror. Whether she could see what I did, I did not know, but I kept my other hand upon the sword and willed that she do so.

"Not so! Not so!" She jerked loose, cowered away so she did not see the mirror. "Lost—I am lost—" She turned that head, which was now a featureless lump, now her own, to look at me. "You—your meddling has done this, as Dinzil warned. I am lost!" She wrung her hands, and never in all my years had I seen my sister so distraught and broken. "Dinzil!" She looked about and with a passion of pleading in her thought-voice: "Dinzil—save me! Forgive me—save me!"

Inside I felt the pain of seeing her so broken. The Kaththea of the past might have suffered deeply, but she would have fought to the end, asking aid only as might one shield mate from another.

"Kaththea—" I tried to put my paw on her again, but she backed farther and farther from me, her eyes wild, her hands warding me off. "Kaththea, think!" Could I reach her anymore? Though I was loath to give that which abode here any deeper rooting in me, yet that I must do, or perhaps lose her utterly.

I held the sword by the blade so that the hilt was between us. Then I said a *word.* Fire shimmered once more, to burn me, but still I held fast to that column of golden flame.

"Kaththea, are you one who harbors evil within you? Those of the Wise Ones often examine their spirits, look well upon their motives, know the pitfalls and traps which await all those who put out their hands to the powers. Long you dwelt with them, and your unwillingness to join with them came from no evil, but because you had stronger ties elsewhere. Since you left Estcarp and came into Escore, what ill have you done by design—or thought on doing?"

Was she even listening to me? She held her hands before her face, but did not try to touch it, as if she feared that the flesh there would not be human.

"You are not evil, Kaththea; that I will not believe! If you are not, then how can it be that you see your inner self? This is only an illusion; we are among those to whom illusion is a common tool. You are only monster on this plane, as I am monster."

"But Dinzil—" she thought.

"To Dinzil this is his place; he has made himself one with it. He has said so, just as he also told me that when you were one with it, not part monster, then you would be locked to him and his cause. Is that what you wish, Kaththea?"

She was shivering, great shudders shaking her squat, unlovely body. More and more her face faded and I saw the eyepits, the ovoid head of the weeper.

"I am monster—lost in a monster—"

"You dwell within a covering forced upon you in this place. For many powers fair is foul, as well as foul is fair."

I thought she was listening now. She asked slowly: "What do you want of me? Why do you come to pull at me with memories?"

"Come with me!"

"Where?"

Where, indeed? I might recross that plain, pass through the remains of the gem barrier, back beyond the weeper's place. But then where? Could I find an exit, leading from the Tower, anchored in Escore? I was not sure, and she knew my uncertainty and fastened upon it.

"Come with you, say you! When I ask where, you have no answer for me. What would you have us do, wander in this place, brother? It holds dangers the like of which you cannot imagine. Do not doubt Dinzil will come hunting."

"Where is he now?"

"Where is he now?" she mimicked me shrilly. "Do you fear that he will come into the here and now to face you?" Then suddenly her eyes changed and the old current flowed between us.

"Kemoc?"

"Yes?"

"Kemoc, what has happened to us, to me?" She spoke simply as might a child bewildered by all she now saw and felt.

"We are in a place which is not ours, Kaththea, and it seeks to mold us into its own forms and ways. There is a way back—do you know it?"

Her blob head on which the traces of her normal face had almost disappeared, turned slowly as if she now gazed about her with new eyes, to which this was much of a puzzle.

"I came here—"

"How?" I believed I dared not press here too hard, yet if she did know of Dinzil's door between the worlds, and it was not the same one through which I had entered, there was a chance for our escape.

"I think—" That hand which was still human raised uncertainly toward her head. Clumsily she turned to face the tapestry covered wall. "This way—"

She shuffled, her hands out before her. Then she picked up one edge of the tapestry, pulled it out. There, set in the wall, glowing an angry purple-red, was a symbol. I did not know it but its far-off descendant I had once seen, and I knew it for a symbol of such a power as I would not dare to summon.

I felt my sister's thoughts writhe to shape a *word,* before I could protest. The symbol in the stone coiled as if a loathsome reptile had been loosed. Round and round it ran, and I would not look upon it, for there was a sickness in me that Kaththea knew that *word.* Then the stone vanished and only those glowing lines ran, and ran, spilling down into a pool of sullen, molten color on the floor, and that began to trickle away.

I stumbled forward, pulling at Kaththea to save her from the touch of that pool. Ahead was nothingness as there had been in that other tower through which I had plunged into this place.

"The door is open," Kaththea's thought was once more chill and assured. "For the sake of what lay between us in the past, take your freedom and go, Kemoc!"

The arm which still bore Orsya's bespelled scarf was about her shoulders before she could dodge me. With the sword in my other hand I plunged on, using the weight of my body to bear her with me. I think she was too surprised to resist. It might not be Dinzil's door, but in that moment I saw it as the only hope for both of us.

Falling—falling—I had kept no grasp on Kaththea after we went over the drop. That she had come with me was the thought I carried along into nothingness.

Once more I awoke to pain and a dulling of mind. But in awhile I noted that no color flashes leapt here, rather there was dimness and chill walls about me. I thought that Dinzil, by some trick, had me again in prison. The sword—where was the sword?

I raised my head where I lay prone on hard stone and looked about. Then I saw a glimmer beyond my paw—Paw? So I was *not* free from that other place. A vast misery of disappointment fell on me as a crushing weight.

But—my head strained higher—the paw was at the end of an arm, a human arm! On that the faint tracing of a scar I knew well; I could remember the fight in which I took it.

Now I levered myself up to look down at the rest of my body. It was no longer that of a toad man; remnants of human clothing covered me from the waist down. But the paws—I hardly dared to touch my face with those misshapen things, as if some of their foulness might rub off. But I must know if I still wore a toad head on my shoulders.

Beyond me, in the gloom of that place, something else moved. On my hands and knees, dragging the sword with me, I went to see what.

A human body wearing the riding dress of the Valley people, a woman's body. At the end of her slender arms were red paws even more formless than mine. Above her shoulders was an ovoid, hairless featureless, save for two eyepits. At my coming the head swung and those pits looked at me as if organs of sight hid somewhere in their depths.

"Kaththea!" I stretched forth my paws to her, but she once more avoided me. Only raised her own paws to set beside mine, as if to emphasize their monster form. Then she cowered away and brought up her arms to hide her head.

What moved me then I do not know, but I plucked at the scarf about my arm, no longer a band of light, but once more silken fabric. I now held it out to Kaththea.

The pit eyes peered at it over the top of one of her shielding arms. Then her paw came forth and snatched it from me, winding it around and around her head, leaving but a small slit open for sight.

Meanwhile I looked around. We were either back in the Tower rooted in Escore, or its double. We sat on the floor near the staircase as steep as a ladder. The doorways through which one could pass into those other worlds were closed, but the sooner we were away the better. I turned to my sister.

"Come—"

"Where?" her thought demanded. "Where can I find a place to hide what I now am?"

Fear touched me that perhaps her terror was rooted in truth, that we had brought back from the place Dinzil knew permanent disfigurement, since we had wrought there with powers of the light, but which, perhaps, had been distorted by the Shadow.

"Come—"

Somehow I got her to her feet, and we went down that breakneck stair and stood in the corridor of the mound. Once more the runes ran red on the sword, and those I watched. But still I set paw to Kaththea and drew her with me. She went silently beside me, moving as one stricken so she cared not where she went, nor to what future.

We came out into a gray day with sullen rain falling heavily. I wondered at how I was to find our way back to where I had left Orsya. But this rutted road we could follow in part.

Kaththea's mind was closed to me, though I tried to get her interested in our escape. She walked dumbly, behind a barrier I could not pierce. I kept my eye upon the sword, though after we emerged from the mound, the runes cooled, nor did they fire again as we passed through the dell and climbed the rise on the other side.

From here I surveyed the ground, marking landmarks I had set in mind when

I came this way. Surely it had been over there that I had slain that monstrous thing which was one of the guardians of the Dark Tower.

The hunger of which I had been aware in that other world was now pain and I brought out from my belt pouch the roots Orsya had supplied. I offered one to Kaththea.

"It is good—untainted—" I told her as I put another to my lips.

She struck it out of my grasp, so it rolled out of sight into a crevice between two rocks. Still her mind was closed to me. My hatred of Dinzil was such that had he stood before me I would have tried to rend him with teeth and nails, as might a woodland beast.

Kaththea began to waver back and forth, stumbling now and then, so I steadied her. Suddenly she twisted and shoved me from her, so I fell. Before I gained my feet she was staggering back toward the Tower.

I caught up with her, and, apparently, that last rebellion had drained her energy. She did not try to throw off the hold I kept on her, though I was alert to any move she made.

We went downslope and the footing was rough. But we might have walked through a deserted world. The sword runes did not light, and we saw no living thing. I thought I knew the brush ahead, though it was not mist-wreathed today. At last we came to the stream and the reef of rock where I had last seen Orsya. Somehow, I do not know why, I had expected to sight her there still, waiting, just as I had seen her last. When she was not I knew a surge of disappointment.

"Did you think you could depend upon the water wench, my foolish brother?" That hard, unknown Kaththea's thoughts cut into my brain. "But it is as well for her."

"What do you mean?"

Laughter now, inside my head—such laughter as I had never thought to hear except from one as far along the path elsewhere as Dinzil.

"Because, Kemoc, my dear brother, I might ask a boon of you and, I think, I could make you grant me that boon, and thereafter it would not be well with your water wench."

"What do you mean?" I demanded again since she had left down the barrier. Only that dreadful laughter rang in my head. I guessed I had lost Kaththea for now, even though she walked unwillingly beside me.

Our road out was the stream and beyond the river. So plain was that I did not need Orsya's guidance. Yet I still worried about her—hoping that she had prudently withdrawn to safety, and not that she had been captured by some roving danger of this land.

We came to the deserted house of the aspt and under my urging Kaththea crawled into the chamber ahead of me. She settled herself against the far wall, as far from me as was possible in such confined quarters.

"Kaththea, in the Valley they know much, more than we. They will know what to do!"

"But, Kemoc, my brother, *I* know what to do! I need only your water wench for the doing. If not her, there will be another. But she is an excellent choice, being what and who she is. Bring her to me, or me to her, and we shall make such magic as shall astonish you—Kemoc who thinks he knows something of mysteries and only cons tatters discarded by those far greater than he."

I almost lost my patience. "Such as Dinzil, I suppose."

She was silent for a long moment. Then once more that laughter rang in my mind. "Dinzil—ah, there is one who climbs clouds to tread the sky. He wants so very, very much, does Dinzil. But whether he will have even a handful from the full measure he thinks upon, that is another question, and Dinzil must come to face it. I think I hated you, Kemoc, for what you wrought when you brought me forth. But now, thinking on it the more, I see you have served me even better than I could have ordered for myself. There I was subject to Dinzil—you were so right to fear that for me. Dear brother, for your services there shall be a reward." The head so closely shrouded in the green scarf nodded.

I was chilled within, wondering what manner of thing had come to dwell within Kaththea, and whether it could ever be expelled. I thought of those two fates Loskeetha had foreseen, though neither had come to pass. In them Kaththea was one with the enemy. Now perhaps I could accept that she would be far better dead.

Only all men cling to hope and if I could get her back to the Valley surely there would be those who could deal with her, taking away not only the monster face, but the monster inner dweller also.

"Sleep, Kemoc; I swear to you that I shall be here when you wake. I want nothing more now than to go where you go."

She spoke the truth, I knew. But now it was not what I wanted to hear. Whether she slept, I do not know. But she lay quiet, her bandaged head upon her arm. At length I could watch no longer, for weariness overcame me.

XVII

*W*e crept forth from that den in the morning. Again I offered Kaththea some of the roots and she refused, saying she had no hunger for such. When I pressed as to what food she needed, she shut herself off from me. Still she went with me without urging.

Once more the mist curdled the air about the stream. I welcomed it, for the water made a path plain to follow and the fog, I hoped, would shelter us. I watched in the stream for any movement which might show Kofi was here, for I held in mind the thought that Orsya might have left the Merfay to await us.

Or had the Krogan girl believed my mission to the Dark Tower so hopeless that she saw no reason to prepare for any return?

The scraps of vegetation looming through the fog were clean of that taint which streaked the land. But they were beginning to wither from nature. It was much colder and I thought winter must be now the closer. I could not control my shivering and longed for a cloak such as I had used to make my puppet along the way.

As we went I also paid attention to the sword for rune warnings. The mist deadened sound in a curious way and I thought that the blade might be our only alert against some dangers.

We could follow the waterways back to the Heights, if we were very lucky. But I would not attempt a return through the underground passages. Therefore, we must somehow win across the land.

To do so was a fool's folly. There was every reason to believe that we could be tracked down between one sunrise and sunset. Still I turned to the Heights and kept on. There was no other way.

Laughter—faintly jeering laughter. I turned my head quickly and looked to Kaththea.

"Impossible, my dear brother? You have an excellent forefuture reading, according to your gifts. But, remember, you do not walk alone, and I can show you some tricks which even your water wench or the Wise Ones of Estcarp could not truly lay name to. We shall get back to the Valley, never fear. If we will it, both together, that we shall do."

Again arrogant confidence in herself, the mocking half-note in relation to others. Yet that confidence carried conviction that she knew whereof she spoke. It was just that, within me, I shrank from any aid she would give me, whereas I had welcomed that of Orsya.

"What . . . !" Her scarf swathed head turned from me; she was staring into the water which was curiously agitated where the mist curtain touched it.

"Kofi!" I cried. "Orsya?" I sent a thought call. But there was no answer. The rippling in the water drew closer as the Merfay treaded water, waiting for us to catch up.

"What is it?" demanded Kaththea. "I cannot thought-scan it. But there is life here. What *is* it?"

"A Merfay. It guided us into this country."

"A friend to your water wench?" Kaththea stopped as if she did not want to approach it any nearer.

Suddenly her designation of Orsya rasped me. "Her name is Orsya and she, too, is a holder of power. With her only did I find you." My reply sounded sharp, even in my own ears.

"Orsya," Kaththea repeated. "Your pardon, brother—it shall be Orsya. So, she aided you to me? That I shall remember also. It is her magic which has strengthened this scarf of mine. But to return to this messenger we cannot see, nor mind-touch—he is a messenger, is he not?"

"I hope so."

I went down on one knee in the shallow wash of the stream and held out my hand—that paw hand—much as I had when Orsya lent her sense of sight to mine so that I could see Kofi. The disturbance in the water drew closer, but this time I felt no light touch of alien flesh on mine. Perhaps Kofi could not bring himself to such contact with the thing which now served me as a hand. For that I could not blame him. But I hoped my gesture of good will would be accepted as a greeting between us.

The splashing moved away, downstream. I did not know whether he wished nothing more to do with us, or was trying to be our guide once again. Since we must keep to the river for now, I was willing to hope it was the latter.

It must have been that, for he did not leave us behind, but kept to a pace which matched ours, though some strides ahead. Once the runes blazed red and I threw up my hand to stop Kaththea, listening, watching that thick curtain of mist. There was a muffled cawing, a series of cries splitting the silence. Then nothing, though we stood very still to listen. After a while, the runes faded.

"He hunts—" Kaththea's thought came to me.

For me now there was only one "he." "Dinzil—for us?"

Again her laughter. "You did not truly believe he would let me go so easily, brother? After he had gone so far to gain my aid? I think now Dinzil needs me more than I need him. Which makes a good point for any future bargains."

"Bargains?"

"I do not intend to go misshapen in this or any other world, Kemoc!" Her confidence cracked a little; behind it I thought I read deep anger.

"I thought you knew a way to help yourself." I pursued the subject even though I knew it was painful, for no other reason than I must learn all I could of what she thought Dinzil might do, or what she was prepared to do. I no longer trusted this Kaththea.

"Oh, I do. But it would be like Dinzil to make trouble afterwards. The road I must take can only be walked once. Also—" She checked her thought flow quickly and once more there was a barrier between us.

I shivered almost convulsively. The chill ate into my half bare body. Kaththea's head swung around so that the slit which gave her eye room faced me. Then she raised one of her red paws.

"Bring me some of those—" She motioned toward reeds growing nearby.

Though my paws were not shaped for such work, I pulled a goodly handful and held them out to her, at her gesture laying them across her two paws. She bent her head and breathed on them. Though her mind was now closed to me, I felt a kind of stirring which came from the use of power. The reeds lengthened, thickened, became part of one another, and she held a thick, wadded jacket, such as we wore in Estcarp in autumn. I took it from her and drew it on. Not only did it shield me from the chill of the wind, but also it appeared to radiate warmth, so I was now as comfortable as if I walked through a warm spring day.

"You see—power can be used to smooth the way in little things as well as big," Kaththea's thought came to me.

I rubbed the front of the jacket. It felt very real. I only trusted that the spell would linger.

She caught that. "As long as you have the need, it will, for it is shaped to your use."

We reached the main river, the mist disappearing. I still kept watch, but Kaththea marched along through the shallows as one who had naught to fear. Before us the vee of ripples marked the swimming Kofi. So he still accompanied us.

Far off sound again. Not the cawing this time, but rather a baying, such as the way the hunted hounds of Alizon (those bred for the harrying of men) sound when they course their prey.

"The Saran ride—"

I only realized since Kaththea went veiled how much one reads in the expression of one's comrades. Could I be sure that the emotions aroused by her thoughts were hers—or mine? I thought she was excited, but not as if the hunt had any connection with her. She might have been an onlooker. Was she so sure that Dinzil valued her to the extent that if his hunters came upon her she need have no fears?

"Dinzil know what he needs." So again she read my thoughts. "Dinzil has not climbed clouds to assault the high skies without being careful of all he must use along the way—until he is finished with it. Dinzil had fitted many tools to his task in the past, but he has never had one from Estcarp. So he now faces a surprise."

The baying grew louder. I saw the vee mark of Kofi dart to the opposite shore. There was a waving in the weeds; the Merfay must be going into hiding. I looked about me, but we were in such a place as had no natural defense spots. We could take to deep water, but when I said so, Kaththea gave a definitive negative.

"Your Orsya likes her mud holes and to slink along the bottom of water reaches. But I am not Orsya, nor do I have gills. As neither do you, dear brother. What of that sword of yours . . . ?" She put out her paw as if pointing a finger and then gave a small cry, jerking it back to nurse against her breast.

"What do you hold there?"

"A weapon and a talisman." Somehow I had no desire to share with her the story of from whence it had come and what it did for me.

The runes were taking fire, standing out upon the golden blade. Not for the first time I wished that I had the knowledge to read them, to know just how much this weapon could do for him who carried it, so that in danger I could call upon all it had to offer and not blunder in the dark.

There was a stirring along the ridge on the other side of the river. I tried to push Kaththea into deeper water, but she eluded me, stood to front what came as if she no fear of it. So, perforce, I had to stand with her, sword in hand, while the runes on it ran so bloody that one might think to see their crimson drip from the blade.

They came: three wolfmen running on all fours, and it was these who bayed. Behind them came men such as the ones who had captured Orsya. In their rear were two more, and they were as those who had used the lightning rods to kill the Krogan.

Again Kaththea's unearthly laughter rang in my head.

"A paltry handful, brother, not meet to think to drag us down! Dinzil forgets himself to offer such insult."

Her paws rose to the scarf about her head of horror and deliberately she began to unwind that covering, all the time facing those who came. In my paw-hand the hilt of the sword heated.

The jaws of the Gray Ones were agape, showing their fangs, while they drooled slaver. Their eyes were red sparks of pure evil. Behind them the others slowed their mounts to a trot. I saw that the animals they rode were not Renthan, but closer in appearance to the horses of Estcarp, save they were larger and more powerful, and all were black. They rode bareback, with no use of bit nor rein. I remembered the Keplian, that horse-demon which had almost slain Kyllan.

So they came to the river bank and looked across to us, the water flowing between. The Gray Ones crouched at the edge of the stream, the others ranged behind them. The swordsmen were, as Dinzil had been, outwardly sons of the Old Race, or enough to pass unnoticed among them. But the two who bore the fire weapons were alien. They rode masked with hoods. But the hands—ah—there I saw paws like those I now was doomed to wear. I thought that, could I pull off those hoods, I might see toad heads. Dinzil must have summoned these henchmen out of that other world to which the Tower was the dread entrance way.

The folds of the scarf dropped away from Kaththea's head. In this open daylight that monstrous face which was not a true face was pitilessly revealed. For the first time I saw it completely and could not help an involuntary shrinking though I fought it instantly.

No mouth, no nose, only those eyepits in the red ovoid of head. Remembering my fair sister, I understood how such a happening could well nigh turn her brain, make her seek any remedy she knew of.

The Gray Ones did not advance into the stream, and I recalled Orsya's saying that running water was a deterrent to certain types of evil. But I had seen the fire weapons of those hooded ones spit across another river and I waited tensely now for one of those rods to point in our direction.

Kaththea raised both paws as high as her shoulders, held them outwards, the paws pointed to that assorted company. She used thoughts and her hands moved as if she waved them on at the enemy. What words they were I did not know. I wanted to run from her, for in my mind was a tearing, a burning, such as no man of human birth could stand. But I held to the sword and the warmth from the hilt traveled up my arm, into me, finally reaching my mind and there set up a barrier against the forces she summoned, so that, though her paws still waved and she continued to hurl her thoughts, it meant nothing to me.

The Gray Ones threw back their heads and broke into a wild, tormented howling, like unto the cries of those damned and doomed. They dashed back and forth, finally away from the river, retreating into the broken country behind.

After them the Keplians neighed, reared. Some threw their riders before they followed the wolfmen. Some of the men managed to keep their seats, but those who fell lay prone, unmoving, on the ground as if struck dead. Only the two hooded ones slid from their unhappy mounts, which plunged off, and stood together, watching Kaththea. But they made no move to turn their weapon tubes upon us.

My sister's arms dropped to her side. She spoke by open mind thought so I understood her.

"Say this to your overlord: the hawk does not hunt when the eagle flies. Nor does one who wears the cloak of power send to an equal less than a Herald of Banners. If he would have words with me, let him say them as we have always dealt—face to face." She laughed. "Remind him of what you see now; it will hearten him, for there can be a bargaining."

They gave no outward sign that they understood, any more than they replied; they simply turned and walked away, presenting their backs to us as if they had no fear of any attack. Now Kaththea again fastened the scarf back in shrouding folds.

"You sent a challenge to Dinzil," I said aloud.

"I sent a challenge," she agreed. "He will not again, I believe, dispatch underlings to hunt us as if some slaves of his were escaping. When he comes, it will be full in the power he thinks he has."

"But—"

"But that is what you fear, brother? You need not. Dinzil thought to make of me a tool, as one uses pinchers of iron to take a blazing coal from the heart of a fire. For a while"—she tucked the loose ends of her scarf into the front of her jacket to keep them tight—"he might have had a small part of it. Only—you see—he exposed me to much he had learned. Since I had already been well taught in another school, I could fit that learning into a new pattern which he does not know. Let him believe I have power and he will be twice eager to treat with us. Shall we go?" She turned her muffled head from one side to the other, and then pointed to our left. "I dislike water walking. I do not believe we shall again be challenged by anything in this land. The Valley lies that way."

"How can you be sure?" Her arrogance was growing. She snapped her thoughts now as a hunter snaps a riding whip against a boot. Surely the Kaththea I had known all my life was further and further from me.

"The Valley is a reservoir of power, surely you cannot deny that. As such it puts forth a signal for all those who can feel. Try it yourself, brother, with that mysterious fire sword of yours."

So much was I under her command at that moment, that I did raise the sword, holding it only loosely to see if it could act as a pointer. I swear that I did not incline it, but it did point in the same direction she had indicated.

Against my will we left the river, though I knew that sooner or later we would have had to do so, since I would not have gone underground again.

We were quickly through that wholesome growth along the stream bed and into the blasted land which laced this rolling country. Kaththea marched straight ahead, as one who has no need to fear, but I held the sword as a guard against what might lie here, avoiding, making her avoid, certain bushes, stones, and the like, when the runes warned. We had not gone far before I knew that we had skulkers to our right and left, also trailing behind. Some of the shapes I sighted were ones I had seen before in the ranks of evil, others new to me. Not all were foul or monstrous seeming. If they were illusions they were proof against my desire for clear sight.

None of these moved to obstruct us in any way, save that they were ready to close in upon the command of their warlord. I kept ever alert, waiting for Dinzil to appear and accept Kaththea's challenge.

For such a battle I was ill-equipped. I had but one ultimate weapon, as Orsya had pointed out. There were those *words* from Lormt which had been *answered*. I might call again on what had so *answered*. Though to do so was a risk only to be taken by one in the depths of despair at a time of complete loss of hope.

Good spots appeared here and there in this seared land, mostly, I noted, about springs, pools, or small runlets, as if water was a factor in holding back the evil which had blasted so much of the country. It was a hard way to follow, for, as I had seen from my rock perch in the Heights, it was very broken, sharp ridges dividing narrow ravines, so that it seemed to me we were eternally climbing, or descending to climb again. Yet Kaththea appeared to be in no way baffled at direction and unhesitatingly took the lead, always bearing to the left. Now I could see the Heights themselves as proof she was right.

We stopped at last beside one of the pools of sweet water. I ate one of the few remaining roots Orsya had given me, though I could have finished them all. But again Kaththea would have no food, seating herself with her back against a great rock, staring downstream. I was well aware that all about us scouts of that company behind watched us.

"We must find a place for night camp." I tried to find a normal subject to discuss with this stranger I found it hard to believe was my sister.

"We shall find one and—" her thoughts were silent. Then she added, "If all goes well, we shall discover thereabouts what is most needed. But there is no time to linger now."

Already she was on her feet, striding away up the cut above the pool. As I tramped after her I suddenly saw, in the soft earth of the bank, the print of wedge-shaped feet, the toes only marked by faint indentations. As I had learned to know them—Krogan! They led from the pool, away from water, which puzzled me.

Orsya? But I could not be sure of that. If the Krogan had allied themselves with the Shadow as they may well have done by now, then any one of them could be among that company now ranging behind us. Only, *why away from water?* That was the one thing they dreaded more than anything else. I saw no other prints to suggest that this wayfarer had been a prisoner, nor even if he or she had been hunted, and thus forced into dry country.

The marks were to be seen now and again in patches of dry soil, smudged but still unmistakable. A Krogan, apparently deliberately, climbing the same way, against all nature and custom. Twice I knelt to examine them more closely, certain I must be mistaken. Once I touched sword point into one to see if the runes would tell me anything. This might be an illusion meant to deceive. But the runes did not light.

It was growing fast into twilight when we came into a narrow dark cut leading upward and Kaththea went into it without faltering. I saw the prints here also, but something made me believe that the maker now walked with difficulty. Was there water ahead? If so, I trusted that the straggler from the river had managed to reach it.

Then I saw in the deep gloom a tiny spark of white fire. It could be nothing but Orsya's horn-rod, set up as she had before, for protection against the evil roaming here. But Orsya away from water—why?

"Because we have need of her, brother!" Kaththea's thought reached me for the first time in hours. "She gave of her magic in this scarf—and that can be a two-way road. Having put something of herself into it, I could reach her so—now she waits us."

"But she is far from water, and she is Krogan. She must have water!"

"Do not worry; she shall have all she needs when we reach her."

I was aching tired but I ran now, stumbling into rocks which choked this place. Then I came to where stood the unicorn horn with its taper of protection. By it lay Orsya. She moved feebly as I dropped on my knees beside her. Water—but I had no bottle of that precious fluid. Could I take her back, down the broken land, to the pool where I had seen her prints first? It would be almost hopeless to try, but if there were no other way of saving her, that I would do.

"It is not necessary." Kaththea stood there, gazing down at the two of us, "What needs to be done can be done here and now."

"There is no water, and without water she will die."

Kaththea was slowly unwinding the scarf. Orsya's head turned a little on my arm. I had an impulse to life my hand, to cover her eyes so that she could not look upon the monster my sister had become.

"Monster—yes."

I was ashamed that my sister had caught that thought. "But now we have the remedy—that which you can do for me, Kemoc. As I know you will—you will— you will—" She repeated the words in my brain with a beat, and I found myself agreeing that what she wanted would be done.

"Take that good sword of yours, Kemoc, and give me blood—blood to wash away ensorcelment, to be Kaththea again."

"Blood!" I was startled out of my acquiescence.

"Blood!" She leaned closer, stretched out her paws. "Kill the water wench; let me have her blood! Or would you have me half monster all the rest of my days?"

Then she spoke other words, meant to bind and command, and I raised the sword. On it the runes blazed high and the hilt burned my hand. I looked to Orsya and she gazed at me, though she made no plea for mercy, nor was there any fear in her large eyes, only a kind of patient waiting for what she could not escape.

I cried out, rammed the point of the sword into the earth so it stood quivering between Kaththea and the two of us. And I heard Kaththea cry in answer. This time not with her mind but aloud, it being so terrible I shuddered. In it I heard that moan of one betrayed by him upon whom she had the greatest right in the world to trust. Her anguish cut through the Kaththea who now was, to reveal the Kaththea who had once been. She cowered away from us covering her face with her forearms.

I laid Orsya back on the ground and reached for the sword hilt.

"If you must have blood," I began and raised that blade to my own flesh.

But she did not listen. Instead she laughed, that terrible, lost laughter. Then she ran away from us, back into the dark. But her thoughts still reached me.

"So be it! So be it! I shall make another bargain. But perhaps it will not be so simple, and you shall rue it even more, Kemoc Tregarth!"

XVIII

I would have gone after her, but Orsya caught at my ankle, so that I tripped and fell. She held tightly, and, when I writhed around to free myself by force, she cried out:

"I do this for you, Kemoc, for you! She is no longer what you think her. Now she would lead you straight into their hands. Look upon your sword!"

I was loosening her hold finger by finger. Now I glanced to the sword which had fallen from my hand, and which now lay, point out into the dark. Never had I seen those runes blaze so fiercely.

"It is Kaththea out there!" I loosed the Krogan girl's hold. "And we were followed by forces of the Shadow."

"She is not the Kaththea of your knowing," Orsya repeated weakly. Her eyes closed, and she forced them open again with what was manifestly a great effort. "Think you, Kemoc; would she to whom you have been bound ask you to do what she did?"

"Why—why did she?" I had my hand on the sword hilt. But I was no longer so driven by the need to follow Kaththea. Thought had returned to me.

"Because it is true. Blood is life, Kemoc. Among the half people, hunters drink the blood of the bravest of their kill, that they may have the life force and courage of those they have vanquished. Do not warriors mingle their blood, that henceforth they may be brothers?"

"Among the Sulcarmen they do."

"Wherever your sister has been, she has been marked. She cannot be whole and herself unless blood draws her back entirely to this world again. Kemoc— your hands!" She was staring at my paws. I held them closer to her unicorn candle for her viewing.

"As she is marked, so am I. It is worse for her. To be a fair maid, and then look upon yourself as—*that!* It is enough to drive one mad!"

"Which is also true." Orsya's reply was but a whisper. "She put the drawing spell on me, did she not?"

"Yes."

I looked from my paws to the Krogan girl, roused from my thoughts. Water— Orsya would die if she had no water. If I followed Kaththea, Orsya would die in this desolate place as surely as if I had done as my sister demanded. If I could not kill Orsya by sword stroke, still less could I leave her to die more lingeringly.

"Water . . . ?" I looked dully about me as if I expected to see it gush forth from some rock at my saying of the word.

"The pool—back there," I added, though I thought that was hopeless. Even if I could find my way back in the dark, carrying Orsya, she might well die before we reached there. If we were able to escape being pulled down by that monstrous army . . .

Her thoughts whispered faintly in my mind: "Over Heights—"

I looked up the cut. Such a climb—in the dark. . . .

She struggled feebly, reaching out her hand for the horn. When I would have taken it up for her, she roused to refuse me.

"No . . . if you touch it . . . virtue departs. . . . Hold me . . . to take it."

I supported her until her feeble fingers closed about the horn. Then I fastened the sword to my belt and got to my feet, gathering her up in my arms. The horn lay upon her breast and the light from it was no longer a narrow candle but a radiance which showed something of the path ahead.

That night was our time of fear, despair, struggle, endurance. Somehow Orsya held to life, and I kept going, carrying her. Now and then the sword would blaze, but I dared not wait to see what followed. The sky was dawn-gray when we came through a pass, blundered through. We looked down into wild lands. Somewhere, farther on, might lie the Valley. But for us both now there was only one need—water.

"Water—" It was not a plaint, that word from Orsya, but, I realized with an inward leap of hope, recognition! "Left, now—"

I wavered to the left, downslope. Brush tore at me and my burden, and I was so weak with weariness that, had I fallen then, I do not believe I could have come again to my numb feet. But when I did stumble forward, it was near a small cup into which fed the merest thread of spring.

Laying Orsya on the ground, I used my paws to splash and throw that precious liquid into her face, along as much of her body as I could. When she stirred I could have shouted aloud my relief. Then I pulled her closer to that small basin, and she plunged her head and as much of her shoulders into it as she could, lying there unmoving as she soaked it into her skin, regaining so its vitalizing energy.

Then she raised her head and sat up, to put her feet into its freshness. This was an act of magic as great as I had ever seen, for the body which had been so light and withered as I carried it, grew firm and young again under my eyes. I half lay now on the opposite side of the pool, sure she could care for herself, so drugged with fatigue that I could not have kept from sleep if Dinzil himself had appeared before me.

I awoke to a kind of singing in which there were sounds which might be words but which I did not understand. The hum was soothing, and held off any terrors night in these haunted wilds might hold—for it was the dark of night which I saw when I opened my eyes. Orsya, much as she had been when we journeyed into the land of the Dark Tower, sat there, facing her candle-horn, holding out her hands to its light as one warms oneself at a fire.

But when I remembered the Dark Tower, then there returned to mind all else, so the content of those first moments was lost. I sat up abruptly, looking over my shoulder, for we were still in the cup of the pool and behind us the Heights from which we had come, wherein Kaththea might still wander lost.

"There is no going back!" Orsya came to me. As she had done to show me Kofi, she knelt behind me and put her hands upon my temples. So I "saw," that the land behind us was a-crawl with the forces of the Shadow, that they were uniting for some great thrust. I knew without her telling that the thrust would be at the Valley. My allegiances, so long divided, I still could not reconcile. I was torn two ways—Kaththea and those to be warned.

"This is not the moment, nor the hour, nor the day, on which you can stand battle for Kaththea. If you return into that caldron of danger, then you shall have wasted your strength and what gifts you have for naught. Indeed, you may do worse; did not Dinzil hint that in you he might find yet another tool? Will he not be more inclined to try that since he can no longer control Kaththea? You might be a rich prize—" Orsya reasoned.

"How know you what Dinzil said to me?" I interrupted.

"While you slept you dreamed, and while you dreamed, I learned much," she returned simply. "Be assured, Kemoc, your sister has stepped beyond the limits where you can call to her."

"There are powers; they can be sought." I closed my mind, or tried to, to that fear.

"But not by you. You know too little to be properly on guard; you might lose too much. Now must be your choice: Throw away all by going back, or take your warning to the Valley."

She was right, but that did not make her words any easier to accept. I had failed, and for the rest of my life I must live with that failure. But, matters now going as they seemed to be, that life would probably not be long. Best spend it doing all I could to withstand the Shadow.

We had to keep to water, which made us vulnerable. Yet I would not do as Orsya urged and leave her to follow alone. I knew too well what might happen to her. I had lost Kaththea through ignorance—for I might have given her my own blood and so won her back—but I was not going to be responsible for Orsya's loss also.

She kept the horn tight against her. It glowed still and gave us light. And, she told me, it had other properties for our protection. But I disliked using it, for power draws power, even if they are of opposite natures.

At dawn we huddled in a niche between two large boulders. The thin rill we had followed from the pool linked here with a larger stream and first Orsya lay long beneath its surface, drawing restoration into her. Once we roused from uneasy dozing, hearing a ring of hooves on stone. I pushed into a crack from which I could see below. Men rode there—not on Keplians, but on Renthans. They might be a scouting party from the Valley, was my first thought, until I saw their banner and read the device on it as one borne by a follower of Dinzil.

But they would be welcome in the Valley, thus opening a door for their fellows. . . . In me now was born a need for speed, to deliver the warning. Orsya's hand touched my paw.

"They ride from, not to, the Valley," she said. "But it is true that time grows short for all of us!"

How short we realized as we moved on. Twice we crouched in hiding as parties of the enemy went by. Once some shadowy things which glowed and left a putrescent odor on the air; then, three Gray Ones who loped with a fast, ground covering stride.

Orsya found food for us, things which she routed from under stream rocks and which I crammed hastily into my mouth and tried neither to think on or taste, as I manfully chewed and swallowed. We kept to the stream which luckily ran in the right direction. Shortly before sundown Orsya pointed to a vee of ripples.

"Kofi?"

"No, but another of his people. Perhaps he has news for us."

She trilled and twittered as she had with Kofi, and then turned to me with a slight frown.

"The forces of the Shadow are spread widely between us and the Valley. They await some word for attack."

"Can we pass them?"

"I do not know. You swim, but not well enough to take the deep ways."

"If I have to, then I shall. Show them to me," I told her grimly.

She seemed very doubtful. But after further twitter speech with the Merfay, she shrugged. "If it must be, it must—"

But we were not to reach her "deep ways." From nowhere, there converged on us shortly after what looked to be, by the troubling of the water, a large school of Merfays. They treaded water about Orsya. I heard their small cries which must have been delivered with great vigor to reach my ears.

"What is it?"

"My people are coming—"

"They have joined the Shadow, then?"

"No. They still believe they can make peace and go their own way, if they pay a price to those they fear the most. That price is you and I. They know we travel the river and their magic I cannot hope to elude."

"You can hide. Surely the Merfays will show you where. I can take to the land again." I was impatient to get on. There was an urgency which burned me as a fever.

Orsya did not appear to hear me. She had turned back to those splashes and ripples and was once more twittering. "Come—" She moved downstream, the invisible Merfays, judging by the disturbance, falling in on either hand as an escort.

"But why? You said—"

"Not far. There is a side way, partly underground . . ."

"Through the tomb caverns?"

"Perhaps it is an outer section of those. But not the portion we saw before. It is one my people do not know."

We did not go much further before the Merfay ripples darted ahead; Orsya paused and held out her hand to grasp that beastly paw which now marked me.

"They go to mislead the others. My people do not know this country and they will come slowly. Also they will listen to the Merfays. Now—we go this way!"

She dropped her hold and used that hand to sweep aside some bushes which trailed in great drooping fronds, the tips floating in the water. Behind that screen was another waterway, shallow as a brook, running through a narrow slit.

Part of that way we went on hands and knees, hidden by the walls of the slit. By luck it was largely overgrown with the trailing branched bushes and, while sometimes those lashed at us stingingly, we could make our way under them. The brook ended in a pool and Orsya halted there.

"The entrance is below; we must dive for it."

"How long underwater?"

"Long for you, but it is the only way."

I made the sword fast to me. Then I pulled off that warm jacket Kaththea had spun out of reeds and illusion. I rolled it into a ball and thrust it beneath the roots of one of the bushes, only to see it dissolve into a frayed bunch of yellowed reeds. I filled my lungs and dived.

Once more that nightmare, wherein I pinned my hopes on Orsya's guiding touch on my shoulder, to steer me. I had reached the point where my lungs were bursting when my head broke water and I could breathe again. There was dark, but out of it came Orsya's touch and voice.

"Thus—" She urged me forward and I swung clumsily, the weight of the sword pulling me down. It is hard to judge distances in the dark and I do not know how long we swam. But I was tiring as we came out, as if through a door, into a gray place and saw in the wall not too far above our heads crevices through which the light came.

Those were not difficult to reach, and then we were out among rocks, looking down at the last of the sunlight on a plain. There mustered an army. It would seem that our side path had led us directly to the enemy.

I did not recognize the land beyond. If this was before one of the ramparts of the Valley, it was a section I did not know. I said as much to Orsya.

"I do not think they move against the Valley yet. Look—"

My gaze followed the pointing of her finger. To our right and not too far away was a ledge and on that stood a group of people. I caught a glimpse of a green swathed head.

"Kaththea!"

"And Dinzil." Orsya indicated a cloaked man, looming tall beside my sister. "There is also one of the Captains of the Sarn Riders, and others who must be of note. And—do you not feel it, Kemoc? They dabble in power."

She was right. There was a tingling in the air, a tension, a kind of ingathering of force. I had felt it once before, on that night when the Wise Women of Estcarp had made ready their blow of doom against the army of Karsten coming through the southern mountains. It sucked at one's life forces, gathered, gathered. . . .

"They will try such a blow, and then, with those of the Valley still reeling under it, move in."

But I did not need Orsya's explanation. I had guessed it for myself. Worst of all—I caught one strong element in that brewing of evil. Kaththea was mind calling—not me, but Kyllan! She was now so utterly of the Shadow that she turned that which was born in us to summon my brother, to use him as a key to the Valley.

Then I knew the true meaning of Loskeetha's fates, that Kaththea was indeed better dead. And that it was laid upon me to kill her. If she could use such calling, then could I also.

"Stay you here!" I ordered Orsya, and I began to creep along the heights so I could find a place above and behind that ledge. It did not take me long to reach it. I think they were so oblivious of anything besides what they did that they would not have seen me had I marched down to them.

I found a place where I could stand in the open. Then I drew the sword and pointed its tip at my sister. All the wisdom I knew went into the call I sent in one lightning thrust.

She swayed, her hands to her swathed head. Then she turned and began to run across the ledge, scramble up to me. They were still so intent upon their convergence of wills and forces that they did not understand for a moment, long enough for her to start the climb. Then Dinzil followed her. She could not reach me; she would not have time. So I did what I had seen myself once do in Loskeetha's sand bowl; I hurled the sword at her, willing her death.

It turned in the air and its hilt struck between her eyes. She dropped and would have fallen back to the ledge, but her body caught against a point of rock and lay there, the sword in the earth, standing upright.

Dinzil, seeing her fall, halted. He looked up at me and began to laugh; it was the laughter. I had heard from Kaththea, only more lost and evil. He raised his hand to me in salute as one salutes a clever bit of weapon-play.

But I was already sliding down beside Kaththea. I took up the sword and then her also, setting her body back in the slit between spur and cliff.

"The hero," he called. "Too little, too late, warrior from overmountain!"

He made a gesture and suddenly the sword slipped from my grip. Nor could I make that misshapen paw grasp it again.

"And now harmless—" he laughed. He stood there, laughing with the rest of that company of the Shadow gathering behind him, watching me with their eyes or whatever organs served them for sight. These might not be of the Great Ones of evil, but they did now strive to reach such heights. I think even the Witches of Estcarp would not have willingly matched strength with them.

"You have found one talisman." Dinzil glanced to the sword. "If you had only known how to use it, you would have done better, my young friend. Now—"

What he meant for me I do not know. But that it was wholly of the dark I understood. Even death does not close some doors. But there was a slide of earth and small stones as Orsya came down in my wake. She held her right hand against her breast, and in it, point out, was the unicorn horn.

Whether by some magic of her own she mystified Dinzil, for the necessary moment or two, I do not know. But she was beside me and he still stood there. Then she plunged the point of the horn into her other hand so the blood welled up about it. As that flowed she reached out and caught my now useless paw, smearing it with the scarlet fluid. There was a tingle of returning life. I saw that foul toad flesh slough away and out of it emerge my fingers. Then I threw myself to the left and reached the sword.

The enemy was moving, not with weapons, but with their knowledge. As one might use a blacksmith's sledge to crush an ant, they were turning on me, on us, the weight of what they had been about to send against the Valley. To meet this I had nothing left but my weapon of despair.

I stumbled to my feet, sweeping Orsya behind me with my sister's body. This was indeed the last throw of fate. The sword I held up, not in a position of defense, but as one saluting an overlord. And I spoke the *words.* . . .

It had been sunset when we had come upon that gathering of attackers. Twilight had crept in as a part of their indrawing of dark force. Now it was instant day, with so brilliant a flash that I was blinded. I felt some of the substance of that light strike the sword blade, run through it and me—then out again. I was deaf; I was blind. Yet I heard the *answer*—and I saw. . . .

No, I can summon no words to describe what I saw, or think I saw, then. There had been many kinds of power loosed in Escore during the ancient struggles, and keys to some long forgot. Just as Dinzil had striven to find one of those keys, so had I, by chance and desperation, found another.

I was a channel for the power which *answered* my summons, and it used me. I was not a man, nor human, but a door through which it came into our space and time.

What it did there neither did I see. But it was gone as suddenly as it had come. I lay helpless against the earth while the heavens were filled with a storm such as I had never seen, and only lightning flashes broke the dark. I could not move. It was as if all the life which had been mine to command was now exhausted. I breathed, I could see the lightning, feel the lash of icy rain over me: that was all.

Sometimes I lapsed from consciousness, then I roused again. Weakly my thoughts moved as my body could not. After what seemed a long time, I called:

"Orsya?"

At first there was no answer, but I persisted, and that became the one tie which held me to the world about me. I felt that if I ceased to call I would slip away into some nothingness and never come forth again.

"Orsya?"

"Kemoc—"

My name in her thoughts! It acted upon me as water upon a man dying of thirst. I struggled to rise and found that I could move a little, though I lay partly covered by a mass of earth and small stones. My numbed body began to feel pain.

"Orsya, where are you?"

"Here—"

I crawled—hardly rising from my belly, I crawled. Then my searching hand touched flesh and in turn was gripped eagerly by her webbed fingers. We drew together while about us the rain poured less heavily. The lightning ceased to beat along the ridges. Gradually the storm died, while we lay together, not speaking, content that both had survived.

Morning came. We were on the ledge where Dinzil had tried to bring power to move the world. There had been a slide down the mountain, half entrapping us. But the enemy I did no longer see.

"Kaththea!" Memory returned to sear me.

"There—" Already Orsya crawled to a body half hidden in a pile of earth. The green scarf was still twisted about my sister's head. I put out my hand to touch it. Then looked at the fingers Orsya had given back to me. Furiously I began to dig free Kaththea's body with those fingers.

When she lay straight upon the ledge, I set her paw hands upon her breast. Perhaps I could hide those so none would ever know why and what she had become. But, under my hand I felt a faint beating—she was not dead!

"Orsya"—I turned to my companion—"you—you gave me back my hands. Can I give Kaththea back hers, and her face?"

She moved away from me, looking about as if she searched for something among the debris. "The horn—" Tears gathered in her eyes, ran down her slightly hollowed cheeks. "It is gone."

But I had seen something else—-a glint of metal. Now I dug there, though my nails broke. Once more my hand was able to close about the hilt of the talisman sword. I jerked it free. But of the blade there remained now but a single small shard and that was not golden but black and dull. I tried it on the ball of my thumb. It was sharp enough and it was all I had.

I went back to Kaththea and tore off that much faded scarf, looked down at the monster head. Then I did as Orsya had done before me, I cut my flesh with that broken sword and allowed the blood to drip, first upon the head, and then upon the paws. As it had for me, but more slowly, the change came. The red skin and flesh melted; my sister's own face, her slender hands, were free of their horrible disguise. I gathered her into my arms and I wept—until she stirred in my hold and her eyes slowly opened. There was no recognition in them, only puzzlement. When I tried to reach her by mind call, I met first amazement and then terror. She fought to free herself from my hold as if I were some nightmare thing.

Orsya caught her hands, held them firmly but gently. "It is well, sister. We are your friends."

Kaththea clung to her, but still looked doubtfully at me.

The Krogan girl came to me a little later where I stood looking down at the havoc the storm had wrought. There were bodies in that wrack, but no man nor creature moved under the rising sun of a fine day.

"How is it with her?" I asked.

"Well, as to her body. But—Kemoc—she has forgotten who and what she was. What power she had is now gone from her!"

"For all time?" I could not imagine Kaththea so drained.

"That I cannot tell. She is as she might have been had she never been born a Witch—a maid, sweet of temper, gentle, and now very much in need of your strength and aid. But do not try to recall to her the past."

So it was that while Orsya and I brought Kaththea back to the Valley, we did not bring back the Kaththea who had been. And if she will ever be that again, no man nor witch can say. But the forces of the Shadow suffered a second defeat, and for a space we could ride Escore more boldly, though the darkness was far from cleansed. And our tale of three was not yet ended.

Sorceress
of the
Witch World

I

∞

$\mathcal{T}$he freezing breath of the Ice Dragon was strong and harsh over the heights, for it was midwinter, and the dregs of a year which had been far from kind to me and mine. Yes, it was in the time of the Ice Dragon that I took serious thought of the future and knew, past all sighing and regret, what I must do if those I valued above all, even my own life, were to be free from a shadow which might reach them through me. I am—I was—Kaththea of the House of Tregarth, once trained as a Wise Woman, though I never gave their oath, nor wore the jewel which lies so heavy on the breasts of those who take it to them. But such learning as was and is theirs was given me, though not by my choosing.

I am one of three, three who once became one when there was need: Kyllan the warrior, Kemoc the seer-warlock, Kaththea the witch. So my mother had named us at our single birthing; so we were. She was of the Wise Women of Estcarp also, and was disowned for wedding with Simon Tregarth. He was no ordinary man, though, being a stranger who had come through one of the other world gates. Not only was he one learned in the stern art of war (which was of vast use to Estcarp, for that torn and age-worn land was then locked in struggle with Karsten and Alizon, her neighbors), but he had that which the Wise Women could not countenance in a man, some of the Power for his own.

Thus, upon her wedding and bedding it proved that Jaelithe, my mother, was not summarily shorn of her witchery as all believed she would be, but rather found a new path to the same general end. This raised the ire of those who had turned their faces from her on her choice. However, though they would not openly acknowledge she had proved tradition naught, they had to lean upon her support when there was great need, as there was.

Together, my father and mother went up against the remnants of the Kolder, those outland devils who had so long menaced Estcarp. They found the source of that spreading evil and closed it. For the Kolder, like my father, were not from our time and space, but had set up a gate of their own through which to spill their poison into Estcarp.

After that great deed the Wise Women dared not openly move against the House of Tregarth, though they neither forgot nor forgave what my mother had done. Not that she wed—for they would have accepted that, feeling only contempt for one who allowed emotion to beckon her from their austere path—but because she remained one with them in spite of her choice.

As I have said we were born at a single birthing, my brothers and I, I being the last to enter the world. And for a long time thereafter my mother ailed. We were put into the care of Anghart, a woman of the Falconers whom fate had used hardly, but who gave us the loving care my mother could not. As for my father, he was so enveloped in my mother's sufferings that he scarcely knew during those months whether we lived or died. And I think he could never, in his innermost heart, warm to us because of the hurt she took to bring us forth.

When we were children we saw little of our parents, for their combined duties in that ever-present war kept them at the South Keep. My father rode the borders there as Warden, and my mother as his seeress-in-the-field and more. We lived at a quiet manor where the Lady Loyse, who had been a comrade-of-war of my parents, kept a small circle of peace.

Early did the three of us learn that we had in us that which set us apart: we could link minds so that three became as one when there was need. And, while we used this Power then for only small matters, we were unconsciously strengthening it with each use. We also instinctively knew this was a thing to be kept secret.

My mother's break with the Council had kept me from the tests given all girl children for the selection of novices. And she and my father, whether they guessed our inheritance or not, set about us such guards against absorption into the Estcarp pattern as they could.

Then it was that my father disappeared. In one of the lulls of active raiding he had taken ship with the Sulcar, those close allies of Estcarp and his old battle friends, to explore certain islands rumored to have suspicious activity sighted on them. Neither he nor his ship were thereafter sighted nor heard from.

My mother rode into our sanctuary and for the first time she summoned Kyllan, Kemoc, and me to a real trial of power. With our strength united to hers, she sent forth a searching and saw our father. With so slender a clue, she went forth again to seek him; we remained behind.

When Kyllan and Kemoc joined the Borderers and I was left, the Wise Women moved as they had long prepared. They sent to the hold and had me taken to their Place of Silence. And for some years I was cut off from the world I knew and my brothers. But other worlds was I shown and there is a kind of hunger for such knowledge born in those of my blood which feasts and grows, until at times it fills one to the loss of all else. I fought, how I fought, during those years not to yield to the temptation of full eating, to keep part of myself free. So well did I succeed that at last I was able to reach Kemoc. Thus, before they could force the final vow upon me, he and Kyllan came to bring me out.

We could not have broken the Council's bond had it not been that all the Power was gathered up for a day and night as one pulls into one hand all the threads of a weaving. They hoarded their strength that they might deal a single blow to Karsten and put an end to their most powerful enemy. They took all their force and aimed it at the mountain lands, churning the heights, twisting the very stuff of the earth by their united will.

So they had none we could not break to spare elsewhere. And we rode eastward into the unknown. Kemoc had discovered a new mystery, that those of the Old Race of Estcarp had been mind-locked in some very ancient time, and therefore the direct east to them did not exist. This had been done when they had come from that direction into Estcarp.

Thus we went over mountain to find Escore. And there, to save us and to learn what we must know, I worked certain spells, almost to the undoing of the whole land. For this was a place where in the past mighty powers and forces had been unlocked by adepts, very ancient, but of my mother's people. And they had blasted the land in their strivings for mastery. At last those who had founded Estcarp had fled, roiling the mountains into a supposedly eternal barrier behind them.

But when I wrought my spells (small compared to what had been done in Escore in the past), forces were awakened, a delicate, hard-won balance was destroyed, and struggle between good and ill once more awoke.

We came into the Green Valley, which was held by those older even than the Old Race, though they had a measure of our blood too. But they were not of the Shadow. As we stood comradely to arms, and sent forth a warn sword to summon all of good will for a combat against the Dark, there came one they accepted as of their kind.

He was of the Old Race, a hill lord who had had for a tutor one of the last of the adepts to choose to stay in Escore and not meddle. But Dinzil was ambitious and he was a seeker. Nor was he corrupted by the love of domination when he first began that seeking. He was long known to the Green People and they met him with honor and good will. He was a man with much in him to draw one's liking—yes, and more than liking, as I can testify.

To me, who had known only my brothers and the guardsmen my father had set about us, he was a new kind of friend. And there was that which stirred in me for the first time when I looked upon his dark face. Also, he set himself to woo me, and that he did very well.

Kyllan had found his Dahaun, she who is the Lady of Green Silences, and Kemoc was as yet unheart-touched. Kyllan did not set hand to sword when I smiled upon Dinzil, and Kemoc's frowns I took, may I be forgiven, for jealousy because our three might be broken.

When Kemoc vanished, lost to us, I yielded to Dinzil's promise for aid in finding him, as well as to the wishes of my heart. The end being that I went secretly with him to the Dark Tower.

Now when I try to remember what was done there, I cannot. It is as if someone had taken water and a strong soap to wash away all the days I was Dinzil's aid in magic. Though I try to force myself to recall it, I have only pain and more pain within me.

But Kemoc, together with the Krogan maid Orsya, came seeking me, as he tells in his part of this chronicle. And he wrought with more than human endurance and strength to bring me forth from what had become an abiding place of the Shadow. By that time I was so tainted with what Dinzil and my own folly had plunged me into, that I stood at the end with Dinzil to do hurt to those I loved best. And Kemoc, daring to see me dead before I fell so low, struck me down with half learned magic.

From that hour I was as one newborn, for that stroke rift from me my learning. At first I was as a little child, doing as I was bid, without will or desires of my own. For a little I was content to be so.

Until the dreams began. I could not remember them wholly when I awoke; it was well I did not, for they were such as no sane mind could hold. And even the faint memory of some portions left me sick and cold, so that I lay upon my bed in Dahaun's feather-roofed hall and could not eat, and dared not sleep. All the protection I had learned against such ills in my days among the Wise Women had been stripped from me, so that I was as one body bare to the winter's blast. Save that what I stood naked before was worse than any sleet-laden wind, for what buffeted me was of the Shadow and very foul.

Dahaun wrought as she could, and she was a healer. But her healing was of the mind and body, and this was a matter of spirit. Kyllan and Kemoc sat by me and strove to keep the Shadow at bay. All the knowledge of those within the Valley was shaped to the end of saving me. But in those moments when I knew what they did, I understood the evil of this. For the Valley needed full protection, not only the protection of visible weapons, but also of the mind and spirit. To fight my battle weakened their defenses.

My child's clinging to the small safety and comfort they offered I must put away. So did I grow older and no longer only an unthinking child. I also knew that the dreams were only the beginning of what might attack me, and through me others. For when my own knowledge had been taken an emptiness had been left, and into that something alien was striving to pour itself.

So, even though I no longer thought as Dinzil had made me, I was still enemy to those I loved best. And I could prove a gate set in their midst through which ill could reach them, breaching their defenses.

I waited until there was an hour when Kyllan and Kemoc went into council of war. And I sent a message to Dahaun and Orsya. To them I spoke frankly, saying what must be done for the good of all, perhaps even for me also.

"There is no rest here for me." I did not ask that, I stated it as a truth. And in their eyes I read agreement. "This is also true: I am fast becoming a door to that which waits only for an entrance to be shaped for it. I am a worse enemy than any monster prowling beyond your safeguards. Strong are you in ancient magic,

Dahaun, for you are the Lady of Green Silences, and all which grows must pay heed to you, all animals and birds. And you, Orsya, also have your own magic, and I can testify that it is not to be lightly thought on. But I swear to you that this struggling to enter through me now is greater than you two joined together.

"I am empty—I can be filled, and with that which we would not like to think on."

Slowly Dahaun nodded. There was a sharp stab of pain within me then. For, though I knew I spoke the truth, yet some small, weak part of me had held a dying hope that I could be wrong and that she, who in her way was so much the superior of anyone I had once been, would tell me so. But rather she agreed with the verdict I had to face.

"What would you do?" Orsya asked. She had come from the stream to my side and her hair was drying, forming a luminous silvery cloud in the air, but there were still droplets of water on her pearly skin, and those she did not wipe nor shake away, for to the Krogan water was life itself.

"I must go forth from here—"

But to that Dahaun shook her head. "Beyond our safeguards what you fear will surely come, and soon. And Kyllan and Kemoc would not allow it."

"Yes, and yes," I answered. "But there is something else. I can return whence I came and find aid. You have heard that the churning of the mountains broke the power of the Council. Many of them died then because they could not contain so long the force they had to store until they aimed it. The Wise Women's rule is done in Estcarp. Our good friend Koris of Gorm is now the one who says this is done or that. But if even two or three of the great Wise Ones still live they can raise this from me and Koris will order them to do that speedily. Let me return to Estcarp and I shall be healed and you will be free to carry on battle here as you must."

Dahaun did not answer at once. It is part of her magic that she is never the same in one's eyes, but always changing, so that sometimes she seems of the Old Race, dark of hair, white of skin, while at other times her hair is ruddy, her cheeks golden. Whether this is done by her will or not, I do not know. Now it seemed she was of my own race as she absently smoothed a strand of black hair, her teeth showing a fraction upon her lower lip.

At last she nodded. "I can set a spell, a spell which may carry you safely as far as the mountains, if your travel is swift, so you need not fear invasion. But you must aid it with all your strength of will."

"As you know I shall," I told her. "But now you must give me aid in another way, the two of you, standing with me when I tell this to Kyllan and Kemoc. They know that I will not be in danger once I reach Koris. . . . We have learned from those coming to join us that he is seeking us. But they may try to hold me here even so. Our tie is as old as our years. So we must be three set firm for this, saying even that I shall return once I am given a new inner shield."

"And this will be the truth?" asked Orsya. I did not know if she thought of me with any charity. When I was Dinzil's I had been an enemy to her, even seeking her life by my brother's hands, so she had no reason to wish me well. But if she were as one with Kemoc as I suspected, then perhaps she might, for his sake, do me this service.

"I do not think so. I might be cleansed. But to return here would be a chance I would not dare," I told her frankly.

"And you believe you can make this journey?"

"I must."

"It is well," she said. "I shall stand beside you."

"And I," promised Dahaun. "But they will want to ride with you—"

"Set your own spells, the two of you. Let them seek the border with me; I do not think we can keep them from that. But thereafter make them return. There is nothing in Estcarp for them, and they have now given their hearts to this land."

"That also can we do, I think." Dahaun replied. "When will you ride?"

"As soon as can be. If I grow too worn with this battle, I shall lose before you are rid of me."

"It is the month of the Ice Dragon; the mountains will be ill going." But again Dahaun spoke as if she were not forbidding the effort, but rather searching in her mind for ways to overcome difficulties. "There is Valmund, who has ridden those trails many miles, and we can call upon the keen eyes of Vorlong and his Vrangs to scout before you, that no great ill may lie in wait. But it will be a cruel, cold trail you take, my sister. Be not overconfident."

"I am not," I assured her. "Only the sooner I am out of Escore, the sooner will what we hold dear be the safer!"

So it was settled among us, and having set our minds firmly upon the matter how could those others stand against us? Hard and fierce arguments they raised, but we showed them the logic of what we would do, even until they were in agreement against their wills. I swore and swore again that once healed I would return, with one of the parties from overmountain. Now and again there came those to join us, their coming always made known in good time by sentinels the Green People maintained where there were passes. The sentinels were of many kinds, some scouts from the Valley, a few former Borderers who had come to serve under my brothers, others the winged Flannan, or Dahaun's green birds, whose messages only she could understand, or once in a while a fighting Vrang, wide-winged hunter from the high clouds.

It was one of those who broke our first plan into bits when he reported that the direct route to the pass over which we had first come into Escore was now closed. Some messenger or liege thing to the Shadow had wrought a sealing there which would be better avoided than assaulted—with me as one of the party facing it. I think Kyllan and Kemoc rejoiced to hear that, deeming that we would now abandon the project altogether.

Only I sweated and shrieked under the dreams more and more, and perhaps they knew that I could not long continue to stand against that which sought to occupy me. Death would have to be my portion then, and I had sworn them to that by an oath they could not break.

Summoned, Vorlong himself came to the Valley. He perched on a rock already well worn by the scraping of his talons and those of his tribe before him, his red lizard head in bright contrast to his blue-gray feathers, his long neck twisting as he turned his eyes from one of us to another while Dahaun made mind talk with him.

At first he would not give us any hope, until, at last, with continued pressure, she brought out of him an admittance that by swinging farther east and north, it might be possible to avoid the pass we knew for a higher, more difficult passage. And he would send us a flying scout. From the Green People volunteered their best mountaineer, Valmund.

In the Green Valley the Ice Dragon was kept at bay. The season there was no cooler ever than late fall in Estcarp. As we rode past those symbols of power which kept that small pocket inviolate, the full blast of winter met us.

There were five of us who rode the sure-footed Renthan—those four-footed beings who were not animals, but comrades of battle as they had proved many times, and who were the equal of all in wit, perhaps superior in courage and resource. Kyllan took the fore, Kemoc rode to my right, Valmund for a space at the left, and behind was Raknar out of Estcarp, who had chosen to go overmountain with me to my final goal, since he sought to find certain liegemen of his and bring them back to swell the host in Escore. He was a man of more years than the rest of us and one my brothers trusted highly.

Beyond the boundaries of the Valley, as the Renthan beat down snowdrifts with their hooves, a shape dove from the sky to become clear in our sight as a Vrang, Vorlung's promised guide.

We traveled by day, since those of the Shadow are more used to the ways of night. Perhaps the severity of the weather had immured them in their lairs, for, though we once heard afar the hunting cries of a pack of wolf-men, the Gray Ones, we did not sight them or any other of the Dark Ones. We wove a way with many curves and small detours to avoid places which Valmund and the Vrang found dangerous. Some were only groves, or places of standing stones. But once we looked upon a somber building which seemed not in the least gnawed by time. In those walls were no windows, so it was like a giant block pitched from some huge hand to lie heavily on the earth. Around it the snow was not banked, though elsewhere it lay in white drifts from which a weak winter sun awoke sparkles of diamond. It was as if the ground was too warm there, so that a square of steaming earth enclosed that ominous masonry.

At night we sheltered in a place of blue stones, such ones as were to be found here and there as islands of security in the general evil of the land. When it grew quite dark pale light shone from these; that light beamed outward rather than toward us, as if to dazzle anything prowling beyond, to blind them from seeing our small party.

I tried not to sleep, lest those crowding dreams bring disaster, but I could not fight the fatigue of body, and, against my will, I did. Perhaps those blue stones had some remedy even greater than the power Dahaun had brought to my succor. For my sleep was dreamless and I awoke from it refreshed as I had not been for a long time. I ate with an appetite, and I took heart that my choice was right and perhaps our trip might be without ill incidents.

The second night we were not so lucky in finding a protected camp site. Had I still the learning I had once made my own, I might have woven a spell to cover us. But now I was the most helpless. Vrang and Valmund between them had brought us into the foothills of the mountains we must cross, but we were still heading north, rather farther to the east than would serve us.

We had rested in a place where stunted trees made a thick canopy, in spite of the fact they had lost their last year's leaves. And in that half shelter the Renthan knelt, giving us their bodies to lean against wearily as we chewed journey cake and drank sparingly from our saddle bottle. It was Green Valley wine, mixed with water from the springs there, a well-known restorative.

The Vrang winged off to a crag of his own choosing and the men settled the watch hours among them. Again I fought sleep, sure that with no safeguard I would be vulnerable to whatever the Shadow sent after us.

I did not think beyond our piercing of the mountains and the coming to Estcarp. Only too well did my imagination create for me what might happen between this hour and that when I was again in the land of my birth . . . though I knew that in the marshaling of such ills I was harming myself.

Valmund sat to my left, his green cloak about him. Even in the gloom, for we dared not light a fire, I could see his head was turned to look toward the mountains, though before him now was such a screen of brush and tree limb that he might not see through. There was something in his stance which made me ask in a half-whisper: "There is trouble ahead?"

He looked now to me. "There is always trouble in the mountains at this time."

"Hunters?" What kind? I wondered. There had been fearsome surprises enough in the lowlands. What foul monsters might seek us out in the heights?

"No, the land itself." He did not try to hide his fears from me and for that I was glad. For what he spoke of seemed less to me than things my dreams brought. "There are many snowslides now and they are very dangerous."

Avalanches—I had not thought of those.

"This is a dangerous way? More so than the other?" I asked.

"I do not know. This is new country for me. But we must go with double care."

I dozed that night and again my apprehensions were not realized. I might not have slept in a protected place, but I did not dream.

In the morning, when the light was strong enough for us to move on, the Vrang came to us. He had been scouting across the heights above since first light and what he had to report was none too good. There was a pass leading west, but we must reach it on foot, and would need a mountaineer's skill to do so.

With a great curved talon the Vrang drew a line map in the snow, went over each point of probable danger for us. Then he rose again, once more to seek the heights and so scout even farther ahead than the distance we could cover in the hours of this day. Thus did we begin our mountain journey.

II

At first our way was no worse than any mountain trail I had yet seen, but by the time the pale sun was up we had reached that portion the Vrang had foretold where we must say farewell to the Renthans and go thereafter on our own two feet. What had been a path, though steep and to be followed warily, now became a kind of rough staircase fit for two feet but not four.

The men packed our scant supplies and brought out the ropes and steel-pointed staffs which Valmund among us knew best how to use, and he now took the lead. We started up a way which was to be a test of endurance.

I could almost believe that we did indeed tread a stairway, one fashioned not by the whim of wind and weather, but by the need of some intelligence. I could not believe that the maker, or makers, had been men like us, however, for the steps were far too steep and shallow, sometimes giving only room for the toe of one's boot, very seldom wide enough to set the full length of a foot upon them.

Yet there was no other indication that we trode a way which had once been a road. And the constant climb made one's legs and lower back ache. At least the wind had scoured the snow and ice from these narrow fingers of ledge so that we had bare rock to tread and need not fear the additional hazard of slippery footing.

That stairway seemed endless. It did not go straight up the slope, although it began that way, but rather turned to our left after the first steep rise, to angle along the cliff face, which led me even more to surmise that it was not natural but contrived. It brought us at last to the top of a plateau.

The sunlight which had been with us during that climb vanished, and dark clouds lowered. Valmund stood, his face to the wind, his nostrils expanded, as if he could sniff in its blowing some evil promise. Now he began to uncoil the rope which had belted him, shaking it out in loops, so that the hooks which glinted in it at intervals could be seen.

"We rope up," he said. "If a storm catches us here . . ." Now he pivoted, looking toward what lay ahead, seeking, I believed, for some hint that we might find shelter from a coming blast.

I shivered. In spite of the clothing which made me move clumsily, the wind found a way to probe at me with icy fingers which wounded.

We made haste to obey his orders, snapping the rope hooks to the front of the belts we wore. Valmund led the line, and after him Kyllan, then Kemoc, and I, and, bringing up the rear, Raknar. I was the least handy. During the border war my brothers and Raknar had had duty in mountain places, and, while they did not have Valmund's long training, they knew enough to be less awkward.

Staff in hand, Valmund moved out, we suiting our pace to his, to keep some slack in the line linking us, but not too much. The clouds were thickening fast, and while as yet no snow had fallen, it was hard to see the far end of the plateau. Nor had the Vrang returned to give us any idea of what might await us there.

Valmund took to sounding the path before him with his staff as if he thought some trap might await under seemingly innocent footing; he did not go as fast as I wanted to, with the wind striking colder and colder.

Just as the climb up the stair had seemed to be a journey without end, so did this become a matter of trudging toward a goal which was hours, days before us. Time had no longer any true meaning. If it was not snowing, the wind raised the drifts already fallen to encircle us with bewildering veils. I feared that Valmund was indeed a blind man leading the blind, and we were as well able to blunder over some cliff as to walk a path to safety.

But we won at last to a place of shelter where the wind-driven snow was kept from us by an overhang of rock. There my companions held council as to the matter of going on or trying to wait out what Valmund feared to be a storm. I leaned back against the rock wall, breathing in great gasps. The cold I drew into my laboring lungs seemed to sear, as if I inhaled fire. And my whole body trembled, until I was afraid that if Valmund did give the signal to return to that battle outside I could not answer with so much as a single step.

I was so occupied with the failure of my own strength that I was not really aware of the return of the Vrang until a harsh croaking call aroused me. The Vrang waddled in under the overhang, an awkward creature out of its element of the upper air. It shook itself vigorously, sending bits of snow and moisture flying in all directions, and then it squatted down before Valmund in the stance of one come to settle in for some time. So I gathered that perhaps our travel for this day was over, and I slid thankfully down the wall which supported me, to sit with my legs out, my back still resting against the mountain rock.

We could not have a fire, for there was no wood to feed it. And I wondered numbly if we would freeze here under the lash of the wind which now and again reached in to flick us. But Valmund had an answer to that also. He produced from his pack a square of stuff which seemed no larger than my hand when he first pulled it forth. In the air, though, as he began to unfold it, it spread larger and larger, fluffing up, until he had a great downy blanket under which we crept and lay together. From this heat spread to thaw my shivering body as it served my companions also, even the Vrang taking refuge beneath one end, its bulk making a hump.

The covering had the soft consistency of massed feathers where it touched my cheek, but it looked more like moss. When I ventured to ask Valmund explained that it was indeed made from vegetation but via insect handling, since a small worm found in the Valley feasted upon a local moss and then spun this in turn, meant to make a weather protection shell. The Green People had long since, in a manner, domesticated these worms, kept them housed and fed, using the tiny bits of substance each produced to fashion such blankets. Unfortunately, as it took hundreds of worms to make a single blanket, each one was the work of many years; there were few of them, those in existence being among the treasures of the Valley.

I heard my companions talking, but their words became only a lulling drone in my ears as I drowsed, because of the fatigue of my aching body no longer trying to fight sleep. It seemed that here all my fears faded, and I was no longer Kaththea who must be constantly alert lest I fall prey to the enemy, but rather a mindless body which needed rest so sorely that lack of it was pain.

I dreamed, but it was not one of those nightmares from which I roused crying out with dread horror, though it was as vivid, or more so, as one of those. It seemed that I lay with the others under that soothing blanket and watched, with a kind of lazy content, the roar of the gathering storm outside, secure and safe with my protectors around me.

From that storm there spun out a questing line, silvery, alive, and this beamed over us, hovering just above our huddled bodies. In my dream I knew that this was a questing from another mind, one which controlled Power. Yet I did not think it evil, only different. And the end of that silvery beam or cord swung back and forth until it came to hold steady over me for a space. Then I seemed to rouse for the first time to a feeling of vague danger. But when I summoned what small defenses that I had, the line was gone and I blinked, knowing that I was now awake, though all was just as it had been in my dream, and we lay together with the storm beyond.

I did not tell my brothers, for my dreams must not be used, I made certain in my own mind, to flog them into dangerous efforts in the mountains. At that moment I decided that, if I did feel the touch of true evil any time as we climbed these perilous ways, I would loosen my fastening on the life rope and plunge, to end my problems, rather than draw them after me.

We spent the rest of the day and the next night in our hiding place. With the coming of the second dawn there was light and no clouds. The Vrang took wing, to soar high, coming back with news that the storm was gone and all was clear. So we broke our fast and went on.

There were no more stairways. We climbed and crept, up cliffs, along ledges. And all the time Valmund studied the heights above us with such intent survey that his uneasiness spread to us, or at least to me, though I could not be sure what he feared, unless it was an avalanche.

At midday we found a place on a wider ledge than we had heretofore traversed, and crouched there to eat and drink. Valmund reported that we were now within a short distance of the pass and that perhaps two hours would see us through the worst of the journey ahead and on the down slope, where once more we could angle east. So it was with some relaxation that we munched our blocks of journey bread and sipped from flasks filled with the Valley brew.

We had crossed the pass well within the time Valmund had set and were on a downward trail which did not seem so bad compared to the way we had come, when our mountaineer leader called a halt. He tested the rope ties and signaled he must reset them. So we waited while he shucked his pack to begin that precaution. It was then that the danger he had foreseen struck.

I was only aware of a roaring. Instinctively I jerked back, trying to flee—what I knew not. Then I was swept away, buried, and knew nothing at all.

IT WAS very dark and cold and a weight lay on and about me. I could not move my arms nor legs as I tried to reach out in a half-conscious fight against that punishing burden. Only my head, neck and half of one shoulder were free and I lay face up. But all was dark. What had happened? One moment we had been standing on the mountainside a little below the pass, the next, so had time passed for me, I was caught here. My dazed mind could not fit that together.

I tried again to move the arm of the free shoulder and found with great effort I could do so. Then with my mittened hand I explored the space about my head. My half numbed fingers struck painfully against a solid surface I thought was rock, slipped over that. I could not see in this gloom, only feel, and touch told me so little—that I now lay buried in snow save for my hand, shoulder, arm, head resting within a pocket of rock. That chance alone had saved me from being smothered by the weight which imprisoned the rest of me. I could not accept that imprisonment, and began, in a frenzy of awaking fear, to push at the snow with my free hand. The handfuls I scooped up flew back in my face, bringing me to understand I might thus bring upon myself the very fate from which the rock pocket had saved me.

So I began to work more slowly, striving to push away the burden over me, only to discover I was too well buried; I could make no impression on that weight.

At last, exhausted, sweating, I lay panting, and for the first time tried to discipline the fear which had set me to such useless labor. There must have been an avalanche, sweeping us downslope with it, burying us—me. The others could be digging now to find me! Or they might all be . . . Resolutely I tried to blank out that thought. I dared not believe that a chance rock pocket had saved me alone. I must think the others lived.

More bitterly than I ever had since I had fallen in that last struggle at Dinzil's side I regretted my lost communication with my brothers. With my magic that had been rift from me also, my punishment for being drawn into the underfolds of the Shadow. Perhaps . . . I shut my eyes against the dark in which my head lay, tried to rule my mind as once I had, to seek Kyllan and Kemoc—to be one with my brothers as had been our blessing.

It was as if I faced some roll of manuscript on which I could see words, clearly writ, but in a language I could not read, though I knew that reading might mean life or death for me. Life or death—suppose Kyllan, Kemoc, the rest of our company had survived; suppose that it would be better for them now if they did not find me. . . . Only there is that stubborn spark of life in us which will not allow one to tamely surrender being. I had thought I might throw myself into nothingness in their service if the need arose. Now I wondered if I could have done that. I tried to concentrate only on my brothers, on the need that I now speak with them mind to mind. Kemoc—if I had to narrow that beaming to one, I would select Kemoc, for always had he been the closer. In my mind I pictured Kemoc's dear face, aimed every scrap of energy toward touching him—to no avail.

A cold which was not from the snow imprisoning me spread through my body. Kemoc—it might be that I tried to reach one already gone! Kyllan then, and my elder brother's face became my picture, his mind that I sought, again to reach nothing.

It was the failure of my power, I told myself, not that they were dead! I would prove that—I had to prove it!—so I thought of Valmund with what I hoped was the same intensity, and then of Raknar. Nothing.

The Vrang! Surely the Vrang had not been included in our disaster! For the first time a small spark of hope flashed in me. Why had I not tried the Vrang? But that creature had a different form of brain channel: could I succeed with him where I had failed with men? I began to seek the Vrang as I had the others.

There was the picture in my mind of the red head swinging above the gray-blue feathered body. Then—I had touched! I had found a thought band which was not that of a man! The Vrang—it must be the Vrang! I cried aloud then and the sound of my own voice in that small pocket was deafening.

Vrang!

But I could not hold that band long enough to aim a definite message along it. It wavered in and out so I could only touch it now and then. Only it was growing stronger, of that I was sure. The Vrang must be seeking us somewhere near, and I doubled my efforts to send an intelligible message. The wavering of that communication band was first irking, and then raised the beginning of panic in me. Surely when I touched that intelligent creature would try to pinpoint me in turn. Yet as far as I could sense it did not. Was the consciousness of that touch mine only, so that the Vrang could *not* be guided to where I lay?

And how much longer could I fight to hold my small sense of communication?

I was gasping. For the first time I became aware that it was difficult to breathe. Had I pulled too much of the snow back on me when I made those first ill-directed attempts to free myself? Or was it that this pocket of rock held only a limited supply of air and that was becoming exhausted?

Vrang! The picture in my mind slipped away. Another took its place. And I was so startled at the single glimpse of a creature I did not expect that I lost contact.

No lizard-bird. No, this was furred, long of muzzle, pricked of ear, white or gray, like the snow about me, but with amber eyes narrowed into slits. The Gray Ones—a wolf-man! I had brought upon me a worse fate than being smothered by snow. Far better to gasp out my life in this pocket than be broken loose by the thing or things now questing for me.

I willed myself into a kind of mind sleep, trying with all my strength of will to be nothing, not to think, not to call—to hide to my death from discovery. And so well did I succeed, or else so bad had become the air about me, that I did lapse into a dark I welcomed.

But I was not to end so. I felt air blow upon my face. My body, playing me traitor, responded. But I would not open my eyes. If they had dug me free there was a small chance they might believe they had brought into the day a dead body and leave me. So small a chance, but it was all I had left to me now with my power gone and no weapons.

Then my ears rang as a baying began from far too close. It was not quite a howl, nor as sharp as a bark, but somewhat between the two. There followed a sniffing; I felt the puff of a strong breath across my face. My body jerked, not in answer to my own muscles, but because there was a grasp on my jacket close to my throat and I was being dragged along. I willed myself to lie limp, to seem dead.

The dragging stopped. There was another energetic sniffing of my face. Could the creature tell I was not dead? I feared so. I thought I heard movement away. Dared I hope—could I escape.

I raised my heavy lids and light was a pain for a moment or two, I had been so long in the dark. It was bright, sunshine. And for a space I could not adjust to it. Then a shape stood well in my line of vision.

So sure had I been that one of the Gray Ones had dug me out that it took me a long instant to see that one of the man-wolves did not crouch there. Wolf it looked, yes, but wholly animal. Its hide was not the gray of the Shadow's pack, but rather a creamy white; its prick ears, a long stripe down its backbone which included the full length of its tail, and its four well-muscled legs were light brown.

Most striking of all, it wore a collar, wide band which gave off small flashes of bright, sparkling color as if set with gems. As I watched it, my eyes now fully open in startlement, it sat on its haunches, its head turned a little from me as if it waited the coming of another. Its well-fanged jaws opened slightly and I could see the bright red of its tongue.

It was an animal, not a half-beast. And it was one who obeyed man or it would not wear that collar. So much did my survey satisfy me. But in Escore one never accepts the unusual as harmless; one is wary if one wants to hold to life or more than life. I did not stir, only slowly I turned my head a fraction at a time, to see what lay about me.

There was a mighty churning of snow, not only of the slide, but also where the animal had apparently dug to free me. It was day, though whether the same day we had come through the pass, I could not tell. Somehow I guessed it was not. The sun was very bright, enough to hurt my eyes, and involuntarily I closed them.

In that glimpse about I had seen no indication that any of our party, save myself, had been dug free. And now, as I braced myself to look again, I heard the animal once more voice its summons (for I was certain it was a summons) to master or companion.

This time a shrill whistle answered, to which the hound, if hound it was, replied with a series of sharp and urgent barks. Its head was turned fully from me as it gave tongue and I used my remaining rags of strength to push myself up. I had the feeling I wanted to face the whistler on my feet, if I could do so.

The hound did not appear to notice my struggles. It was on its feet now, running away from me, throwing up the loose snow in its going. I got to my knees with what haste I could, then to my feet, where I stood weaving dizzily back and forth, afraid to take a step in the snow lest I tumble again. The hound still floundered away, not looking back.

Now! Balancing with care lest I fall, I turned slowly, striving to discover some small shred of proof that I was not the single survivor of the slide. I swayed and stumbled eagerly to it, falling there to my knees, brushing and digging with my hands to uncover the pack Valmund had shucked moments before the catastrophe had struck.

I think I wept then, my eyes blurred, and I stayed where I was on my knees, lacking the strength to pull up. My hands rested on the pack as if it were an anchor, the only sure anchor left, in a world gone wrong.

So it was that the hound and its master found me. The animal snarled, but I would not have had the energy to raise a weapon even if I had one to hand. I stared blearily up at the man wading through knee-high snow.

He was human as to body. At least I had not been found by one of the nightmare things which roamed the dark places of Escore. But his face was not that of the Old Race. He was dressed in garments of fur unlike any I had seen before, a wide gem-set belt pulling in the loose tunic of bulky fluff about him. A hood, beruffed about the face with a band of long greenish hair like a tattered fringe, had slid back on his head to show his own hair, which was red-yellow, though his brows and lashes were black, and his skin dark brown. So wrong in shade did that hair tint seem that I could believe it a wig colored so in purpose.

His face was broad instead of long and narrow as those of the Old Race, with a flat nose having very large nostrils, and his mouth was thick-lipped to match. He spoke now, a series of slurred words, only a few of which bore slight resemblance to the common speech of the Valley, which in turn was different from what we used in Estcarp.

"Others"—I leaned forward, bearing my weight on my arms braced against the pack—"help—find—others—" I used simple words, spaced them, hoping he would understand. But he stood with one hand reaching to the hound as if to restrain that animal. Measured beside the man I could mark the huge size of the beast.

"Others!" I tried to make him understand. If I had survived that fall, surely the others might. Then I remembered the rope which had linked us together and fumbled to find it. Surely that could be a guide to Kemoc, who had been before me. . . .

But there was nothing, save a tear which had cut into my jacket where the hook must have been pulled out with great force.

"Others!" My voice spiraled up into a scream. I crawled back to the tumbled snow where rocks showed here and there, ripped loose by its sweep. I began to dig, without guide or purpose, hoping that if the stranger did not understand my words, though I used the intonation common in the Valley, he would follow my actions.

His first answer was a quick jerk which nearly brought me over on my back again. The hound had set its teeth into the fabric of my jacket near the shoulder. With those fangs locked it was exerting its strength to pull me back to its master. And at that moment the animal had more strength than I could resist.

But the man made no move to approach me, nor to aid the hound in its efforts. Nor did he speak again, merely stood watching as if this was no affair demanding his interference.

The hound growled in its throat as it pulled me back. And my position was such that I could not have beaten it off, even if I had had a weapon. A final sharp jerk and I sprawled on my side, sliding down and away from where I had tried to dig into the debris of the avalanche.

There was a shrill whistle again. This was answered, not by the hound which stood over me still growling, but by a barking in the distance. Then the man waded down to me, though he did not try to touch me, only waited.

What he waited came: a sled which was a skeleton framework, drawn by two more hounds, their collars made fast to thongs. The hound which had found me stopped growling and wallowed through the snow to the sled, where he took a position slightly to the fore of his fellows as if waiting to be hitched in turn. Then his master reached down and put a firm grasp on my shoulder, pulling me up with surprising ease. I tried to struggle out of his hold.

"No! The—others—" I mouthed straight into his expressionless face. "Find—others—"

I saw his other hand lift, but I was still astounded as it flashed at my jaw. There was a moment of shattering pain as it met flesh and bone and then nothing.

III

*T*here was an ache running through my whole body. Now and then I was shaken so that the sullen, constant pain became a twinge of real agony. I lay upon something which swayed, dipped, was never still, but which added to my misery by movement. I opened my eyes. Before me, across ground where the sun made a blaze to set tears gathering under lids, ran the three hounds, straps from their collars fastened to the sled on which I now lay. I tried to sit up, to discover that, not only were my wrists and ankles trussed tightly together, but over me was an imprisoning fur robe made fast to the framework of the sled.

Perhaps that was meant for warmth as well as a safeguard, but at that moment of realizing my helplessness, I saw it as another barrier between me and freedom.

The sleds I had known in Estcarp had always been more cumbersome, horse-drawn. But at the pull of the huge hounds this one moved at what seemed to me a fantastic speed. And we traveled more silently. There was no jingle of harness, no chime of bells which it was customary in the west to hang on both harness and sled frame. There was something frightening in this silent flight.

Slowly I began to think more clearly. The pain was centered in my head and that, added to the shock which had come with the avalanche, made any planning now a task almost too great. My fight against the bonds was more instinctive than reasoned.

Now I ceased to struggle, slitting my eyes against the too bright sunlight, enduring the misery of my aches and pains, as I set myself to the needful task of piecing together what had happened.

I could remember rationally now up to the blow the stranger had dealt me. And it was apparent I was not rescued, but his prisoner, on my way to his dwelling or camp. Also all I knew of Escore, which I was ready to admit was very little (even the Green People did not stray far from their Valley stronghold), mostly came from rumor and legend. Yet never had I heard of such a man and such hounds.

I could not see my captor now, but thought his place must be behind the sled. Or had he sent me on alone in the care of his four-footed servants, to be made sure of before he turned his attention to other survivors?

Other survivors! I drew a deep breath, which also hurt.

Kyllan . . . Kemoc . . .

There was this, which I clung to with all that was within me, as a mountain climber might cling to an anchoring rope when his feet slipped from some precarious niche: so deeply were we united, we three, that I do not think one of us could go from this world without the others knowing instantly that a fatal blow had been dealt. Though I had lost my power, yet there was still such a need and hold that I could not believe my brothers dead. And if not dead—

Once more I fought against the cords holding me, to no avail, thumping my head against the frame of the sled behind me, the answering stab of agony was so intense that I nearly lost my senses again. Now—now I must override fear, bring to what lay before me such coolness and mind alertness as I could summon.

Among the Wise Women I had learned such discipline as perhaps even warriors need not bend to. And I called upon what was left to be my armor and support now. One thing at a time. I could not hope to aid, if aid they needed, those who were the most in the world to me, unless I won my own freedom. And to present myself as a captive who needed constant watching was to defeat any chance I might have.

I knew so little about my captor, what role I must play to outwit him. My best chance at present was to be what he had thought to make me, a cowed female whom he had beaten into submission. Though this would be difficult for one of the Old Race, especially from Estcarp, where the Wise Women had been considered the superiors of males for so long that it was bred into them to take the lead without question. I must indeed seem worse than I was, weak and easily overborne.

So I lay motionless in the sled, watching the bobbing of the hounds pulling it, trying to marshal my thoughts. Had I been able to tap the Power as once I did, I would have been free from the moment I roused, for I had no doubt that I could have brought both hounds and master under my domination. It was as if someone who had always depended upon her legs now found herself a cripple, and yet was faced with the necessity of walking a long and perilous road.

Twice the hounds came to a halt and sat panting in the snow, their long tongues lolling from between their fangs. The second time they did so their master came up beside me to look down. I had had warning enough from the crunch of his feet on the snow to shut my eyes, presenting, I trusted, a most deceptive picture of unconsciousness. I dared not look about again until the hounds were once more running.

When I did, cautiously, I saw that the surface over which we sped was no longer unbroken ahead, but that there were signs that other sled runners had here beaten down the snow. We must be nearing our goal. Now more than ever I must fix my mind on the part to be played—that of a broken captive. But as long as I could I would sham unconsciousness, that I might learn more of these people, for, by the number of tracks, I thought I could assume that my captor was not alone, but had companions in plenty ahead.

The hounds ran downslope into a valley where trees showed dark fingers against the snow, stark and clear, though the sun was now down, leaving only a few lighter streaks in the sky. The trees sheltered those we sought, but I saw the leap of flames marking more than one fire. And there arose a chorus of howling, which the hounds pulling me answered in full throat.

It was a camp, I noted between almost closed lids, not a place of permanent dwellings such as the Green People had. Though it was already dusk among the trees I could make out tents, ingeniously set to make use of the trees as part of their structures. I was reminded of Kemoc's tale of his stay among the Moss-wives, whose dwellings were walled with moss hanging from the branches of age-old trees.

But these were not moss walls, rather sheets of woven hide, cut into strips and then remade in large sections, supple and easy to handle, draped and staked to form irregular rooms, each about some tree, the fire set before the door and not inside.

At each there stood, barking furiously at our coming, two, three, four of the hounds. Men came out to see the cause of their clamor. As far as I could detect in the limited light, they were all of the same general cast of feature and coloring as my captor, so much so that one could believe them not of just one tribe or clan but from a single inbred family. As the sled slowed to a stop on the fringe of the wood, they gathered close about it, which was my warning to counterfeit as best I could one who had never regained her senses.

The cover which had been part of my bonds was thrown off and I was picked up, carried to where odors of cooking fought with those of fresh hides, hounds, and strange bodies. I was dropped on a pile of stuff which yielded under me enough to cushion my aching body, yet not enough to spare me an additional throb of pain.

I heard talk I could understand, was pulled around, felt warmth, and saw light even through my closed lids as some torch must have been held close to my face. I had lost my cap somewhere during my journeying and my hair hung free. Now fingers laced in it, pulled my head even farther to one side and I heard excited exclamations as if they found my appearance surprising.

But at last they left me and I lay, not daring to move yet, listening with all the concentration I could summon to learn if I was still in company. If I was not, I wanted very much to look about.

I began to count in in my mind. At fifty—no, one hundred—I would risk opening my eyes, though I would not turn my head or otherwise stir. Perhaps even such a limited field of view would give me aid in assessing my captors.

When I reached that hundred further caution kept me still for another. Then I took the chance. Luckily the last inspection of the tribesmen had left me lying with my head turned toward the open flap of the tent and I could see a small measure of what lay beyond.

Under me was a pile of furred hides tucked over fresh cut branches which were still springy enough to give an illusion of some comfort. To my right I had a quarter view of some boxes covered also with hide from which the hair had been scraped, the resulting leather painted with bold designs, though that paint was now faded and flaking. I did not recognize any symbols that I knew.

Against the other side of the doorway was a shelved rack, made of uprights notched to have the narrow shelves set sloping toward the back. These were crowded with bags, wooden boxes, and unpainted pottery which was well shaped but bore no decorative patterns. There also hung two hunting spears.

The light by which all this could be viewed caused me the greatest amazement. From a center pole stretched two cords running from one side of the tent to the other. Along these were draped strips of filmy stuff which was like the finest of the silken strips Sulcar raiders sometimes brought from overseas. Entangled in this netting of gauze were myriads of small insects, not dead as one might see them in a spider's larder, but alive, crawling about. And each insect was a glowing spark of light, so that the numbers together gave to the tent a luminance, dimmer, yes, than that familiar to me, but enough to see by.

I was staring at these in surprise, which betrayed me when the stranger came in and caught me open-eyed and plainly aware. Angry at my own foolishness, I tried to play my chosen role, assuming an expression I hoped he would read as fear, wriggling back on the bedding as one who would flee but could not.

He knelt by the side of the bed and stared down at me critically, appraisingly. Then he suddenly thrust his hand inside my jacket with brutal force, in a manner I could not mistake. Now I did not have to play at fear; I knew it, and what he would do, as well as if I could still read minds clearly.

I could no longer hold to my role of cowed female. It was not in me to allow without a struggle what he would do. I bent my head vainly, trying to snap my teeth into the hand which was now joined by his other, ripping loose my jacket and the tunic beneath. And I brought my knees up, not only to ward him off, in an effort but to battle as best I could.

It would seem that this was a game he had played before and he took delight in it. He sat back on his heels and there was such a grin on his face as promised evil of another kind than I had known. Perhaps drawing out and prolonging my degradation was also pleasing to him, for he did not proceed as I thought he would. Instead he sat watching me as if he would think out each step of what he would do, savoring it in fantasy before taking action.

But he was never to have his chance. There was a sharp call and the head and shoulders of another appeared under the tent flap, letting me view my first tribeswoman.

She had the same broad features as my captor, but her hair was coiled and pinned into an elaborate tower on her head, the pins being gem-set so that they glinted in the light. Her fur coat was not tightly belted, but swung loose to show that under it, in spite of the chill of the weather, she wore nothing above the waist but a series of necklaces and collars of jeweled work. Her breasts were heavy and the nipples were painted yellow with petals radiating from them as if to simulate flowers.

While she spoke to my captor she stared at me with a kind of contemptuous amusement, and her air was one of authority such as would set on a minor rank Wise Woman. Somehow, I had not expected to find this among these people, though why I had deemed it a male-dominated society I did not know, except for the way the stranger had served me.

Their words were oddly accented and they spoke very fast. I thought that here and there I caught a part of speech I did dimly recognize, yet I could make no sense of it at all. Again I yearned for my lost power, even a small measure of it. Only one who has held such and lost it can understand what I felt then, as if a goodly half of me had been emptied, to my great and growing loss.

Although I could not understand their words, it was plain that they speedily grew to be ones of anger, and that the woman was ordering my captor to do something he was loath to do. Once she half turned to the door behind her and made a gesture which I read as suggesting that she call upon someone else to back her commands.

The leering grin had long since vanished from his fat-lipped mouth. There was such a sullen lowering there now as I might have feared to see had I been the woman. But her contempt and impatience only grew the stronger and she swung again as if to call that help she had indicated stood outside. Before she could do so, if that was her intent, she was interrupted by a low, brazen booming which rang in one's ears as if the air reechoed it.

And, hearing that, I for a short instant of time forgot where I lay and what ordeals might yet be before me. For that sonorous sound awoke in me something I thought I had lost forever—not only a bit of memory but instantaneous response which was for me so startling I wondered that I did not cry out as one suffering a sore wound.

Though my Power had seemingly been rift from me, memory had not. I could call to mind the skills, spells, domination of will and thought which had been taught me, even if I could not put them to use. And memory told me that what had sounded through this barbaric camp was a spirit gong. Who might use that tool of sorcery in such a place I could not guess.

The woman's triumph was plainly visible, my captor's scowl uneasy. He drew from his wide belt a long-bladed knife, stooped over me to saw through those twisted cords which held my ankles tightly together. When I was free he hoisted me to my feet, his hands moving viciously over my body in a way which promised ill for the future if he could not have his way now.

Placed on my two feet by his strength as if I had no will of my own, he gave me a push forward which would have sent me helplessly on into the wall had not the woman, with muscles to match his, not caught me by the shoulder.

Her nails dug in in a grip which was cruel. Holding me, she propelled me out of the tent into a night which was alight with fires. Those about the flames did not look up as we passed, and I had the feeling they were deliberately avoiding sighting either of us for some reason. There still hung a trembling in the air, a vibration born of the gong, which had not died with the sound.

I stumbled along, both upheld and forced forward by the woman, past the fires, other tents, deeper into the woods, by a winding way which the trees gave us. With the fires well behind us now it seemed very dark and our path completely hidden. But my guard—guide—never faltered, walking confidently as if she could either see better in the dark than I, or had come this way so many times that her feet knew it by heart.

Then there was the wink of another fire, low, with flames which burned blue instead of crimson. And from it rose an aromatic smoke. That, too, I knew of old, though then it had spiraled from braziers and not from sticks set in the open. Had I been brought to a true Wise Woman, perhaps some exile out of Estcarp come overmountain even as we in search of the ancient homeland?

The fire burned before another tent and this was larger, almost filling the small glade wherein it had been pitched. A cloaked and hooded figure did sentry duty at its door, stretching forth a hand now and then to toss into the flames herbs which burned sweetly. Sniffing those, knowing them well for what they were, I was heartened by this much: this was no power from the Shadow. What was fed, or could be summoned to such feeding, was not of the dark but the light.

Magic stands in two houses. The witch is one born to her craft, and her power is of the earth, of growing things and what is of nature. If she makes a pact with the Shadow then she turns to those things of evil which abide on earth—there are growing things to harm as well as heal.

The sorceress may be a born witch who strives to climb higher in her craft, or she may be one without the gift who painfully learns to use the Power. And again she chooses between light and dark.

Our Wise Women of Estcarp were born to their craft and I had been one of them, though I had not vowed their vows, nor taken on my breast the jewel as one of their sisterhood. Perhaps I could once have been deemed sorceress, since my learning went far beyond the simple witchcraft I could have wrought without struggle and preparation.

Which did I front now, I wondered as my guide bore me on toward the tent doorway? Was this a witch, or a learned sorceress? And I thought perhaps I should be prepared for the latter, judging by the evidence of that gong.

While the tent in which my captor had put me had been wanly lit by his entrapped insects, this was brighter. There were the strips of gauze with their prisoned, crawling things, but there also was, on a low table meant for one who knelt or sat crosslegged rather than in a chair, a ball of glimmering crystal. I was impelled to enter and that light which seemed to swirl fluidly within the container flared to sun brightness.

"Welcome, daughter." The accent was archaic by Estcarpian standards, but the words were not the gabble I had heard used elsewhere in this camp. I went to my knees before the globe, not compelled by my guide, but the better to see who spoke.

The Old Race do not show signs of age, though their span of years is long, until they are close to the end. And I had seen few—one or two among the Wise Women—who ever showed it so plainly. I thought that she who huddled, bent and withered, beyond the table of the crystal must indeed be very close to death.

Her hair was white and scanty, and there had been no attempt to twist and pin it into the style favored by the tribeswoman. Instead it was netted close to her skull, and that I knew, too, for it was common to the Wise Women. But she was not lengthily robed as was their fashion. Around her shoulders was the bulk of a fur coat and that hung open showing a necklace with a single large jewel as a pendant lying on her bared body where her ancient breasts were now unsightly flaps of leathery skin. Her face was not the broad, thick-lipped one of the tribe, but was narrow, with the cleanly cut features I had seen all my life, though very deeply wrinkled, the eyes far sunken in the head.

"Welcome, daughter," she repeated (or did the words just continue to ring in my head?). She reached forth her hands, but when I would have completed that old, old greeting and put mine palm to palm with hers I could not for the bindings on me. She turned to my guard, spitting words which made that woman cringe hastily down beside me, slitting at the cords with a knife.

My hands rose clumsily, the returning circulation prickling in their numbness, but I touched her skin, which was hot and dry against my own. For a moment we sat so, and I tried not to flinch from the mind which probed mine, learned my memories, my past as if all had been clearly written on an oft read roll.

"So that is the way of it!" She spoke in my head and for so little I was cheered, that I had received her thought so clearly, as I had not been able to do, even with Kyllan and Kemoc.

"It need not remain so for you," she was continuing. "I felt your presence, my daughter, when you were still afar. I put into Sokfor's mind, not openly, but as if he had thought it for himself, to go seeking you—"

"But my brothers—" I broke upon her sharply. With her power could she tell me now the truth? Did they still live?

"They are males, what matters it concerning them?" she returned with an arrogance I knew of old. "If you would know read the crystal."

She dropped my hands abruptly to indicate the glowing globe between us.

"I have no longer the power," I told her. But that she must already know.

"Sleep is not death," she answered my thought obliquely. "And that which sleeps can be awakened."

Thus did she echo that faint hope I had held when I had started for Estcarp. I had not only feared that my emptiness might be filled by some evil, but I wanted, I needed, to regain at least a small part of what had been so rift from me.

"You can do this?" I demanded of her, not truly believing she would say yes, or that it could be so.

I sensed in her amusement, pride, and some other emotion so far hidden and so fleeting that I could not read it. But of them all pride was the greatest and it was out of that she answered me now.

"I do not know. There is time, but it is fast being counted bead by bead between the fingers." Her left hand moved to her waist and she dangled into my sight one of those circlets of beads which, each strung some distance from the other, are smooth and cool and somehow soothing to the touch. Wise Women use them to govern the emotions, or for some private form of memory control. "I am old, daughter, and the hours are told for me swiftly. But what I have is yours."

And so overjoyed was I by this offer of help, never thinking then that I might be enspelled by her power, or that no bargain benefits but one alone, that I relaxed, and could have wept with joy and relief, for she promised me what I wanted most. Perhaps some of Dinzil's taint remained within me, that I was too easily won to what I desired, and had not the caution I should have held to.

Thus I met Utta and became one of her household, her pupil and "daughter." It was a household, or tenthold, of women such as was fit for a Wise Woman. I do not know Utta's history, save that, of course, that was not her true name. An adept gives that to no one, since knowing the true name gives one power over its owner. Nor did I ever learn how she came to be one with this band of roving hunters, only that she had been with them for generations of their own shorter lives. She was a legend and goddess among them.

From time to time she had chosen "daughters" to serve her, but in this tribe there was no inborn gift to foster and she had never succeeded in finding another to share her duties even in the smallest part, or one who could comprehend her need for companionship. And she was very lonely.

I told her my tale, not aloud, but as she read my thoughts. She was not interested in the struggle for Escore, light against dark; long, long ago she had narrowed her world to this one small tribe and now she could not nor would not break the boundaries she had so set. I accepted that when I found she might help me regain what I had lost. And I think that the challenge I represented gave her a new reason to hold to life. She clung to that fiercely as she set about trying to make of me again at least a ghostly copy of what I once had been.

$\mathcal{T}$he Vupsall, for so these rovers named themselves, had only vague legends for their history. Nothing that I overheard while dwelling among them suggested that they had once had fixed abodes, even when Escore was an untroubled land. They had an instinct for trade and Utta, in answer to my questions, suggested that they may have been wandering traders as well as herdsmen or something of the sort, before they turned to the more barbaric life of hunters.

Their normal range was not this far to the west. They had come here this time because of the raids of a stronger people who had broken up their larger bands, reducing most to fleeing clans. And I also learned from Utta and her handmaids that to the east, many days' travel by tribal standards, there was another sea, or leastwise a very large body of water from which these enemies had come. As the Sulcar of the west they made their homes on ships.

I tried to get more exact information, a drawing of a map. Whether they were honestly ignorant of such records, or whether they were, out of some inborn caution, deliberately vague, I never knew, but all I learned was hazy as to details.

They were restless and unhappy here in the west, and they could not settle down, but wandered almost aimlessly among the foothills of the mountains, camping no longer in any one place than the number of days to be told on the fingers of both hands, for so primitive were they in some things that was how they reckoned.

On the other hand they were wonder-workers with metal and their jewels and weapons were equal to the finest I had seen in Estcarp, save the designs were more barbaric.

A smith was held in high esteem among them, taking on the role of priest among such tribes as had not an Utta. And I gathered that few were provided with a seeress.

While Utta might rule their imaginations and fears, she was not the chieftainess. They had a chief, one Ifeng, a man in early middle years who possessed all the virtues they deemed necessary for leadership. He was courageous, yet not to the point of recklessness; he had a sense for trail seeking, and the ability to think clearly. He was also thoughtlessly cruel, and, I guessed, envious of Utta, though not to the point of daring to challenge her authority.

It had been his sister's eldest son who had found me via his hound's aid. And early the morning after Utta had appropriated me to her service, he came to her tent together with my late captor to urge the latter's rights, by long custom, over my person.

His nephew stood a little behind, well content to let the chief argue in his favor, even as I sat crosslegged the length of a sword behind my new mistress, the dispute being left to our elders. He watched me greedily and I thanked what Powers beyond Powers that there are walking the far winds of the world that Utta was here for my shield.

Ifeng stated his case, which by custom was clear and could not be gainsaid. I could not follow his speech, but I knew well the purport of it from the frequent glances in my direction, the gestures at me and in the direction of the mountains.

Utta heard him out and then with a single sharp-voiced sentence broke his arguments to bits. Her thought at the same time rang in my mind:

"Girl use your power. Look upon yonder cup, raise it up and bear it to Ifeng by your will."

A feat easy to do in the old days but beyond me now. But such was the strength of her order that I obediently raised my hand and pointed to one of the cups wrought of silver, focusing my will on the task she demanded of me.

I shall always think that it was her will working through me which brought results. But the cup did rise and travel through the air, to come to rest at Ifeng's right hand. He gave an exclamation and his fingers jerked from proximity to it, as if it were molten hot.

Then he swung to his nephew and his voice arose in what could only be berating before he turned again to Utta, touched his hand to his forehead in salute, and went from us, urging the younger man before him.

"I did not do that," I slowly said when they were safe gone.

"Be still!" Her order rang in my head. "You shall do far more if they will be patient. Or wish you to lie under Sokfor's body for his pleasure?" She smiled, and all the thousand wrinkles of her face creased as she read my instant reaction of disgust and horror. "It is well. I have served the tribe for long, and neither Ifeng, nor Sokfor, nor anyone else will rise to cross me. But remember this, girl, and get you to our work together, I alone am your buttress against that bed-service until you relearn such skills as shall protect you on your own."

Such logic gave me even more reason to plunge into the training she devised, which began almost at once.

There were two other members of her tenthold. One was a crone almost as old as Utta in appearance, though much younger in years for she was of the tribe. She was, however, far stronger than she looked, and her bone-thin arms, her crooked fingers, accomplished a vast amount of labor in the general work of the tent. It was she, cloaked and hooded, whom I had seen feeding the herb fire on my first night in camp. Her name was Atorthi and I seldom heard her speak. She was totally devoted to Utta, and I think the rest of us did not exist for her except as shadows of her mistress.

The woman who had brought me to Utta was also of the Vupsall, but not of this clan. She was, I learned, the widow of a chief of another tribe the Vupsall had overrun in one of the fierce feuds which kept them from becoming a united people. As spoils of war she had been claimed by Ifeng as a matter of course, only Ifeng already had two wives under his tent and one of them was very jealous.

After two or three tempestuous days of domestic altercation he had made a ceremony of presenting this human battle spoil to Utta as a servant. Within the seeress' establishment Visma had found a place which suited her as perhaps Ifeng's would not, even if she had been the first or only female there. She was a woman of natural dominating qualities, and her new position as liaison between Utta, who was seldom seen outside her tent except well muffled in furs on a sled during a march, and the rest of the clan, gave her just what she wanted. As a guard and overseer she was perfectly placed.

I think at first she resented me bitterly, but when she saw I was not in any way a threat to her own sphere of authority she accepted me. And finally she used reports of my growing power as a new accent to her standing in the tribe.

There was a duality within the nomadic community. Utta and her tenthold reproduced a way of life I had known, a community of women using the Power to bolster their rule. Under Ifeng the rest of the encampment followed an opposite pattern of a male-dominated society.

I soon saw that Utta was right that I must make haste in learning or relearning what I could, for she could not be far from death. The wandering life of the clan was not good for her in this cold, though she was surrounded and tended by every possible comfort that Atorthi and the rest of us could offer.

At last Visma went directly to Ifeng and stated firmly that he must soon locate a more permanent campsite and there settle for a lengthy period or she could not say how long Utta would yet live. That suggestion so frightened him that he straightaway sent out his best scouts to find such a place. For Utta's service had for generations kept this clan "lucky," as they termed it, far beyond the general lot of their kind.

They had been traveling eastward again for a space of some ten days since my taking. I had no way of telling how many leagues we had put between us and the mountains, which still loomed high behind. I had begged many times of Utta a reading in her seeing globe for some news of my brothers, but she said repeatedly she was no longer able to waste her strength on such a search. Until I learned enough to lend my winging thought to hers it was a useless exhaustion for her which might even bring about her death. So it was to my self-interest, if I wished to use the globe, to protect her from such a drain and obey her commands to learn, cramming into me all she could give. I grimly noted, though, that when she was following her own desires in any matter she was far more strong and able than when I pushed for my own wishes.

I saw that I must humor her if I would gain what I had lost. And not to have her as a buffer between me and the men of the clan, especially Sokfor, who continued to follow me with his eyes whenever we were in sight of one another, was a danger indeed. Could I relearn certain parts of my Power I would be free of that peril at least: a true witch cannot easily be forced against her will—as my mother once proved in the Hold of Verlaine when one of the arrogant nobles of Karsten would have claimed the role of bedfellow.

So I bent my will to Utta's. And she was not only content but triumphant in an almost feverish fashion, working me for long hours with a hectic need, it would seem, to make me as much her equal as she could. I thought at that time it was because all these years she had sought for an apprentice and found her not, so that all the frustrations which had so long haunted her were now fastened on me.

She had few of the techniques of the Wise Women; her talents were more akin to witchcraft than sorcery, so perhaps the easier for me to assimilate now. I soon found it irking that her mind seemed to skip erratically from one piece of knowledge to another which appeared to be no kin to the first, so that what I accumulated (at the best rate I could) was a vast mass of odds and ends I never seemed to have a chance to unravel and put into any order. I began to fear that I would be left like this, an aide to her when she needed, but without enough straight knowledge in any direction to serve myself. Which was very well what she might intend.

Twice after those first days of traveling we established longer camps, one to the extent of ten days, while the hunters were out to replenish our supplies. Before each of these hunts Utta worked her magic, drawing me in to lend my strength to hers. The results of her sorcery were detailed descriptions to be set in the minds of the hunters, not only for the locating of game, but listing those places under the influence of the Shadow which must be avoided.

Such sessions left her exhausted, and we would not work together for a day or so thereafter. But I could understand how valuable was her gift for these people, and what dangers and losses lay in wait for any clan who had no such guardian.

I had kept track of the days since my awakening under the fringe of the avalanche. And it was on the thirtieth thereafter that our sleds swept into the mouth of a narrow valley between two ridges of very rough cliff seamed here and there by frozen runnels of water. As we descended farther into a narrow end of a funnel-shaped area, that water thawed and dripped. And the snow which had been heavy and thick-crusted became slushy and light, so that those who had ridden the sleds, save for Utta, now walked, that the struggling dogs would have lighter loads.

Finally the snow disappeared altogether. Two of the younger men trotted closer to add their strength to the pull lines of Utta's sled. The brown earth showed bits of green life, first a coarse moss, then tufts of grass and small bushes. It was as if coming down that way we had advanced from one season to another, all in a few steps.

It was warm, so much so that we must first open our outer coats, toss back their hoods, and then take them off; the men and women of the tribe both went bare to the waist and I found my under tunic sticky with sweat, clinging dankly to my body.

We came to a stream and had I not been warned by the steam which hung above it I might have tried to drink, since my throat was dry and the damp heat made me very thirsty. But this was hot water, not cool, and must arise from some boiling spring. It was its breath which made the core of the valley into near summer.

Our traveling pace had grown slower, not just because of the lack of snow for the smooth passing of the sleds, but we also paused for intervals while Ifeng conferred with Utta. That this was a place the clan longed to enter was plain, but that it might hold some great danger for them I also guessed. At last Utta gave the signal that they might advance without fear, and so we came into what had manifestly been a favored camping site—if not for this clan, then for others, and for a long time.

There were the scars of many old fires, and lengths of bleached wood had been set upright to form posts for tents. Walls of loosely piled rocks were also ready to be used as additional security. And the Vupsalls speedily set about making a more permanent settlement than I had seen.

The hide walls of the tents were fortified from the outside by new walls of stone until finally the hide was only visible as a roof. In the steamy mildness of this place, however, there appeared to be less need for such protection than there had been in the snow waste through which we had come.

Pools and eddies of the hot steam provided us with water that needed no heating. And in the privacy of our hut-tent we washed our bodies thoroughly, which to me was a great comfort and joy.

Visma brought fresh garments out of those painted chests and saw that I was clad as a tribeswoman in breeches with painted symbols, a wide jeweled belt and many necklaces. She wanted to paint my breasts, having so redecorated her own, but I shook my head. I later learned from Utta that my instinct had been right, for a virgin did not so adorn herself until she chose to accept some warrior, and I might have unwittingly given an invitation I was not prepared to follow in a way acceptable to a proud clansman.

But I did not have much time to consider the formalities of daily living for once more Utta plunged me into learning, hardly giving me time to eat or sleep. I grew thin and strained, and had I not earlier known the discipline of the Wise Women I might have cracked and broken. Yet it seemed to me that Utta throve, not suffered as I did.

What she taught me was the same knowledge she used for the welfare of the clan. And more than once in the following days she put me to service answering some need of those who sought her out, sitting by to watch, but allowing me to follow through the spell by myself. To my surprise the clanspeople did not resent this as I well believed they might, asking for mistress instead of student. Perhaps it was her sitting by which led them to trust me more.

Healing spells I learned, and those for hunting. But as yet she had not brought me into direct foreseeing as she used when Ifeng needed it. And I began to suspect that she did this of a purpose, not wanting to give me the chance to contact any beyond this camp as I might well do, since the method of such foreseeing and the long-looking of straight mind search was largely the same.

My struggles on my own behalf seemed to be hampered in that direction; the haze which had covered my last days with Dinzil lifted enough to let me know that this was the portion of the Power which I had truly misused, and so perhaps I might never regain it. I remembered with a shiver and a feeling of hot guilt what Kemoc had told me, that, fully in the grip of the Shadow, I had used the calling to try to summon Kyllan for the betrayal of the Valley. No wonder it was now forbidden me. It is of the very nature of the Power that once misused, or used only for a selfish purpose, it can recoil or be drained past recovery.

And all my pleas to Utta to let me know whether my brothers lived or died went unanswered, save for some enigmatic statements which could be interpreted many ways. I could only cling to my belief that so strong was our birth tie I would have known it if they were dead.

My toll of days, marked on the innerside of my jacket by pinprick, reached forty and I reckoned up what I had accomplished during that time. Save for the forereading-mind search, I had as much now at my service as I had had in my second year of schooling among the Wise Women, though what I had learned was more witchcraft, less sorcery. And there were still gaps Utta could not, or would not, bridge.

Although the surroundings of our camp were much easier for the clan than the harsh necessity of travel had been, they were not idle. Now they turned to craftsmanship. Furs were tanned and made into garments, and the smiths set about the mysteries of their calling, attended by their chosen apprentices.

Hunting parties ranged out from the valley of the warm springs in greater numbers, always assured by Utta that they had naught to fear. I gathered that though the raiders were many in autumn, the winter months were not good for seafaring. Free of that danger, as well as encroachment from other clans, who had been earlier exterminated by the raiders or also driven west, the Vupsalls had an empty land to themselves.

Here it was almost possible to forget one was in Escore: we saw no ruins; there were no near places of ill repute where the Shadow taint lingered. In fact, there were no traces of the Escore I had known. And the tribesmen were so unlike the Old Race or those mutants who were allies of the Valley that I sometimes speculated as to whether they were native to this world at all, or had come through one of those Gates which the adepts had opened to make passage from one world to another possible.

We had a healing session, a child brought by its mother. A fall among the rocks had injured it beyond the knowledge of the people. I used the inner seeing and made right what was wrong, plunging the little boy into the deep sleep of healing so that he could not undo with movement what had been done. And Utta had in no wise given any aid, but had left it all to me.

When the mother had gone carrying the child, the seeress sighed, leaning back against the padded rest she now used all the time to support her skeletal frame.

"It is well. You are worthy to be called 'daughter.' "

At that moment her approval meant much to me, for I respected her knowledge. We were neither friends nor unfriends, but more like two chips hewn from the same tree whirling together in a pool to float side by side; there was too wide a span of years, experience, strange knowledge separating us for there to be more than need, respect, and agreement to bind us.

"I am old," she continued. "If I looked into that"—she gestured at the globe which ever sat at her right hand, and which she now never used. "If I looked into that I would see naught but the final curtain." She fell silent but I was held to her side by a strong feeling that there was more she must say and that it was of great importance to me. Then she raised her hand a little, signing with her fingers toward the doorway of our hut, and even that slight effort seemed to exhaust her.

"Look—beneath the mat—"

It was a dark mat, not fashioned of woven strips of hide and fur as were the others in the hut, but rather of some fiber. And it was very old. Now at her bidding I went to lift it, to look upon the underside, which I did not remember having seen before.

"Your—hand—above—it—" Her mind words were as whispers, fading.

I turned it all the way over and held my hand above its surface. Straightaway there was a glowing of lines there and runes came into being. Then I knew what bonds she had laid upon me, not by my will, but by hers. For this was a spell which would only affect those in tune to such mysteries. It would tie me to her and this way of life. And in me resentment was then born.

She hitched herself higher on the rest; her hands lay on the ground on either side of her body.

"My people—they need—" Was that an explanation, even the beginning of a plea? I thought so. But they were not *my* people; I had not accepted them ever. I had not tried to escape because she had offered me the regaining of my lost knowledge. But let her indeed pass behind the final curtain and I would be gone.

She read my thoughts easily. In our relationship I could not shut her out. Now she shook her head in a slow, wavering movement.

"No," she denied my plan, elusive as it was. "They need you—"

"I am not their seeress," I countered quickly.

"You—will—be—"

I could not argue with her then, she was so shrunken, so fallen in upon her wisp of body, as if even that slight clash of wills between us had drained her almost to death.

I was suddenly alarmed and called Atorthi. We gave her what restoratives there were, but there comes a time when such can no longer keep a struggling spirit within worn-out clothing of flesh and bone.

She lived yet, but only as an anchor to her spirit, which pulled impatiently at this useless tie with the world, eager to be free and gone.

And through all the rest of that day and the next so did she lie. There was naught Atorthi and Visma could do to arouse her. Nor could I reach her via the power any more to know that she still had a faint tie with earth and us. And when I looked outside the tent-hut I saw that all the clan was sitting in silence, their eyes fixed upon the door.

At the midnight hour there was a sudden surge of life, as a high tide might flood a bay. I felt once more her command in my head as her eyes opened and she looked at us with intelligence and the need to bend us to her desires.

"Ifeng!"

I went to the doorway to signal to the chieftain who sat between two of the fires they had built as men erect defenses against that which prowls the dark. If not eagerly he came, neither did he linger.

Visma and Atorthi had braced her higher on the backrest so she almost sat upright with some of her old vigor. Now her right hand gestured me to come to her—Visma withdrawing to give me room. I knelt beside her and took her cold claw, the fingers closing about mine in a tight and painful spasm, but her mind no longer touched mine. She held to me but she looked to Ifeng.

He had knelt, a respectful distance from her. Then she began to speak aloud, and her voice, too, was strong as it might once have been when she yet kept age and eventual dissolution at a goodly distance.

"Ifeng, son of Tren, son of Kain, son of Jupa, son of Iweret, son of Stoll, son of Kjol, whose father Uppon was my first consort, the time has come that I step behind the final curtain and go from you."

He gave a low cry, but her hand raised, as the grip of the other on mine tightened yet more, and she held out both to him, drawing my hand with hers.

Now he put forth both his hands to her and I saw there was not so much personal sorrow to read on his face, but fear such as might be felt by a child threatened with desertion by an adult whose presence means security against the terrors of the dark and unknown.

Under Utta's grip my hand was brought to his and she dropped it between his palms where he closed upon it with a hold harsh enough to make me cry out, had I not steeled myself against such a display.

"I have done for you the best I might," she said and the gutturals of this language I had learned were as harsh in my ears as his grip. "I have raised up one to serve you as I have"—she made a mighty struggle to complete that, the effort bringing her forward from the rest, wavering weakly from side to side—"done!" She got the last word out in a cry of triumph as if it were a war shout to be uttered into the very face of death. And then she fell back, and that last thin thread holding her to us was broken forever.

V

*U*tta's burial was a matter of high ceremony for the Vupsalls. I had never witnessed such before and I was astounded by their preparations: there was such ritual as one would not associate with a wandering clan of barbarians, but rather a civilization very old and pattern-set by years. Perhaps it was the last vestige of some age-old act which was all they had brought with them from a beginning now so hidden in the foggy past they could not remember it.

She was dressed by Atorthi and Visma in the best her traveling boxes had to offer, and then her wisp of body was bound round and round with strips of dampened hide which were allowed to shrink and encase her withered flesh and small bones for eternity. Meanwhile the men of the tribe went south for almost a day's journey and there set about digging a pit which was fully as large when they had done as the interior of the tent in which she had spent her last days. To that pit the tent was taken, along with sleds full of loose rocks, all to be set up again.

I tried to watch for my chance of escape during all this, but the magic Utta had laid upon me held and I had not enough power to defeat the runes I had so unknowingly set foot on when I crossed into her tent. Let me try to venture beyond the boundaries of the camp alone and there came upon me such a compulsion to return as I could not fight, not unless I gave my full will and purpose to it, which a fugitive could not do.

During the four days of preparation I was left to myself in a new tent set a little apart. Perhaps the tribe expected me to make some magic beneficial to their purpose, for they did not urge me to help with the labors for Utta, for which I was thankful.

On the second day two of the traveling cases were brought by women and left just within my tent. When I explored these I found that one contained bundles and bags of herbs, most of which I identified as those used for healing, or to induce hallucinatory dreams. In the other was Utta's crystal, her brazier, a wand of polished white bone, and two book rolls encased in tubes of metal, pitted and eroded by time.

The latter I seized upon eagerly, but at first I could not master their opening. They were carved with symbols, some of which I knew, though they had slight differences from the ones I had seen many times before. On the ends of each were deeply set a single design or pattern. The markings seemed to have been less affected by time than the cases. There were fine twists of rune lettering—but I could not read it—surrounding as a border a small but very distinct picture of a sword crossed by a rod of power. Hitherto I had never seen two such symbols in close combination, for among the Wise Women the rod was the sign of the sorceress, the sword that of the warrior, and such were considered unseemly in contact, one female, the other male.

By very close study I finally found the faint cleavage mark which was the opening of the cases, and by much labor sprung their very stiff catches. But my disappointment was great to discover, though the rolls inside were intact, that I could read neither. Their runes might be the personal jotting of some adept who had devised a code for the better keeping of secrets.

At the beginning and end of each roll the crossed sword and rod were clearly drawn in colors: the sword red, the rod green touched with gold. This at least reassured me that what I held was not of the Shadow, for green and gold were of the light, not the dark.

The drawing surprised me, for here, as was not so apparent in the pattern on the cases, the sword was laid over the rod, as if suggesting that action was the first interest of the user, to be backed, not led, by the Power. And printed with a broad pen beneath it were letters which did make sense—or at least they formed themselves into a readable name, though whether of a people, a place, or a person, I did not know. I repeated it aloud several times to see if by such sounding I could awake a spark of memory.

"Hilarion."

It meant nothing, and I had never heard Utta mention it. But then she had told me very little of her past; she had concentrated instead on my learning what she had to teach. Baffled, I rewound the rolls, slipped them once more into the cases.

For a space I sat with my two hands pressed to the surface of the crystal, hoping against hope that I would feel it warm beneath my palms, glow, become a mirror to show me what I would know. But it did not, and that, too, I returned to the chest with the wand which I knew better than to touch, since such rods of power answer only she who fashioned it for service.

On the fifth day two women came to my tent; not waiting for permission, they boldly entered. Between them they bore a heavy jug of steaming water, together with a bathing basin. A third followed them, garments laid across her arm, a tray with several small pots and boxes on it in her hands.

While the two who carried the basin and jug were commoners, she with the robes and tray of cosmetics was Ifeng's newest wife, Ayllia. She was very young, hardly more than out of childhood, but she carried herself with stiff arrogance, thrusting forward her small breasts thickly coated with paint. She had chosen so to depict two scarlet blooms, her nipples at their centers glistening as if tiny shards of gemstone were mixed with the pigment. It was a very garish display, more barbaric than those worn by the others.

Her glance at me was sharp, surely more unfriendly than any I had met since Utta had taken me as her pupil and companion. Ayllia's lips pushed forward in what was close to a pout as she swept me with a long, measuring stare which was wholly hostile.

"It is time." She broke the silence first and I think she liked me even the less that she must do that and that I had asked no questions. "We take the old one to her time house; we do her honor—"

Since I did not know their customs, I judged it best to follow their lead. So I allowed them to bathe me in the water, to which they added a handful of moss which expanded in the moisture to be used as a sponge. It gave off a faint odor, not unpleasant but strange.

For the first time I was not given the breeches of hide and fur which were the common wear, but the garments Ayllia brought, a long and wide skirt of a material very old, I thought, but preserved by metal threads woven into it in a pattern of fronds or lacy leaves. These threads were tarnished so that the design was now a very faint shadow, to be seen only by looking carefully. In color it was dark blue, and it had a border of the same metal thread, a palm's width deep, which weighed it down, swinging about my ankles.

Under Ayllia's orders they painted my breasts, not with flowers, but with radiations of glitter pigment. They did not add to my clothing any of the necklaces which she and the other women wore; instead a veil was draped from the crown of my head, a netting of the tarnished metal thread. Once I was so clad Ayllia waved me out of the hut, taking her place behind me.

The tribe was drawn up in a procession headed by a sled. This was not drawn by dogs—the four which had served Utta walked on leashes held by tribesmen—but carried shoulder high. And in that lay, covered with choice skin robes, the body of their seeress. Directly behind that was a gap into which Ifeng's gestures urged me. Once I had obeyed, Visma and Atorthi fell in, one to my right, one to my left. They were newly clad and painted, but when I looked from one to the other, thinking to say some small word, not of comfort, perhaps—who could comfort their loss?—but of fellowship, they did not answer my glances, for each had her eyes fixed upon the sled and its burden. And each carried in her two hands, held high against her breast, a stone cup which I had not seen before. Dark liquid frothed and bubbled in the cups as if troubled by internal fire.

Behind us came Ifeng and the more important hunters and warriors. Then the women and children, so that we moved out and toward the grave in a line of the whole tribe. Once beyond the steaming pools and river of the valley it was cold and there was snow underfoot. I shivered within my ancient robe, but those walking beside me, half naked as in their tents, gave no sign of discomfort.

We came at last to the side of the excavation. And those bearing the sled went down a side ramp of earth to the tent set up below, coming from that empty-handed. Once they had returned Visma and Atorthi raised their bubbling cups and drank as women who thirsted for a long time and were now given the sweetest of water. Still carrying the now empty cups they went hand in hand down to the tent and we saw them no more.

I did not realize the significance of what they had done at once, not until I saw those who held the sled dogs use their knives to kill quickly and painlessly. Then those furred servants were taken to join the human ones below. I started forward—perhaps it was still not too late . . . Visma, Atorthi—they must not—

Ifeng caught my shoulder and his strength was such that he held me helpless as the warriors laid the dogs outside the tent in the pit and fastened their leashes to stakes, as if they slept and did not darken the earth with seeping blood. And, though I wanted to run into that hole and bring out those two who had been Utta's women, I knew there was no use in trying. They had already followed their mistress beyond that last curtain from which there is no return.

I no longer struggled against Ifeng, but stood quiet in his grip, though I shivered now and then with the cold of this barren place. So I watched the members of the tribe, men, women, children, to the youngest baby at a painted breast, walk or be carried past the pit. And into it each threw some token, even the baby's hand being guided by his mother to do so. Weapons fell from men's grasps, the glint of gold from women. Small treasured boxes of scented ointment, dried delicacies of food, each gave a treasure, their greatest personal possession, I believed. I knew then the full of their regard for Utta. It must have seemed to them that a whole way of life had died with her, since she had dwelt among them for generations and was a legend while still in their midst.

The men drew then to one side and they had with them the bark shovels, the ropes for pulling stones, all they had used to dig this place and would now need to cover it from the light of day. But the women gathered around me and they took me back with them to the camp. However, they did not leave me alone in my tent.

Ayllia came with me, and several of the older women, though among them was not the chief's first wife, Ausu. When I had seated myself on one of the cushions sewn of hide and stuffed with sweet grass, Ayllia boldly pulled up another equal with it. At her move I saw several of the others frown uneasily. While I did not understand what lay in the future, I thought it well then to assert myself. Utta had named me seeress before Ifeng; I had no intent, however, of binding my future to the Vupsalls as she had done. Once I broke the rune ties on the mat I would be away.

But to achieve that desire I must have quiet and leisure to study with what power I had regained. And it looked as if that was about to be denied me.

At any rate, for a Wise Woman to accept Ayllia as an equal, chief's wife though she was, would be a grave error. I must make certain from the start that they held me in awe, or else lose the small advantage I did have.

So I turned swiftly to look full at the girl, and my voice was sharp as I asked, though perhaps my grasp of their tongue was halting: "What would you, girl?" I copied such a tone as I had heard Utta use upon occasion, which was such as the Wise Women brought to their command in the Place of Silence when a novice strove to be more than she was.

"I be she who places hand to hand." She did not quite meet my gaze; in that she showed uneasiness. But her answer was pert and had a defiant note in it: "So I am beside you."

If I knew more of her meaning I might have been prepared. As it was I could only move by instinct and that told me that I must preserve my superiority before any of the tribe.

"To One Who Sees Before do you so speak, girl?" I demanded coldly.

By ignoring her name and speaking as one who knew it not because such small matters were of no concern, I put upon her the shame of lessening in the eyes of the others. Perhaps I was doing wrong in making an enemy, but she was already my unfriend, as I sensed when we first came face to face, and I might lose more by a try for conciliation.

"To one who needs me to place hand to hand I speak," she began, when someone else entered the tent.

She walked with difficulty, leaning on the arm of a young girl with unpainted breasts and a plain face marred by a red brand down one cheek. The newcomer was an older woman, her towering pile of hair streaked with gray which silvered the bold red coloring. Her broad face was additionally swollen, as her ungainly body was fat, her breasts great puffy pillows. It was not a natural stoutness but a bloat, and she carried other signs of ill health which made me wonder why she had not been among those who sought out Utta's aid during the weeks I had trailed with them.

Two of the women by the door made haste to rise and draw forward the cushions on which they had been sitting, piling one upon the other to give greater height for the stranger, it being manifest that she would find it difficult to get to her feet otherwise.

To this seat she was lowered by her attendant and she sat there for a long moment breathing heavily, both hands pressed to her huge breasts as if to ease some pain there. At the sight of her Ayllia came to her feet, moving back to the wall of the tent, her sullen pout more pronounced, yet that slight uneasiness with which she had faced me had become almost fear.

The maidservant went on her knees to one side so that she could look from her mistress to me.

"This be"—her voice was barely to be heard above the harsh breathing of her mistress—"Ausu of the Chief Tent."

I raised my hands and made a gesture of one tossing or sowing, which I had learned from Utta. So I acknowledged the introduction.

"Ausu, mother of men, ruler of the Chief Tent, be blessings and more good than can be held in the two hands of all, on you!"

Her panting breath seemed to ease somewhat and I remembered now that alone of the tribe she had not been among those who had ushered Utta to her last resting place. It was plain to see why: her great bulk, her poor state of health would have made such an effort impossible. Now she parted her blubber lips to speak for herself.

"Utta spoke to Ifeng; she left you behind to smooth our paths." She paused as if expecting some answer or confirmation from me. I gave her what I could.

"So Utta said." Which was true but did not admit that I agreed with the seeress's high-handed ordering of my future.

"As with Utta then you come under Ifeng's hand," Ausu continued, her voice wheezing sometimes so it was difficult to understand her words, each of which whistled from her with visible effort. "I come to place hand for you. And you, being what you are, will now be head in Ifeng's tent."

Her head turned a fraction on her ponderous shoulders, just enough to allow her to favor Ayllia with a glance so cold and menacing that I was startled. Ayllia did not drop her eyes.

But it was no time to mark any byplay between these two wives of the chief. For, if I understood them aright—marriage! I was to wed with Ifeng! But did they not know that as a Wise Woman I would forfeit the power they needed by coming under any man's hand? Or would I? My mother had not. Perhaps that was superstition only, enlarged upon and nurtured by the Wise Women to keep themselves and their rule invulnerable. It was unknown in Escore. I knew that Dahaun did not anticipate any lessening of her gifts when she gave her final word to my brother and became the core of his house as well as his heart. And Utta herself had spoken of being the consort of Ifeng's long ago predecessor in the chieftainship.

Whether or not such a union was in truth a threat to my partly regained power, it was a threat to myself and one which I would not yield to unless this barbarian overlord took me by force. And there lay within close distance of my hand now such measures as would render me cold meat in his bed should the worst come. But before that last extremity there were other ways of escape, and at least one came to my mind now. None of these women could read my thoughts and I might prepare—if I had the time—such an answer as would satisfy all concerned for a space.

So did I trust I had not betrayed my surprise, which I might have well anticipated had I been only a little quicker of wit. But rather I again made a gesture of good will toward Ausu and said, "The Mother of Many does me honor as is meet between two who are as sisters," making a claim of equality as I would not do with Ayllia. "Though we have not shared the same cup as becomes those born of one mother, yet there shall be no forewalker or aftergoer between us."

I heard a murmur from the women about us as that refusal of her offer of headship over Ifeng's household was spoken, and I knew they would accept my words as binding.

She continued to eye me for a space, those eyes, half buried in her cheek and nose, on mine. Then she sighed, and the stiff erectness of her shoulders sagged a little. I was able to understand the iron will which had brought her to me, the determination which had led her to do what she believed right.

I hastened to make sure that what I needed most, my privacy, would be allowed me.

"I am not as Ausu," I told her. I leaned forward and dared to take her puffy hands gently into mine. "As Utta I talk with spirits and so must have a tent to offer them room when they would visit me."

"That is so," she agreed. "Yet a wife comes to her master. And Utta abode part of the night with Ifeng when there was need."

"As is the custom," I agreed in return, my mind busy with my own answer for that. "Yet do I live apart. And, sister, is there not something which I can do for you? Your body ails, perhaps the spirits can find a cure—"

The oily rolls of fat making her face twisted. "It is the evil from the north. You have not been long enough with us, sister, to know. This is a sending upon me for foolishness I wrought. Ah—" She broke my hold and put her hands once more to her breasts as she cried out in sudden pain. And her handmaid hurried to bring forth a capped cup made of horn, unstoppering it quickly and giving her to drink. Some of the colorless liquid dribbled from her lips to leave sticky trails across her wealth of chins. "A sending," she repeated in a whisper. "There is no answer save to bear it to my grave pit."

I had heard of such curses—illness of spirit attacking those who wittingly or unwittingly intruded upon some one of the pools of old evil, reflecting in the body the ill of soul. It would require very great power to defeat such. But this was the first time among the Vupsall I had come across any sign of some brush with the ancient ills of Escore.

There was a sudden clashing from without a loud, metallic clatter which startled me. From the women arose in answer a crooning song. Ifeng? Had my bridegroom come to claim me? But not yet! I had not had time to prepare. What might I do? And I lost most of my sureness in that moment.

"Ifeng comes." Ayllia pushed closer, though I noticed she did not go too near her superior in the household. "He seeks his bride."

"Let him enter." There was dignity in Ausu in spite of her grotesque body.

The other women drew back against the wall, with them Ausu's maidservant.

When Ayllia did not follow them Ausu turned on her once more that glare which had force enough to move her.

Then the head wife raised her voice in a call. The flap was raised and Ifeng bowed his head beneath it, coming to Ausu's right. Her puffy hand groped out and he held his hard brown one where she might take it, though neither of them looked to the other, but rather to me.

I did not read in his face what I had seen earlier in his nephew's—that which promised me shame. Rather he was impassive, as one who went through a task set upon him by custom and which was part of the dignity and responsibility of chieftainship. But over his shoulder I saw Ayllia's face clearly and there was no mistaking her expression: jealous rage which burned with a fierce flame.

Ifeng knelt beside the vast bulk of his first wife and now she held her left hand to me and I set mine within it, so that she brought my palm against his as earlier Utta had done. Her wheezing breath formed words I did not understand, perhaps in some archaic speech. Then her hands dropped away leaving us joined in our own grasp. Ifeng leaned farther forward and with his other hand pulled aside the metallic veil which I had draped as closely about my shoulders as I could striving to gain from it some small measure of protection against the cold. Then his fingers came down on my breasts, stripping away the paint there as one would strip away clothing. At that moment the women about the sides of the hut gave a cry which had a queer ring—not unlike that Utta had given at her death, so might they have marked some victory.

How far Ifeng proposed to go now was my growing concern. I had had no chance to take the precautions I had planned. But it seemed that the ceremony was now at an end. And, perhaps because she knew I did not know their customs well, Ausu courteously gave me the clue I needed as to the next step, and one which would carry out my own desires.

"The plate and cup now to be shared, sister. And to this tent blessing. . . ."

The maid and women swooped forward and hoisted her to her feet. I arose also to do her honor, bowing her out of the tent. Ayllia had already vanished, probably so angered by my new tie with her lord that she had no wish to witness more.

Ifeng was seated on one of the cushions when I returned and I went straightaway to Utta's chest of herbs. From it I took some dried leaves which could turn one of their ordinary brews into a fine feast-drink. These I added to the goblets which were brought on a tray to the door of the tent and shoved under the flap as if no one would now disturb us.

When he saw what I did Ifeng's eyes lighted, for Utta's stores were relished. And he waited with greedy eagerness while I dropped a few more leaves into his goblet, stirred them well with a rod.

It is not always necessary to say a spell aloud; the will being directed toward the needed result is what matters most. And my will was firm that night, the firmer for my need. I added nothing Ifeng could see except an herb he knew well, but what I added by thought was the first step in my plan of salvation.

At least Utta had not tied me in this as she had with the mat runes. Ifeng drank; he ate from the plate we shared. Then he nodded and slept. And from Utta's chest I took a long thorn of bright red. About that I wrapped two hairs pulled living from my head, and I spat upon it, saying certain words against which Ifeng's ears were now safely closed.

When it was prepared I thrust it deep into the hide cushion which supported his head, then I began weaving a dream. It was not easy to imagine that which one has never experienced, and I dared not let myself doubt that I was succeeding. But as Ifeng turned and muttered in his sleep he dreamed as well as I could set in his mind that in truth he had taken a wife and set his hand and body upon her.

Had it been so with Utta? I wondered when I was done and sat exhausted, watching him sleep in the thin glow of the netted insects. Was this how she had been wife to chiefs and yet still a Wise Woman? It would be tested when he awoke, the sureness of dream weaving.

VI

*T*he night was long and I had much time for thinking, also to foresee some of the perils which might now lie in wait. Utta had taught, or retaught me much, that I knew. But she had left, either by design or because we were not originally of the same order of Wise Women, blanks in my knowledge which could make me as a wounded warrior striving to defend a stretch of wall where he could only use one arm, and that the left, when the right was natural to him.

She had not given me back my foreseeing. And of all the talents the Vupsall might call upon me to display, that was perhaps the most important. I wondered more and more concerning that lack of preparation on Utta's part. Had she feared I might use the mind touch which was a part of it to bring aid from the Valley? Yet she had made no seeress of her people, bereft of the gift which would mean the most to them.

Ifeng slept on. I crept across the tent, reversed the rune mat, to read again the lines set there which bound me to those people. At the same time I searched my memory for all which pertained to such spells, their making and breaking.

There are many ways for a Wise Woman of Power to bind one (especially one who has lesser talent than herself, or who may be ignorant of such matters altogether). Such as to present something of value to the victim. If he accepts, then he is yours until you see fit to release him. But for the lesser dabbler in power that has one side danger—if he chances to refuse the gift the spell recoils upon the sender. There is a kind of overlooking with the proper spells, a weaving of dreams to drive someone from his body and make two entities slave to the witch, the soulless body and, in another world, the bodiless soul.

But mainly these were matters of the Shadow, and I knew that Utta, one-minded as she had been for the welfare of her adopted people, had not depended upon the light, nor the dark for her powers. No, if I were to break these runes to escape (and that I must do speedily) then it must be by some of Utta's own learning.

And I doubted whether my newly awakened skills could do that—yet. As in all arts practice is an aid; one advances in skill by the use of it. I crept back to Ifeng, listened closely to his breathing. He no longer dreamed the dreams I had sent him; rather was he now in a deep sleep which would hold him yet awhile. Moving with what care I could, I put off the bridal robe, folding it carefully. Now I stood with none of their making on my chilled body, scraping the remains of the paint from my breasts, putting aside all that was of the tribe. I must have nothing about me to tie me to these people, for I would try a piece of magic which I feared too great for my limping skill, but which was my only chance to foresee even a little.

There is this: any object which has been used by a human being takes to itself some impression of that owner. Though most of Utta's personal belongings had gone with her into the tomb pit, yet I had what lay in the two chests, which were part of her magic.

Shivering in the cold, I knelt by the box where I had found those scrolls with the unreadable runes. At least in handling all from the chest I had learned this much, that of all Utta had left there was the greatest concentration of Power in those.

I brought them forth, and sat, holding one in each hand, trying to make my mind an empty pool, a mirror, waiting to be filled, to bear some reflection which could come from these things.

There was a stir—slow, reluctant, thin—as if so long a time had passed between that day and this that only a shadow of a shadow of a shadow could be summoned, despite all striving to bring it into clear focus.

I was not a mirror, rather did I look upon a mirror which was befogged by mist. Yet in that things moved dimly; dusty, dusky figures came and went. It was no use! I could not make them clear.

The containers in my hands grew heavier, dragging down my arms. Against the uncovered skin of my body they were icy cold, so that I shuddered.

If not the encased rolls, then what of the rolls themselves? One I laid aside, the other I opened, brought forth the scroll. This I took in both hands, lowered my head that I might press my forehead to a surface which felt like a long dried leaf.

Now—

I might almost have cried out at the sharp picture leaping into my mind had not long discipline warned me. It was a filling right enough, but such a filling, whirling about wildly, scenes which flashed so fast I could not grasp their significance. Lines of formulas, columns of runes came and went before I could guess their meaning. There was no reason, logic, nor sequence to this. It was as if someone had emptied a vast amount of poorly related material into an empty bin, and stirred it vigorously about.

I dropped the roll, thrust it back into its container. Then I put my hands to my head where that whirling of ill-timed, ill-sorted odds and ends of learning started such a pain as I had felt upon my first coming to the Vupsall camp. Nor could I at that moment advance further in my trial and error searching for Utta's secrets. I was suddenly so tired that I could not keep my eyes open. Almost, I thought with a small surge of unease, as if I had drunk such a cup as I had put in Ifeng's hands and was now about to follow him into a dream world.

I pulled myself together long enough to dress in the clothing I had laid aside when they had given me the marriage robe, though I moved sluggishly. Drawing one of the hooded cloaks about me, I fell back rather than laid me down, to sleep. And I had been right: I dreamed.

There was a castle, a keep as great, or so it seemed, as that citadel which centered Es City. It was the largest work of men's hands I had ever seen. In parts it was as solid as the stones of Es, yet other parts shimmered, came and went, as if they had substance in this world, yet in another also. Though I knew that, I did not understand the why or how of it.

And there was one who wrought all this, both by the work of the hands of those he commanded, and by Power. The master here was no Wise Woman, but an adept who was far more than warlock or wizard. And the castle was only the outer casing of something which was strange and of greater power than the walls about it.

I saw him, sometimes as only a shadow thing, as I had seen when I held the tube to me, and again as clear as if he stepped at intervals from behind some veil held about him by spells. He was of the Old Race, and yet there was that about him which argued that he was partly of another time and place.

He was working with Power, and I saw him do things as if he gathered up the raw strings of force to weave them and shape them this way and that into a pattern obeying his desires. He moved confidently, as one who well knows what he would do and has no fear that it shall not follow his desire. Watching him I knew a bitter envy. So once had I almost known the same sureness, before I had become one to creep blindly where I would have run.

Under his feet runes burst in lines of fire, and the very air about him was troubled by the words he uttered, or the strength of his thought sendings. This was greater than aught I had ever seen, though it had been given me once or twice to watch the most powerful of the Wise Women at their spelling.

Now that I saw all his weaving and building was centered in the hall in which he worked, the lines of the runes, the troubling and stirring of the air gathered into one place. Finally there was to be seen there, standing straight, an archway of light. And I knew that what my dream showed me was the creation of one of those gateways to another world which are to be found in this ancient, sorcery-steeped land. That they existed was well known, but that they were created by adepts, that we had learned only after we had come into Escore. Now I had witnessed the opening of one.

He stood there, his feet planted a little apart, his arms suddenly flung up and back in a gesture which was wholly human, one of triumph. The calm concentration on his face became fierce exultation. But, having his gate, he did not hurry to enter it.

Rather did he retreat from it step by step, though I saw no sign that his confidence ebbed. I believe that he felt then some unease which kept him from any rash leap into the unknown. So he seated himself on a chair and sat there, looking at the gate, his hands folded palm to palm, raised so that his steepled fingers touched his pointed chin, his look of one deep in thought or planning.

While he sat so considering his creation, I continued to watch him, as if the man himself and not the sorcery in which he had been engaged had drawn my dreaming. As I have said, he was of the Old Race, or was at least a hybrid of that breeding. Was he young—old? No age touched him. He had the body of a man of action, a warrior, though he wore no sword. His robe was gray and belted tightly about his narrow middle with a sash of scarlet along which rippled lines of gold and silver. If one fastened attention on them long enough, these lines seemed to take the form of runes, yet they glowed quickly and faded before one could read them.

He appeared to come to some decision, for he arose and held up his hands a little apart. As he brought them together with a sharp clap I saw his lips move. And in answer that gateway disappeared and he was in a steadily darkening hall. But it was in my mind that having so wrought once he could do it again, that his triumph remained.

But it would seem that my dream had only this much to show within that hall. Then I was outside, going down a passage, and between great towering gates on which crouched creatures out of nightmares; they turned their heads to look solemnly upon me as I passed, yet I knew they were bound against harming such as I.

That journey was in such detail that I thought, should I, waking, come upon that same place I would know it instantly and be able to find my way again into that hall, as if I had been born within those walls and lived there through my childhood.

The reason for my dream I did not know, though such dreaming is always sent for a purpose. I could only believe, when I awakened, that it had sprung from my attempt to "read" the scroll. My head still ached with a pain which made the morning light a torment to my eyes. But I sat up with a jerk and looked to where Ifeng slept. He was stirring and I lurched quickly to him, drew forth the thorn, hiding it in the hem of my cloak, and then sank back as he opened his eyes.

He blinked, and, as intelligence came back into his face, he smiled oddly with a kind of shyness which sat oddly on such a man.

"Fair morning . . ."

"Fair morning, leader of men." I gave him formal greeting in return.

He sat up on the cushions and looked about him as if he were not quite sure of where he had rested that night. For a moment or two I was wary, wondering if the dream I had spun for him had been so badly woven that he would know it for a dream. But it would seem that I need not have feared, for now he bowed his head in my direction and said, "Strength grows strength, Farseeing One. I have taken your gift to me and we shall be great always, even as it was under Utta's hand." Then he made a gesture with two fingers crossed which was common to his people when they spoke of the dead, so warding off any ill from naming those gone before. He went from me as a man well satisfied in the doing of some duty.

But if the dream satisfied Ifeng and those of the tribe he must have reassured with his account of that night, it also made me an enemy—this I was not long in discovering. For, after the custom, I was visited during the morning by the senior and chief women of the tribe, all bringing gifts. Ausu did not come to me since I had made it clear that we were equal in Ifeng's family, but Ayllia was the last to visit my tent.

She came alone, and when I was alone, as if she had waited until there was none to witness our meeting. And when she entered, her hostility was like a dark cloud about her. So much had my powers advanced that I could so read danger when I met it face to face.

Alone among her people she seemed in no awe of my sorcery. It was almost as if she could herself look into my mind and know how little I really knew. Now she did not sit, nor did she give me any formal greeting. But she flung with force, so that it struck the ground before me and burst open, spilling forth its contents, a small box cunningly and beautifully fashioned. And the necklace it had held was a great work of art.

"Bride price, elder one." Her mouth twisted as if the words she spoke tasted bitter. "With Ausu's welcome—"

I dared not allow her this insolence. "And yours, younger sister?" I asked coldly.

"No!" She dared that denial, though I noted she held her voice prudently low. For some reason she was wrought to strong anger, but she still had prudence in that she did not want those who might listen to know ill feeling lay so nakedly between us.

"You hate me," I put the matter bluntly; "why?"

Now she did come to her knees so that her face was nearer on a level to mine. She thrust her head forward so that I could see the congestion of fury darkening it, the small flecks of spittle at the corners of her wide mouth.

"Ausu is old; she is ruler in Ifeng's tent only in small things. She is sick—she no longer cares." The words came forth in a rush bringing mouth moisture with it to touch my cheek. "I"—her fist beat against her gaudily painted breast—"I am chief in Ifeng's sight, or was. Until your witchery stole his mind. Aye, dealer in spells, blast me, turn me into a worm to be crushed beneath the boot, to a hound to draw a sled, to a stone to lie unheeding—better would that be to me than what I am now in the tent of Ifeng."

And I knew she spoke the truth. In her rage of jealousy she would rather have me enchant her as she believed I could rather than take her place and leave her to watch what she believed to be my triumph over her. It was the courage of complete despair and envy past bearing which led her to defy the person she thought I was.

"I want not Ifeng," I said steadily. Once I might have taken over her mind, her will, made her believe what I said was so. Now I strove to impress her with the truth, but I feared with small success.

At least she sat silent, as if she were thinking upon my answer. And I hastened to use any small advantage I might have gained.

"I am a dealer in spells, as you have said," I told her. "I do not depend upon the good will of any man, be he chief or warrior only. It is within me—me—do you understand that, girl?" I brought my hands to my breasts, took upon me with what I hoped was good effect a semblance of the arrogance the Wise Women wore as easily as their robes and jewels.

"You lay with Ifeng," she said sullenly, but her eyes dropped, seemed to study the open box and tumbled necklace which lay between us.

"For the good of the tribe. Is it not the custom?" I might—just might—have disarmed her completely with the true version of the night, yet I decided against it. To keep one's secrets well is the first lesson of any seeker after knowledge.

"He—he will come again! He is a man who had tasted a feast and goes hungry until he eats so again!" she cried out.

"No, he will not come again," I told her, and hoped I spoke the truth. "For this is true of those of us who walk the path of Power: we cannot lie with a man and use still our learning. Once—to make sure our strength passes to the chief in part as it should—but not again."

She met my eyes and this time her anger was dulled, but her stubbornness did not yield. "What cares a hungry man for words? They but sound in his ears and do not fill him. You have one mind, yes, but I tell you Ifeng is of another. He is as one who dreams—"

I tensed. Had she hit upon the truth of this without my telling? If so, what harm could come in her resentment?

"Tell me"—she leaned still closer, until her breath mingled with mine—"what sorcery do you Wise Ones use to ensnare a man who has always thought clearly and was not bemused by such things?"

"None of my making." But was it so? I had dealt quickly, and perhaps not with clear thought when I had laid Ifeng under my spell. If that was what mattered I had the answer now. My hands pressed on that part of the cape I had pulled about me, and through the fabric I felt the prick of the thorn I had concealed there. "Be assured, Ayllia, that if he was bespelled by chance, then shall I break it, and speedily. I want this no more than you do!"

"I shall believe you when Ifeng goes with clear eyes and comes to my bed place as eagerly as he did two nights agone," she told me bleakly. But perhaps she did believe in me a little.

Now she got to her feet. "Show me, Wise Woman, show me that you are not unfriend to me—perhaps to all of us!"

She had turned on her heel and went from me. When I was sure she was gone, I dropped the tent flap and made it fast to the inner stake set as a kind of lock to insure privacy. With the flap down, no one by custom would enter.

I had no servants such as had waited upon Utta, nor any novice learning my mysteries. Yet I moved with caution, still fearing that I might be in some way overlooked.

One of the braziers still held a coal not yet completely dead and I blew on that, fed it some bits of shaved wood, then some of the dried herbs. As the fragrant smoke puffed out I dropped my thorn into the heart of that handful of fire. A pity, since I would have to make another if the need arose. But Ayllia was right; if Ifeng held me so firmly in mind I wanted the dream tie broken quickly.

It worked, for the chief did not approach me, nor was I troubled with any visitors for a space. It seemed that another move was in their minds. Though I had believed them well settled, perhaps for the rest of the winter, amid the warmth of the hot streams. This was not to last. It was a matter of game, which had become more and more sparse in the general vicinity. In addition I think some restlessness was a part of the spirit of these people, that they were not long happy nor content in any one place even though that promised an easier life.

Left to myself, save that they brought food and firewood to my door each morning, I spent hours in striving to recall with the aid of Utta's things more which could help me. Sooner or later, probably sooner, Ifeng and his men were going to demand a casting of foreknowledge of me. I could pretend such, but that was a piece of deceit which I dared not enter upon. It was a betrayal of the Power to claim what I had not. And in the present I wanted no more misuse to cancel the small gains I had made.

For all my desperate trying foreknowledge continued to elude me. Mind search efforts came to nothing at all. Perhaps had there been another learned in the

Power to aid me, I might have made contact. But at last I came across another of Utta's tools, well wrapped and at the very bottom of her second chest as if it were something long forgotten or overlooked. I sat with it in my hands studying it.

This was a thing such as the novices in the Place of Silence use. It was a child's toy in comparison with more complex and better ordered aids, but I was certainly a child again in such matters and it would be better than nothing . . . I must be humble and use what I could.

It was a board of wood, runes carved on it in three rows. Traces of red paint, hardly to be detected now, were in the deep cracks of the first row, gold in small tarnished lines in the second, while the third was deep shadowed and must once have been painted a dire black.

Providing I could make this work, even a little, I would have an answer for Ifeng's asking and yet not practice deceit. I could no more than try it now. What of my own question, to which I so yearned to have an answer? What better beginning than that?

Kyllan, Kemoc! I closed my eyes, pictured those two nearest to my heart, my other selves, and under my breath I began a chant of words so old they had no meaning, were only sound to summon certain energies.

Laying the board on my knee, steadying it with my right hand, I touched its graven surface with the fingers of my left and began sweeping them from top to bottom, first the red row, then the gold, and then, though I had to force them to that task, the black. Once, twice, I made that sweep, then a third time—

So did my answer come. For suddenly my fingers were as fast to the uneven surface as if they had sunk into it, had become one with the wood. I opened my eyes to read the message.

Gold! If I could believe it, gold—life, and not only life but well-being for those I had so tried to reach. Straightaway, when I allowed myself to believe that, my touch on the board loosed and I could withdraw my fingers.

A burden I had not measured as I carried it was lifted from me. And I did not in the least disbelieve that I had read aright.

So . . . now for my own future. Escape—how, when?

This was more complex. I could not draw a sharp picture in my mind as I had of my brothers' faces. I could only try to build a strong desire of being elsewhere and wait for an answer.

Again my fingers adhered, but this time close to the foot of the red column. So escape was possible but it would come through peril and not in the immediate future.

There was a scratching at the flap of my tent.

"Seeress, we seek." Ifeng's voice. Had my countermagic failed? But surely as a husband he would not wait outside with such a call.

"They who seek may enter." I used Utta's formula, slipped the flap cord from its peg.

He was not alone; the three warriors who were the senior members of the tribe and acted as an informal advisory council were at his back. At my gesture of welcome they knelt and then settled back on their heels, Ifeng acting as spokesman.

"We must go hence; there is need for meat," he began.

"This is so," I agreed. And again I kept to Utta's formula. "Whither would the people go?"

"That we ask of you, Seeress. In us it is to go east again, down river to the sea where was our home before the slayers came over water. But will that bring evil upon us?"

Here it was, a demand for foreseeking. All I had was my tool of board and my finger. But I would do what I could and hope for a good ending.

I brought out the board and saw that they looked at it in a puzzled way as if it were something new to them.

"Do you not look into the ball of light?" Ifeng asked. "Such was the way of Utta—"

"Do you," I countered, "carry the same spear, wear the same sword as Toan, who sits at your right hand? I am not Utta, I use not the same weapons she did."

Perhaps that seemed logical to him, for he only gestured and did not question me again. I closed my eyes and considered the matter of journeying as clearly as I could arrange my thoughts. Again it was a question that was hard to form as a mind picture. At last I believed my best results were to fix upon myself, on such a journey. And in that choice lay my mistake.

I ran my fingers and they were caught and held swiftly. I opened to see them but halfway down the first column.

"Such a journey lies before us," I told him. "In it is some danger but not the greatest. The warning is not strong."

He nodded with satisfaction. "So be it. All life holds dangers of one kind or another. But we are not men to walk without eyes to see, ears to hear, and we have scouts who know better than most to use both. East it is then, Seeress, and we shall travel with the sun two days from now."

VII

J had no wish to travel eastward, farther and yet farther away from that portion of Escore which meant the most to me. Even should I now manage to break the rune bonds and be able to escape, leagues of unknown country would lie between me and the Valley, a country full of traps—many sly and clever traps. But Utta's magic left me no choice and when the Vupsalls marched so did I. My only resource was to memorize our path so that I might have some guides on my return. That I would break the rune spell and be free I did not doubt; it was only when I did not know.

We—or I—had forgotten the bite which winter held while we camped in the place of hot springs. Going out from there was stepping from early summer into midwinter.

Utta's sled and dogs had gone with her into the burial pit, but Ifeng, according to custom, furnished me with a new sled and two well-trained hounds, and sent me Ausu's maid to help in packing. As yet I had no servant from the tribe, nor had I asked for one, since I wanted no spying eyes when I strove to remaster my former skills. However I could see now that Visma and Atorthi between them had saved much labor during our travels. And since work with tents was new to me, I would have to ask for such an addition to my tenthold.

There were castes among the tribe, small as it was, and they had been set long ago. Some tentholds were always free from demands from Ifeng or the other leaders; others obeyed naturally. And I learned that the latter, as Visma, had been war captives, or the descendants of such.

I watched those particular families with new attentions as we moved out, striving to see one of the younger women among them whom I might bring into my own tent. And my choice was undecided between two. One was a widow who lived with her son and his tenthold. She had a dull, time- and circumstance-beaten face, and moved among the family almost as did the Kolder slaves of my mother's long ago tales. I did not think that curiosity was still alive in her or that she would be a spy menace, but perhaps would learn loyalty to me if taken from the tent where she was a cowed drudge.

The other was a young girl who seemed biddable enough. She had a clubbed foot which did not appear to interfere with her work, but put her outside the hope of marriage unless she went as a second or third wife, more servant than mate. But perhaps she was too alert of mind to serve my purpose.

I had already learned to guide the dogs with the called commands to which they were trained from puppyhood. And, once all was laden on the sled, I took my place in line, just behind the sleds of Ifeng's household.

The men ranged out, flanking us through this stream country, busy at keeping the heavily loaded sleds going, lending their own strength, pushing and pulling. But we were not long in that place of sand, stones and warmth, moving upslope into the snow and ice of the outer world. When our runners struck the easier going of the snow, our escort fanned out and away on either side of the main body of travelers, setting a protective screen between us and attack.

Once more we moved through a deserted country in which I saw no signs of old occupancy such as one marked easily in the western part of Escore. I wondered anew at this. For the country, even hidden under the burden of winter storms, gave the appearance of being one able to support garths and farms, to nourish a goodly population. Yet there were no marks of ancient fields, no ruins to say that the Old Ones had ever had their manors and lands here.

It was on the second day of travel that we came to the river. An icy crust lay along each bank, extending out over the stream save for a wide dark band marking the center. There I saw the first signs that this had not been a totally forsaken wilderness. A bridge spanned that way, its pillared supports still standing except at midpoint of the stream.

Guarding either end of that broken span was a set of twin towers, looped for defense, large enough perhaps to provide garrison housing. One was intact; the other three had suffered and were crumbling, their upper stories roofless and only partially walled now.

But midpoint between these two guarding our side of the river was a stone arch which was so deeply carved that its pattern could still be read. And the symbol it bore was one I had seen before—on Utta's rune rolls—a sword and rod crossed.

On the other side of the bridge a smoothness in the sweep of snow suggested that a pavement or roadway extended on. But it was certainly not the choice of the tribe to make use of its convenience. Though I did not detect any taint of the Shadow about the ruins, we made a wide arc out and away, avoiding any close contact with those crumbling walls.

Perhaps the Vupsalls had long ago learned that such could be traps for the unwary and avoided all remnants of the past on principle. But I kept my eyes on the bridge and that suggestion of road, and wondered where it led, or had once led, and the meaning of those symbols above the gate. To my seeress' knowledge they had no rune significance, but must once have been a heraldic device for some nation or family.

The use of such identifying markings had long since vanished from Estcarp. But some of the Old Race who had managed to escape the Kolder-inspired massacres in Karsten and had fled for refuge over the border still used them.

We did not cross the river and on this side appeared no vestige of roadway. We paralleled the stream, once more heading due east, whereas we had angled northward out of the warm valley. I thought that this river must feed into the eastern sea my new companions sought.

I finally made my choice of tent aid and asked Ifeng at our second night's halt if I might have the aid of the widow Bahayi, which request he speedily granted. I believe the first wife of Bahayi's son was none too pleased, for Bahayi, in spite of her dull-witted appearance, was a worker of excellence. When she took charge of my tent all went with some of the old ease that had surrounded us when Utta's women had organized our travels. Nor did she show in the least any interest in my magical researches, rolling herself in her coverings to snore away the night. And I learned to ignore her as I sought a key to my prison.

With a growing intensity of need I made that search. There was almost a foreshadowing of danger to come. Each time that warning hung over me I would consult the answer board and always that reassured me. However, again I made the grave mistake of asking for myself alone—a mistake I have since paid for with much regret.

Our course along the river did bring us to the sea; under the wintery sky that was a bleak and bitter place where winds searched out with fingers of ice any opening in one's cloak or tunic. Yet this seemed to be the place the tribe sought and under the winds they walked as people who had been in exile but are now returned to their own place.

It was along that shore that the ruins I had missed inland were to be seen. The major pile lay on a point which thrust like the narrow blade of a sword into the sullen and metal gray sea. What it had been—a single castle of fortification, a small walled town, a keep such as the Sulcar sea rovers had once built on Estcarp's coast—I could not tell from a distance.

And distance was what the Vupsalls kept between themselves and it. Their camp lay about midpoint of the bay into which the river emptied, and that pile of rocks was on the north cape protecting the inner curve, leagues away, so that sometime it was veiled from us by mists.

For the first time the Vupsalls made use of the remains of other structures. These were waist-high walls of well-set masonry. We may have been camping in the last vestiges of a town where men of the Old Race had once met shipping from overseas.

Our tents were incorporated with those walls for hybrid dwellings which gave us better shelter and such warmth as I, for one, welcomed. I noted that the tribe must have known this spot well and used it many times before, since each team and sled made its way to a certain walled foundation as if coming home. Bahayi, not waiting any direction from me, sent our own hounds to one of the foundations a little apart, the last intact one to the north of those chosen for dwellings. Perhaps this one was Utta's when she had been here. I accepted Bahayi's selction, for it served my purpose well, being away from the rest.

I helped her rather ineptly to use the tent walls plus those of a good-sized roofless room. Then she made an improvised broom of a branch, sweeping out sand and other debris, leaving us underfoot a smooth flooring of squared blocks. She brought in armloads of branches with small aromatic green leaves. Some of these she built into beds along the wall, others she shredded into bits and strewed on the floor, so that the scent of their crushing arose pleasantly to mask the odor the stone cell had had at our coming.

At one end was a fireplace which we put to good use. And when we were settled in I found this to be more comfortable than any abode I had been in since leaving the Valley. I sat warming my hands at the fire while Bahayi prepared our supper. I wondered what manner of man had built this house whose shell now sheltered us, and how long it had been since the builders had left the village to sand, wind, rain, snow and the seasonal visits of the nomads.

There had never been any way of reckoning the ages since Escore fell into chaos and the remnant of the Old Race had fled west to Estcarp, sealing the mountains behind them. Once I had, with the aid of my brothers, given birth to a familiar and had sent it forth questing into the past that we might learn what had happened to turn a fair land into a lacework of pitfalls set by the Shadow. We had seen through the eyes of that child of my spirit the history of what had passed, how a pleasant and seemly life had been broken and ravaged through man's greediness and reckless seeking for forbidden knowledge. The toll of years, of centuries, had not been counted in our seeing, and age beyond telling must now lie between our fire this night and the first ever lit on that same hearth place.

"This is an old place, Bahayi," I said as she knelt beside me putting forth into the heat of the flames one of those long-handled cooking pots which served at camp fires. "Have you come here many times?"

She turned her head slowly; her forehead was a little wrinkled as if she were trying to think, or count—though the counting system of her people was a most primitive one.

"When I was a child . . . I remember," she said in her low voice, which came with a hesitation as if she spoke so seldom she had to stop and search for each word. "And my mother—she remembered, too. It is a long time we have come here. But it is a good place—there is much meat." She pointed southward with her chin. "And in the sea, fish which are sweet and fat. Also there is fruit which can be dried and that we pick in the time of the first cold. It is much good, this place, when there are no raiders."

"There is a place of many stones there—" I pointed north. "Have you been there?"

She drew in her breath with an audible sucking sound, and her attention was suddenly all for the pan she held. But in spite of her manifest uneasiness I pursued the matter, for there was something about that wind and water assaulted cape which stayed in my mind.

"What is that place, Bahayi?"

Her right shoulder raised a little, she averted her head even more, as one who fears a blow.

"Bahayi!" I did not know why I insisted upon an answer; I only know that somehow I must have it.

"It is . . . a strange place—" Her hesitation was so marked I did not know whether it was born of fear, or if her dull mind could not find words to describe what lay there. "Utta—once she went there—when I was a small child. She came back saying it was a place of Power, not for any who were not of the Wise Ones."

"A place of Power," I repeated thoughtfully. But of which Power? Just as there were pools of evil left by the passing or abiding of the Shadow in some places of this ill-treated land, so there were bastions from which one such as I could draw sustenance and aid. And if the ruin on the far headland was like one of those refuges of blue stones, could a visit there be a strengthening of what I had regained?

Only it stood so far from us that I thought the rune spell would not permit me a visit. I had experimented from time to time, trying to discover how far I could travel from the tribe, and the distance was small indeed.

Suppose I could persuade some of them to accompany me, at least to the boundaries of the place, if they held the interior in too great awe or fear to go all the way? Would that lengthen my invisible leash to the point that I could go exploring?

But if it were a dwelling place of the Shadow, then the last thing I must do would be venture there in my present poorly defended state. If only Utta had left some record of her days with the tribe. By all reckoning she had been with them for generations. Perhaps if she had begun any such account the dust of many years had long since buried it. Living among a people who recorded only by some event she had doubtlessly lost her own measurement of time.

I thought of those two enigmatic scrolls in Utta's chest. Perhaps they had come from this cape citadel. And if that pile was the one shown in my dream . . .

There were two scrolls—I had used only one when I saw the adept and his open gateway. Suppose the other held some secret to give me what I now wanted, my freedom? With that thought I experienced a vast surge of impatience to get at such an experiment, to try to dream again and wrest from such dreaming the learning I needed.

I had to call upon hard-learned discipline before Bahayi. For though I was almost certain she was what she appeared to be, incurious and slow of wit, such dreaming could carry one out of one's body for a space. And so defenseless I wanted no witnesses.

Thus I called upon the same device I had used with Ifeng and brought out Utta's herb to turn our water-wine into a pleasant drink. Bahayi was so surprised that I offered her such a luxury that I reproached myself for not having done so before. And I set in my mind that I must do something for her. What better time than now?

Thus when she slept I wove a dream spell for her—one which would give her the pleasure she would enjoy the most, leaving it to her own mind and memory to set up the fantasy once I had turned the key to unlock the door for it. Then I set a lock spell on our door and stripped myself. I held the second scroll against the warmth of my breast, bent forward to lay my forehead to its upper end, opening my mind to what might enter.

Again there was a flow into my mind, so much of it incomprehensible, too obtuse for my unlocking; had I the time to puzzle it out, though, I might have gained very much. But I was in the position of one placed at a table on which there lay a vast heaping of gems, under orders to sort out those of one kind in a short time, so my fingers must quest for all the emeralds, pushing aside rubies, sapphires and pearls, beautiful and rare as those might be, and as much as I coveted them.

My "emeralds" I did pick here, there, and again here. Those bits and scraps were more to me as I awoke than any real gem. I returned the scroll to its container and looked to Bahayi. She lay upon her back, and on her face was the curve of a smile such as I had never seen before on that dull face.

As I drew my cloak about my shivering body and reached out to lay more wood on the fire, I thought again of what I might do for my tent fellow. A small spell might give her for the rest of her life this ability to enter happy dreams each night. To one who wanted more of life than sleep and dreaming it would be a curse rather than a gift. But I thought that for Bahayi it would be a boon. So I brought out what would best reinforce my thought commands and I wrought that spell before I turned to what else I must do that night.

For my "emeralds" had proved treasure indeed. As I had known from the first Utta's magic was more nature allied than the learning of Estcarp. And her rune ties were a matter of blood. But blood can cancel blood under certain circumstances. Though it would be painful and perhaps dangerous for me, I was willing to try that road.

I unfolded the mat with the runes, passing my hand across the dull surface so they blazed. Then I took one of the long tribal knives. Its point I put to a vein upon my arm and I cut so that the blood flowed red and strong. From Utta's hoard I had that rod I had discovered on my first delving. This I dipped into the blood and with care and my own red life, I repainted each rune, its blaze being smothered and darkened by what I had laid upon it. Often I had to stop to press the knife deeper, increase the flow by so much.

When I had done I bound a healing paste of herbs about my wound as quickly as I might, so that I could be about the rest of the spell. I did not know just which of the forces Utta might have called upon in the setting of those bounds, but I had for rebuttal those the Wise Women had known. And now I named them one by one as I watched the blood congeal, the runes hidden by those splotches. When I believed it was ready, I wadded it into a mass and thrust it into the fire.

This was my moment of testing. Had I not wrought aright my life might answer for such destruction. In any event it would not be easy.

Nor was it, for as the flames licked and ate at the mat, so did my body writhe and I bit my lips against screams of agony searing me. Blood trickled down my chin as well as my arm as my teeth met through my own flesh. But I endured without an outcry which might have awoken Bahayi. I endured and watched the mat until it was utterly consumed. Then I crawled to Utta's chest and brought out a small pot of thick grease which I smeared, with trembling fingers and many catches of breath, at the hurt, up and down my body, which was reddened and sore as if I and not the mat had lain unprotected in the heart of the coals.

So was the spell broken, yet the breaking left me in so sad a state that it would not be that day which was now dawning, nor even the one to follow, which could see me on my way. Also there were other precautions I must take, for any hound in the camp put to my trail could nose out my way and run me down were I to be found missing.

Bahayi roused with the daylight, but she was as one who moved in the afterglow of a dream, going about her duties with her usual competence but taking very little note of me save when it was necessary to bring food. And we were further aided in our solitude by a blizzard which made such a cloud about our ruins that those of each tenthold kept to themselves and there was no coming nor going.

By late afternoon my hurts were healed to the point I could move about, if stiffly and with some pain. And I set about my own preparations for flight. The thought of the cape ruins held steady in my mind. Utta had visited there and had said it was a place of Power, warning off the tribe. But she had not said of evil Power. And if I took refuge in such a place I might escape pursuit.

Were I to vanish there they might well take it to be an act of magic and be too frightened to come seeking me with hound and tracker. I could shelter therein and wait for better weather to start west again.

It seemed to me as I sorted through all of Utta's belongings, packet by packet, box by box, jar by jar, that all was very much for the best and that I was coming out of this venture very well. While I had certainly not regained all I had lost through my companionship with Dinzil, still I knew enough now not to be a menace to those I loved. And I might return safely to the Valley.

I made up a small pack of healing herbs and those I needed for such spells as I could use for defense during a journey. And, after Bahayi went to sleep again, I put aside a store of food choosing those things which would last longest and give the greatest strength and energy in the least bulk.

If I went openly, with the knowledge of the clan, to visit the ruins, I could have a sled for the first lap of my journey. However, after that it might well be a matter of carrying only what I could pack on my back. All the more reason to be sure I was fully cured of my ill taken in destroying the rune mat.

The storm came from the north and it held steady for two days and the night between. The howl of the wind overhead was sometimes strangely like voices calling aloud and Bahayi and I looked uneasily at each other, drawing closer together before the fire, which I fed with some of the herbs as well as from our fast dwindling pile of wood.

But at dusk on the second day the wind died and soon after there came a scratching at our door flap. Ifeng stamped in at my call, shaking snow from his heavy furs. He had brought with him a pile of driftwood gathered from along the shore and dumped it by our hearth place, together with a silver scaled fish Bahayi welcomed with a grunt of pleasure.

Having so delivered supplies he looked to me. "Seeress," he began, and then hesitated, as if not knowing quite how to put his request into words. "Seeress, look into the days to come for us. Such storms sometimes drive the raiders to shore—"

So I brought out my board and he squatted on his heels to watch. I questioned him as to the form of ship to be feared and his halting description gave me a mental picture not unlike those of the Sulcar ships of my childhood. I wondered if these other sea rovers were not of the same breed.

Holding that picture in mind I closed my eyes and read with my fingers. Down the red line they slid rapidly, and down the gold. But on the third ominous black column they caught fast, as if the tips were clotted with pitch. I looked—they were fastened so close to the top I cried out in alarm.

"Danger—great danger—and soon!" I gave warning.

He was gone, leaving the door flap open behind him. I threw aside the answer board to follow, to see him in the dusk of early twilight floundering along the drifts between the ruined walls. Now and again he stopped at some downed flap to yell a warning, so he left all stirring behind him.

Too late! He wavered suddenly, as if he had trod on a treacherous bit of icy footing, falling back against a wall. He had drawn his sword but he never had a chance to use it. I saw in the half gloom the hand ax which had struck him between neck and shoulder, biting out his life. A thrown ax—another Sulcar trick.

Before he had more than fallen to the ground there was a flitting of gathering shadows racing between the low crumbling walls; I heard screaming from the other side of the settlement, where the raiders must have already forced their way into some of the shelters.

I turned on Bahayi, catching up the pack I had prepared.

"Come! The raiders—"

But she stood staring at me in her most stupid way, and I had to throw her cloak about her, pull her to the door, push her ahead of me. The sled dogs had been loosed from their common kennel in the center of the settlement and were at grim work, buying time for their masters. I pulled and dragged at Bahayi, trying to urge her along with me northward.

For some moments she came. And then suddenly, with a sharp cry, as if she were awakening from a dream, she struck out at me, freeing herself. Before I could catch her again she was out of reach, on her way back to the very heart of the melee.

I looked back. Had I been such a one as Utta, with natural forces at my command, I might have been able to aid the tribesmen. Now I was the least in any defense they might summon.

So I turned resolutely north, struggling from one patch of cover to the next, leaving the fighting behind me, just as snow began to fall again.

VIII

*T*he swirling of the snow not only hid what was happening now in the village, but the rising of a savage wind also drowned out the cries. Within minutes I thought I had chosen the worse of two evils in my flight, for I was completely lost. But I kept blundering on, until I staggered into a half seen brush from which I recoiled. That told me that I was out of the ruins and into the beginning of the growth which masked my distant goal.

This brush was tall and thick enough to shelter me once I had fought a little way into it, and I half fell through a slit in it, which must mark a trail. The way was so narrow that I deemed it a game path. It ran with so many twists and curves that it certainly did not follow any ancient road, since mankind has a way of imposing his will on nature in the building of roads not yielding to her quirks.

Some of the taller spikes of brush, which were close to the stature of trees, held off the fury of the storm, and I was able to stumble along at a goodly pace. I believed that my sense of direction had not altogether deserted me and I was heading for the mysterious pile of timeworn masonry on the point.

Perhaps it would be better to strike directly away from the sea westward—but not in such a storm and with perhaps raiders on my trail. I believed that the building on the cape would be an excellent hiding place.

So far I had kept my mind on my own escape and the immediate future, trying to shut from my thoughts the probable fate of the tribe. It was the custom, as I had learned during my short time among them, for them to live in a continual round of blood feuds and raids. But the sea rovers were the worst of their enemies. The males of a defeated people faced certain death, the women, if they were pleasing enough, would be taken as minor wives; if uncomely they would be slaves. It was a hard life at best, but one they were bred to.

In my short life I had lived constantly with war, being born into the midst of Estcarp's death struggle with Karsten, my mother and father both serving on the border from which the greatest of threats came. I had seen my brothers ride off to battle before they had more than a faint shadow of beard on their cheeks. And I had been impressed thereafter to fighting of a different sort. Since we had fled into Escore, fleeing the wrath of the Wise Women, struggle had been ever sitting on our left hand, sword striking in our right. We had hung arm shields in childhood and we had never been allowed to put them off.

Therefore such a raid now did not come to me as a blow. Had my power been as great as it once had been, I would have used it to encircle the tribe against this ill before I left. I would have brought Bahayi with me had she allowed it. And I thought of Ausu with some regret. But there were no others among the tribe to whom I owed any allegiance, nor whom I would have drawn steel to defend.

My wandering trail came out suddenly under an arch of leafless growth into a wider path, crossing that at an angle. I guessed that under the drifted snow was a road leading to the point and I turned into it. They might run me down with hounds, the Vupsalls, always providing they won the battle in the village. But if the hounds did lead them here, would they be bold enough to push in after me? I thought not, at least until they had built up their courage somewhat. And since I had proved a poor seeress, they might follow me in revenge, but not for wish of more of my company.

The storm was growing worse and now such winds buffeted me, such veils of snow closed me around, that I grew alarmed. I would have to find some shelter and soon, or else I might fall and be covered with that white harvest, and so end ignominiously.

Brush grew on either side and among it, scarcely to be seen, were dark outcrops. I staggered to one of the nearest and found it to be a pile of rubble, debris of some structure. There was a hollow in it which my searching hands rather than my snow-blinded eyes discovered, and into that I pushed my way.

What I had found was a cave-like space between the tumble of several walls. It gave me the feeling of safety and, as I faced around to explore, the curtain of snow sealed me in. I knew I had done the best that I could for my protection.

Time and wind had deposited dried leaves here. I made good use of them, hollowing out a nest of sorts, pulling them over me when I settled into it. Then I practiced the small art which was part of my inheritance from Utta. I chewed a palmful of herbs and lulled my mind by will.

It was not a true trance—I would not have dared to enter one under such circumstances—but akin to it. In this state the cold meant little to my body; I would not slip into that icy induced sleep from which there was no waking.

I was aware of where I lay, of the dark and storm, but it was as if all that had no meaning, as if I had withdrawn into a small portion of my body, leaving the rest lulled into tranquil waiting for an end to outer discord.

There were no dreams. I willed myself to no mental activity such as planning ahead or speculating as to what the next hour, the next morning might bring, for that would break the spell I was using as a buffer between me and the ills of exposure. This was endurance only, and one who had lived long in the Place of Silence knew how to hold steady in that state.

Toward morning the wind slackened. Snow had drifted against the door of my pocket, so that I had view of only a small slice outside. It was enough to tell me that the storm was past, or else in lull.

I pulled out of my nest and took out some of the dried meat that was pounded with berries and hardened into cakes. One had to suck this rather than chew it, lest one's teeth splinter. With some in my mouth I shouldered my pack and started out.

Only the lines of brush protruding above the snow marked the outline of the old road, and this was a series of drifts, with wind-scoured places in between. To wallow through the drifts was exhausting and I tried that for only a short time, then sought a way nearer the brush.

The struggle left me panting and blowing. And, in spite of my struggle to keep well aware of my direction, it was not long before the labor of merely walking, or rather skidding, slipping and falling, filled most of my world.

So it was that I nearly died. But the ice and snow which was my bane also was my enemy's. Ayllia, instead of impaling me neatly on her hunting knife as she had aimed to do, lost her footing, struck against me, carrying us both down into a smother of drift where I floundered free in time to meet her scrambling rush, prepared to kick the knife from her hand and send her sprawling a second time. The knife was gone, lost in the deep snow now furrowed by our scuffling. But she was at me with nails and fists in a whirlwind of fury, and I had to defend myself as best I could.

A hard cuff to the side of her head sent her down again. And this time I followed, kneeling over her, holding her down while she squirmed and spat and showed her teeth like a frantic animal.

I summoned my scraps of willpower, beamed them at her with all the decision I had in me, and at last she lay quiet under my hold. But in the stare she used to meet my eyes there was hot hate.

"He is dead!" She mouthed that as if it were both an accusation and an oath. "You killed him!"

Ifeng—had he meant that much to her then? I was a little surprised. Perhaps all my life I had depended too much on mind talk. I had not learned to judge people well by other signs as must those who do not have the ability. It had been my thought that Ayllia loved her place as second wife (perhaps almost first wife since Ausu's condition left her mainly a figurehead in Ifeng's tent) rather than the chief who had given it to her. But perhaps I had so wronged her and it was a true grief which had driven her to hunt down one who, by her reasoning, had as much blood debt as the raider who had actually loosed the ax to cut her husband down.

With some hatreds there is no reasoning and if Ayllia had gone past the point where I could reach her with logic, then I was given a burden I did not know how to solve. I could not kill nor disable the girl and leave her here; I was certainly not going to return to the tribe; and to go on with an unwilling prisoner was a very unhappy third choice.

"I did not kill Ifeng," I said with what reasoning force I could summon, seeking to impress also her mind.

"You—" she spat. "Utta was his shield; she foresaw rightly. He believed you do likewise. He depended upon you!"

"I never claimed to have Utta's powers," I told her. "Nor did I by choice choose to serve—"

"True!" she interrupted. "You wanted free of us! So you let the raiders come so you could run while they let their swords drink! You are a dark one—"

Her words bit into me as if they were the sharp edge of one of the blades she spoke of. I had wanted above all to escape the tribe; had I unconsciously therefore betrayed them to that purpose? Had I not remembered to consult the answer runes, take other precautions, because I wanted them rendered helpless? Dinzil had served the Shadow, and under his influence I had come very close to such deeds as would have damned me forever. Did the taint of that linger deep in me, rendering me now liable to such cold choices as Ayllia had accused me of?

I had been so keen on regaining my powers—for my own gain—as now I saw. And there is a balance in such things. Used for ill, good becomes ill, and that effect snowballs until even when one desires it greatly one cannot summon good, only something scarred and disfigured by the Shadow. Was I so maimed that from now on when I did aught with what I had in me it would injure others?

Yet one who has the Power is also constrained to make use of it. Such action comes as naturally as breathing. When I had been emptied of it I was a ghost thing, a shell walking through a life I could not feel or touch. To live I must be me, and to be me I must have what was my birthright. Yet if that also made me a monster who carried a fringe of the Shadow ever with me—

"I wanted my freedom, yes," I said now, and I was as much seeking an answer for myself as for Ayllia. "But I will swear on the Three Names that I meant no ill to you and yours. Utta kept me captive, even after her death, by her arts. Only lately was I able to break the bonds she used. Listen, if you were taken by raiders, kept a bondmaid in their camp, would you not use the means to freedom when it lay ready to your hands? I did not bring the enemy upon you, and I never had the means of clear foresight Utta controlled. She did not teach it to me. Ifeng came to me just before they struck; I used the answer runes and gave him warning—"

"Too late!" she cried.

"Too late," I agreed. "But I am not of your blood, nor sworn to your service. I had the need for freedom—"

Whether I could have made her understand I do not know, but at that moment there came a brazen sound, carrying. She tensed in my grasp; her head swung to look back down the drifted road where the marks of our scuffle broke the smooth dunes of snow.

"What is it?"

"The sea hounds!" She signaled for silence and we listened.

That keening was answered from our right, to the west. There were already two groups and we might well be caught between them. I got to my feet to look ahead. There was no sun, but, though the day was cloudy, it was clear enough. Ahead was the beginning of the cape ruins and there my mind visualized many hiding places. It would take an army in patient search to find us there. I held out a hand, caught at Ayllia's wrist and drew her up beside me.

"Come!"

She was quick enough to agree and we pushed on for a step or two until she realized that our way led to that pile of buildings Utta had warned against. Seeing that, she would have fled, I think, had not the horn sounded closer from the west. The east was now walled against us by so thick a hedge of thorny growth as would need a fire to eat a path for us.

"You—you would kill—" She tried to break my grip. But barbarian though she was, tough and bred to struggle and warfare, she could not free my hold. And, as I propelled her along, the horns sounded again, much nearer.

There is bred into all of us a fear of such flights, so that once we began that retreat fear grew, swallowing up lesser terrors. Thus now it was with Ayllia, for she struggled no more, but rather hastened for the dark pile promising us refuge.

As we went I told her what I believed possible, that such ruins could not be easily combed and we would have a hundred hiding places to choose from until our pursuers would give up and leave us alone. In addition I assured her that, though my powers were crippled when compared to Utta's, they were still strong enough to give us fair warning of all Shadow evil.

I half feared, though this I did not tell her, that this might be wholly a place of the Shadow and so barred to us. Yet Utta had gone here and had returned. And a Wise Woman would not have risked all she was by venturing into a cesspool of ancient evil.

The road we followed led us between two towering gates. Their posts were surmounted by figures of fearsome nightmare creatures. As we set foot between those pillars on which they crouched there was a loud roaring. Ayllia cried out and would have fled, but I stood firm against her, shaking her sharply until a portion of her fear subsided and she listened to me—for such devices I knew of old. One of Es City's gates was so embellished. It was the ingenuity of their makers, since it was caused by the wind blowing through certain cunningly set holes.

I do not know whether she believed me. But the fact that I stood unshaken and that the creatures, in spite of the roaring, gave no sign of clambering down to attack us, seemed to reassure her so I could pull her on again.

Once within the gates some of the need for haste left me and I went more slowly, though I did not pause, and my grasp on Ayllia did not slacken. Unlike the village, these were not ruins, though, as in Es City, one had the feeling of long aging, as if many centuries weighed upon the massive stones, driving them yet farther into the earth. They did not crumble, only took on a patina of eternal, unchanging existence.

The outer walls were very thick, and seemed to have rooms or spaces within, for the passage through showed grilled openings on either side. Perhaps at some time guardians not human had lived there, for each had the appearance of a cage.

Then we were in a paved way which sloped up to the mighty pile of high towers and many rings of walls which was the heart of the whole city or fortress. Perhaps it had been a city, for between the outer gates and the inner core of castle many buildings were crowded. Now they turned dead window eyes, gaping mouths of doors, to us. Here and there, standing among the paving blocks, was a wizened, withered stalk of weed. Pockets of snow added to the dreariness of long desertion.

The stones were all uniformly gray, lighter than those of Es City. But above each door was a spot of mute color my eyes delighted in—the blue sheen of those stones which, throughout Escore, stood for protection against all which abode in the darkness we feared most. Whatever this stronghold had been, it had sheltered once those with whom I could have walked in safety.

Now I was conscious of something else: this street, sloping gently upward to a second pair of gates marking the keep, was somehow familiar to me, as if I now walked a way I had known of old and half forgotten. But it was not until we reached the second gate and I saw what was carved in the blue stone above it that I knew. There was the wand and the sword laid together. And this was the way I had walked in my dream when I had watched the opening of the gate.

Nor could I turn aside now and not complete my journey, for we were both drawn forward, following the same tracing of ways I remembered from the dream. I heard Ayllia give a small frightened cry, but when I looked at her her eyes were set and she moved as one under compulsion. That pull was on me, too, but not to the same extent, perhaps. I recognized it for the attraction of Power to Power. Whatever that adept had wrought here in the long ago had left a core of energy which would not be gainsaid.

As we went our pace grew faster, until we were half running. We entered doors, threaded corridors, crossed lesser rooms and halls, in greater and greater haste. Nor had Ayllia made another sound since her first cry.

We came at last into a high walled chamber, which must have been taller than a single story of that massive inner bailey. And, as we entered, it was into life, not dreary death. The weight of countless years felt elsewhere was lighter. There was a sense of awareness and energy, so strong it would seem the very air about us crackled with it.

Along the walls near us there were still some furnishings. Tapestries hung, their pictured surfaces now dim, but woven with such skill that here and there a face of man or monster peered forth with the brightness of a mirrored reflection, as if they were really mirrors and creatures invisible to us, marching up and down eternally viewing themselves on the surface of the cloth.

There were carved chests with symbols set in their lids. And those I knew for the keep-sake of record rolls. Perhaps it was from one like these that Utta had plundered her two. To go to the nearest, lift the lid and look upon such treasures was a vast temptation. But instead I linked hands with Ayllia and drew her with me in a slow circuit around the wall of that vast room, not venturing out upon the middle portion which was so clear and empty. But there was light enough to show the designs set in colored stones and metal strips which covered most of its surface.

Deeply inlaid, not just drawn for a single ceremony, were the pentagrams, the magic circles, all the greater and lesser seals, the highest of the pentacles. These lay a little out from our path around the walls. But beyond these symbols which were keys to so much knowledge were vaguer lines, not so well defined—as if when one advanced toward the center of the hall one advanced in knowledge, and concrete symbols were no longer needed as guides. Of those I did not know so many, and those I recognized had small differences from the ones I had seen before.

This might almost have been a school for the working of Power, such as the Place of Silence. But so much greater was this, and such suggestions did I read in those vague lines near the center, that I thought those who labored here might well look upon the Wise Women of Es as children taking their first uncertain steps.

No wonder a sensation of life lingered here. The stones of the walls behind these mirrored tapestries, those under our feet, must have been soaked in centuries upon centuries of radiation from Power; so that, inanimate though they were, they now reflected what had beat on them so long.

We were a good distance from the door we had entered when I noted the chairs set out on the patterned floor. They were more thrones than chairs, for each rose above the surface of the pavement on three steps, and each was fashioned of the blue stone, having deep-set runes which glowed faintly, as if in their depths fire smoldered, unwilling to die.

They had wide arms and high, towering backs in which were set the glowing symbols. Laid across the seat of the middle one was an adept's wand, as if left there only for a few moments while its owner went on an errand elsewhere.

The symbol in the back of that chair was one I had seen on the seals, the broken bridge, the door of this citadel—the wand and the sword. And I was sure it stood for the man—or more than man—under whom this pile had held domination over the countryside. I did not doubt that this had been the principal seat of some ruler.

As I glanced at the chair I again remembered the details of my dream. This was where he had sat to watch the glowing presence of the gate he had opened. What had happened then? Had he, as legend told us was true of so many of the adepts, gone through his gate to seek what lay on the other side?

Now I looked past the chair, seeking for some trace of the gate itself, so vividly had the dream returned to my mind. Where that arch had presented itself there was bare pavement; no symbols, not even the vaguest, were discernible on the floor. Had the master of this hall indeed reached a point where he needed none at all for the molding of energy? I had thought the Wise Women, then Dinzil, represented heights of such manipulation. But I guessed that had I met the sometime master of that third and middle chair I would have been as Ayllia, as Bahayi, one simple and lost. And in me that was a new feeling, for though I had been emptied of much which had once been mine, I could remember how it had been at my command. However, here I was conscious of something else, the belief that all I had ever learned would be only the first page of the simplest of runes for the master of gates.

Realizing that, I suddenly felt very small and tired, and awed, though the hall was empty and what I reverenced was long gone. I glanced to Ayllia, who at least was human and so of my kind. She stood where I had left her when my hand dropped from her arm. Her face had a strange emptiness, and I knew a flash of concern. Had bringing her here, into a place where such a vast residue of Power was still to be sensed, blasted her as I with my safeguards need not fear? Had I again, in my stubborn self-centeredness worked evil?

I put my hands gently to her shoulders, turned her a little to look into her eyes, used my seeking to touch her mind. What I sensed was not the blasting I had feared, but a kind of sleep. And I thought this was her defense, perhaps it would continue to work as long as we lingered here. However it was well to go now lest that seeping of old Power was cumulative and would enslave us.

But to go was like wading through a current striving to sweep us in the opposite direction. To my alarm I discovered that there *was* an unseen current rising and that it swept around that third chair as if its goal lay somewhere near where I had seen the gate.

Ayllia yielded to it readily before I was fully aware that we might be in real peril. I had to grasp her tightly, pull her back, though her body strained away from me, her eyes stared unseeingly at that central emptiness. The arm I did not grasp swung out, the fingers of her hand groping blindly as if to seek some hold which would aid her to pull out of my determined grip.

I set up my mental safeguards. I was not strong enough to put a wall about both our minds, but if I could hold, surely I could keep Ayllia with me, work us both out of the hall. Beyond the door I thought we would be safe.

Only now it was all I could do to hold against that drag. And Ayllia pulled harder and harder until we were both behind the middle seat and I could have put my hand to its high back. There was the wand on the seat—could I snatch it up as we reached that point? And if so, what could I gain? Such rods of Power were weapons, keys governing shafts to be used in spells. But they also were the property of one seeker alone. What could I gain by trying to use it? Still, it remained so sharply in the fore of my mind that I knew it had some great importance, was not to be lightly overlooked in my present need.

We were level with the seat now. I must make my move to seize the wand or be pulled out of reach, for Ayllia was beginning to struggle against my hold and soon I must keep both hands on her.

I hesitated for a second and then took the chance. With a sharp jerk I dragged Ayllia closer to the chair, took the first step in a single stride, and groped for the end of the rod with my left hand.

IX

My fingers closed about the wand, and then nearly did I drop it, for it was as if I had grasped a length of frosted metal, so cold it burnt the skin laid against it. Yet I did not release it—I could not—for at that moment it clung to me more than I grasped at it.

At the same instant Ayllia broke from my control. She threw herself forward, out of my reach before I could catch her again. As her feet touched the pavement she staggered and went down, falling on her hands and knees. Her weight upon those stones must have released some hidden spring, for a flash burst upward. As it had been in my dream, there stood the gate marked in fiery lines.

"No Ayllia!" If she heard my shout it meant nothing to her ensorcelled mind. She scuttled forward, still on hands and knees like some tormented beast, and passed between the gateposts of that weird portal.

Though through it I could see the hall beyond, Ayllia vanished utterly once she went through the arch. Still clutching the wand, I leaped after her, determined that no more lives would be lost because of my lack of concern or courage.

There was a feeling of being rent apart, not altogether pain but rather a hideous disorientation because I passed through some space which a human body was never meant to penetrate. Then I was rolling over a firm surface, and I found myself moaning with the punishment I had taken in that brief instant of time or out of time.

I sat up dizzily. Though I was now silent there was still moaning and I looked around me groggily. Against a tall object looming high in the gloom lay a crumpled bundle which cried out. I crawled to Ayllia's side, raised her head upon my arm. She lay with her eyes closed, but her body twitched and quivered. Now her head began to turn restlessly from side to side as I have seen in one who is deep in some burning fever. And all the while she uttered small sharp cries.

Pulling her closer to me, I looked back and up for the gate. To see—nothing!

I had oftimes heard of my father's coming into Estcarp through such a portal, and on this side he had found two pillars set to mark the entrance on Tor Moors. When he and my mother had gone up against the stronghold of the Kolder, that gate, too, had been marked in both worlds. But it would seem that this entrance or exit differed, for I could see nothing but a stretch of open land.

It was day here, but clouds hung low and the light was dusky. Whereas snow and ice had clothed Escore on the other side of that vanished doorway, here the atmosphere was sultry and I coughed, my eyes tearing, for the air seemed filled with noxious puffs of invisible smoke.

There was no vegetation. The ground was as uniformly gray as the sky, a sand which looked as if it had never given root room to any healthy growing thing. In some places there were drifts of powdery stuff which looked like ash. This might be a land cleared in some great burning. I glanced at the pillar Ayllia had fallen against.

It was tall, taller than any man. But it was no seared tree trunk nor finger of stone, but rather metal, a girder or support, now pitted and scaly as if something in the acrid air was reducing it little by little to flakes of its former self. Had it once been set to mark the gate on this side? But it stood too far from where we had come through.

I settled Ayllia on the ground, her head pillowed on my pack. Then I got shakily to my feet and I saw something gleaming on the ground and staggered toward it. The wand lay there, so white against this drab sand that it was like a beam of light.

Stiffly I stooped to pick it up. The icy cold of it was gone—now it was like any other smooth rod. I tucked it carefully into the folds of my belt sash. Then I made a slow turn, viewing what lay about us, hoping for a clue to the gate.

The sand was heaped in ashy dunes, each so like the next that it would be very easy, I believed, to be lost among them. There was no marker except the pitted pillar. But when I faced that squarely and looked beyond, I saw another one some distance away, in a straight line with the first.

Ayllia stirred, pulling herself up. I went to her hurriedly. Once more her eyes were blank; she was lost in some inner wilderness where I could not reach her. She clawed her way to her feet, holding to the broken pillar for support. Then she faced about, in the same direction as that second column. Her head was up and back a little, turning slowly from side to side, almost like a hound questing for some familiar scent. Then she began to stagger on, in the direction of that next pillar.

I caught at her shoulder. She gave no sign she knew me, but she struggled, with a surprising return of strength, against my hold. Suddenly, when I least expected it, she swung around and struck out with a shrewdly aimed blow which sent me sprawling.

By the time I got to my feet again she was well ahead, her first staggering giving way to as firm a run as one could keep over this powdery footing. I scrambled after her, though I was loath to leave that spot without further exploration. I dared not believe that the gate was totally lost and we had no hope of return.

The second broken pillar stood near to a third and Ayllia was on her way to that. But it did not seem to me that she was being guided by them at all, but rather that she once more was led by something within her mind, an unseen compulsion.

We passed six of those columns, all as eroded and eaten as the first, before we came out of the place of sand dunes and into another type of country. Here there was a withered growth of grass-like vegetation, in sickly patches, more yellow than green. The line of pillars continued in a straight march across this landscape, but now they were taller and seemed less eaten—until we came to two which were congealed and melted into blobs of stumps. Around these were growths of the first vigorous vegetation I had seen, unpleasant looking stuff with a purple tinge, fine filaments of dusky red fluttering from the leaf tips, as if questing for life to devour. I had no desire to examine it closely.

Beyond the melted columns lay a road. Unlike the pillars, this showed no signs of wear: it might have been laid down within the year. Its surface was sleek and slick looking and of a dead black. Ayllia came to the edge of that and stood swaying a little, though she did not look down at what might be a treacherous footing, but still stared ahead.

At last I caught up with her. And, from behind, I grasped her shoulder, held her. But she did not try to attack me this time. I did not like the look of that road, nor did I want to step on it. And I was hesitating as to what to do next when I heard the sound. It was a rushing as if something approached at great speed. I set my weight against Ayllia, bearing her with me down against the gritty ground, hoping our dull colored garments would be one with the gray-brown soil.

It came along the road at such a speed as to leave me unsure of the nature of what had passed. Certainly not an animal of any kind. I had an impression of a cylinder, perhaps of metal, which did not even rest on the surface over which it skimmed, but perhaps the length of my arm above. It followed the roadway at a great speed, leaving a rush of air to cover us with dust as it vanished in the distance.

I wondered if we had been sighted. If we had, those controlling the thing had not bothered to stop. Perhaps they could not in this place. The speed with which they had swished by would not answer to a sudden halt.

But what manner of thing was it which would race so, not touching the ground, yet manifestly traveling by the roadway? The Kolder had lived with machines to do their work. Had we broken into the Kolder world, even as my mother and father had once done? If so we were in great peril, for the Kolder gave their captives to a living death such as no one could imagine without skirting madness.

I had in my pack very little food. And I carried no water, for I had intended to travel where snow and river could have satisfied my thirst at will. Here the acrid atmosphere and the dry blowing of the wind had awakened a thirst to parch my mouth, as if I had tried to swallow handfuls of the ashes about me.

We must have water, and food, to keep life in our bodies. From the look of the land so far we could not expect to find either—which meant we must risk the worst and travel along this road, perhaps in the same direction as the rushing thing.

I put my hand to Ayllia, but she had already turned in that direction, her eyes still staring blankly. Now she began to march along the edge of the road, while for want of a better guide I followed.

We saw it from far off. I had looked upon the towers of Es City, upon the citadel of the unknown eastern cape, and both had I thought major works of man's hand. But this was such as I could not look upon and believe that man alone had wrought. The towers, if true towers they were, arose up and up to tangle with the gray clouds of the sky. And they were all towers, with little bulk of building below to support them. From tower to tower there was a lacing of strung ways, as if their makers put roads high in the sky. And all this was of the same dun color as the ground. They might have been growths out of the ashy soil by some fantastic cultivation. Yet they had the sheen of metal.

The fluid-looking road we followed fed directly into the foot of the nearest tower. Now we could see other such roads spreading out from the city, running from other towers. I have watched the webs of the zizt spiders with their thickly woven center portions, their many radiating threads of anchorage. And the thought came to me that if one were able to soar elsewhere overhead and look down on this complex, it would seem from that angle to be a zizt web—which was not a promising thought, for the zizt spiders are such hunters as it is well to avoid.

I ran my tongue over lips which were parched and cracked, and saw that Ayllia was in no better state. She had begun to moan again, even as she had when she first came through the gate. Somewhere there was water and it looked like we would have to enter that web of metal to find it.

There was another warning rushing sound and once more I pulled my companion to the ground. A carrier swept by, not on the road we had followed, but some distance away. And, as I levered myself up when it was safely past, I saw something else, a dark spot in the sky, growing larger at every beat of my thundering heart.

It could not be a bird. But what of my father's stories of the past? In his world men had built machines, even as did the Kolder, and in such they rode the sky, setting the winds to their commands. Had we—could this be my father's world? Yet such a city—he had never spoken of that, nor of a land reduced to cinders and sand.

The sky thing grew and grew. Then it halted its flight to hover over a space between two of the towers. I saw a platform there, more steady than the lacy ways which provided passage between height and height. With caution the sky thing settled on that platform.

It was too far away for me to see if men came out of it to enter any of the four towers at the corners of the landing space. But it was so strange as to make me a little afraid.

Kolder lore, their machines and the men they made into machines to do their will, had so long been evil tales that we of Estcarp were tuned to an instant loathing for all their works. And so this place had the stench of vileness which was not like the evil of Escore which I could understand, since that came from the wrongful use of talents I was aware of—but this was of a monstrously twisted way of life wholly alien to all I stood for.

Yet we must have food and water or die. And there is always this: one does not willingly choose death when there is even a small chance of grasping life. Thus we stood and looked upon that fantastic city, or rather I looked, and Ayllia stared as if she saw nothing.

At ground level the only entrances to the nearer towers seemed to be those tunnels fed by the roads. In fact, there were no breaks in the walls until the first of the airy ways and those were higher than the highest spires I had known in Es City. No windows at all.

Therefore if we would enter we must do it by road. And I shrank from putting foot to that slick surface. Yet how long would my strength, or Ayllia's, hold without supplies? To delay was to weaken ourselves at a time when we must harbor all the energy we could summon for survival.

It was growing darker and I thought that it was not a coming storm but night which brought that dusk. Perhaps the dark would be our friend. I could see no lights aloft. But, even as I watched, there was a sudden outburst of sparkling radiance to outline each of the inter-tower ways, glistening like dew on a spider web.

There was a duller glow outlining the cave holes into which the roads fed. And light in there could be more unfriend than aid. But I thought we had no choice, and what small advantage might lie with us grew the less with every passing moment.

So I took Ayllia's arm. She no longer led the way, but she did not hang back nor dispute with me when I pushed ahead, still beside the road, the glow of the entrance before us.

As we drew closer I saw, with some small relief, that the opening was wider than the span of the road so that there was a narrow walkway beside it and we need not get down on its surface. But was that wide enough to save us should one of those carriers make entrance when we were attempting the same? The wind of their passing had twice proved forceful; in the confined space of the tunnel it might be fatal.

I halted at the mouth of that opening and listened. There was certainly no warning of such a coming, and we could not hesitate here for long. Best get inside and seek out a side way off the course of the road.

The surface under our feet as we passed into the base of the tower was, I believe, some sort of metal overlaid with a slightly elastic spongy stuff so that it gave with every step. We were in a tunnel as I had expected, and I hurried Ayllia along that narrow walk, hoping for a break in the wall beside us, some door opening from the tube.

We found such an opening, marked by a very dim light burning above it, and below that light a symbol foreign to me. The passage beyond was as narrow as a slit, leading off at a right angle. Once into it I breathed a little freer, relaxing my need to listen for destruction rushing from behind.

So relaxed, I sensed that other feeling in this place. The air was not as sultry as it had been outside, but it was still unpleasant to breathe, and now it carried odors which I could not identify, but which made me sneeze and cough.

At lengthy intervals along the wall were other patches of light; but so dim were they that the spaces between them were pockets of dark. We were midway in the second of those when I realized we had found this side burrow just in time. For there was a mighty roaring from behind and the walls and floor quivered. One of the carriers must have entered the tunnel. There were blasts of air so fume-filled that we strangled in our coughing fight for breathable air. Tears streamed from our eyes until I was blinded, I only staggered along instinctively, still pulling at my companion, trying to escape that pollution.

When we reached the haven of the next light I leaned against the wall, trying to wipe my eyes, regain my breath. And so I saw that the footing under our boots was drifted with a feathery deposit, as soft as the ashes of the outer world, but black. Along the way we had come we had left a well-marked trail. But ahead there were only untroubled drifts. By such signs no one had passed this way for some time—perhaps for years. And that thought was heartening, but it did not bring us any closer to what we must have to sustain us.

The narrow passage ended in a round space which seemed like the bottom of a well. I could put my head far back on my shoulders and look up and up into eye straining distance, as if this well space extended from here to the far-off crown of the tower. There were openings along it at intervals, as if it bisected various floors. Some of these were dim of light, others shown brilliantly. There was no ladder, though, no sign of any steps which would lead to even the lowest of these openings. We had no choice, I decided, but to retreat to the dangerous tunnel and try along it for a second possible escape route.

Ayllia stepped forward suddenly, jerking me with her. I threw out my hand to retain my balance, my palm slapping hard against the wall.

There was an answer to that unplanned action. We were no longer standing on our two feet at the bottom; instead we were rising, our bodies soaring as if we had sprouted wings. I think I cried out. I know my hand went to the wand at my belt. Then I clawed at the smooth side of the space through which we rose, striving to win some hold to stop our going. My nails scraped and broke, but they did not even slow that ascent.

We floated past the first opening, which must mark the level immediately above the one we had entered. This was one of the dimmer lighted and I saw there was space on either side, as if this hole bisected a passage somewhat wider than the entrance into this trap.

I began to move my feet, kick out a little, and so I discovered that I could so push myself toward the side of the well. I must now make an effort at the next level to pull out, taking Ayllia with me. And to that I bent all my energies. We finally won free of the well, somehow pulling into another passage on the opposite side from where we had entered.

This was much better lighted and there was sound—or was it vibration, which seemed to come, not from any one direction, but from the floor on which we lay, or out of the walls about us. There was still a spongy coating on the floor, but no longer any drifts of sooty ash. We could have come into a portion which was in use. And that must make us more wary in our going.

I was conscious that Ayllia was sitting up, staring from me to the walls about us, then back to me again. That fixed look which had masked her for so long was gone and she shivered, her hands going to cover her eyes.

"The Paths of Balemat," she whispered hoarsely.

"Not so!" I put out my hand, not to lead her this time, but rather to give her what comfort might lie in human touch. "We live; we are not dead." For she had spoken then of their primitive belief in an evil spirit who waited beyond the final curtain for those whose rites were not properly carried out.

"I remember—" She still did not take away the fingers she used to blind herself. "But this is surely Balemat's land and we walk in his house. No place else could be so."

I could almost agree with her. But I had one argument which I thought would persuade her she had not joined the dead.

"Do you not hunger, thirst? Would the dead do so?"

She dropped her hands. Her expression was one of sullen hopelessness.

"Who can say? Who has ever returned to say this is this, that is that, behind the curtain? If not the House of Balemat, then where are we, witch woman?"

"In another world sure enough, but not that of the dead. We found an adept's gate and were drawn through it into one of the other worlds—"

She shook her head. "I know nothing of your magic, witch woman, save that it has ill served me and mine. And would seem to continue to do so. But it is true that I hunger and thirst. And if there is food or drink to be discovered I would like to find it."

"As would I. But we must go with care. I do not know who or what lives here.

I only know it is a place of much strangeness and so must be scouted as we would a raiders' camp."

I opened my pack and brought out the remains of the food I had carried and we managed to choke some mouthfuls of it until our thirst proved too strong for us to swallow more. That little meal did give us a lift of energy.

As we went on we discovered that this hall was broken by the outlines of what must be doors. But all were without latches or ways of opening them. And though I was finally emboldened to push at one or two, they did not yield to pressure. So we finally came to the end of that way, which was a balcony open on the night. From it swung one of the skyways connecting the tower with the next farther in toward the heart of the city. And, looking at that narrow footway, which seemed to be the most fragile of paths, I knew I could not cross it. Ayllia covered her eyes and pushed back into the corridor.

"I can not!" she cried.

"Nor can I." But what else could we do? Trust again to the well and its upward pull to waft us to yet another corridor aloft where we might fare no better?

I asked her then what she remembered of our coming this far. And she replied with most of it, but said that it was all to her as a dream of which she was a spectator, not a part—save that earlier she had been moving by a drawing which ceased when we came to the road.

We started back toward the well, having no hope but to trust to it again. But before we reached that end of the hall there was a small snap of sound which sent us both into what very poor cover this way offered, flattening ourselves against the wall, standing very still.

One of those doors which had been so tightly shut opened and a figure stepped out. Stepped? No, it did not step; it rolled, or rather hovered above the floor even as the carrier had on the road. And that figure—

I have seen many mutants and monsters. Escore is plentifully inhabited by creatures who are the end results of long ago experimentation by the adepts. There are the Krogen, who are water men, born to live within that liquid at ease, and there are the Flannan, who have wings, the Gray Ones, who are an evil mixture of beast and man, and many others. But this—this was somehow worse than anything I had seen or heard described.

It was as if one had begun to make a machine which was also a man, metal and flesh grafted together. The lower half was an oval of metal, having no legs, though folded up against that ovoid shape were jointed appendages which ended in claws, now closed together as one might close fingers into a fist.

There were similar limbs on the narrower upper section of the body, but above that was a human, or seemingly human, head, though there was no hair, only a metal capping ending in a point. And behind that ball-with-a-head came another mixture of man-machine, though this one walked on two legs, and had human arms. But the chest and the body were all metal, and the head again ended in a metal point.

Neither of the things looked in our direction, but one floated, one walked, toward the well; there they simply stepped or rolled out into the empty space and were borne upward, past the roof of this level and out of our sight.

X

*N*O!" Ayllia's denial of what she saw did not rise above a whisper. But she stood with some of the old blankness back in her eyes.

Meanwhile, I wondered how the magic force of that well might be reversed, talking us down the shaft and not up. After seeing what must inhabit the reaches of this tower city I had no desire to explore it further. And my hopes for finding supplies were already gone. Those things which were such an unholy mixture of flesh and metal could certainly not eat nor drink, nor furnish us with provisions even if we managed to find a storeroom in this maze.

I tried now to remember what had begun our float upward. My hand had fallen on the wall and now, as I tried to recall that memory more distinctly, I thought I had seen a plate of differently colored metal set there. My hand had scraped down it—but we had risen *up!* Could it be a uniform signal?

If so, could I find a plate somewhere which would reverse our course and send us safely down? We could only try. To remain where we were, I believed now, was only waiting to be discovered, and my whole being shrank from the thought of any close contact with those half and half things. It was just by the vast favor of fortune they had not looked in our direction.

"Come on—" I reached for Ayllia's arm in the old way.

She tried to elude me. "No!"

"Stay here," I told her grimly, "and they will find you."

"Go there"—she pointed to the shaft—"and they surely will!"

"Not so." Though I could not be sure of that. Hurriedly I explained what I thought had brought us up the shaft and the chance we might reverse the process.

"And if we cannot?"

"Then we shall have to try our fortune across the bridge." But that to me was almost as great an ordeal as facing one of the half-monsters of this place. And the only bridge we had access to led deeper into the city, not out of it.

I think that Ayllia liked that no better than I did, for she started on toward the shaft without further urging. But we went slowly, listening at each door marking, testing it with our hands before scuttling to the next, fearing each might open and we would have to face some inhabitant. When we reached the last opening, through which the two had come, we found the crack more pronounced. Under my fingers the barrier moved a little.

That hum which had been a part of the walls was louder and I saw, through a very narrow slit which was all I dared to open, sections of metal wrought into incomprehensible objects. But I did not linger for more than one hurried glimpse.

We reached the side of the shaft and I looked right and left. It was hard to detect the control plate, but it was there and I saw two depressions in it, one set above the other. I had passed my hand down before, now I would try up. So I did. But thereafter I lingered for a long breath or two, not quite wanting to put my guess to the test.

If we stepped out and were carried further aloft, following the grotesque metal pair, it might well be that we would be taken past any concealment straight into the hands of those who dwelt here. Then I remembered the pack. I could use that for a test. Though to part with the few supplies we had . . .

I loosed its straps and tossed it out. It reached the center of the shaft with the force of my throw and began to sink. I was right!

"In!" I ordered and stepped out, though that took some force of will, conditioned as I was to the fear of falling.

Ayllia gave a small, choked cry, but she followed me. Our descent was faster than our rise had been, though not to the point of actual falling. I worked my body until I reached the wall of the shaft where the openings were, ready to swing in, for I remembered that other dim level we had passed in our ascent. Now that I had a possible second exit I was emboldened to explore further where the lack of strong light suggested a deserted, or near deserted, level. And I said as much to Ayllia.

I think she would have refused, but she was in no mind to be left alone. We reached the level and I caught at its opening, while Ayllia, who had grasped my cloak, swung in beside me. We were perched in that opening as a Vrang might roost on a stone crag, the pack having gone past us to the bottom of the shaft—though I did not worry about that now.

We were not, I speedily discovered, in another corridor as we had been above, but rather on a narrow walk which ran out a short distance over a vast space. So dim was the light we could see little except that immediately around us, and of that I could make little sense. There were a number of large objects on the floor, each standing a little apart from its neighbor. Finally I decided that these were the carriers we had seen in swift passage on the road, though they were now at rest.

They were cylinders, perhaps twice the height of a tall man, and each was pointed into cone shape. I could see the marks of openings along their sides. But, as with the doors in the upper corridor, these were tightly shut, save for one in the nearest.

And that had not been easily opened. There were stains and sears and the metal was torn and rent, sticking out in points. It plainly had been forced and heat had been used in that forcing. Now, looking further, I could just perceive a similar tear was in the next cylinder. Though why the inhabitants of the city needed to break open their own containers, if that was what these were, was a puzzle.

Were they storehouses? Or were they used to transport supplies to the city as the wains from the manors of Estcarp crawled at harvest time to Es? If so there might be food in them. I told Ayllia that.

"Water?" she asked hoarsely, "water?"

Though I could not believe any water supply was so housed, I was tempted to explore in that faint hope. We had to have water and soon, or we would not have enough strength to leave the city.

There were no steps nor ladders to descend from the balcony on which we stood, but the drop to the floor below was not too great and I made it. This time Ayllia did not follow. She swore she would remain where she was but not explore. And since I was already down there was no reason to return without at least a closer inspection of the nearest transport.

I longed for a torch—the half light was even less around the carrier. But now I saw something else. From that jagged cut in the side trailed a line, good proof that whoever had forced the opening had explored within.

It was not a braided nor woven cord I discovered, but fashioned of a mesh of small metal links, very strong for its size. And it had loops spaced along it in which I could just set the toes of my boots as an aid to climbing. So small were those loops I thought they had been made to support a foot less long than my own, unless they were only intended for handholds.

I looked back. Ayllia was pressed against the rail which walled the walkway. I raised my hand and she waved back before I climbed. When I reached the seared edge I crouched to peer in. And was so startled I nearly lost my balance. For when I set hand on the wall inside there was an answering shaft of light in the interior of the cylinder.

There was a mass of tumbled boxes and chests, the covers of which had been torn away or beaten in, plainly for the purpose of plunder. But the contents were a disappointment, at least to me, for they consisted mainly of metal bars or blocks. And there was a foul smell coining from a sticky pool where a large drum had fallen on its side.

So strong were those fumes, even though the pool was almost dried to a greasy scum, that I feared to stay longer in the close interior. My head began to swim and perhaps I had breathed in some poison.

I backed away, wondering if it was worth my while to try one of the other plundered transports further on in the cavern. But I was beginning to cough and wanted nothing more than to be free, not only of this transport and the place where it was parked, but of the towers into the bargain.

Just as I reached the opening, set my hand to the rope again, I froze. From deeper in the cavern came a flash of light so vivid as to blind me temporarily. Yet

I could not remain where I was; the fumes seared my throat and lungs. Blindly I went through the break, swung out and down to the floor. Then I was racked by such a spell of coughing that I could do no more than lean against the side of the transport, my hands pressed to my chest, my eyes blinking.

There was another flash of light, but this time I had not been directly facing it so was spared the assault on my eyes. This time it became a steady glow, and I guessed that perhaps those who had come to plunder were still at work, burning their way into another carrier. The determination of their search suggested that what they sought was of prime importance.

Were there others just as human as ourselves who also sought food and drink? After all, the gate in the citadel could have entrapped more then just we two throughout the years. And my mind fastened on that with a pitiful hope, so that I was determined to put it to the test here and now by spying on whoever was using that fire.

But to reach the place of the light I must go well away from the entrance, leaving Ayllia. To return to explain might be a waste of valuable time. . . .

I think now my mind was affected by those fumes I had breathed, but at the time all my decisions seemed logical and right. I did not return to Ayllia but instead rounded the nose of the transport I had entered, and began to work my way toward that distant glow.

At least enough sense remained to me to make that advance cautiously. I kept to cover with all the skill I had learned in Escore. The dim gloom of the place was an aid and the rows of transports provided many pools of shadow in which to halt before making a dash to the next.

My cough disappeared as I got into this air which, lifeless though it was, yet was free of that sickly odor. It had also increased my thirst to the point where I was frantic for water. And it seemed to me then that I need only reach those ahead to find it.

At last I huddled at the tip of another transport to watch the workers. Two of them clung to a webbing draped on either side of the door they were attacking. They hung there, watching the efforts of two more at floor level, aiming up at the metal beams of light which struck, to spray out, eating slowly into its substance.

I made the mistake of again looking at the light and so was blinded momentarily. I shrank back and waited for my sight to clear. A glimpse of those working to force the entrance had been enough to make me think they were not the same breed of half-things as I had seen above. They all appeared to have normal bodies, legs and arms.

Now I peered between my fingers, using them to shield against the glare. Was it fire they used as a tool, I wondered, or a force of light with the strength of fire? Fire I could and had summoned to answer my will, for it is a thing of nature and so must come at the call of a Wise Woman. But this was a different thing, for the

beam issued from a pipe these workers held in their hands, and the pipe was connected by a limber hose to a box sitting on the floor between them.

The fire suddenly died, and now those on the webs swung closer. They
smashed bars against the glowing opening, prying and working at the metal now
softened a little.

But I no longer watched them. One of those who had held the pipe laid down
the strange weapon and went to a pile of packs. He picked up a small container
which he held to his mouth—drinking!

Water!

At that moment all the wealth of knowledge could have been mine for the taking and I would have passed it by for what the stranger held. What I was going
to get!

He put down the container and went back to the pipe. As he raised that, ready
to shoot the beam again, I moved, running along the side of the transport which
sheltered me from their eyes. They were so intent upon what they did, though
working openly as if they need have no fear of any inimical onlooker, that I did
not believe I was in any danger then.

My world, my future, narrowed to that container. I made my way toward it,
sparing only a short, searching glance now and then at the workers, to be sure
none came my way. But they were engaged once more in burning, their attention
all for the stubborn metal. My hand closed upon the container and I raised it to
my lips.

It was not pure water, unless water in this world had a sour taste. But it was so
refreshing to my cracked lips, parched mouth, and dry throat, that I had to fight
myself not to swallow more than a few sips.

There was a cry from the working party and I turned in fear, sure they had
sighted me. I discovered instead that the door had given away and those on the
webs were kicking it loose.

I fumbled throught the packs they had stacked here. There were some packets
which might contain food and two of those I took. But I could carry no more for
I had chanced upon three more of the water containers, by their weight nearly
full.

Slinging two carrying straps over my shoulders, clasping the third tightly to
me with the packets, I faded back into the shadows, intent now on reaching
Ayllia. We were in a good position by the door to watch these workers when they
withdrew. If they were of our own kind, earlier victims of the gate, we could then
claim meeting. Having drunk, my caution returned and I was not minded to surrender to any who prowled this world until I was sure it was not the enemy.

When I gained the entrance to the cavern there was no Ayllia. I dare not risk
calling: my voice might carry back to the working party. And, burdened as I now
was with the food and water I carried, I was not sure I could regain the upper
level of the balcony.

At last I was forced to return to the ladder, reclimb into the fumes to unhook it, and drop in a jarring fall to the floor. Ayllia still did not show and I worked as fast as I could lest those beyond miss their water ration and trail me. There was a hook at the end of the ladder and I whirled a length around my head, let it fly, so it caught on the railing of the balcony. With this anchored I was able to climb, draw after me the containers I had made fast to the lower end.

Equipped with supplies, I sped down the short space to the well, but saw no sign of Ayllia. I hung over to peer down to the bottom of the shaft. She was not there either. But I was almost certain she had gone this way.

As my boots rapped against the floor of the shaft I looked around for the pack which had fallen ahead of us. There were many marks on the pavement, the gritty dust of these lower levels stirred and scuffed—more than could result from just our coming and going. The working party, had they come this way? I had not noticed too much on our entrance, but now I studied each foot of the way with care as I retraced the passage to where it gave upon the road entering the base of the tower.

I was now away from that sound or vibration which made floors and walls sing faintly on the upper levels, so I heard a sound ahead. Not the warning roar of the arrival of a transport, but a cry which I thought must be human. And I was greatly tempted to call out to Ayllia, save that suspicion warned me she might be in some danger which it was better not to walk into blindly.

As I started down the dusty passage leading to the entrance I thought I saw movement ahead. I slowed, listened. If something or someone was coming toward me perhaps I would have to retreat, but if it went the other way I could follow.

Then in a small pool of glimmer I saw Ayllia. She was being dragged along by two figures shorter than she, creatures I could not see clearly. As I watched one of them dealt her a vicious blow across the shoulders which sent her staggering on. And they straightaway closed in on her again. She kept her feet but she went as one who was either only semiconscious or completely cowed, offering no resistance.

They were very close to the road tunnel and a moment or two later they were gone into it. I started to run, the heavy water bottles inflicting bruises as they banged my ribs, battering me as that blow had done for Ayllia.

At the tunnel I hesitated once more. Not only did I listen for the roar which would precede one of the transports, but I was undecided as to which way Ayllia and her captors had gone. Deeper into the towerways, or out into the country?

Though I listened and peered, I could find no clue. But at last I decided that it would be out. I hardly thought that those who inhabited the city would, by choice, take the dangerous road here. It was more likely to be the way of some invader.

Yet I was plagued as I began backtracking with the fear that my logical reasoning was at fault, that instead of following Ayllia I was heading in the opposite direction.

It was not until I was safely off that narrow footway and out in the night that I had confirmation as to the wisdom of my reasoning. That came when my foot struck against an object in the dark and sent it spinning into a shaft of moonlight—for I had not emerged into the blackness of complete dark but into a silvered world where a moon hung full and very bright.

What I had kicked into view was a packet I knew well, seeing as how I had made it up with my own hands, some of Utta's healing herbs tied into a small sack. That had not fallen from my pack when we had entered this place because, until I had opened it to share the food with Ayllia, the carrier had been well tied. Therefore, someone had opened the pack hereabouts and dropped this.

I went to one knee and felt around. If anything else had been dropped, I did not find it. I could only believe that those who had taken Ayllia also had the pack, had opened it for inspection and lost this.

The workers in the cavern, the shadow figures I had seen with Ayllia—I decided they were alike. They certainly had human bodies, even if they were over-small. I had an impression, when I took time to call to mind and assess all I had seen, of very thin legs and arms. And I thought of those of Escore—the Thas—bloated bodies, spider limbs, creatures who veered so far from the human they were now utterly loathsome to us who dwelt in the outer world above their tunnels and burrows.

Had Thas found their way through the gate? But their use of fire as a tool—that was no Thas doing.

So those I had trailed had come this way, but now where? In the bright moonlight, and I could not be too far behind them, could I track them? The packet had lain well beyond the edge of the road turning to my left as if those I sought had struck out between that highway and the next tower.

The ground had a hard surface, but across it were drifts of the ashy sand. Neither was good for my purpose but I quested on, searching for any hint of trail. And I found it, far plainer than I had hoped. This was another roadway, though cruder than those feeding into the towers. It was apparent that heavy weights had passed here to wear ruts in the soil. And where that upper crust had been broken, I found prints of feet. Some of the sharpest were from boots—Ayllia's, or so I believed. The others were smaller and narrower. The toes, instead of being rounded, speared out in points, unlike any I had seen. But they all pointed ahead and I followed.

That trail ended in a space where a new marking began and more and wider ruts cut very deep. I could only think of some vehicle which had carried a weighty cargo. There was no attempt to hide it and I marched along beside it.

The ruts approached the next road but did not cross it, rather paralleled it back into the country through which we had come on our way to the towers. This part of the land was more rolling and rougher than that we had traversed. The road was cut through hills, whereas the ruts veered and wove a way around such obstructions. It was impossible to see far ahead; I listened, hoping to hear something to tell me those I trailed were near, needing a warning if I were not to march blindly into captivity.

The hills rose higher all the time and crags of rock protruded from them—or what I thought to be rock, until taking shelter behind one when I thought I heard a noise, my hand rested on its surface, and detected a pattern of seam. And a closer look told me that these were not of nature's forming, but the work of man or some intelligent creature. These hills were not of earth but the remains of buildings half hidden by the shifting of the ash-sand dunes.

I had little time to think of that, for my belief that I had heard a noise proved to be true. There was a hissing, and then a soft crunching. Into the moonlight below my perch crawled a new form of transport. Beside the swift cylinders speeding along the highways this was a clumsy, ill-constructed thing, as if born from another type of brain and imagination.

It had no wheels as the carts of my own world, but huge bands which ran from the front to the back, turning so, their treads spinning on rods projecting from the box body. If it carried driver or passengers they were in that box which was ventilated only by a series of narrow vertical slits spaced evenly around it.

The pace it held was slow, ponderous, steady, and it gave such an appearance of a fortress able to move across the land that I wondered if that was how it had been conceived. But the route it followed was the rutted way to the towers; perhaps it had been sent to fetch those who plundered the cavern.

I kept to my hiding place in the corner of the half-buried wall and watched it crawl on out of sight.

XI

*C*an one say that there is a "smell" to Power? I only know that one can sniff the evil of the Shadow; whether that be done by the nostrils of the spirit, or ones of flesh I have never learned. But it is true that in Escore I could sense the places of the Dark to be avoided. In this world, however, there was an acrid stench always with one and foreseeing, even to the small extent I had regained it, was blunted. It was as if in passing through the gate I had shed the right to call upon what had once been a shield on my arm.

Now I had no more than my own five physical senses to depend upon, and it was like losing half of one's sight. Still I tried to see if I could not use even a little of my skills. Since Ayllia was also of my world there was a faint chance that there might exist a mind bond between us, and, using that, I could either gain from her some idea of where she went and the dangers which lay between us, or even, in a good meeting of mind, see through her eyes.

It was a very forlorn hope, but now I settled farther back into the ruined wall and concentrated upon Ayllia, building my mind picture of her, willing an answer.

Only—

What!

I sat up tense, gasping. Not the Vupsall mind. No! But had touched, merely touched, on the edge of a mental broadcast so powerful that that small contact expelled me, buffeted me from its path, for it was aimed in another direction.

Not Ayllia, of that I was certain. Yet, was I also sure that what I had touched was of my world, trained in the Power? The gate—had my thought that others had come through it been right? But . . .

Part of me wanted fiercely to seek again that reassuring contact with the familiar. Another warned caution. I knew Escore history, and over and over had it been said that those who had used the gates were often of the Shadow, or the birth roots from which the Shadow had grown. To open communication with some dark power would doubly doom me.

I could not believe that those half-men of the city, nor those who had crawled past in the movable fortress, were of Escore. We have never depended upon machines. That is what we abhorred in the Kolder, who were in a way half-men, part of the machines they tended. And the Wise Women had believed us right in our choice, for in the last great battle at Gorm it had been mind power which had burnt out and vanquished those welded to metal.

But somewhere and not too far away was at least one from my world. And I longed to go seeking, but dared not until I knew more.

The rutted road of the crawler was very clear in the moonlight. And the sound of its crunching had died away. That was the road Ayllia had gone and the one I must follow. I drank sparingly from one of the water containers and slipped out to walk the ruts.

More and more of the hillocks and mounds around that roadway showed signs of being the remains of buildings. I could well believe that this had once been a city, unlike the tower one, but of some size and importance.

Then the ruts began to run between taller walls and suddenly into a vast open space like a huge crater or basin pocked deep into the earth. Here there were no remains of buildings, rather stretches of glassy material which the crawling tracks dodged around as if the treads of the fortress could not pass over their slick surfaces.

The ruts led to the center of the basin where there was a gaping blackness as if it were a mouth of such a shaft as we had found in the city, but as large as the base of one of the sky-reaching towers.

There was no cover to be found here. If I approached the well in the moonlight I would be as visible as if I sounded a warn horn at the verge of a manor. Yet it was into that hole Ayllia had surely gone. And it was laid on me, as heavily as if it were a geas, that I had a responsibility for her and must free her if I could.

I could not tell what spy searches might be laid about. But just perhaps—

Once more I hunkered down in the shadow of the last vestige of ruined wall. This time I covered my eyes with the palm of my left hand. With the right I touched the wand still thrust through my belt. I had no other thing of Power with me, and if it could add to my limited efforts I needed it badly.

I set the picture of Ayllia in my mind and sent out a search thought.

What I met was blankness. But it was a blankness I recognized and again I was startled into breaking my concentration. Ayllia was mind-locked against any such search. So alerted, I tried, very cautiously, as one might touch with only the tip of a finger, to find the source of the mind-lock. But what I fingered so very lightly was not what I expected to find, rather something entirely alien to all I knew.

A machine with Power? That was an anomaly I could not accept. Power was utterly opposed to machines and always had been. A Wise Woman could handle steel in the form of a weapon if some urgent need arose, as my mother had done upon occasion, though one relied mainly on the Power. But even so much a modification as a dart gun—that meant careful preparation in thinking patterns. We could not ally with a machine!

Yet touch here told me Ayllia was held in a pattern of mind-lock familiar to me, but that it was created by a machine! Could there have been some welding here of Escore knowledge with that native to this world to produce a monstrous hybrid?

To enter that hole ahead knowing no more than I did of what faced me there was utter folly. But neither could I turn my back on Ayllia. So was I one torn in two directions, unable to make up my mind. And such a state was so alien to my nature that I was perhaps easy prey to what followed, my mind so occupied with my dilemma that I was not ready, my safeguards down.

What struck was that seeking I had met before edge on. For a moment I received an impression of shock to the sender as great as that I had earlier experienced. And after that slight recoil, came a pouring out of a need so great that it actually pulled me on, out of the hollow where I had taken refuge, into the open. It was a current such as I had felt to a lesser degree in the hall of the gate.

My resistance awoke and I tried to fight with all I could summon, so I was a swimmer floundering in water rushing me madly toward sharp rocks of perilous rapids. And that which drew me on seemed triumphant, showing a kind of impatience which would not allow me any return of my own will.

Thus I came to the hole, which was a great mouth to gulp me down. And I saw a platform a little below me. But that did not fill the whole expanse, only a small wedge of it. Perhaps it was awaiting the return of the crawler that it might be lowered into the depths. Below I could see nothing else and it seemed to me this well reached so far toward the core of the earth that it was the length of one of the towers in reverse.

Beyond the waiting platform was the beginning of a stair circling down, hugging the wall of the shaft. I tried to fight the compulsion which drew me on, but there was no chance to free myself and I began the journey into the depths.

I discovered quickly that I must not look into the dusk below, but must keep my eyes on the nearer wall to fight the giddiness which struck at me.

Time had no meaning; my world narrowed to the wall, the abyss on the other side into which I must not look. And it seemed to me that this lasted for hours, days. The wall was smooth in parts, with the slick look of those glassy patches in the basin; then again it would be rock, but rock dressed to a uniform surface.

The moonlight which had been silver bright in the outer world no longer reached me, and now I went more slowly, feeling my way from step to step. But never was I released from that drawing.

At last, when I felt for the next step, I met solid level surface. I leaned, shaking, against the wall, daring now to turn my head and look up to where the outer world was a segment of light, then around me in the dark. I was afraid to venture away from the wall I could touch and which so afforded me a sense of security, if there could be any security in such a place as this. But the pull on me never faltered.

So I began to feel my way along, hand to wall, testing each step before I took it. I was, I thought, perhaps a quarter of the way around that space from the point where I reached the bottom, before my hand on the wall met empty space. And it was into that opening the current drew me. But again I sought frantically for a wall and kept my fingers running along it, tapping one boot toe ahead, lest I end up in a pit trap.

After that first burst of recognition the mind beam which had entrapped me took on a mechanical sending. I longed to probe for what personality might lie behind it, but I was afraid to so open myself to invasion. It was known that an adept could take over a lesser witch or warlock, and such bondage was worse than any slavery of the body. It was what I had feared and fled in Escore, and to succumb to it here would mean I was wholly lost for all time.

There was a sound ahead, a faint hissing. Then there appeared a line of light which widened as I blinked against the glare. I had an open door and I walked through in spite of a last resistance to the pull. But, as I stepped into the light, the compulsion vanished and I was free.

Only I had no time to take advantage of my release, for as I swung around to retreat, the halves of the door were already nearly shut—too narrow a space was left for me to wriggle through. I stood, wishing for some weapon. . . .

As in the cavern of the stored transports, I stood on a balcony or narrow upper runway; before me was a scene of activity I could not take in all at once. There was a board or screen on which lights flashed, flickered, died, or flashed again in no discernible pattern. From that came a tinkling which was not of human speech.

The screen appeared to divide the whole of the space below into two parts, though there was an aisle with a low wall running from some point immediately below where I now stood, to a narrow arch in the screen.

On either side of that wall were cell-like divisions, all having partitions about shoulder-high and each like a room. Some of these were occupied, and seeing those occupants I recoiled until my back struck against the door now tightly closed behind me. I had thought those figures in the cavern, and with Ayllia had had some odd outlines which half denied humanity. Now I saw them in full light and knew that, though they might be travesties of men, they were such as made them worse than the monsters of Escore. My last hope that I might find here some others caught by the gate vanished.

They were small, and their skin was a pallid gray which in itself was repulsive. Where the half-men of the towers had had heads capped with metal, these had a thin thatching of yellow-white hair, but it had fallen from the scalps in places, to leave bare red splotches which looked sore and scabby. They wore clothing which fitted so tightly to their bodies and limbs that it was almost a second skin. This was uniformly gray, but of a darker shade than the flesh beneath it, so that their hands showed up as pallid sets of claws, for they were thin to the point of near skeletons.

I saw, when I forced myself forward a step or two again to look at them, that their faces had a great uniformity, as if they were all copies of a single model—save that here or there they were further disfigured by puckered scars or rough and pitted skin.

They moved sluggishly when they moved at all. Most of them lay on narrow shelf bunks within their individual cubicles. Others simply sat staring ahead of them at the low walls as if awaiting some summons which dim wits could not understand but would respond to. One or two ate from bowls, using their fingers to cram greenish stuff into their mouths. I averted my eyes hurriedly from them as they slobbered and sucked.

Men they might be in general outline, but they had become less than the animals of my own world.

The pattern of lights across the great board suddenly made a symbol and there was a clap of sound. Those lying on their bunks roused, stood straight by the doors of their cells. The eaters dropped their bowls to do likewise.

But only a few of them issued from their small private sections, gathering in the aisle. The line then faced in the opposite direction and marched, to file out of sight beneath the place where I stood.

The rest remained standing where they were. Nor did they show any sign of impatience as time passed and they were neither dismissed to their interrupted meal and rest, or alerted for some errand or labor.

The symbol on the board dissolved once more into running lights and I began to wonder about my own immediate future. It was plain that I was not going to break out through the door now closed so firmly behind me.

There was no sign of Ayllia in any of the cells below, though there remained the section behind the lighted screen—I did not know what was there, or beyond the exit through which the marchers had gone. Would any of those now at attention sight me if I were to go down to their level? I could not determine how unaware they were. And I was afraid to try to reach Ayllia by mind touch.

But I was not to be given time to put even my wildest half-plan into action. If it had seemed that the mind touch which had drawn me here had stopped at the door, there were other precautions in force at the command of he who ruled this underground enclave, as I speedily discovered. For, without warning, I was caught by a rigidity which would not yield to any of my attempts to break it. I could only blink my eyelids. For the rest I was frozen as if one of the legends of childhood had come true and I was turned to stone.

So imprisoned by a force new to me, I had to watch four of those standing at attention below turn and march, again under the shelf where I was. But now an opening appeared near me and through it raised a platform with the four guards. They crowded about me and one of them aimed weapon not unlike a dart gun at my feet and legs. As he thumbed it the bonds which held that part of my body had vanished and I was free to move as they steered me to their platform, and on it we were lowered to face the aisle of the screen arch.

Seen from floor level and not from above, that screen with all its rippling lights awoke awe. It was alien, totally so to me, but there was that about it which I could recognize as well as a force influence wielded by a Wise Woman. Only this was not aimed at me, and it was not part of the current which had drawn me hither.

Shepherded by the guards, I went through the arch of the screen. Here were no cells, no divisions, just a four-step dais. Around the bottom level of the dais were small screens: only two of those facing me sparkled with light. Below each screen jutted a ledge sloping toward the floor at an angle, and those were covered with buttons and small projecting levers. More and more was I unpleasantly reminded of the tales of Kolder strongholds.

Each of these ledges had a fixed seat before it. Gray-clad men sat at the two which flashed lights, their eyes fixed upon the screens, their hands resting on the edges of the ledges as if ready at any moment to press one of the buttons, should the need arise.

On the dais itself, however, stood that which drew and held all my attention—in part the answer to the mystery which had entangled me. There was a tall, pillar-shaped box of clear crystal. And completely embedded in its heart stood a man of Escore. Not only one of the Old Race, I realized as I looked closer, but this was the man I had seen in my dream, he who had opened the gate and then sat to watch it.

Entombed, yes, but not dead! No, not mercifully dead. From the crown of that crystal coffin there fountained a series of silver wires which were never still, but quivered and spun, sparkling in the air as if they were indeed not metal but rising and falling streams of water.

The eyes of the prisoner now opened and he looked straight at me. There was a fierce brightness in his gaze, a demand which was cruel in its intensity, its force bent upon me. He tried in those few instants to beat down what was me, to take me over to do his will. And I knew that to him I represented a key to freedom, that he had brought me here for that purpose alone.

Perhaps if I yielded at once to his demand he might have achieved his purpose. But my response was almost automatic recoil. None of my breed yielded to force until we were overcome. Had he pled instead of tried to take—but the need in him was too great, and he could not plead when all life outside his crystal walls had become one with the enemy in his mind.

The silver strands tossed wildly, rippling as he fought to possess me as his slave thing. And I heard a startled cry. From before one of those ledges arose a man. He leaned forward and stared at the captive in the crystal. Then he swung around to look at me, astonishment speedily changing to excitement, and then satisfaction.

He was as different from the gray men as I was. But he was not of the Old Race. Nor had he any of the Power; I knew that when I looked upon him. But there was life and intelligence in his face and with that a detachment which said, though he looked human, he was not so within.

Standing a head taller than his servants, he was lean of body, though not reduced to such skeleton proportions as they. Nor did his face and hands have the gray pallor, though the rest of his body was covered by the same tight-fitting clothes as they wore, distinguished from theirs by an intricate blazon on the breast worked out in colors of yellow, red, and green.

His hair was almost as brightly yellow as that blazon, thick and long enough, though he wore it tucked behind his ears, to touch his shoulders. That was the hair of a Sulcarman. But when I studied his face I knew that here was no sea-rover trapped by the gate. For his features were very sharply angled about a large and forward thrusting nose, giving him almost the appearance of wearing one of the bird masks behind which the Falconers rose into battle.

"A—woman!"

He touched a button on his board and then he came around to face me, standing with his hands on his hips, eyeing me up and down with an insolence which made my anger rise.

"A woman," he repeated and this time he did not speak in surprise but thoughtfully. And he glanced from me to the prisoner in the crystal and then back again.

"You are not," he continued, "like the other—"

He gestured to the other side of the dais. I could not turn my head so I saw no more than the edge of a cloak. But I knew that to be Ayllia's. She did not move and I thought perhaps she was caught in just the sort of web as now held me.

"So"—now he addressed the prisoner—"you thought to use her? But you did not try with the other. What makes this one different?"

The man in the crystal did not even turn his eyes to his questioner. But I felt that deep wave of hate spread from the box which held him, hate that froze instead of burned, a hate such as I had at times sensed in my brothers, but never in such a great tide.

His captor walked around me, though I could not turn my head to see him. I had learned this much, however, that he could not instantly recognize Power as his prisoner had done. Therefore he was devoid of any trace of that talent. And that thought gave me a spark of confidence, though looking upon the prisoner, I could not hope too much. . . . For as he had known me as witch, so did I know him as more than warlock, as one of the adepts such as no longer existed in Escore and had never been known on Estcarp, where the Wise Women carefully controlled all learning lest just such a reckless seeker after forbidden learning rise.

"A woman," the stranger repeated for the third time. "Yet you aimed a sending at her. It would seem she is far more than she looks, bedraggled and grimy as she is. And if there is any chance that she is even a little akin to you, my unfriend, then this is indeed a night when fortune has chosen to give me her full smile!"

"Now"—he nodded at my guard and they crowded in upon me, though there seemed to be some barrier so they could not really lay hand on me—"we shall put you in safekeeping, girl, until we have more time for the solving of your riddle."

They continued to crowd me along the steps until I was on the opposite side of the room from the entrance, behind the prisoner in the crystal, so he could no longer see me, though I knew he was as aware of me as I was of him. The guards then stepped away and from the floor arose four bars of crystal like the pillar, but only as thick as my wrist. They slid up above my head and then they began to glow. As they did so the force which had held me rigid vanished, but when I put out my hand I found that there was an invisible wall between one bar and the next and I was boxed.

There was room within my square of unseen walls for me to sit down and I did, looking about me now with the need to learn all I could of this place—though I could not begin to guess the reason for it, what great project it was necessary to.

I could see Ayllia now. She sprawled as one unconscious or asleep on the second step of the dais, her head turned from me. But I could see the rise and fall of her breast and knew she still lived.

I needed sleep too. As I sat there all the strain and fatigue of my hours in this world closed about me as a smothering curtain and I had to have ease and relaxation of mind and body. Thus I concentrated on setting certain safeguards to alert me against any new attempt on the part of he who stood in the pillar to take command. With that done I rested my head on my knees.

But between my palms, hidden from sight, I held that wand I had brought out of Escore. Did it belong to the man in the pillar? If so, it might have been what he had noted instantly at my coming and wanted to get, though how he might reach it through his walls I could not see. That he was of value to my new captor was certain. And it might be that I would also end so. This thought I willed away, for sleep I must have if I would be quick of wit when such was needed.

XII

*W*hile I slept, I dreamed. But this was no second assault upon my will, no harsh order to obey. Rather a hand slipped into mine to lead me to a place of safety where one could speak mind to mind without chance of being overheard; it was the prisoner of the pillar whom I faced in that place which was not of our waking world. Somehow he seemed younger, more vulnerable, not filled with white hate and the need to burst bonds and rend the world about him to satisfy the revenge his spirit craved, all of which I had read in him before.

That he was an adept I already knew, one above the Wise Women of Estcarp as I was above Ayllia in the scale of Power control. Now I learned his name, or rather the name by which he went, since that old law that the naming of true names was forbidden lest it offer some enemy a straight course into mastery held. He was Hilarion, and once he had dwelt in the citadel of the gate.

He bad created the gate because his seeking mind ever pushed on and on for new learning. And, having opened it, it followed that he was constrained to explore what lay beyond. So he came, arrogant and proud in his power—too arrogant, because of the past years of his supremacy in his own sphere, to take precautions.

Thus he had been caught in a web which was not spun from such learning, learning that would not have held him for an instant. But this danger was born of a machine, or a different path of Power, and one he did not understand. Only it was a strength which could incorporate him into it, even as I had seen the half-men in the city of towers, part flesh, part machine.

Between the towers and this underground hole was a long war. It would seem that the present inhabitants of the towers made no overt attacks against the underground; but the gray men, under the orders of he who dominated this chamber, raided in the cities, bringing back the supplies which were needed to sustain this installation. And this life of raid and struggle had lasted for untold years—so many that Hilarion could not list them, for it was old before he had been entrapped, and he had dwelt here long. This I well knew, for the days of the adepts in Escore were past perhaps a thousand years ago.

The machines here had been set in place a millennium ago for the waging of a great war and had continued to function although the world on the surface had been blasted so that nothing remained there save the towers. The machines had been faltering when Hilarion had come, but at his capture they took on new life from his Power, so that now he in a measure controlled them, though in turn he was controlled by Zandur, who was master here, who had always been master. At hearing that I showed disbelief that a man could exist so long.

"But he is not truly a man!" countered Hilarion. "Perhaps he was, long ago. But he has learned to make other bodies in a growth vat and transfer to them when the one he wears grows old or ails. And the machines weave such a protection around him that he cannot be reached by any impulse I have been able to summon. Now he will soon know that you are of a like nature to me and he will imprison you to add to the power of his machines—"

"No!"

"So said I once: 'No' and 'No' and 'No!' Yet my 'Nos' could not stand against his 'Yes.' There is this, that together we may—I need only be free of this crystal which negates anything I send against him, and then we shall see which is stronger, a man or machine! For now I know these machines as I did not before, all their stresses and weaknesses; I know they can be attacked. Loose me, witch. Give me your Power for my backing, and we shall both win free. Deny me your aid and you shall be entrapped as I have been for all these weary reaches of time."

"He has me entrapped now," I pointed out warily. Hilarion's arguments were well ordered, but I had not forgotten his first try at making me, not an ally in his struggle, but a weapon in his hand.

He read that now and said, "Such imprisonment is said to build impatience in a man. But if that same man sees before him a key to his cell, perhaps in easy reach, will he not put out his hand to seize upon it? You brought here what is mine, and which, in my hands, will be worth more than any steel, any fire-spitting rod such as these people turn upon each other in their deadly dealing."

"The wand."

"The wand, which is mine and which I had never hoped to see again. It will not serve you to any purpose. But me—to me it will give the power this world withholds!"

"And how do you get it? I do not think your pillar will be easily broken—"

"It looks solid but it is a field of force, force which can be seen. Put the wand to it—"

"Then so I can also loose me!"

"Not so! You know the nature of such a wand. It will obey the one who wrought it, in the hands of another it is a feeble thing. It is not your key, but mine!"

And he spoke the truth. Yet was I now a prisoner and so his wand was as far from him as if it too were encased in crystal.

"But—" What more he might have said was lost. For suddenly he was gone, out of my dream, as a candle might be blown out in a puff, and I was alone. Whether I slept then, or whether my waking thereafter was as quick as it seemed, I do not know. But when I opened my eyes all seemed just as before. I sat guarded by the pillars of light, even as Hilarion was in his casing, and I could not look upon his face, only his back.

However, there was this much of a change: those silver trails which sprouted from the top of the pillar were weaving rhythmically, and I saw the flicker and flash of lights on more than one board which, when I had fallen asleep, had been dark and untended. There were gray men at them now. And around the dais paced Zandur, pausing now and again behind one of those lighted sections, as if he read the lights as runes. There was a tenseness about him, though the gray men worked automatically, as if they were concerned by nothing but their immediate labors.

There was a loud crack of sound, and Zandur spun about to face the large screen which walled this division from the cells of the gray men. A rippling of light ran across its surface, glowing in portions that had been dead and dull moments earlier.

Zandur studied that display and then ran to an empty seat before one of the small boards. His fingers sped across the buttons there. Instantly, in response, I felt such a blow as if someone had laid a lash across my bared body. We were not in the dream now. What demand or disciplining torment was given Hilarion, I also felt, though, I thought, in lesser extent.

So this was how Zandur used controls to make his captive do as he desired. And yet Hilarion had not told me of that. I marveled at the spirit of a man who had been kept so long captive by such pressures.

There are measures one may take in one's mind to elude the pains and needs of the body, a discipline my kind learns early, for if one would use Power one must learn rigid self-control Hilarion had these to call upon for his protection, unless the machine, being wholly alien, could negate them. And I thought that perhaps that was at least partly so.

Not only for pity, though that was awakened in me, must I do what I could to aid Hilarion, since there was an excellent chance of my being set with him, to be played upon by the same demands and stresses. I had the wand; now I turned it over in my hands. Hilarion had warned that it would not serve me, only him. But I had little chance of getting it to him now. And I was sure that when Zandur released me, he would be well prepared to counter any bid for freedom I might make.

There remained Ayllia. I glanced at where she still lay. How much of mind sending could Zandur detect? I had respect for the machines here, the more so because I did not understand them in the least.

Were there among them some to pick up mind sending, alert our captor to any efforts in that direction? And mind send itself was the part of my own talent which I had not regained to any extent. I was a cripple forced to rely on my maimed talent for support.

There was this, that unless Ayllia was also locked in some invisible cover, then she was teachable. That she was unconscious might perhaps be in my favor. The Wise Women's hallucinations and dreams were principal ways of moving others to their purposes. Now—if I could work on Ayllia, and *if* my mind send was not detected . . .

As far as I could see Zandur was completely absorbed in what was happening on the screens. The Vupsall girl still lay where I had seen her last, but now she had turned upon her side, her head pillowed on her crooked arm, much as one in a natural sleep. If that were so it was even better for my purpose.

I began to blank out, bit by bit, the room about me. This was the traditional method of thought control, and I went at it as cautiously as I had walked in the dark of the outer passage leading here, now testing the strength of my forces, as I had then tested for pitfalls ahead.

This was an exercise known to me for years, but never before had I to hold to it with such uncertainty. Good results depended upon the receptiveness of the person to be influenced. And in Estcarp there had been no such distractions as surrounded me here. I did not want to touch the band Hilarion operated upon, lest such interference be instantly apparent in some way to Zandur.

I closed my eyes, not in truth, but as I had been taught, upon all but Ayllia's body. There was no need for the mental picture; she was there before me. I began to reach, questing for the right line to her brain. Seemingly they kept no watch on her, but that, too, might be deceptive.

The strain was very great; I was forcing my mutilated power. "Ayllia!" I beamed my call at her as if I shouted that aloud.

"Ayllia! Ayllia!"

I have seen many times a patient fisherman casting out a line, letting it drift, bringing it back, to cast again, and yet with no result. And so it was with me. I fiercely fought the rising despair, the feeling that it was no longer in me to succeed in this thing which had once been such a small exercise.

"Ayllia!" No use—I could not touch her. Either I was lacking in force, or else something blanked my questing.

But if that was so how had Hilarion been able to make me dream true? Or had I? Was that all a hallucination spun by Zandur?

Some of the adepts had not walked in the Shadow, but more of them had. Could I believe that he was one of the Dark Ones? I wavered, lost, drew in' upon myself, and knew bitterness from my failure.

For a space did I so retreat, and then once more I began to think, with more clarity. My fellow captive was a part of whatever Zandur did with these machines. To be such a part it was necessary for mental contact, since his body was imprisoned. And it was plain to my eyes that the gray men who pressed buttons below the dais did that by rote and not because they thought. Therefore there was an energy here, enough akin to our Power to be able to link to it. Suppose I could so link in part, build thus a backing for my crippled mind sending.

Such a course was tempting, but there was danger in it, too. For such a touch might well draw in the whole of me, as a magnet draws steel. And it was plain that what chanced here now was demanding from Hilarion a high amount of force. Did Zandur have a need for sleep, or was his synthetic body without fatigue known to the human kind? Did there ever come a time when the energy here was at a low ebb? And if so, how far were we from such a period now? Too long for me, that Zandur might be reminded he had a second captive and turn to my humbling?

I set myself to watch what was going on—and discovered that in the time I had been concentrating on Ayllia there had come a change: the extra boards which had been alight and tended by the gray men were once more dark, the seats before them empty.

Zandur—I caught sight of him on the other side of the dais, where he must be facing Hilarion. He looked up at the adept and there was a satisfied smile on his face. He spoke then and his words, though low-pitched, reached me.

"Well done, my unfriend. Even if not by your will, yet you have added to our accomplishment. I do not believe those in the towers will try that again: they have no liking for losses." He turned his head slowly from side to side as if he surveyed all within that huge chamber with pride. "We wrought better than we first guessed when we set these here. Machines they were then, extensions only of our own hands, eyes, brains. Now they are more. But still"—his face was suddenly convulsed; he grimaced as if some inner pain gnawed at him—"but still they are ruled, they do not rule! And that is how it must be as long as one tower stands! They wrought worse than they thought, those builders of towers, giving themselves to the machines. We knew better! Man"—he beat one fist into the palm of his other hand—"man exists, man abides!"

Man, I wondered. Did he speak thus of himself, who Hilarion had said was certainly not human as we judged human, or the gray men who were but things operating under orders with no will or minds of their own? He spoke as one waging a battle in a rightful cause, as we spoke in Escore against the Shadow, as they spoke in Estcarp when they mentioned Karsten and Alizon.

In such bitter struggles there is a pitfall which few seldom avoid. The time comes when to the fighters the end justifies the means. So it had been when the Wise Women had churned the mountains and put an end to Karsten's invasion; but they had been willing to pay a price in turn, giving up their lives to that end. It was a very narrow path on which they had set their feet and they had not overstepped—they had summoned the Power to that blow, but they had not trafficked with the Shadow.

Here it might have gone otherwise. Perhaps in the beginning Zandur had been one such as my father, my brothers, and then he had taken Dinzil's road, seduced by the thought of the victory so badly needed, or by the smell of power, which, as he handled it, became more and more sweet and needful. He could also still deceive himself that what he did was for a high purpose, thus making him the more to be feared.

"Man abides," he repeated. "Here—man abides!" And he threw up his head, looked to Hilarion as if he taunted his captive with that, dared him to deny his saying.

The silver wires which had stood so erect and had rippled with force and energy now hung limp, with no life at all, about, the pillar providing a thin veil for the prisoner within. And if Hilarion had any way to answer he did not.

For the first time a new thought crossed my mind. How was it that I so understood Zandur's speech? It was certainly not the tongue of the Old Race, even modified and changed as it was in Escore. Nor did it resemble that of the Sulcarmen. Why should it? This was another world—unless Zandur, too, was one who had passed through a gate.

Then it came to me that this was some magic of the machines. They must pick up the words he said, then translate them for us. The machines—what could they not do? I had been momentarily shaken from my plan by what happened here, but now I turned to it. The energy of the machines was linked to Hilarion. My need of it—

But time—I needed time! Zandur moved away from the dais, coming toward me. Luckily I had not altered my position. If I could deceive him into believing me still sleeping . . . even so small a deception should be to my advantage.

I closed my eyes. With most of the thrumming lights stilled I could hear the sound of footfalls drawing closer. Was he standing now to stare at me? Though I did not look to see, I thought that he was, and I waited tensely for some word to tell me that this was the end of what small freedom I still possessed.

But he did not speak, and, a moment later, I heard footfalls again, this time receding. I counted fifty under my breath, and then another fifty to make sure. When I opened my eyes it was to find him gone. A single gray man sat at one bank of buttons, the screen before him alive. But, left to right, all others had been shut down. And, save for Ayllia, the prisoner in the pillar and myself, there was no one else in the chamber I could see.

Hilarion—no! To mind touch him with purpose would be to bring the very recognition I must be most careful to avoid. However, I did not quite know how to go about my search, except to conduct it as the mind quests which had once linked me with Kyllan and Kemoc when we were at a distance from one another.

There are bands of communication which perhaps one can best visualize as bright ribbons laid horizontally edge to edge. To touch these is indeed a kind of search. My brother Kyllan had always been able to find those of animals and use them; but I had never sought any save the bands best known to those of my own craft.

Now I must range higher or lower and to do so took time, which perhaps I could ill spare. For the sake of a beginning point I chose the old one so well known to me, my brothers'.

I do not think I cried out. If I did the gray man at the one live bank of buttons did not turn his head to show that the cry alerted him. I had touched for an instant so clear and loud a call that I was shocked into relinquishing touch, even as I had when Hilarion's mind had earlier met mine.

Kyllan? Kemoc? Once before Kemoc had followed me into the terrors of an unknown world, far more alien to those of our heritage than this one. Had he been drawn after me again?

"Kemoc," I called.

"You—who are you?" The demand was so sharp that it rang in my head as loudly as if the words had been shouted in my ears, deafening my mind for an instant the way my ears could be dulled.

"Kaththea," I answered with the truth before I thought. "Kemoc—is that you?" and a part of me wanted *yes,* a part of me feared it. For, I thought, to have the burden for his safety laid on me once more was more than I could bear.

I was not answered now in words, rather did I seem to look, as through a window, into a room with rock walls, gloomy and dark. There was a stone bowl set on a pedestal. In that bowl blazed a handful of coals, giving limited light to that portion of the chamber immediately about it. Standing in that light was a woman. She wore the riding dress of the Old Race, breeches and jerkin of dark, dull green, and her hair was braided and netted tight to her head. At first I could not see her face: it was turned from me as she looked down into the fire. Then she turned around as if she could look through that window at me.

I saw her eyes widen, but her surprise could be no greater than mine.

"Jaelithe!"

My mother! But how—where? Years lay between our last meeting, when she had ridden forth to seek my father, vanished apparently from the sea. She had searched for him by a trail of magic in which all three of us had played a part, the first time we had been drawn into a formal use of our gift.

Time had not touched; she was the same then as now, though I was a woman and not the girl child. But I saw that she was not confused by the change, but knew me.

"Kaththea!" She took a step toward me, away from the brazier, lifted her hands as if across that strange space between us we might touch fingers. Then her face took on an urgent expression and she asked quickly: "Where are you?"

"I do not know. I came through a gate—"

She made a gesture with her raised hand as if to wave away unimportant things. "Yes. But now describe where you are!"

I did so, making as short a tale as I could. When I was done she gave a sigh which might be half of relief. "So much it is to the good; we are in the same world at least. But now—you searched with thought for us?"

"No, I did not know you were here." And I went on to tell her what I must do.

"An adept who wrought a gate kept prisoner!" She looked thoughtful. "It would seem, my daughter, that you have stumbled by chance on that which may save us all. And your plan of using the girl, that is well reasoned. But that you need help from outside is also true. And we shall see what can be done. Simon," she called with her mind, "come quickly!" Then she turned her full attention to me again. "Let me see this girl through your eyes—the room as well . . . ."

And I did for her what I would not do for Hilarion; I surrendered my will so that her mind linked fast to mine and I knew she viewed all I saw. I turned my head slowly from side to side for her benefit.

"Are these Kolder?" I asked.

"No. But there is a likeness. I think that this world was once close to the Kolder and something of their Power spread to the other. But that is of no consequence now. I know where lies the entrance to the burrow in which you are. We shall come to you with what speed we can. Until then, unless you are in great need, do not link. But if this Zandur would work on you, as he has upon Hilarion, link at once."

"Ayllia?"

"You have read rightly that she may be your key to freedom. But again we cannot use her as yet, not if we are to have time. Above all, the adept is necessary. He knows the gate; it was of his creation and will answer him. If we are ever to return to Estcarp we must have that gate!"

Suddenly she smiled. "Time seems to have run more swiftly for you, my daughter, than it has for us. Also, I appear to have borne one who is as I wished for, a child of my spirit as well as my body. Take you care, Kaththea, not to throw away now, by some chance, that which will work to save us all. Now I will break link, but you shall be in mind and if you have need, call at once!"

The window into that place of stone was gone. And I was left to wonder—how had my mother and father come here? For she had spoken to him as if he were some distance from her but no world away. Had he stumbled on another gate into this world, she following him thereafter? If so, it would seem that portal had been closed to their return.

That led me back to Hilarion. The gate he created must answer to him, my mother had said. Then we must free him in order to win back. But time—was time our friend or enemy? I fumbled in my cloak and drew out the packet of food I had taken from the gray men's supplies. It was a square of some dark brown substance which crumbled as I pinched it. I smelled the scrap I held in my fingers: a strange odor, not pleasant, not unpleasant. But it was the only sustenance I had to hand and I was hungry. I crunched it between my teeth. It was very dry and gritty, as if made of the ashy dust which covered the surface of this world. But I drank from one of the containers and swallowed it somehow. There was now only the need to wait, and waiting can be very hard.

XIII

*B*ut I could think and speculate. Time, my mother had said, ran less swiftly in this land than it had for us. It was true that in the mind picture she seemed no older than she had when she had ridden forth on that quest for my father. But then we three had been children not yet started upon our life paths. Now I felt immeasurably older than I had at that hour.

It would seem that she and my father, having once reached this world, were imprisoned for lack of a gate. So her eagerness concerning Hilarion. But if they dared to come to this pit, could they not also be sucked into the same net? It was in me to call a warning by mind link—until I remembered that she had spoken of knowing this place in which I was captive. If she did, then surely she also knew of the perils it had to offer.

I finished the food and drank sparingly. About me the pillars still blazed, the silvery strands continued to veil the adept's prison. Perhaps he slept.

But suddenly I caught slight movement on the dais where Ayllia lay. They had apparently put no bonds on her, no visible ones. Now she was rousing from whatever state of consciousness had held her for so long. She sat up slowly, turning her head, her eyes open. As I watched her closely I thought she did not seem wholly aware of her surroundings, but was still gripped in a daze, as she had been during our journey to the tower city.

She did not get to her feet, but rather began to crawl along the step on which she had lain. I watched the gray man on duty. He sat inert before his board, as if he could see nothing but the lights on the screen.

Ayllia reached the corner of the step, rounded that, began to crawl at a sluggish pace down the far side. In a moment or two she would be out of my sight. And perhaps out of reach when I needed her. I sent a thought command to halt. But if it touched her mind there was no answer. Now she was out of my sight on the far side of the dais.

Then I noted that one of the silver tendrils about the pillar stirred, enough to touch the one next to it to the right, and that to the next, and the next, before those, too, were hidden from my observation. That movement carried with it a suggestion of surreptitiousness, as if it must be hidden from any watcher. I could not remember whether there had been any movement of the tendrils before Ayllia's apparent waking, or if it had begun only when she moved. Was Hilarion putting into practice what I had earlier attempted, contacting the barbarian girl's mind and setting her under his orders to try a rescue attempt?

Two sides of the dais were hidden from me. The third I faced, where Ayllia had lain, and the fourth I could also see. But any advance along that would be in plain sight of the gray man. And he could hardly fail to notice if she passed directly before him.

I waited tensely to see her come into view. But she did not. The arch in the big screen was in my view; if she tried to leave through that I could see her. Then— then I must contact Jaelithe in spite of the danger lest my one possible aid be taken from me.

But Ayllia did not creep to that door. Instead there was another bright ripple of lights along the screen, followed by that sound which had earlier alerted the gray men to march. I saw the tendrils on the pillar stir and rise slowly, so slowly that watching them one had a feeling of a great weight of fatigue burdening each and every one of them.

Through the arch in the screen now marched a squad of the gray men, while from some point behind me came Zandur. I did not have time to play asleep, it was too sudden. And I was frightened when I saw that the gray men marched straight for me, making a square about the lighted rods of my small prison.

Zandur approached more slowly, but he came to a stop directly before me, and stood as he had earlier before Hilarion, his hands on his hips, staring at me intently. Instinctively I had risen to my feet as the guards closed in. Now I met his gaze as steadily as I could.

It was not a duel of wills as it might have been with one of my own kind, as it had been with the adept, for we had no common meeting of Powers. But I was determined that he would not find me easy taking for his purposes. Yet I also waited before beaming a call to my mother, since I would not do that unless I had no other course.

Zandur appeared to come to a decision. He snapped the fingers of his right hand and one of the gray men crossed to the other side of the dais, to return, pushing before him what looked like a chest set upon one end. Down one side was a narrow panel of opaque substance, not unlike the screens, and this was put to face me.

Behind it Zandur stood and his fingers played across its surface, first hesitatingly, and then with an air of impatience, as if he had expected an easy answer and had not received it. He said nothing, nor did the gray men even show interest in their master's action. Rather they simply stood around me as a guard fence.

Three times Zandur touched his panel. Then, the fourth time he did so, that opaque length came to life. Not with the rippling patterns of the screens but with a weak blue glow.

That color! It was—it was that of the rocks which spelled safety in Escore! To look upon it now was almost reassuring. I had a strange feeling that could I but lay my hand to the screen over which it crawled, I would be far more refreshed than from the food I had just eaten.

But Zandur jerked his fingertips away from the block with a sharp exclamation. He might have been burnt where he expected no fire.

He hastened to press a new place. As the blue spread it also became darker. And I thought he must be focusing upon me some test of Power. For long moments he held fast until the color reached the top of the panel. There it remained steady, neither darkening nor lightening again. Zandur gave a nod of satisfaction and took away his finger. Straightaway the color disappeared.

"The same, and yet not the same." For the first time he spoke. He could have been addressing me, or only speaking his thoughts aloud, but in either case I saw no need to answer.

"You,"—he gave another wave of hand which sent one of his followers moving off the box—"what manner of thing are you?"

Manner of thing! It seemed that he now equated me with his machines. To him I was a thing, not a person. And I felt some of the rage which ignited Hilarion. Did Zandur only recognize force as coming from machines, and therefore see us, because of what we held in us, as machines?

"I am Kaththea of the House of Tregarth," I made answer with those words I could best summon to underline the fact that perhaps I was even more human than himself.

He laughed. There was that in his scornful mirth which fed my anger. But a warning alerted me within: *Do not let him play upon your emotions, for in that way lies danger. You must guard each step you take.* So I fell back upon the discipline of the Wise Women and ordered myself to look upon him objectively as they would have done. Perhaps it was their old feeling that the male was the lesser creature which now came to my aid. I had not accepted such a belief—I could not when I knew my brothers and my father, all of whom had a portion of my talents—but when such an idea is held constantly before one, it is easy enough to accept it as a pattern of life.

This was a man—at least one who had been a man. He was not born to the Power, but must depend upon lifeless machines to serve him as our minds and spirits served us. Therefore, for all his trappings, he was not really one to stand full equal to a witch out of Estcarp.

Yet there was Hilarion, an adept, who had fallen into Zandur's web. Yes, my mind rationalized swiftly, but Hilarion had come here unprepared, had been entrapped before he was truly aware of the danger. I—I could have safeguards.

"Kaththea of the House of Tregarth," he repeated as one would mock a child by reiterating a simple statement. "I know nothing of this Tregarth, be it country or clan. But it would seem that you have that which I can use, once we fix you even as we have this other—" He waved to Hilarion.

"And it is best for you, Kaththea of the House of Tregarth, that you do as we would have you, since the penalty for doing otherwise is not such as you would wish to face a second time—though it is true you are a stubborn lot if you are akin to this other."

I did not answer him; best not be drawn into any argument. Many times is speech weakness, silence strength. I was sure that Zandur could not read my mind without his machines, which I distrusted deeply. Thus I could plan and not be uncovered in that planning.

It would seem that his gray men did not need spoken orders; perhaps he controlled them as I had tried with Ayllia. They split into two parties and marched into the obscurity of the chamber somewhere behind me. I did not turn to see them go, not wishing to lose sight of their master.

He seated himself before one of the small boards, releasing the chair to turn and face me. There was about him an air of ease which to me spelled danger . . . . If he deemed me so well in his control perhaps I had against me more than I could imagine.

Ayllia? She had not come into sight at the far corner of the dais, nor had she headed for the arch. Therefore she must now be before Hilarion. And Zandur and a single gray man, still in his own seat, were alone—for the moment.

I did not close my eyes in strict concentration, but at that moment I aimed my call, seeing that I might have no better moment for attack.

"Jaelithe—Simon!"

Instantly came their answer, full, strong—as if protecting arms were about my shoulders, a shield moved to stand between me and sword point. There is an old tale that if one with Power wishes to sever two who have caused tears and heartache to one another for all eternity he or she shakes a cloak between them. I could almost believe in that moment that the cloak was before me, that I could see, feel it. Still that sense of protection, though it continued to abide with me, did not cloud my present purpose.

"What need you?" came my mother's quick question.

"To deal with Zandur—now!"

"Draw." She gave both consent and order in that word.

I drew because of my crippled need, and there flowed into me such strength as

I had not known since the days I walked with Dinzil. All I had regained through Utta's teaching and my own seeking was as a single pale candle's shine compared to the full sun of midday. And that power I pulled and shaped into a beam of command, seeking again my answer to Zandur.

"Ayllia!"

This time there was no failure: my command, my enveloping force swept into the barbarian girl. I filled her with my purpose, not daring in my extremity to remember I was doing this to a living person, for she was my only weapon for all our safety.

There were a few moments of strange disorientation when I looked through my own eyes at the lounging Zandur and the dais, but I also had another glimpse of the fore of the pillar as Ayllia must be seeing it.

Then I concentrated on that second seeing. I had never before ruled another so, save under carefully controlled experimentation in the Place of Silence when I was a novice. This was so dire a thing that one's spirit sickened as might one's body if put in a place where no human had a right to be. But I fought that sickness and kept my place in Ayllia.

At first her body answered me clumsily. It was as if I were one of the traveling puppet masters who used to come on harvest feast days to the manor markets— yet an inept one, as I handled the strings controlling the arms and legs awkwardly, making them slew in the wrong directions.

Still, I dared not be clumsy if I could help it. So I did not try to totter to my feet, but turned and crept as Ayllia herself had earlier crept, heading in the direction from which she had come. If I could so reach the same step where she had been I would be able to make my move at the right time.

Now I was no longer conscious of Jaelithe and Simon, only of the strong, ever-flowing current they gave to me. And I hurried faster, each passing breath of time giving me more control over Ayllia's body, though I did not try as yet to do more than take it back to the spot not far from Zandur.

I came to the far side of the dais, and along that to the corner from which I could see Zandur in his chair still facing the four blazing rods which held—*me*.

Seldom is it given one to look upon one's self save in a mirror. And now when I tried it I had a sensation of dizziness, of whirling into some space which was neither here nor there, that I speedily averted my eyes and kept them fixed on Zandur.

Fear marched forward with every measure I gained. Why the master of this prison had not already turned to sight me I could not understand. It seemed to me that the generation of such energy as had brought me to this desperate move would touch him. It was almost as if an invisible line spun across the open air tying the me in the cage of light rods to the me who crawled in Ayllia's body.

At last I came to the place where Ayllia had lain when first I saw her. There I paused for some long breaths. If Zandur turned now and sighted me, I might still be safe. But if I proceeded, as now I must, to a point behind him, I had a long, or what seemed a very long space of open to cover—during which journey I would be instantly suspect if sighted.

He stood up and, involuntarily, I cringed. But he did not turn his head. He was instead looking into the depths of the chamber to a point beyond the cage of rods. There was a stir there as his gray men returned. Now he came to stand before the cage. Could he tell that I was not in my rightful body? I must depend upon the fact that he had none of the real gift, and things instantly visible to an adept would not be so to him.

Now I must dare my last move along the step, rising to my feet at last and running to a point directly behind him, willing all the way that he would not turn to see me. Now much would depend upon expert timing. I made my last impressions on Ayllia's sleeping mind. This must she do when the time came; I set that command as deeply and strongly as all the renewed strength I could call upon gave.

Then I returned to myself. Between my hands, ready, was the wand. The gray men had reached an area where I could see them without turning my head. They bore, some singly, some together, a number of objects. And these Zandur went to sort, sending some to one side of the dais, assembling the burdens of others closer to my cage.

Instinct told me that I would only have a few moments at the best, no more than a heartbeat or two at the least. And for that I must be ready. I waited. I could see Ayllia standing on the dais. Her eyes were open, fixed on mine, and a touch assured me that she was filled with the need to obey the last command I had left in her.

Zandur came to stand before me again.

"Now, my Kaththea of the House of Tregarth," he said mockingly, "and well do I call you mine, since you shall do my will from this hour forth. But be not downhearted at such a fate. Will you not now be one to live forever, knowing life as you have not been privileged to taste it before? No, you will have much to thank me for, once you have learned to accept my wisdom, Kaththea of the House of Tregarth."

He must have given one of those voiceless orders to his followers for they began to open boxes and casks and set out on the corner of the dais a gleaming circle, making it fast to that base.

It pleased, or amused Zandur to explain what they did for two reasons: to let me know there was no escape from what he planned for me, and to have an audience. Perhaps he had long gone lonely for one still sentient enough to match him in brain power, for it was plain to see that the gray men were no companions, rather servants and extra hands and legs for his use.

What they were doing was preparing a second pillar, this to encase me as Hilarion was held. And so encased I would add what Power I held, even as the adept did, to protection and renewing of Zandur's precious machines. He seemed almost to believe, as he talked, that once it was all explained to me I would indeed understand the justice and need for this action, and go docilely into the cage which would be far more permanent than the one which held me now, going so because I agreed that this was necessary.

The very ancient war between the towers and this place had existed so long as a way of life that he could not think of any other pattern. And aught which would make more secure his position was to be seized upon and incorporated in his defense. Thus I was another sword for his hand.

His followers worked with precision and no wasted motions, as if they were so much a part of the machines here that they needed little direction to the task. They had embedded the ring in the floor of the dais, and now they set certain small machines about it.

When they had done and stepped away, I made ready. They must release the force of my rod cage to free me from one trap before putting me in another. I would have seconds then to act. I tensed, ready, the wand now in my right hand. Yet I strove to give Zandur the impression of one cowed and easy to control.

Perhaps he thought speed best, to use surprise as a counter to any attempt at escape on my part. The glow from the rods flicked out without warning. Only I had been watching, was ready.

I did not try to leap away as he probably expected. Instead I hurled the wand and joyfully saw Ayllia catch it. Then, without hesitation, she turned and leaped up the last step to the top of the dais, dashing for Hilarion's pillar with the wand held point out, as she might hold a sword against a human enemy.

Perhaps Zandur was not aware at once of what I had done. Or he could have been so sure of his own defenses and safeguards that such cooperation between me and one he believed utterly useless came as a shock he did not at first absorb. I think that absolute control for so many centuries had given him such confidence in his own power to rule his world that he could not foresee nor understand what had happened.

The point of the wand struck the pillar. In that moment all the installations in the chamber went wild, as if some vast storm, such as the Wise Women working in concert could summon, burst upon our unsheltered heads.

Flashes of raw light which blinded and hurt the eyes, noise as might have been thunder multiplied a thousand times, swept down and held us. Smoke rose in acrid clouds to make a stinking fog.

I moved now, running for the arch in the wall screen. I heard Zandur shouting, saw gray men blundering here and there as light whips of raw energy struck at them. There were things I saw only briefly, marveled at afterward, when I remembered them. There were worms of fire crawling on the floor, or dropping from air to writhe with a semblance of living creatures. I leaped over one and reached the front of the dais.

"Ayllia!" With mind call I pulled her and she came stumbling down to me. I need not so summon that other; he was already running for the arch, free as he had not been for untold centuries. In his hand was the wand, which he used as a pointer, aiming with it to send those serpents of fire hither and thither behind us. Whether they attacked Zandur and his men I could not see, for the stifling smoke was a yellow fog to set one coughing, with streaming eyes, but they did build behind us a formidable rear guard.

Hilarion looked at me and I read in his eyes something of what he felt in his moment of triumph. With his free hand he gestured us on toward the opening through the big screen; there was an alert wariness about him which told me that we were far from rid of what Zandur might summon.

On the other side of the screen we met the first of these ranks of the gray men, in their hands fire tubes such as I had seen used by those who cut their way into the transports. I drew upon the tripled power within me and built an hallucination. It was hastily contructed, unfinished, but for the moment it served. Ayllia, by my side, took on the appearance of Zandur. Seeing him with us, the gray men did not loose their fire, but fell back to give us an open passage, down which we fled.

We came to a plate in the floor beneath the balcony and huddled on this at Hilarion's gesture. Once we were upon it, it rose under us, taking us to the higher level. None too soon, for the gray men had taken heart, or learned the deception, and were firing at where we had been only seconds earlier. As those fiery trails whipped back and forth under the rising plate, I saw smoke float out from behind the screen and heard the clamor of that storm Hilarion's freeing had induced.

"Well done, sorceress." For the first time he spoke. "But we are not free yet. Do not think that Zandur is one as easily handled as this girl you have so aptly used."

"I do not underrate any enemy," I told him. "But help comes—"

"So!" It appeared that with that I had startled him. "Then you did not come through the gate—you two—alone?"

"I am not alone." I made him an answer, but more than that I did not say. Hilarion was a key now as Ayllia had been the key earlier, and I did not trust him. Only with my mother and father to stand with me would I dare to set any demands on him . . . for the old question stirred and dwelt ever at the back of my mind: some of the adepts, many, had turned to the Shadow. Was Hilarion even faintly so tainted, though he might not have been wholly of the dark? I had believed in and trusted Dinzil, who had in turn seemed one with the Valley people, been accepted as friend by them. And yet he had proved in the end to be one with the enemy. So it would seem there were those on the other side of our war who could take on the semblance of light while they were truly of those choosing to walk in the great dark.

A common danger can make temporary allies of unfriends and this might be true here. Suppose Hilarion did return us through the gate he had created, enter with us into Escore, and then prove to be such a one as those there had to fear? No, we must be ever on our guard until we knew—and how could we learn?

XIV

*W*e faced now what seemed a solid wall, and I remembered how that had parted when I had been drawn here and closed behind me. How could we force our way out when this must be controlled by Zandur's machines, and we had not even the fire-shooting weapons of his followers? It would not take them long to reach where we stood, and then we might be crisped to ashes with no escape.

But Hilarion had no doubts. He approached the wall, though I noticed how he moved stiffly, as if long imprisonment in the pillar had frozen his body. But even if his muscles obeyed him slowly, he had every confidence in his Power. As Ayllia had done he used the wand in a swordsman's move, laying its tip against that portion of the wall where we could see a fine line of division.

And I felt, though I did not add to it, the surge of will which emanated from him at that moment. From the tip of the wand leaped a blue spark which fastened to that line, sped down and up, running along it. There was a trembling through the floor on which we stood. Then the portal gave, very grudgingly, affording us only a narrow slit of passage. I pushed Ayllia through and followed myself, to have Hilarion bring up the rear.

We were in the dark passage through which I had groped with such care nights—days—earlier. In the narrow strip of light from the door I saw Hilarion aim the wand once more at the portal. Again blue light moved, and, as falteringly as it had opened, the door began to close. When a slit only the width of a finger remained, I saw a flash of blue, this time not aimed at the opening but along the floor, rising to run in the same fashion overhead.

"I do not believe they can force that too soon." There was satisfaction in his voice, but something else, such a spacing of words and slurring of them as I have heard in the voices of men who have been pushed very close to the edge of endurance in both body and spirit.

"Kaththea?" he called. I could not see him in the dark.

"I am here." I answered swiftly for it seemed to me that this was a call for either reassurance or aid. It astonished me greatly—unless the battle he had waged for his freedom, and incidently ours, had truly exhausted him.

"We . . . must . . . reach . . . the . . . surface—" The hesitation, the slurring were stronger. And I could now hear heaving breath, a rasping as a man might make after he had just climbed a steep rise at his best speed. I put out my hand, touched firm, warm flesh, and felt my fingers taken into a grasp which was not strong, but which held. Straightaway I sensed a draining from me into him.

"No!" I would have broken that hold but, weak as it seemed to be, there was no loosing of my fingers.

"Yes, and yes!" There was more energy in his denial. "My little sorceress, we are not yet out of this pit, and perhaps our first skirmish was the least of those to be faced. I must have what you can give me, as I do not think you could carry me if you would. Nor do you know the pitfalls herein as I do; remember I have been an unwilling part of them. I have been too many ages pent within that prison to be as able on my feet, or as fast as a master swordsman. You will give me what I need, if you truly wish to be free of Zandur."

"But the machines—the fires—" I drew upon what had happened in the chamber to add to my stubborn resistance.

"No worse hit than they have been many times before. There are fast methods of repair, and Zandur will have already put those into action. Remember, this place was made to wage war, such a war as I do not believe you have dreamed of, my lady sorceress. For it is not a war those of our blood have ever seen. This place has many defenses and most of them shall now be turned on us, as speedily as Zandur can make the repairs to activate them. So give me of your strength and let us hurry."

Then I, recalling that long descent which I had made, wondered if we could reclimb it. Ayllia came willingly enough, but as at first, she must be led. I did not try to control her mind again.

"Let him have what he now needs," my mother's thought rang in my head. "Feed, and we shall feed you! He speaks the truth: time now marches, heavily armed, against us all!"

So I let my hand remain in his grasp as we went on down that dark way, and felt the energy flow out, to be soaked up by him as a sponge soaks up water. But into me came what Jaelithe and Simon released to my aid, so that I was not drained as I might well have been. Again I wondered whether, had that not been so, Hilarion would have indeed plundered me, and then what he would have done with Ayllia and myself. My distrust of him grew the stronger.

We reached the foot of the long climb, but the adept did not turn to the stair. Instead, in the half-light (for there was no moon above, rather a clouded sky, very far away, gray and forbidding), he again raised the wand, pointed it at that part of the well which seemed to be cut by a half cap.

As slowly as the doorway had obeyed him, so did that segment begin to descend, and I recognized it as the platform which ferried the vehicles up and down. But it moved very slowly, and, though he said nothing, I knew that Hilarion was disquieted. He turned his head now and then as if listening. I could hear a humming, feel a vibration such as I had heard and felt in the tower. But of the clamor we had left behind there was no whisper, nor could I hear anything moving after us. I was afire to be away, and would even have attempted the curve of the stair had not a dependence upon the superior knowledge of Hilarion and the guess that he chose now the best and easiest way, kept me where I was.

The platform finally reached the bottom and we three scrambled onto it. Then it began to rise again, this time more swiftly than it had descended, and I felt a small relief. Once we were in the open we might be able to use the broken nature of the land as a cover for our escape—if we could cross the basin fast enough.

But we were not to reach the surface. We were still well below the point of possible leap or climb when the platform stopped. For a very short space I believed that halt only temporary. Then I saw Hilarion pointing his wand to the center of the surface beneath our feet. Only this time the spark of blue from its tip was gone before it touched. He tried again and the effort he made was visible. Yet the quickly dead flash did us no service. At last he turned to me.

"There is a choice left us," he said, his face expressionless. "And it is one I shall make. I advise you to do the same."

"That being?"

"Leap." He pointed into the well. "Better that than be taken alive."

"You can do nothing?"

"I told you, there are strong defenses here. We are now trapped, to await Zandur's pleasure as surely as if he had put his force fields about us. Leap now— before he does do just that!"

Having said this Hilarion moved to carry into action exactly what he had suggested. But I caught at him and such was the drain which exhausted him that, though he was the larger and normally stronger, he swayed in my hold and nearly fell, as if my touch had been enough to destroy his balance.

"No!" I shouted.

"I tell you yes! I will not be his thing again!"

But my call had already gone forth and I was answered.

"The help I promised—it comes," I told him, dragging him back to the center of the platform. "There are those who bring us aid."

Though at that moment I could not have told what manner of aid came with my parents; I only had confidence that they would have it to give.

"This is folly." His head dropped forward on his breast; he lurched against me as if at that moment the last drop of his strength had run from him. I was borne to the floor under the limp weight of his body. So I sat there, Ayllia dropping down beside me, Hilarion resting against my arm and shoulder. And I stared up at the rim of the well, tantalizingly out of reach, waiting for the coming of the two who sought us.

What outer defenses Zandur might have I did not know, and I began to fear that perhaps they were too many for any quick rescue. It could well be that

Hilarion would be proved right and his solution, grim though it was, was the better one. As my mother said, time was our enemy.

And time, as it has a way of doing in moments of great stress, walked or crept on leaden feet as I watched that rim and waited. I listened, too, for sounds from below. And I watched the wall in quick sideward glances to mark whether we might be descending on some order from Zandur. To lose what distance we had gained might mean we had lost all.

Then I marked movement above. I waited in fear to learn who or what leaned over there to view us. The light was less dim than it had been. Perhaps we had come here at dawn and the day now advanced. So I at last saw what dangled toward us from above, striking the wall with a sharp metallic clink that I longed to order to silence lest it alert some lurker below.

When it came a little lower I saw it was a chain ladder such as had been in use in the transport cavern. And, as it touched full upon the platform, my mother's mind send reached me.

"Up, and speedily!"

"Ayllia—" First I turned my mind control on her. She rose and went to the ladder without question, began to climb.

"Well enough!" my mother applauded. "Now, hold to the adept."

That I was already doing, but now I felt that inflow and outflow. This time it was not my own strength being so drained, but that which came from the two aloft. Hilarion struggled out of my hold, got slowly to his feet.

"The ladder—" I guided him to it. But once his hands closed on it he took on new life and, as Ayllia, he climbed, steadily, if more slowly than my impatience wanted to see him go.

As soon as he was well above my head I put my own feet and hands to use. I could only trust that the chain would support the weight of the three of us at once, for Ayllia, though continuing to move, was still well below the rim.

"Hold well!" My mother's command came for the third time and I held. Now the ladder moved under me, not me over it, as if that tough but slender strand to which we all clung was being hoisted.

There sounded a grating noise from below. I looked down, startled, at the shadow which was the platform. Surely we were not ascending that swiftly? No, the platform was sinking, down into the depths where Zandur's forces doubtlessly waited. We had left it just in time.

Up and up we went. I soon found it better not to look up, and surely not down, but to cling as tightly as I could to that swinging support and hope it would hold for time that was a measurement to lessen my fear. Thus it was that we came at last, one by one, into a gray and clouded day.

And for the first time in so long I looked upon those two from whose union I had come. My mother was as she had appeared in my mind picture, but Simon of Tregarth was so long lost in the past I had half forgotten him. He was there beside her, his head bare of helm, but about his shoulders the mail of Estcarp. He, too, had not aged beyond early middle life, yet there was a thin veil over his features which could be read as much weariness and endurance under great and punishing odds. He had the black hair of the Old Race, but his features were not the regular ones of inbreeding you saw in those men, being blunter, a little heavier. And his eyes were strange—to me—startling when he opened them wide to look intently upon one. As he did at me now.

It was a constrained meeting between the three of us. Though these were my mother and father, as a child I had never been close to either. Caught up as they had been in the duties of border guardians, they had spent little time with us. Then, too, our triple birth had prostrated our mother for a long time, and, Kemoc had once said, that had earned us our father's dislike. Therefore, while our mother lay fingering the final curtain, not sure whether or not she would lift it to go beyond, he had not been able to look upon us at all.

Anghart of the Falconers had been our mother by care, not Jaelithe Tregarth. So that now I felt strange and removed from these, not racing to open my heart and my arms to embrace them.

But it would seem that it was not in their minds to make such gestures either, or so I then thought. My father raised one hand in a kind of salute, which straightaway altered into a gesture beckoning us all on to where stood one of those crawling machines which I had seen moving toward the towers.

"In!" he urged us, stopping only to coil together the ladder and carry it over his shoulder as he shepherded us before him. There was a door gaping in the side of the box and we scrambled in.

The interior was indeed cramped quarters. My father slammed the door and pushed past us to take his seat at the front behind such a bank of levers as I had seen under the screens below. There was a second place to his right, and in that my mother settled. But she turned halfway around to face the three of us where we sat upon the floor.

"We must get away fast," she said. "Kaththea, and you, Hilarion, link with me. It will be necessary to maintain the best illusion we can lest we pull pursuit after us before we dare to turn and fight."

In the half-light of that small chamber I saw Hilarion nod. Then he gripped his wand by one end, allowed the other to touch the back of Jaelithe's seat. His left hand he put across Ayllia to me and I grasped it.

As we had linked, Simon, Jaelithe and I, so now did the four of us combine when my mother put the fingers of one hand on my father's arm. And our minds came together with one purpose, though for Hilarion and myself it was merely a lending of thought force to be molded and used by those other two as they saw best. I do not know what they wrought outside our crawling box, but at least no attack came. I guessed that perhaps they had chosen to produce a simulation of our machine headed in another direction.

There was a screen set before the two seats at the front, and on this appeared a picture of the basin over which we traveled, so that while the window slits were too narrow to see through, the outer world was thus made plain to us.

I had been so intent upon what lay before me when I had tracked Ayllia hither that I had not noted much of the country. But I could see on the screen the crunched tracks of the transports that had gone out from the well and returned to it. We soon veered from that course, heading at an angle over ground which was not so marked. Would we not then leave tracks doubly easy to follow? one part of my brain questioned as I bent my energy to supplying what was needed for the weaving of the hallucination.

My father had a reputation for being a wily and resourceful fighter, a leader of forlorn hopes which usually ended in success, as he had gone up against the Kolder to bring an end to them. One must have confidence now that he knew what he was doing, even though it seemed errant folly to the onlooker.

Ayllia had lapsed into the same sleep or loss of consciousness which had held her in the underground, lying inert between Hilarion and myself. The adept sat with his back against the wall of the cabin. His eyes were closed and there were signs of strain on his face, even as they were painted upon my father's. But his hold upon the wand, his grip on my hand, were firm and steady.

That we could depend upon his aid as long as we were in this haunted land I was certain, for failure would mean an even worse fate for him if we were taken. But what if he did activate the gate again and we won back into Escore? Could it be that his return would then bring upon my brothers and the people of the Valley such danger as they could not stand against?

I had no globe of crystal for foreseeing, nor had I Utta's board to summon the *possible* future—for no one can see the future exactly so and say this and this shall be. There are many factors which can change, so one can see a possible future and perhaps alter it thereafter by some action of one's own.

But I determined that I must speak in private with my mother, not trusting mind speech, which Hilarion could easily tap. And I would beg her aid and that of my father to make sure we did not bring new danger through the gate—always supposing that Hilarion *could* find and unlock it once more for us. I did not believe that I could find the place where we first burst into this world (unless by some concentration it could be traced by a mind search—such troublings of the fabric of time and space ought to leave a "scent" which the talented could perceive).

It was not an easy ride in that box, for once we crept from the basin there was a jolting, a slipping, a sickening up and down swing of the floor under us. Meanwhile, we were deafened by a throb which marked the life of the thing, and the acrid air of this world was rendered even worse to our nostrils by fumes which gathered in our close quarters. But all these discomforts we had to ignore, concentrating only on supplying the energy necessary to provide our flight with what cover we managed to maintain.

The screen now showed again those remnants of ancient buildings which ringed the basin. They were even more noticeable on this portion of the rim than they had been where I came in. Truly this must have been a city of such size that Kars or Es would have been swallowed up in one small district.

We followed a weaving path, keeping to what lower and clearer ground was visible. Our pace could not be any faster than a man's swift walk. I thought we might make a better escape if we trusted to our own feet and not to this stinking box which swayed and rumbled over the blasted ground.

Then, suddenly, we ground to a stop. And a moment later I saw what must have alerted my father, movement on the top of a crumbled wall. Not a man, no, but a black tube which now centered its open core upon us. My father stood on his seat, his boots planted firmly, his head and shoulders disappearing into an opening directly above. What he did there I could not guess, until fire crackled across the screen, struck full upon that tube. Under that lash of flame the tube was no longer black; it began to glow, first dull red, then brighter and brighter.

After that our weapon began a wide sweep over the ground from side to side as far as we could see on the screen. And it was several long minutes before my father settled back at the controls.

"Automatic weapon," he said. "No hallucination can confuse that. It was set, I think, to fire at any moving thing which did not answer some code."

In the world in which he was born my father had known such weapons, and it would seem that in this nightmare country he was fitted to conduct such an alien type of war.

"There are more?" asked my mother.

I heard my father laugh grimly. "Were there any around here we would know it by now. But that there are more between us and open land I do not doubt in the least."

On we crawled and now I watched the screen for the least hint of movement which would mark the alerting of another metal sentry. Two more we found and destroyed in a like manner, or rather my father so destroyed them. Then we left behind the traces of that forgotten city and crawled into the open country he sought, where that ashy ground was broken only here and there by the withered vegetation which seemed either dead or filled with loathsome life.

Our journey appeared to continue forever. And the cloudy sky began to darken. Also, I was hungry and thirsty, and the supplies which I had drawn upon in the caverns had been left behind in our dash for freedom.

At length we stopped and my mother shared out some sips of water and a dried meat with a bad smell. One could chew and swallow it, and hope it would mean strength and nourishment. My father leaned back in his seat, his hands resting on the edge of the control board, a gray tiredness in his face. Still he watched the screen as if there were never to be any relief from vigilance.

My mother spoke to Hilarion. "We seek your gate," she said straightly. "Can it be found?"

He had raised a water container to his lips; now he made a lengthy business of swallowing, as if he needed that extra time for thought or to make some decision. When he spoke he did not answer her but voiced a question of his own: "You are a Wise Woman?"

"Once, before I chose to take another path." She had turned as far as she could in her seat that she might see him the better.

"But you did not so lose what you had had." This time it was no question but a statement of fact.

"I gained more!" My mother's voice held pride and a kind of triumph.

"Being who you are," Hilarion continued deliberately, "you understand the nature of the gates."

"Yes—and I also know that you created the one we seek. Indeed, we have long been hunting you, having some small hint you were where you were. But they kept you lapped in something hostile to our seeking so we could not speak with you—until Kaththea reached you and so opened a channel of mind seeking between us. Having created the gate you can control it."

"Can I? That I shall not know until I try. Once I would have said yes, but I have been warped by that which is alien to my own learning. Perhaps it has twisted me so askew that I cannot again summon the true Power to answer me."

"That rests on one side of the scales," agreed Jaelithe. "But we do not know what lies upon the other until we set to the weighing. You were truly adept or you would not have made the gate. That you have been a prisoner to other purposes is your bane; it need not be your end. Can you take us to your gate?"

His eyes dropped from hers to the wand, and he turned it about with the fingers of both hands, looking upon it as if he now held some new and totally strange thing he did not recognize.

"Even that," he said in a low voice, "I cannot be sure of now. But I know this much, that I cannot have a guide to follow if I remain in this machine: the taint of the other is too strong and able to warp what I would try."

"Yet if we leave it"—my father for the first time took part in that exchange— "we go out as men naked to a storm. This has defenses enough to provide us with a moving fortress."

"You asked me," Hilarion returned in sharp impatience, "and I have told you the truth. If you want your gate we must be away from this box and all it stands for!"

"Can you go forth a little," I began, "and do what must be done to find the direction, then return?"

Both my father and mother looked at Hilarion. He continued to slip the wand back and forth for a long moment of silence but at length he answered.

"There can be but a trial to see. . . ." There was such hesitation in his voice, such weariness there, that I thought that any seeking of that nature would be a task he must force himself to. Yet a moment later he asked, this time speaking directly to my father, "If you name this country safe as you can see it, there is no better time for my efforts. We cannot wait and hope and let Zandur loose his might on our tail. Also, those of the tower have their own brand of terror when dealing with aught walking the surface here. And since you travel in this thing which is of Zandur's people, their air scouts will be ready to use lightning against us if they sight it."

So it was that we came forth from the crawler into the darkening night and stood looking about us at the desolation which was the countryside here.

XV

*T*he bare bones of this land, which was all that was left, were stark under a night sky. And the moon, so bright and full when I had come into the basin, was now on the wane. Yet it gave enough light for us to see what was immediately about us. My father waved an order to stay where we were for the time being while he flitted—I can find no words to really describe his swift movements—blended with the landscape, spiraling away from the halted vehicle. And I realized that he now put into use the training of a border scout. He had disappeared when my mother spoke.

"There is no danger close by. Which way?" This she asked of Hilarion.

He lifted his head; I thought I almost saw his nostrils expand as might a hound's testing scent. Then he raised the wand, setting its tip to his forehead midpoint between his eyes, which were closed, as if he must see the better inwardly instead of outwardly.

The wand swung, pointing to the right from where we stood. When he opened his eyes again there was a spark of new life in them.

"That way!" So certain was his pronouncement that we did not doubt he had managed to find us a guide through this ash-strewn wilderness.

When my father returned, which he did shortly (I think in answer to some mind search call from my mother, not within my range), he studied the direction Hilarion's wand had indicated and then, within the crawler, made adjustments to the board of controls.

But we did not set out at once, taking rather a rest period, with one of us, turn about, on guard. I slept dreamlessly. When I awoke the moon had vanished, but so clouded was the sky that the light was that of dusk. Once more we ate and drank sparingly from our scanty stores. And my father said that he was sure that we had not been seen in any way, especially as the mechanical sentries of the crawler machine also registered naught.

We crept on, now following the path Hilarion had set us. But within the hour my father turned the nose of the machine abruptly and, at a rocking pace we had not used since we left the basin, sent it under a ledge, or at least most of it into that protection. There came a loud buzzing from the controls until he swept his hand down, hastily thumbing buttons and levers. The throb of life stilled, we sat in silence unable even to see much, for the screen now displayed only the bare rock of the crevice into which we were jammed.

My father's back was rigid and he did not turn to offer any explanation, only stared at the controls. I feared some danger he thought beyond his ability to counter. And I found myself listening, though for what I had no idea.

It was Hilarion who moved as if to ease his long body, cramped in the inadequate space beyond the still sleeping Ayllia.

"The tower people." He did not ask that as a question but made it a statement of fact.

"One of their flyers," agreed my father.

"This machine," Hilarion continued, "it answers you easily, yet she"—he pointed with his chin to my mother, not loosing his grip on the wand—"is of the Old Race and those love not machines. . . ."

"I am not of Estcarp," my father answered. "Gates upon gates seem to tie worlds together. I entered through such a one into Estcarp. And in my own time and place I was a fighting man who used such machines—though not exactly like this one. We found this on the shore of the sea when first we came here through a gate which would not open to us again. And since then it has been our fortress."

"Only if you keep away from the towers," Hilarion commented. "For how long have you roamed so, hunting a gate to take you back?"

Simon shrugged. "The days we had numbered, but it would seem that time here does not march at the same pace as it does in Estcarp."

"How so?" Hilarion was surprised. How much more stunned would he be when he discovered just how many years had passed in Escore if or when we returned?

"I left a daughter who was a child," my father said, and he turned to smile directly at me, shyly, ill at ease, but somehow as a plea, "and now I face a grown woman who has gone her own way to some purpose."

Hilarion looked to me, more surprise in that glance, before he stared again at Simon and my mother.

Jaelithe nodded as if she were answering some unvoiced question.

"Kaththea is our daughter. Though we have long been apart. And"—now she spoke to me—"it would seem much has happened."

I must pick and choose my words well, I thought. To tell them of what had chanced in Estcarp and perhaps somewhat in Escore, that I could do. But while

I distrusted Hilarion, and there was no chance to talk apart with my parents, I must speak with care.

Now I told them of what had chanced with the three of us after Jaelithe had gone seeking my father—of my own taking by the Wise Women and the years spent in the Place of Silence. Then of that last blow which the witches of Estcarp aimed at Karsten, and of how Kyllan and Kemoc had come to free me and of our escape into Escore. Thereafter I did not change the truth, I only told part of it— that we had come into a land which was also under the cloud of an ancient war, and that we had united there with those akin to us in spirit, though I mentioned no names or places.

My own misfortunes I dealt with as best I could, saying mainly that I had been ensorceled by one deceiving us and had headed back to Estcarp for treatment. Thereafter I spoke of the Vupsall and of the raiders, and lastly of how Ayllia and I had come to the citadel on the cape and of our passing through the gate.

I dared not use mind touch, even to let my mother know there was more which should be known between us. But something in her eyes as they met mine told me that she had guessed it was so and when opportunity arose we would speak of it.

Mostly I feared that Hilarion might be one to turn on me with questions of how Escore had fared since his leaving there. But strangely enough he did not. Then I began to see in that abstraction a suspicious silence, and I liked even less the thought of his return, though without him we could not go either.

When I had done my father sighed. "It would seem that indeed our carefully numbered days here are not to be trusted. So Karsten is now behind a barrier and the Wise Women brought themselves to naught in so building it. Who then rules?"

"Koris, by our last hearing, though he suffered an ill wound in the latter days of the war—so that he no longer carries Volt's ax."

"Volt's ax," my father repeated as one who remembers many things. "Volt's abiding place and the ax . . . . Those were brave days. Their like will not come again for us, I believe. But if Karsten lies low, what of Alizon?"

"It is said by those who have come to join Kyllan," I told him, "that Alizon, having seen what chanced with Karsten, walks small these days."

"Which will last only for years enough to match my fingers." He held out his right hand. "And then they shall think big and begin to rattle swords out of sheaths again. Koris may rule, and well will he do so, but he can also do with old friends at his back or right hand. And if he holds not Volt's ax, he shall need them even more."

As well as if I could read his mind I knew my father's thought. Though he was not of the Old Race born, yet by will he had become one of them. And between him and Koris of Gorm there was a strong tie forged by blood and sweat during the struggle with the Kolder. He willed with all his might now to ride once more into Es City and be there at his friend's need.

"Yes," agreed my mother. "But before we ride west to Es, we must be in the same world."

So she summoned us back to the matter at hand. My father shook his head, not in denial, but as if to thrust away thoughts which were now a hindrance. Then he looked at the control board, seeming to read plainly there what was a puzzle in my sight.

He asked of Hilarion, "Have you any knowledge of how far we are from your gate?"

"This will tell." Hilarion spun the wand between his fingers. "We have yet some distance before us. And what of your flyer?"

"It is going." Once more my father's attention was for the board. "We can travel as soon as the alarm ceases."

It was indeed not long before the crawler backed out of the pocket in which my father had set it. Then it trundled on its way and all we saw was the unchanging bleakness of this world.

This was a place of dunes and hillocks and we were forced to pick a roundabout way among them; our view of what might lie ahead was thus foreshortened. But my father had other warnings built into this machine and upon those we depended.

It seemed long, that night during which we bumped along until our bodies were as one huge bruise, though in the seats my mother and father fared a little better. Then we pulled to another rest stop and Hilarion thereafter took my mother's seat, as the wand now showed that we were not too far from our goal. Jaelithe came to sit beside Ayllia. We had been able to dribble water into the girl's mouth, but she had not eaten since she and I had divided our supply in the corridor of the tower city, and I wondered how much longer she could exist. My mother reassured me that, remaining in this unconscious state as she had for so long, her body had less demands.

We lost the crawler up a ridge, teetered there for a minute, and began a downward slip. I heard my father give a shouted exclamation and saw his hands move quickly on the controls. The screen showed us what lay ahead—one of those black ribbon roads. And we were sliding straight for it as my father fought to halt our precipitous descent.

He managed to turn the blunt nose of the vehicle sharply left so we skidded to a stop pointing in that direction parallel to the road. I heard what I was sure was his sigh of relief as we came to rest without touching the pavement.

"What now?" But he might be asking that of someone or something beyond our own company.

"That way!" Hilarion squirmed impatiently in his seat, pointing the wand directly across the highway.

My father laughed harshly. "That takes some considering. We cannot cross in this—not and want it to be of service thereafter."

"Why?" Hilarion's impatience was stronger, as if, so close to the goal, he would not be gainsaid in making a straight line to reach it.

"Because that is no ordinary roadway," my father returned. "It is rather a force broadcast meant to keep the tower transports in motion. This tank was never designed to touch it. I do not know what will happen if we crawl out upon it, but I do not think that it would survive such a journey."

"Then what do we do? Seek a bridge?" demanded Hilarion.

"We have no promise any exists," my father answered bleakly. "And to hunt a bypass or overpass may take us many leagues out of our way." He turned away from the screen to look directly to the adept. "Have you any knowledge of how close you now are to the gate site?"

"Perhaps a league, or less. . . ."

"There is a chance—" my father began hesitatingly, as if while he spoke he was measuring in his mind one ill against another and trying to assess which was the least. "We might perhaps use this tank as a bridge. But if it fails, and leaves us caught midway . . ." Now he shook his head a little.

"I think, Simon," my mother broke in, "that we have little choice. If we seek a way around there may be none, and we shall only be putting such a length of journey between us and the gate as will defeat us. If this half plan of yours has any merit at all, then we must prove it here and now."

He did not answer her at once, but sat looking to the screen as one studying a weighty problem. Then he said, "I can promise you no better odds than if you throw the tip-cones with Lothur."

My mother laughed. "Ah, but I have seen you do that very thing, Simon, and thereafter, having made your wager, take up two handfuls of round pieces from the board! Life is full of challenges and one may not sidestep even the worst of them, as we well know."

"Very well. I do not know the nature of this force but I think that it flows as a current. We must set the controls and hope for the best."

But there were more preparations for us to make. Under my father's orders, we climbed out of the crawler, taking Ayllia with us; and then we loaded into that small section where we had crouched as passengers, and into the seats in front, all the loose rocks we could gouge from the ground about us, setting such a weight in the interior as would give the vehicle some anchorage against any flow of force. My father brought forth the chain rope which had aided us out of the well. With that we made handholds on the flat roof of the crawler, taking with us what was left of our supplies and water. Once we were all atop, save for my father, he entered the cabin, crawling through the small space he had left for that purpose. Under us the machine came to life, edged back and around to once more face the road directly. It was partly upslope, tilted toward the black surface on which my father read such danger.

As it began to crawl and slide down again, my father swung out and up to join us. He had been right in his foreboding. As the heavy vehicle rammed out onto that surface it was struck with an impact like the anger of a mighty river current, half turned from its course.

Would it be entirely turned, bearing us, as helpless prisoners on and on to the towers this road served? Or would the power my father had activated win across for us? I lay grasping the rope until its links bit painfully into my flesh, while under me the machine trembled and fought. It traveled at an angle to the right, but it still had not been sucked into the complete turn which would mean disaster. I could not be sure that we were still making any progress toward the other side.

We had already been swept on, well away from the point where we had entered. And what would happen if one of the transports for the towers came down upon us? So vivid was the picture of that in my mind that I fought to blank it out, and so perhaps missed the turning point of our battle.

I was suddenly aware of the fact that my father was no longer stretched flat beside me, but was on his knees freeing the packs of supplies. With a quick toss he hurled them both to his left so that, raising my head, I saw them strike the ground beyond the road, on the side we wished to reach. Then his hand gripped my shoulder tightly.

"Loose your hold!" he ordered. "When I give the word—jump!"

I could see no hope of success. But this was a time when one must place faith in another, and I struggled with my fear long enough to indeed loose my frantic hold and rise to my knees, then, with my father's hand drawing me up, to my feet. I glanced around to see my mother and Hilarion also standing, Ayllia between them, stirring as if awaking.

"Jump!"

I forced my unwilling body to that effort, not daring to think of what my landing beyond might mean. But luckily I struck on the edge of a dune of ash-sand and, while I sank well into it, I was uninjured, able to struggle out, spitting the stuff from between my lips, smearing it out of my eyes and nostrils.

By the time I was free of it and able to see, I marked other dust-covered figures arising from similiar mounds. And, as I stumbled toward them, I discovered we were no worse off than bruises, choked throats and grit-tormented eyes.

But the tank had now been turned wholly about, caught tight in the mid-current, and was fast disappearing from our sight, whirling on to the distant goal of the towers.

We slipped and slid back through the dunes to find and dig out the supply packs. Then Hilarion took out the wand which he had stowed in his tunic for safekeeping. Once more he held it to his forehead.

"There!" He pointed into the very heart of the dune country.

Ayllia was walking, though it was needful to hold her by the hand, and I knew my mother had taken over her mind to some extent. This was a burden on Jaelithe, so that I straightaway joined with her in that needful action.

Footing in the shifting ash-sand was very bad. Sometimes we waded in the powdery stuff almost knee-deep. And the dunes all looked so much alike that without Hilarion's wand we might have been lost as soon as we left the side of the road, to wander heedlessly.

But all at once I saw something tall and firm loom up and I recognized it as one of the metal pillars which I had seen when we entered through the gate. With that in sight part of my fears were lost. Only, would Hilarion really *know* when we reached the proper spot? There had been no marking on this side that I had been able to perceive.

However, our guide appeared to have no doubts at all. He led us in a twisting hard-to-travel path, but always he came back to the way the wand pointed. At last we stood at the base of another of those pitted pillars. I could not be sure, for there was a terrible sameness to this country, but I thought that we had indeed reached the place we had first entered.

"Here." Hilarion was certain. He faced what seemed to me merely air full of dust (for a breeze had arisen to blow up whirls of acrid powder).

"No marker," commented my father. But my mother, shielding her eyes with her hands half cupped about them, stared as intently ahead as the adept.

"There is something there," she conceded, "A troubling—"

Hilarion might not have heard her. He was using the wand in quick strokes, as an artist might paint a scene with a brush, moving it up and down and around, to outline a portal.

And in its track the dust in the wind (or was it dust? I could not be sure) left faint lines in the air following the path of the wand tip. This outlined an oblong which was center crossed by two lines each of which ran from the two upper corners to the two lower ones. In the four spaces thus quartered off the wand tip was now setting symbols. Two of these I knew—or at least I knew ones like them, as if those I learned had somewhat changed shape in time.

The others were new however, as was the last, drawn larger to cross all the rest. When Hilarion dropped his wand we could see what he had wrought, misty and faint, yet remaining steadfast in spite of the rising wind and swirling sand.

Now he began again, retracing each and every part of that airborne drawing. This time that wispy series of lines glowed with color, green first, darkening into vivid blue—so that once again I saw the "safe" color I had known in Escore. But that color did not hold and before he had quite completed the entire pattern the first of it was fading, as a dying fire leaves gray-coated coals behind.

I saw his face and there was a grimness about it, a set to his mouth as you may see on a man facing odds which will try him to the dregs of his strength. Once more he began the tracing, with the color responding to the passing of his wand. A second time it faded into ashiness.

Then my mother moved. To me she held out one hand, to my father the other. So linked physically we linked minds also. And that energy which was born of our linking she sent to Hilarion so that he glanced at her once, startled, I think, and then raised the wand for the third time and began again that intricate tracery of line and symbol.

I could feel the pull upon my power, yet I held steady and gave of it as my mother demanded. This time I saw that there was no fading, the green-blue held, glowing the brighter. When Hilarion once more lowered his wand it was a brilliant, pulsating thing hanging in the air a foot or so above the sand. Around it the wind no longer blew, though elsewhere it spread a murky, dust-filled veil.

For a moment Hilarion surveyed his creation critically, I thought, as if he must make sure it was what he wanted, having no flaw. Then he took two steps forward, saying as he went, though he did not look back at us: "We must go—now!"

We broke linkage and my mother and I snatched up our packs, while my father gathered up Ayllia. Hilarion put wand tip to the midpoint of those crossed lines on the door, as one would set a key in a lock. And it opened—I saw him disappear through. I followed, my mother on my heels, my father behind us. Again was that terrible wrenching of space and time, and then I rolled across the hard stone of pavement and sat up, blinking with pain from a knock of my head against some immovable object.

I was resting with my back against the chair which had dominated the hall of the citadel. And the glow of the gate was the only bright thing in that room where time had gathered as a dusk.

Someone near me stirred; I turned my head a little. Hilarion stood there, his wand in his hands. But he was not looking toward the gate through which we had just come, rather from one side of the long hall to the other. I do not know what he had expected to see there, perhaps some multitude of guards or servitors, or members of his household. But what or who he missed, that emptiness had come as a shock.

His hand went to his forehead and he swayed a little. Then be began to walk away from the chair, back into the hall along the wall, walking as someone who must speedily find that which he sought or else face true fear.

As he went so I felt a lightening of my inner unease, for it was plain he had no thought of us now—he was caught in his own concerns. And what better chance would we have for a parting of the ways?

So, in spite of the wave of dizziness which made me sway and clutch at the arm of the chair, I somehow got to my feet, looking around eagerly for the rest of our party. My father was already standing, Ayllia lying before him. He stepped over her body to join hands with my mother, pulled her up to stand with his arms about her, the two of them so knit together that they might indeed be one body and spirit.

Something in the way they stood there, so enclosed for this moment in a world of their own, gave me pause. A chill wind blew for a single instant out of time, to make me shiver. I wondered what it would be like to have such a oneness with another. Kyllan—perhaps this is what he knew with Dahaun, and this was what Kemoc had found with Orsya. Had I unconsciously reached for it when I went to Dinzil, to discover in the end that what *he* wanted was not me, Kaththea the maid, but rather Kaththea the witch, to lend her power to his reaching ambition? And I also learned, looking upon those two and the world they held about them, that I was not enough of a witch to put the Power above all else. Yet that might well be all which lay before me in this life.

There was no time for such seeking and searching of thought and spirit. We needed to be aware of the here and now, and take precautions accordingly. I stood away from the supporting chair to waver over to my parents.

XVI

*P*lease—" I felt shy, an intruder, as I spoke softly, for I feared that my words might resound through that hall, perhaps awaken Hilarion from his preoccupation and bring him back too soon.

My mother turned her head to look at me. Perhaps there was that in my expression which held a warning, for I saw a new alertness in her eyes.

"You are afraid. Of what, my daughter?"

"Of Hilarion." I gave her the truth. Now I had my father's full attention as well. Though he still had his arm about my mother's shoulders his other hand went to his belt as if seeking a weapon hilt.

"Listen." I spoke in whispers, not daring to use mind touch—such might be as a gong in a place so steeped in sorcery.

"I told you part of the tale, but not all. Escore is rent, has long been rent by warring sorcery. Most of those who wrought this have either been swallowed up in the darkness they summoned, or else have gone through gates such as this into other times and places. But it was they who started this trouble in times far past, and upon them rests the blame for it. We do not know all concerning Hilarion. It is true that I do not believe him to a master of darkness, for he could not control the blue fire were he such. But there were those here who followed neither good nor ill, but had such curiosity that they worked ill merely in search of new learning. Now we battle for the life of Escore . . . and I had a hand in reviving this old war when I unknowingly worked magic to trouble an uneasy old balance. Also, I did other damage and that not too long since. I will not have a third burden to bear, that I brought back one of the adepts to meddle and perhaps wreck all that my brothers and our sworn comrades have fought to hold.

"Hilarion knows far too much to be loosed here and taken to the Valley. I must learn more of him before we swear any shield oath for his company."

"We have a wise daughter," commented my mother. "Now tell us, and quickly, all you did not say before."

And that I did, leaving out nothing of my own part in Dinzil's plans and of what came of that. When I had done my mother nodded.

"Well can I understand why you find this Hilarion suspect. But . . ." Her face had a listening look, and I knew that she was using then a tendril of mind search to find him.

"So—" Her gaze from looking inward was turned outward and we had her attention again. "I do not think we need fear his concern with us, not for awhile. Time must be far different between this world and that other. Even more so than we had guessed. He seeks that which is so long gone even the years themselves have lost their names and places on the roll of history! Because he must believe this is so, he is now lost in his own need for understanding. Ah, it is a hard thing to see one's world swept away and lost, even while one still treads familiar earth. I wonder whether— Do you really believe, my daughter, that Hilarion can be so great a menace to what you must cherish?"

And I, remembering Dinzil, crushed down any doubts and said yes. But it would seem that my mother was not yet fully convinced. For, at that moment, she opened a mind send between us that I might read, though maybe only in part, what she had learned from Hilarion. And the pain and desolation of that sharing was such that I flinched in body as well as mind, to cry out that I did not want to know any more.

"You see," she said as she freed me, "he has his own thoughts to occupy him now and those are not such as we can easily disturb. If we would go—"

"Then let us do it now!" For in me arose such a desire to be out of this place which was Hilarion's, and away from all thought of him (if I could so close my mind on part of the past), that I wanted to turn and run as if rasti or the Gray Ones hunted behind.

But though we did go it was at a more sober pace, for we still had Ayllia with us. I began to think about her and what we would do with her. If the Vupsalls were still at the village perhaps we could awaken her sleeping mind and leave her nearby, maybe working some spell which would cloud the immediate past so she would not remember our journeying, save as a quickly fading dream. But if the raid had indeed put an end to the tribe I saw nothing else but that we must take her with us to the Valley wherein Dahaun and her people would give her refuge.

My father left one of the packs of food and water where it had fallen on the floor. But the other he shouldered, letting my mother and myself lead Ayllia. So we went out into the open. Then I, too, learned the surprises time can deal: I had entered here in the coldest grasp of winter, but I came out now into the warmth and sun of spring—the month of Chrysalis, still too early for the sowing of fields, and yet a time when the new blood and first joys of spring stir in one, bringing a kind of restlessness and inner excitement. Still, to my reckoning, I had only been away days, not weeks!

The snow, which had lain in pockets in this long deserted place, was long since gone. And several times our passing startled sunning lizards and small creatures, who either froze to watch us with round and wary eyes, or disappeared in an instant.

I was a little daunted by the maze of streets and ways before us, for I could not clearly remember how we had found our path through the citadel. And after twice following a false opening which brought us up to a wall, I voiced my doubts aloud.

"No way out?" asked my father. "You came in without hindrance, did you not?"

"Yes, but I was drawn by the Power." I tried not to remember each and every part of how Ayllia and I had come here. Looking back it seemed that our road had been very easy to find from the time we entered twixt those outer gates where the carved guardians gave tongue in the wind. This sprawl of passages and lanes I did not recall.

"Contrived?" I asked that aloud.

We had come to a halt before that last wall when an opening which seemed very promising had abruptly closed. About us were those houses with the blue stones above their doors, their windows empty and gaping, and something about them to chill the heart as winter winds chill the body.

"Hallucination?" my father wondered. "Deliberate by bespelling?"

My mother closed her eyes, and I knew she was cautiously using mind seek. Now I ventured to follow her, fearing always to touch a cord uniting us to Hilarion.

My mind perceived, when I loosed it, what the eyes did not. Simon Tregarth was right, that a film of sorcery lay over this place, erecting walls where there were none, leaving open spaces which were really filled. It was as if, upon closing our eyes, we could see another city set over the one which stood there before. The why of it I did not know, for this was no new spell set for our confounding by Hilarion; it was very old, so that it was oddly tattered and worn near to the first threads of its weaving.

"I see!" I heard my father's sharp comment and knew that he in turn had come to use the other sight. "So . . . we go this way—" A strong hand caught mine, even as with my other I held to Ayllia, and on the other side of the Vupsall girl my mother walked. Thus linked we began to defeat the spell of the city, going with our eyes closed to the light and the day, our minds tuned to that other sense which was our talent.

So we came to a street which sloped to the thick outer wall, and that I recognized as the one up which we had come on our flight before the raiders. Twice I opened my eyes, merely to test the continuance of the confusion spell, and both times I faced, not an open street, but a wall or part of a house. I hastened to drop my lids again and depend upon the other seeing.

One without such a gift could not have won through that sorcery as we discovered when we came at last to the gate. For within an arm's length of escape lay a body stark upon the ground, arms outflung as if to grasp for the freedom the eyes could not see. He had been a tall man and he wore body armor, over which thick braids of hair lay, while a horned helm was rolled a little beyond. We could not see his face, and for that I was glad.

"Sulcar!" My father leaned over the corpse but did not touch it.

"I do not think so, or else not of the breed we know," Jaelithe returned. "Rather one of your sea rovers, Kaththea."

As to that I could not swear for my glimpses of them on the night they had come to Vupsall had been most limited. But I thought her right.

"He has been dead some time." My father stood away. "Perhaps he trailed you here, Kaththea. It would seem that for him this trap worked."

But for us it failed and we passed through the wall, between the brazen beasts who would howl in the tempests. There we found signs that this was indeed a place others found awesome: set up was a stone slab, dragged, I thought, from the ruined village. And on it lay a tangle of things, perhaps once placed out in order and then despoiled by birds and beasts: a fur robe now stiff with driven sand and befouled by bird droppings, and plates of metal which might once have held food. Among all this was something my father reached for with a cry of excitement, a hard ax and a sword. He had never been more than an indifferent swordsman, though he had put much practice into the learning of that weapon's usage, swords not being used in his own world. To a warrior, however, any weapon, when his hands are empty, is a find to be treasured.

"Dead man's weapon," he said as he belted on that blade. "You know what they say—take up a dead man's weapons and you take on perhaps also his battle anger when you draw it."

I remembered then how Kemoc, when he came to seek me in Dinzil's Dark Tower, had found a sword in the deep hidden places of a long vanished race and had taken it, to serve us well. And I thought that since a man's hand reached instinctively for steel, one had better judge it for good instead of ill.

But my mother had taken something else from that offering table and stood with it in her two hands, gazing down into it with almost a shade of awe on her face.

"These raiders plied their looting in odd places," she said. "Of such as this I have heard, but I have not seen. Well did they treasure it enough to offer it to the demons they believed dwelt here!"

It was a cup fashioned, I think, of stone, in the form of two hands tight pressed together save for an open space at the top. But they were not altogether human hands: the fingers were very long and thin; the nails, which were inlaid with gleaming metal, very narrow and pointed. In color it was red-brown, very smooth and polished.

"What is it?" My curiosity was aroused.

"A mirror for looking, to be used as one does a crystal globe. But into this one pours water. I do not know how it came to this place, but it is such a thing as must not remain here for—Touch it, Kaththea."

She held it forth and I laid fingertip to it, only to cry out. I had touched, not cold stone as I expected, but warmth, near to the heat of a live firebrand. Yet my mother held it firmly and seemed not to feel that heat. Also from that light touch I felt an instant inflow of Power, so I knew it for one of the mighty things which could be as a weapon for us, even as the sword came naturally to my father's hold.

My mother pulled loose a wisp of tattered silk which also fluttered on the offering table and wrapped it about the cup, then she opened her tunic a little and stowed the bundle safely within. My father belted on the sword openly and also thrust the ax into that belt for good measure.

The finding of that pile of plunder outside the gates suggested one thing, that the raiders and not the village people had been the victors in that snowbound struggle. I was sure that the raiders had left this here; never had I seen the Vupsall willing to leave their treasures behind, save in the grave of Utta. Yet I must make sure Ayllia's people were gone before we left this place.

When I explained, my parents agreed. It was mid-morning now and the sun was warm, pleasantly so. As in the city, there were no pockets of snow left, and some early insects buzzed lazily; we heard the calls of mating birds.

Until we were well down the cape, setting foot on the mainland, I walked tensely, expecting at any moment to be contacted by Hilarion, to feel his summons, or his demand as to where we went and why. But now that we were back in the budding brush and in a world normal in sight and sound, a little of that strain ceased. I was still aware, however, that we might not be free of that companion I wanted least to see.

It was plain, when we scouted the village, that it was deserted, and not by the regular wandering of the tribe. The torn skins of the tent-roofs of those tumbled stone walls flapped here and there.

As scavengers in search of what we might find to make our journey westward easier, we went down into the ruins. I found the hut from which I had fled— when? Weeks, months earlier? To me that period was days only. The sea raiders had been here. Utta's chests had been dumped open on the floor, her herb packets torn, their contents mixed as if someone had stirred it into a perversely concocted mess.

My mother stooped to pick up a leaf, dry and brittle, here, a pinch of powder there, sniffing and discarding with a shake of her head. I looked for those rune rolls which had guided me to the citadel. But those were gone, perhaps snatched up as keys to some treasure. We did find, rolled into a far corner, a jar of the journey food of dried berries and smoked meat pressed together into hard cakes. And at the moment this meant more to us than any treasure.

Ayllia stood where we had left her by the outer door, nor did she seem to see what lay about her, or understand that we had returned to the village. My father went to hunt through the other tent-huts, but he was quickly back, motioning us to join him.

"A place of death," he told us bleakly. "One better left to them."

I had had no friends among the tribe, but rather had been their prisoner. Neither would I have willingly been their enemy, yet in part would these deaths always rest on my shoulders; they had trusted in my gift and I and it had failed them. My mother read my thoughts, and now her arm was about me as she said, "Not so, for you did not willfully deceive them, but did what you could to leave them to their own destiny. You were not Utta, nor could you be held to a choice which she forced upon you. Therefore, take not up a burden which is not yours. It is an ill of life for some that they feel blame lying upon them when it comes from an act of fate alone."

. . . Words which were meant to comfort and absolve and yet which, at that moment, were words only, though they did sink into my mind and later I remembered them.

We had no snow sleds with mighty hounds to drag them, nor real guide except that we knew what we sought lay to the west. But how many days' travel now lay between us and the Valley, and what number of dangers could lie in wait there was a guess I did not care to make as a challenge to fate.

I thought I could remember the way upriver and across country to the place of the hot stream. But my father shook his head when I outlined that journey, saying that if the hot stream valley was so well known to the nomads it was better we avoid it and instead strike directly west. This was thought best even though we could not make fast time on foot, especially with Ayllia, who walked to our control but must be cared for as a mindless, if biddable, child.

So we turned our backs upon the sea, and upon that cape with the citadel black and heavy between sea and sky when I gave a last glance northward to it. Our supplies were very few, the ill-tasting meat we had brought out of the ashy world, and the jar we had found in the village. At least there was no lack of water, for there were springs and streams throughout this land, all alive now in the spring, having thrown off their winter's coating of ice.

My father, picking up two rounded stones from the ground, fashioned an odd weapon such as I had never seen before, tying them together with a thong, and then swinging the whole about his head and letting it fly in practice at a bush.

There it struck and with the weight of the stones the cord wove around and around, to strip small buds from the twigs. He laughed and went to unwind it.

"I haven't lost that skill, it seems," he said. And a few minutes later he sent the stones winging again, not at a bush, but at an unwary grass dweller, one of the plump jumpers which are so stupid they are easily undone. Before we stopped for the night he had four such, to be roasted over a fire and eaten with the appetite which comes when one has been on sparse and distasteful rations for too long.

The warmer air of the day was gone. But after we had eaten we did not stay by the fire in spite of its comfort. My father fed it a final armload of the sticks he had gathered, and then led us to a place he had already marked for our night camp, well away from that beacon which might draw attention to our passing.

He had chosen a small copse where the winter storms had thrown down several trees, the largest landing so as to take several others with it and providing a mat of entangled limbs and trunks. In that he hacked out a nest, into which we crowded, pulling then a screen of brush down to give both roof and wall to our hiding place.

I wished we had some of the herbs from Utta's store, but those had been so intermingled by the raiders that I could not have sorted out what was needed most. So the spell barrier they might have given us was lost.

But my mother took from her belt a piece of metal which glowed blue, very faintly, when she passed her hands caressingly up and down its length. This she planted in the earth to give us a wan light. I knew it would blaze if any of the Shadow's kin prowled too near. But against the common beasts or perhaps even the raider and nomads, we had no defense which was not of our own eyes and ears. Thus we divided the night into three parts; I had the first watch while the others slept, so closely knit together that we touched body to body. And I grew stiff because I feared to move lest I rouse those who so badly needed their rest.

My eyes and ears were on guard and I tried to make my mind one with them, sending out short searching thoughts now and then—but only at rare intervals, since in this land such might be seized upon and used to our undoing. There were many sounds in the night, whimperings, stirrings. And at some my blood raced faster and I tensed, yet always did it come to me at testing that these were from creatures normal to the night, or the winds . . . .

And all the time I strove to battle down and away the desire to think of Hilarion and wonder what he did at this hour in that deserted pile which had once been the heart of his rulership. Was he still lost in his memories of a past time which he could never see again? Or had he risen above that blow, and drew now on his talents—to do what? He would not chance the gate again, of that I was sure: his long bondage to Zandur had decided that.

Zandur . . . I turned eagerly, defensively, from those dangerous thoughts of Hilarion, to wondering what had chanced with Zandur. Had our ripping forth from his place of Power put far more strain on his machines than Hilarion believed, perhaps crippling his stronghold? We had expected him to follow us; he had not. Suppose he was left so weakened that the next time the tower people struck they would put an end to his underground refuge, finishing the immemorial war that had caused a world of ashes and death.

But Zandur's memory, too, might be an opening wedge for a searching by Hilarion, so I must put it from me. There remained the farther past, the Green Valley, Kyllan, Kemoc—I had been months out of Escore. Was the war still a stalemate there? Or were those I cared for locked in some death struggle? I had regained my mind search in part—enough to reach them?

Excitement grew in me, so much so that I forgot where I was and what duty lay upon me. I closed my eyes, my ears, bowed my head upon my hands. Kemoc! In my mind I built his face, thin, gaunt, but strong. There—yes, it was there! And having it to hold, I reached beyond and beyond with my questing call.

"Kemoc!" Into that summons I put all the force I could build. "Kemoc!"

And—and there was an answer! Incredulous at first, then growing stronger. He heard—he was there! My faith had been right: no death wall stood between us.

"Where? Where?" his question beat into my mind until my head rolled back and forth and I strove to hold it steady in my hands.

"East—east—" I would have made more of that, but my head was not moving now with the struggle to mind send; it was shaking with a shaking of my whole body. Hands on my shoulders were so moving me, breaking by that contact my mind touch so that I opened my eyes with a cry of anger.

"Stupid!" My mother's voice was a cold whisper. I could not see her as more than a black bulk, but her punishing hold was still on me. "What have you done, girl?"

"Kemoc! I spoke with Kemoc!" And my anger was as hot as hers.

"Shouting out for any who listens," she returned. "Such seeking can bring the Shadow upon us. Because we have not sniffed out its traces here does not mean this land is clean. Have you not already told us so?"

She was right. Yet, I thought, I was right also, for with Kemoc knowing that I lived aid might come to us. And if some gathering of evil stood between us and the Valley we would be warned by those wishing us well. As I marshaled my reasons, she loosed the hold on me.

"Perhaps and perhaps," she said aloud. "But enough is enough. When you would do this again, speak to me, and together we may do more."

In that, too, she spoke what was right. But I could not put from me the exultation which had come with Kemoc's reply. For in the past, ever since I had shared in Dinzil's defeat, I had been severed from that which made one of three. As I had painfully relearned my skills from Utta it had been working alone. But to be again as I was—

"Will you ever be?" Again it was my mother's whisper, not her thought, to strike as a blow. "You have walked another road from which there may now be no returning. I demanded for you three what I thought would serve you best in the world into which you were born: for Kyllan the sword, for Kemoc the scroll, for you, my daughter, the Gift. But you shared in a way I had not foreseen. And perhaps it was worst for you—"

"No!" My denial was instant.

"Tell me that again in the future," was her ambiguous reply. "Now, my daughter, trouble us with no more sendings. We need rest this night."

Although it went sore against my impatient desires, I made her that promise. "No more—tonight."

Again I settled to scanning only the outer world, that of the night about us, until that hour when Jaelithe roused to take the watch and I willed myself resolutely into slumber.

Shortly after dawn my father awakened us all and we ate of the jar cakes. It was more chill than it had been the day before. Now there was a rime of frost on the branches about us.

Though my father had been much afield along the borders, my mother riding with him as seeress for the rangers, yet they had not gone afoot. Neither had I ever before this time traveled for any space in that fashion, for the nomads had made use of their sleds, walking and riding in turn when they were on a long trek. So now we all found this a slow method of covering the ground, one which wearied us more than we would have guessed before we began it. We tried to keep an even pace, slowed as we were by Ayllia.

The Vupsall girl would walk at our direction, just as she ate what we held to her lips, drank from the cup we gave her. But she went as one walking in her sleep. And I wondered if she had retreated so far from reality that she might never be whole again. As she now was we could not have left her with her people, even had we found them. They would have given her only death. Such as she were too much of a drag upon a wandering people. Utta had lasted so long only because of her gift, and Ausu, the chief's wife, because she had had a devoted servant to be her hands and feet.

XVII

S imon Tregarth had the skill of one who had long laid ambushes, or avoided those of the enemy, in the wild lands of the Karsten mountains. He scouted ahead, sometimes ordering us to remain in hiding until he had explored and then hand-signaling us on. I could not understand what had so aroused his suspicion, unless it was something in the very lay of the land, but I trusted in that suspicion as our safeguard.

We did not use mind touch because this was a haunted land. Twice my mother ordered us into hasty detours around places where her arts told of the lurking of the Shadow. One of these was a hillock on which stood a single monolith of stone, dusky red under the sun. No grass or shrubs grew there; the earth was hard and had a blackened look as if it might once have been burnt over. And the pinnacle itself, if one looked at it for more than an instant, flickered in outline, appeared to change shape. I averted my curious eyes quickly, knowing it was not well to see what might reform from that misty substance.

Our second detour nearly plunged us into disaster. It was caused by a spread of wood wherein the trees were leafless, not as might normally be because of the early season, but because the foliage had been replaced by yellowish lumps or excrescences with pinkish centers, sickening to behold. They might have been open sores eating the unwholesome flesh of the vegetation. One had a queasy feeling that not only were those trees deformed and loathsome, but that something crawled and crept in their shade, unable to issue forth into the sunlight, but waiting, with an ever ravening hunger, for the moment it might grow strong enough to leap.

To pass this ulcerous mass we had to strike south, and the wood proved then to be much wider than we had first suspected, with fingers of leprous vines and brush. It was like a beast, belly-down on the earth it contaminated, crawling ever forward by digging those fringe growths into the soil to drag its bulk along. At one point those holds were on the river bank and we halted there in perplexity.

We would either have to batter our way through them, a task we shrank from, or take to the water, unless we could negotiate a very narrow strip of gravel below the overhang of the bank. And with Ayllia to care for that would be far from easy.

Then sounds carrying over the water set us all to lying low on the earth of the upper bank, a thin screen of growth between us and the water below. I choked as a breeze blew toward me, passing over the tainted growth nearby—the stench nearly drove all the wholesome air from my lungs. Yet we had no chance to withdraw, for out on the far bank of the river came those whose voices carried, not with distinguishable words, but rather as a rise and fall of sound.

For a moment or two I believed them survivors of the village raid, as they were certainly of the same breed as the Vupsalls. But as the newcomers splashed into the shallows to fill their water bags, I did not recognize any face among them. And I noted that while their dress was generally the same, they wore a kind of brightly woven blanket folded into a narrow strip across one shoulder, rather than the cloaks of Utta's clan.

They were in no hurry to move on; in fact the women and children settled down, preparing to make a fire and set up their three-legged cooking pots. Some of the men pulled off their boots and took to the water, crying out as they felt its chill, but persevering, to spread a net among them and sweep it for water dwellers.

For the first time I felt Ayllia stir on her own and I turned quickly. That blankness of now expression was fading; her eyes focused with intelligence on that busy scene, and I saw recognition in them. She raised her head, and I feared that, though these newcomers were not Vupsalls, yet she knew some among them, and would call out for their attention. I tried to grasp her hand, but she twisted away, striking out at me, her blow landing on the side of my head to momentarily daze me. Then she was on her hands and knees, not trying to reach that party overstream, but scuttling away from them, as if she saw not friends but deadly enemies—which could well be with the many feuds in existence.

Had she merely headed back, away from the river's edge, all might still have been well. But in her blind haste she went west, straight for that nightmare growth. And we all knew that she must be stopped before she reached it.

My father threw himself in her direction and an outstretched hand managed to close vise-tight about her ankle, jerking her flat on her face. At least she did not cry out—perhaps her fear of the tribesmen was such that it kept her silent. But she curled around to attack her captor with teeth, nails, all the natural armament she possessed.

But what was worse than that fierce struggle (in which Simon was plainly winning the upper hand) was that the evil vines toward which their battling carried them began to stir. Not as if any wind had brushed them into motion, but as if they had serpents' awareness of what moved close by and were preparing to attack.

In that moment both my mother and I united in a blanketing mind send meant to subdue Ayllia, whose frantic struggles might not only betray us to those across the stream, but could carry her and my father into the grip of those vines now poised in the air as if about to strike.

Ayllia went limp as our mind bolt struck her deeply into bondage. My father lay an instant or two panting, half across her. But it was the vines which frightened me.

They, too, were studded with those loathsome bulbous knots. And now, as the stems set up a wild writhing, the bulbs cracked open. My mother cried out and rose to run forward, with me following.

We caught at whatever portion of the two bodies was the nearest, jerking them away from proximity to the vines. And we were none too soon, for at least one of the knots burst across, loosing in the air a stream of menacing motes. Luckily they did not float toward where we scrambled frantically to get out of range, but drifted to the ground under the writhing stems.

It seemed we had escaped some grave danger only to fall into another. There were sudden shouts from the river bank and I looked hastily around. The fishermen had dropped their net, were splashing toward us, steel in hand.

"Link!" My mother's command rang in my head. "Link—hallucinate!"

I do not know what manner of picture she had selected to give us cover, but what came out of our joining of Power was indeed enough to stop the tribesmen short in midstream, set their women and children screaming and running. Before my eyes, and I was one who was giving Power to raise that guise, my two conscious companions became monsters. Such was their being that I knew these mental pictures had not taken shape by any will of ours. Nor did I doubt that I, myself, must equal them in horror. Of us all only Ayllia, lying as if dead under my father's hands, remained in human seeming.

There was a sudden faltering, lasting only for a breath, in my mother. Her astonishment must have been equal to my own. She stood erect on two misshapen clawed feet, great taloned paws swaying menacingly, her demon's mask of a face turned upon those in the stream. And from her throat came a roar which was enough to crush eardrums.

Seeing her, the tribesmen broke and ran after their womenfolk. And we were left, trying to avoid viewing one another.

"Break." My father pulled himself to his feet, stooped to swing Ayllia up over a horn-plated shoulder. "We have served our purpose—so break."

Break the illusion? But we had instinctively tried that as soon as the tribesmen ran. However, though we no longer fed the hallucination, it remained in force. The monster who had been Jaelithe turned slowly to stare at the hideous wood.

"It would seem," she mouthed between thick purple lips, "that we have wrought our spell too close to that which could twist and turn it to unsightly purpose. We did not achieve invisibility but went far too far in the opposite direction. Also, I do not see the means of breaking this yet—"

And in me then arose a sharp sword of fear to cut and thrust, so that I shivered and quailed. For once before I had worn the stigmata of the Shadow, and so harsh had been that burden that it had driven me to things I hated to remember. Kemoc, by his own blood, shed in mercy, had won me back then to human kind. But at first I had known terror and self-disgust. Were we doomed again to carry such befoulment?

"Let there be a time for shedding later," my father agreed. "I think we are better off the farther we get from this growing cesspool of vileness."

We trailed him down to the river wherein he boldly splashed. I thought that for now we need not fear the return of the tribe. The water rose about us, and in a way that was reassuring, as it is one of the fundamentals of the Power as opposed to the Shadow, that running water can, in itself, be used as a barrier to evil. I almost expected my monster-seeming to vanish as that current washed strongly about my warted and scaled skin. But it did not and we came ashore unopposed in the half-set camp of the tribe.

Seeing some of their packs lying there I became practical and went hunting, finding and filling a sack with what dried foodstuffs were spilled out and around. But my mother passed me, her horned and horrible head down and bent as if she sniffed a trail. At last her taloned paws rent open a tightly lashed basket, turning out dried herbs, which her long and filthy nails sorted until she scooped up a scant handful of twigs and leaves, dried and brittle.

We lingered no longer at the river, but turned westward again. Now my father did not scout ahead, relying on his monster-seeming to be a defense, carrying Ayllia, while we flanked him on either side. A strange and forbidding company we must have made if any of the tribe lurked in hiding to watch our going. I doubted that for even the great hounds had caught the contagion of their masters' panic and had joined in the rout.

"When it is safe"—my mother's words were almost as distorted as the new mouth which formed them—"I think that I have that which will return us to ourselves again."

"Good enough," was Simon's answer. "But let us have more distance traveled behind us first.

On this side of the river the country opened out into a meadowlands. Perhaps these had once been farms, though we came across no signs of walling or any hint of buildings. But my belief that man had once lived here in peace and plenty was affirmed when we came to lines of trees. These were not the twisted, evil things of that terrible wood, but were flushed with the petals of early flowering, and they formed an orchard which had been planted so.

Some were dead, split by storm, battered by the years. But enough still flowered as a promise that life did continue. And life did, for birds nested among them in such numbers as to surprise, unless they depended upon early fruit to sustain them.

Just as that other wood had been a plague spot of evil, so here was a kind of benediction, as if this had been a source of good. I could smell the scent of herbs, faint but unmistakable. Whoever had once planted or tended this orchard had also set out here those growing things which were for healing and good. There were no blue stones of security set up, only a peace and wholesomeness to be felt.

And there we took our rest. While Ayllia slept, my mother brought out the cup made as clasped hands. Holding it in her talons, she turned her head slowly from side to side, until as one who sees a guide point directly ahead, she went down one of the lines of trees until she came to a dip in the ground. I went after her, drawn by the same elusive scent.

A spring bubbled in a basin which my two arms might have encircled. About it stood the first tender growing green ringed by small yellow flowers—those which in my childhood we had called "stareyes" and which are very frail and last but a day, but are the first blooms of spring.

My mother knelt and filled the cup half full from the spring. Carrying it with care, she returned to our temporary camp under the trees.

"A fire?" she asked my father.

His horned and fanged head swung from side to side. "Is it necessary?"

"Yes."

"So be it."

I was already gathering from under the dead trees their long shed branches, choosing those I knew would give forth sweet-smelling smoke, dry enough to burn quickly and brightly.

My father laid a small fire with care, and once done he put spark from his lighter box to it. At my mother's nod I fed to the rising flames some of those herbs she had taken from the tribe's packets.

Jaelithe leaned above the fire, holding the cup in her two hands. Now she stared into its depths. I saw the water it held cloud, darken, then serve as a background to throw into bright relief a picture. It was my father who stood in the depths of that cup, not as the monster who tended the fire, but as the man. I realized what we must do and joined my will to hers. Even so it was a struggle. Slowly that picture in the cup changed. It grew misshapen, monstrous, as we watched and willed. Finally it was completely the thing which had led us across the river.

When that was so my mother blew into the cup so that the picture was broken and only water remained, as clear as it had been at her first dipping. But when we raised our heads and tried to straighten the cramp in our shoulders, my father was again the man.

Then my mother passed the cup, not to me, but to my father. Though she looked at me somewhat ruefully, if such an expression could be read on the twisted countenance which was now hers, and she gave me an explanation: "He who is closest—"

I was already nodding. She was right—to my father would the mind picture be the sharpest now.

So in turn I lent my will to his, while she rested. But I was growing more and more tired, must force myself to the struggle. In the cup my mother slowly changed from a woman of great and stately beauty to monster, until we were sure it was safely done, and my father blew the demon mirrored on the water into nothingness.

"Rest," my mother then bade me, "for what is left we two shall do together, even as we gave you life in the beginning."

I lay back upon the ground, saw my mother and father lean above the cup, and knew that therein they would paint me as they had seen me. But we had been so long separated, was the "me" they would build there the "me" I myself would see in any mirror? It was an odd thought, a little disturbing. I looked away from where they wrought their spell, up into the flowering branches of the tree under which I rested. In me arose such a great desire to remain where I was, to lose all the burdens I had carried, that I yearned to remain here always at rest.

There was tingling along my body, yet I did not care. My eyes closed then and I think I slept. When I awoke the sun was far warmer and lay in slanting beams which told me that a goodly portion of the day must now be behind us. I wondered that we had not gone on.

But as I raised my head and looked along my body I saw that I had indeed returned to my proper guise. My mother sat with her back to the trunk of a tree, and my father lay prone, his head in her lap. He slept, I thought, but she was awake, her hand stroking his hair gently, smoothing it back from his forehead. She did not look at him, rather into the distance, though there was a smile on her lips which softened her usual stern expression—it was even tender, as if she remembered happy things.

In me awoke again that faint desolation, that sense of emptiness which had come before when I had witnessed the expression of their feeling for one another—as if I were one who looked into a warm and comfortable room from outside, where the dark of a chill night closed about me. I almost wanted to break that contentment which I read in my mother's face, say to her, *what of me, of ME? Kyllan has found one who is so to him, and Kemoc, also. But me*— I thought I had such in Dinzil. Is it true, what I learned from him, that any man who looks upon me sees only a tool to further his ambition? Must I turn my mind resolutely from such hopes and follow the narrow, sterile road of the Wise Women?

I sat up and my mother looked to me. I had indeed broken her dream, but not by my full will. Now her smile widened, reached also to me, in warmth.

"It is a thing to weaken one, such spelling. And this is a good place in which to renew body and spirit."

Then my father stirred also and sat up, yawning. "Well enough. But it is not good to dream away the whole day. We need to make more distance for what remains of the sun and light."

It seemed that our rest period had been good for Ayllia too, or else my mother had released her from the full mind block that she might not be so great a drag on us. She roused enough to walk after we had eaten a portion of the supplies we had taken from the tribe.

So we left that oasis of good in the old orchard. As I passed beneath the last of the flowering trees I broke off a twig, holding the blossom close to my nose so I could smell its fragrance, tucking it then into my hair that I might bear with me some of the peace and ancient joy of that place. Oddly enough, the fragrance, instead of growing less as the flowers wilted, became stronger, so that I might at last have laved my whole body in some perfume distilled from their substance.

Our camp that night was on the top of a small hill from which we could keep watch in all directions. We did not light any fire, but when the dark closed about us we could see a distant point of light which was a fire, or so Simon believed.

And since it lay to the south he thought it might mark the camp of the tribe, though it was well away from the river; perhaps they had not returned there, even to gather up what they had abandoned in their flight.

Again we slept in turn. But this time I had the middle hours of the night. And when I was aroused by my mother to take that watch, I found it chill enough to keep my cloak tight about me. Ayllia lay a little beyond, and it was shortly after my mother had gone to sleep that I heard the barbarian girl stir. She was turning her head from side to side, muttering. And that mutter became whispered speech as I leaned closer to listen. What I heard was as much a warning of danger as if she had rung some manor alarm.

"West—to the evil wood—across the river south—west again—to the orchard—then west to a hillock among three such, but standing higher than the other two. West—to what they name the Green Valley—"

Three times she repeated it before she was silent. And I was left with the belief that she herself was not trying to memorize our route, but rather reported it to another. Reported it! To whom, and for what reason?

Her people had been killed or scattered and taken captive by the sea raiders, and I did not believe that any among them could evoke the mind send anyway. Her actions today had been those born in fear when she had seen the other tribe. Did they by chance have some seeress like Utta who had traced us thus? It could be true, but that was not the first and best answer I imagined.

Hilarion! He would not have tried to contact me, or my parents, knowing that any such contact, be it the most tenuous, would have been an instant warning. Then he would have had to try complete take-over. But Ayllia, by our standards, was a weakling, to be easily played upon by anyone learned in sorcery. Therefore he could reach out and work upon her—and now he was using her to keep track of us.

All my fears of what he might be or could do flooded back. But at the same time there was a weakness in me also, for I remembered that touch my mother had made for me, how I had tasted the terrible loneliness which had rent him as he understood what had happened to the world he had known and dreamed of returning to while he stood in Zandur's pillar.

I had never believed him actively evil, only one of those who, following a trail which interested them, could be ruthlessly self-centered, acting recklessly out of curiosity and confidence in themselves. So had he been once, and if he remained so, then he was a threat to what was being built here anew in Escore. If he could track us to the Green Valley . . . !

We could mind block Ayllia completely again. But if we did so she would be only an inert bundle, needing to be carried and constantly tended. And there surely lay many dangers ahead which would make such a captive our bane and perhaps even our deaths. We could abandon her, but that, too, was unthinkable.

And the final decision was not mine but to be shared by the three of us.

During the rest of my hours of watch I listened, not only to the noises of the night, but to any sound from Ayllia. She slept untroubled, however.

When I roused my father to take the final watch I warned him of what I had heard, that he might be alert in turn, even though there was certainly little more that she could report.

In the morning we took council together. My mother was very thoughtful as she considered my ideas.

"I do not believe in a tribal seeress doing this," she said. "Your Utta must have been unique among those people. Hilarion *is* the more reasonable answer. Upon us may now rest an error in judgment for leaving him behind."

"But—" I protested.

"Yes, but and but and but. There are many ifs and buts to be faced in every lifetime and we can choose only what seems best at the moment when the choice is to be made. We have the Power, which makes us more than some, but we must be ever on the alert not to think that it makes us more than human. I think we dare not mind block her. It would render her too great a burden on us. Also, I would set no rearguard cover spell. Such can be as easily read as plain footprints in muddy earth by one like Hilarion. Better to let him think we suspect nothing while we plan ahead for a defense needed at our journey's end."

My father nodded. "As ever, you put it clearly, my witch wife. Our first need is to cross this country to where we shall find friends. To be thought less than we are, not more, is a kind of defense in itself."

They were logical, right. Yet as we started on in the first daylight, I had a feeling that I must now and then look behind me, almost as if some barely perceptible shadow crept behind, always fluttering into hiding just upon my turning so that I never saw it, only sensed it was there.

XVIII

*W*e found no more sweet and sunlit spots such as the orchard; neither did we again chance upon a pool of vileness as the wood. Rather we journeyed over what might have been a land where man had never set foot before. A wild country, yet not too difficult to travel. And for two days we headed steadily west over this. Each night we listened also as Ayllia reported in whispers her account of that day's traveling, as if she had walked with a knowing mind and open eyes scout-trained to see. Nor when I urged that she be blocked did my parents agree, for fear of rendering her helpless that we could not transport her.

On the third day distant blue lines against the sky to the north and west broke into individual mountain peaks. And I was heartened, for by so much were we closer to a land I knew, at least in part. And perhaps I could, within this day's journeying or tomorrow's, pick out some landmark which would guide us into a land the Valley riders patrolled.

We surmounted a ridge at midday, to look down and away into a meadowland, though the grass was now a drab, winter-killed mat through which only a few spikes of early green stuff broke. But man had been here, for there were very old stone fences, so overborne by time that they were mere lines of tumbled rocks. Yet those lines in one direction marked out a road, and the road ended in piers water-washed by a languidly flowing river, some planted in the water, jagged stumps above its surface, and one on an island midway between the two shores.

But it was what occupied that island which froze us, startled and staring, on the ridge crest, until my father's fiercely hissed warning sent us down flat, no longer to be noted against the sky. What we had chanced upon was a sharp skirmish between two bands of sworn enemies.

On this side of the stream reared, pawed, galloped up and down, black Keplians—those monsters with the seeming of horses that served the Sarn Riders. The Sarns—I had thought them all dead in the defeat of Dinzil, but it would seem that enough had survived to make up this troop at least—were human appearing, their hooded cloaks flapping about them. Padding along the margin of the water were the Gray Ones, pointing their man-wolf muzzles into the air as they slavered and screeched their hatred. But, as ever, running water kept them both from full attack. Not so the others of that Shadow pack. From the air shrieked the rus, those birds of ill omen, flying with talon and beak ready to harry the party on the island. And I saw, too, the troubling of the water as rasti swam in waves of furred and vicious bodies, struggling out into the jumble of rocks which was the only defense the island party had.

And running water did not hold others of that foul regiment. Well above its surface floated a swirl of yellowish vapor which did not travel fast, yet made purposefully for the island. Only the sharp crackle of the energy whips of the Green Riders on the island kept all these at bay. Yet perhaps what the forces of the Shadow fought for was only to hold until support came, since we could see movement on the ground at the other side of the river, an ingathering of more of the Sarn Riders and the Gray Ones. Behind those something else moved with intent, but was so covered by a flickering of the air that I could not truly see it. I believed it, however, to be one of the strong evils.

Once Kemoc and I had been so besieged in a place of stones, with a monster force ringing us in. Then Kyllan and the Green People had broken through to our rescue. But here it would seem that some of the Green People themselves were at bay.

Kemoc! His name was on my lips but I did not cry it aloud, remembering that such a betrayal of my recognition might be caught by one of the Shadow and used as another weapon against the very one I would protect. Now I saw a boiling of water about the island and wondered if the Krogan, alienated as they had been, had also now come fully under the Dark Ones' banner.

My father had been surveying the scene below with critical measurement. He spoke now.

"It would seem wise to provide some diversion. But these are not Kolder, nor men—"

My mother's fingers moved in gestures I understood. She was not really counting those of the enemy between us and the river; rather she was in a manner testing them. Now she answered him.

"They do not suspect us, and among these there is knowledge of a sort, but they are not of the Masters, rather creatures born of meddling in pools of the Power. I do not know whether we will turn them by spelling, but one must try. An army . . . ?" And of those last two words she made a question.

"To begin with, yes," he decided.

She brought out of the fore of her tunic some of the herbs which she had used to break the counter spell of the monster-seeming while my father and I clawed loose the earth of the ridge about us. Using spittle from our mouths, we made of it small balls, into which Jaelithe pressed some of the bits of dried leaf and broken stem. When she had done so, she set them out in a line before us.

"Name them!" she ordered.

And my father did so, staring long and hard at each one as he spoke. Some of the names he uttered were ones I had heard:

"Otkell, Brendan, Dermont, Osboric."

And a great name that last was! Mangus Osberic had held Sulcar Keep and taken its walls and Kolder attackers with him when there was no hope of relief.

"Finnis . . ." On and on he spoke those names, some of Old Race Borderers, some of Sulcarmen, one or two of Falconers. And I knew that he so chose men who had stood beside him once, though now they were dead and so could not be harmed by our magic.

When he had done, and there were still some balls remaining, my mother took up the tale. The names she called sounded with a particular crackle in the air. Thus I knew she raised, not warriors, but Wise Women who had gone behind the final curtain.

She was done and a single ball remained unnamed. I was—possessed? No, not in reality, for another will did not enter into me to direct my hand or take over my brain, yet I did that which I had no forethought to do. My finger went out to the last ball and the name I gave it was not that of the dead, but of the living, and a name I would never have voiced had not that compulsion out of nowhere brought it to my lips.

"Hilarion!"

My mother sent a single direct and measuring glance. But she said naught, rather put then her force to the summoning, and my father and I joined with her. Then from the small seeds of soil, herbs and spittle, gathering form and solidity as they did rose, came the appearances of those named.

In that moment, they were so very real that even putting forth a hand one might feel firm flesh. And one could indeed die under the weapons they carried, ready for battle.

But that last seed, that which I had so intently named, did not bear fruit. And I had a fleeting wonder if it had been only my fear of him, perhaps a desire to think him dead and safely removed from us, which had led me to that act.

There was no time left for idle speculation as down from the ridge marched the army we had summoned, the warriors to the fore, behind them a half a dozen gray-robed women, each with her hands breast-high, holding so her witch jewel, in its way as great or greater a menace to the enemy than the steel the others bore.

So great was the hallucination that, had I not seen the spell in progress, I would have accepted the sudden appearance of a battle-ready force as fact. Yet that one ball of mud remained. I would have pinched it into nothingness but I discovered that I could not, so I left it lying as we four got to our feet to follow the army our wills commanded down the slope to the river.

I do not know which of those in the lines of besiegers first looked up to see us coming, but suddenly there was an outward surge, mainly of the Gray Ones leaping at us. Among them our warriors wreaked slaughter, though at first I thought that perhaps the enemy could sense they were not normal and meet them as illusions.

Now the Sarn Riders wheeled and rode, and from them sprang lance points of fire. Yet none of those at whom they aimed shriveled in the flames or fell in death. And as our warriors had met the Gray Ones, so did the Wise Women of the second line send forth beams from their jewels. These touching upon the head of Keplian or rider appeared to cause madness so that Keplian ran screaming, stopping now and then to rear and paw wildly, throwing riders who had not already been crazed by the touch of jewel beams.

Our advantage was a matter of time, as I knew well, and I struggled along with my parents to hold fast the flow of energy which fed our illusions. For, if we faltered or tired, they would fail. And soon we marched less quickly, and I felt drops of sweat gather on my forehead, to roll as tears of strain down my cheeks. But still I gave all I had to this task.

The regiment of illusions reached the river bank. Then the drifting swirls of mist floated back from the island toward us. These were in fact so insubstantial they were naught which could be hewed nor did the jewel beams appear to harm them, though they would swing away from any aimed at their centers.

And, if these were not enough, that curious "thing" we had seen advancing on the other side of the river was drawing closer. But the Sarn Riders and the Gray

Ones on that side of the water made no attempt to cross and join the fighting here, nor even to reach the island. It could be they only waited to cut off retreat, leaving the strange thing to do the battling.

Suddenly my mother flung out her hand, and, as suddenly, my father was at her side, his arm about her shoulders, supporting her. I caught only the sidewash of that chaotic confusion which struck at us obliquely, so that my mother must have taken far more of its force. And I knew without being told that it was a blow from that flickering unseeable. However, if it had thought to contemptuously sweep us into nothingness by such tactics, it was soon to learn that we had more, or were more, than it expected.

Our illusionary troops did not fall dead, nor fade away; they simply ceased to be, as we withdrew that energy which gave them life and being in order to defend ourselves. Still, they had cleared a path to the river bank and those on the island were quick to take advantage of what relief we could offer them. I saw Renthan arise from where they had lain, men swing onto their backs, energy whips lashing, to sweep the rest of the rasti away. Then, with great leaps through the water, they came to us.

Kemoc was well in the van, and sharing his mount was Orsya, her hair and pearly skin still water-sleeked. Behind them were six of the Green People, four men, two women.

"Mount!" My brother wheeled his Renthan close, his order clear. I saw my father half throw Ayllia to one of the Green Riders, and then aid my mother to mount behind another. I took the hand of one of the women and rose to sit behind her, seeing my father behind another.

The Keplians and Gray Ones who had been so scattered by our illusions were not united to stand yet, and we rode southeast, keeping along the river bank. We rode knowing that behind us that flickering menace was coming, and, of all the enemy we had fronted this day, that was the most to be feared.

I glanced back, to see that it was out over the stream now—though it made that journey quickly, as if it cared little to cross running water. Then it was on the same bank. And how swiftly it might travel could mean the difference between life and death for us. We dared not halt again to make a new army, even if we could summon strength anew to call it into life.

I had never really known just how much speed the Renthans could summon, but that day I learned, and it was such learning as I would not care to face a second time unless the need was very great. I only clung to the one who sat before me and centered all my determination on holding that seat, while I closed my eyes to the wild sight of the world flashing by so fast that it would seem we bestrode a flying thing which never touched hoof to solid earth.

Then we were running not over land but in the river's wash, and still east, away from our goal. With the water-covered gravel under them the Renthan slowed, though they kept a pace the fastest horse of Estcarp could not have bettered.

I dared not look behind again, for ever and anon something reached out at us, a kind of nibbling rather than a blow designed to bring us down. To me that insidious touch was worse that a sword cut. There was a tenacious spirit to it which meant that once it had set upon a chase nothing would turn it from the trail.

The Renthan could not be tireless, and what would happen if they must mend their pace or were forced to rest?

Our river travel ended as suddenly as it had begun, the renthan having crossed the stream at a long angle, to come out on the opposite shore, miles from the island. Now they faced about to run west again. But there were long shadows lying across our path and sunset could not be too long ahead—and night was the time of the Shadow. It could then summon to our undoing creatures who never dared face the light of day. We must, I was sure, find some stronghold we could defend during the dark hours. And I only hoped that those with whom we rode had enough knowledge of this land to do so.

When the Renthan came to a halt I was amazed, and could only believe that their energy had at last failed, to leave us in as great, or almost as great, a place of danger as we had fled. For we were now in the midst of open, level land, with dried grass brushing knee-high on our mounts. There was no sign of any outpost of the Light—no blue stones, not even such a memory of good as had hung in the orchard. We were in the open, naked to whatever attack our enemies might launch.

But the Green People slid down from the backs of their allies, and perforce we did the same. Then I saw the meeting of Kemoc and our parents. Kemoc stood as tall and straight as Simon, though he was more slender. And he looked my father eye to eye until he put forth both arms and my father caught them in the grip of the Borderer's greeting, drawing him close till their cheeks met, first right and then left. But to my mother Kemoc went down on one knee and bowed his head until she touched it, and he looked up, to have her make one of the signs upon his forehead in blessing.

"A good greeting at an ill time," said my father. "This seems a place in which we have no defenses." That was a half question.

"The moon is at full," my brother answered. "In this night we need light, for that which follows can twist dark to its own purposes."

But we had more than the moon to serve us. The Green People moved with the swift sureness which said that they had done this many times before, marking out a star upon the ground by laying the fire of their whips accurately, a star large enough to shelter our whole party. Upon its points they set fires which were first kindled from twists of grass and then had planted in the heart of each a cube of gum as big as a man's clenched fist. This took fire but did not blaze fiercely nor was it quickly consumed; from it instead pillared a tall shaft of blue radiance, making us safe against evil.

So sheltered we ate and drank, and then we talked and there was much to say. Thus I learned that Kemoc and Kyllan had been flung by the force of the avalanche well to one side, and with them Valmund, but he had been sore injured. They had later found Raknar's crushed and broken body, but me they could not locate. And they had been forced away by a second avalanche which buried deeper that part they had frantically dug into. In the end they had returned to the Valley, but, as I had done, they clung to the hope that because of our bond they would have known of my death.

Thereafter, in the winter, matters grew more difficult for the Valley. Cold brought boldness to the evil things and they kept such a patrol about the borders of that part of the land the Green People and their allies had cleared, that each day saw some struggle or clash—as if the Shadow force planned to wear them down by such a constant keeping of alarms ringing them in. To my brothers this was the old way of Borderer life and they fell back easily into its pattern.

It appeared that those besieging them weakened with the coming of spring, however, and patrols from the Valley ventured farther and farther afield. Kemoc had been on one such mission when my mind touch reached him. And instantly he had ridden to seek us. We were well outside the influence of the Valley here and we must ride swift and hard to gain its shelter.

So had life been with him. Then we must add our own story, both separately and together, and this took time to tell, though we kept to the bare bones of fact. He was startled to hear of Hilarion and straightaway looked at me. I knew what moved in his mind, that he wondered if again we must arm ourselves against another Dinzil, and one perhaps ten times more powerful. And I could not say yes or no, for I had fear only, not proof.

By his side sat Orsya, also watching me. I flinched from her eyes remembering only too well how, tainted by Dinzil's teaching, I had once wished her so much ill. Could I ever be sure that she, too, could look at me and not see the past rise as a wall between us?

But when we would sleep at last, she came to me and in her hand she had a small flask, no longer than the smallest of her fingers. She unstoppered it with great care and held it close so that a delicate fragrance reached my nostrils.

"Sleep well, sister, and be sure that such dreams as may come will have nothing of the Dark rooted in them." I knew she was giving me of her own magic. And now she put fingertip to the vial and moistened it. With that moisture she wet my forehead, eyelids and, at last, my lips.

I thanked her and she smiled and shook her head, restoppering the vial with the same care. Then she gestured to Ayllia, who sat staring at nothing with unseeing eyes.

"This one needs a safe world for a while," Orsya commented. "She is not of our breed and what she has seen rests too heavy a burden on her. Once in the Valley Dahaun can bring her better healing than we can offer." She lifted her head higher and turned her face to meet a breeze out of the night.

There was no effluvia of evil in it, though it was chill. But in it was the hint of renewing life. Breathing deeply of that air, and doubtless helped by Orsya's cordial, I felt as one from whose shoulders a weight of burden was loosened.

I saw that most of our party was already at rest, the Renthans kneeling to chew their cuds and think their thoughts, which are not those of my kind, but as meaningful. Orsya still sat between me and Ayllia, and now her hand came and we clasped fingers.

She looked at me searchingly. "It is better with you, my sister."

As if she had meant that as a question, I answered her with perhaps more firmness than I was inwardly sure was the truth. "It is well. My Powers have well nigh returned."

"Your Powers," she repeated. "If you have regained or found what you treasure, cherish it well, Kaththea."

I did not understand what she truly meant by that but, bidding her then good sleep in turn, I rolled in my cloak and sought that state myself.

If there was virtue in Orsya's fragrant liquid, it did not seem to work for me. For straightaway when I closed my eyes I was back on that ridge where we wrought in mud to raise our small army. Once more my finger touched that last ball and I uttered the name I did not want to say.

But this time those other small balls remained earth only, and he whom I so summoned arose—not as I had seen him last in his deserted and time-worn citadel, but rather as I had viewed him in that other dream, when he had sat upon his chair and looked at the gate he had opened.

He turned to look at me with something in his eyes that made me wish to turn away and quickly, only I could not.

"You have named me in the field of death." He did not speak those words but I read them mind to mind. "Do you then hold me in such fear—or dislike?"

I brought all the boldness I had into my answer, giving him the full truth. "I fear you, yes, for what you may do, being who and what you are. Your day is past in Escore; seek not to raise your banner here again."

As if my very thought conjured up what I feared the most, I saw then a banner form in the sky behind him. It was as yellow as the sunlight across gold sand, and on it were the wand and sword crossed.

"Raise not my banner," he repeated thoughtfully. "For you think my day done, do you, Kaththea, sorceress and witch maid? I lay no geas on you, for between us there must never be ruler or ruled. But this I foresee, that you shall wish for this banner, call for it in your need."

I marshaled my thoughts to drown out his, lest he influence me. "I wish only that you keep your own place, Hilarion, and come not into ours. No ill will do I call upon you, for I think you are not one who has ever marched with the Shadow. Only let us go!"

Now he shook his head slowly. "I have no army, naught but myself. And you owe me a boon, since you death-named me. The balance will be equaled when the time comes."

Then I remembered no more, and the rest of the night I did sleep. I awoke with a vague foreboding that this day, new come to use, would be full of trial and danger. For the first hour or two after our leaving the star camp, though, it would seem I was wrong.

We rode steadily westward. The Renthan did not race as they had the day before, but they covered ground at an awesome pace, seeming not to feel the burden of their riders. Before long, however, we knew that if Sarn Riders and Gray Ones did not sniff behind us, that flickering thing did. And we also knew that it was more than matching our speed, though it labored to overtake us.

I saw the two Green Riders who formed our rear guard look now and then behind. When I did likewise I believed there was the flickering to be sighted far off. It also cast some influence ahead, slowing our thought, clouding our minds, and affecting even our bodies so that each gesture became a thing of effort. And under that drain the Renthan, too, began to give way.

The sunshine which had seemed so bright was now a pale thing; there might have been a thin cloud between it and us. Cold gathered about our shivering bodies as if the Ice Dragon breathed, months after he had been driven to his den.

Our run became a trot, then a walk in which the Renthan fought with great effort to achieve some of their former speed. Finally their leader, whom Kemoc rode, gave a loud bellow and they came to a halt as his thought reached us.

"We can do no more until this spell is lifted."

"Spell!" My mother's reply came quickly. "This is beyond my skill. It is born of another kind of knowledge than I have dealt with."

Hearing this, the cold of my body was matched by the chill of inner fear. For she was one I believed stood ready to challenge and fight aught which walked this tormented land.

"Water magic I do have," Orsya said. "But it is no match for what hunts us now. Kemoc?"

He shook his head. "I have named great names and have been answered. But I know not what name can deal with this—"

And at that moment there came into my mind that I alone knew what—who— might face our pursuer. I had named him to death on that ridge, not understanding why. If I called him now it was to death—for the breath of that lay on us, and whoever faced it in battle must be mightier than any I had thought on. Even the Wise Women of Estcarp must work in concert for their great bespelling.

I could call. He would answer—and death would be the end. So did my fear tell me. To summon one to his death—what manner of woman could do that, knowing before that she did so?

Yet it was not my life I bargained for if I did this thing; it was the lives of those about me, together with what might well be the future of this land. So I slipped from the back of the Renthan and I ran out from them, facing that thing we could not see.

As I went I called for help as one might who was lost: "Your banner— I summon—"

Why I framed my plea thus I could not tell. But I was answered by a flash of gold across the sky, seeming to bring with it a measure of the sun's warmth, which had so strangely gone from us. Under it Hilarion stood, not looking back to me, but facing the thing, with no bared sword but a wand in his hand.

He raised the wand as a warrior salutes with his blade before he gives the first stroke in a measured bout. Formal and exact was that salute, and also was it a challenge to that which came behind us.

But of the rest of that battle I saw nothing, for there was an increase of that flickering, vastly hurting to the eyes so I had to shield my sight or go blind. Only, though I could not look upon what chanced there, there was one thing I might do: what Hilarion had demanded of me as Zandur's prisoner, now did I give freely, and not for his asking. I allowed to flow to him all that was in my Power, emptying myself as I had not wanted to do since I regained what I had lost.

I think I fell to my knees, my hands pressed to my breast, but I was not really aware of anything but that draining and the need for giving. So did time pass without reckoning.

Then there was an end! I was empty with an emptiness which was deeper than the wound Dinzil had left in me. And I thought feebly that this was death, what death must be. But I had no fear, only the wish to be at peace forever.

But suddenly there was the warmth of hands on my shoulders and I was drawn up from where I crouched. Through that touch there flowed back into me life, though I did not want it now, knowing what I had done with my summons.

"Not so!"

Thus I was forced to open my eyes, not on the terrible blinding chaos I had thought, but to see who stood by me. And I knew that this was not one of Dinzil's breed, those who do not give, only take. Rather it was true that between *us* there was neither ruler nor ruled, only sharing. There was no need for words, or even thoughts—save a single small wonder quickly gone as to how I could have been so blind as to open the door to needless fear.

We walked together to those who had watched and waited. And the opener of gates so became a defender of life, while I had an ending to my part in the saga of Escore.

WE WROUGHT well together, and with our combined Power we rode and fought, and rid the land of the Shadow, driving it back and back. And when it crept away into holes and hiding places we used the Power to seal those. When most of the cleansing was done my parents rode for Estcarp, for it was there their hearts were bound. Yet between us roads would now be opened and our thoughts would also move faster than any messengers could hope to ride.

My brothers and their people came forth from the Valley to take up lands their swords had bought. But I looked out upon a many-walled citadel thrusting boldly into the sea. And out of the dust of years came a new awakening which was very rich and good.

About the Author

Andre Norton is one of the most distinguished science fiction and fantasy writers of all time. She was the recipient of a Life Achievement Award from the World Fantasy Convention and was honored as a Grand Master by the Science Fiction Writers of America. Her books have sold tens of millions of copies worldwide and have been translated into more than a dozen languages.

Miss Norton was born in Ohio, where she lived for many years. She also lived in central Florida for some time before moving to Murfreesboro, Tennessee, where she presides over High Hallack. Discover more about Miss Norton, her work, and High Hallack at her Web site *www.andre-norton.org*.